RAMSES
WARNING

RAMSES WARNING

STEPHEN FRANCIS MONTAGA

ARPress
45 Dan Road Suite 5
Canton, MA 02021

Hotline: 1(888) 821-0229
Fax: 1(508) 545-7580

Ordering Information:
Quantity sales. Special discounts are available on quantity purchases by corporations,associations, and others. For details, contact the publisher at the address above.

Printed in the United States of America.

ISBN-13:   Softcover   979-8-89389-246-8
                eBook   979-8-89389-247-5

Library of Congress Control Number: 2024906313

CONTENTS

PREFIX

Three thousand, two hundred years ago, the all powerful and well feared Ramses walked the banks of the Nile River. He was looking for a special place to build a sacred Temple to honor the Gods he believed protected the life giving waters of the mighty Nile River. As he slowly walked along the River's edge, walked countless times in the past by his great ancestors, he was being closely followed by eleven of his most trusted priests, a number of Royal Guardsmen, and his beloved lady, Queen Nefertari.

Ramses walked by himself, at times allowing his foot to actually slip in the cool waters of the Nile. Occasionally, his wife would walk up to his side and she would lightly touch the cheek of his weathered beaten face, and he would smile back at her warmly. She would then retreat back to her appointed place two steps behind her great husband. At one point, a priest ran over to his side, and he offered the Pharaoh some fresh cool drinking water. The great Ramses savored the sweet taste of the water, and then the priest quickly disappeared back in the procession as they continued to follow the wandering Ramses and his ongoing search for the right place to build his temple.

On this wonderful day while the Pharaoh of both the Upper and Lower Egypt, walked along the muddy edge of the mighty Nile River. Ramses suddenly slipped and he almost fell into the water he loved and respected so much throughout his life. Whereupon, two of the priests immediately rushed up to his side and they helped right the falling

Pharaoh. Ramses looked away from the harsh glare of the sun and back onto the waters of the river. Then he looked back to the sun itself again. Then to the water and he smiled. The harsh glare reflected at the side of the mountain bordering the mighty River, as if the sun itself was trying to show him where the Sun God Re Harakhte, wanted his Temple to be built.

Suddenly, Ramses turned to his horde of priests and ordered them in a commanding voice. "Here is where I shall build my great Temple to honor the powerful Sun God Re Harakhte, to give him many years of thanks and respect for the precious life the Nile waters give to all the faithful children of Egypt. I shall give my special thanks to Osiris, the god of the Nile River, and the Ruler of the Nether World, and the final judge of the dead. I shall command a second, but smaller Temple be built there as well." The powerful Pharaoh pointed to a spot a few hundred yards further down river on the side of the mountain of Adu Simbil.

"I demand this Temple to be dedicated to the God Hathor, the Goddess of love, in honor of my wife Nefertari, who has given me so much love." Ramses took in a huge breath, and then spoke again to the gathered. "Re Harakhte will forever shine over and protect the great waters of the mighty Nile River, the life and body of all Egypt and her children yet to come. The Goddess Hathor will smile pleasantly upon this place, and bring forth many new children to nurture and protect these sacred waters for Egypt's future history."

At the dedication ceremony to his Temple once completed eleven years later in which all peoples of Egypt attended, Ramses stood between the gigantic statues of his own likeness. Ramses looked over the horde of Egyptians gathered to honor Re Harakhte and himself, and smiled with his inner soul because he was so proud of his accomplishments to honor his Gods. His people were pleased, there were no wars raging in his lands and children were smiling and happy and enjoying themselves. Looking over the mass crowd he noticed numerous babies protectively held in mother's arms, and children feeding at their mother's breasts.

The waters of the Nile River were clean and blue as the sky. As the solemn leader of all Egypt looked over the peaceful waters, he watched a huge Nile crocodile basking in the warm waters, and he took this vision as a good omen, adding to the importance of the day.

The massive crowd was extremely noisy at best, with many people of Egypt talking amongst themselves at the same time, and many countless babies crying and fussing. Adding to the most upsetting noise drowning out his words, Ramses lifted his mighty hand over his head, and the crowd immediately quieted down, even the babies were still now. With his hand still raised over his head he spoke in a commanding voice to his people. "Here me my children of Egypt, faithful children of the Nile River. We are here to honor the waters of the Nile River. I shall now bless these most sacred waters."

The greatly respected Pharaoh paused for a brief moment as twenty priests quickly ran over to the banks of the Nile, and poured in a good mixture of blood drained from four virgin priestess, along with a number of different herbs and petals from flowers that adorned the banks of the Nile. When this was accomplished, the priests returned to their places of honor and waited. Then, the god like Ramses continued speaking to the gathered as he looked over the masses with great pride displayed upon his face.

"I warn every Egyptian man, woman and child standing here before me on this great day of days, and to those Egyptians of future generations yet to come. If the sacred waters of the mighty Nile River ever stop flowing, even for one full day. Then the land once known as Egypt will shrivel up, and will be slowly blown away by the hot breath of the desert winds. It is the sacred duty of every Egyptian man, woman and child to protect these precious waters of the Nile River with his life. Or I warn all gathered before me here today, there will be no life left throughout all the lands of Egypt if any of you fail on this quest I lay out before you.

"We cannot possibly allow any other nation of the world to block the flowing waters of the mighty Nile River for any reason whatsoever. Nor can we not take all the precautions to safeguard ourselves against the many whims of nature itself. For she might take it upon herself someday, to punish the good people of Egypt for their many past sins and aggressions committed against Geb and the river itself. We must take action now and keep taking action every day of our lives to protect the waters of the Nile. We have to make great pockets of water, so as to save us through the hard times of the days of future drought, or the more need of these sacred waters. Remember my faithful people of Egypt. We have to fight to keep the waters of the mighty Nile River flowing for all times to come, or your lives, and the lives of all your children and family will cease to exist in this world."

The powerful leader Ramses, suddenly stopped speaking at this point, and then he slowly and proudly turned away from the massive crowd, and he quickly disappeared into the center of the new Temple. He was followed closely as always by his beloved Queen, Nefertari. Many of his main and trusted council members also followed the two revered leaders into the great Temple, and the Royal Guard, and many of his special priests and priestesses.

The great Pharaoh Ramses was never seen again for the rest of the day by the gathered crowd. Soon, the masses grew bored with standing and baking out in the hot blazing sun, and one by one they slowly left the great Temple area for the safety of their homes. Because the sacred Temple was not open to any of the commoners and poor of Egypt, or their personal pleasures offered to the sacred Gods that the Temple was constructed to honor.

CHAPTER 1

PRESENT DAY - Nowhere on the face of the earth, other than along the great path of the mighty Nile River, can one understand more dramatically the true meaning of the phrase, "Water is life." The true path of the Nile River, the longest river in the world over four thousand, one hundred and forty miles long, traces through many different boundaries and countries of Africa. The Nile River gathers its waters from nine other countries. Burundia, the true source of the White Nile, Rwanda, Tanzania, Kenya, Uganda, Zaire, the Sudan, Ethiopia and Egypt share one million, one hundred fifty thousand square miles of water coming from the Great Nile River.

Over forty percent of the Nile River has no true tributaries adding to its waters, so its water level and flow was determined by the heavy rainfall season in the highlands of the Ethiopia mountain ranges, where the Blue Nile River is truly born and given life. Over sixty five inches of rainfall hits this one major mountain range yearly, and it drains down into the waters of the huge and deep Lake Tana, or the flowing water from the rains finds its way down to the much smaller Atbara River, and between these two sources of water, makes up over eighty four percent of the Nile River's life giving water.

One of the principal tributaries to the waters of the Nile River is Lake Tana, sometimes called the Blue Nile which contributes over sixty four percent of the Nile's waters. In addition, are the Atbara River, contributing nearly twenty percent, and Lake Victoria which supplies twelve percent of the waters of the Nile River, along with the Semliki and Sobat Rivers. These waters join the main flow of the waters of the White Nile around the town of Malakal. Together, these three flows of water contribute over sixteen percent of the Nile River's powerful water flow.

The White Nile, one of two main branches of the great Nile River, begins its long journey to the Mediterranean Sea through Africa originating from Lake Victoria, which is around four thousand feet above sea level. The massive lake covers well over twenty six thousand square miles of the earth's surface with water coming from over five hundred miles down river from the true source of the great Nile River which has three main tributaries to its water flow.

The true source of the Nile River is born in the highlands of southern Burundi. From there, the Ruvironza River flows north down to become the narrow Ruvubu River. This river's joined together by the Nyabarongo River which has many small tributaries constantly feeding the flow of water coming from the southern side of Virunga mountain ranges in the nation of Rwanda. The Virunga Mountains are sometimes referred to as the "Mountains of the Moon," because of its ever present and low hanging clouds, which covers the mountains almost all the year round.

Also, this vast mountain range is located in the wettest area of the world. Ice caps forty five feet thick, are constantly melting and helping to feed the White Nile River year round. The valleys of the mountain ridges are swamp land and are perpetually muddy, with the richest deposits of nutrient laden silt on the face of the earth, and this mud slowly finds its way to the Nile River flow. Its river line helps the farmers situated along the Nile River when the rich silt is deposited anew during each flood season on their lands. Any reduction in the flow of this silt would cause the farmers in Egyptian land, hardships. Any reduction whatsoever in the flow of the water would totally destroy Egypt, whose very life depends on these most vital waters.

Many other smaller tributaries making up the flow of the White Nile River, include the Kagera River and Lake Edward situated three thousand feet above sea level. Lake Edward is a long and narrow lake some fifty miles long, and over one hundred, and thirty feet deep at its deepest point. The Lake is well noted for its great catches of huge white perch, tiger fish, and also the mud fish. The waters of Lake Edward pour into the Semliki River, and then it flows down until it finally ends up in the tiny Lake Albert, at two thousand feet above sea level, and there it mixes in with the vast water of Lake Victoria. At this point and beyond, these rivers and lakes add their life giving water to the flow of waters of the Sobat River, and this makes up the waters of the White Nile River flowing fifteen hundred feet above sea level.

The great waters of the White Nile River overflow their banks every year during the heavy rainy seasons, back washing and then replenishing the valuable swamp and marsh lands developed from many prior floods periods, and thus washing the rich deposits of this new silt into the flowing waters of the Nile River, only to be left behind lying on the banks in Egypt.

The White Nile River continues to meander down until it finally reaches the capital of the Sudan, Khartoum. Here, the waters of the White Nile mix in with the much faster, and more powerful flowing waters of the Blue Nile. The Blue Nile River which is the largest feeder of the true Nile River, is born in the large, ice cold waters of Lake Tana. Lake Tana is situated six thousand feet above sea level in the vast mountain ranges of Ethiopia. These floodwaters born in this region, are the chief source of the powerful flow of water of the Blue Nile, and the source of the Egyptian Sudan irrigation systems. The Blue Nile River actually serves as a water highway for the people of the Sudan, Egypt and many other nations and their peoples who live all along her unending river banks.

The unpredictable waters from the River Atbara also joins the water flow of the two Nile Rivers some two hundred miles downstream from the capital city of Khartoum, and these waters finish the flowing waters of the Nile River, with over ninety eight percent of its water supply in the Nile River. Eight smaller rivers and streams also help to make up the rest of the two percent of feeding waters of the Nile River.

The Atbara River does not flow all year round though. In mid winter, the sun heats the earth to over one hundred and twenty degrees Fahrenheit, and the Atbara River slowly dries up, becoming a number of stagnated pools and ponds for fish, crocodiles and hippopotamuses to survive in until the waters flow once again in the river. By late August the rain waters again roar out of the high mountains of Ethiopia, thus turning the Atbara River back into a mighty river of over one thousand feet wide, and ripping the dried lands apart, and carrying off more rich deposits of silt and top soil to the Nile towards Egypt.

The vast Nile River's surrounded by many mysteries of Egypt's ancient past as well as having its riverbanks dotted by many exquisite temples from the time of the great Egyptian Pharaohs. The Pharaohs of Egypt's great past realized the importance of the waters of the Nile River, and many of them chose to honor the life giving waters of the Nile River by building great Temples to their Gods along her banks for the River's protection.

The Nile River was the true cause of many great explorers to lose their lives, as well as their credibility, in the search for the true source of the Nile River. The search for the source of the Nile River caused many explorers to go mad or bankrupt. A source that would be found many times over, only to be proven wrong by later explorers. The Nile River does not give up her secrets easily.

In Ethiopia's highlands, a strange and silent lake looms in the dense jungle. Few people lived that high up in the mountains because of the thin air which made the lake look like a throwback to prehistoric times of the past. When the lake was first discovered, it was surrounded by thick growth of vegetation, and the water was covered by low heavy hanging clouds throughout most of the year. In 1603, a Portuguese priest, Father Pedro Pase discovered the lake after escaping from the Arabs holding him prisoner because of his religious beliefs.

The priest wrote in his diaries he felt he was lost in another time, and quite apparently he was the first European to ever see the great lake. The priest stayed in this mystical land of savages and converted many once heathens over to the Catholic Religion. Father Pase had also helped the poor living near the lake to cultivate the shores of the massive Lake Tana. Then in 1621 the Father built the first Roman Catholic Church on the shore of the lake, and it helped to colonize the Lake Tana region. His great work created a foothold for the Catholic Church and religion inside Ethiopia.

Lake Tana measures around one thousand two hundred square miles of surface water, and is believed to be over a thousand feet deep, with a constant overflow of water to feed the Nile River. Many explorers who read the papers from the priest, searched for the true source of the Nile. The first was the English team of Richard F. Burton and John Speke.

The two Englishmen set out to find the source of the Nile River in 1856. They landed on the island of Zanzibar in the Indian Ocean, some twenty miles from the African coast. Here the two explorers brought slaves, and set out to find Caput Nile, the source of the Nile. They both wanted to be the ones who discovered the source of the Nile

Trade was used to pay the tariffs for the explorers, so they could pass safely through many tribal lands. Both men made maps and used local tribesmen to help find the way through the uncharted and extremely dangerous territories of the countries they traveled through. The ragtag caravan fought Malaria, pneumonia, dysentery and open sores to their exhausted bodies. For five months Burton's caravan climbed, crawled and dragged themselves through the harsh and unforgiving land, sometimes traveling just five miles for the entire day.

But on November 7th, 1857 the ragtag group entered the village of Kazeh. Speke and Burton spent a month healing their wounds and fatigued bodies and questioning the local Arabs, making new maps of the land further to the west from their information. In December the explorers headed out again to Kigoma on Lake Tanganyika. After they explored the shore of the lake, Burton knew he had not found the true source of the Nile River.

By June of 1858, the explorers found themselves back at Kazeh. But here, Speke was not satisfied and he set out anew to the north to find a larger lake than Tanganyika. As Speke headed north, he noticed the air changing after traveling two hundred and twenty four miles. The air smelled like rain all the time. Speke came across vast fields of cotton and millet. His pace quickened then, until his trek ended at Mwanza. Here, he stood on the shore of Africa's largest Lake. He was positive he found the true source of the Nile River, and named this lake, Victoria. Now his fight began, Burton argued it was not the true source of the Nile River, and upon their return to England the discovery was contested by scholars. But Speke was not without his staunch supporters, and thus the heated debates over the source of the Nile raged for years.

The debates raged on until another explorer finally came along and started his quest to find the true source of the Nile River. In 1937 a German explorer, Doctor Burkhart Waldecker traced the River to its true source at a tiny spring that makes its way directly out of the earth's surface. Here, the southernmost source of the Nile River made its appearance in the mountains outside Burundi, the capital of the nation of Bujumbura. The question of the true source of the Nile River was finally answered after all these years and countless debates. But still, to this day, mysteries still surrounds the Nile River, with scholars unrelenting in their argument the true source of the Nile River remain undiscovered.

Adding more fuel to the fire to the many countless mysteries of the Nile River are the numerous Temples dotting the River's banks. Great Citadel walls, vast grave yards and early Christian churches constructed at Gebel Adda, a city occupied since before the second century A.D. The beautiful Temple dedicated to the Egyptian Queen Hatshepsut, sits in Nubia. A number of smaller Temple remains constructed at the villages in Kumna and Semna, with another ancient Temple built at Danbur. There is the large Roman Temple built at Kalabhand. The masterpiece of all ancient Egyptian Temples sits at Abu Simbel, and the Pyramids on the west bank of the Nile River at Giza which served as the tombs for the ancient Pharaohs, as well as the Temples at Medinet Habu and Deim el Bahri.

In 1902, the first real attempt to try and control the highly unpredictable waters of the Nile River took place as a number of barrages, or low Dams were built to raise the water level to feed irrigation baskets and fields. The first Dam of the Nile River was completed in Asyut in the year 1902, and it was comprised of concrete and earth. A second Dam was completed in Isna, and a larger Dam of concrete was completed in the Nag Hammadi area in the mid thirties.

But even before these attempts to control the Nile water took place, the Egyptians built the Muhammad Barrage in 1861. This barrage lifted the waters of the river, so water could be supplied to the hand dug canals lying behind the Dam, and irrigates the land for their crops, and receives some of the nutrient rich mud.

The next attempt to control the waters of the Nile River took place in 1954. A large Dam and hydroelectric plant was built at the Owens Falls. This Dam backed up the water flow of Lake Victoria, thus making the lake the largest reservoir in the world. Through the years that followed, more Dams sprang up all along the Nile trying to harness the power of the river. The Roseiries Dam, Senna Dam, the larger Jebel Aulia Dam outside Khartoum, and the Aswan Dam which gave birth to the vast Lake Nasser.

The old Aswan Dam was the first one ever built which raised the mighty waters of the Nile River that it actually threatened the ancient ruins of Egypt's great Pharaohs which dotted the land of Egypt that were built along the river's edge. The Dam has been added to twice, thus raising the flood waters and threatening even more of the ancient ruins of Egypt's past. The first works of the ancient past to be threatened by the rapidly rising waters of the Nile River, were the shrines of Philae Island. The water leaves its staining marks on the pylons of the Temple of Isis, as well as on the colonnades of the unfinished Kiosk.

The ever fears of concerns of their water needs for the future of Egypt, led to the consideration of a much larger Dam to be constructed before the old Aswan Dam. The new Aswan High Dam was going to be a modern technical achievement, accomplished with the help of the nations of the United States and England. But with the Egyptian government's attitude leaning more towards the influence of Russia, the United States and England suddenly pulled their support of the project, and it opened the door for the Russians who quickly seized the opportunity, and they moved in. The Aswan High Dam was initiated in the year of 1960, and it was going to stand three hundred and sixty four feet above the ground, and twelve thousand five hundred and seventy feet long at its crest, and the water was going to be six hundred feet above sea level once the Dam was completed.

The larger reservoir was to be formed by this new damming of the Nile River, was going to be called Lake Nasser in honor of Gamal Adbel Nasser, the then President of Egypt. Nasser believed the damming of the Nile River was absolutely necessary for Egypt's future food and water supplies because of its ever increasing population and their future demands. The Dam was going to also produce electricity for Egypt as a byproduct of the dam. The massive generators were supposed to produce two thousand megawatts of electrical power, and the Dam would increase agricultural land along the Nile by over three million acres.

Lake Nasser was one of the largest manmade lakes ever created in the entire world. The new lake measured over three hundred miles long, and it held back five thousand, five hundred and thirty two trillion cubic feet of water when the Dam was finally completed. This vast amount of water was enough for two years consumption by the Egyptian people, as long as other waters flowed in the manmade reservoir, even though the Dam once completed, would not be the highest, nor longest Dam in the world, or would the reservoir be the biggest ever built by man.

One more important accomplishment that came about by the creation of this Dam, has been the recognition of being the only Dam built that would reclaim the entire cost of the construction in just two years of operation. A much more productive Dam will never be built on the face of the earth again. This great Dam contributed to all the strides in shipping and communication along the Nile River and its people of different nations, and with the added advantages of electrical power for new industries soon to develop at a cheap rate, and permanent protection for Egypt against the constant threat of flood and drought, Egypt began to become prosperous.

The Aswan High Dam was scheduled to be completed by the year of 1968, but it was delayed because of many different problems with land, and the massive concrete footings for the Dam's construction, along with the unforeseen problems of losing, under many feet of water, a number of Egypt's extremely important national shrines. The most important shrine to be threatened by the raising water of the Nile River, was the Temple Ramses. The second was built to honor his father and revere the great waters of the Nile. Now, it would be the very waters Ramses blessed that would soon cover his Temple.

After Egypt let the world know she was more than willing to flood many of the great past of ancient Egypt in order to protect the future of modern day Egypt and her people. A multi national band of scientists and engineers were quickly sent to Egypt to study the situation. The work teams were led by Sweden, and it was funded mostly by the United States, to see if there was a way to save Egypt's great ancient past. After many months of studies, a mammoth project was set in motion. The multi nation workforce planned to carve up the great Temple of Ramses, and move it two hundred feet further up the side of the mountain, well above the encroaching waters of the Nile River.

The great Temple of Ramses the Second, was built in the side of the mountain, compounding the problems of dissecting the ancient Temple encountered by the horde of modern day workers so it could be moved. The Temple was carved by Egypt best stone carvers and artists over three thousand years ago, at the height of Egypt's power. The Temple's stone cutters labored nine years to complete their task.

Modern day workers labored long hours in order to cut up, and then move the great Temple as other workers built earthen Dams and high walls to stop the encroaching water from flooding the Temples before the new construction was completed. It was decided to move Ramses Temple completely, before any work was done on the much smaller Temple of his Queen Nefertari, who's Temple was dedicated to the great Egyptian Goddess of love, Hathor. The project engineers were more than willing to allow Nefertari's Temple is lost to the rising waters of the Nile River, if it rose before they were able to start work on her Temple after they have completed work on the larger temple.

Late in 1963, the first phase of the great Dam was completed. The work on the Temple of Ramses started in earnest in the year of 1964, and it was completed on April 17th, 1966. The great Temple was carved two hundred feet into the side of the mountain, and it was situated right on the side of the mountain so that twice a year, the Sun's powerful rays would penetrate the full length of the deep Temple. To shine right on the face of this God King of Egypt's past, carved into the likeness of himself. Ramses' image was surrounded by many worshipped and well respected gods of the Egyptian religions.

The water that forms the vast Lake Nasser reservoir was to be filled by 1975, giving the modern day workers enough time to move both ancient Temples the two hundred feet up the mountain's side. Other shrines that had to be moved were the Sphinxes at the three thousand year old Temple of El Sibu, and the Lions of Protection. Ramses the Second, built the Temple El Sibu, and he listed his numerous children's names on the walls of the structure. The Temple was scheduled to be moved to the new shores of this immense soon to be reservoir, a little over three miles away from where they stood watch over the Nile River for thousands of years past.

Another unforeseen problem soon facing the workers trying to save some of Egypt's great ancient past, was not even considered until the many difficulties of this operation had first started. When man made this immense lake, no one took into consideration what other problems would quickly arise when this much weight from the water was added to a small surface of the earth. The enormous weight of this great new lake, well over twenty trillion pounds, had a rather unexpected effect on the earth. Months after the vast lake was filled to capacity, the area of the Dam was suddenly hit by its first ever earthquake. The earthquake was a major one which measured just five point four on the Richter scale, and since the first quake had struck the area, there have been two other but much less violent earthquakes, which occurred under the lake's vast surface.

The lake waters lose over three billion cubic feet of water yearly to the evaporation from the blazing sun. This evaporation adds greatly to the ecology problems suddenly facing this region of the earth, and it also affects the climate. Scientists did not understand the full affects of this much water being added to the atmosphere, but one effect noted is this much evaporation caused the Nile River waters to become much more saline over the past years. Coupled this with the disappearance of some native species of fish and certain water birds. Ninety five percent of Egypt's thirty four million people live on just seven percent of the country's four hundred thousand square mile area. Most Egyptian people live right on the very edge of the Nile River.

The Aswan High Dam was completed in the year of 1970, and it took almost another five years for the Nile River waters to finally fill the vast Lake Nasser. The Dam is now producing nearly twelve billion kilowatts of electricity a year from the twelve massive turbine generators installed at the Dam site.

There are many other countries the waters from the Nile River flowed through their land boundaries, and each of these countries depends greatly upon the waters of the Nile River in order to sustain life, and grow their crops in their fields.

The Sudan's extremely dry in its northern section, while its southern area is wet. The southern area of the Sudan is a lush and green area filled with much wildlife, while to the north it's a yellow span, with vast oceans of sand for its soil. This area is a vast clay plain, which is bordered by huge mountains on its east, west and southern borders, with an endless desert to the north. The Sudan covers twelve percent of Africa's land surface.

From the Egyptian border all the way down to the capital city of the Sudan, Khartoum. The land is mostly desert land, spotted here and there with small sanctuaries of life known as Oasis. In Khartoum, Arab speaking Moslem Nomads drive their foul tempered camels across the great and ancient trade routes for countless years. Just south of where the White and Blue Nile Rivers merge their waters together, the old farmers raise cotton, millet, corn and peanuts as their main staple crops. Southward, beyond the capital city of Khartoum, there are huge Nile crocodiles who basked calmly along the banks of the Nile River, while huge herds of hippopotamuses, water buffaloes, and also great herds of elephants wallowed in the warm and clean waters of the Nile River.

The Sudan's most important industry is the Gezira irrigation project, which got underway in the early twenties. Watered by a very complex maze of connecting canals and waterways, which is fed by the dammed up reservoir of the Nile River at Sennar River. The Gezira project produced a million and a half acres of productive farming lands, in which wide oceans of cotton, millet and beans are grown. The Gezira project produces more than half of the government of the Sudan's revenues.

The railroads, which transports the cash crops produced in the Gezira project, leads to the coast through Ethiopia, and it makes up the rest of the revenues of the Sudan's economy.

From the ancient acacia trees of the Kordofan province west of the Sudan capital of Khartuom, come over ninety percent of the world's supply of gum Arabic. To the south of the capital, the Sudan's land is infested with the dreaded tsetse fly, along with great swarms of hungry mosquitoes, mostly because much of this land is prone to severe flooding in the wet season of the year. The countless stagnated pools of drying water are vast breeding pools for the bothersome pests. However, Lake Nasser created by the Egyptian's Aswan High Dam, extends the flooding area out to the third step or cataract of the Nile River, some one hundred and fifty miles into the lands of the Sudan.

Through many minor irrigation projects and manmade canals, the water from Lake Nasser actually doubled the land the Sudan was able to cultivate and grow crops. The Sudan covers nine hundred and seventy thousand square miles of land, with a population of over fifteen million people, its largest city being her capital, Khartoum. Its climate is extremely hot throughout the year, and extremely dry in the northern lands, arid, barren regions with a moderate summer rainfall dominate the south.

The poorer lands of Ethiopia, which lies to the east of the Sudan and it shares its borders, its friendly neighbor, and with Somalia to the west. Ethiopia's a mountainous land, and is inhabited by friendly and practical, independent people who had been isolated from outside influences of modern technologies for many past centuries, mainly because of the vast deserts to its north, east and west that successfully cut the nation off from other nations of the region.

The land of Ethiopia divides itself into three distinct, and extremely different climate regions in which to live and try to grow crops within, each region faces its own agricultural and habitual uses and problems. The lush rich region of the Dega steps slopes, range from eight thousand feet above sea level. The land in this region is mostly green, and it is an extremely rich and fertile grassland area which is primarily used for feeding its vast herds of live stock of cattle and goats, as well as for the production of certain cereal grains and other cash crops that only grow in extremely fertile lands.

The Voina dega region ranges of Ethiopia extends from six thousand to eight thousand feet above the sea level, with temperatures constantly hovering in the range of sixty to seventy degrees all year around. This area contains most of the population of Ethiopia, and it also produces the major cash crop of the country which is coffee, as well as the lesser grown crops of cotton, tobacco, grapes and olives that the country mostly exports.

The vast wastelands of Ethiopia are the Quolla region which consists of everything below the six thousand foot level of the nation which includes the barren, extremely arid areas of the Danikil lowlands. Danikil is an endless sea of yellow, unforgiving, steaming hot sand that stretches northeast to the massive Afar Depression which borders the Red Sea to the east, and encompasses the lower reaches of the Ogaden Plateau in the Hararge Province of Ethiopia. This vast expanse of angry and extremely hostel land is spotted with thorn trees, and the scorched ancient stream beds in the quolla region of this nation. Many Arab Nomad bands wander throughout the vast parched lands, driving their herds of goat, sheep and camels while trying to scratch out a rough living in this forbidding region.

Few raw minerals of any great value have even been discovered or successfully worked in this poor land that makes up much of Ethiopia, and there is a serious lack of any concern by its people to try and locate any other deposits, and with none of the minerals developed to any extent. Although the Ethiopians started to mine some gold and platinum in Yubdo, Akobo, and Ugaro, but with very little if any real zest for the work at hand.

Ethiopia's main export is one that has no real income benefit to its poor people at all. It's the endless flow of waters of the Blue Nile River which arches into a great curve from the River's true source, Lake Tana. The flow of this water tumbles down the great waterfalls and plateaus, and then it travels west, taking along with the flowing waters a rich, and well irrigated silt for the farmers of the Sudan and Egypt to claim for their crops.

Ethiopia also covers a land mass of over four hundred and sixty five thousand square miles, along with a rapidly growing population of over twenty three million people. Its largest city also serves as the capital city of the country, Addis Ababa. With a climate that is generally hot throughout the entire year, but with much cooler and more comfortable temperatures in the higher up mountain regions of the nation. Ethiopia has extremely dry and hot winters, and she also enjoys more moderately wet summers, with little if any rainfall in the endless desert regions of the country for the entire year.

Somalia, which does not border or feed the Nile River with any tributaries, has an average annual rainfall of about twelve inches for the entire year. But Somalia enjoys an extremely strategic location, situated on the eastern hook of the African coast south of the Red Sea. Somalia's main harbor at Mogadishu, Somalia's capital, is badly blocked by shallow sandbars, and wrecks of countless ships that had failed to navigate the poor harbor properly.

The familiar coastal ships was well aware they must lighten their loads by the use of rafts, and shore them through the crashing surf while maintaining their ships out to sea to avoid being trapped and sunk in the shallow waters of Somalia.

Between the rivers of Wabi Shabala River and Juba River of Somalia, there is a cash crop of bananas grown primarily for export. Somalia also grows crops of cotton, millet and sugar cane. Somalia's only claim to fame is that she supplies over sixty percent of the world's supply of frankincense and myrrh. Somalia's small land mass only measures a mere two hundred and fifty thousand square miles, with a population of over six point five million people. Its climate is extremely hot and dries the full year round. The rather small nation of Somalia is constantly being plagued with countless wars raging between the many different warlords and gangs, all fighting for control over the extremely poor nation.

There are at least five other countries that border the Nile River below the Sudan. But not one of these other countries depends much on the waters of the Nile River for survival more than the country of Egypt. Because without the waters of the Nile River, Egypt would surely die. Egypt's land is made up primarily of endless deserts. To her west lies the Great Sand Sea, and further west lays the Rebiana Sand Sea in Libya. To her south lies the vast desert of the Sudan, which is part of the Great Sand Sea. To Egypt's east lies the Arabian Desert, with the only caches of life being on the very banks of the Nile River. That is why ninety five percent of the population of Egypt lives along the very banks of the Nile River.

The vast desert that makes up most of the land mass of Egypt has very limited the industrial development, and the growth of the country. Egypt produces oil primarily in Port Said, situated along the shores of the Red Sea. Iron ore is mined from the Aswan area. Egypt's main staple is cotton and rice, along with crops of millet which the Egyptians grow mainly for export.

Egypt covers over three hundred and ninety thousand square miles of land mass. Its capital is Cairo which overlooks the great pyramids, and is also guarded by the ever watchful Sphinxes, and is a mere ninety eight feet above sea level. Egypt's climate is very hot, and her scorching summers having temperatures reaching up and over one hundred twenty degrees during the worst of the months, cooling down to mild winters. It is extremely dry most of the year around as well.

CHAPTER 2 - EGYPT

In the closing months of 1995, a new threat suddenly came glaringly to light for the rest of the world to witness, and it caused Egypt, who is one of the most stable countries in the Middle East. To rise up on her toes and warn the other nations of the world of her intent to go to war.

Ethiopia at this time, was suddenly threatening to detour over eighty percent of the life giving waters that flowed from Lake Tana down to the Nile River, and use this water for a number of planned irrigation projects in the deserts of the lowlands of their country, to help feed the nation's ever expanding population.

Egypt demanded a special session of the United Nations, and they got it in order to air her complaint if Ethiopia cut the flow of Lake Tana, it would cause the collapse of Egypt. Egypt let it be known in no uncertain terms she was well prepared to fight to stop this from happening.

JANUARY 5th, 1996 UNITED NATIONS BUILDING,
NEW YORK CITY, 8:30 A.M.

At a specially scheduled meeting of the emergency Security Council members of the United Nations, a rather heated debate raged on the main floor, with the Egyptian Delegate standing tall on the floor screaming at the top of his lungs be heard by the other members of the meeting. He threatened to start a fire in the Middle East and Upper Africa that would rage for years to come, and burn out the very heart of Central Africa. If Ethiopia was allowed to deprive Egypt of the waters of Lake Tana which fed the Nile River.

Egyptian Ambassador Mohammed Kheir, the likable and well respected Delegate from Egypt, was currently addressing the President of the Security Council, recently placed in power over the United Nations meeting. The original President of the Council was from Egypt, and he was asked to step down in the interest of finding the best possible solution that would suit everyone concerned without prejudice. The new President of the Council was from Sweden.

Ambassador Mohammed Kheir warned the Ethiopian Delegate, and the rest of the Council in no uncertain terms with a pointing and threatening finger, that he would see his country of Ethiopia burned to a cinder before his country would ever allow the Ethiopians to stop any flow of waters from Lake Tana. This warning brought an instant and extremely angry reprimand from the fuming Delegate from the Sudan, who placed his country in the position of backing Ethiopia if war came to the region.

The extremely angry and young Egyptian Delegate pointed his finger at the Ambassador from the Sudan, which instantly brought on his ire, and a flood of curses flew between both men. The President from Sweden banged his gavel on his desk loudly but to no avail. The two men continued to scream at one another, and finally the Council President drew the meeting of the Security Council to an immediate end, and he reset it for eight o'clock the following morning.

That night after the meeting, brought about a number of private and secluded meetings held behind closed doors between many countries involved in the present turmoil, if war broke out between Ethiopia and Egypt. Some private meetings lasted well into the middle of the night, leaving many groggy and extremely tired Delegates sitting at their chairs the next morning.

The Swedish President, Aaron Ostberg, again banged his gavel on his desk, and called the meeting to order. This time the meeting was being held between all the member nations of the United Nations. He took time to warn the Delegate from Egypt before he gave him the floor to speak to the rest of the representatives of the meeting. "In the interest of searching for a more workable solution to this very difficult situation we find ourselves mired in. I expected you gentlemen to refrain from any further name calling, or cursing at any Delegates."

This request from the President of the Council brought a promise from the Ambassador of Egypt, and a rather nervous chuckle from many other Delegates gathered at the Council meeting.

Nevertheless, the Egyptian Ambassador Mohammed Kheir did not mince his words in the least, as he immediately started his conversation off by angrily reading from a list of countries that had already vowed they would back his country in an attack against the nation of Ethiopia, if that nation stanched the flow of water from Lake Tana. If Ethiopia was allowed to reroute any waters from Lake Tana. He read off the names of the countries, "Libya, Algeria, Nigeria, Uganda, Tanzania, the Somalia Republic and Iraq, along with Mali, are in complete sympathy for Egypt's just cause, and for her ancient right to the waters of Lake Tana that she had enjoyed since the beginning of time."

Reading this list of countries brought the Delegate from the Sudan to his feet as he bellowed angrily at not only the President of the Council, but also at the Egyptian Delegate. "Is this a declaration of war sir? Or a search for peace from Egypt, Ambassador Kheir?"

Ambassador Kheir glared harshly at the Sudanese Ambassador as he hissed at him angrily. "Why you old son of a filthy camel eater you, your worthless nation will die long before Egypt dies. I'll assure you of this as I..."

The Sudanese Delegate cut Ambassador Mohammed Kheir off from any further comments as he snarled just as angrily back at him. "You young dung eater, you are forcing me to stand and fight on the side of the nation of Ethiopia as I have already warned you I would yesterday, fool." The Sudanese Ambassador looked around the Council room as he cried out in a bellowing voice to all gathered in the meeting room. "Who among all the countries gathered here today, will join us in our fight against these godless jackals?"

The Delegates from Chad, Niger, Mauritana, and the Central African Republic, along with the Ambassadors of Kenya, Saudi Arabia, Turkey, Sicily and Spain, all stood as one. Along with the Delegates from Iran, standing and promising not to fight unless absolutely necessary. But he let it be known if his country was forced to fight, he would stand behind the nation of Ethiopia. The Delegates from Israel and Jordan also stood. The Sudanese Delegate waited, and once he was certain no one else was going to stand, he sat down along with the other Delegates attending the meeting. Then Syria's Delegate yelled out from his seat that his country would join Egypt in their battle with these godless and lowly dogs of Ethiopia.

All eyes drifted over to the Delegates from the larger countries of the world, all looking for their leadership, and hopefully for a solution to the new threat of war threatening to be released upon the face of the earth again. England's Ambassador was the first one to speak up. She offered that her country wanted to stay neutral in this situation for the time being, as well as did France, and the Baltic Alliance States. Ethiopia's Delegate looked to the Representative from the United States with pleading and questioning eyes.

Ambassador Walters face took on a hard set as he looked from the Ethiopian envoy to the Delegate from Egypt. He wiped his brow and then stated to the members of the United Nations. "Gentlemen and ladies, when this emergency Council was called to order, I was under the impression we were called here looking for a more peaceful solution to an extremely serious problem, and it was our sworn duties to stop a possible march towards another World War. Now, I look at my colleagues gathered here, and I see them using this meeting to choose sides, and to set the stage for war. I suggest we step back and take a breath for ourselves, and see if we can avert this possible war. Please gentlemen, ladies, let's keep the lines of communication open, and use this meeting place for what it was created to be used for, and that is for keeping world peace." He sat back and then stared at the Egyptian Delegate.

The Libyan Delegate suddenly jumped to his feet and cursed the American politician, calling him an "Infidel," and worse before the other members of the Council, and then he quickly stormed out of the great meeting room in a rush, followed closely by the Iraqi Delegate.

The polite Egyptian Ambassador stood again, and he moved to the center of the floor this time. He looked at the many faces of the envoys staring directly at him as they waited for him to speak again. He drew in a breath and then let it out slowly as he flexed his hands and then stated, "I shall continue to speak with anyone in this room to try and stop this soon to be war in this region of the world. I'll continue to talk until all words and understanding are used up. But I warn every country represented here today. If Ethiopia and my country cannot come to a mutual understanding, and if Ethiopia stops the flow of water from Lake Tana in any way, shape or form, my country will have no other alternative but to declare war on Ethiopia, and all who support her in this crime threatening to be committed against my nation of Egypt." With these words spoken, Mohammed Kheir sat down again.

The Ethiopian Delegate stood slowly and then he waited to be recognized by the Council President before he dared to speak further.

The President of the Council looked at the stunned acting Ethiopian Delegate and announced in a calm tone of voice. "The chair now recognizes the Delegate from Ethiopia. You may speak if you so choose, Mohammed Aidid Sir."

"Thank you Mr. President Sir." He bowed towards the Egyptian Delegate as he remarked to him. "I just wanted to assure Ambassador Mohammed Kheir that my country has no intention whosoever of cutting off the flow of water to her friends in Egypt. As everyone here is well aware of, we the people of Ethiopia are locked in our fourteenth year of severe drought. All we are saying is, we're going to divert some of the waters of Lake Tana, and see if we can convert some of the dry lands of my nation into food producing tillage.

"I stand before all the members of this establishment and promise we will not do anything before we consult with Egypt first, and of this Council. Ethiopia begs help from any country who would help her in this project, so we can better feed and care for our own people. But one thing everyone here has to understand. Lake Tana, and all its water truly belongs to the nation of Ethiopia alone. We promise to share this life giving water with Egypt for all times to come. I thank you at this time for hearing me out." The Delegate fell silent as he sat down again.

Ambassador Mohammed Kheir stood quickly and then he walked over to the Delegate from Ethiopia and he put out his hand. Both Ambassadors' shook hands as many other members of the Council clapped as they stood looking at the two men smiling at each other now.

Ambassador Walters from the United States smiled to the other members of the Council as he put his hands up, and the clapping and conversations took a few minutes to stop. Ambassador Walters then said to the other Delegates. "Now this is what this Council is all about. The system does truly work after all. Ambassador Aidid, my country wishes to inform you my country's resources are at your government's disposal, sir. We'll be willing to supply your country with our engineers and machinery, as well as the monies needed to accomplish this great undertaking. It's a good idea to try and get water to the lowlands of your great country sir. Thank you."

England's Delegate stood and she made the same offer, as well as did France's Representative.

Again the Council chamber was flooded with applause and many conversations now, and the remaining Delegates stood and looked at the Ambassador from the United States.

It was now Ambassador Aidid's turn to put up his hand, and he wait for the other Delegates to become quiet before he spoke to the gathered. "Ambassador Walters Sir, my country wishes me to inform you, and the other members of the esteem Council that we knew we could count on the great peoples of the United States for their future assistance in this matter, sir. I offer your country my country's sincere thanks for your kind offer to help, and also for averting a possible war I am most certain no one wanted, sir. Once again I promise you my country will not be the cause of any future war between my nation and the nation of Egypt. I assure you we only want peace, and to feed all our children, sir."

Egyptian Ambassador Mohammed Kheir started to speak when the Delegate from Ethiopia became quiet. "Ambassador Walters Sir, my country also wants to thank the United States and her people for its offer to help with stopping a possible future war in this region of the world. I'm pleased it was all a misunderstanding, and with the help of your country as well as the other nations of the world, and with my own nation's help. I'm quite certain we can get the needed water down to the lowlands and help the people of Ethiopia feed themselves, without hurting my countries interests in the process. Thank you Ambassador Walters Sir."

With these comments made, the applause started again at the meeting. As some Delegates turned to the Representative on either side of them, and they shook hands together as they smiled at one another. All the envoys were jubilant war seemed to be averted, because the people of the world were growing tired of war, from watching all the small wars waging on and tearing old Russia apart. One by one, the many Delegates slowly left the auditorium. Just as fast, the news reporters of the world not allowed in on the closed session, pounced on the Delegates as they left the chamber. The reporters taped and they jotted down every word said.

Every Representative left the Council pleased, all except for the Ambassadors from Libya and Iraq. Even though the Egyptian Delegate did not allow it show, he was deeply distressed over the outcome of the

United Nations meeting. Because he understood down deep in his heart, it was only a matter of time before his country was forced to go to war with Ethiopia. The Egyptian delegate also understood Egypt could ill afford to lose even one drop of water from Lake Tana. The warning from Ramses rang loudly in his ears. 'You must protect the waters of the Nile River at all cost, or Egypt will cease to exist as a nation in this world'.

Ambassador Mohammed Kheir walked past the news reporters and newscasters as if they did not exist, he smiled and waved pleasantly at them, but nevertheless he continued to walk right past the gathering as he rushed out of the building. He outright refused any comments, even when one reporter actually shoved his pocket recorder in his face. Mohammed Kheir wanted to shove the small recorder up the man's ass, but he only smiled and continued to walk, but not before he gave the arrogant reporter a hard shove back, and causing him to almost lose the small recorder along with his balance.

Mohammed quickly made his way to his apartment, and then he placed a call to the Egyptian Consulate on his special phone line hookup. He quickly informed his government official of all that had transpired at the meeting. After finishing his report, Ambassador Kheir was ordered to make contact with the Delegate from Libya. The government official informed Mohammed the Libyan Delegate placed a call to the Consulate, and he requested there be a special meeting setup between the two of them.

Mohammed informed the official of his feeling about being associated with Libya, because of their past involvements with terrorist groups which caused embarrassment for the Arab nations.

The Consulate official snarled nastily back at Ambassador Kheir over the phone. "I don't remember asking you for your god cursed opinion of any of these miserable jackals, sir. I have given you a direct order to meet with the lowly jackal, because in their worthless hands might well rest the future sake of all Egypt, sir. Mohammed Kheir, Egypt's future is more important to me than any mere embarrassment over our association with these Libyan dog eaters, sir. Do your job as you have been ordered and keep your opinions to yourself, sir. Or I shall simply have you replaced, and then your bones will be laying bleached white on the hot desert sands, Ambassador. Do I make myself perfectly clear to you, sir?"

"I hear and I shall obey, wise and great one." Was the only response Ambassador Mohammed Kheir hissed as he slammed the receiver back in its cradle, and then he stared at his reflection in the mirror before him.

The Egyptian politician suddenly leaned back in his chair and took a deep breath for himself, he did not like being talked to in this manner by anyone, especially a representative from his own country. His attendant came in and brought him a shot of Cutty Sark chased with an ice cold beer, and he placed them on the desk in a small silver tray. Then the young man quickly retreated to the kitchen. The young Egyptian aide knew Mohammed was in an extremely foul mood, and he decided to make himself scarce.

Ambassador Mohammed Kheir took the cold beer and rubbed the container over his aching forehead as he let out his breath in a rush, and then took the chilled glass of scotch and downed it in one quick gulp. This caused his body to actually shudder in rejection of the harsh fluid running down his throat. Mohammed threw the glass to the floor and took a sip of beer to wash the foul taste down. He dreaded his next phone call, because once he placed it, he would be trapped and Egypt would be on a fast slide to war, and perhaps her own destruction. He was certain if war came, Egypt would not survive remembering what the United States done to Iraq during that past war, and he understood America would fight as they always did for the right side.

Egyptian Ambassador Kheir fumbled around with the paper he held so tightly between his fingers, on which he wrote down the private number to the Libyan Delegation. As he looked down at the paper, he shook his head sadly and mumbled to himself an angry curse. Then he looked from the paper to the antique French telephone sitting on the edge of his desk, as if it was bidding him to make the call. The Egyptian leaned forward and picked up the receiver, and then dialed the number as if his fingers were going to fall off his hand.

The phone rang three times before it was finally answered by a most threatening sounding voice which growled into the phone angrily. "Libyan Delegation to the United Nations. How may I be of assistance to you and direct this call?"

"Yes. This is The Egyptian Ambassador to the United Nations Mohammed Kheir, and I wish to speak with your Ambassador as I was instructed to do by my..."

The still angry sounding voice instantly cut him off in mid sentence as it snapped back at him over the phone. "You shall wait sir, your call has been anticipated, Ambassador Kheir Sir."

He was placed on hold, as the Arab music instantly replaced the voice on the receiver. Mohammed took this time to take a sip of his warming beer as he waited on the phone.

"Allah Akhbar Mohammed." The not very well liked Libyan Delegate Kamal, offered rather cheerfully into the phone.

"Ambassador Kamal Sir, my Consulate aide has informed me to get in contact with you at once sir. What do you wish to speak to me about sir?"

Ambassador Mohammed Kheir demanded to know from the other Ambassador in a rather hot tone of voice.

There was a slight and quick laugh on the other end of the line as the Libyan offered. "Mohammed, do you dislike me and my country so much that you cannot be civil with me, sir? Have you now lived so long in the world of the god cursed lowly infidels in the United States, that you're so much like them yourself, sir?" Ambassador Kamal snapped in the phone in an obvious attempt to embarrass the Egyptian politician.

"Please forgive my terrible insult and lack of manners to you, Ambassador Kamal. I'm truly sorry and can only offer I wasn't thinking properly, sir. Allah Akhbar my old friend Ambassador Kamal. Perhaps I have lived too long in the world of the loathsome and hated infidels, that I'm forgetting my good manners to be displayed before a fellow brother Arab, sir. What is it you wanted to talk about with me sir?"

Ambassador Kamal had known Mohammed for many years, and he has disliked him as much as he understood Kheir hated him. He truly enjoyed embarrassing Mohammed, and he did it whenever he got the chance. He smiled in satisfaction as he spoke again to the Egyptian over the phone. "Mohammed Kheir, I want to set up a private meeting with you as soon as possible. We have a lot to discuss my friend. We Arabs have to protect ourselves from these foul camel eaters, and I have many ideas to explain to you. When can we meet?"

Mohammed looked at his watch and then grumbled at the Libyan Delegate. "It's now six o'clock, please give me some time to eat and to take a quick shower. I shall be pleased to meet with you later tonight, if that is all right with you, Ambassador Kamal?"

"This time will work out just fine with me Mohammed. We shall meet tonight at eight o'clock at my hotel. But not in my room, sir. We'll meet in a second room, 1432. You shall see the reason for this request later tonight I assure you sir."

"This is fine with me Ambassador Kamal. I shall be there at eight o'clock tonight. Allah Akhbar Ambassador Kamal."

"Thank you for your kind hospitality. Allah Akhbar Ambassador Mohammed."

"It is given in the name of true friendship for my Arab brother," Mohammed Kheir said as he hung up and then slugged down the rest of his beer, in an attempt to wash out the foul taste of speaking to Kamal left in his mouth. He was aware Kamal was responsible for the deaths of thousands of fellow Arabs throughout his country of Libya, and the Middle East.

This knowledge made it almost impossible for him to forgive, and to treat this most ugly man with any sort of proper respect. He believed only animals killed their own kind, and Ambassador Kamal liked killing, even if his targets were fellow Arabs. This Libyan jackal went against all the words of the Holy Qu'ran, and its sacred writing of the Great Prophet Muhammad Himself, which stated an Arab should never kill a fellow Arab. He could not help despising this evil man, and everything he and his country stood for.

Without looking up, or without asking his young man servant had setup the table and placed Mohammed's food out when he hung up the phone. His servant was good, and he could anticipate what he would want to eat and when he would want it served. The servant put out a thick New York cut steak with his favorite, French fries along with Italian bread and butter. He put out another bottle of cold Michelob light beer. The servant poured the cold beer in a chilled glass as Ambassador Mohammed said. "One good thing the foul land of the lowly infidels have, and we can never have in Egypt is good beer."

Both men laughed and then the man servant quickly disappeared from the room. Leaving Mohammed Kheir by himself for the moment.

The powerful Egyptian Ambassador looked at the golden liquid as it bubbled in his glass and mumbled to himself. "You better have all the beer you can get now, because once the fighting starts you'll immediately be pulled out of the United States, and this American liquid is not offered for sale back home." Then he thought again as he took a sip of beer. 'They will not dare send me home. My government will have to keep me here to negotiate a peace to the fighting surely coming.' He settled in enjoying his meal. Once he finished, he left the table and moved to the living room. From out of nowhere, the servant appeared and cleaned off the table and then brought another beer to his master as he sat in the soft chair. The servant put on the RCA television, and he asked Mohammed what he wanted to watch.

"I don't have much time to spare, fool." He looked at his watch that read six forty five and then replied. "Put on one of the cursed X rated tapes for my pleasure, let's see. Put on the one with three men and two women." He watched as the television suddenly came to life, and a young blonde performed oral sex with two men at the same time. Then he looked to the young man servant smiling as he watched the film with him.

"Another great invention from these lowly infidels in the great land of sin and no respect, no wonder they're in such trouble in their own foul country. Warn me when it's seven forty five. That shall give me enough time to get over to the cursed room One, Four, Three, Two and meet with this lowly jackal from Libya." The Egyptian Ambassador then settled down and watched the tape. He promised himself to order two women when he got back from his soon to be most upsetting meeting with this dog politician from Libya.

At exactly seven forty five, the Egyptian man servant cautiously interrupted Ambassador Kheir as he offered in a soothing tone of voice. "Ambassador Kheir Sir, it's time for you to go sir."

"Thank you Salim, and that'll be all for now. This meeting should not take any longer than three hours, so I want you have two young women for hire here when I return. Blondes, young, Americans at that. Get them good and drunk and warmed them up for me, young fool. I want to be treated well tonight when I get back to my room. I shall need it I'm afraid after this forced meeting with that lowly jackal from Libya." He went out of the double doors and down the hallway. He had to go to the elevator, and up two floors to get to room 1432. He left his prayer rug behind which was rare, because he never went anywhere without it. But he never gave it a second thought this time because he was so upset meeting with the Libyan.

Within minutes he stood in front of the doors of Suite 1432, and then he knocked on them. Another man servant, who obviously also served as a bodyguard as well for the always angry Libyan Delegate, opened the doors and he immediately ushered Mohammed in the room and said to him at the same time. "This way please sir."

The large Arab servant led him to a room with two men already seated at a table. Mohammed saw the bulge under the man servant's left arm, obviously made from a hidden weapon he carried. The room was large and strangely it seemed filled with a most annoying vibration, and there was a distinctive hum to it also.

The Libyan Ambassador Kamal, sitting at the table with his Kaffiyeh headdress on, and his prayer rug laid out facing Mecca, noticed Mohammed looking around and commented. "That hum and vibrating you're experiencing is coming from an anti bugging device system, my dear Mohammed. This is so no one can listen, or possibly tape anything of what we're going to talk about here tonight, sir. A great invention by one of our little yellow friends from the Far East, Ambassador Mohammed. Please, sit down Mohammed and make yourself comfortable, I believe you already know the Iraqi Representative, Mohammed Ahmed Nimeiri here, sir."

Mohammed Kheir nodded towards the Iraqi Representative who nodded back in return.

"Have something to eat please, a drink to help settle you down some Mohammed? What is your, excuse the Americanism please, poison? If I remember right my old friend, Michelob light is it not sir?" With this the man servant automatically reappeared with a cold Michelob, and he offered it to Mohammed, who took the bottle. There was no glass offered him which made Kamal laugh and add. "Alcohol is forbidden to us Arabs. But here in the great land of sin, by Allah's great will everything is allowed to us. But we have to give up some of these creature comforts offered here to remember our great customs. Therefore, no glass, Mohammed." All three men laughed as the man servant offered a scotch to Nimeiri, and a martini to Kamal.

The Egyptian politician looked at the food, hot tea, and goat cheese wrapped in baked pita bread, grilled fish and olives covering the surface of the two large serving trays. The three politicians toasted each other's health, and they placed their half finished drinks on the end table in front of them.

Ambassador Kamal sat back and offered with patience in his tone of voice. "I guess you're wondering why it was so important for you to meet with us here tonight, Ambassador Kheir. Please allow me to explain further to you my fellow Arab brother. Mohammed Nimeiri and his followers are going to overthrow the useless and hated Saddam Hussein within the next three days or so. Most of the Iraqi military is going along with the overthrow, because the people of Iraq are fed up with the mad dog eater, and all his useless ways. Besides, this is imperative to our future plans at the same time. Plans that include your nation of Egypt, and with your country, our plans will be complete, Mohammed.

"As you may be aware of by now Ambassador Mohammed, my country has been having some serious problems with that little shit of a country of Chad. We intend to destroy this god cursed miserable country completely once and for all, and now with Ethiopia threatening to cut off your water supply to Egypt. This latest threat also adds to the reasons why to fight the loathsome people who try and call themselves fellow Arabs, my brother. Iraq is willing to help us, as well as the other countries who have already offered you help at the recent United Nations meeting earlier today, sir. You understand well Mohammed, the Sudan is made up of many unclean Arabs who bred with the foul and cursed blacks, and they have destroyed their true bloodlines of all the Arab people, Ambassador.

"Ethiopia is less of an Arab nation than even the worthless Sudan is. So we offer no excuses for attacking Ethiopia, but merely to help you and your country in her times of greatest needs. There are many other Arab countries who say they're against us and our beliefs. But once they see we'll easily win this upcoming war, and becoming a world power in the process as well. They'll come together and join us in our holy cause against all lowly infidels of the world, and we can complete the great prophesy of old, a total Arab world. We have the means at hand of destroying any country we chose. Yes Ambassador Mohammed Kheir, this includes the once all powerful United States if we so desire, and we'll get the job done properly sir."

Ambassador Kheir laughed as he snapped back at the man he disliked so much. "Ambassador Kamal, you were always a dreamer as I remember. You live in a world all your own, fool. How could you possibly offer the threat you can destroy such a power as the United States? You, Ambassador Mohammed Nimeiri, you above all others should know the oversight of this dream better than anyone of the other Arab States. Look at what the United States military forces have done to your country a few years back, sir. Your country is still trying to rebuild the awesome destruction created by the might of the United States forces. And now you try and tell me your foolish country is willing to risk the powerful hand of the United States to close tightly around the throat of your foul country and its people once again, sir? Obviously I'm truly in the presence of madmen who live in a fool's world. Your bones will be bleached white in the burning sands of the desert by the angry Eye of Allah."

Ambassador Kamal hissed nastily as he interrupted Kheir's defaming words. "Dog of a lowly infidel. How dare you mock us when we're offering your country life, and you seem to be leaning towards death, you godless pig? I warn you Mohammed Kheir, the only other door that'll be left open to you and your foolish nation, only if you do not take the help we propose to you. Is the blazing sun, the always angry Eye of Allah, and the slow death of your country and all its foolish people, if you don't stand and fight side by side along with us. Your cities will turn to dust, as will your people die of thirst in the sand that'll cover all your foul cities, fool."

"Ambassador Kamal, I assure you many foolish countries have tried to destroy the Great Satan of the United States throughout the steps of history, and she is still here and she is still strong as ever. Or the fools tried to take over the world with the empty and useless threats of the new weapons of terrible worldwide destruction. Always new weapons that would've destroyed the countries fighting against them. But as you can plainly see from history, none of these great weapons of death or useless threats have been successful, because the United States is still alive.

"What the devil makes you believe for one second of time that you can possibly accomplish what other foolish countries have tried and failed in? Besides, we in Egypt are not interested in fighting, or taking over the world. All my country is interested in and wants and demands, is the continuous flow of water from Lake Tana and the Nile River, and that is all sir. I'm willing to leave world conquest to madmen like you foul fools, with your crazy dreams of great weapons of mass death and destruction. As it has been said for centuries past, 'Follow the filthy Vulture and he will surely lead you to death'." Mohammed said as he laughed.

Ambassador Kamal glared harshly at the Egyptian Ambassador for a moment, and then he snapped angrily. "Fool of a non-believer, it's only because you're a fellow Arab brother that you're still alive and able to laugh, pig. Because no one talks to me like you just have, and lives to laugh again, fool. I shall try once more to point out your errors in judgment in not choosing to join forces with our two nations. Because like it or not Ambassador Kheir, we're the very salvation of Egypt and all her children. I intend to unite all the Arab nations of the Middle East and Africa in one great force, and then lead them against Jerusalem and the Jews who slaughter our fellow Arab brothers and sisters. Where the Zionists will fall to the ever consuming yellow fire, and what is left of them will be bleached by the all powerful Eye of Allah.

"Mohammed, allow me to inform you of something about some of our new weapons in our possession, and how we have come upon them. Many foolish Russian scientists have fled the dying lands of Russia, and they have refused to join the Baltic Alliance, or give their vast knowledge to the hated United States, or other nations of the world but my nation.

"Hatred of the loathsome imperialist country of the evil devil and home of Satan is still felt by many Russian people. Little by little, all these foolish scientists have found their way to our Arab countries. All we had to do was offer these lowly dogs of the desert some money and female friends, and they were willing to do anything for our country, and it's just cause. We procured some extremely angry Japanese technicians who have helped the hated Russian scientists develop some of these new weapons of mass destruction.

"Mohammed, we have two hundred nuclear warheads currently in our arsenal, and the missiles to deliver them to any part of the world we so choose to attack with the evil things. We also have a hundred warheads from the Russian missiles, before they were moved from their silos, and dismantled by the Ukrainian fools. In addition to these weapons, we have the means to destroy all the Jew tanks that had dealt us the fatal blow in our numerous wars waged against the despicable Jews of years past. But we'll need your country in order to accomplish the part of operation we're proposing to you at this meeting, fool. I shall explain all of this to you later on, if you join our countries to rid the world of its trash.

"We also have a good number of chemical weapons in our possession that had been developed many years ago in Russia. But they were so powerful and hard to control that even the Russian fools were afraid of them, and they decided not to continue developing them any further. Now the worthless Russian scientists are here with us, and the fools are free to work on any type of weapon of mass destruction they may choose to continue to develop for our use, Mohammed. The foolish Russian scientists gave new birth to these once forgotten weapons of mass death, and we now have them resting in our arsenal, and are ready to be employed against any enemy of our nations. I warn you we're not afraid to use them either sir.

"We have also developed a number of new and specialized anti personnel weapons to employ to stop any possible invading enemy troops, as well as new weapons to knock out entire wings of warplanes and attack helicopters while in flight. Mohammed, we have also developed an anti ship missile that is more than capable of destroying the great warships of the United States sending their hated warplanes or missiles out against our Arab nations of the world. What has happened to Iraq, is not going to happen to us I assure you if we engage the fools in combat, Mohammed. The enemy ships and planes or tanks are not going to get at us this time around. If your country joins forces with us, you shall be on the winning side of the war this time, my Arab brother. We're not even afraid of the once feared United States.

"These lowly god cursed infidels are no longer the power they once were, they now have to rely heavily on volunteers to man their worthless Armies who are the scum of the earth that could not get a real job in the civilized world. Mohammed, you have to believe us, we'll win any fight we engage in sir. The United States does not have the belly for fighting a real war any longer, and the Russian dogs are no longer a threat against any nation of the world. The yellow devils of China will eat each other, and that'll leave only the Arab nations in complete control of the world. Not even the hated Jews stand a chance against our might, not with these new weapons we possess and will employ in any war." Ambassador Kamal stopped speaking and looked at Mohammed staring at his tightly clasped hands as he held his breath, not willing to speak at this moment for fear of what he might tell this madman to his face.

Mohammed's mind was working like it had never worked before. He hated the position he found himself locked in, having to dare consider working with these son's of the jackal.

Ambassador Kamal grew impatient and finally barked at the Egyptian politician. "Mohammed Kheir what do you think? Are you going to fight on the side of Allah? Or are you going to side with the lowly infidels of the world, the loser in this case, and stand by and watch as your great country slowly shrivels up and blows away in the hot desert winds of the night, sir?"

Egyptian Mohammed Kheir glared angrily into the pitch black eyes of the Libyan Kamal, and then hissed angrily at him. "So this is what you meant by the consuming yellow fire, the hated nuclear weapons. I fear this much, death by nuclear weapons."

Kamal repeated his words rather confidently. "Are you going to stand by and watch your great country slowly dry up from the lack of water. Or will you fight for her and her children?"

"Lowly sand flea, how dare you think I would ever sit by for one second of time, and watch my great country die before my burning eyes, fool. May Allah strike me dead if I dare so commit such a foul sin. I'm not in a position to make such a decision on my own accord, sir. I'm going to have to report to my President and inform him of all you have informed me of tonight, and then get his permission to join forces with your little Army."

"Mohammed, you fool yourself most unwisely here I fear." Kamal hissed as he interrupted and then went on with his angry words. "This is no game and I assure you we're no small Army I'm asking your country to join forces with. We're the future of the world, like the great Satan of the Americas once was. Allah is on our side, the side of right Mohammed."

Mohammed Nimeiri decided to speak for the first time since the two Ambassadors started sparring with each other. "My dear Ambassador Mohammed Kheir, many weapons Ambassador Kamal speaks about here have not yet been revealed to me until this very moment, sir. Now I know I and my nation is on the side of right and might. Once my country's revolution is complete, and I take over power of my country of Iraq, I shall wreak my revenge on the miserable countries of Kuwait and Saudi Arabia. For daring to assist the cursed American dogs who have destroyed my country. I remember your country has also joined the enemy of Iraq, but I'm more than willing to forgive your country's error in good judgment, Mohammed.

"I understand completely your nation was forced to assist Saudi Arabia, because many of your people worked in that miserable coun¬try of lowly traitors to the Arab world. I promise if you join forces with us in our future quest, your country will never have to worry about money again. Because we'll put your people in charge of the Saudi Arabia's vast oil fields once that country is destroyed. There are many other reasons for your country to join forces with us which will become much clearer to you in the near future, once the fighting is over with and we divide up the countries that we want for our own needs. Just think of it Mohammed, think of what you might end up with yourself, if you talk your great government into joining forces with us."

Mohammed looked into the cold eyes of this brother of Allah from Iraq. He never wanted to kill a man like he wanted to kill this hated jackal. His hands actually shook, angry over having to be in the company of these two animals who talked of the annihilation of many Arab countries as they would talk of killing a wild boar. He cursed his luck and the gods for knowing he was going to be forced to deal with these two evil types of people. This thought was the only reason he did not kill these two foul dogs this very second.

The fuming Egyptian politician drew in his breath and then spoke slowly. "Again, I have to repeat that I'm not in the position to make this grave a decision on my own accord, sir. I shall inform my government of your kind offer of assistance, and they'll give me their determination, and then I shall inform you what that decision is."

The Libyan Ambassador Kamal stared back at this middle aged Egyptian for a long moment and he thought before replying. "Very well then Mohammed Kheir, I shall trust you to deliver my message to your government leaders, and I'll wait not so patience their response, fool. A simple word of warning to you though on this day, Mohammed. Don't allow their answer be too long in coming, or we shall withdraw our offer of life to you and your nation, and then your country will become our enemy in the upcoming war. Another warning I must issue to you my dear Arab friend. If I find out that you have talked against me or my plan to your leaders. I shall have your foul bones bleaching white in the sands of the desert before another day passes." Kamal stopped talking and he glared harshly at this tall Egyptian who returned his stare with as much hatred as the Libyan politician held in his eyes.

Ambassador Kamal was the one who suddenly broke the intense stare down, by standing up and then he walked over to a chest of drawers and opened the second drawer, and then he removed a small black box covered with a number of dials and switches. He brought it over to Ambassador Mohammed Kheir and held out his hands and offered it to him, and then waited for the Egyptian Representative to take possession of the box.

Mohammed looked at the Libyan politician with questioning eyes. At first, he thought it might be a bomb of some sort.

The Libyan politician noticed the fear suddenly etched in Mohammed's eyes, and he added to him in a sharp tone of voice and a smirk on his lips. "No Mohammed, it is not a bomb, I have no interest in ending your worthless life at this time and this easily, fool. This little beauty here is the invention of our little yellow Asian friends. This box is the thing creating this slight humming and vibrating you have been feeling throughout our entire conversation, sir. I warn you to use this device when you and your President speak of our plan. This is the only way no one will be able to listen in or tape your conversations, sir. It shall also insure the secrecy of our plans until we put them in action. You may leave us now Mohammed, because I know how you feel towards me and I understand this emotion, be assured my friend the feelings are mutual."

Ambassador Kamal actually turned his back on Mohammed at this point with sheer distain in his actions and thoughts, and then he started a conversation with Ambassador Nimeiri.

Neither man made any further acknowledgment of Mohammed presence within the room, while he stood holding onto the small box, and he slowly turned and left the room. But before he was completely out of the room, Ambassador Kamal called out without turning to him. "Allah Akhbar Mohammed, I'm afraid you're getting to be a most uncivilized Arab after all I fear, my old Arab friend."

Mohammed felt terribly embarrassed, because he forgot his manners a second time with the Libyan. He allowed his personal feelings for this ugly man to rule over what was good for his country. He stopped and replied in a calm voice. "I see I beg your pardon once again Ambassador Kamal, may Allah be with you my friend. Allah Akhbar."

Ambassador Kamal stopped speaking to the Iraqi Ambassador for a second as he listened to the response from Mohammed, and then he smiled to Ambassador Nimeiri as he offered him. "Well, maybe there is still some hope remaining for this Egyptian dog after all sir."

Mohammed left his meeting with Ambassador Kamal fuming, and he hurried to the bank of elevators, and within seconds he was standing at the door to his private apartment. He opened the door only to find two young and beautiful American looking naked blondes. One of them was busy riding on Salim's lap. The blonde riding Salim looked over her shoulder as he entered the apartment and said to him. "Get out of your clothes and come and join us for some fun and games." She purred sexily without missing a stride on Salim's shaft, while the other blonde snorted up a long line of cocaine Salim had laid out for the two young women, and she chased it down with cold beer. As she saw Mohammed, she walked over to him and began to fumble with his clothes while staggering as she tried to kiss him.

The large and good looking and powerful Egyptian politician gave her a slight shove backwards which caused her to stumbled, and then she fell to the floor. Lying with her legs spread apart the way she landed, she looked up at Mohammed and then laughed hauntingly at him. Then she eyed him for a moment then beckoned him to come and join her on the floor with her finger and a huge grin on her lips.

The blonde riding on Salim's lap was soon done with the young man, and then she offered to get Mohammed ready for her friend with a special gift of oral sex.

He looked to the young woman still sitting on the floor. The other blonde who was now sitting on the edge of the bed next to the exhausted Salim, and she saw him looking at the other naked blonde and she said to him in a slurred voice. "Oh sir, Cathy will also help me bringing you great pleasure of the body and mind on this wonderful night, sir. She just loves to help me with someone who I want to entertain."

This kind offer brought a quick smile to his lips as he replied to the two women. "I shall take you two ladies up on that kind offer you have just made to me, but first I have to make a very important phone call. While I do this, please feel free to show Salim even more of your great pleasures of the body you hold within yourselves. Salim will give you more of the white powder of the head, and more beer for your enjoyment."

With this said, Ambassador Mohammed Kheir went into his massive bedroom, but he had to bodily stop one of the young blondes who actually tried to following him into the other room. He merely smiled at her, he was still amazed because this was the first time he had ever seen a young female without pubic hair. This turned him on more than the offer of oral sex with the two girls at the same time.

When he closed the door to his bedroom, he cried to himself. "May Allah forgive me for my many weakness of the soul and body and mind while I live upon this good earth." As he allowed his thoughts to linger on the lovely vision of the young blonde without hair between her legs. He then carefully laid out his prayer rug properly facing Mecca and prayed for the life of his country. After five Salaams he rose to his feet and rolled the rug up carefully, and then quickly setup the small box Ambassador Kamal gave him moments ago and plugged it into the wall socket. A instant and most annoying low hum and vibration immediately emitted from the small box while he held it in his hands.

He placed the small box on the top of his chest of drawers and then quickly dialed the number also given him by Ambassador Kamal. As the phone rang he was busy listening to the sounds of the pleasure coming from the outer room of his massive apartment, and wished no one would answer the phone so he can get to know the two blonds and he could go out there and join in the fun and games with the two naked and beautiful women. But his hopes were dashed when on the third ring, a nasty sounding voice answered sharply. "Faisal Sadat's office."

Ambassador Mohammed Kheir was shocked and confused at the same time as he replied to the voice on the other end of the phone. "Err... please forgive me sir, but I must have dialed the wrong number by accident I believe sir. I wanted to speak to Minister Amr Moussa. I shall try to ring him once again. Thank you and I'm sorry for dialing the wrong number sir."

The voice on the other end of the phone growled back at him in an extremely angry tone of voice. "I assure you that you have dialed the correct number Ambassador Mohammed Kheir. Amr Moussa no longer represents any interests of Egypt and her people, sir. The son of the great leader Sadat, now rules over the two Egypt's as one, sir. You shall remain on the foul line Ambassador Mohammed Kheir, while I get the new President of Egypt for you to speak with, sir. He was expecting your call for quite a while now I warn you sir. You have taken your time with calling him as you were ordered to do. The President has been in a rage for over an hour, while waiting for your call to come to him, Ambassador. Hold the line please sir."

The stunned Egyptian Ambassador looked into the end of the receiver while wondering what was happening to his country he was unaware of. He had no idea the other President of Egypt was in any trouble in his country. A long second passed as the sound of his own breathing filled his ears, until the phone finally came back to life, and someone on the other end offered him in a sharp tone of voice. "Well Ambassador Mohammed Kheir, whatever took you so long to get in touch with me after your god cursed meeting with the great Libyan fool and his worthless cohort who held the private meeting with you, fool?"

"Sir, the meeting had lasted a little longer than I had first expected it to, and I also took a few minutes to myself, to think about all that I have been informed of at this foul meeting of tonight. I was extremely confused by what was offered to me, and I'm further confused by hearing Egypt has a new President, and I..." He started to offer but he was immediately cut off by the angry sounding voice on the other end of the phone.

"Please you foul fool you, don't try and compound your sins and evil ways against your country and religion by lying here, to the rather long list of the other crimes you have committed against me and your country, Ambassador Mohammed Kheir. I happen to know you currently have a pair of young American whores in your apartment at this very moment sir, as well as the forbidden drugs and even liquor. Perhaps it's time you return to our country, and you become retrained in the many Egyptian ways and beliefs again, fool. You're fast becoming more than an embarrassment to your own country, and to myself also, Ambassador. You're becoming one of the lowly infidel yourself, sir. What is this god cursed humming I'm hearing now over this phone? Are you playing a game with me Mohammed? It's not very wise to anger me so, it could cost you your worthless life, fool." President Sadat suddenly screamed in the receiver.

Ambassador Mohammed Kheir was stunned this man on the other end of the phone knew so much about his private escapades. But as a good politician as he was, he recovered quickly and replied to the angry sounding voice without knowing his man servant was reporting his every move to the new Egyptian President. "I have been ordered to report to Minister Amr Moussa, and to no one else on this earth, sir. He's the man who gave me this assignment in the first place, and to only him I will answer to sir."

"I assure you dog of a fool, you'll have to speak loud to the vast sea of sands of the desert and earth, because he now rests under them, Ambassador Kheir. He was a man of ill health for quite a while now Ambassador, and it finally caught up with the great fool and his foul lifestyle he chose to enjoy. And if you're not much more carefully with the way you're daring to speak to me, you might soon join him, you foul and cursed son of a filthy sand flea. You'll give me your report, or I shall feed your heart to a lowly camel, Ambassador Kheir."

There was deadly silence on the phone from both men for the moment.

Ambassador Mohammed Kheir sighed deeply as he replied in total submission to the angry sounding voice on the other end of the phone this time. "Very well then sir. May Allah protect you at all times, sir. I have met with this hated Libyan Ambassador Kamal as I have been instructed, he is an extremely upsetting and most evil man and..."

"What is this cursed hum I'm constantly hearing over this foul phone while I'm speaking with you, fool! It's most annoying, Ambassador!" The new President of Egypt, Sadat growled as he actually stuck his finger in his ear and wiggled it.

"My President, that's the sound being emitted from a special scrambler device given to me by the terribly upsetting Libyan Ambassador. It was given to me by Ambassador Kamal himself, sir. It's to help safeguard us against anyone listening in on our conversation and..."

"Don't speak another foul word to me over the cursed phone then, you're ordered to report to the Egyptian Consulate immediately, and bring your foul new machine along with you, Ambassador Kheir. If you have to talk to me in this foul a matter that you feel you need a special scrambler device to help protect our conversation's privacy. Then I want you in a better secured area and on a secured line at the same time, fool. You're to leave immediately for the Consulate. It's almost eleven thirty your time in New York City. I shall be in the United States by no later than ten o'clock tomorrow morning, Ambassador. I want to hear your full report of that foul meeting that you attended personally, sir. That is all I have to offer to you at this present time, Ambassador Mohammed." With this said, President Sadat hung up, leaving Mohammed with a dead receiver held in his hands.

For a fleeting second, Mohammed Kheir actually gave some thought about going over to the United States Consulate, and requesting political asylum, and then inform the American authorities of all that was going on behind the closed doors in the Arab world. But this thought was quickly driven out of his mind, because no matter how corrupted he had become lately in the ways of the West. He still loved his country above all else, and he was no traitor to his country or his fellow Egyptians either. He sat back and then listened to the sounds of pleasure still coming from the next room.

Then he stood and walked over to his closet and removed the Arab dress, which he was required to wear to enter the Egyptian Embassy when he visited it. He removed his western style clothes and dressed in his robes, and then walked out of his room and surveyed the scene being displayed before him. Salim was seated on the couch, sound asleep, and the two blondes were servicing one another and paid no attention to him.

The Egyptian Ambassador Mohammed Kheir watched the interesting spectacle of twisted and naked female bodies, and then cursed himself for having to leave the situation. He walked over to Salim and slapped the young man hard on his bare leg. Salim's eyes immediately flew open from the force of the blow to his leg, and he instantly saw Ambassador Mohammed Kheir leaning over him, and he jumped to his feet and staggered a bit on his feet.

"Fool, when the two young ladies are done with one another, you shall give them each one thousand American dollars apiece, and then you shall usher them out of the door, Salim." Mohammed Kheir held out a fist full of one hundred dollar bills and offered it to the young and confused man. The two women stopped what they were doing to each other and looked up at him. Then they thanked Mohammed for the money as they took the cash and quickly folded and held on to it, as the Egyptian politician ordered the two women.

"I want the both of you young ladies to return to my apartment tomorrow night at the same time, and I want the both of you to be as hot as you were here tonight. I want to see if you two young ladies can wear me out, like you have obviously done to poor little Salim here. I'm of much more stemma than he is in possession of."

The youngest looking blonde woman who shaved herself clean in the private area of her body, laughed pleasantly as she said with a huge grin on her lips to the Egyptian politician. "We shall be back here tomorrow, and tomorrows tomorrow for you kind sir. With bells on if you so wish of us, and we shall exhaust you with even more pleasures than you have ever dreamed possible in your lifetime, kind sir. Of this I promise to you with all of my heart and soul sir."

With this said to the large and good looking young Egyptian politician, she bent her head down again and then she went back to what she was doing to the other young woman moments ago, before Mohammed had interrupted them and their lovemaking to each other. This display made him laugh as he turned and then left his apartment, closing the door behind him quietly as he left. He was still extremely upset that he was forced to leave the two young women to head over to the Consulate.

At a second emergency meeting of the United Nations was called for, this time by the nation of Japan. The new Japanese Delegate addressed all the other Council members, with Mr. Genshiro Nangaku venting his sheer outrage before the other members as he almost roared at them. "I have come here to demand a seat for Japan at the Security Council meetings, and again the United States has chosen to block our request, and our right to sit in on and be part of current world affairs, as a permanent member of this most esteem Council. The United States has forgotten the fact that in 1992. They sent their then President, and many of their big business representatives to our country with their hats held in their hands, begging for Japan to buy more of their inferior American made products. My country did this as an ally to the United States, and it has led to the complete collapse of much of Japan's own economy.

"My government shall never forget, nor will she ever forgive the terribly ugly slur tactics employed by the United States workforce over the passing years that quickly followed. The worse of all was the one that still turns my stomach ill, 'Out of work, eat your Toyota'. Or that other extremely nasty remark, 'If you want to buy Japanese products then you better be ready to apply for Japanese welfare.' And many other nasty remarks far worse than these two, but I'll not repeat them here before you. The United States has also blamed Japan for its countless problems, and we were made to suffer the humiliation we are still suffering even to this day."

These sharp remarks caused a slight mumbling throughout the gathered Delegates of the meeting, and it prompted the United States Representative to stand in protest over Nangaku's last remarks made against his country and her people. But he was immediately waived back to his seat as the gavel fell, and the President of the Council demanded quiet in the chamber. Then the Secretary General asked Ambassador Nangaku to continue with his remarks.

"Gentlemen, is it a no wonder that Japan is presently marred with violent protests, demanding American companies and their interests and holdings be forced to leave Japan. I'm certain every one gathered here today remembers when Japan allowed the United States automobiles into our most honorable country, and what those Viet Nam veterans did in return against us. They started a movement to stop buying Japanese cars and products in the United States. In just one year's time, our car exports have went from six million cars a year, down to under one million vehicles.

"This year's export of our cars and trucks to the United States, is expected to be a mere twenty five thousand vehicles. And what has happened to Japan when we were forced to come to the United States with our hat held in our hands? All our pleas for help have fallen upon deaf ears, and now the United States leadership is refusing to help us in the least. Is my country still being punished because of the war that most of the civilians of my country never raised a weapon against the United States? Now my country is mired in vast debt owed too many other countries of the world, and the United States is strong and powerful militarily and economically.

"We need help, and we also demand to be allowed to join the Security Council as a full member of the Council, over the United States constant objections against our request. We have paid our dues to the world, and Japan feels she is entitled to a full membership with the Council. If we're not allowed to join this Council then Japan will withdraw her support for the United Nations, and what it stands for in the flow of the world. Thank you gentlemen for hearing my words." Ambassador Nangaku then bowed to the members and then sat.

When the Delegate from Japan sat down, the Representative from the United States requested permission to address the Council members next. Ambassador Ostbery looked at the Delegate, and then he gave him a simple nod, and Ambassador Walters immediately took the floor and began speaking right off. "Thank you for allowing me to address this esteem Council Mr. Secretary General Sir, fellow members of this Council. I cannot tell you how pleased and honored for me to have the honor to address the members. It seems our esteemed friend from Japan has made the comment we're still punishing Japan for her part in the war in the Pacific.

"Please allow me ask the learned Gentleman from Japan a question. Why is it Japan makes no mention of this war she started in any of her history books for her children to learn from? Could it be they still don't want the youth of their own country to know what their once proud ancestors have allowed lose upon the civilized world? Could they possibly still be ashamed of what they have done, or are they just trying to ignore what they did, sir?"

The Japanese Ambassador Nangaku jumped up to his feet again, red in his face as he shouted angrily at Ambassador Walters, and the rest of the members of the Council. "How dare you, how dare you speak of Japan in this foul a manner, Ambassador Walters! I shall have you know that Japan is not ashamed over any actions now, or for the past history of my country. Japan owes no explanations for past situations that once faced my country, and.."

The Japanese Delegate was cut off by the banging of the gavel, as Council President Ostbery drowned him out by shouting from his seat, the Delegate from the United States had the floor, and the Delegate from Japan was to take his seat and remain silent. It took a moment to get order restored and for Ambassador Walters to start speaking again.

Ambassador Walters spoke once the Japanese Ambassador was seated and quiet again. "Yes it's true, I must admit that the United States did go to Japan for economic help back in 1992. But Japan has to realize they had flooded our American markets with their vehicles in the past. While doing their best to keep our automobiles out of their country, sir. When our automakers were having their economic problems, the Japanese took full advantage of this situation and yes, they did finally open their shores somewhat to our businesses. But only after we forced the issue with the Japanese government.

"But on the other hand, if the Japanese leaders had opened their shores to our companies at the same time we opened our shores to their commerce. Then the present problem Japan's facing at this time, wouldn't be happening to them now. Yes, we went through our times of economic crisis and problems, and Japan's presently going through their own situations as we speak today, sir. I'm quite certain the United States will do everything in its power, to help our friendly nation of Japan out of their present problems, just as they have done for us in the past. Now is the time for helping, not finger pointing. That is all I have to offer to the members of this Council for the time being. But my office door is always open to the Japanese Delegate, anytime he wants to speak of these problems to me or to my government leaders. I would be honored to set up a meeting with the Ambassador and my President."

After a shot period of silence inside the vast meeting chamber, other issues were soon brought up on the floor at this meeting. But no other issues were of the magnitude of the problem quickly growing between the two superpowers of the United States and Japan. Neither Delegate spoke to the other for the rest of the meeting, and after the meeting was over nor did many news reporters stop the United States Delegate to interview him. The Japanese Ambassador just rushed past the horde of reporters in a huff, and refused any further comment or discussion with the other Delegates being interviewed. A fact that did not go unnoticed by any reporters who tried to make more out of the story than there was. This caused the United States Delegate to call a quick end to his news interview.

At his private office at the United Nations Headquarters in Manhattan, Ambassador Walters placed a call to the Japanese Representative who refused to answer it. Walters then placed a call to the White House, and he made a report to the President of the United States, which he then informed the American Leader he felt Japan would give them some serious problems in the near future. The President told the Ambassador he would handle Japan.

EGYPTIAN CONSULATE, MANHATTAN. NEW YORK CITY

The Egyptian Ambassador's meeting with his new President of Egypt never took place. Instead, he was immediately placed under arrest at the Egyptian Embassy upon entering the complex. He was never informed why he was arrested, he was just placed in a dank, dark cell in the basement of the Embassy. President Faisal Sadat never turned up at the Embassy that day, and he felt as if he was arrested because his name was linked with this conspirator.

Mohammed Kheir heard a slight commotion upstairs and within moments the commotion was over, and then silence filled the air again. As he sat alone in his cell, he heard footsteps coming down the marble stairs leading to his prison cell, he held his breath as they came closer. An Embassy security guard suddenly appeared at the cell door while holding a rifle threateningly in his arms, and he opened the steel door. The guard then ordered Muhammad to follow him. The Egyptian politician followed the angry acting guard to an office on the third floor, they used the steps and not the elevator. Once there, he noticed a young Egyptian man sitting behind the desk of the old Egyptian Ambassador. The young man smiled as he entered the office, and he offered Mohammed a chair with a simple wave of his hand.

Ambassador Kheir sat in the chair but he did not recognize this young man. So he sat in silence for the moment to see what was to happen to him next. Also to see if he could find out whom this man was. As they sat in silence, another man suddenly entered the room and sat in the chair right next to Mohammed Kheir. It was the Libyan Ambassador, Kamal. Mohammed felt the hairs on the back of his neck standup on end as his anger immediately built for this evil man while staring at him with undisguised disdain.

The smirking Kamal waved his hand out before him, and then removed a napkin from the fold of his robe and put it up to his nose as he complained of a terrible stink suddenly in the room.

The man seated behind the desk ignored Ambassador Kamal's latest crude remarks as he sat smiling, and then he spoke when Ambassador Kamal was seated and comfortable. "I see by the expression on your foul face Mohammed that you don't know who I am. Hmm... Then please allow me introduce myself to you, fool. I'm the voice on the phone of the other day. I'm Faisal Sadat, my father was President Sadat, and now I'm President Sadat. I'm the new President of Egypt, Mohammed."

He was stunned as he mumbled. "How could you be the President of Egypt? What has happened to President Hosni Mubarak, sir? What are you trying to pull off here sir?"

"President Mubarak has died, it was the end of his time upon this earth, and all is as Allah wills it to be. He has died because he was too old, and chose to back the United States in their Desert Storm War of years ago against the Arab nation of Iraq. We Arabs have long memories, no Mohammed Kheir? Besides, he was going to allow that miserable foul country of mix blooded animals to dictate to Egypt, and to cut off our much needed water supply from the mighty Nile River that flows from Lake Tana. Soon, Ethiopia would be in power and dictating terms on which Egypt would receive the waters of the Nile to survive. Well, the Egyptian people have decided to put their backs up and ousted the old man, and he died in this process. It'll take some time for us to build up our military forces and prepare them for war.

"So we shall allow the loathsome Ethiopia people and her allies to build their god cursed Dam. But I assure you Mohammed Kheir, by the time their construction project is nearing completion, we should have our military forces set in place as well as our military defenses. Then we'll spring our trap against the worthless fools and put a quick end to the troublemakers to our south. With the help of our other brother Arabs such as Ambassador Kamal here, we should have no trouble with taking over all of northern and central Africa. We can depend on South Africa to follow our lead, once we have acted against Ethiopia. They'll declare war on the blacks in their country, and eliminate them to the Sudd in southern Sudan.

"This will quickly end the many difficulties taking place inside Africa once and for all, because all the trouble here is caused by these cursed black Arabs. Who do you think started the foul trouble in Ethiopia, the lowly black Arabs. Soon, all Africa will be Arabs and South Africans, and you know once everything settles down. We'll then attack South Africa because our overall plan is to make all Africa an Arab country. We're going to get back at the nations of Saudi Arabia, Iran and Kuwait as well. The only Arabs that'll be left alive in the world will belong to our organization. Israel will be a country of the past times. We'll give that lowly country of filthy mongrels, or what will be left of it to the Palestinian fools who'll surely help us rid the Arab lands of all cursed infidels."

Mohammed looked from this man to Ambassador Kamal and grumbled at him. "I guess you are happy with this situation, Ambassador Kamal?"

Sadat immediately snarled nastily at Mohammed. "I'm speaking to you Mohammed, not Ambassador Kamal. You'll address me directly if you wish to comment during any of this conversation! If you have anything to say to Ambassador Kamal, you'll address it to me first. The reason you're here is because I need you to be my envoy in this upcoming operation. I picked you because you know all the worthless Delegates of the United Nations, and they seem to trust you for some reason. I'm counting on many friendly Delegates delaying any possible military action that might be taken against Egypt by that cursed waste of an establishment, once we go to war. The horde of filthy jackals know and trust you, and they'll cling to your every word for hope of a peaceful solution to the turmoil we shall start.

"Mohammed, I'm banking on this delay, and hoping it'll give us the time we need to get our weapons and troops set in place. Once this is accomplished, no power in the entire world, not even the mighty United States! Will be in the position to stop us, I'm counting this door will remain open, by using you to keep it open for me. You, as a well known peace loving man, the great fools will trust you to all ends. I'm going to give you ten minutes of time to think this over. Then you'll have to decide if you're going to do what is asked of you? Now I order you to do as I ask of you. Remember all this is for the good of Egypt and her faithful children."

Mohammed spoke right away in a clam tone this time. "I don't need any time to think of my reply to your words, sir. If whatever is asked of me is for the good of Egypt and her children. I shall do it without hesitation, sir. But I have to believe it's for the good of Egypt, and not for the good of a madman." He turned and glared harshly at Ambassador Kamal.

President Sadat instantly growled back just as harshly at Mohammed as he kept him locked in his angry glare. "I resent that last remark of yours while you're staring at one of my faithful allies, Ambassador Kheir. You can be assured anything I do, or ask of you to do. I do for the good and sake of Egypt, and not for the good of any one individual's gains, sir. I personally will kill any man who tries to gain personally from this terrible situation we're currently facing, sir."

"What would happen if I was able to work out a plan that'd be in the best interest of Egypt, sir? Would we still have to go off to war which is what you seem to be preparing us for sir?" Ambassador Mohammed Kheir asked of the new President of Egypt in a concerned sounding tone as he stared at the man while waiting is response.

"My dear Ambassador Mohammed Kheir, water is in the best interest of Egypt and her children, and without it, all Egypt will be history, sir. So I shall not accept anything less than the exact amount of water from Lake Tana we have been enjoying up until now." President Sadat hissed angrily back at his Ambassador.

"I'm well aware water is what this situation is about, President Sadat." Mohammed cried and then went on with his response to his new President. "But you're talking about getting even with the countries that went against Iraq in their war with the United States. And that's not about water or for Egypt's sake, sir. You seem to forget one important fact President Sadat, and that is Egypt fought against Iraq in that war. After many discussions, we felt Iraq was a serious threat against the Arab world peace, and we were well aware how Egypt fit in Saddam Hussein's future plans. He planned to attack us after he had taken control of Saudi Arabia and Iran, and he was even thinking about attacking the new Russia in his near future.

"We know this was that lowly jackal of a madman's wants for a fact, because we discovered countless papers confirming his evil plans aimed at Egypt. If anyone was going to start a World War, it was surely going to be that madman of Iraq. Now, I'm listening to all these men. One of whom I hate with a passion, and another who never witnessed the horrors war can unleash upon the lands of those who started it, and who says he's now in full control of my country of Egypt, and offers me no other proof than to sit in a chair in Egypt's Embassy. Before I give my full support to you, I need more proof than what you offer to me is the absolute truth. Even if you are who you say you are, I want a peace guarantee from you if I'm able to stop the Ethiopians from building this cursed Dam, or give us a promise the flow of water from Lake Tana will remain the same, if we allow the construction of this Dam.

"If there is no significant water lost to Egypt. I must be able to stop this march to war we're marching to. I want you to swear by the hand of Allah, you'll stop this insane talk of war if no water from the Nile River is diverted. If I can accomplish a just settlement for both countries involved in this situation, and this agreement is completely backed by the members of the United Nations. With a promise that they'll step in if Ethiopia goes against her agreement with us." Mohammed looked at the both men then added to his words.

"I want correct that, I demand proof and promises, and if I don't get them. I'll not life one finger to help you, because I have no intention of being a pawn, and a buffer to blind the good faith members of the world, while you buildup your armies, and make your traps. If you want my help, you must give me your word things will never go so far out of hand, that they'll not be able to be stopped in time before the world is destroyed, sir." Mohammed demanded angrily.

The Libyan Ambassador Kamal suddenly threw his hands in the air and jumped to his feet and started to pace the room, and then he snarled at the Egyptian President. "There, you see, I told you he wouldn't be able to be relied on, this filthy scum of a dog's hair, this shit eating sand flea. President Sadat, he's not to be trusted for one moment of time, sir. He knows too much for him to continue to live. I say we kill this motherless son of the lowly jackal, and get someone we both can trust to do our bidding without question or hesitation."

Mohammed also jumped up to his feet, but just as fast the doors to the office flew open, and four heavily armed soldiers scurried into the room with their weapons held at the ready pointed directly at the chest of Mohammed, who instantly froze in his tracks.

Sadat looked at Mohammed, and then he warned him in no uncertain terms. "Sit down Mohammed Kheir, and remain seated until I'm finished speaking with you. Any sudden foolish movements on your part, could prove to be fatal to your health." Sadat then turned his attention to Kamal and barked at him this time. "You Kamal, will sit down as well! I shall not tolerate any further childish outbursts from either of you foolish jackals. Both of you are supposed to be professionals, and I suggest you start acting like it, while you're still able to act at all."

Mohammed sat down, but not before he had his say. "I've been in the service of my country for ten years, and I don't have to stand for the terrible insults this filthy shit eater is hurling at my person. I'll kill this uncouth foul animal, before I allow him to threaten me so again."

Ambassador Kamal again was on his feet and roared his reply at the Egyptian politician. "How dare you call me a shit eater, you cursed sand flea? I'll show you, you son of a scarab to respect me at all times when in my presence." Ambassador Kamal suddenly produced a sharp edged Jambiya knife and made a threatening move against Ambassador Kheir.

Mohammed again jumped to his feet and made ready to fend off the knife attack from Kamal.

Sadat also jumped up as he yelled at his four guards staring at the threatening men and not knowing what to do next. "You guards are to shoot the first man who harms the other."

Two guards instantly dropped to one knee while the other two guards remained standing, as all four of them aimed their machine guns at the pair of threatening Arab men.

The two Delegates looked from one another then to the guards, and then back at each other and then they turned to President Sadat who was now smiling at them. Ambassador Kamal slowly lowered his knife and put it back in a fold of his robe as he offered to the Egyptian Ambassador. "I see I'm forced to put off the pleasure of killing you until later in life, dog born under the shadow of a filthy camel." Ambassador Kamal snarled without taking his eyes off of him.

Mohammed glared back at the Libyan Representative, because he was no dummy. He was caught unarmed, and with the soldiers aiming their weapons at him, he would be the fool of fools to continue on with his threat against Kamal. He decided to wait and listen to the rest of the nightmare these two men had dreamed up. To see if he was going to help them, or somehow put a stop to their crazy dreams and evil intentions.

When the two Arab politicians finally stopped their threatening moves against each other, and calm was ultimately restored to the meeting, and they were both seated again. President Sadat looked at the four soldiers, and then he waved his hand dismissively at them. The soldiers immediately left the room without comment or hesitation.

President Sadat spoke in a very calm tone of voice this time. "Gentlemen, we are Arabs here, and we have too many enemies outside our world to worry about, so we can ill afford fighting against each other. But make no mistake about my threat to you two fools, I shall have any troublemaker killed, and that means the two of you. Each of you fools are too important to this future operation, for either of you to be trying to kill the other within my presence."

The new Egyptian leader looked to Ambassador Kheir for a long moment, and then he offered him. "Mohammed Kheir, I order you to put your ill feelings towards Ambassador Kamal out of you heart and mind, and to think of only Egypt and her children for the time being, sir."

President Sadat then turned to Libyan Ambassador Kamal and warned him in a threatening tone of voice. "Ambassador Kamal, you shall stop trying to goad Mohammed with your angry words and actions aimed at him, you know of his foul temper. We need him, and I intend to use him. Now you two fools are going to have to get along for no other reason than for the sake of this operation, and of my country. Once this operation is over, you two will be free to kill one another whenever you see fit. I'll happily supply the weapons to the both of you to get the job done properly." President Sadat said as he ended up looking at Mohammed.

Ambassador Kamal bowed while sitting in his chair, as he put his right hand to his forehead then to his lips and then he swung his hand to his right. President Sadat looked to Mohammed who did the same, a sign of respect towards Sadat, and to each other.

"Very good. Mohammed, you have just asked me for some kind of proof of my being the new President of Egypt. I have little proof to offer to you at this time. But perhaps you'll recognize the official seal of Egypt that rests upon my finger, fool." President Sadat extended out his hand so Mohammed could see his ring, and then he added to his words as he calmed down further. "Also Mohammed, I have a number of news clippings from our trusted newspaper of Al Mussawar, that informs all their readers of the recent coup, and the results putting me in command of Egypt. Other than this, I have little else in the way of proof with me that you seek, sir. You'll have to take a trip back to Egypt, or wait for the United States newspapers to print the story for you, sir. The world should be informed of what happened in Egypt within the next few days, sir." President Sadat stopped speaking and just stared at Mohammed.

The Egyptian politician shifted his weight nervously in his chair and replied to the obviously new President of Egypt. "I have no reason to doubt what you have just told me is true, and I'm more than willing to do whatever is necessary that my country and my President asks or demands of me, sir. What is it you want me to do sir?"

"That is much better Mohammed. As I have just stated Mohammed, I have an important operation for you to complete for me and our country, sir. Ambassador, I don't profess to know the many confusing ways or language of the Diplomats, nor do I wish to learn of them, sir. You people are in a world of your own I'm afraid. That is why I have you, and if you refuse to do as I say and order of you, I have no further need of you. Do we have an understanding between ourselves, Mohammed?" President Sadat did not wait for a response as he added. "As I started to offer to you, I want you to make contact the Israeli Delegate, what is the loathsome Jew's foul name, err..., yes Haetzni. That is the godless dog's name, Haetzni. Mohammed, you're to ask him for permission for our people to enter the Sinai Peninsula, sir."

President Sadat took a quick breath for himself, and then he went on with his explanation for the stunned looking Egyptian Ambassador.

"Mohammed, you're instructed to inform this lowly Jew dog that we're going into the Sinai Desert in an attempt to explore that region for water, in hopes of replacing the water we'll be losing to the hated Ethiopians plan. You're to inform this Jew this exploration is a search for water, and you will assure him it's not a military expedition. You'll also inform this lowly fool he can accompany our search teams out in the desert, and even assist us in our search if he wishes. You'll freely answer any questions he may ask of you, and make the answers sound convincing for the lowly jackal's ear to accept. If he agrees and allows our work teams to enter the desert, this will give us free rein in the Sinai Desert, because you know these cursed Jews have no intention of helping us for any reason.

"So this free rein will allow us to build an active military defense no Israeli force on the face of the earth will be able to penetrate with their worthless armies. You see Mohammed Kheir, it is up to you if we're to be successful in this future operation. A warning though to you, if you fail your task it will not only cost you, but it shall cost your entire family, your father, your mother and wife and three children, those you chose to leave in Egypt, yes, it'll cost all of you your heads." President Sadat sat back in his chair and took a deep breath, and then glared at him as he waited for an answer from the frightened and angry looking man.

"My President, I assure you that I'll do the best I possibly can for you, President Sadat Sir. But you cannot hold me responsible sir, if the god cursed Jews will not hear of us going into the Sinai Desert in search of water, sir. Also, what happens to the operation in case the Jews want to have a surprise inspection of our units supposedly looking for this water in the Sinai? What happens if the Jews discover what we're truly up to in the foul desert? I feel I should know of all of what is going on with this operation, sir. So I know better of any possible pitfalls to stay away from, when I'm speaking to these damn Jews, my President."

The new Egyptian President grunted at his Ambassador nastily as he warned him in an extremely angry reply. "Mohammed, first off, you better do a lot more than your best in convincing the god cursed hated Jews that you're truthful for your family's sake. You'll learn what you have to know of our future plans to sound right to the lowly Jews. Nothing more and nothing less, it's that simple my dear Mohammed. The less you know and say, the less you'll be able to hurt this future operation, and if you dare betray us in any way, shape or form, your entire family will suffer greatly and long for it.

"Once I'm certain where your alliance truly lays with my plans for the future of Egypt and her children then and only then will I inform you of the entire operation we plan, sir. A word to the wise to you though Mohammed. If this operation happens to succeed, and I have no doubts it will, there'll be a place in high office for you in Egypt's future. Of this I promise, you'll become the third most powerful man in all of Egypt, Ambassador. Think of the unlimited power I'm offering to place within your foul hands.

"Along with this unlimited power I offer to you, you shall also be allowed to have your own Harem of filthy whores even in Egypt, Ambassador. You'll have access to all the liquor and drugs you'll ever need for life. You'll also deal with the men we choose to leave in power throughout the many different Arab countries we shall conquer, who'll beg you to be Egypt and Libya's friend. Yes Ambassador Mohammed Kheir, you know how many of these other cursed Delegates pay their foul respects to the other Ambassadors. And the women Mohammed, you'll have all the god cursed women coming out of the sands for your pleasures. The world will paid at you feet, if you play your cards right with me my friend."

Mohammed Kheir puffed up his chest as he growled at the new President of Egypt. "My country means more to me than all the worthless whores in the world, President Sadat. I'll do anything my country asks of me, sir. The only thing I'd like to know from you, is to assure me that you'll allow me to install a cut off switch."

"A cut off switch? What the devil are you talking about Mohammed? Switch? What kind of switch do you want?" President Sadat demanded of him.

"I want you to promise me that you'll allow me to install a switch, sir. A cut off switch that once thrown, will immediately stop any and all aggression from our two countries. A cutoff switch to stop all fighting instantly if started. Someone is going to have to be there to talk, and to shut down everything so the big boys don't start throwing around their god cursed nuclear missiles, and kill the whole world off in one nuclear exchange…"

President Sadat cut Mohammed off in mid sentence as he growled at him. "We fear no such threat of nuclear weapons as you have offer, thrown around Mohammed. You seem to forget something here, my friend. We too can now throw around nuclear missiles if we so choose, sir." President Sadat looked at Mohammed for a brief moment as he rubbed his hand across his brow, and then he looked at the sweat in his hand as he continued speaking with his Egyptian Ambassador. "I see and understand your concern Mohammed, and they are just concerns I must admit. Yes, I think I shall install a switch as you have put it at that, designed to shut down any fighting if started. But the power of this switch will depend on how well you pull off your part of this operation, sir. I might give you control of this switch, if you accomplish what I want from you. Now leave us at once Mohammed, I wish to speak to Ambassador Kamal further in private.

"Go back to your apartment of sin and wait there for further communication from me. Mohammed, I have a little present waiting for you there when you return to your apartment, this was given to you for the inconvenience I have caused to you last night by holding you in the cell. Remember this at all times my dear Mohammed, in your hands you have the power to make the future of the world much easier to stay at peace, by using your diplomatic words and means. After all, this is what you were trained for sir. Now leave me and wait for my call." President Sadat suddenly looked down at his hands. Thus, dismissing Mohammed, who looked at Libyan Ambassador Kamal still sitting in his chair smiling. He so desperately wanted to smash his fist into the smiling decaying teeth of this lowly jackal. Instead, he offered his hand to Ambassador Kamal, but he did not offer his hand back, so Mohammed merely left the office in a huff.

Mohammed's body actually shook with anger as he quickly left the Egyptian Embassy for his apartment. His robes smelled from sweat from being locked in the damp cell, so he was looking forward to a steaming hot bath, and his Michelob beer. He hailed a cab and in less than five minutes he found himself waiting for the elevator to carry him to his apartment, another two minutes, and he was standing at his door. Even before he retrieved his key, the door suddenly flung open, and Salim stood in the doorway with a worried face and a million questions.

Mohammed held up his hand and mumbled at his scared man servant. "Not now Salim, I want a shower. Get me a beer." He grumbled as he entered his apartment. But he stopped when he noticed two different blonde women sitting on the floor. When the women saw him enter, one started a sexy strip show for him.

He turned to Salim who merely shrugged and quickly explained. "The two women knocked on the door less than an hour ago, and they said they were a special gift sent to amuse Ambassador Mohammed Kheir, who was on his way home."

He looked to the blonde one now completely naked and noticed she also had no pubic hairs on her body. She noticed he was looking at her womanhood, and said with a giggle. "It was told to me that you were thrilled to see a women naked, and with no hair below. So in your honor, I shaved myself to increase your great pleasure, Mohammed Kheir. Whatever I do will be for your pleasure alone sir. Do you like what I have done for you?"

"Who the devil has sent you here, and how did this person know of my likes and desires?" He demanded hotly of the young and extremely pretty woman.

The naked blonde immediately explained to the confused Egyptian politician. "The same person who has sent the other two blonde women to you the other night, sir. Every woman who has came here over the past five years now, have come from the same stable as I am from, Mohammed. Each woman tried to gather as much important information as they could from you, but you would never give any, and that is why you're still alive, sir. You have held your tongue very well throughout your employ, Mohammed. Please, allow me explain further for your edification. The people, Gail on the floor and I, JoAnne work for, know you're a man of great honor and respect, who is to be trusted, and you'll not divulge any state secret information to anyone who searches for it from you, sir."

JoAnne looked at Mohammed and then added with a slight smile on her lips. "You look a mess Ambassador Kheir, please allow me to draw a bath for you satisfaction sir. I'll be most pleased to wash you, and then Gail and I will drive you crazy beyond your wildest dreams all night long, sir. Follow me please sir." She purred as she headed off for the bathroom.

He watched as she headed off for the bathroom. In seconds he heard the water running in the shower. He followed her in the bathroom a moment later, smiling as he entered the steaming hot room already, and she closed the door behind him. He swiftly turned and instantly grabbed the naked woman by her hair, and violently yanked her head back as he took a bottle of hair rinse and broke it on the edge of the sink. Then he placed the jagged edges of the shattered bottle under her left breast and snarled at her savagely. "I asked you who sent you here to me and you have failed to respond to that question properly, bitch?"

The young and beautiful blonde looked into his extremely angry face of the Arab politician while struggling to breathe properly with cold blue eyes, and then she smiled again at him without showing any fear whatsoever in her eyes of him.

"If you want your fucking body to remain looking like it does right now bitch, you'll tell me what I demand to know from you. Or I'll cut your breasts from your god cursed torso, and then I'll start work on your lovely face until you tell me what I demand of you. Who the hell sent you here to me, you fucking bitch you." He actually pushed the broken bottle edge under her breast up until the jagged points lightly touched her tender flesh, and it slightly cut into the soft skin. Causing her to cry out slightly and he immediately added to his angry words aimed at her. "I just asked you who the hell sent you here bitch?"

"I shall tell you who sent me to you, Mohammed. It was President Sadat who sent me and Gail to you, who did you think it was, you great fool? He sent us here to please your pleasures. He knows how much you enjoy women, so he sent us as a special gift for you to play with. Just think of Gail and myself as your private little play toys, until President Sadat calls you to the Embassy once again, sir. One thing I feel I must warn you about though, Mohammed Kheir. I don't particularly enjoy any rough stuff from anyone, mister." JoAnne said this with a slight sigh, and then she quickly reached up with her right hand and she grabbed his hand, and applied surprisingly strong and painful pressure. Then she bent his hand against the grain until he was forced to drop the broken bottle, or end up with a broken wrist. He now cried out in pain.

With surprising speed, skill and strength, the young and stunningly beautiful naked blonde pulled his arm around to his back, and she skillfully got behind him herself. Then she next wrapped her other surprising strong arm under his neck, completely cutting off the air supply to his body, and causing him intense pain. She then moved her firm body from behind his with the speed of a large cat, still with her arm locked under his neck, and she roughly shoved him backwards and down to the tile floor and he ended up on his hip.

The stunned Ambassador was slammed hard against the tile floor with a breath robbing thud, knocking what little breath he still had in his body, out with a grunt. He hit his head on the floor and ending up landing on his back and right leg. He found himself sprawled out on the bathroom floor while drawing in large gulps of air while trying to catch his breath.

JoAnne still naked, stepped over his body and bent down at the waist, and placed her both her hands flat on his belly, and then she pushed down fast twice on his stomach. He was forced to roll over on his side, because he felt like he was going to throw up by the sudden actions of this woman, but in a second or two he was breathing normally again.

She then offered the prone Mohammed her hand as she laughed. "Oh please Ambassador Kheir. I have forgotten to inform you another thing about me and my lovely little sister, sir. We both are your private bodyguards. Nothing will ever happen to you while we're around and protecting you. Just think of me as your protective little play toy sir."

Ambassador Mohammed Kheir hesitated for a brief moment while taking in the lovely view he had as she straddled him. Finally, he took the offered hand as he laughed himself. "Yeah, and who is going to protect me from you and your friend, young woman? By the way, is there anything else you might have forgot to inform me of young woman?"

"No, that is about it I'm afraid sir." She replied with a very sexy purr in her tone.

They both laughed as they finally relaxed a little with one another for a moment.

She helped him back to his feet and then out of his robes as she added more at him then to him. "After what I intend to do to your body on this night, with the help of my sister as well, you just might need some added protection for your body at that, sir. Ambassador Mohammed Kheir Sir, both my sister and I am here solely to give you great pleasure of the body and mind, and relieve any stress you might suffer from, and not pain sir. Please, don't make me protect myself again against you and any of your foolish actions, sir."

She helped him slowly lower his aching body into the steaming hot water of the tub, he had to suck in his breath because the water was so hot. She then jumped in with him, and then she washed his rock hard body. When she was done, he stood and she toweled him off, she then rubbed lightly scented oil over his body. Taking a clean robe from the hanger in the bathroom, she offered it to him as she quickly dried herself off. Then she rubbed her own body down with the same scented body oil and offered. "This is only the beginning of what is in store for you, if you work for President Sadat, Ambassador Kheir Sir."

She led him from the bathroom and took the beer from Salim, and took a swig of it herself, she then offered it to the good looking Arab politician. Gail was now naked, she also had no pubic hair. Her motor was running as she played with herself, wiggling around on the floor. Salim quickly disappeared as JoAnne led Mohammed over to the other girl. JoAnne laid on the floor and pulled on the Arab's arm until he sank down to the rug also. The night was long, but very enjoyable. It was the best night he ever spent on the earth with a woman, let alone two. He awoke the next morning at nine o'clock, and Salim offered him a cup of coffee.

He sat up sitting between the two naked women, and smiled at Salim as he said. "I think we're going to enjoy ourselves with these two new little play toys of ours, fool."

JoAnne rolled over and laid her arm lightly across the Egyptian's legs, and then she nestled up tight against his body, immediately falling back to sleep. He slowly wiggled out from between the two young women, and went into the kitchen where Salim was busy setting the table for his morning meal already. The young and good looking Egyptian politician sat down to enjoy his morning meal.

CHAPTER 4

Egyptian Ambassador Mohammed Kheir was a rather large man who stood over six foot five inches tall, who, at one time in his life, worked out regularly with iron weights. He was well developed, even though his belly was starting to stick out a bit on him. His arms were large, capped off with a mitt like hand, and a thick neck. He enjoyed strikingly good looks like most Arab people with a sharp chin, large nose, and beautiful white teeth. His eyes were black, and grew even blacker whenever angered, and they were outlined by thick bushy eyebrows, and dark brown wavy hair. He had a thin mustache which he kept neatly trimmed, and no beard. He skin looked like he always had a rich even tan. His commanding figure led to his success in dealing with the other Delegates from the United Nations.

Mohammed told Salim after he ate he was going to do some shopping, and from behind him JoAnne warned the Egyptian politician. "You'll go nowhere until you hear from President Sadat, sir. I shall accompany you wherever you go, but only if it's an emergency sir."

Mohammed turned and glared harshly at her as he snarled savagely. "What the devil am I to believe, that I'm under house arrest?" He looked at this beauty that could not weigh a hundred pounds soaking wet standing naked in front of him and laughed and added. "I don't see anyone here powerful enough to stop me from going if I wanted to leave."

JoAnne removed her arm from behind her back, and carefully aimed her stainless steel Glock nine mm pistol directly at his head and warned him in no uncertain terms. "I fear you enjoy a rather short memory my dear Mohammed. You must have forgot what happened to you in the bathroom a little earlier today, sir. Make no mistake about it Mohammed Kheir. I'm more than capable of killing you, and I will if you leave me no other choice but to do so, and you dare try to leave my sight for a moment, sir. Please Mohammed, enjoy your breakfast and come and enjoy me again. Let's be friends until President Sadat calls for you. I'd truly hate to be forced to handcuff you to the plumbing sir." She smiled at him, exposing her perfect white teeth.

He went to his feet and smiled as he offered in an extremely confident voice. "I don't think you'd really shoot me young one."

Gail suddenly appeared from behind JoAnne's back, and she too was still naked as she hissed just as savagely at the Egyptian politician. "Maybe she will not kill you fool, but make no mistake about it. I'll blow your fucking head off your shoulders if I'm forced to, Mohammed Kheir Sir." She instantly cocked the hammer on her Glock pistol, and placed the barrel of it against Mohammed's forehead, and then she added to her stinging words aimed at him. "As the young lady offered you fool, why do you not enjoy your food and then us, sir. It might be the last fuck you'll ever enjoy for a long time to come, Mohammed."

He had no other choice in the matter and he sat down hard in his chair as he started to eat again. He called over his shoulder without looking at either of the two women. "You girls will have to service each other, because I'm in no mood for either or both of you now. It wrecks the shit out of my desire to have guns aimed at me before enjoying sex."

The girls laughed as they left the kitchen. JoAnne bantered back. "It's your loss, tough guy."

After he ate, he went in the living room and found the pair of beautiful women fully dressed. They sat on the couch, one on either side of it, with their weapons lay threatening on the side tables, well within in easy reach of their owners.

The still angry Egyptian politician sat down in the chair directly across from the couch. The three of them spent the rest of the day, and most of the evening just staring at each other. Any time he moved around the apartment, whether it was to go to the bathroom, or to retrieve himself a beer, he was followed closely by either of the two beautiful women who would carry their weapons with them. As he watched the female when she walked, he could easily tell she had some sort of military training in her life. The trio sat in the living room, they ate and then they watched TV until late into the night.

The young Egyptian politician snapped in sheer disgust at his pair of female jail keepers he was going to sleep. It was then JoAnne suddenly asked him which one of them he would prefer to spend the night with. She offered the both of them for his service for this night.

He laughed aloud as he grumbled because he did not want to spend the night with any female who could kick the shit out of him. This remark caused JoAnne to laugh as she then announced she was going to take the duty from Gail, and then she followed him into his bedroom. He growled again he did not want to sleep with either of them tonight, but she completely ignored him as she prepared to lay in the bed with him.

JoAnne laughed again as she explained he had no choice in this matter. She told him they were bought for him, and it was her duty to sleep with him, and to please and informed him it was unhealthy to go to sleep unrelieved and frustrated. She warned he better get used to it, because one if not both of them were going to be with him for the rest of his life if need be.

"We both are assigned to you, and ordered to protect you, and to service your every wish and desire, Ambassador Mohammed Kheir. So why do you not enjoy yourself while you still can sir?" She offered politely as she placed her weapon down on the small night table, and quickly stripped as he watched and enjoyed her little strip show. She then slid under the covers and pulled back the sheet, and motioned for him to join her in the bed, which he did. Once under the blankets, she warned him not to make a try for her weapon, because she liked him and it would be a terrible shame to be forced to kill someone she liked.

"Besides, Gail is sleeping outside the bedroom, and if you were lucky enough to dispatch me. Gail would deliver the kill to finish her orders to your President Sadat, and avenge my death at the same time. Remember Ambassador Mohammed Kheir, you might be able to kill one of us, but you'll never be able to kill the both of us, no matter what you try against us. No man is that good sir." Again she laughed as she added and then pulled the big man close to her with surprising strength fitting a well developed man, as she slid beneath the covers.

The next morning did not come fast enough for Mohammed, as he jumped up and headed for the shower. No sooner did he get the water temperature right to his desire, and he slip under its flow of water than did he find JoAnne joining him in his shower. He thought this might not be too hard for him to get used to after all. As she carefully washed his body, paying special attention to his manhood. When they were done washing and coming out of the bathroom, Gail passed by them on her way for a quick rinse off herself.

Salim met Mohammed down the hallway, and let him know breakfast would be prepared within five minutes and then asked him. "Should I set three places for the meal sir?"

He told Salim to set one place, but JoAnne overrode his order by saying. "I think three places will do just fine if you don't mind, thank you Salim." As she looked to Mohammed.

Salim did not know what to do now. So he merely looked to his master for an answer.

"Three places will do Salim." He said as he looked at JoAnne, who smiled at him.

The trio ate pretty much in silence, and Salim kept the coffee cups full as he hovered over the table like a bee hovering over a flower. Finally the phone broke the strained silence of the room. Mohammed stood to answer it, but he found his way blocked by Gail who rose also. This was to give time for JoAnne to answer the phone. By the way she spoke in the phone, he realized the call was from Sadat. JoAnne was on the phone for a few minutes, she then hung up and ordered Gail and Mohammed to get dressed. They left the building in five minutes of the call. Outside, they were picked up by a stretch limo. Inside were President Sadat, Libyan Ambassador Kamal and another Arab man. The women got in the front seat of the vehicle.

Egyptian Ambassador Mohammed Kheir corkscrewed his six foot frame in the seat of the vehicle, he could easily hear the scrambling machine running, because of the constant hum emitted from the machine. He also felt the vibration from it. There was another object sitting on the table between President Sadat and Mohammed. When President Sadat noticed Mohammed looking at it, he offered. "That Mohammed, will eliminate the hated Jew Army from the face of the earth for us, sir. It's called a fog or fuel air explosive and this is a much smaller version of the actual weapon. Allow me to explain it a little further to you how it operates.

"As you can plainly see for yourself, the body of this weapon is made out of heavy and hard plastic. It's actually a land mine, new, and made of plastic components that makes it completely undetectable to most, if not all conventional mine detecting equipment commonly employed by most armies in their search for such mines. In addition Mohammed, the weapon is simply detonated by fiber optic connections controlled by an operator constantly monitoring the mine field at all times while the weapon is being deployed against our enemy.

"The mine will not go off even if a tank runs directly over it. So with just fifty of these new weapons we can wait until enough of the hated Jew tanks were in our circle of death then we'll fire them off. Dammit Mohammed we could wipe out a whole column of enemy tanks with one blow. Just think of it, over a thousand tanks could be burnt to a cinder in one white hot flash with a couple of hundred of these weapons." Sadat said as he tapped the box on the table.

"I'm impressed that is if it'll do what you said it does sir. But I don't know how this thing works, and I fear what the world would say of us attacking the Jews like the other crazy Arabs of the Middle East always do." Mohammed replied with a sharp snap in his tone.

President Sadat displayed his displeasure with his Ambassador as he grunted angrily. "The only dead Jew the world ever cared about was their Christ, fear not world opinion this time, fool. The fuse detonates when the operator sends the firing impulse to the weapon. Then a fine cloud of fuel oil a hundred feet across and fifty feet wide is instantly sprayed into the air about five feet over the ground, this rapidly spreading fuel is then ignited by a secondary smaller explosion. Thus a massive fireball is produced, consuming all oxygen and incinerates everything within its range. The fireball will set off secondary explosions caused by the ammunition stored inside the tanks, or carried by foot soldiers caught in the blast."

The sound of the scrambler machine was driving Mohammed up the wall as he offered in an angry tone of voice. "This sounds fine to me sir. But how are you going to set the things where the Jew tankers would blunder over them sir?"

"That is where you come in, you fool." President Sadat said with obvious nervousness in his voice as he went on. "As I told you before Mohammed, you're going to be the one who'll get permission for us to look for water in the Sinai Desert. We'll take the appearance of units actually searching for water. The units will be equipped with drills and other machinery to make it look to the world we're truly workers searching for water in the desert. But in reality, we'll be planting many of these such mine fields on, or near the old routes we feel the Jew tankers will employ. Along with their cursed support vehicles and hated foot soldiers when they're forced to invade the Sinai Desert once they see our tanks and troops on the move.

"The worthless Jews have taught us a very valuable lesson along the Suez Canal in the war of 1973, and the foul Americans finished the lesson of training in their Desert Storm War with Iraq. With these weapons and the help of the detonation strips, we feel we could stop, or even destroy enough Jew soldiers and tanks to neutralize them for the remainder of the war against them. Of course that is unless Iraq decides to finish the Jews off once we crippled them.

"Ambassador, we intend to have a number of civilian trailers with water accompany all the workers who go in the Sinai Desert. These tanker trucks will have a false bottom constructed inside them. If the Jews open the ports in the trailers and they happen to look into them, all they'll see is water. Even if they stick a probe in the water, all they're going to feel is water. But in truth, each of the trailers will contain four hundred of these mines stored in water tight containers accessible through the bottom of the tanker truck. While the workers pretend to look for water, in reality, they'll be setting these mine fields and anti personnel strips for us. This plan is foolproof Mohammed Kheir, one that is if you do what is asked of you sir." President Sadat said as he looked deeply into the steel black eyes of Ambassador Mohammed Kheir.

Mohammed absentmindedly played with the end of his mustache as he mumbled barely over a whisper to his President. "It seems you have most everything figured out very well, President Sadat. I hope you know what you're doing to the world once you start."

"Mohammed!" President Sadat hissed as his angry glare narrowed. "Allow me worry about the rest of the foul world. I had enough of your constant voice of doom. Let me warn you Mohammed, Egypt will be doomed if she is deprived of the life giving waters of the sacred Nile River. You better make up your mind if you want to leave this car alive. I need you and it'll take much too long for me to train another fool Diplomat who'll be as trusted by most of the other worthless Delegates as you are. But if I cannot rely on you one hundred percent then you shall leave me no other choice. I'll kill you myself in the name of Egypt, and have someone else trained. Oh, one other thing Mohammed if I have to go this route.

"I shall eliminate your so called cut off switch you had requested, such as you call it. In case you don't understand by now, you're the switch you asked for Mohammed. We'll go along with the plans we already decided upon, but if you stop the Ethiopian dogs southeast of us with words, we'll not instigate any attacks. My dear Ambassador Mohammed Kheir, you yourself are the shutoff switch, without you there is nothing in Egypt's future but war and death." Again, President Sadat stopped speaking, and looked at Mohammed as if to see in his soul, knowing the next words spoken by this man, would let him know if he would help him in his quest.

Mohammed took a deep breath, he was having trouble breathing, it felt like the air closed in on him in the car. "When do you want me to make contact with the Israelis, and setup a meeting between myself and their Delegate? I don't understand why we have to ask their permission to explore the Sinai Desert. After all, the Sinai Desert is our territory is it not sir?" He found it hard to believe this man was an Egyptian because he sounded so American.

Sadat answered Mohammed's question in an extremely angry voice. "This is something most Egyptians don't understand, fool. When my father signed that god cursed peace accord in Camp David with the American President Carter, he promised never to send any Egyptian troops into the Sinai Desert without informing the Israeli government first, as a sort of courtesy, and to prove we intend no future attack against the Jews. It was never written on paper, it was a handshake and a word given. But this handshake is going to close tightly around the Jew snake's neck, and it'll squeeze until the Jew threat to the Arab nations is dead forever in all the Middle East."

It was true Sadat sounded American, but this was a result of his father, the young Sadat was always around Americans, and he picked up many mannerisms and phrases of them.

Kheir looked at this frail, smallish man who looked so much like his honored father, and he could not help but wonder what the history books were going to write about this son of the great man of Egypt. He wondered if this man was going to destroy all his father labored hard to accomplish with his ambitions, along with destroying the country of Egypt itself. He had to shake his head to clear the troubling thoughts he was thinking, and then he replied to the new President. "With your permission President Sadat, I shall call Haetzni, the Israeli Delegate and request a private audience with him, so we can commence with your plans, sir."

President Sadat took note of the angry tone in his voice and responded just as nastily. "I hope that anger I'm detecting being displayed in your foul voice, is because you don't enjoy dealing with the Jew dogs, and it's not directed at anyone here, especially me you fool? I know I ask a lot of you Mohammed, having to deal with some of our country's worst enemies like they're our friends, but it's absolutely necessary for the success of this upcoming operation. Remember my friend, your job is to keep the loathsome Jews off balance while we plant our deadly mines. Mohammed, I'm finish speaking with you, you're free to go, and take your new toys with you. They serve many other purposes in your arsenal. These women not only serve you, they'll serve anyone you want power over. Whether it be female, or male. The women will do anything you ask of them. But remember this at all times Mohammed."

President Sadat said as he leaned forward and looked deeply into Mohammed's eyes and added. "They serve me first, and you second. They shall report to me on any and everything you say or do, or have them do for you, fool. Also, you'll be in their sight twenty four hours a day. Another warning to understand Mohammed, they have orders to kill you over the slightest infraction you might commit against me. If they deem it a threat to me, or my operation.

"I rather lose you just like that Mohammed." Sadat said while snapping his fingers, and making a spitting motion as he continued with his words aimed at the Ambassador. "Than to take a chance of you giving away our plans to our hated enemy. When you're with any other Delegates, you're to take the one called JoAnne with you. You'll introduce her as your private secretary. She'll wear the clothes that'll confirm why she's truly with you, fool. Leave my side now Mohammed. You're to inform me when you make contact with the Jews and what their response is to our requests from them." With this said, Sadat sat back and folded his arms across his chest and stopped speaking. The car came to a stop and JoAnne open the door.

Mohammed looked out the door, only to see he was right in front of his building again. He got out, and was followed into the building by both JoAnne and Gail who followed the two out.

JoAnne opened the doors for him, she got the elevator for him as well. Mohammed could not help but feeling important, just by the way the two women were treating him. JoAnne opened the door to his apartment now using her own key this time.

Mohammed showed a quick flash of anger at knowing of her having her own key.

She smiled at his obvious displeasure as she offered pleasantly. "We're ordered to do whatever was necessary to keep control over you, and anyone else you come in contact with, Mohammed. I needed my own key, that simple, I'm sorry if you're insulted. You have no privacy from now on, at least until your mission is completed, sir. I promise you Mohammed, I'll make up everything, all the inconveniences I may cause you. You're worth a hell of a lot of money to me, enough, so I'll not have to turn anymore tricks when this is over with. Please come, allow me and my little sister show you some of the benefits of having us around you, Mohammed. Allow us show you how grateful we are to you and your people."

Egyptian Ambassador Mohammed Kheir followed her in the apartment in silent rage.

She announced she was going to take a quick shower, and she invited Mohammed to join her, but he declined the offer while stating he had some paperwork to catch up on, which he did. He left JoAnne heading for the bathroom, and he turned for the office he setup in the spare bedroom of the large apartment. Gail followed him and she stood over his shoulder, as he made numerous memos to himself and Salim. Mohammed decided to talk to Gail as he wrote down some last minute assignments for his many aides to do the following day. He asked Gail what her nationality was, as well as that of JoAnne's.

The second young female bodyguard smiled pleasantly as she started to speak. "We're both Scandinavian, and we're true blondes. We've been in the United States for nine years now. We came over at the same time as Nannies, if you can believe that, Mohammed. But there was so little money in that field, we both looked for something else to do with our lives. Soon after we were here, we were discovered by a man who offered us much money to do a number of private strip shows for some of his very wealthy clients. Well, one thing led to another, and when we started fucking, oh excuse me please. I know how you Egyptians feel about a woman cursing. Anyway, when we started to make love to the many clients, we quickly found out we could make much more money by doing this, than by just merely stripping for the fools.

"Viola, so here we are, making money by fuc, err... making love, and also by watching over you sir. There is more to our story, our benefactor had us trained in hand to hand combat, to enable us to protect the more important clients he wanted us to make love to. I'll not go into all our training, but we could hold our own with any foolish man. I have never killed a man before, but make no mistake about it sir. Both my sister and I would do it without a second's hesitation if we were forced to sir." She suddenly announced in a very combative tone.

He looked at Gail straight in the eye that stood over him and then he offered to her in a very calm voice. "Why do you call yourselves sisters? Are you true sisters? You don't look very much like each other to be sisters."

She took a quick breath, smiled and then offered. "We call ourselves sisters as a matter of respect to one another, as well as because we've been together ever since either of us can remember, Mohammed. We come from the same town, and share an apartment together on the eastside since we came to New York City, sir. After this operation is over, we'll be able to buy the whole eastside if we so choose to do." She laughed.

He said while staring at her. "You looked like you and JoAnne had some military training. I could tell by the way you hold yourself and by the way you move, I guess I was right."

She sighed as she stated. "You're very observant for a man I see Mohammed. I didn't want to go into this end of our lives, but since you asked me sir. When we were approached for this operation, if you want to call it that for the lack of a better word to describe it. We were told we were going to have to go through some very intense military training so we could better protect your life, Mohammed. Your government somehow got us special permission to go off to Israel of all places sir, for our specialized training.

"The Israeli government was informed we were going to be special bodyguards for some of Egypt's most important and well respected Delegates and other politicians, and they wanted us to be well trained to protect the lives of the Ambassadors we were going to be assigned to protect, sir. The Israeli government was more than pleased to train us for Egypt, Mohammed. We spent eight full weeks in the desert, learning how to kill a person with our bare hands, our legs, fingers, teeth, and even our breasts if needed, Mohammed Kheir Sir."

He laughed at her words as he stared at the stunning beauty for a moment.

"You laugh, but do you know I could actually smother you to death with my breasts if I was forced to dispatch you, as well as with anything else we could pick up, and use as a weapon against anyone who has threatened me or my sister or even our ward. After our training was completed, we were sent back to the United States, and then placed in a special stable with other women from all over the world, trained in much the same way as we were. Then we were sent out every so often on special dates for your government. We were used whenever your government wanted us for some special protection purposes, or for blackmailing by taking pictures of the date in very compromising situations if you know what I mean, sir. One other thing about your government, they pay very well for our services Mohammed."

"How many dates were you sent on since you started your work with my government?"

Again she sighed as she offered to the young Egyptian politician in a calm voice. "This is our fourth assignment working together, sir. Usually, JoAnne and I go out on the same dates because we click so well together, and we're able to bend any foolish man around our little fingers nice and easily like, sir. This assignment with you will last until your government pulls us off this present duty, or we're forced to kill you for some reason or the other, Mohammed. That is the only way it'll ever end for us before we're relieved by your President, sir."

Their conversation was cut off by Salim as he entered the room. Mohammed looked at the servant and then he offered. "Sir, it is late, would you like me to prepare you something special to eat. It's afternoon, and I'd not like for you to eat a big lunch at this time, it's getting close to supper, Mohammed. I could always offer you and the ladies something to nibble on that'll not spoil your appetite, sir."

He thought for a brief moment and then smiled as he said to his man servant. "Very good Salim, some nibbles would do just fine please. I guess I'd starve to death if it wasn't for you constantly looking after me. I'd like a beer, and bring one for the lady also."

"I don't drink, I never did sir. JoAnne does all the drinking for the both of us, Mohammed. Although I sometimes have a drink when I just meet someone to help me relax the situation, and to also start the conversation rolling. I like to have my wits as sharp as possible about me at all times, and I'm afraid booze causes me to fall asleep, sir. Once I wake up after drinking, I can never remember if I had a good time or not, and I don't like that feeling."

"One thing you said puzzles me greatly young woman. You said you were specially trained by the Israeli soldiers. I never knew we were that friendly with the god cursed hated Jews, for them to be so willing to train some of our people for special service activities." He asked while he cocked his head to the side and waited for Gail to reply.

"Then I guess there are a awful lot of things you really don't know about your government Mohammed Kheir. I guess I could tell you some of it and not betray any trust. I don't think I'd be giving away any national secrets to you. Well here it is Mohammed, ever since the Jews and Egyptians signed that peace accord between them years ago. Israel had taken to training one squad of Egyptian soldiers a year, as a condition to the signing, sir. No matter how she tried, Egypt couldn't bring out the true soldier in her soldiers, so naturally your government turned to the Jews who are the best soldiers in the world. The Jews were more than willing to assist in this request from your government. Maybe in this way it was a method for the lowly Jews to keep a closer eye on the progress of the Egyptian soldiers and their training, and to keep some kind of control over these soldiers at the same time, Mohammed. I don't really know why the Jews took to training the Egyptians in the first place sir.

"I know they, the Jews have trained JoAnne and myself, and they also tried a number of mind games on us which didn't work. Now, word has it Egypt is sending whole companies of soldiers to train with the hated Jews. From what I was led to believe, when we are scheduled to do our training there next year. Egypt is going to send something like a thousand soldiers to be train in combat tank and ground tactics with the wise Jews.

"In fact Mohammed, the Israeli's were going to train these new Egyptian troops in tank assault tactics, because your government made the Jews think Egypt was worried about an attack from Libya or Iraq. Because the Egyptians chose to join forces with the Allies in their attack on Iraq in the Desert Storm thing with the United States. I have no proof of this, but I was led to believe Saudi Arabia is also sending a large number of their soldiers to Israel for this special training program. I have also heard a number of stories many other countries were likewise involved with the Allies in Desert Storm War, are training special troops in advance attack and quick response tactics, sir. Many, if not all the same countries are suppose to be banding together, and vowing to lend assistance to anyone of these other countries who end up feeling any wrath or attack from Iraq, or any of her Allies for their involvement with the United States.

"I understand the Egyptians soldiers going through this added training in Israel right now, have orders from your government. If and when Egypt starts the war with Israel, these units are instructed to attack Israel from inside the border of that country. These soldiers have their targets picked out. Mohammed, I cannot tell you more without betraying my oath to your President. If you want to know more, you're going to have to speak to Sadat, and if he wants to tell you, he will." With this she sat in a chair across from him and watched as he wrote more memos.

It seemed like Salim was waiting for their conversation to end, because he came in the office with a tray of cut carrots, black and green olives, and a pile of raw spinach on warm pita bread the moment Gail stopped speaking. This tray was one of Mohammed's favorite afternoon snacks. Salim placed the beer on the desk, and then he setup a small folding table, and placed the tray on it. Then he offered Mohammed the newspaper.

He laughed as he remarked to his young man servant. "I don't have the foul time to read the god cursed paper at this time Salim, but thank you anyway."

He took a quick breath, fearing not to overstep his bounds as he stated. "Sir, I think you should make the time to read the newspaper today. There is a story I believe you should look at, it starts on page two if I remember right sir." Salim bowed politely from the waist as he left the room leaving the paper on the top of his desk.

The Egyptian Ambassador Mohammed Kheir picked the newspaper up and opened it with a deep sigh of disgust, as he turned to page two and began to read. There, the headlines read in bold, large black print. 'Coup recently established in Egypt, President Hosni Mubarak ousted as the leader of Egypt, and the only son of the great Egyptian Leader Anwar el Sadat, Faisal Sadat has taken over power, and the Presidency and control of Egypt'.

He bolted upright as if he was just stuck with a pin as he quickly read the small print of the article. 'Even though the young President Sadat has vowed to the world to keep his country a Democracy, the United States holds her breath. The new and rather young Egyptian Leader announced he was going to keep the same Diplomats in place, and let it be known he was willing to hold negotiations with any other country of the world, to try and put to rest all the usual fears of changing his country's policy. The new President Sadat made this statement to the world. "It is Egypt as usual'."

Gail looked at his ashen face and then asked him. "You look suddenly troubled Mohammed, it is not like you didn't realize this was not going to take place, Ambassador Kheir. You were made aware of this change in your government in advance sir. Here, take this please." She held out her hand and offered him a small brass key.

"What is this?" He asked the young female, as he rolled the tiny key in his fingers.

"It's your own key to Suite One, Four, Three, Two sir, where you have recently met with the Libyan Ambassador Kamal the other day along with President Sadat. I'm instructed to inform you it's now your private room to hold special meetings in with other Diplomats, whether they are friend or foe to us. I was also instructed to inform you this room is equipped with the disrupter or scrambler, and tape machines so you can tape your conversations to go over them at your leisure, sir. The Japanese have developed a new type tape machine that has the ability to tape over, and omit the sound produced by their own scrambler system, Mohammed. We'll therefore be able to tape all conversations you have with anyone in this room, while no other nation will be able to tape, or even eavesdrop on your conversations, sir.

"It's a extremely well secured room in which to deal out of, Ambassador Kheir. JoAnne is to be your private secretary in the room at all time, and she'll control the tape machine from her seat by means of a number of hidden controls. Again Mohammed, I must warn you that you'll have no life of your own, until this operation is completed, and your government pulls us from you, or the other option transpires which I hope to God truly does not take place sir."

"It looks like my government has thought of everything?" He asked of his tormentor.

"There is always that unknown factor which all the great masterminds have overlook in any operation. That is why we're here with you Mohammed. Our job is to overcome that one hidden factor, which could prove an embarrassment to your country and your President, sir."

JoAnne walked into the office wearing just a towel wrapped waist high around her exquisite body after showering. She looked at Gail, who immediately stood and reported her entire conversation with Mohammed to the younger woman who Mohammed suddenly realized was in charge of everything the two women did or said.

"Does the foolish thickhead understand everything you told him my little sister?" She asked her partner as she shot her a quick and warm smile as she stared at her.

"If he doesn't then he's even dumber than he looks, my little sister." This remark brought laughter from the two women, and a slight smiling protest from Mohammed.

JoAnne took a piece of cut carrot and pointed it at Mohammed's chest and reminded him. "I think you had better place a quick call to the Israeli Delegate my dear Mohammed as you were instructed to do. Your government wants you to get this part of the project underway as soon as possible, sir." She commanded as she took a bit of the carrot.

"I intend to call the Ambassador after supper. I know he'll be in his office by then."

"I think you should try a call to the Jew right now as you were instructed, Mohammed." She outright ordered him with a glare as she straightened up.

"And I think you should back off my ass a little bitch. You might be in good with my government, but you're not going to dictate terms to me, young woman. I'll do things how and when I so choose, not when you say to do them, got it? Besides, you're not trained in the war of politics. Some things cannot be rushed woman." He hissed with as much venom as he could possibly muster in his voice as he glared back at the young blonde now.

She backed off, and merely shrugged at Mohammed. Then she bowed slightly as she stated. "Please forgive me impertinence Mohammed, I stand corrected by you sir. Maybe I have overstep my bounds a little with you sir. I'm only guilty of trying to serve and protect you in your quest while you're carrying out your government's orders, sir. I don't want to hurt you, or your feelings either. All you have to do is tell me what you want, and it shall be done sir."

He laughed as he replied to the stunningly beautiful young woman. "I never thought I'd be saying this to such a beautiful and half naked woman. But will you please cover your breasts, woman. So I can stay angry at you without such a exquisitely beautiful distraction being waved in my face?" This remark caused the trio to laugh, and it broke the tension between them.

She pulled the towel over her breasts, and then she sat down on the edge of his desk.

"I'll call the hated Jew right after supper as I have offered. But first I'm going to take a shower myself. Then, I want a thick steak with French fries to help build my strength. These last few days have been pure hell on me and my body and sleep." He griped, with this he stood and went into the bathroom.

Salim had a steak cooked which he was going to feed every one with, but since his master's demand for a big dinner, he threw on three smaller steaks for the women and himself. As always, Salim would eat when his master was asleep, or involved with the women.

This time Gail followed him to the bathroom and went in the shower with him. Mohammed did not protest to being washed by her. When they finished, she dried him and they again returned to the office. JoAnne sat on the love seat fully dressed as he sat in his chair. It was too early to eat, so he reached for the newspaper he was reading, now lying on the floor. He again turned to the second page, but another story caught his eye. It was a story on the nation of Algeria. It seemed again a flare up was occurring just as it did in the early part of 1992.

The Muslim Fundamentalists of that nation were urging all Algerians, including the soldiers of the nation's army backed government to revolt, because the government was going to cancel all nation's elections. The Muslin's complained the cancellation was an act of treason. The Islamic Salvation Front called for open combat between the People's Republic, and the puppets of colonialism. These calls for national unrest and defiance heightened fears of opened warfare breaking out between the Muslim, and the government of Algeria, which took power of the nation in late 1992. He read the capital, Algiers remained calm for the most part yesterday, even though hundreds of tanks and armored vehicles were deployed at all government building, and intersections spread throughout the city and nation.

Foreign reaction poured in and it was a mixed reaction at best. France, Algeria's former colonial power, said she was keeping a close eye on the present situation. France let it be known she was more than willing to commit combat troops to help preserve, and restore the calm and peace if the Muslim Fundamentalists requested any help fighting the Socialist government.

At a closed door meeting which lasted for the entire day, the New Islamic Salvation Front leaders issued a news release in the Islamic Eye newspaper. Stating the clique in power had proven its treasonous acts against their country and her people. The Muslim group called on the people of Algeria to rise up and protect their right of choice, and reject the lies presently coming from the government, and destroy their will. They went on to urge the Muslim Fundamentalists, soldiers, intellectuals, and the civilian population in general, to unite in a common cause, and to also be prepared for any and all eventualities, in order to try and save their country from this present government of tyranny, even if it meant all out war.

Mohammed through, now it's going to start, war between many of the Arab nations, as he scanned the rest of the paper with renewed interest. On page four he read more bad news for the Arab world. The Chad military had successfully destroyed most of the rebel forces within its borders, and now the deposed President, President Hissen Habre, was threatening to level new attacks aimed at the surviving rebels, who chose to remain loyal to his deposed government, both inside the nation of Chad and other rebels who fled to the Sudan to avoid being hunted down and meeting their death.

The military officials of Chad stated President Idris Dedy who overthrew the President of Chad, Habre, with the Libyan government backing the coup which drove Habre from power in December of 1990. Was asking for help from the Libyan government for a second time, if the new threaten attacks were perpetrated against his government. Libya stated in their newspaper Al Fajr El Jadid, that she was more than willing to commit a number of combat troops to help the real government of Chad, in its fight against the new rebel threat.

On the same page of the newspaper as this report he was reading, he read a story about some new fighting taking place within the country of savage lands of Somalia. Whose troops were now engaging troops from Ethiopia seeking a truce in their ongoing fighting between the warlord Mohammed Aidid, the military leader of the United Somalia Congress, (and a distant cousin of the Delegate of Ethiopia, General Farrah Aidid) and the ex-president turned warlord of Somalia, Mohammed Ali

Mahdi, in the fierce clan based urban battles raging unchecked between the tribal Militias of the beleaguered and lawless country.

Somalia was locked in the grasp of a terrible famine and severe drought, and the two powerful warring warlords, and their once population of six point five million people. Was presently down to just four million, and one was rather hard pressed to find any young children under the age of twelve, still alive in the almost completely destroyed country. At night, the sky was set aglow from the great pyre fires burning the bodies of the dead, mostly of young children and women slaughtered by the warring sides. Or they were beaten to death, or starved to death because of this ungodly, senseless, and ever on going war. The massive airlift of food stuff coming from the United States and other concerned nations of the world started in the summer of '92, and was still in operation to this day. This year's airlift was scheduled to be well over nine hundred thousand tons of food stuffs and other medical and much needed supplies. The airlift, and use of Marine soldiers to feed the starving backfired on them, because it undermined the Somalis will to even try and help themselves.

The United Nations saw little if any hope of settling the tribal wars still raging in Somalia, citing Somalia's problems to be more of an internal problem than a National one, and the warring did not presently fall under the guide lines of a civil war. They also saw it more as a class struggle than anything else. The United Nations stated it hoped other Arab countries, would refrain from acting and allow the country settle its problems without interference. However, the United Nations offered mediators to get both sides to a peace table, as they did every year to the warring sides in Bosnia Herzegovina. Many other countries of the United Nations were giving monies to Israel who got involved in the fighting, once it was proved the Serbs were trying to eliminate a race of people much in the same way Hitler himself had attempted to do.

As he continued to read the most disturbing newspaper, another article soon caught his eye. It was one about the nation of Iraq. The remaining Kurds still alive in that shattered country, discovered a number of mass graves hidden in the hills of northern Iraq. One grave contained the bodies of well over two thousand Kurdish men, women and children, while another grave recently discovered, contained the bodies of another four thousand more slaughtered by the madman of Iraq. Many of the dead bodies were examined, and most showed sever acts of violence lead to their deaths. Body's skulls were shattered by bullets fired at them at close range. A picture in the newspaper showed part of the mass grave which there could be seen many bodies of young children lying in it. A Kurdish official said they were presently looking for even more mass graves spread throughout the mountain range of the nation.

The Kurdish official showed even more proof by holding up fistfuls of photos and other documents, as he gave his interview from Ankara, the capital of Turkey. The speaker, a member of the Patriotic Union of Kurtishstan, wanted to show the rest of the world, the proof of the terrible atrocities constantly being committed by the Iraqi secret police and their foul government right under the noses of the civilized world against the Kurdish population of Iraq.

The United States released a statement condemning the past actions of Iraq and her madman of a leader and government, and America hinted at the possibly of taking some kind of military action against the Iraqi government for these latest atrocities that just came to light.

Israel was appalled at the actions Iraq took aimed against the ravished Kurdish population, and they wanted to show the correlation between the atrocities perpetrated against the millions of Jews in World War Two, and the atrocities currently being carried out against the Kurdish people of Iraq by the madman in control of that country. Israel condemned the Iraqi government's actions, calling Iraq another Nazi state. Israel warned Iraq they were no longer going to stand idly by, and watch another race of people being erased from the face of the earth. She hinted she was prepared to take military intervention if the killing continued.

This statement caused the Libyan government to warn Israel and the United States if they were to take any action against Iraq, Libya would react this time to any attack from either nation.

Ambassador Mohammed Kheir cursed as he thought the world had nothing to worry about from the Arab nations. All the world had to do was sit on the sidelines and wait until the Arab nations destroyed each other as they were constantly doing. Then the other nations could just step in, and destroy the remaining Arab countries, and the Arab's would be a people of the past, as sure as the Kurds are now. He shook his head in disgust at the thought of Arabs killing Arabs. He remembered what was written in the great book of the Holy Qu'ran, which told an Arab would never get in Paradise if he lifted his hand in anger against another Arab and he cursed. "Look at what we're doing to each other for the love of Allah. I'm certain the great Prophet Muhammad Himself would be rolling over in his grave, if he ever witnessed what we Arabs are doing to each other."

Egyptian Ambassador Mohammed Kheir's temper almost got the best of him as he thought of actually ripping the newspaper to shreds out of disgust over what some of his people were doing to themselves. When the heavy print from yet another story suddenly caught his eye this time and it read. "Islam Fundamentalists Conquest Stops At The Very Border Of Egypt."

The story was a collection of many other different Arab organizations busy threatening the very fiber of Egypt herself. The first story was about the organization of Arab fighters calling themselves The Holy War. This group was directly linked to the assassination of the former and well respected President of Egypt, Anwar el Sadat, and they challenged the seat of government after the murder. But now they were reduced to sitting in the smoke filled back rooms of small stores and shops around the capital of Egypt, to talk about what was.

A splinter group of Muslim Fundamentalists, which led to the Holy War and losing its power was the Muslim Brotherhood. This group made up the largest block to the Egyptian Parliament. The Brotherhood was outlawed in the country, when some of its members tried to assassinate the late President Abdel Nasser in 1954. But this group was given its recognition when President Hosni Mubarak was elected to power over Egypt. Another mistake the Fundamentalists did was oppose the involvement of Egypt with the United States, and Saudi Arabia in their attack on Iraq. Much of their monetary support and respect dried up, and they found themselves on the outside.

But the Brotherhood of the Islamic Fundamentalists persisted in their existence. They took over some of the smaller labor unions, and also the teaching facilities throughout Egypt, and these leaders denounced the rampant government of Egypt's corruption. The Brotherhood was staunch defenders of the true faith, hassling unveiled women walking the streets of Cairo. Other problems they caused the Egyptian government, were throwing firebombs into liquor stores and bars, as well as attacking many Christian shops and churches in Egypt. Some Fundamentalists even advocated the violent complete overthrow of the Egyptian government, thus leading to their own prosecution throughout all Egypt by the Egyptian Military forces.

Once these Muslim Fundamentalists were arrested, they were subjected to terrible tortures, more than any other state prisoners throughout Egypt. This was because they were politically outspoken and extremely violent in their beliefs. It looked like Egypt was preparing to tear herself apart from within, Mohammed thought angrily to himself. He suddenly threw the newspaper to the floor out of a new rage against it and what was happening in the Arab world.

Gail, who was sort of daydreaming as she sat by the table, was startled by the sudden angry outburst from Mohammed, and she jumped to her feet and immediately drew her weapon as she moved away from the small table and checked around herself.

JoAnne, who was also in the room, asked him what was wrong. But he was so angry he could no longer help himself, he took his uncontrolled anger out on his man servant before he realized what he was doing to the young man.

"Salim, you'll get your miserable ass in here right this minute, you young fool you!" He snarled harshly at the young man.

Gail put away her weapon before Mohammed even noticed it was out and she had it aimed directly at his chest.

As the slender and rather young man appeared in the room with concern causing lines on his forehead. He yelled at him harshly. "Where the hell is my supper at god dammit! I'm hungry you useless piece of shit you. Get me some food before I beat you for failing in your duties for me, you lowly worthless jackal." He was so upset he dared to slap the young man across his face in front of the two stunned looking young women in the room.

Salim staggered back in stunned disbelief as he rubbed the side of his face with his hand.

"Get my supper out now dammit!" Were his final words to the staring young man.

This was not the first time he struck the frail young man. But this was the first time he did so in front of anyone else who might have been in the room with them. The embarrassment hurt him much more than the blow itself. Salim moved as fast as he could to the kitchen and within moments, he had the diner resting on the plates, and then on the table.

His meat was a little raw, but he ate it without complaining further. He felt terrible about losing his temper and striking the poor Salim, especially before the two women in the room. But his position kept him from apologizing to the young man.

The group ate in silence, the women afraid to speak, and he was to angry to speak. After they finished, they moved to the living room and sat for a moment, before he announced he was going to place his call to the Israeli Diplomat. He stood, than went to his bedroom office, followed by JoAnne. She sat down on the edge of the desk, allowing her dress fall from her legs.

He had no trouble seeing she did not have underpants on. He picked up the receiver and aimed it at her and said. "Will you excuse me for a moment please."

She shot back at him. "Not on your life." As she settled in to listen to the conversation.

Mohammed Kheir shook his head slowly, hating the lovely prison he found himself locked within, and dialed the phone to the Israeli politician as he ignored the beautiful young female still in his private office, and sitting on the edge of his desk before him.

CHAPTER 5

The phone rang three times before it was finally answered. A young sounding male voice responded politely. "This is the Israeli Ambassador's private office to the United Nations. How may I be of service to you please?"

"Yes, and this is Ambassador Mohammed Kheir from the Egyptian Delegation, sir. I wish to speak to Ambassador Haetzni if he's available that is, sir." The young Egyptian politician nearly growled in the phone in a commanding tone before he caught himself.

"Yes, I recognize your name sir. I shall have Ambassador Haetzni on the phone in a few seconds for you Ambassador Kheir Sir. Please hold the line sir, and thank you very much for your patience sir." Immediately, music came on the line as Ambassador Mohammed Kheir was forced to wait for the Delegate from Israel to finally answer the phone for him.

The music was disconnected and the voice of Ambassador Haetzni came in on the line as he spoke pleasantly to his counterpart on the phone. "Ah yes Mohammed Kheir Sir, it is a real pleasure to hear your voice once again sir. It has been a long time since the last time we spoke together sir. How is your wife and children doing Ambassador Mohammed Sir?"

"Fine they are all fine thank you for asking about them sir." He responded as he calmed down even more now. He kind of liked this

VJew politician, because he was so pleasant to speak with, and he always tried to stay to his word once he gave it to anyone.

Ambassador Haetzni smiled because he knew as well as most of the other Delegates from the United Nations that he was a real womanizer, and he gave little thought for his wife or children living in Egypt. It did not matter to him a bit what he did with his life, because it was standard practice for many delegates to have a woman or two on the side. In order to take away some boredom of the long lonely nights while so far away from home and family. Most women used by the Delegates were supplied by the governments they represented. An added perk, if you will. "How can I be of help to you Mohammed?" Ambassador Haetzni asked pleasantly.

He decided to get right to the point with the Jewish Ambassador and he offered. "Ambassador Haetzni Sir, my government has asked me to place this call to you to inform you we're requesting permission from your government, to move a small unit of engineers, and workers into the Sinai Desert. In hopes of exploring this region for any possible hidden water stores, sir. As you know, within the next two year's time we in Egypt will lose a certain amount of Nile water to Ethiopia, and we have to make up the difference somehow sir.

"We're looking into the use of desalination plants much like the ones presently in operation in Saudi Arabia and Kuwait. We sent a number of our engineers there to explore the use of these systems. But this is far in Egypt's future. Many of our engineers think it'd be far easier and faster to find the water we'll need in the Sinai Desert. So my President would appreciate all the assistance your government might want to offer in Egypt's quest to search for newly discovered sources of water, sir." He stopped talking and held his breath, while waiting for the Israeli politician to respond to his last words.

A nervous laugh and then the Israeli politician offered to the Egyptian Delegate in a calm voice. "Slow down a little here Mohammed Kheir. You know if this request came from any other person on the face of the earth. I'd think there was an ulterior motive hiding behind this request sir. I'll tell you this much Ambassador Mohammed. The mere presence of your Egyptian engineers moving into the Sinai Desert would cause my government great distress, sir. We'd have to monitor these workers extremely carefully, sir. If they're allowed to enter the Sinai Desert that is sir. As you 're aware, our countries have always used the Sinai as a sort of buffer zone between our two great nations, Ambassador Kheir. I don't know about this latest request coming from you and your nation, Mohammed.

"Is there any other possible way for your government to try and locate the water they're going to need in the future, other than by sending your people into the Sinai Desert, sir? I'm afraid I have to be quite honest with you Mohammed. This request of yours will scare many of my people, especially with the latest unrest currently happening throughout many of the other Arab countries, sir. My government remembers the terrible threats your country had issued against the nation of Ethiopia at the last Security meeting, sir. Mohammed, I seriously doubt if my country will go along with your request, I'm sorry."

He sighed deeply as he replied. "I'm terribly sorry also Ambassador Haetzni Sir. But I'm going to have to insist for your permission to enter the Sinai Desert region to try and search for water there, sir. Look at it this way Ambassador Haetzni, if you withhold your country's permission for us to search for water in this area of the desert, and if Ethiopia goes through with her plans with this Dam they plan to construct, and they cut down the flow of the Nile River waters to my country, sir. These terrible decisions will leave my country with little if any other choice but to think about a military response to the situation, in order to acquire the water we'll need to survive as a nation, sir. Don't get me wrong Ambassador, I'm not making any threats here sir, you have known me for more than eleven years now, sir. I know you as a man of your word sir. I hope you think of me in the same light sir."

The Israeli Delegate cut him off as he stated back to him. "I do Mohammed, and I have nothing but the greatest of respect for you as a person, and a man of your word, sir. And it is important for me to know that you think of me in much the same manner, sir."

He cut him off this time as he added. "I'm pleased we can speak to each other in this manner Ambassador Haetzni. I want you to understand that I'm not threatening anyone with a fact my country is ready to go to war. I want you to comprehend if your country chooses to block our request to explore for water in the Sinai, my country will have no choice but to fight for our very existence. We need water to survive sir!"

"Mohammed, don't misunderstand me sir. I didn't think for one minute you were threatening me or my country with war, sir. I understand of Egypt's need for water, and I'll do everything in my power to help your country out with this problem. I'm quite certain we could work out something that'll be most satisfactory to our countries as long as we talk, and if you were to send the units into the desert, maybe we could send some of our engineers and workers to accompany your workers, and assist you in your search for any new sources of water there. I hope you know you're not the first government to search for water in the Sinai Desert, a number of your great Pharaohs searched the desert, but they didn't have much luck finding water, sir."

He sighed deeply again and then he replied to the Israeli Delegate. "Of course they didn't find any water, but they didn't have the modern day equipment, or the technology we currently have at our disposal, when they initiated their search for water the first time in this region of the world, sir. Ambassador Haetzni, I want to be completely frank with you on this problem, sir. All I and my government wants, is to head off a possible war in the future, and save our people, that is all. I'll do everything in my power to make sure peace in this region is preserved, sir. But I do have to warn you sir, if my country loses Nile water to Ethiopia, and you refuse permission for us to explore the Sinai Desert for a new source of water. I don't know how long I can possibly hold my country from striking out at the countries trying to destroy her sir.

"I further promise you Ambassador Haetzni that Egypt has no ulterior motive for our people wanting to go out into the desert, other than looking for our much needed water, sir. There is nothing more important to my country and her people than water, and peace with your country. If we have water, we have peace it is that simple. There is another option left open to us, and that is if you don't want us to explore in the Sinai Desert for water then maybe you could use your influence with the United States and her President, and see if she could stop Ethiopia from cutting off the flow of water from the Nile River to Egypt, sir. Then everything will be back to the way things were before Ethiopia started this latest trouble with our water supply, and Egypt's future sir." He held his breath while waiting for the Israeli Delegate to say something more positive to him this time.

"Ambassador Mohammed Kheir, you have just given me something to think about, and try to work out for you sir. I shall surely speak to my people tonight sir. I don't know how long it shall take for them to come up with a possible working solution to this problem of yours, correct that, with all of ours. But I'm certain my country won't let your people down sir. My country will remember the Egyptian government, and her great and respected people were the first Arab State to ever offer, and then make peace with Israel. I feel personally, your country has nothing to worry about. As always, I like your attitude Ambassador Kheir. I'm pleased you're so interested in keeping the peace in this region, and between our two great countries, sir.

"I shall inform my government of this surprising offer you have made of me, sir. Thank you again Ambassador Mohammed Kheir, and I assure you I'll be in touch with you when I get word from my people, as to what they would want to do about your present request, sir. I should warn you in advance though Ambassador Kheir, my people might put some restrictions on your people, if they were to allow your engineers and workers to explore the Sinai Desert for water. You might be forced to take some of my engineers along with your workers, I know you offered this solution sir. I'm sorry for this, but after all these years of fighting the Arab nations, I know my government would have a hard time trusting your country's intention."

Ambassador Haetzni stopped speaking at this point, he hated speaking to Mohammed in this harsh manner. He knew deep in his mind he would allow the Egyptians to do whatever they needed to do, to find their needed water supplies. He had known Mohammed for many years now, and he trusted him emphatically, and he was going to suggest to his fellow countrymen as a sign of good will that they should allow the Egyptians to go into the Sinai Desert with their blessing and even help. If the Egyptians declined an offer of help from Israel. Israel should still allow them go on their way, or maybe reinforce some of their troops along the Negeu and Sinai Deserts, if they had not learned as yet to trust the Egyptians.

Ambassador Haetzni shook his head slowly as he mumbled to himself, someone sooner or later will have to start trusting the other side, and it might as well be Israeli's turn to try some of that trust and goodwill. After all, we Israelis wanted the Arab nations to trust Israel, and yet we have not learned to offer them any trust in return, even to the friendly Arab governments who has accepted Israel as a nation in the Middle East.

Mohammed broke the silence as he offered to the Israeli politician. "Ambassador Haetzni Sir, I thought after all these years of peace between our two great nations, there would be some manner of trust shown from both sides. I'm quite certain my government understands you'd want to put certain restrictions on us, but to want to send your people with mine into the desert, I don't understand this. We in Egypt are no threat to your country, sir. Please my old friend, if you have to place some of your people with mine, have your government tell mine they're being sent with us to help, and that is all. It'll make a most bitter pill that much easier to swallow, if you know what I mean, Ambassador. This bit of advice is just between us." He said as he tried to keep the anger from creeping into his voice, he knew this wise Jew could sense his feeling of anger growing over the thoughts of sending Jews along with his people.

"Ambassador Mohammed Kheir, I feel your anger and I don't blame you one bit for being so upset sir. I shall inform my government of what you have proposed to me, and I'll try to have them show the trust your government should have from us, sir. I'm quite certain I can convince them to show some good faith to your country Mohammed, and allow your people do what they have to in your search for water. I know if we send our people along with your workers, all they'll do is serve to be in your way every time your people turned around. I'll point this out to my people. Give me some time to try and work this out, I'm quite certain I'll have a solution, one that'll not insult your government or its people. Good night Ambassador Kheir. If there were more understanding people in this world like yourself, I'm certain peace would rule the Middle East in my lifetime, and many lifetimes to come."

Mohammed let out his breath in a rush, knowing if anyone could get the Israeli government to listen to them, it was this Jew he was speaking with over the phone. He understood if he could send his engineers out in the Sinai Desert without the Jews interfering with them, his people could hide the land mines they had to. If Israel put their nose into the business of Egypt, Egypt would lop it off like it should have been done in the 1973 war. He could not believe he had this type of thought, all this time he thought he was well above this type of reaction towards the Jew state. He looked at the receiver and offered. "Yes, good night Ambassador Haetzni Sir, I shall wish you all the luck in the world on your task. I knew I could talk to you sir." With this, he hung up and took three quick breaths.

The instant the receiver hit the cradle, JoAnne cried out. "I see you are very good at what you do Mohammed, you're going to pull this off for us with the lowly Jews. You're going to get the Jews to trust you, an Arab. Who would have ever thought this possible. Jews trusting Arabs, and it's going to cost them their worthless necks for that trust. Sonofabitch Mohammed, no wonder your government didn't want us to kill you, and President Sadat trusts you so much. Come on

Mohammed, tonight is your night to enjoy, you have made me much money today, and you have also made me happy, and when I'm happy, I'm pleased. So I want you happy. I want to make love to you in a way you have never made love before. Gail, I want your help. Let's show this poor Egyptian fool what it means to make us happy."

JoAnne stood and she pulled Mohammed to his feet then led him to the master bedroom of the apartment, as she quickly undressed while walking with him. The night was long, and it was a maddening blind meld of twisted, wiggling hot bodies combined with sweat and words of praise for Mohammed, mumbled by both young women as they fulfilled his wildest dreams. Yet he was not very happy, because he was still deeply troubled by the deceit he was perpetrating on a well trusted and long time friend, even if that friend was a Jew.

He was the first one to wake and take his morning shower. He enjoyed having the shower to himself for the first time since the two beautiful but extremely deadly women came to stay with him. Salim was up already and had his breakfast ready when he emerged from the shower. A folded newspaper sat by his place.

Gail appeared in the kitchen dressed as he seated himself. She sat opposite him and Salim gave her a cup of coffee without being asked for one, and she sipped the steaming brew. She did not talk, just stared at nothing in particular.

The Egyptian politician figured she was not totally awake yet, and she was just going through the motions out of habit. He had no doubt in his mind these two women would keep a close eye on him even in their sleep, and possibly shoot him without thinking about it. He picked at his eggs and did not bother to eat the toast as he unfolded his newspaper. Today, the headlines stated many pollsters picked the New York Giants to win this year's Super Bowl. Sports did not interest him in the least, so he turned to the second page of the paper, where there was an article about the quarterback of the newly rebuilt Giants, a John Resse. The article read he was going to be the third black quarterback to ever be picked to win the famous Super Bowl game.

He shook his head as he thought how most Americans, especially after all these years, still referred to a man or woman by the color of his or her skin. Who gave a care if this young football player was black or not. Why did the paper just say the young man instead of the young black man. He laughed at the proud Americans who run around every day of their worthless lives saying they're color blind and proud of it, and yet they still write about and refer to this man as a black quarterback. "How stupid these foolish Americans truly are." He grumbled.

Gail looked up in sort of a stupor and asked him with a little concern in her voice. "What was that you just said Mohammed?"

"Nothing, I forgot you were sitting there you are so quiet young woman. I just read something out loud that is all woman."

Gail did not wait for his explanation, and she went back to her private little world locked away in her daydream.

The Egyptian politician looked to the third page of the newspaper and read; The Baltic Alliance was getting their food prices under somewhat of control, as they put most of the black marketers out of business in their countries. It now cost a black marketer his life if he was caught selling goods illegally. There was a story about another coup attempt in the old part of Russia. On the same page of the newspaper, there was a story stating the United States was sending the Army Core of Engineers to Ethiopia, to put the construction of the Dam in full operation. He read there was continued trouble with the warring tribes, and the civilian workers falling well behind in their work on the purposed Ethiopian Dam, mainly because of the minor attacks leveled against the workers.

The American Army Core of Engineers were being sent to the country, to help the Ethiopian's with the construction of the Dam, and to further help the civilian workers form good work crews, and offer protection from the insurgent constantly attacking on them. He was angry as he thought of these rat people, who could not stop fighting amongst themselves for one minute. They were even fighting the people working to help their own country survive. The United Nations wanted Egypt to trust these people biting the hand trying to feed them.

He understood the Army Engineers had special CIA Agents mixed in with the American workers, as well as military advisors, and probably fighting soldiers. He turned to the next page, almost threatening to put down the paper, if he read another story which distressed him. But just as fast, he read a headline printed in bold print on the fourth page and his blood ran cold.

IRAN TRAINS SUDANESE SOLDIERS IN GUERRILLA WARFARE IN THE SUDAN

The article went on to read. 'Fearing a possible unprovoked attack from Libya, the Sudanese President has appealed for help from the other Arab countries in the region, and Iran was the first nation to respond to the cry for help even though she was not an Arab country. Iran sent two thousand military advisors to the Sudan, to train the Sudanese military in guerrilla warfare tactics to be fought on their land. The Iranian government intended to send a number of aircraft, both French and American made warplanes to the Sudan.

The Iranian government also planned to train the Sudanese flyers on how to fly, and intended to sell the Sudanese military their surplus tanks, armored vehicles, and long range artillery pieces. The United States let it be known she was going to send the Sudanese, planes, tanks, and artillery pieces to help them protect its borders against the growing threat from a possible invasion by Libya. The article went on to mention Libya was also threatening to go after the deposed President of Chad, supposedly to be in exile in the Sudan. No one knew where President Habre truly was hiding out, but Mohammed knew the deposed President of Chad was somewhere close to Chad, and he was still causing unrest through his supporters.

Mohammed Kheir wondered about Iran, he both fears and hated that country and what her intentions truly were in this region of the world. He wondered if Iran knew of Libya and Egypt's plans to attack Chad, the Sudan and Ethiopia in the near future. Over the passing years, after her wars with Iraq, Iran turned into a some what stabilizing force in the Middle East. Iran was the first country to call for peace throughout the Arab world, ever since the American hostage releases of late 1991, and early 1992 years. Iran also took the role of the Arab peacemaker. Iran's President Hashemi Rafsanjani was still in power, went so far as to resume diplomatic relations with the United States, and America sent help to Iran when she was hit by the devastating earthquake late in 1993.

Iran offered to sit in on any meetings as a none interested mediator between the two countries of Libya and Chad's deposed president, which caused Libya to level threats towards Iran. Libya accused Iran of being a puppet government for the United States, and she further accused Iran of helping the United States to get a foothold in the Sudan. Thus threatening Libya from the southeast in the Sudan, and the north from the sea. Libya even went so far as to threaten to attack Iran if she helped the Americans or Sudanese military and government any further.

Iran ignored the threats from Libya, but she responded to the accusation of Libya calling Iran a puppet government for the United States. Iran sent a stinging letter off to the Libyan President, warning Iran was more than capable, and would defend her shores against a Libyan threat.

Egyptian Ambassador Mohammed Kheir understood the United States was well prepared to help Iran if Libya carried out her latest threat to attack the Sudan or Iran. He was also aware the United States was secretly supplying Iran with the military hardware, and America was also training the Iranian fighters in the operation of this military equipment they were receiving.

The Egyptian politician laughed while saying out loud. "If only the world knew of the back door politics going on because of this Middle

East situation over Egypt's the need of water." He wondered how the United States was going to react, if she ever found out the Japanese were selling war components for electronic warfare to Libya, and the Russians were selling old nuclear warheads and missiles to Libya as well. Many of Russia's weapons and nuclear specialists were now in Libya, and they were helping Libya become a super power in her own right.

He breathed a deep sigh of relief, and then continued to scan the newspaper until he came across yet another article that caught his attention in the paper. Again the civilian Kenyan government cracked down on the pro democratic movement as it did back in 1992. The article informed the reader the democratic movement was rapidly gaining momentum throughout the entire state, but the totalitarian government of Kenya slaughtered any troublemakers without mercy. Hundreds of civilians who wanted freedom and change their government, died in terrible and unprovoked attacks against them by heavily armed soldiers. As he read on, Libya's name was mentioned again, as to commit troops to help the Kenya government put down the troublemakers making problems for their government.

The concerned Egyptian politician was certain Libya had secretly committed hundreds of her troops, and they were already stationed in Kenya, and they were most likely the ones slaughtering the insurgents and civilians who got in their way. He was not very concerned with the fate of the Kenya people, because no Arab countries classified these people as Arabs. He felt these god cursed people were poor blacks, just waiting for the world to pick up their tab for their being lazy, which was far from the truth. Because there were no harder working people in all of Africa, than the Kenyan's. He hoped Libya could take over the country, that way it could become a true Arab country in due time.

Ambassador Mohammed knew if Libya took over the nation of Kenya, the blacks would be a people of the past, as the Arabs permeated the population and rapidly took it over. He thought that's probably the best thing that could ever happen to this miserable lowly country of poor misfits. He had it with the newspaper and all the disturbing news he was reading and crumpled up the newspaper and then threw it to the floor in anger.

The next three days passed boringly by for the Egyptian Ambassador. He was ordered by President Sadat to stay put in his apartment until he heard from the Israeli Delegate. The women were worse than pests to him. They were everywhere he wanted to be, and constantly getting in his way or disturbing his concentration. He never saw JoAnne contact Sadat, but the few times he spoke with him, Sadat knew everything he did, or was doing for the past few days. He took to reading the newspaper everyday, to keep up with the current events occurring in Central Africa.

On the forth day of his unofficial house arrest, the Israeli Ambassador Haetzni placed a return call to him. "Mohammed Kheir." The voice on the other end of the phone requested.

He was actually surprised Ambassador Haetzni had placed the call to him in person as he offered. "Yes Ambassador Haetzni, this is he. How are you today sir." He replied politely as he shifted nervously in his chair.

"Just great Mohammed, and how are you today sir?" Ambassador Haetzni's voice was rather upbeat and slightly excited while he was speaking to the Egyptian politician.

"Fine, fine." He did not bother to mince his words as he started right off with the Israeli. "Has your government reached a decision on my government's request to all our workers to enter the Sinai Desert in search of water, Ambassador Haetzni Sir?"

Haetzni laughed as he replied just as excitedly as the Egyptian was acting on the phone. "I'm certain your ears must have burned over the past few days, sir. Yes, I learned many new curse words over the past few days I assure you, Mohammed. In all my years, I thought I have heard every curse in every language there was to hear or be called. There were a few times in our discussions I thought some members of Parliament was going to demand my resignation, and I thought some others were going to have a heart attack over my words.

"They became so red in the face with anger, before the meeting came to a close. Never mind all this, it's nothing but politics as you well understand, and it does not concern you in the least. You're only interested in the outcome of these most heated discussions. Yes Mohammed, we have come to a decision about your government's request, sir. At first, the Security Council demanded any expedition into the Sinai Desert have five Israeli police, or troops accompany the units into the desert. But then I pointed out we're dealing with the only Arab country with whom we have a peace accord, and we had to start showing trust if we're going to demand trust in return. That statement set off another round of new and unfamiliar curses to me."

He laughed, causing the Jew to stop speaking and laugh with him.

The Israeli politician then continued with his words to the Egyptian. "As I was saying Mohammed. When the yelling and cursing calmed a little, others of the Council started to sympathize with me, mostly the young new members, sir. There were many who didn't want to trust any Arab nation, mostly the hardliners at the meeting. The ones who fought in the wars of the past against the Arabs were the hardest to convince to start trusting any Arab country. You had to deal with some of these people on many occasions, sir. But thank the Almighty there were some who wanted to show faith, and after heated discussions. The Parliament voted, and they decided to put their trust in the Arab nation who showed their trust in our country.

The Egyptian politician was hanging onto every words the long winded and stalling Jewish politician was dragging on.

"Mohammed, my government gave its permission for your government to enter the Sinai Desert whenever they so choose to do so, sir. However, there are some requirements and restrictions attached to the allowance I'm afraid, sir. They request your government to inform us when and where your engineers will be working before they even enter the Sinai Desert. Also Mohammed, I must request your engineers and camp be open to spot searches at any time of day or night. Mohammed please, before you get angry, between you and me. I don't think my government would ever dare stop and search your workers, sir. But please, in case it does happen sir. I beg of you that your workers open themselves to these investigations, sir.

"Failure to do so could open the way to our military forces taking over any work in the Sinai Desert your workers were completing, and also might lead to hard feelings between our two countries, sir. I trust you can see the importance for your workers to hide nothing from my people in they happen to want to search your workers in the desert, sir. Mohammed, we say we trust Egypt, but you know neither side really trusts the other. I'm afraid we have a long way to go yet. Mohammed, look at what we have accomplished here today, sir. If my government sent some of my people into the desert to check on your workers sir, and nothing was wrong, or nothing threatening the security of Israel was found. It could well lead to more trust from my government, and who knows where this could all lead, sir? We could actually be reshaping the way the Arab nations, and Israel look and think about each other, maybe even change the face of the Middle East all together if you will.

"Yes, and maybe this will even lead to the acceptance of Israel's presence within the Arab countries and the world, sir. Mohammed, this is the first time since the collapse of the Middle East peace talks of 1992 and 1993 that almost forced peace which Iran was able to bring around, that any Arab country talked with Israel. We could be opening the lines of communications once again. And who knows, with all the young blood in our Parliament at this time, and the youth taking power in many of the Arab states where this could lead, we could be seeing the long awaited peace of the Middle East, Mohammed.

"Mohammed, I stuck my way neck out for you and your nation of Egypt in the past few days my friend, and I think this entitles me to ask you this question and expect an honest answer to it, sir. I hope I don't insult you with this question, but it does have to be asked, and you being who you are, and a well trusted and honorable Diplomat, sir. I shall put my faith in your answer, and it'll stand on its own merits, and the question will never be asked of you again once answered, sir. Mohammed, your people are not up to anything in the Sinai Desert, except for merely looking for water as you have told me they were, right?"

There were a few seconds of silence on both ends. Mohammed took a deep breath and then let it out slowly which was easily heard by the Israeli as he responded. "Ambassador Haetzni, I assure you sir we are only entering the desert looking for water, nothing more and nothing less, sir. We need water to survive as a nation and people, and with Ethiopia threatening to cut off some of the supply of Nile water from us, we have to look elsewhere for it, sir. Ambassador Haetzni, I'm not insulted by your question, quite on the contrary I understand it was a question which had to be asked of me. I hope I have answered it to your complete satisfaction sir. Now that it has been asked and put aside, maybe we get down to the real problems and seek their solutions. When can we think about going into the desert and start our exploration for this needed water, and how much trouble can we expect from your soldiers when we do go in, sir?"

Israeli Ambassador Haetzni was angered by his last remark aimed at him, but he chose to ignore it as he went on with his words to the Egyptian. "Mohammed, as far as I know, my government is not going to give any of your people difficulties, sir. I wish you would get that thought out of your mind all together sir. All my government plans to do at this point is maybe, just maybe check on a unit or two every once in a while, sir. Just for the first few months or so of your operation, Mohammed. Until the trust is firmly established and then you'll not know we exist. As far as I'm led to believe at this point, when your engineers are ready, you can start you search for water. Mohammed, I wish your people the very best of luck in their quest. Because I feel I can trust you, and your aim is truly peaceful sir.

"This work will ensure peace between our two countries sir. One other thing you must be made aware of Mohammed, my government wishes me to inform your government, if there is anything we can possibly do to aid in your search for water, don't hesitate for a second to ask us sir. We'll be more than pleased to do anything to help your people during these trying times. Thank you for your interest in keeping the peace in this region, Mohammed. Can I expect you here later today to sign this agreement between our two countries, sir?"

He breathed a great sigh of relief as he replied to the Israeli politician. "On behalf of the government of Egypt Ambassador Haetzni, I thank the good government of Israel for its kind understanding of this situation. I appreciate your kind offer to help the people of Egypt in her time of most need, sir. If we need help with this project, I shall be the first one to let you know, sir. Once again, thank you Ambassador Haetzni for your kind help, and yes, I'll be there later today to sign this agreement between our two nations, sir. What time would you want me to be at your office? Would it be all right for me to bring my secretary to the meeting?"

"One o'clock would work out just fine with me Ambassador Kheir, and please feel free to bring along your private secretary if you care too, sir."

"One o'clock it is then sir. Thank you once again Ambassador Haetzni." With this said, Mohammed Kheir hung up the phone, and then he sat back in his chair and took a quick breath for himself, and held it before letting it out slowly. He turned to his left and saw JoAnne was staring at him and said to her. "I didn't know you were standing there. I guess you heard?"

"Yes. I'm very pleased you had the wise foresight to ask the Jew permission for me to come with you on your visit to his office later today, Mohammed. I would've found it extremely awkward to just show up without the Jew knowing I was coming. This was good thinking on your part Mohammed. I shall inform President Sadat I trust you completely. This should get some pressure off your shoulders, and it should also help in your relationship with your new President. I'm sorry it had to be done this way, but President Sadat didn't know if he could trust you or not and it was up to Gail and myself to find out. I'll assure him he can trust you sir. If you'll please excuse me, I'm going to have to get ready for the meeting. I want to look my best for our meeting with the lowly Jew." She said with a smile as she quickly left the room.

He yelled to Salim for coffee, which he brought quickly. He looked around the room for the other woman who was nowhere to be seen, so he enjoyed his coffee in peace.

Seconds later, he heard the water in the shower running, and knew JoAnne was going to be out of his hair for the time being. His ears perked up because the water stopped, and he looked in the direction of the bathroom. But JoAnne did not appear, he heard singing from behind the door. As he thought, he found himself liking having these two beautiful young women at his beck and call, but he did not like losing his freedom though. Then he reasoned it out by thinking, if one had to lose his freedom, there could be no better way to lose it than to have these two beautiful female jailers who would do anything he asked of them. A smile suddenly crossed his lips as he thought about last nights activities with both of his blonde jailers. Then his thoughts went back to the Jew politician.

Anger showed in his eyes as he thought, who did this Jew think he was, to dare tell him or any of his people that his people could not go out into a certain area of their own nation, without the permission from the Jews first. Even though he truly liked this Israeli politician, he could not help but feel some resentment towards him and the rest of his people. Anger rose from deep within his chest as he thought about how his country had to bend over backwards, to try and keep the peace between their two countries, and it always seemed the Jews were constantly doing something to rub the Arabs noses into the sand.

Ambassador Kheir remembered the chance his country took to achieve the peace between the two nations of the Middle East. But

Israel had to go and build their homes in the occupied territories taken during the wars of the past times with the other Arab nations of the Middle East. Dashing all hopes of peace in the almost wars of '93 and '94 over these same lands. He thanked Allah that Saudi Arabia was wise enough and gave some of their land to the Palestinian peoples. So the Palestinians could have a land under the guise they cause no more trouble with the Jewish state, in a effort to force peace in the area between the two nations. The Palestinians had not caused any further trouble in the region, and Israel was supposed to start talks again about the possibility of giving the Palestinians, Jerusalem as their homeland.

The Egyptian Ambassador could not help but feel the Israeli government caused most of their own hell for themselves. By fighting constantly with the other Arab nations of the Middle East at every twist and turn they took. He really hated having to deal with them. He remembered how many times he had prayed to Allah to strike all the Jews of the world dead with a simple wave of his mighty hand. But he also understood the Israeli people deserved a place to live in peace in this world. He marveled at how Saudi Arabia and his country had gotten along with these most arrogant of people. But he also wondered how his people would act, if the Egyptian people were killed like the Jews were in World War Two.

Maybe they had earned their arrogance at that. Hell, he thought, am I giving them a crutch to hang onto here? Enough. The Jews have to make it in this world on their own, like all other nations of the world, and stop collecting the sympathy of the other nations for what had happened to them in the long ago past. They have to earnestly try to fit in with the Arab countries of the area, or there will never be a true peace in this region of the world.

Putting his head back for a brief moment, he rubbed his burning eyes as he thought about what was happening in the rest of the world today, and he found himself wondered if there ever was going to be anything left of the world for his son if he made it to adulthood. What would be left for him if he made it? Was the world going to be made up of ash and dust, with ninety percent of the world's population dead, and the rest who survived the war, locked in a nuclear winter, or forced to live like rats in dark cellars and underground for the rest of their lives? Or are the so called adults going to finally come to grips with their hatred, and put a stop to all this killing. We are killing people in the name of religion, nationality, color of skin, or any other reason we could possibly come up with to justify killing people.

"Maybe it's time for the Christian belief of another coming of their Christ Savior. Maybe we should remove all the people off the face of the earth, and give it back to the lowly animals of the world. How ironic all this sounded to him, to wipe out the human so called civilized people acting like wild animals, and give the earth back to the wild animals who were acting more civilized than the humans were. This thought made him laugh just as JoAnne placed her hand on his shoulder, making his eyes fly open as he jumped from his chair.

JoAnne jumped and then offered to Mohammed as she tried to stifle a laugh. "Oh, I'm sorry I scared you Mohammed. You must have been deep in thought, and didn't hear me come in, you were laughing. I thought you must have read a joke in the paper and I wanted to know it."

Ambassador Kheir did not say anything back to her. Instead, he stood there staring at her with his mouth hanging open. Mainly because she was standing before him dressed in a deep, blood red, skin tight dress which barely covered her ample breasts. It looked like her breasts were actually fighting to be free of the rather restrictive fabric.

The Egyptian politician wondered how her breasts were ever being held inside the dress like they were. He looked at the sides of the dress which were slit up both sides to where she was unable to wear underpants, or they would have shown in the slits. She wore thigh high black nylons and the front of her hair was put up in a bun, but her long blonde hair was allowed to flow free on her back and over her shoulders. Her lipstick set off her well tan face perfectly, and her blue eyes were ringed with a matching eye shadow. She was strikingly beautiful, and her mere presence would dominate any conversations which might take place at the meeting with the Jew politician. He knew if any other women were going to be present at this meeting, their tongues were going to be set to wagging over his stunningly beautiful weapon accompanying him. He felt proud to be with this total weapon and beautiful young woman.

"I see you approve of my choice of dress. Err... you can start breathing again if you like."

"My dear young woman, in that dress you could ever arouse a gauze wrapped mummy who had been dead for three thousand years. You look great today woman. I believe I like my new assignment after all." The Egyptian politician offered with much conviction in his tone this time.

"If you like this dress, you just wait until we come back to the apartment from our meeting with the Israeli politician. You'll not believe what I have in mind to do to your poor body on you, Mohammed Kheir. You'll not believe it even while it's happening to you, lover. If all goes as well as is planned today, sir. Then we're going to be making love like you have never dreamed possible in your entire life Mohammed Kheir, all three of us. Because once this meeting is finally over, all that'll be left for Gail and myself to do, is guard you, and to make love to you and anyone else you want us to entertain. Someone you might want to get extra power and command over, Mohammed. We'll be yours to command at your will sir." Again she laughed at Mohammed and the looked he was wearing, and she was joined by Gail who just walked into the room with them.

He announced with a snap in his tone that he was going to and take a shower, and then change in his suit and then go to their scheduled meeting with the Israeli politician. He offered to take JoAnne out to lunch before the meeting, but she refused, saying she would much rather eat after the meeting was completed, which he fully understood after seeing how she was stuffed into her very restricting dress.

The Egyptian went in the bathroom next and took a steaming hot shower. JoAnne put out his favorite suit on the bed in his room, and then waited for Mohammed in the bedroom. He dressed while declining the offer of oral sex from his young female bodyguard. Once he was dressed, he and JoAnne left the apartment for their meeting with the Jew politician. It was twelve fifteen p.m. already, and the Israeli Embassy was some fifteen to twenty minutes drive from them, depending on the flow of the downtown Manhattan afternoon traffic.

Salim sent for Mohammed's limo, and it was waiting outside the building as the pair came out. The doorman opened the door while taking a good look at JoAnne, who made a big deal out of getting into the car. Showing as much leg as she possibly could, and driving the poor man crazy with her flashing legs, and her breasts dangling in front of the old man's face.

JoAnne smiled at Mohammed, knowing he was fully aware of what she was doing to the poor doorman. The limo slowly pulled away from the front of his building, and they sat in silence, with the Ambassador looking out the side window of the car while deep in thought of the upcoming meeting with the Jew, and JoAnne was sort of thinking to herself, as the car headed for the Israel Embassy. Minutes later the limo pulled in front of the pair of gates, and two Israeli guards open the iron gates for them, and the car was allowed to pull into the courtyard, and then park in the designated parking place for all visitors to the embassy. Once there, they were met by a young Israeli man who obviously was a soldier dressed in civilian clothes.

The slight bulge under the side of his suit was made from a pistol he was obviously carrying, and he easily noticed it as he got out of the car and then waited for JoAnne to join him. They were expected and then quickly lead into the embassy and over to the Ambassador's private office. After all the usual formalities were done with, he and the Israeli politician signed the necessary documents and then shook hands.

Then they shared a glass of fine French wine together. The Israeli Ambassador was having a real tough time with keeping his eyes off the front of JoAnne's dress throughout the entire meeting with the two. With every move she made, JoAnne exposed just enough of her breasts to keep his attention locked in place, and this pleasant distraction kept the Israeli politician off stride throughout the entire meeting which made Mohammed feel like he was one up on the Jewish Delegate. He quickly realized he was going to enjoy putting to use the weapons he was now armed with in the form of two lovely young women.

The meeting went off with much strain between both men, because they both felt they were giving into the other, and neither one liked the feeling in the least. When the signing of the agreement was completed, and the wine drank. Ambassador Mohammed Kheir made his excuses he had to leave, and the Israeli politician could not wait to have this man finally leave.

Once the two were back in the long black limo, JoAnne remarked to Mohammed. "I thought the Jew was going to trip over his tongue, and I made certain he saw all he wanted to see whenever he looked at me." Her laughter was joined by Mohammed, who saw the Jew almost fall out of his chair when JoAnne uncrossed her legs in front of him at the meeting.

Ambassador Kheir ordered the driver to take them to the best restaurant he knew in this section of New York City. There they enjoyed lunch, and the extra attention the waiters showed them. He was certain this was because of the dress JoAnne almost wore, and was mostly coming out of. It seemed every time JoAnne moved, every male in the restaurant held their breath and stared at her, hoping to see her charms she was clearly putting on display for all to see.

The United States kept their word, and sent two thousand Army Core of Engineers and special advisors to Ethiopia to help search for the best possible location to position the new Dam on the tributary which flowed from the mighty Lake Tana. After three months of research, it was finally decided to place the Dam a quarter of a mile down river from the great Tesissat Falls. This area was covered with deep, blue hard as steel granite stone miles deep and wide. A great base for any Dam to be constructed on.

The water going over the falls here fell two hundred feet from Lake Tana down to a flat plateau. The Dam would be placed at the first turn of the river created by the falls, and it would have to be a mile and three quarters long at this point, and over three hundred feet high. It would be built with a special concrete wedge designed in the center of the water's flow behind the Dam. This wedge system was added by the Ethiopians without the permission of the United Nations, and if turned in the flow of water it was able to divert more of the water Ethiopia needed for her own purposes, while leaving enough of the flow to the Blue Nile River intact. The wedge would move, in case even more or less water was needed for the people of Ethiopia.

Army Captain, Edward (Popeye) Campanelli was in complete command of the American engineers, and the few protective military forces also dispatched to Ethiopia for the civilian engineer's protection, and all the workers employed in the construction of the Dam. Before landing on the site, Captain Campanelli ordered the pilot to fly around the entire area of the projected construction site. The project was at least three miles away from the closest native village which pleased the Captain greatly. Now he did not have to worry too much about his people messing around with the young local native female population of the area, and getting the clap, or even worse, AIDS from the natives.

Captain Campanelli received his nickname of 'Popeye' when his only son Francis was born. Edward put his face close to his new born son, and the baby happened to swing his hand, poking him in his eye. Thus making his eye tear and he kept it closed for a few seconds. But in those few seconds, one of his lesser officers happened to come in to see his new child, and he laughingly said to the Captain. "What's up with you Captain. You look like Popeye with your eye closed like that sir."

As anyone who ever went through the service knows, a name spoken some times in jest, will most likely end up being your tag name for the rest of your life in the service. Thus Edward 'Popeye' Campanelli was tagged. The young Captain had no other choice in the matter either, for his wife liked the name also and she laughed when the other officer called her husband Popeye. So it set in with her, and then her son using the nickname also.

Captain Edward Campanelli was in command of just over one thousand five hundred military personnel, and a thousand American civilian workers, with more civilian workers scheduled to be sent to the project once it got off the ground. He was being helped by a young and pretty female Second Lieutenant named Renee Mendoza, a real hot headed, and even more hot blooded Latino woman, whom he had some trouble at times controlling, because of her pigheadedness, and her set ways and temper. She was a damn good military officer who commanded much respect from her subordinates, and she was a real looker too. Campanelli was pleased he did not understand much Spanish, because when he got in an argument with her, she would immediately blow up and start he was sure, cursing him in Spanish. He did not mind as long as he did not understand the angry words. He would just smile at her and let her get it off her chest.

The Captain's other military officer was another Lieutenant, and a very dear and close friend, John White. Campanelli laughed when he thought of Lieutenant White, because he was as black as the ace of spades, and he was having a hard time calling him Mr. or Lieutenant White. The Captain felt at ease with his fellow officers. The most important aspect of his command, was there was no bigotry being carried out between them. At times, he would forget and call Mendoza a spic, or White a nigger, but they both knew it was not out of bigotry, just anger over a dumb move they created. Both officers knew if they were to call the Captain a Whop because he was an Italian, it would be taken in the same light that he screwed up something, and he would take the criticism as well as dish it out.

It was one of his unwritten laws that allowed his officers know exactly that they all stood on the same level as their commanding officer at all times. This attitude also transferred over to their troops, who knew if the screaming was flavored with some ethnic slurs. It was not aimed at them with any malice intended, just out of anger for a screw up or another reason. The officers and men shared a good camaraderie between themselves at all times while they served under Captain Campanelli's command.

Campanelli was not very pleased with his present operation though. His last orders were boring for him also, and they had him in charge of protecting the lives of some foreign Diplomats being threatened by some rebels in their own country. Now he was sent off to the middle of the jungle, with a bunch of angry civilians blaming him for everything wrong with their situation from the cold, damp weather, to the lack of most modern conveniences and enjoyment.

His soldiers, who were not referred to as such for this supposed civilian mission, were much easier for him to control and handle. If they complained about anything, they received extra duty for their gripe, period. The Captain could not wait until the battalion of naval construction Seabees finally arrived on his new base, because then he could have these men erect a number of structures instead of tents for the workers and soldiers to live in. The Army Engineer of Core were there strictly for work on the new Dam.

Edward Campanelli was just a Captain though he was in the service long enough to be a Colonel or even a possible General. He was overlooked for promotion many times in his past because of his none program attitude. He was military and a good officer, but he did things his own way rather than the government's approved way. Try as they might, his superiors just could not change him of this sort of anti service habit. The Captain suffered from the age old Italian curse, not knowing when to keep his big mouth shut. He was happy to stay Captain, because lately he was thinking of getting out of the service anyway, and try to save his shaky marriage heading for a divorce down the road.

Through it all though, the Captain found himself dishing out orders once again at the civilian workers he was in command of, as well as the soldiers ordered to help the civilian workers. He had his first meeting with the Ethiopian General, Mengistu Mariam, who wanted to know if all his men were just civilians, or if he had any military personnel mixed in with them. After a brief but rather heated conversation, the Ethiopian General understood who was who, and what these men were there for. The Ethiopi¬an General left the American Captain with a warning there seemed to be some kind of trouble heading for Chad from Libya. He also warned the American Captain something about the deposed President of Chad, was planning to reenter Chad and takeover power in that country for a second time.

The Ethiopian General Mariam also warned Captain Campanelli that Libya would not allow this work to continue without raising a finger, not after all the money and favors Libya did for the puppet government presently running the nation of Chad. When the very dangerous Ethiopian General left Campanelli, he went to his communications tent to place a call to the Joint Chiefs of Staff. Once connected he informed General Weidenbacher of this new possible threat. The powerful General promised to get back to the Captain within the day, and he decided to stick around the communications tent, and watch the engineers survey the area of the proposed new Dam site. Over an hour later the general was back on the line and he asked the Captain if he thought the air strip would take the C 5 Galaxy transport plane for landing.

Captain Campanelli assured the Chairman of the Joint Chiefs of Staff the massive transport aircraft could land without much problems. To which he informed the Captain to expect three of these huge aircraft packed with a horde of Seabees then. He also informed the Captain there would be a number of extra equipment coming other than bulldozers on these planes. He was ordered to be expecting two thousand other personnel, and the General also warned Campanelli these people were to be referred to as civilians, but in essence, they were going to be crack highly trained Special Forces troops from the Third and Fifth Marine Corps. The General further stated to his captain. "They're being shipped out to you along with their equipment, and they're to be employed mainly for the protection of all civilian workers on the project."

"General Weidenbacher Sir, I already have fifteen thousand soldiers on site, and I think this many more soldiers would only serve to get..."

The General cut him off in mid sentence by barking at the Captain. "I don't give a shit what you think Captain. Those men you have are fucking engineers, and they're to work on that Dam and nothing else, mister. These soldiers I'm sending you are troops highly trained to protect and defend their positions and fellow soldiers, and they're also trained to attack, and they'll have the necessary military equipment with them to accomplish their orders. If what I fear happens in Chad comes true, we'll need an operational military base from which to operate from, Captain. So we're able to lend immediate support to the Chad defenders or any of our other allies who might come under attack from the many different rebel fractions operating in the region, sir.

"You know as well as I do if Libya attacks the nation of Chad again, they'll also attack the damn Sudan in the same operation. I would, if I had to attack one, Libya might as well attack the other thorn is in her backside. It'd be a perfect way for the Libyans to get the nation of Nigeria to put in with them, and if that happens, it could lead to the other Arab nations choosing up sides, and all hell breaking lose in the damn region, sir.

"Captain Campanelli Sir, I have ordered the Aircraft Carrier Strike Group headed by the USS Theodore Roosevelt, whose designated call numbers are CVN 71, and she's presently stationed in the Indian Ocean. To sail to the Gulf of Aden to lend air support to your people if needed. She'll be our main command center if anything goes wrong in your area of responsibility, sir. The Roosevelt's our newest by means of her recent refit, operational nuclear Aircraft Carrier under commission, sir. She has over six thousand sailors and Marines on board her at all times, and the Carrier has an air wing of eighty six aircraft, and ten assault helicopters. The aircraft are split up between fighters and bombers, but either wings could be converted easily, so they all could become either fighter or bomber aircraft, sir.

"The Carrier also enjoys our latest attack fighter bomber with her, the YF 23, twelve of these fighter/bomber aircraft, and the Carrier also has three E 2 Hawkeye advance warning and control aircraft on board, as well as the F/A3 18 Hornet fighter bomber, and a wing of the new F 14C3 Tomcat fighters. The Roosevelt's equipped with the latest in ship defense, the `Hard Rock' systems. The Hard Rock system got its name because of the effect of the noise, which had the same effect on the developers as rock and roll music. This weapon was developed by a young engineer playing around with the firing mechanism of a Mark 48 torpedo. He loaded it for the fifth time, but before he made it fire, the mechanism fired by itself. He looked around until he found the source that made the torpedo activate. On his television set on the Discovery channel, there was a movie about an earthquake. This vibration caused the firing of the torpedo, sir.

"This kid took his discovery to the Navy, and after a number of years of refinement, the Navy developed this idea into an operational weapon system used against a possible torpedo attack against any of our warships. The Roosevelt has five speaker stations below the waterline on each side of the ship. When the Hard Rock systems are activated, it emits a rumbling sound, a wall of sound if you will, two hundred yards from the ship. This sound causes any torpedo fired at the ship to detonate harmlessly well away from the ship under attack. The Navy's trying to develop a cousin to this weapon which would work in the air. So they could aim this weapon at any incoming missiles, thus detonating them before they could hit any United States ships.

"The Navy's also deploying the X 117, the Navies version of the F 117 Stealth fighter bomber to Saudi Arabia. There's talk the Airforce is developing a version of the Hard Rock system for their aircraft to employ in a dogfight or attack from SAM ground to air launch missile. And I have technicians installing a deployed Skylight system as we speak, sir. It should be fully operational within the week or maybe even less I'm told, sir."

"General Weidenbacher, I have already heard some scuttlebutt about the Hard Rock system before, sir. But I never heard anything about this Skylight system, sir. What's this one about?" Campanelli inquired from his Commanding Officer.

"I'm not very familiar with the damn thing myself Captain. But I have some papers on it here somewhere. Where the hell's that damn report on this system they're installing on the Carrier Roosevelt?" The General bellowed at someone working in his office.

Captain Campanelli heard the rustling of some papers and he decide to wait until the General found what he was looking for.

"Yeah. Here we go Captain Campanelli, I got them damn things now sir. The Skylight system or Mid Infrared Chemical Laser System, MIRACL for short, couples a beam director with a rather advanced powerful energy chemical laser system. It's based around a sort of

Magneto Hydrodynamics system, which employs a rocket engine to mix various chemicals together, and exciting the molecules to a much higher state of energy.

"The molecules are then rapidly cool off, and drop back to a normal, or ground state, sir. There, they emit protons in an ultra concentrated beam of high light energy. This powerful beam of energy's then aimed and it tracks a target, like an inbound missile say, and it rapidly burns through the missile's body at the point of aim, thus destroying the missile while in flight, sir. The computer can also lock onto as many as up twenty different targets at the same exact time, and when one target's destroyed by the weapon, another one can be instantly picked up to replace the destroyed missile, sir.

"Hell, I'm informed if there's a weakness in this newly developed weapon system, this is it, Captain. It can track up to twenty inbound missiles at one time. But it takes the system four seconds to burn through, and then destroy the one target once the beam hits it while in flight." The well respected General stopped speaking at this point to get his breath back.

"Sounds pretty good to me General Weidenbacher Sir." Campanelli offered back to his well respected Commanding Officer.

"Yeah, the Roosevelt's commanded by Commander Robert J. Owens, and she can launch three aircraft at once every forty seconds, and land one in under a minute at the same damn time, sir. The Roosevelt's battle group consists of twelve ships in all, the USS White Plains AFS 4, a combat store ship, the Cimarron Fleet Oiler, the USS Flint Ammunition ship, the USS Guam Amphibious Assault Ship, the USS Barbey, a Frigate with two other missile Frigates, the USS Robert G, Bradley and USS Vandegrift, the USS Charles F. Adams' a guided missile Destroyer used mostly for anti-submarine warfare, and the two missile Cruisers, the USS Princeton and the USS Yorktown, Captain Campanelli." The General did not inform his officer just ahead and behind the Carrier Strike Force lurked two Los Angeles class attack nuclear submarines.

A third nuclear submarine paralleling the same exact course as the Carrier Strike Force, off to her port side. The nuclear Trident Class submarine with twenty four long range nuclear tipped, Trident missiles with a seven thousand five hundred nautical mile range, and a graphite body and glass nose casing housing the nuclear warhead, it cruises at five hundred feet below the surface. The submarine was ready to add her might to the destructive force that is the Aircraft Carrier Battle Group.

The Chairman of the Joint Chiefs of Staff continued with his words to the young Captain. "It's a hell of a formidable force of ships as you can plainly see for yourself, Captain Campanelli. But I want the damn Arabs to know we mean fucking business in this region of the world, sir. These things are difficult to choreograph precisely, Captain. I want to get enough of our military forces in this region to cover any contingencies that might crop up against us. I'm also ordering the 71st and the 22nd Tactical Fighter Wings presently stationed in Sicily on a twenty four hour upgrade alert level, and I'm further ordering the Strategic Bomber Wing 21st, stationed in England out of mothballs, Captain. I'll place them on a one hour standby alert notice.

"The President has no intention of getting caught flatfooted on this one sir, not since the fricking terrorists killed those damn civilian hostages last year on us, Captain Campanelli. I'm not going to allow your group to become new possible hostages in this damn mess, sir. You're instructed to put your troops on a twenty four hour alert status at all times while this construction project is in operation. One sleeps while the other watches, sir."

"Sir, how the hell am I supposed to get any work done on the Dam, if I have to have my people stuck on such an alert status, General Weidenbacher Sir?"

"That's your problem to deal with, I never promised you a rose garden on this operation, mister. These orders are to stay in effect until your Marines arrive at the site for deployment, sir. Their Commander will know how to set his troops up, and that'll leave your people free to work on that Dam after they arrive at the site, sir. Other orders will come your way when we know what, if anything's going to happen in Chad, and what fucking Libya's going to do about it sir. Captain Campanelli, you have your orders, and you'll follow them out to a tee, sir.

"Don't be afraid to call for any extra help if needed, Captain. The ships should be arriving off the coast of Ethiopia within twelve hours, sir. I want you to check in with the Roosevelt every eight hours to make certain orders didn't change on you, Captain Campanelli. If we fail to hear from you in a nine hour time period sir, I'll have the Roosevelt launch a number of fighter aircraft to find out what might have happened to your ass, so you'll only have to hold out against any possible attack against you and your troops and civilian workers no longer than an hour before help arrives on site. Captain, you're in an extremely volatile area in the world and things can go sour in an hour. Keep your eyes open and stay on your fucking toes, sir. Any questions?"

"No Sir General Weidenbacher Sir." Captain Campanelli snapped confidently back at his Commanding Officer as he breathed a sigh of relief.

"Good, good, one more thing I feel you must know about before I leave you, Captain Campanelli. In view of your present situation, you're to accept no fire from any possible attackers without returning that fire. Right now, the Ethiopian government's our friend. But that can change within the hour with a simple coup. I repeat, don't accept any incoming fire without returning it, sir. Protect your troops and civilian workers at all times, Captain. You're authorized to have a closed camp sir, and protect those damn civilians at all costs, sir. No one enters without permission, setup perimeter lines marked out with concertina wire and claymore mines, and don't forget to set the sensors out, sir. You have permission to shoot to kill any hostiles, sir. We'll extract if the situation demands it. Air supports only an hour away at the most, sir. Good luck Captain." With this the secured, special scrambler line went dead.

He looked at the Sergeant sitting by his side, and then offered. "It looks like we have some fucking work to do people."

The concerned Captain left the so called command tent and he immediately started to look for Lieutenant Mendoza. He saw her standing near a number of civilian workers looking over papers a little while ago.

"Lieutenant. Hey Lieutenant Mendoza. I wanna see you for a few moments, Lieutenant." Campanelli yelled out to her from the command tent.

Mendoza looked up to see who was calling out her rank and name, and then she headed to the Captain. She could tell something was bothering him because if everything was fine, he would have called her Mendoza.

Lieutenant Mendoza saluted the Captain as she ran up to him. "Trouble sir?" She asked him.

He smiled as he quickly informed her. "How well you read me Mendoza, yes, we have some trouble Lieutenant. I want perimeter lines established, place a number of M-60 machine guns out to cover all trails leading up to the base, have the mortars we took with us setup as well. No one is allowed on or off of the damn base unless they identify themselves first and have papers. We have permission to fire if fired on. We're to trust no one. Issue M 18s with five extra clips and side arms to all non working soldiers. Working soldiers are to have side arms issued to them, and they're to carry the fucking things on their person at all times from this point on. No one's allowed to leave base without permission. We have to hunker down until a detachment of Marines arrive on site. Then, security will be handed to them, Lieutenant.

"Use the civilian equipment with setting up the perimeter defenses. Any civilians who give you any trouble are to be directed to me, or placed under arrest without question. We have air support an hour away, as well as a nine hour time limit of non communication, and troops will arrive without request. Let's hop to it and get Whitie to help you some."

"Are we expecting a possible attack, and if so, from who Captain Campanelli Sir?" She asked him with sudden concern in her tone of voice.

"No attack, all precautions are just that, precautions for the time being, but I'll tell you this much Mendoza. If trouble comes, it'll come from Chad and the Sudan, but no one knows how the damn Arab nations will react if a conflict breaks out in this stinking region, so we can't trust any countries. So shove off Mendoza and get the perimeter lines up."

"Right away sir." She saluted her Commanding Officer and then she turned on her heels and barked out orders to some of the other soldiers she picked up doing nothing. She screamed at the civilian workers as well. Bulldozers started up and dug long pits along established perimeter lines. Other soldiers strung out lines of razor backed concertina wire, while others placed claymore mines and hand grenades on the wire. The Captain watched as a pair of M-60s was quickly setup in strategic positions in order to rack across any paths leading towards their base. They were setup to overlap the firing and killing radius of the weapons. The mortars were setup to hit the only major road leading to the camp. Within five hours after giving out his first orders, Captain Campanelli was examining the finished perimeter defenses which he found to be laid out perfectly. He looked at the sweat covered Mendoza and announced to her in a commanding voice. "Well done there Lieutenant."

Everywhere the concerned Captain went, he noticed soldiers standing on full alert and armed with weapons, he also picked up less and less natives walking around on the securing base. The Captain found himself wondering if the natives left because the soldiers were armed, or if Mendoza ordered them off the base. Again he turned to Mendoza walking alongside him while he inspected the security and he offered. "Mendoza, did you order the damn locals off the base? I'm seeing a lot less of those pains in the asses hanging around."

She drew in some air, and then she replied in a sharp tone to her Commander. "Yes Sir Captain, I took it upon myself and ordered them off base until we can issue new identification cards with their picture printed on them to the trusted ones, and this present emergency's over with sir. Quite frankly Captain, I'd much rather keep them off the base altogether if you don't mind, sir. I don't trust them in the least, they're always looking for something to steal from base. Hell sir, yesterday I caught one of the damn buggers trying to steal a jeep. Remember what happened in Nam, we allow those bastards on base during the day, fed them and looked after any injuries they suffered from, and they would turn around at night and use the information they scooped up during the day, in their attack against us at night. I'd much rather protect our base from any such attacks like that sir."

"Now I know why I keep asking for you whenever they send me out on another stinking shitty duty mission, Lieutenant. Carry on with your present orders Lieutenant Mendoza, you're doing fine work here. I know you'll pick up my slack for me Lieutenant."

She stared intensely at her Commanding Officer for a long moment, and then she snapped at him. "Why you sonofabitch you, and here I thought it was just my dumb luck to be stuck with you every time they send me out on another mission, sir. Dammit sir, what a fool I was. I should've known it was you all the time Captain." She looked in the wonderful brown eyes of this good looking Italian man and then she added. "I wanted to thank you for the trust you have showed in me sir, to keep asking for me sir. I feel very proud to serve with you anytime and anywhere. Thank you sir."

She continued to stare at this man in a new light, because she felt at best, he just tolerated her presence, and at worse. He disliked her because he never showed very much interest in her romantically, or professionally for that matter. She touched his face with a slender finger and then smiled up at him.

The Captain suddenly felt a little nervous as he remarked to the beautiful female Lieutenant. "I'm sorry I never told you before that I needed you, Mendoza. That I never told you you're the best officer I had under me." He immediately blushed at his poor choice of words,

`Under me' as he went on with his words to his lieutenant. "I requested the second bar for you because of your outstanding work, it's pretty tough to find officers willing to serve, and put up with me and my temper and all, Lieutenant. I'm not the easiest SOB to get along you know. Mendoza, you're a good officer and soldier, you do me proud Ma'am." He continued to walk as he headed to the armory the engineers constructed of concrete. Outside, it looked impenetrable, and when they entered the damp building, he saw no one getting in unless they belonged there.

"Very good Mendoza, this place could stand up to anything thrown at it. But I think it's awful damp in here. I feel the weapons might rust, no? Maybe we can have the SeeBees install a dehumidifier in here to remove some of the dampness inside the building, Lieutenant?"

"I already took care of that sir. When I first inspected the building I felt the same way as you did. I have the electricians running wires underground from the generator building setup by the Dam structure sir, and I ordered heaters placed inside the building, sir. The heaters should stop any rusting, Captain. I could use this problem as K.P. duty. If someone screws up, I'll have him work on the weapons being stored inside the building, you know, oil them and remove any possible rust, and make certain everything is in proper working order, sir."

"I should have known you were on the top of the damn situation, Lieutenant. I'm sorry for bring it up to your attention. Come on Mendoza, I'll buy ya a cup of coffee."

She followed the young Captain over to the mess building. It was the only building made of wood so far on the entire worksite and rapidly shaping military base. Here the soldiers ate with the officers, and civilians had to eat with the soldiers whether they liked it or not. The Captain was a real stickler about this order. He ate the same food as his soldiers did, and never asked for anything made special for him to eat. He said if he had to rely on these men and women to protect him then the least he could do was eat with them, and the same food as they ate. He would laughingly say, 'if his troops had to survive on this mess then he would suffer the same fate along with the soldiers.

This attitude made all his troops respect him more, but it also made the brass cringe, and talk about the spirited officer behind his back. It was no wonder his unit had the largest reups in the Army. Some of his unit were on their fourth, or even their fifth tour of duty with the Captain they proudly referred to as Popeye. He was a good officer who looked well after his troops as if they were his own children.

As soon as he sat at a table, a immediately private brought him and Mendoza a cup of coffee. He never asked to be served, but no cooks would have him standing on line for food. It was embarrassing to be waited on, but he was starting to get used to it, and now he did not give the practice a second thought. It was accepted no officers were to stand on line, unless they wanted something special other than what the cook brought over to them at their table. After all, the cooks would do just so much for the officers.

The Captain sipped his coffee. Lieutenant John White, who caught up to the two other officers just as they sat down, sat and a second later the private showed up with a cup of coffee for him.

She was the first one to speak. "Captain Campanelli, do you think trouble's coming at us sir?" She would never use his nick name before any of the other troops.

"Sure as I'm sitting here Mendoza, and I know the damn Libyans will be behind the mess when it happens. I wish Muammar al Qaddafi was still in control of that crazy ass country, instead of this other nut who is more content in leading their country right down the barrel of a fucking weapon. It's a damn shame he was forced out of power."

Lieutenant White spoke up next as he remarked with a little concern in his tone of voice. "Yeah, and I thought we were in for all sorts of fucking hell to break out when Egypt threatened Ethiopia for cutting off this fucking Nile River feeder on them as well, Captain. I don't know what the hell's keeping the Egyptians in check, sir."

The Captain added to their conversation. "I think Egypt's too damn civilized to go off to war if you were to ask me. I hope the Ethiopians stick to their word and they don't try and stop too much of the god damn water from going to Egypt. This wedge design was something recently added without informing the damn Egyptian government."

Mendoza looked at the Captain with concern as she asked. "What the hell does this damn wedge design do anyway, sir?"

"Mendoza, the wedge system can be moved in the water before the Dam's gates and once it's moved, it diverts more water from the waters leading down to the Nile River, and it sends it down the mountain to Ethiopia. I know it's Ethiopia's water, but I don't know just how far they're going to be able to push the Egyptians, before they have to finally put their foot down and attack Ethiopia over this damn mess. Yes Mr. White, you're right as rain here with your words, sir. I fear the next fucking war we get involved in, is going to be against Egypt this time around sir. I'd sure hate like fucking hell to have to fight the god damn Egyptians. They're such a proud and beautiful people. Dammit to hell and all the way back again, I'd surely hate to fight these people, but I fear the cards have already been dealt out, and it's only a matter of time before all hell breaks out in this area of the world and we're forced to react, sir.

"Furthermore people, I believe we're going to be on the god damn spot when it finally does come down the chute. I'm quite certain that's why our government's sending the Marines out to protect our stinking asses while we're working on this Dam project, sir. This will give the United States a land base from which to work from." He finished off his gripe.

Lieutenant White spoke up again. "One thing you just said puzzles the shit outta my ass though sir. You said you wished Qaddafi was still in power in Libya, sir. Why is that sir? He was a royal pain in the ass from the get go."

"Mr. White you have to understand. Qaddafi was a real smart sonofabitch. He knew exactly when to rattle his saber, and when to sit tight with his mouth shut. He would never attack the United States, in fact he helped us in many different ways while he was in command of his country. As much as he ranted and raved, he was a rather stabilizing power also. No Arab countries would ever act up until they saw what he was going to do first. He would carry on and by the time he finally quieted down, the other Arab countries that should've been up in arms, were calmed down and forgot what was itching them in the first place. Look at what happened when he ran into trouble in his country, what did he do? He turned to us for help, and where is he now, in Miami soaking up the sun while waiting to return to his country. He's now a guest of the United States, and I'm sure our government's helping him out one way or the other."

"You think we'll be involved in another war? And do you really think it'll happen in the Middle East, sir? I thought it'd take place somewhere in Central America, Captain. Or we declare war on Columbia because of the stinking drug thing down there. I was glad they put an end to that mess themselves, once drugs started to show up in the Alliance States, and Russia and what was left of Russia, threatened to blow Columbia off the face of the earth. I was kind of hoping war was a thing of the past, god dammit." Lieutenant Mendoza cried.

He looked at Mendoza for a second or two, and then he remarked. "What a helluva thing for a soldier to say. War, a thing of the past. Hell Mendoza, if wars were over then soldiers wouldn't be needed, and you and I would be out of a stinking job, baby. A soldier's job is killing, that's what a soldier does best. What he's born and bred for young lady."

Her Latin blood immediately got hot and she snapped angrily at her Commanding Officer. "I thought a soldier's job was also teaching the poor and helpless to fend for themselves, and teaching them to protect themselves, like we're doing in Somalia, sir."

Captain Campanelli laughed as he added while he smiled at Mendoza. "What the hell do you think we're here for, the god damn peace corps or some shit like that, Lieutenant? Look at that stinking mess we got ourselves into in Somalia, dammit. We've been there almost four fucking years now, and the damn situation's the same shit, if not worse. The poor still starve, and no one really gives a flying shit about them poor bastards. No, we're fucking killers tried and true. Killers, and sooner or later, we will kill again at our government's request or orders. That's why we were trained, and that's why we were deployed to this nation, Lieutenant."

The female Lieutenant jumped to her feet, causing everyone sitting in the mess hall to turn to her, because of her sudden aggressive move as she nearly roared at her Commanding Officer. "I don't intend to be known as only a fucking killer and that's that sir. We're doing some good in Somalia and soon or later it's show, Captain Campanelli Sir."

The Captain laughed again as he continued to smile at his Lieutenant and added to his young and pretty female Lieutenant. "Look Mendoza, we're nothing more than god damn walking targets in fucking Somalia. We lost a hundred good Marines in that damn place already. Their youth throw stones at any Marines they see, and the damn United Nations is still dragging their feet in the god damn area. Any time their units come under fire, they pull back and request our Marines to clear their way for them, and yet they take all the stinking bows when something good happens there. When it's the blood of our Marines which caused the breakthrough in the first place. It's all bullshit and bad manners if you were to ask me."

She ignored his remarks and replied in a huff to her commander. "I think a soldier can be known for other things than just being a damn killer, Captain. No, I won't accept this for a moment sir. True, I'm a soldier, but I'm no killer, Captain Campanelli Sir. Don't get me wrong Popeye." She blushed at calling the well respected man by his nickname to his face.

"I'll kill if I had to, or if I had no other choice in the matter, or my government orders me to do so, and I wouldn't think twice before I kill either, sir. At least the government gives me a much better choice than they give the poor cops back in the States, Captain Campanelli. I know if I'm forced to kill, I won't be brought up on charges of murder like the poor bastards find themselves being charged, whenever they're forced to use their weapon in either self defense, or to protect some civilian or property. I know we're going to have to start protecting the police officers of our country, while they take their lives in their hands each and every day they strap on their bulletproof vest while protecting the god damn civilians of our country. We have to stop protecting the scum of the world like we are constantly doing lately, sir.

"Shit, it's getting so bad lately now if the god damn criminals go off to jail, they get a stinking high school or college education, all their damn medical needs are taken care of at taxpayers expense, and yet there's thousands of good, hard working Americans who can't afford their own damn medical coverage and schooling. Yet they're forced to pay for this shit to get the damn criminals healthy and smart, only to go out and hurt or kill someone whose trying to make a living in a rough world, and pay for his own health care and education. It doesn't make any fucking sense to me, sir. Remember the headlines when those assholes put that bomb under the Trade Towers. It read, 'Day of Terror', Dammit, it should have read 'Day of Heroism'.

"I saw the faces of the police and firemen, in fact, anyone who helped with the injured, with compassion etched in their eyes. It made me feel good to know those men and women were out there helping the injured of our country, sir. These people are the special breed of people of the world, the first responders, sir." She ended her conversation with a few Spanish curses.

"C'mon Lieutenant Mendoza, you're getting far from the point you were trying to make here. We all agree the cops are getting shafted by the ways their hands are tied dealing with a criminal, I'd never want to be a cop in the States. But, what are you trying to say here young lady? Get it done now soldier. I want another cup of coffee, besides, everyone's looking at you, waiting for your point to be brought across." Campanelli offered as he smiled at her from his seat.

The Lieutenant knew what he was doing. She knew she was caught up in a no win conversation going nowhere fast on her, and he was offering her a way out of this mess.

"Oh hell, Popeye, err..., Captain Campanelli Sir. I don't want to be known as just a god damn killer. I didn't join the Army to be a stinking killer, sir. I wanted to do something more than just kill people. Maybe make a difference in this crazy ass world, help someone who needs help." Mendoza looked at this smiling man staring back at her, not as a Commanding Officer, but as an equal. An equal in every respect with something to say.

"Dammit Captain Campanelli, I don't know what the hell I mean any longer, sir. I just don't want to be known as only a killer, sir. I'd truly be hurt to feel people just look at me as a god damn killer. I guess that's what I really wanted to say, Captain." As she sat down, a cook showed up with coffee for the officers. The private looked at the Lieutenant and then offered. "Lieutenant, I just wanted to tell you that I think you're more than just a killer Ma'am. You're a good person, besides, a stinking killer wouldn't have a heart like yours."

Lieutenant Renee Mendoza looked back at this young man and then she smiled at him. Then she looked at the other two officers sharing her table, who were smiling back at her.

Captain Campanelli lifted his cup up to toast her as he said. "The private shares our feeling Ma'am. You're a good person."

The upset female Lieutenant looked around the mess hall, half expecting to see all the other soldiers and civilians laughing at her, but to her surprise everyone offered her a salute with their cups. They even smiled and nodded at her.

"There you go Lieutenant Mendoza. It looks like you're more than just a fucking killer to them, Ma'am. I believe I might have been wrong, there's more to it than just being a stinking killer with being a soldier I guess. I thank you for pointing this fact out to me, Lieutenant. I guess a Captain's never too old to learn from his lesser officers I see. I guess

I have to be a little more open minded when it comes down to the way I look at some things around here young lady." The Captain never informed Mendoza that he was only trying to make a joke when he first said a soldier was just a trained killer for his country. He did not realize he was going to hit a nerve with his young and pretty female officer.

"Mendoza, you too, you're involved in this mess as well Whitie, we have a hell of a lot of work ahead of us. We have to be prepare to receive this new batch of mud Marines heading for this project. From the sounds of it, it seems we're in for a lot of company coming in over the next few days." With this said, Captain Campanelli stood and quickly left the mess.

Lieutenant Mendoza followed the Captain shortly afterwards, she wanted to check on what all her other troopers were doing at the present moment. The young and pretty female Lieutenant watched and soon she saw no civilians were allowed to go anywhere on base without an armed escorts of soldiers in tow. This was her top priority, the protection of the civilian workers for the Dam project. Because she knew if one of them were to get hurt then it would cause many other problems with the rest of the civilian workers on the site.

CHAPTER 7

The next three days were sheer hell for the military officers concerned with the Dam project. Captain Campanelli was notified the strike force lead by the Aircraft Carrier Roosevelt was now set in place, and already the base had nine flyovers by American warplanes. This was to show their full support of the workers and soldiers at the site. The Marines were scheduled to arrive later on that day. The Captain looked in the sky, searching for the first sign of the incoming troop transport planes. At eleven thirty five a.m., the first massive transport aircraft showed up. The black body of the massive C 5 Galaxy came out of the haze three hundred feet above the ground. He saw another transport aircraft some twenty minutes behind the first aircraft.

Within minutes, the first massive aircraft circled the newly enlarged airstrip twice. Campanelli watched as the plane lightly touched down, but before it came to a full stop the tail ramp dropped, and soldiers jumped out of the still moving plane. The Captain immediately heard the familiar sound of tank engines starting up inside the plane. Seconds later he saw the new Abrams M-63 anti missile tank roll out of the tail end of the massive plane. This tank was followed by a second one, the newer and massive M-65 Abrams Blackfoot 3 tank, the largest tank in the world, and it replaced the already outdated Abrams M1A1 tank.

The Blackfoot with her newly developed electronics and night vision capabilities, made her the best fighting tank in the history of military warfare. The tank had an automatic main mount ammunition feeder, and it could fire a round that could knock out the very best of the enemy tanks, from over six full miles away with pin point accuracy, while the tank was traveling at over sixty miles an hour.

He was aware of this tank's existence, but this was the first time he ever saw one of these new tanks in person, it was huge. He knew about the porcelain mesh add on the reactive, round absorbent armor, along with its tungsten pointed side ribbing under the specially plated armor to deflect any enemy round fired at the machine. Especially the armor piercing Sabot dart round, which might make it through the reactive plating. The thing he found most interesting about the new machine was the water sprinkling system the tank employed.

This newly developed recycling water sprinkler system was fully self contained, and it sprayed a fine mist of cool water all over the tank's entire outer surface. This mist quickly cooled down the surface of the metal skinned monster, which in return hid the camouflaged tank from most of the best infrared, and also heat seeking detection and aiming weapon systems. The system also reclaimed most of the water it used, by means of a number of small ports built right in the sides of the tank, which funneled the water back to the reserve water tank inside the massive war machine to be cooled down by the condenser. This system operated by electric, so the tank's engine could shut down, also helping to erase its heat signature from detection by any enemy forced out to destroy the machine of war.

In seconds, this massive tank was followed out of the aircraft by a second tank of the same make and size. The Marines instantly deployed a squad of troopers around them, and they followed the deadly war machines to where they were ordered to setup for any possible action. The plane was emptied within fifteen minutes, and was just taking off as the second Galaxy aircraft circled the airstrip for a landing. Only moments after the first aircraft was in the air, did the second transport plane come in for a landing.

This second mammoth transport aircraft held the rest of the Marine troops, and two more Blackfoot tanks. It took longer to empty this one, because it contained ammunition and many small arms and other military equipment. A large number of Stinger Three missile systems, and two portable Vulcan rotating machine gun track machines were also on board this second plane. It looked like the Marines could now hold off a very sizable attacking enemy army with the equipment they were unloading from this aircraft. The Lieutenant in charge of the Marine units searched out Captain Campanelli and he reported to him. But the Captain kept the young man at bay while he watched as the plane was rapidly unloaded.

The scheduling of the aircraft was working out perfectly, because as this aircraft was rapidly emptied, a third transport aircraft showed up circling over the ever expanding military base and construction site. The same procedure was carried out with this one, as the second plane lifted off, the third aircraft prepared for landing.

The third massive aircraft landed carrying more Marines. But this plane also carried the five Seabee units, along with their construction and defensive equipment. This load was boring to the Captain, because he knew he was not going to see any new armament. So he put his hand on the shoulder of the Lieutenant, and offered to buy him a cup of coffee. The young Marine Lieutenant followed the Captain over to the mess hall.

Campanelli called out to the young soldier over his shoulder. "What's your name son?"

"Lieutenant Peter Gates, sir." He snapped to attention and saluted the young Captain.

"Never mind that shit. Don't ever fucking salute me out in the fucking field, mister. Most of the troops call me Popeye, if they got the fucking balls too. The rest of them just call me Capt. This is one hell of a duty we pulled for ourselves Lieutenant. That's why we have relaxed regs here, sir. But make no damn mistakes about it mister, I'm in command here. What are your orders soldier, I want to see if anything changed?"

The young Lieutenant and Captain stopped as the Marine informed Campanelli of his orders. "Sir, I was ordered to station my troops outside your present defense setups, sir. We're to meld in with the damn jungle and stay well out of sight of any possible recon birds, sir. Captain Campanelli Sir, we also have orders to setup our own mess and heads for our troops. The less your people and natives see and have to do with us, the better off we're all going to be, and the less trouble our presence will cause anyone concerned, sir. We had an escort of four F 18 Hornets coming in, and we passed a fleet of American warships stationed in the Gulf of Aden, a great sight to see sir. I think we can secure this area even if the worst happens, sir."

Captain Campanelli looked at the young man with the fine chiseled features that seemed to be standard to the Marine code of looks then he offered. "Have you heard anything about what the hell's going on in Chad? I feel we're more or less cut off from the rest of the world out here. I'm sure command isn't telling me everything about what's happening around us. I guess command's operates under the less you know, the less scared of the situation you'll be, sir."

The Lieutenant offered his opinion with a smirk. "Captain Campanelli, the last I heard was. The leader we recognize as President of Chad reentered Chad from the south, where he had most of his support for his deposed government. His people started a number of riots which forced the old President, Idris Dedy to commit troops to restore peace to northern Chad. So far, he's giving southern Chad a wide berth. I heard Libyan planes are doing some flyovers in the south near the capital but for now it remains just flyovers, no attacks yet sir."

The suddenly concerned Captain looked at the young Marine's face while he went in thought for a moment, and then he replied. "I want your true assessment of the present situation, Lieutenant. How long before the shit really hits the fucking fan, son?"

"Err..., my personal evaluation of the growing situation, sir. I figure in less than a week, President Dedy will be forced to attack the southern end of Chad, and possibly make some attacks on the Sudan, in order to cut off the aid to Habre's rebel forces from that nation, sir. I know the Iranian troops training the Sudanese soldiers in trench warfare, have deployed to the Sudanese border with Chad, and took a lot of their armor and aircraft with them, Captain. Yes sir, I figure no more than a week before all hell breaks loose in the region, Popeye."

Captain Campanelli looked at the young Lieutenant for a long moment, making him sweat a little for daring to use his nick name so quickly, and then he smiled as he replied. "I'm pleased to see you got the balls I thought you had, boy. I don't want some pussy ass yes soldier protecting my stinking can during any possible attack. I agree with your last assessment Lieutenant, and I think you'll need every bit of your balls before this action comes to a conclusion on us. We're going to have to setup an intelligence net, do you have any S 3 officers with you? I want to setup a threat board and an intelligence network. I don't really think I'm going to have the god damn time to monitor all the fucking information that'll soon come in by myself, soldier."

The Marine Lieutenant thought for a second and then he replied to his new Commanding Officer. "Err... yes Sir Captain Campanelli Sir. I have two S 3 soldiers with me, but they're noncoms, not officers, sir. I'll setup an intelligence CP (Command Post) and have them setup the threat board in there, Captain. At your request sir, they'll pull up the latest information available to us about this present situation going down in Chad, as well as all our troop and enemy positions, if and when it happens against us sir. I'll also setup for communications with the Strike Force, and Wing Commands stationed in Sicily, England and NORAD.

"I'll have a line open to the Joint Chiefs of Staff and President, which is SOP sir. The Opts tent will be the only way you'll have to communicate with me once we're dug in out in the field, Captain Campanelli Sir. I have direct orders to do recon trips to the Sudan border, to monitor the happenings going on there sir, and I was given the power to fight my way out of any possible situation or engagement in either in Ethiopia, or on my recon patrols to the Sudan. My units only answer to yourself, or the President. Of course he overrules your orders as you well know sir."

Captain Campanelli gave a deep sigh as he suddenly barked at the young Marine. "You're starting to get on my last fucking dick nerve buster. Of course I know the President overrides my fucking orders, mister. What the hell's your call name going to be while you're out in the stinking Bush, Lieutenant?"

"I'm going by the call name of Grave Digger sir, and your base is?" The Marine Officer replied confidently to the concerned Captain.

"Our base is 'Easy Money' for now. I want to stay as far away as possible from making this fucking operation look and sound anything like a god damn military one on the field phones, Lieutenant. You got that sir?"

"Sir, I was informed to make this operation not to look like a military one unless absolutely necessary. I have five hours in which to establish my positions and temporary base, and then my troops are ordered to be invisible to all eyes in this region, Captain Campanelli Sir. We expect five AH 64 RS Apache gunships to be shipped out to our present position in the next day or so, so don't be surprised when you see them come in, sir. They'll disappear in the jungle also sir. Captain Campanelli Sir, I have work, so if you'll excuse me I have to get to my troops."

The two officers never got to the mess for coffee, instead, they headed back to the airstrip. The Captain saw the strength of the battalion size Marine Units standing at attention along the side of the airstrip. The men were packed and ready to move out. The Lieutenant took command and screamed at his soldiers. "Okay listen up people, you know the fucking routine. Assholes and elbows, we're ordered to disappear and only come out when needed. Let's get hot people. Sergeants move your units to their designated positions. Let's move it, let's go."

The Marines turned as one and headed off in the jungle smartly, all of them wore their skin and jungle uniform camouflage. The Captain watched as young soldiers split off, and headed in three different directions in the thick bush. In less than ten minutes, all the Marines were gone, he could still hear some movement in the jungle every now and then. But for the most part, he could not detect hide nor hair of the soldiers.

Captain Campanelli looked to where the tanks were parked. The only tanks sitting in the open were the two Abrams M-63 anti missile tanks. The four massive M-65 Blackfoot tanks were nowhere to be seen. As he looked over the airfield, he could find no traces of the Marines, or any of their equipment. The Captain could not help but admire how well these soldiers were trained. He felt secured knowing the Marines were his backup for this operation.

The Captain's attention was suddenly drawn to the sky, another huge C 5 transport aircraft was coming in and as the monster landed, more Navy Seabee's unloaded bulldozers and building and war supplies. He looked to the end of the air¬field and noticed many Seabee's were busy clearing a large area of trees and brush, in order to build barracks and living quarters for the soldiers and the civilian workers, as well as communication installations and water tanks for drinking water reserves. Captain Campanelli surveyed the entire area of the base and thought his camp and work area was taking shape. At least the civilians would get off his back, now that the living conditions were going to improve drastically for them.

One thing Captain Campanelli did not like about his present situation though, was all the booze starting to show up on his base ever since the transport aircraft started coming in. He expected this, and there was little he felt he could do about it at this time. It happened every time there were civilians on any military bases. Besides, if the Marines did not bring it with them, he was certain the Seabee's would have plenty of it with them. He dealt with Seabee's before, and they always seem to have an uncanny way of finding everything that should not be on a military base, and getting it there, from booze to women. He laughed as he shook his head at the thought of what he was going to be facing soon.

Captain Edward Campanelli heard the Seabee's having an argument with some of the civilian workers on the base. The controversy came to a quick conclusion when a Seabee started up a bulldozer, and he then proceeded to crush whatever the men were fighting about. The wise Army Captain allowed the Navy Construction Seabees to fight their own battles with the civilian workers, after all, the Seabee unit's came with their own Commanders set in place, and it was their responsibility with the Seabees. He knew it was only a matter of time before the Seabee officers would contact him as well as the civilian workers, who also had gripes about the Seabee's terrible attitude being displayed towards the civilians.

The Captain laughed again as he headed back to his tent to lay down for a little bit, he was beat out and hot. As he headed for his private quarters, his attention was drawn to the sky as a wing of F 14s flew over the base. The fighter aircraft dipped their wings in a kind gesture of acknowledgment to the soldiers toiling below them. He laid down on the cot, but no sooner did he close his eyes then he heard the voice of Lieutenant Mendoza asking for permission to speak with him. He called for her to come in. It was the hottest part of the day, with the temperature outside reaching well over the ninety degree line.

She came in wearing an undershirt and camouflage trousers. Her undershirt was soaked through with sweat, and she had no bra on so the undershirt was just about transparent.

Captain Campanelli could not take his eyes off her lovely breasts, and she knew what she was doing to him with the shirt. He stuttered as he wiped the sweat from his eyes and he stared at her while waiting to hear what she had to offer.

Lieutenant Renee Mendoza smiled as she asked the Captain if he was having a slight problem with his breathing suddenly. As he tried his best to straighten up and give himself some added room between his legs, without being too obvious about his growing problem. She decided to make her move on him and remarked with a grin.

"Here, let me help you with that there little problem, Captain Campanelli." She said as she placed her hand between his legs. She was happy to find him stiffer than a new boot.

Lieutenant Mendoza let go of him and took a step back, she then reached for the ties of the tent flaps and pulled them free and allowed them close then she pulled the wet shirt over her head.

Campanelli drew in air in a rush, because he could not take his eyes off her stunning beauty. He had no idea her breasts were so well formed and firm. He could not help himself as he suddenly reached out and rolled the beautiful flesh around in his hands and he mumbled at her at the same time. "Shit, you don't know how long I wanted to do this with you, but why now Mendoza? We had many other opportunities before this to make love to each other, especially when I was having all that trouble with my marriage, and I was crying on your shoulder all the time. Why now baby?" He reached for both breasts now.

"I guess I didn't want to take advantage of you then. You were so hurt and then when your baby came. I thought you'd never take notice of me after that. But when you told me it was you who was always requested me, and you were the one who put me up for my second bar. I just had to find some way to thank you, didn't I? Shit Popeye, I always wanted to see if I could melt your god damn socks for you, mister." She smiled at her intended lover now.

The Captain standing now, stepped back and he looked at her lovely breasts for a moment.

"Do you like what you're looking at there, sir?" Lieutenant Mendoza laughed as she made her breasts jiggle slightly before him by shaking her shoulders a little. Then she unbuckled her belt and allowed her pants to fall from her waist. She did not have on any underpants and she said to him. "This isn't sweat baby. I just took a quick shower then I got dressed without drying myself off. I figured once my shirt got good and wet, you'd see all you wanted to see. Then I'd know if you wanted me. Well, from the looks of that bulge in your pants, you must want me sir.

Let me see, to coin a phase, 'is that a rabbit in your pocket, or are you glad to see me baby?'"

The Captain laughed at the very pleasing touch of humor, it was just what this situation called for. He could not help but continue to stare at this strong, well shaped woman standing naked before him. Her dark skin shined in the light entering the tent through the slit in the flaps, adding a glow to her wonderful beauty. She turned to the side so he could see the side view of her breasts and shape.

Lieutenant Renee Mendoza stood about five feet seven, and she had beautiful breasts with a small waist, and a Latino's ass. Her legs were long, perfect and very strong, and her skin was free of any blemishes, and she also had the Latino pigment which made her look like she had a golden tan all year long. Her form was very muscular from the many years in the service, and the Captain felt she could probably kick the shit out of many men, maybe do him in also if she had a mind to. Her face was small, and she had a little mouth which always seemed to be smiling no matter what was going on around her, and her eyes were jet black with heavy eyebrows, and a small nose and beautiful white teeth, which looked even whiter because of the dark color of her skin.

She broke Campanelli's trance by suddenly stepping a little forward, and then undoing his pants, and then letting them fall down around his ankles. She knelt before him and took his member in her mouth and stared working him over.

The Captain almost fell to the floor from the wonderful feeling of her on him. This was something his wife had never done to him. Many time he would get his wife drunk as a skunk on purpose, so he could try and slip his member in her mouth. But she never allowed herself to get drunk enough to allow him do it like this mad Latino woman was doing to him. He had to stop her from doing him, or he was going to come. He pulled her up to her feet by her shoulders. He kissed her then he returned the favor to her. He lowered her down on the cot and then made love to her. They were in the tent for over an hour, and in that hour two more transport aircraft landed, unloaded and took off again.

When the well pleased Captain came out of the stuffy tent, he was pleased to see his base could operate without him overseeing everything happening on it. He was outside for ten minutes before Mendoza showed up standing behind him. She placed her hand on his shoulder, he turned and looked at her and turned red and said. "Look Mendoza, I'm really sorry for what happened in there. I guess I kinda lost control, and I…"

She looked at him like he had two heads and then she complained. "What the hell is that shit about mister? You're sorry? You poor little baby you. What the hell are you sorry about, sir? You didn't enjoy what we just did in your tent, sir? That's the only reason you should be sorry. Baby, I really enjoy myself, and I hope we can have an instant replay whenever either of us wants one sir." She said with a smile which could melt ice if she looked at it.

"I was only saying I'm still married, and nothing could come of us now. I think I still love my wife, and I don't think I'm being fair to her and my son, or to you for that matter…"

"You know something Captain Campanelli, you think too much mister. You'll drive yourself crazy one day, sir. Isn't it possible for you to just sit back for once in your life and enjoy yourself a little, sir? I'll let you know if you're being unfair with me or not. Look at it this way Captain. I needed you and you were there for me sir. I knew what I was doing in there all along sir. I came to your tent with this exact intention in mind sir. I'm a big girl sir, and I hope we're going to do it again and real soon at that Popeye."

Campanelli looked at this stunningly beautiful young woman who he was sure, could have her pick of any man in the entire world, and yet she chose him. He was ten years older than she was and he grumbled at her now. "Mendoza, if you want me, please, take me. I'm all yours to do with whatever you want of me, just one thing though. Please be gentle with me." He tried to sing these words to her, but he sounded more like a cat with its tail caught in a car door than anything else.

Mendoza laughed at his singing, as she said she was going to check on her people. She turned and almost skipped towards the airstrip, she was so happy.

The Captain could swear he heard her whistling as she walked away. He looked at her back and thanked his lucky stars to have the good fortune of having such a beauty chasing him. He felt he was ten years younger and invigorated. Suddenly, he wondered if he loved his wife, his mind was flooded with questions. Questions he knew he did not want the answers for, for fear of the answers he might get. He felt like doing something, so he followed one of the paths the Marines took out to jungle base. He wanted to see if he could spot any of them. He wanted to see how good these mud jumpers really were.

The Captain strolled down the path, his mind clouded over with thoughts of making love to Mendoza and thinking of his wife, when he came to an abrupt halt, and found himself staring at two Marines who appeared from out of no where. They were dressed in bush blankets, their guns leveled right at his chest and they were ready for any action.

The Marines did not speak, they just continued to aim their weapons at his chest. The Captain did not hear any noise, when from out of nowhere. The young Lieutenant stood in front of him, he smiled and shook his head and offered. "Captain Campanelli Sir, can I be of service to you sir? Err... if you don't mind my asking you sir. What the fuck are you doing out here, god dammit? Trying to get yourself killed or something like that sir."

The concerned Captain sort of laughed as he responded to the young soldier. "Well Lieutenant, I felt like taking a little walk that's all." He lied.

Now it was the Lieutenant's turn to laugh, because he knew he had the Captain dead to rights and offered to his Commanding Officer. "Shit Captain, I was wondering how long it was going to take you, before you came around to check us out sir. You lasted much longer than I had first expected, I'm pleased you didn't disappoint me any sir. Well how did we do so far sir? Did we pass your inspection, Captain?"

He understood he was caught dead to rights as he replied. "Was I that obvious sir? Lieutenant, I didn't mean to check on you and your people. You're a good Commander, and have good control and obvious respect from your troops. You're doing a fine job here sir. I'm sorry I had the compulsion to check you out like I did, sir. I'll leave now with my tail between my legs Lieutenant." The Captain saluted the men, turned and walked back to base.

The Lieutenant called after the Captain. "Sir, I don't feel threatened by you checking on us in the least, sir. In fact sir, I would've been kind of disappointed if you didn't come by and check up on me soon or latter sir. If I was in command, I surely would've checked your ass out by now Captain Campanelli. I too, like to know just how good the people I have under me are. Sir, please feel free to check us out anytime you feel the need sir." The Lieutenant laughed slightly as if to rub it in, as he quickly disappeared silently back in the bush, followed by his people.

The Captain had no fear the Marines who just caught him, would have surely killed him if he made a stupid move against any of them. Now he wondered if it was such a good idea to have so many heavily armed and highly trained soldiers prowling around in the jungles so near his base and the civilian workers, and they were so ready to kill anyone they came across and looked at them the wrong way. He feared the first incident, and how much trouble it was going to cause him and the rest of the people on his base.

There were just too many weapons hanging around for this not to happen some time in the near future. The Captain absentmindedly walked back to his base, his mind now flooded with this new fear and concern when he suddenly noticed some civilian workers doing something near where the Dam was being constructed. He walked over in that direction to try and discover what was going on over there. His troubled mind letting up a little on him as he had this new concern to deal with.

The workers were laying out the massive footing forms for the great base of the Dam. One of the workers who was obviously the one in charge of the operation. Told the other workers he wanted to make the footing with five continual pours of concrete. He said something about some kind of expansion joints and the likes. Campanelli listened to the conversation, and he was just going to ask him when the other worker asked his question for him.

"It'll take seven thousand yards of concrete to pour continually to make the footings in five continual pours, and also keep the concrete flowing before it has a chance to cure on us."

The man in charge of the other workers asked another worker if it was possible to get this much concrete moving at one time. He also wanted to know where they were going to get all this concrete from if they attempted this big a pour.

"Sure thing man," The other worker replied confidently and then he went on with his words. "It's just going to take all the concrete trucks we have at our disposal, plus all the Ethiopian trucks as well. I just hope the three batching plants can keep up with our demands for the concrete though. You know once we start pouring the cement in the forms, we'll have to finish the complete job without stopping for any reason. We're going to run into some serious trouble with cracking and cold joints in the concrete, if we stop the pour for any reason whatsoever. I have already figured it out, and I came up with this, we'll have to keep the concrete flowing inside the forms at the rate of just over seven yards per minute, in order to avoid any possible cold joints and also prevent any cracking in the footing."

Campanelli looked at the man speaking, and then asked him with some concern in his tone. "What the hell's a god damn cold joint, mister?"

The worker looked at Captain Campanelli with a smirk on his lips as he replied to his question. "Say Captain, a cold joint occurs when the concrete inside the forms starts to dry, we call it setting up, sir. It happens when the concrete stops being poured in the forms and then it starts cooling off. When the concrete flows again it won't stick very well to the concrete already drying and cooling in the form. Thus you end up with two separate pours in the same form. This cold joint will lead to cracks in the concrete in the future, and it'll also take away half the life expectancy of the concrete sir." The concerned sounding worker turned back to his boss and added to him this time. "I estimated the batching plants output, and they should cover our needs okay, barring any complications at the plants. Shit, I just remembered those fucking Seabee's said they had a portable batching plant due in some time tomorrow I believe.

"If we could possibly get our hands on that god damn batching plant, which should take a day or two to setup. I see no problem with getting all the concrete we'll need for the entire pour. That's if we could use their equipment and they don't like us much."

The worker in charge said to his lead foreman. "That's exactly what I wanted to hear from you, man. If we can get all the concrete poured by the end of next week for the footings then we'll be well ahead of the schedule already. You know, while we're pouring the cement for the footing, we're going to have to work around the god damn clock for the entire pour, until we're done with it. I just hope we have all the damn manpower available that's needed to get the job completed, without having to stop in the middle of the god damn pour."

Campanelli butted in this time as he offered to the lead foreman with a grin on his lips. "Would the Seabee's be enough help to you to complete this pour, mister?"

The engineer looked at the Captain and then he offered. "Hell sir, if I can have those arrogant bastards helping us with the god damn pours. Then I'll have no problem with it in the least, sir. Is it possible to get these men, and are they going to mind taking orders from us civilians, Captain? I can't afford to have any friction happening between the working crews during this important pour. This is one of the most important of the entire Dam project, sir."

"You'll have all the men you'll need for this concrete pour, mister. I'll see to it personally, and I promise the people I send you will take orders from you guys, and there'll be no stinking problems from them either, or it'll cost them their stinking hides. I'll also give you Lieutenant John White as their field boss. Anything you want the stinking Seabees to do for you people, all you have to do is tell my Lieutenant, and he'll make it happen and get the job done for you guys. Shit, just the size of this Lieutenant will be more than enough to keep any damn Seabee's in their proper place for the entire time they're working with you people, sir. I'll have the men I have available to report to you at exactly Oh Six Hundred Hours tomorrow morning, and then you can have them until you're completely done with the extra work you need them for, sir.

"But I want you to understand this is going to set back the housing project on the base the Seabees were working on a few days. As well as any other minor conveniences the Seabees were already working on for you guys, before you pulled them from their present duties, to be of assistance to you and the rest of your workers for this stinking concrete pour, sir." Captain Campanelli offered as he looked at the pack of civilians now staring at him.

"Shit sir, if I can use your men to get this first pour in. Then I swear to you that you'll never hear any further complaints from us again, until this god damn job has been completed, sir."

The Captain smiled at the rather large civilian, and then he replied. "You got yourself a fucking deal there mister." The two of them shook hands, and then the Captain left them. He went out looking for Lieutenant John White, and found him talking to a few of the Seabees.

"Mr. White Sir, hey Whitie can you come over here for a second please? I want to speak with you for a second. I have a slight problem and you have to straighten it out for me, my friend." The Army Captain called out to his Lieutenant as he waved him over to his side.

"Uh oh, I really don't think I like the sounds of this one very much sir. What the devil's on your evil mind this time around, Eddy."

Lieutenant John White remarked as he quickly made his way over and made Captain Campanelli laugh over his last comment that was said just loud enough for him to here it as they met and Campanelli slapped White on his back and began speaking the moment they were together.

"Come on Whitie, I'll try and make this as painless as possible for you to absorb, my old friend." The Captain replied while wearing a huge grin on his lips as he stared back at his old friend, and then he slapped him on his back a second time.

The two young military officers spoke between themselves, and when Lieutenant John White finally heard what Captain Edward Campanelli wanted from him, he cried like a child who just got caught with his finger sticking in the cookie jar. All this crying from the angry Lieutenant stopped immediately the instant Campanelli suddenly pulled rank on him, and he just then ordered the Lieutenant to do as he was just ordered to do.

Captain Campanelli left the rather upset Lieutenant still steaming over the last orders from his commanding officer, and then he called over the Seabee Chief, whose job it was to control the Seabees under his command, and to also make certain they were working and caring for their construction equipment properly. The older Chief stared back at the military officer walking directly at him as he waited for the Captain to reach where he was standing. The wise Chief knew immediately he was not going to like what his commanding officer was going to tell him. He could see it in the way the Captain was walking towards him, and he set his stance for the confrontation he knew was coming his way from the Captain.

CHAPTER 8

Events happened fast in the week of February 21st, 1996. As was expected, the deposed President of Chad, Hissen Habre reenter Chad, and the forces loyal to him rallied around him and they were joined by other civilians and soldiers also unhappy with the way the Libyan puppet government currently running the country of Chad. Within days of his return, the deposed President Habre demanded the President of Chad immediately step down.

President Dedy vowed to fight to the bitter end, and when Habre turned his rebel forces loose inside Chad. Every town and village the rebels entered, they were quickly joined by many of the residents of those villages, until the size of his rebel army was staggering and overwhelming, and President Dedy was actually forced to flee the country to the safety of Libya, because of the enemy forces being mounted against his Administration.

Libya in turn called up her Army, and stationed the soldiers on the borders of Libya and Chad, pausing there for an all out attack on the small country of Chad, if requested by President Dedy. Libya vowed to place President Dedy back in power over the small country of Chad. The world held its collective breath as they waited for the outcome of the continuing threats being bantered about by both sides involved in this situation.

If Libya attacks Chad, many other countries would immediately come to the aid of the tiny nation of Chad this time. This action could easily and rapidly escalate into World War Three with little effort, because of the turmoil presently happening in Central Africa.

CAIRO, EGYPT

The new Egyptian President Sadat sent for Ambassador Mohammed Kheir to come back to Egypt by February 16th, just a few days before the deposed President of Chad reentered his country. Egypt had advance warning about the move from Libya, and the Libyan leader wanted to know how far Egypt was with her mining of the Sinai Desert with the deadly fuel air land minds and anti-personnel weapons in the sands of the desert.

Egypt just sent in her first unit of Egyptian workers and engineers into the Sinai Desert, but they had no mines with them at this time. This one crew was sent in to see if the Jews were going to inspect any workers and their equipment. The unit was in the desert for eleven days, and no Jew military units came anywhere around their base of operations. Egypt begged Libya to hold out for a while longer even if it cost them the nation of Chad.

President Sadat informed the Libyan government that he sent for Ambassador Kheir, and he was going to send another unit of Egyptian workers in the Sinai after all the hubbub calmed down over the first unit sent in the desert. He assured the Libyans this time the unit would have mines on them, and they would start to seed the sands of the desert with death.

The Libya government wanted to attack Chad on that very day, but President Sadat would not throw in with them just yet, until he was absolutely certain he had all the specialized mines and anti personnel strips planted in the Sinai Desert, and his defenses were set in place and fully operational. So he could assure his people they could not possibly be attacked, without being well able to defend themselves against any invaders to their country, and they could also beat back any attack carried out against them. Even if it came from the United States, before any major damage was done to Egypt.

The Libyan Ambassador Kamal was insistent, and he requested the Egyptian President Sadat come to Libya for a special meeting between the two of them. President Sadat simply refused to come to Libya, and he informed Ambassador Kamal to come out to Egypt instead.

Ambassador Kamal assured President Sadat he would arrive in Egypt the next day which he did. Kamal was not in Egypt for an hour, when a very irate Israeli Ambassador Haetzni placed an angry call to Ambassador Mohammed Kheir which he had to field cold, because he did not have a chance to be briefed about the present situation happening in Chad, or what was going on between his President and the Ambassador from Libya.

"Mohammed Kheir Sir!" Ambassador Haetzni demanded hotly of him as he stared back at the phone with concerned looking eyes before continuing. "What the hell is going on around here sir? Is your country going to back Libya in its present aggression against Chad, sir?"

Egyptian Ambassador Kheir had to think quick on his feet as he offered back to the highly upset Israeli politician over the phone. "Please Ambassador Haetzni Sir, I have just returned to my country from the United States, and I don't know what is currently happening in the nation of Chad at this time I'm afraid to offer. But I assure you sir, my country's only interest in this present situation, is peace. I know my government invited Ambassador Kamal, the Delegate from Libya to Egypt, in an attempt to reestablish peace in this area, and until I had a chance to speak with my President Sadat in person, sir. I cannot possibly tell you much more than what I know for certain at this time, sir."

Ambassador Haetzni was still as angry as hell and he did not try to hide his anger in the least, because he felt like he was being taken advantage of by this Egyptian politician as he barked at the Ambassador over the phone. "Mohammed Kheir, I have put my neck way out on a line because of you, and you have always proved yourself a trusted friend. I hope you're not going to betray the trust I hold for you." Haetzni fell silent to empathize his concern over this situation.

"Ambassador Haetzni Sir, your insinuation of a possible sinister plot committed by my nation of Egypt against your country is highly unfounded I assure you sir. Your country has nothing to worry about from Egypt or her people, sir. All your fears are unwarranted, this situation will work itself out in a peaceful way, you have to trust me over this matter, sir."

As Ambassador Kheir and Ambassador Haetzni spoke, the Israeli government took matters in its own hands. They immediately dispatched three American made UH 60A Blackhawk troop helicopters out to the Sinai Desert where the Egyptian workers were toiling. They were sent to search the Egyptian workers operating in the desert to make certain the Egyptian workers were not up to something that would threaten Israel and her security.

THE SINAI DESERT

The three Israeli helicopters hovered over the Egyptian workers and their encampment for a few moments, and then they suddenly descended like three prehistoric insects on the attack. They landed in three separate areas around the site, completely surrounding the unarmed Egyptian workers trying to take cover from the driving sand that was being kicked up by the powerful rotor blades of the three helicopters.

Eleven extremely angry Israeli soldiers armed to the teeth, immediately piled out of each of the American made helicopters, and they quickly rounded up all the frightened Egyptian workers, and then the Israeli soldiers forced them to sit in a circle on the sand in the center of the camp. Their hands were clasp behind their heads, and their legs were folded underneath them, while the Israeli soldiers commenced to ransack their trucks and tents, and then the angry Israeli soldiers searched the Egyptian's persons, looking for anything that might be a threat against them or their nation. One Israeli soldier remained on station inside each of three helicopter along with the pilot and co pilot of the machine, his job was to aim the mounted M-60 machine gun at the shaking Egyptian workers while the Israeli soldiers searched through the entire camp.

The leader of the Egyptian workers was a Colonel in the military, and he held his breath as the enemy soldiers examined a water tanker truck parked away from the rest of the vehicles under his command. The truck was the same one to be used to smuggle the land mines into the desert. This truck had the hidden compartment installed inside it. The worker who watched was a Colonel in the Egyptian Secret Service.

The three Israeli soldiers went over every inch of the large water truck, they even opened up all six of the scuttles and then they shined a flashlight into the body of the truck. As well as poking the Egyptian drinking water supply truck with a short pole they found at the campsite. The Israeli soldiers did a thorough check of the truck, and the Egyptian Colonel breathed a deep sigh of relief when the Jew soldiers finally walked away from the lone vehicle without further examining the machine. Now, the Egyptian Colonel knew the truck would be a safe way in which to carry the land mines into the desert for them.

After two hours of searching the entire Egyptian work camp, the Israeli soldiers reported back to the Commanding Officer, and they disclosed their finding just one small caliber hand gun. The Israeli officer then extended their his apologies to the Egyptian workers for the intrusion into their camp. The Israeli Officer ordered his troops back in the still spooling helicopters, and in an instant they disappeared in the bright noontime sun of the desert as quickly as they appeared.

When the Israeli helicopters were gone from the worksite. The Egyptian Intelligence Officer immediately pulled a small pocket radio out from a specially hidden compartment in the water truck. He then reported to his superior that the work unit was just checked out by the Jew soldiers, and they did not find the hidden compartment inside the water truck.

The report went directly to President Sadat's private office, and once he read it, he was pleased the Jewish soldiers did not discover the hidden compartments on the special truck. President Sadat ordered three more units to load up, this time with the land mines hidden on board their caravan, and then they were ordered to head out to the Sinai Desert. President Sadat also placed a call to Ambassador Mohammed Kheir, and he immediately informed him to launch a stinging complaint aimed at the Israeli Ambassador at how their god cursed soldiers had roughed up his frightened workers in the desert. "You know how to do it, make it sound good Mohammed." The angry Egyptian President warned his Ambassador

Egyptian Ambassador Mohammed Kheir did not have a chance to place the call, because the Israeli Representative called him first. His aide came rushing in his private office while he prepared himself to place the call the Jewish politician. The aide informed him the Israeli Delegate was on the phone, and he wanted to speak with him immediately.

He put off answering the phone as he thought for a few moments, and then he ordered his aide to inform the Jew he was on a conference call with the President and Ambassador Kamal and he could not be disturbed at this time, and he asked him to hold the line and that he would be with the Israeli Delegate momentarily. After making the Israeli politician wait for nearly five full minutes, he finally picked up the phone and he said quickly. "I'm most sorry that I kept you waiting so long Ambassador Haetzni. If you'll please excuse this bit of Americanism, I just got my ass chewed out by my extremely angry President for that little stunt your government has pulled in the desert against our workers, Haetzni Sir."

He left off the Ambassador title this time when he spoke to the Jewish politician on purpose, to show the Delegate he was angry at what had taken place in the desert.

Ambassador Haetzni spoke while overlooking the minor insult the Egyptian just offered to him. "Mohammed, this is why I'm calling you sir. I wanted to inform you what happened in the desert before you heard it from anyone else, sir. I was only informed of the incident after it had happened, sir. I guess I was too late to get to you sir. I'm terribly sorry for this intrusion and if it helps any, I shall registered a stern complaint with my government against any further such actions, which could only be thought of as acts of aggression aimed against Egypt and her workers in the desert, sir. Mohammed, I hope you take the current actions in Chad, and the threats coming from Libya, and the sudden appearance of the Libyan Delegate in your country, to try and soften the anger this most unfortunate circumstance caused all concerned, sir."

He allowed his anger remain in his tone as he replied to the deeply concerned Israeli Ambassador. "I assure you Ambassador Haetzni, all your suspicions are founded in pure fantasy, sir. The timing of your government's raid against my workers could not have come at worse timing with the Libyan Delegate coming to my country to speak with my President, sir. I knew his appearance here would cause a reaction from your people, sir. But you have to understand it was your military who just invaded the sovereign lands of Egypt, sir. In paramount, your government has just invaded Egypt, sir. I know we spoke of this event happening beforehand Ambassador. But I had never thought your government would ever carry it out though, sir. What am I supposed to tell my President and people now Ambassador?

"What with the current happenings occurring inside the nation of Chad and Libya gave the Israeli government the right to invade my country, and assault her civilian's rights? I must warn you Ambassador Haetzni that certain elements in my country want Israel punished severely for her sudden intrusion into our land, and their assault on our unarmed and defenseless civilians by heavily armed Israeli soldiers.

Quite frankly Ambassador Haetzni Sir, I find myself agreeing with some of these elements and their desires. I also find myself wondering what the reaction would be in Israel, if three Egyptian helicopters invaded your country, and our soldiers pushed your unarmed civilians around like a gang of gangsters or common thugs, sir. Ambassador Haetzni, I ask you sir. What would the Israel government have done if we Egyptians carried out such an unprovoked action in your country, sir?" He asked the Jewish Delegate, knowing the only answer to his question.

He heard the Israeli politician draw in a huge gulp of air, and then he replied to his last question of him in a rather calm voice. "In all likelihood sir, we would have most likely attacked Egypt in force if this had ever happened to us on our soil, sir. Ambassador Mohammed Kheir, again, I must say I'm truly sorry and deeply sadden for this terrible mistake, and I shall try to stop it from ever happening again in the future sir. I must inform you Ambassador Kheir, a good number of my people are extremely upset, and they understand this was a very foolish action taken on our part against your peaceful workers in the desert, sir.

"I have no possible and logical explanation to offer you that would take away this terrible insult to your fine Egyptian workers, Ambassador Kheir. I can only hope you're still the man I have come to know, and you're still willing to do whatever it takes to keep the peace in these most trying of times between our two nations, sir." The Israeli Ambassador stopped speaking, hoping his sincerity would make the difference, and force Mohammed Kheir to see it was a just a foolish action taken on the Israeli government's part.

"Ambassador Haetzni Sir, I'm certain I can smooth out the ruffled feathers of my government and her people. We'll not demand your government make a public apology to my country, sir. As far as I'm concerned, this incident never happened sir. I promise I shall speak with the Libyan government, and put a quick end to the problems created between Libya and Chad. Ambassador Haetzni Sir, one thing I have to request from you though sir. When you want to check on our other work units we have operating in the Sinai Desert, sir. Incidentally, we have just sent three more units out to the desert today, sir. I hope you'll use your civilian operators to check on them, sir. I don't care if you dress your military in civilian clothes, just make certain it is civilians who search my units from now on sir. Is this acceptable to you sir?"

The Israeli Ambassador Haetzni suddenly breathed a deep sigh of relief as he replied to the Egyptian politician's request. "If this insult ever happens again, it will most certainly be civilians who'll inspect your work teams in the desert, sir. I'll talk my government into refraining from searching your workers altogether sir. I hope you're going to inform my people where these new units will be operating in the desert, as per our original agreement sir."

"I shall send your government their entire work schedule, so you know exactly where the workers are as to our agreement, Ambassador Haetzni."

"Thank you for your kind understanding in this matter, Ambassador Kheir. I wish you much luck in dealing with the always troublesome Libyan government, sir. I really hate to tell you, but you know if Libya attacks Chad, my government soldiers would have no choice but to intervene. The United States will also intervene militarily, as will Saudi Arabia and a few other Arab nations as well, Ambassador Kheir. So please, do your best with them Mohammed. Also, I repeat, if any of your people need help in the Sinai Desert, we'll be most pleased to lend your government all the assistance you might need or request, sir." Ambassador Haetzni listened cautiously in hopes Mohammed would ask him for help, this way they would not be forced to send other troops out to search the Egyptian workers, but no request ever came from the Arab.

"Ambassador Haetzni Sir, this is something my government has to do by itself, sir. It's not like I would not appreciate your kind offer of assistance, but at times we Arabs can be as stubborn as your people are. I shall relay the offer of your help again to my government, sir. By the way Ambassador Haetzni Sir, if you could find it in your power, I think it be a good idea if your government would find a way to apologize to my government, for their callous actions aimed against the civilians of Egypt, sir. I know I said I wasn't going to ask your government for a public apology, but I think in the interests of peace, it should be done." He laughed to himself, because he knew he had the Jew over a barrel, and he would have to make a public statement which would make the Israeli government look bad in the eyes of the world.

After a few moments of dead silence, Ambassador Haetzni finally agreed to make a public statement, apologizing for this mistake made by the Israeli soldiers. The two politicians then broke off their conversation with Mohammed laughing, and Haetzni cursing this Egyptian.

He immediately placed a call to President Sadat, and he quickly informed him what transpired with the Jewish government. Sadat ordered Mohammed to report to his office immediately and Kamal was there, and he wanted Egypt to help with their fight against Chad.

It took him ten minutes to get to the President's office. The hairs on his neck immediately stood on end at the sight of the Libyan Ambassador Kamal sitting in a chair smiling at him as he entered the President's private office. He nodded slightly at Kamal and had to suffer the humiliation and anger of his president for not acknowledging Kamal in the civilized Arab way.

"You are becoming very uncivilized I see of late, Ambassador Mohammed Kheir. I don't enjoy it in the least and you better change your foul ways or suffer the consequences of your foolish follies, Ambassador. Did you forget the proper way to greet a fellow Arab brother when laying eyes upon him again, sir?" President Sadat hissed angrily as he sent a harsh glaring stare at his confidant.

Ambassador Mohammed Kheir instantly bowed politely towards President Sadat, and then he turned to Ambassador Kamal and offered him pleasantly. "It seems once again, I have forgotten my good manners. Please forgive my error Ambassador Kamal. Allah Akhbar my friend."

"Allah Akbar back to you Ambassador Mohammed Kheir." Ambassador Kamal replied while adjusting his Kaffiyeh without standing up, but he remained smiling at Mohammed that ever evil sneer he always flashed as a smile at anyone he disliked.

President Sadat pointed towards a seat for Ambassador Kheir. He made certain he could see the faces of both of these troublemaking politicians without turning his head to either one of them during their conversation. While the two Delegates would have to turn in order to look at each other, if they were to speak to one another before him.

The new Egyptian President Sadat stared at his Ambassador, and then said to him in a commanding voice. "Mohammed, Ambassador Kamal wants us to attack Chad, and then the Sudan as of this minute. I have informed him that Egypt was not ready to join in on any such attack as yet, sir. Mohammed, you know we intend to attack Ethiopia and the Sudan soon. If we could talk Libya into holding off her attack until we're truly ready to begin our own military action against these two foul nations of inferior Arab fools, sir. Then I feel we'll stand a much better chance of defeating these filthy mongrels that live to our south and east, while Libya settles her concerns with the hatful nations of Chad and the Sudan, sir."

Ambassador Kamal butted into the conversation nastily, as he clasped his fingers together and asked the Egyptian leader. "President Sadat, if we were to put off our attack against Chad until you were better prepared for military actions yourself. How much time would your country need, before she is ready to join the attack with us, sir?"

President Sadat looked at Mohammed, and then he waited for him to reply to Ambassador Kamal's last question for him.

He felt extremely uncomfortable as he responded. "I hoped we would not have to attack any nation at all, President Sadat. I always hoped that we could work out our differences with Ethiopia, and I didn't know we were having trouble with Sudan. I..."

Ambassador Kamal cut him off by saying in a very sarcastic tone of voice. "Ah, my dear friend, you are a true romantic I see. Let me explain the facts of life to you, sir. There is no way out of this present situation for both our governments, but to fight our way out of it with soldiers attacking soldiers, sir. Without water, Egypt dies plain and simple, and if Libya allows Chad to be ran by the West, Libya will never have a secured border, and this Libya will not stand for it for one moment. So you better see the light at the end of the tunnel, and act like you should in your country's best interest, sir." Ambassador Kamal openly glared harshly at Mohammed this time, which took his challenge and quickly took a defensive stance against the Libyan politician, while returning his harsh stare with one of his own now.

President Sadat immediately jumped to his feet while pointing his finger directly at the two upset politicians as he yelled at both of them at the same time. "Our countries have enough enemies to fear out there, without us fighting amongst ourselves here, you two fools. For the love of Allah's grace, will you two grow up please. Look at you Mohammed Kheir, you're ready to kill Ambassador Kamal, a fellow Arab brother. And you Ambassador Kamal, you are no better than he is! You stand ready to do the same to Mohammed. You both should know better than this. I order you two lowly jackals to sit down and behave yourselves, or I'm going to call in the guards. Arabs cannot fight fellow Arabs, or all is lost to us."

The Libyan Ambassador Kamal was the first one to retake his seat, he was no fool and he did not really want to tangle with the much larger and stronger Mohammed, because he would easily destroy him. Egyptian President Sadat had to actually glare at Mohammed before he finally relaxed his fists, and then he retook his seat and remained silent.

"That is much better, if you two fools cannot get along better than you are at this time, Ambassador Kamal. I'll request your government replace you at once if you don't start reacting mush better and control your foolish temper before me. Mohammed!" President Sadat warned his own Ambassador while glaring at him now as he added. "I shall have you replaced as well Mohammed, and you'll be shot as a traitor against Egypt. We have important issues to discuss here. Let's get down to business and not argue between ourselves. I shall ask the questions, and both of you will answer them truthfully. Or I'll order the guards to come in, and they'll be ordered to shoot the first one of you two jackals who causes a commotion or disrupt this conversation, do you understand me?" President Sadat looked threateningly at the angry men.

Both men mumbled they understood the warning, and they were willing to place their personal animosities for each other aside for the sakes of their governments and countries.

"Very good this time Mohammed. The question I have asked you before this most childish outburst happened, I believe was. How soon will Egypt be ready to join Libya in an all out attack against our enemies to the south of our country, sir?" President Sadat asked his Ambassador.

He thought for a long moment and then he replied. "I don't see us being ready for any possibly military attack for the rest of the year at the earliest, sir."

Ambassador Kamal let out a deep sigh of sheer disgust which brought an instant and stern glare in his direction from President Sadat, followed by another warning aimed against him this time as he hissed at the same time. "Ambassador Kamal, I warn you in no uncertain terms sir, don't dare to start anything that you cannot handle once again here, or I shall finish it for you this time I assure you, sir. Mohammed, you said by the end of the year we will be ready to joining our Libyan's brothers in their war against our common enemies to our south. What will be set in place by the end of this year to enable us to being our military conquest of our enemies, sir?"

"I'm quite certain all the land mines and anti-personnel strips will be set in place by that time in the Sinai Desert sir, and we will also have the shore batteries setup by that time as well, my President. This way we can easily beat back any possible invasion forces sent from Israel with the land mines and strips, and with the shore batteries in place, any other country that may chose to attack us, sir. We'll easily be able to stop the once feared United State military from attacking us from the Mediterranean Sea side, as well as establishing a beach head on our soil against us.

"I feel and believe many other Arab countries not committed now, will be on our side by then. I'm just as certain Libya will have no trouble stirring up any number of incidents with the United States or the Sudan, and even with the worthless nation of Chad, to cause the non committed Arab states to join our just cause. I feel we should have all our forces set in place by this time in the Sinai Desert, and along the Sudan and Ethiopian borders. One thing, I thought you were to install an off switch to stop this war if we can come to terms with the Ethiopians, sir?"

President Sadat grunted as he snapped angrily at his Ambassador. "Still the optimist I see Mohammed. Yes, you're still the off switch in this coming drama, but I demand your patriotism to go through with whatever your country demands of you, sir. I as you, truly don't want war, but if war is to come to Egypt, then we have to be well prepared for that war at all costs, sir."

Mohammed hissed back at his new young President of Egypt. "I told you before, that I'll do whatever my country asks of me without thought or hesitation, sir."

The Egyptian President Sadat glared harshly at Mohammed as he snarled at him. "You'll do wise not to take such a tone in your voice against me, Ambassador Kheir. It could cost your worthless life, you cursed son of the lowly jackal."

Ambassador Kamal interrupted the slight confrontation raging between the Ambassador and President of Egypt with a laugh as he asked the Egyptian politician mockingly. "Mohammed, I ask you this question sir. Is there any way you can possibly step up your time table of attack? I'd like to attack, excuse me, my country wishes to attack as soon as possible."

President Sadat was angry again as he snapped at the Libyan. "Ambassador Kamal, if you cannot wait for us to be better prepared for war then I suggest you attack Chad and the Sudan now if you truly like, sir. I will not, I repeat this for your knowledge, I will not be forced to attack anyone before my forces are ready to attack and are set in place, sir. I'll not put my country or her soldiers in peril unnecessarily because of you and your country's wants and desires. If I cannot guarantee myself neither Israel nor the United States will not get a foothold on my soil, I will not attack at all. At all, I warn you Ambassador Kamal! You'll not have Egypt on your side if I do not feel protected and able to carry out our attacks successfully."

The Libyan Ambassador Kamal looked at the young Egyptian President for a long moment, and then he said to the angry looking Egyptian Leader. "My country has sent to Egypt twenty thousand fuel explosive land mines, and by the end of this week, you'll receive thirty five French ANS missile launchers which will keep any enemy ship of war far away from your shores, President Sadat. Plus you'll receive a good number of pieces of military hardware to better protect your banks from invasion. The rest will be up to your fine soldiers to carry out, sir. A question President Sadat? How are your soldiers doing inside Israel? What are the statistics on those specialized troops? Do they know what is expected of them when war breaks out?"

President Sadat smiled and replied confidently to the Libyan. "There are two thousand Egyptian soldiers presently being trained by the foolish Jews in Israel, to be a great fighting force. Commandos if you will sir. These troops have already received orders to request political asylum when Egypt joins forces with Libya on her attack against Chad and the Sudan. We're certain Israel will happily grant asylum to these Egyptian soldiers they're training for me.

"The soldiers when able, will then set out to attack selected targets assigned to them for destruction inside the borders of Israel, dealing the fatal blow to the retreating Jew soldiers being slaughtered in the Sinai Desert. It's a fool proof plan, and the Jews will be caught in a vice in which there will be no escape from for them. Ambassador Kamal, I want those anti aircraft missiles you promised shipped out to Egypt quickly. How are you doing with my soldiers being trained in Libya? Are they going to be able to hit any incoming planes or ships? You know the United States will be committing their warplanes stationed in Sicily and Spain as well as in England against both our nations once we declare war on Chad and the Sudan, and then Ethiopia. I want to knock them out of the sky when they are over Egypt."

Kamal smiled this time as he offered to the Egyptian Leader. "President Sadat, you have not been told about another weapon our Russian defectors have developed for us, have you sir?"

"No. What type of weapon are you talking about now Kamal?" Sadat demanded from him.

"The foul and god cursed useless Russian dogs have developed a special anti aircraft weapon that'll all but assure our success in destroying our enemy aircraft aimed at our countries, sir. The weapon is called a 'Drift Bomb', it uses the magnetic forces of the earth in order to float into the path of any incoming enemy warplanes. It'll even change height as the incoming aircraft do while in flight. The special weapon is constructed of a plastic housing, making it just about non detectable to any plane's radar, or even their infrared systems, and the bomb will explode right in the midst of the enemy formation. The one thousand pound blast will knock down as many as twenty enemy aircraft, depending on how tight the formation of aircraft is. We're producing these weapons in great numbers, and we'll have well over ten thousand of these weapons in Egypt's hands by the end of this month, sir. With these weapons in our possession, we'll remove the American warplanes out of the air war."

Ambassador Mohammed Kheir shook his head slowly, because now he understood the so called off switch was something that President Sadat gave him, just to keep him quiet. But he had no real intention of allowing him employ it to possibly stop the coming war. No one is going to stop this upcoming war already fluttering its wings of death in the near future. There has been too much preparation by these two men to stop the war now.

Sadat turned to Mohammed and asked him. "What do you think about our chances now?"

He stared at President Sadat, and then he mumbled. "I think if these weapons of Libya's work like Ambassador Kamal has suggested they do. Then I believe we have a very good chance of living through this war you're so set on starting, my President."

President Sadat instantly jumped to his feet and snapped at Kheir. "Why you impertinent bastard you! Who the devil do you think you are to dare speak to me like this, one of your lowly whores? I can have your head taken for your impertinence at the drop of my hand, you foul desert jackal you. What do you mean by a chance of living through this war, Mohammed? In case you have not realized it as yet sir, we Egyptians are in the driver's seat in this possible upcoming war, and other countries will beg us to cease all hostilities, and that is when we'll name our terms to stop the fighting. Explain yourself to me, you foul fool!"

"President Sadat, I said we will stand a chance of not living through this possible war, because of one thing you seem to have forgotten in discussing what is in our future, sir. If we create the death that the Libyans are speaking about here. Then we'll force the United States' hand to commit their nuclear weapons against our country. If I was the Chad government, and I was losing my country to Libya, I'd surely beg the United States to pop off a few of their nuclear weapons in strategic locations, in order to stop the Libyan's from destroying the entire nation of Chad. After all, half a country saved is better than none left at all, sir." He grumbled as he glared at President Sadat, whose eyes were equally ablaze.

After hearing Mohammed's summation, President Sadat turned his glare back to Ambassador Kamal and he immediately demanded a further explanation from him in no uncertain terms. He wanted to know why nuclear weapons were never brought up to his attention before this time.

Ambassador Kamal smiled sheepishly now as he offered to the young and new Egyptian Leader in a reassuring tone of voice. "Calm down a little please President Sadat. If it comes to where the United States threatens us with their nuclear weapons. We will merely counter with threats of powerful chemical and biological weapons we have stored in our arsenal, thanks to our Russian scientists. This will stop the threat of nuclear weapons used against us. Because any land that will be spared nuclear attacks, will be hit by biological and or chemical weapons fired by our side, leaving nothing but complete devastation for anyone who might have survived the nuclear attack. Thus, a no win situation for either side, and we know how the American fools feel about a no win stance. We know they'll simply not enter this type of situation as was proven by Russia, and the United States stand down during the cold war years of the past."

The suddenly confused President Sadat was scared as he replied to this stunning information just brought up to his attention by his Ambassador. "I don't know about using such god cursed hated weapons of mass destruction as you have just offered, Ambassador Kamal. I don't want Egypt destroyed by either of these God awful weapons you speak of."

"President Sadat, what is the true difference if Egypt is destroyed by either chemical or nuclear weapons, or if Egypt is destroyed by a drought and no water to offer to their population. Either way, Egypt is destroyed and no longer exists in this world, no? And dead is dead no matter how that death had been created." Kamal warned solemnly as a smug smile appeared on his lips.

Now it was President Sadat's turn to think before replying to Ambassador Kamal's last words spoken to him. "Yes, I guess you have a good point there, Ambassador Kamal. Dead is dead no matter how you get there, there is no future for Egypt if she is dead. I pray once the world knows we posses these most unspeakable god cursed weapons in our arsenal, they'll immediately sue for peace with us." President Sadat stared at both politicians as if to be looking for one of them to give him the answer he was so desperately searching for.

Ambassador Kamal laughed his sarcastic laugh as he offered to the Egyptian Leader in a smug tone of voice again. "I assure you President Sadat that we'll give the world no other choice in the matter but to look for peace wherever they can find it. I'll bet the world will be more than willing to allow Chad, the Sudan and even Ethiopia to dissolve in the vast sands of the endless desert, to establish peace in this region of the world again. Thus, Egypt and Libya will be the super powers of all the Middle East, even bending the will of the worthless Saudi Arabian jackals and the loathsome Iranian fools. We'll own the entire Middle East, and we'll pick the countries we shall allow in the area to trade and buy our oil. We'll put the all powerful United States on her knees." Kamal started laughing again as he looked to the angry Muhammad.

Mohammed's stomach churned, leaving the very sour taste of bile in his mouth.

President Sadat stared at Mohammed as if he was trying to read his mind as he snapped at him. "Do you have anything else you want to add to this conversation, Kheir?"

He stiffened as he responded to his President last words. "I have nothing else to add to this conversation. You have obviously made up your mind to go to war."

Sadat hissed at his Ambassador. "You're excused for this conversation then, I have other items to discuss over with Ambassador Kamal. Leave my presence Ambassador Kheir."

Both men waited until Mohammed left the room. Then President Sadat looked to Kamal and offered. "Well Ambassador, we must keep this fiction of peace alive for as long as possible before we dash all dreams of peace in this region. We must keep this farce alive until we attack the countries giving us problems in order to keep the hated United States from leveling suspicion upon us, until it is far too late for them to react against any of our future actions. Can I give my government your word you'll fight on the side of Libya when asked? And if so, when can we expect to commence our attack on these lowly infidels?" Kamal asked the Egyptian President.

President Sadat spoke quietly, as if scared to death to speak the words he wanted to offer to the Libyan politician. "Yes, we will fight on the side of our Arab brothers, Ambassador Kamal. It's now February sir. I think Egypt will be ready for the attack to begin in October. I'll inform our operatives working inside Israel and the United States of my decision, and they'll be prepared to attack when the time is dictated to them. I shall move around my armies disguised as civilians, until the Israeli armor and soldiers has moved into the Sinai Desert. Then the world will know what Egypt is up to. Ambassador Kamal, I hope this fits in with your plans."

Ambassador Kamal warned the new Egyptian Leader sharply. "President Sadat, don't be fearful, be joyous because you're about to witness a new Islamic freedom sweeping over the entire world. Egypt will have to be ready to act by then. Libya will start our attack against Chad on October 5th, 1996. I too will inform our operatives of the day war starts for them. During the hot months of July, August and September, we'll create many other incidents which will enable Libya to step up her war footing against Chad until we finally attack that worthless nation.

"Now President Sadat, your government will have the pleasure of informing the rest of the world that your government had successfully talked our government into stepping down from a war threat against Chad at this time. Also President Sadat, your government was setting up peace talks, which will be scheduled to take place between our two governments, and the governments of Chad and also the mongrel nation of Sudan. Omit Ethiopia from any discussions of peace talks. Let them cry like a wounded pig, so the rest of the world thinks they're just trying to stir up trouble in this region again. President Sadat Sir, I suggest you will allow the great fool Ambassador Mohammed Kheir to issue this news release to the world, it'll make Egypt look good in the eyes of the rest of the world for the time being sir."

President Sadat agreed with the Libyan, and Mohammed was sent for after Ambassador Kamal left for his country. Mohammed was informed to announce the peace talks with Libya, and the reestablished government of Chad, and Libya was willing to recognize President Hissen Habre as the new President of the nation of Chad at this time.

Mohammed Kheir returned to his office and sat down in his chair thoroughly exhausted and then he put on the TV so he could see what was happening in the world. Anger instantly overtook him as he stared intensely at the screen. He tried to control the mounting rage rapidly building up in his chest, and actually making it hard for him to swallow or even breath properly. His eyes went pitch black, betraying the anger that made his body absolutely rigid. Because on the TV it showed huge bulldozers and cranes digging in the dense jungle earth, just a half a mile away from Lake Tana in Ethiopia. The camera showed all the elaborate measures the American engineers had taken in order to reroute the powerful flow of water from the great Lake Tana.

By building a huge temporary earthen Dam, and thus forcing the vast amount of water flow through a number of huge pipes around the entire worksite. The camera spanned the huge construction site. An American engineer slowly came into view as he looked through a transit, and he directed another person way off in the distance by waving his hand at him. The other man was carrying a long measuring stick in his hands.

A number of small blasts could be heard going off in the background as the workers dynamited stones and ledges out of the way, and they cut footing holes in the rock base. Huge dump trucks could be seen moving thousand of yards of dirt and crushed stone off, to be used in the making of concrete for the intended Dam.

Mohammed Kheir's blood pressure rose as he stared at the scenes being played out before him on his TV. He shifted his weight in his leather chair angrily as he glared at his TV. More scenes of work on the Dam clearly came on the screen as the cameras turned their attention to where the Army Core of Engineers were busy with carving a rough trough right through the once lush jungle floor, which would carry the heavy water flow from Lake Tana, down to the great Afar Depression in the lowlands of the vast Ethiopian desert.

CHAPTER 9

Egyptian Ambassador Mohammed Kheir watched as huge blade dozers pushed down age old trees, and cut massive deep scars through the virgin earth. The soil was pitch black and very rich, dirt any good Egyptian farmer would give his right hand for growing his crops in. He shook his head sadly, because in his heart he knew this god cursed Dam was going to cause a war between many Arab nations of the region, and maybe even leading to another World War at the same time. Perhaps, the last the earth could possibly take before she finally closed down and lost her atmosphere, thus causing the death of the entire human race.

Mohammed Kheir grunted in an angry gripe. "Human, now there is a play on words if I have ever heard one I see." He forced his troubling thoughts away from this nightmare and focused them back to reality as he watched the TV again. There was a sudden and huge blast, and the camera immediately flashed to the area. It showed a massive cloud of dirt, stones, broken trees and brush being violently torn from the earth, and thrown high up in the air. When the uprooted earth returned to the ground, massive bulldozers and cranes quickly moved in, and then loaded up the fill and destroyed trees and brush and killed animals into a column of earth movers, and then the huge machines quickly carted it away. The bulldozers shaped the sides of the trough, and an army of workers covered them with riprap. Large stones were positioned on the raw earth in order to stop the strong flow of water from eroding the manmade river bank away.

Mohammed laughed aloud as he watched the black Ethiopian Arabs working with white American workers. "Only the American jackals could ever get these black bastards to do any real work for themselves, and their work is going to destroy the entire world at the same time. If only Allah would have moved his mighty hand and erased all these black Arab fools from the face of the earth, the world would survive in peace."

Ambassador Kheir could watch no more of this nightmare being displayed before his eyes, and he pulled the power cord from the socket, causing the TV to go black. He sent the message Libya was going to recognize the new government of Chad. He cursed and then he left his office, angry at the world. He headed for an apartment where another Egyptian Diplomat stayed. He knew Mohammed Azia would have something there for him to drink.

As he left his office in anger, JoAnne followed him without word. She knew what he was doing, because she monitored all his movements through a small peephole leading from the outer office to his. She understood and felt his anger, but knew she was going to stop him before he got too drunk, in case President Sadat unexpectedly called for him. She knew President Sadat's wrath would fall heavy on her shoulders if Kheir showed up at his office drunk.

As the world held its collective breath and it waited for Libya to react to the situations rapidly occurring in this region of the world, and President Habre took over command of Chad, the United States forces stationed throughout the Middle East reacted.

The Carrier Strike Force led by the Nimitz's Class Nuclear Aircraft Carrier for her first action. The USS George Washington, commissioned in May of 1992, along with nine of her escorts and support ships were ordered to the Indian Ocean, to add her support to the strike force led by the Aircraft Carrier USS. America, and her eight ship support group.

The Carrier USS Independence and her twelve sister ship support group, were ordered to the Mediterranean Sea, to take up position some twenty seven miles off the coast of Libya.

The massive battleship USS Wisconsin, along with of her support and escort ships were ordered to the Indian Ocean also. Nine nuclear submarines were also ordered to take up defensive positions in the Indian Ocean waters, as were three other submarines ordered out to the Mediterranean Sea. The Aircraft Carrier USS John F. Kennedy and her fifteen support ships were already stationed in the Indian Ocean.

England also reacted and ordered her three Harrier Jump Jet Carriers out to the Mediterranean Sea for added support to the American ships. France also ordered her seven Guided Missile Destroyers out to sea, to help support England and the United States in their bid to maintain peace in this region. The Baltic Alliance ordered her Nuclear Cruiser the Vladimir, and the Missile Cruiser Kirov, along with the Admiral Kuznetzov, the only Aircraft Carrier Russia had in her Navy. She was equipped with the long range nuclear tipped SS N 19 anti ship missiles which were positioned under her flight deck, along with the SA 9 surface to air missiles, and the RBU 1200 anti torpedo systems. She was followed by her support ships to the Mediterranean Sea, to lend the Baltic Alliance support to the American warships gathering there.

The American warships appearing in the Mediterranean Sea and the Indian Ocean, reminded everyone of the multi nation task force stationed off the shores of Saudi Arabia and Kuwait during the Iraq war. Protesters were driving hundred of small speed boats between the massive warships in an effort to try and slow their forward progress down. But this stopped as some of the ships of war started to ram some of the small speed boats, and occasionally opening fire on those becoming a little overly persistent and too close to the ship they were harassing.

For nine full days, the world watched as many other nations of the world posed for war in and around North Africa. On the tenth day of the tensions, a statement was suddenly released from the

Egyptian government. 'Due to the timely intervention of the Egyptian government, the new threat of war has been eliminated.' The statement went on to offer to the world. 'Due to Egypt's last minute negotiations with the nation of Libya, she has been able to talk the new Libyan government into sitting down and talk out their differences with the new government of Chad.

"The Libyan government is also willing to recognize this new government of that country which is presently being led by President Habre as the ruling government of the nation of Chad. If the two governments are able to reach a final peaceful agreement between themselves.' The statement went on, but the rest was left up to the politicians to sort out the finer details of the agreement. The world breathed a deep sigh of relief.

Immediately, the concerned Israeli Representative placed a call to Mohammed in Egypt at his government's request. Ambassador Haetzni praised the Egyptians for getting Chad and Libya talking. Haetzni assured Mohammed he was going to get his people to show more trust in the Egyptian workers looking for water in the Sinai desert. Before he hung up, Ambassador Haetzni reiterated he knew his trust was well placed. "Mohammed, the words of our Torah say, `He who saves one life, saves the world entire'. You have saved the world a terrible fate sir."

The Egyptian Ambassador shook his head sadly and mumbled to himself. 'If only you knew what will happen to the world within the next few months, and I'm completely powerless to stop it'. He sat in his chair while staring at the receiver of his phone, wishing he could call every other Diplomat of the world and warn them of the upcoming disaster that is going to strike the world because of the actions of Libya and his country.

EASY MONEY BASE LAKE TANA, ETHIOPIA

Captain Edward 'Popeye' Campanelli heard the loud roar coming of the powerful engines of the Apache fast attack helicopters start before seeing them lift off, he actually sprang out his tent while still naked. He got out just in time as the three helicopters formed a tight formation, and then they quickly headed off in the direction of the Sudan. The worried Captain noticed the sixteen Hellfire missiles hanging ominously down on both sides of each of the helicopter and he grumbled angrily at himself. "This is not good, this is not good at all god dammit."

A passing soldier remarked he was going to get it sunburned if he was not more careful about himself. This remark caused the Captain to look at himself and he realize he was naked. He immediately ran back in his tent and quickly dressed.

Lieutenant Renee Mendoza, who was also sharing the bunk with Captain Campanelli said to him. "You look like you have just seen a ghost my dear. Is there trouble out there Edward?"

"Shit yeah there's fucking trouble going on out there god dammit! The three fucking Apache helicopters have just left for the damn Sudan in a fucking fast hurry it up, young lady. Dammit to hell and back again, I have a bad gut feeling the shit has just hit the damn fan on us. Baby, you better get ready for some shit coming our way."

"How could you say that Edward? The choppers could just be on some training maneuvers, that's all." She watched him got dressed quickly. The concerned Captain took a second and looked at her light brown body glistening in the light of his tent and then he bitched.

"Mendoza, the damn things were loaded for fucking bear, and they took off in a tight attack formation as well. You better get dressed, I really think there's going to be a helluva lot of shit happening real soon. I have to head over to the damn Intelligence Tent and see if they know what the hell's going on around here, baby." His attention was suddenly drawn to the sky, even though he could not see it from in the tent. He heard the wing of fighter aircraft flying over the base while also heading for the Sudan.

"Shit, it's happening now dammit. You had better snap to it some, will you please Mendoza." He yelled at her as he quickly left the tent with his shirt still open, and he doubled timed it over to the Intel tent.

Once inside the communication tent, he noticed the young Marine Corporal wired to the computers. He knew the reason for the wire hookup. If this man's heart stopped beating for any reason, or if he should become disconnected from the computers during a threat or attack. The computers would automatically self destruct. This way if they were overran by the enemy troops, they would never get access to his intelligence net or communications. The second noncom (non commissioned officer) sat by the table, he was busy writing down all the information and any plans they received from the command center.

The noncoms jumped to their feet as the Captain entered the tent and they snapped to attention.

"Never mind that shit. What the fuck's happening out there god dammit?" The excited Captain demanded to know as he moved near the bank of computers.

"Captain Campanelli Sir, I was just about to send a runner out for you, sir. We're on full Red Alert Captain. President Habre has just attacked Dedy, and he's kicking the shit out of him and the rest of his damn supporters. Err..., beg your pardon sir."

"Cut the fricking shit out will ya please and finish with your damn report, soldier."

"Yes Sir Captain Campanelli Sir. Libya has just threatened to attack Chad if President Habre didn't pull out and back off their attack. Sir, our President has just ordered four more strike forces to position in the waters off the coast of Africa, Captain. I have their coordinates here sir. A Libyan Representative's in Egypt, and our President thinks Egypt might help Libya in her attack against Chad if it happens, sir. We're ordered to stand by communications by CIC on the Command Carrier, on a one on one off basis, sir. The Sudan talking about attacking if Libya went after Chad. The Marines were just ordered to send their helicopters out to the Sudan, and take orders from the Sudanese military there, sir. Aircraft from the Carrier Roosevelt are on their way to the Sudan as well at this present time, sir. That's where we're up to now, sir."

"Patch me through to the fucking CIC Roosevelt right away soldier." He hissed angrily at the young man and then he waited for the kid to complete his orders.

Seconds later the call was through and the angry Captain found himself speaking to a young Lieutenant stationed on the Roosevelt. He received the same information that the noncom just reported, but it was his duty to double check the orders. He was ordered to place his entire base on full alert, and informed by command his base was closed to all civilians again.

Campanelli knew he should name his base, so he told the Lieutenant to refer to his base as 'Easy Money' from this point forward. The Captain was further ordered to place his men in their military uniforms, so they could be detected by the aircraft, and separated from the civilians, if they were forced to come to the aide of the base, militarily. He informed the Lieutenant he was going to issue military uniforms to all personnel, even the civilians working on the construction of the dam for easier identification.

The Lieutenant wished the Captain luck because he knew how hard it was going to be, to get the civilians to do anything the government wanted, let alone getting them dressed in military uniforms. The Lieutenant informed Captain Campanelli to sit tight, because no military action had yet been taken or ordered by either side, except for the fighting going on in Chad. So far, it was classified as a civil war by all interested parties.

When the still excited Captain finished speaking with the Lieutenant stationed on the Carrier, he ordered a meeting of the lead civilian Dam workers, and the soldiers under his command. He informed them of the current events taking place around them, and when he ordered the civilians to dress in the military uniforms. The arguing began, and went on until he realized the complaining was going nowhere. So the upset Captain ordered his Sergeants to arrest anyone not in uniform on the base and put them in the brig. This order put a quick stop to the bickering.

Campanelli further ordered two soldiers to be with the civilians day and night. This brought more protests from the civilians who cried they would not be able to get much work done if they had to work around the soldiers just ordered to protect them from any attacks.

The Captain growled angrily that he did not care how hard it was going to be for the civilian workers to get their work done for the project. These were his orders, and his troops were to carry them out, period. If any civilian workers did not like the order, they was free to leave the base and start walking home.

It was hell to work on the Dam project for the next three days, and by the fifth day of the full base alert, all regulations slackened as some reports filtered on base that were less threatening to world peace. On the tenth day, some reports came in that of all nations, Egypt got both warring governments to talk instead of fight. Military Units were ordered to stand down. It took three days for Campanelli's base to get back to normal.

The civilians kind of grew accustomed to working in military uniforms and they continued to wear them to save their civilian clothes. It was no secret there were American military units working with the civilians. This pleased him to all ends because he was never able to tell his men from the local population as long as they refused to work in military uniforms. As he watched, the workers resumed work on the Dam. His attention was drawn out to the jungle as the returning Apache helicopters landed and then disappeared as they waited to be needed again, which the Captain hoped would never come. He hated to have a horde civilians hanging around his base during a fight, they had the tendency to get in the way more than help.

There was a full stand down order issued by the twentieth day of tensions, and the work progressed on the Dam at a rapid pace. The footings were set in place and dried, and the first pour of concrete for the walls of the Dam was prepared. The local population was hanging around the base again, or the working area trying to steal anything they could get their hands on, or to beg to become part of the workforce.

The noncom tethered to the computers was released, and he was able to walk freely around the base again. Campanelli gave both his intelligence men a field raise to the rate of Sergeants, which pleased them, because they would make more money and command more respect from the other soldiers on base. One of the new Sergeants was always stationed inside the Intel Center constantly monitoring the computers, and radio in case something went down.

The Captain suddenly noticed one of the new Sergeants running at him, and for a second he thought the hell of war started all over again. But this time the Sergeant informed him the CAG, (Commander of Air Group) who oversees the wing squadrons stationed on board the Carrier, wanted to speak to him.

Once inside the intelligence tent, the concerned Captain picked up the receiver and said into it. "This is Captain Edward Campanelli, the Commanding Officer of Base Tana Easy Money, sir. What can I do for you, sir? Over."

"Yeah Captain Campanelli Sir, this is CAG, Commander Owens' is in command of the CIC. I wanted to inform you that I'm calling in one of the AWACS aircraft. (Airborne warning and control planes) I have to send it out to Egypt sir. I'll keep the advance warning umbrella over your base at all times, sir. One of these aircraft is more than enough to accomplish this umbrella, sir. Between you and me sir, I want the other aircraft to keep a better eye on Libya, sir."

Captain Edward Campanelli did not even know the AWACS planes were in the air over his position as he replied to the CAG officer. "I guess you people know what the hell you're doing out there sir. I didn't even know we had the damn things up there in the first place sir."

"Stand by for a second Captain Campanelli Sir. Here's Commander Owens now sir."

"Captain Campanelli, Commander Owens here sir. Your damn Intel Officers didn't inform you of this shit beforehand, sir? You didn't know the damn AWAC planes were up and keeping an eye on your damn civilian pet project, what the hell are you running over there sir? You better get your act together mister, weren't out of the woods yet sir." The Commander growled.

"Commander Owens Sir, I have two Sergeants as my Intel Officers. This is because I just raised them up to the rank of Sergeants, sir. They're green, and I'm not coming down on them sir. They did the best they could with what they had to work with, Commander. What the hell difference does it make anyhow sir? I didn't know the damn AWACS were there that's all, sir. I knew everything I need to know, the Marines sent up their damn Apaches, sir."

"You're not in command of those damn Apache helicopters, Captain Campanelli Sir? What the hell is this crap, dammit?" The Commander raged on the connection.

"No sir, the Marines are a separate Unit from the troops I have under my command at the present moment, Commander Owens Sir. I guess it'll remain that way until the damn orders are changed by someone, sir." The Captain offered to the powerful Naval Officer.

"Dammit to hell and back again, shit! Now you listen to me, Captain Campanelli. You're in charge of all the fucking military units stationed on this Lake Tana project no matter which they are, sir. You get those damn Marines to man your Intelligence Post for you sir."

"Commander Owens Sir, I just got them from the damn Marines, and I think I'd like to keep the people I have as my Intel people, sir. I think they done an outstanding job throughout this whole stinking mess that just took place for me, Commander." Captain Campanelli offered back to his Commanding Officer this time.

"Very well then Captain Campanelli Sir, I'm afraid it's your fucking base to run any way you deem fit, Captain. But you'll give the two fucking soldiers a full field commission immediately sir. These soldiers have to be Lieutenants or better, to be allowed to operate any Intel Network, Captain. I'll contact the Marines and have them give you an Officer to assist these two damn soldiers out until they can handle the fucking job properly, sir."

"I already told you the Marines gave me these men in the first place, Commander Owens."

"You did say that didn't you Captain? You should have informed me that you didn't have an officer in command of your Intel network, Captain Campanelli Sir. I'll contact my Intel people, and have them ship you out an Officer to straighten out your two people, sir. He'll stay with them until your people know what the hell they're doing in the damn intelligence field. Captain Campanelli, this bullshit will be logged in my report to the Joints. Your ass will be put on the fucking carpet for it mister." With this the Commander broke off communications.

"Commander Owens Sir, we thought we did pretty good here sir. Sorry we got you in the soup Commander Sir." The Captain added to an empty mike this time.

The Captain turned and looked at the two young men and then remarked. "You two did real fine, don't worry about the damn Commander, he's my problem to deal with. I guess you men heard, you two are Lieutenants now. Congratulations, I'll have your orders cut by the end of the day, you can start wear your new stinking bars as of now though." He smiled as he saluted the two men who saluted him back with smiles.

He quickly left the intelligence tent, and no sooner did he walk twenty feet, than he looked towards the sky and he picked up an aircraft streaking for his base. It was the new F-18R Hornet. The aircraft landed moments after one circle of his ever expanding military base and construction site, an officer then climbed out of the Wizzo or rear seat of the plane, and a second later, the aircraft was taxiing to take off again.

The officer, a young Lieutenant dressed in a Navy uniform watched as the aircraft lifted off. When it was out of sight, he turned and he saw the army captain watching him. He walked over to the rather larger Captain, he then snapped to attention and saluted then offered him his hand.

"For Christ sake, don't ever fucking salute my damn ass out in the fucking field mister." Captain Campanelli growled at the new man harshly.

They looked at a jeep with a couple of Ethiopians staring at them as if they wanted to eat them. Then Campanelli said with a laugh. "Those damn buggers over there would just as soon kill us and cook us up for dinner if they had their fucking way about it, mister."

Both officers laughed over the comment. "Who the hell are you anyway soldier?" The surprised Captain growled as they turned from the jeep.

"Good day Captain, please allow me to introduce myself to you sir. My name's Lieutenant John Byner, sir. I'm your new Intel Officer for the time being. I was ordered by CAG to assume control of your intelligence network, and train the two new officers who don't know their ass from a hole in the ground about the intelligence game. I was told to stay with your people until I felt they could handle any event properly. Sir, do you mind showing me to the tent sir?"

The Captain did not like this skinny Second Louie from fleet right off the bat, he rubbed him the wrong way as soon as he opened his mouth. So he started to walk over to the Intel tent in silence. He noticed the Butter Bar was not following him, so he turned and saw the man standing where they shook hands.

"What the hell's wrong with you Lieutenant? Are you going to stand there all fucking day until your feet root to the stinking ground? Or are you going to follow me over to the damn OD tent, mister." The upset Captain hissed at the young Lieutenant.

"Well sir, I don't know your name, and I didn't know I was supposed to follow you, sir."

"Sorry sir, my mind was miles away on me son. My name's Captain Edward Campanelli, come on man and I'll take you over to the damn Intelligence Center myself." He waited for the Lieutenant to catch up with him. The two then walked side by side for the rest of the way in silence. The Lieutenant knew the Captain had a bug up his ass, and he hoped he was not the bug.

They entered the tent together, and Captain Campanelli immediately introduced the Lieutenant to his two new officers. The three of them then talked and laughed for a few seconds when the Captain took the older man aside and offered. "You're to keep me informed about this lousy new prick, mister. I don't trust him as far as I can throw him. I wonder if he wasn't sent out here to check on how I'm running the base. Keep a close eye on the bastard and let me know what's up. I want to know everything he says and does." With this, the Captain left the tent.

The young Fleet Lieutenant carefully started to explain the proper operations of the intelligence game to the two extremely eager to learn inexperienced younger men. He showed them how to correctly run the deciphering machine, and how to operate the specialized lock box system, while running the computers and also listening to all the reports as they came in over the radio at the same time. He also went over all the coded and un-coded channels through video, microwave, and satellite dish means for the two young trainees, so they better understood what they were supposed to do during any serious times facing them.

The two new Lieutenants were obviously overwhelmed by the new information the Fleet Lieutenant was showing and explaining to them. They quickly realized how untrained they really were on the intelligence operations, and they were pleased for all the information this Fleet

Officer was sharing with them. They studied everything he did with the machines.

The Captain went back to his tent, and sat down on the bunk in total exhaustion, in an attempt to catch his breath and relax a little. He was thoroughly worn out from the stress of thinking that a war was going to breakout in his area of responsibility. Moments later, Lieutenant Mendoza came in his tent and she said to him. "I saw the new arrival land, sir. What's the story with him and what's he doing on our base, Captain Campanelli Sir?"

"Arrr… he's a fucking snot nose fleet fag from the CIC center, sent out to us by Commander Owens to get our intelligence operations properly on line, Ma'am. The two kids I have running our damn Intel operations don't know their ass from a hole in the ground about what they're to do with the systems." He moaned as he rested his head heavily in his hands for a brief moment, and then let out his breath in an exhausted rush and disgusted sigh.

"I guess you're on the shit seat again my lover." Mendoza tried a smiled on the Captain.

"So what else is fucking new Mendoza. I'm getting kind of used to being in the hot seat lately young lady." He grunted as he shook his head, and tried to offer Mendoza a weak smile as he added. "He's teaching our guys the operation of the Intel system. I have a stinking feeling he's hawking my stinking butt, to see how I'm running the base, and to try and bury my ass as well."

"Come on Edward will you please, you know damn well there's no better person in the whole damn service to command a military base better than you are sir. So please stop feeling so sorry for yourself all the time sir. It don't suit you so well you know. You stay on top of everyone and thing that's going on this damn base at all times, Captain. Nothing gets by your ass no matter how small the problem might be. You notice it instantly and you take care of it before it gets out of hand on you sir." Lieutenant Renee Mendoza said as she slowly opened her blouse, and then she walked the few feet separating them and placed her hands on his head and pulled him to her. His head rested between her breasts, and she moved them slowly on his face as she offered to the concerned looking Commanding Officer.

"Come on and let me take all these nasty troubling worries out of your troubled mind for you, Edward. I can make all your troubles disappear for you in a blink of an eye. If you'll allow me to that is sir." She kissed him on the forehead as he grabbed for the offered breasts which made Mendoza giggle, and she responded to his sudden interest in her. He pulled her down to his bunk and they made love. He forgot about the young Lieutenant and all the trouble he might be in with command for the moment.

CHAPTER 10

Three units of Egyptian engineers and workers set out for the Sinai Desert from Egypt, each work crew had two water trucks with them, because the Egyptians could only hide three thousand fog mines in each truck. They figured it would take three days to plant this number of mines, so each empty truck was scheduled to be replaced on the third day. The workers were given a map of the proposed path that the Israeli army took when they first invaded the Sinai Desert, when Egypt and Israel were at war during the Suez war of 1973.

Each unit was ordered to mine certain different passes throughout the vast Sinai Desert. The Sudr Pass, Mitla Pass, Giddi Pass, and the Khatmia Pass, as well as the smaller roads leading to Katia, Bir Gifgafa, and the cross road from Bir Gifgafa to Katia, were to be mined. After the workers had accomplished this, they were to move their operation to the desert flats, and mine any areas which looked like it was packed hard enough to support tanks crossing it. The Egyptians were warned once the Israeli tankers realized the roads were mined, they would move their remaining tanks off the roads, and move them to the sand flats to get them up to support their ground troops. They were ordered not to leave an area without a ring of death near the roads. The object of the mines were to deal a fatal blow to the Israeli tanks.

Once the Israeli tanks were destroyed, and along with them most of the foot soldiers and other armored trucks supporting the tank columns. Israel would be totally defenseless, and easy picking for the commandos who would then move out and destroy the Israeli airfields, and the planes inside Israel on the Jews. The Egyptian workers were ordered to plant miles of detonation strips wherever they thought any enemy foot soldiers might deploy against them. Again, many locations were made known to the units from the actions taken by the Israeli soldiers during the past Suez Canal conflict of years ago.

The Egyptian engineers and workers were well aware where the Israeli soldiers had setup their past command posts and base camps, and from where they ran their attacks against the Egyptian Armies they so soundly destroyed. They were to mine and lay down the deadly detonation strips at the old garrison know as Gaby, near the road leading to Katia and Mandler, and the main garrison once stationed outside of Bir Gifgafa. The Egyptian units were further ordered to mined the Dan Garrison which used the Mitla Pass, and the old garrison positions near the Great Bitter Lake, as well as the old Jerusalem and Amnon sites, and the Sharon site just south of Tasa. The Bren Adan Garrison, ten miles north of Tasa was also to be mined by the workers.

The mining of these selected sites and others that the Egyptian workers thought the Israeli soldiers might make use of in their opening attack against Egypt, would eliminate any safe area for the Israeli soldiers to setup their command posts, and also any of their staging areas. In addition to mining these areas of the Sinai Desert, every Oasis throughout the vast desert was to be mined, and then prepared for sabotage if necessary.

This time, Egypt planned to leave nothing of use for the attacking Israeli soldiers. Not like the last time when the Jews setup their military staging areas near the few Oasis in the desert, and they enjoyed all the water they needed for drinking, and also feeding their deadly war machines. Where as the Egyptian soldiers were forced to carry their water needs on their backs with them. There were forty Oasis spread throughout in the vast desert. The Egyptian units were further required to make hidden caches of water and ammunition at designated areas, so their armies would never be cut off from military supplies and water.

The Egyptian workers were working on the third week without any interference from the Israeli soldiers or government.

On the start of the fourth week of work, the unit of Egyptian workers mining the Oasis at Bir al Hadiratt, was suddenly intercepted by an Israeli patrol. The Israeli soldiers felt the Egyptian workers were getting a little too close to the Israeli side of the border. The soldiers were thirsty and knew the water at this Oasis was there, and they were heading for water more than anything else, when they happened to come across the Egyptians working in the area of the Oasis.

The Israeli soldiers stormed into the Egyptian work camp with their weapons held at the ready, and they quickly ransacked the entire site on the scared Arab workers. Looking for any hidden weapons and maps, worried these men were making maps of their present installations, in preparation for a possible guerrilla attack on Israel later on if war broke out in the region. Two young Egyptian workers resisted the Israeli soldiers attack on them just long enough for the technicians to close up the secret compartments on the water tankers and secure them properly.

The Israeli soldiers quickly grew angry at the slight resistance being offered from the Egyptian workers and they shot a few of the Egyptian workers giving them trouble, and in the same instance a report immediately went out to Egypt, informing Ambassador Mohammed Kheir what just happened, and two Egyptian workers were shot with one dead and the second worker was severely wounded by a Jew patrol. Another report went out to the Israeli command, sent by their soldiers who checked the Egyptian worksite. Instantly, three UH 60A Blackhawk helicopters were dispatched from El Auja to the work site. One was a medic chopper, and the other two picked up the small Israeli patrol, and removed them from the area immediately to avoid any further trouble between the Israeli soldiers and the Egyptian workers.

One Egyptian worker was dead, and the second one was being treated at the scene of the attack and was expected to survive but he was in serious condition.

Again, Ambassador Haetzni placed a call to Mohammed, in which he instantly apologized for this most unfortunate incident. But this time Mohammed Kheir was not to be appeased so easily.

The Egyptian Ambassador was angered at the lose of life to one of his worker crews and the wounding of a second worker. He actually screamed at the Israeli politician that the Jewish soldiers killed an Egyptian civilian on Egyptian soil, and he demanded the Israeli patrol be brought up on charges and tried for murder. He warned Ambassador Haetzni in no uncertain terms that this was the only settlement Egypt would accept because of the unprovoked attack against their civilian workers operating in the desert, and he also told the Jew politician. He was going to arm the workers, and might even put Egyptian soldiers with the work units searching for water because of this attack against his civilian workers.

The concerned Israeli Delegate did his best in an attempt to try and calm down the extremely infuriated Egyptian politician, but Mohammed Kheir was not going to calm down that easily for the Israeli Ambassador this time around. He demanded to know how Israel would react, if an Egyptian were to kill an Israeli civilian on Israeli soil. Ambassador Haetzni had no other answer for him but to say that Israel would retaliate immediately, and attack Egypt for any unprovoked attack against their civilians anywhere in the world.

Mohammed thought fast on his feet, because he understood he had the Jew politician over a barrel and he was going to make the best of it. The still extremely angry Egyptian politician warned Ambassador Haetzni the Egyptian government would accept no further incidence's without reacting to, and then against them.

Ambassador Haetzni assured Mohammed there would be no further searches on any of his work units operating in the desert. He promised he would make his people give the units the widest berth possible. He also informed him that his soldiers would head the other way whenever they came across an Egyptian working unit.

Mohammed allowed himself to calm down just a little, because he got what he was aiming at.

The new Egyptian President Sadat, was all out pressuring him to send another five work units out, to get the job done much faster for them. Armed with this new promise from the Jew politician, Ambassador Mohammed Kheir felt he could get this accomplished a lot faster with the other work units working the area a little closer to the Canal opening.

The Israeli politician was not stupid either. When Ambassador Haetzni gave into the demands of Mohammed, he knew he just placed the safety of Israel at risk. When he finished speaking with Mohammed, Ambassador Haetzni placed a call to the intelligence network of the United States, and he spoke directly with an officer in the CIA. Israeli Ambassador Haetzni requested the officer reroute one of their spy satellites to fly directly over the Sinai Desert. Along with the surrounding areas of Egypt that bordered the Sinai Desert.

Ambassador Haetzni informed the Special American Agent he wanted to watch the Egyptian work units dispatched into the desert supposedly searching for water. He told the special agent even though he informed Ambassador Mohammed Kheir his government trusted the Egyptian government, though neither government really trusted the other. With the help of the United States satellite, it was the only way Israel could possibly keep a close eye on the Egyptian workers without having to search the units personally.

The Israeli politician also informed the agent what happened the last time an Israeli patrol searched an Egyptian work unit operating in the Sinai Desert. It resulted in the death of an Egyptian worker and the wounding of another, and the Israeli government apologizing to Egypt, and having to give up more concessions to try and keep the peace between the two countries. Ambassador Haetzni continued to explain the Israeli government had no other choice opened to them but to publicly apologize for the terrible mishap in the desert. Ambassador Haetzni stopped speaking and then listened for a response from the American agent.

For a few seconds there was dead silence. Finally, the agent offered the Israeli he would bring up this situation to the proper authorities, and assured Ambassador Haetzni something would be worked out one way or the other to assist their only true ally in this region of the world. The American Agent further informed Haetzni he would be back to him when he got an answer.

The Israeli Ambassador hung up with the agent and then he worked on drafting a public apology to Egypt. He worked on the report for three hours and as he added the finishing touches to it, his phone rang, almost scarring him out of his skin. He reached for the screaming phone and snapped into it. "Yes, this is Ambassador Haetzni, who is this please sir?"

"Yes Sir Ambassador Haetzin Sir, this is Agent Davidson of the CIA, sir. You just finished speaking with one of my Agents earlier today Ambassador Haetzhi Sir. Yeah, I was informed about your situation sir, and your requests for a number of flyovers by one of our birds in the area in question, Ambassador Haetzni Sir. After a discussion with my people, we have decided to offer the Israeli government one of our satellite observation platforms, the GR-113 bird for the duration of this present situation, sir." Agent Davidson did not inform the Israeli Delegate about the heated arguments that had taken place at the meeting, because of this most unusual request for Israel to have direct access to one of the United States latest spy satellites.

Agent Davidson also informed Ambassador Haetzni his government was sending to the Israeli's a special linkup computer, and told him he could talk directly to the Platform, a Keyhole satellite called NIGHTBIRD 7, a special Spy Satellite controlled by a secret base stationed in Maryland. "The bird will afford you perfect vision, and you'll be able to observe all the Egyptian workers in the desert, sir. The Nightbird is so powerful you can actually read the license plates of the work trucks if you wanted to, sir. The Nightbird will make six passes over your target area in the daylight, and six more passes at night. Our bird's fully equipped with infrared and night vision capabilities, sir. The Egyptian workers shouldn't be able to hide anything from you.

"Ambassador Haetzin Sir, I also wanted to inform you my government wants to allow your people to understand we're doing them a mighty large favor here sir. My government would like to share any intelligence you pick up with our bird with us, sir. We lose communication with our bird while you're speaking to her, sir. The computer we'll sent you gives you very limited access to the bird's intelligence. You'll be totally blacked out from any observations when the bird's out of range of this region and is over Russia, or any other countries, just as we're blocked off when the bird's over Egypt, and you're talking to her. We trust your government won't use this information to aid in any possible attack on Egypt or any of your neighbors, sir."

"Agent Davidson Sir, my government has no claims on any Egyptian land or nay intentions of going to war with that nation, or any other nation of the world for that matter. This operation is strictly to keep a closer eye on the Egyptian workers operating in the Sinai Desert sir, and to also make certain what they say they're doing in the desert is indeed, what they're doing, sir. We don't need any hidden surprises in case we have to attack them in the future, sir. This is the only reason why we need your satellite platform, sir. My government has instructed me to thank your government for her kind and much needed assistance in this present matter sir. When can I expect to receive this specialized computer of yours, sir?"

"Okay Ambassador Haetzni Sir." The special agent complained, but he said it the way a man says something when he's afraid to acknowledge that he may have been wrong. "Ambassador Haetzni Sir, this is what I have for you so far, sir. The special computer's on its way to you via diplomatic pouch as we speak sir, and it should be reaching you by no later than eight o'clock tonight sir. Please Ambassador Haetzni Sir, you must guard this computer with your very life at all time while it's in your possession, sir. The eye of this bird can be focused down to a ten foot field of vision, to an overall viewing area with a mile radius, with high resolution and clarity sir. Once again I must repeat this to you sir, you will keep us informed about what you're viewing when we're unable to make contact with our bird, sir?"

"Yes Agent Davidson, my government will keep you informed of our observations over Egypt."

"Yeah, Oh… one more thing before I let you go Ambassador Haetzni Sir. If anyone tries to fuck around with this computer in any way, shape or form, you know, to see how it works I mean. It'll self destruct and anything or one within a twelve foot radius of the computer will be dead or destroyed. We can't possibly have this computer fall into the wrong hands or be duplicated, sir. Thank you for your understanding of this situation, sir. Good luck Ambassador, I'll expect to hear from you once a day, every day with a full report of the day's flyover reports until you no longer need our bird, sir." With this Davidson broke off communications.

The Israeli was left holding a dead receiver in his hand. He cursed because of the situation he now found he was locked in. He was being forced to eat shit not only from the Egyptians, but now from the United States. He made a special note to himself to bring up a request at the next meeting of the Israeli Parliament, for more money to launch one of Israel's own recon satellite, so Israel did not have to beg any other country.

SECURITY COUNCIL, THE WHITE HOUSE.
WASHINGTON D.C.

In the United States, even before Israel was informed she would be given direct access to an American spy satellite, a special meeting took place, which happened whenever another country requested use of one of our spy satellites. CIA Agent Davidson fought tooth and nail against the Israeli government getting direct access to one of his special birds. He offered the Israelis would be privy to top secret and extremely sensitive information at the same time.

The debate went on for some time, until the President of the United States finally intervened and he just ordered Israel to have the requested access to their bird. He wanted to know if Israel knew something that the United States should known and it did not. So the President merely ordered two surveillance satellites to change course, and make a slow flyover of Egypt and the surrounding countries, especially Libya. Orders were cut, and the two spy birds altered their course in mid flight, and made their first pass over the contested area over Egypt, within an hour after the orders were passed, and directed at the satellites.

President Albert Cole warned his Intel people that he wanted to be the first one to know immediately if something was afoot with the Egyptians, or any other country in the region. The President being ex CIA Director himself, let his people know he did not trust the Egyptians any more than the Israeli's did. The American President was promised he would be kept well informed, when information became available deemed out of the ordinary to the region.

THE SINAI DESERT, EGYPT

The salting of the so called fog mines and detonation strips in the Sinai Desert by the Egyptian workers was progressing at a much better pace than Mohammed had ever thought possible. Five of the eleven original Israeli encampments from the old war were well mined, and any army taking these positions as their standoff positions, would immediately be annihilated if the fog mines were set off while this area was occupied by those troops. Just one, the old Sudr Pass was mined as ordered. Another Egyptian work unit was ordered to mine the road which led from the Negeu Desert, all the way to the town of Katia in the Sinai.

The mining of the desert was well ahead of schedule. A few Egyptian work units were busy placing anti personnel strips out, while other workers set up the MBR-3 off road anti tank mine triggered when a tank ran over a narrow glass tube placed across the road planted just under the surface of the sand. The weight of a tank would instantly crush the fragile tube, thus exploding a rocket buried just below the sand. This rocket could easily destroy any tank Israel has in her service. The way the mine and anti personnel weapons were placed in the sand, they would surely eliminate any safe haven for the Israeli Army to operate in the Sinai Desert.

For once, the Arabs set a trap which would destroy the Israeli Army. This, combined with the attacks from commandos inside Israel, would stop any reinforcements from getting to the trapped soldiers, and they would destroy what was left of the Israeli bases, from inside her own borders.

Egyptian Ambassador Mohammed Kheir read through the many reports coming in his office almost constantly now. He was extremely pleased by the progress his desert work units were making with their salting the desert sands with land mines and detonation strips. His trend of thought was suddenly interrupted by one of his female weapons JoAnne, who came strolling in his office as if she owns it. She was followed closely by the smug looking Ambassador Mohammed Ahmed Nimiri, the United Nation's Delegate from Iraq.

"Allah Akhbar Ambassador Mohammed Kheir Sir." Mohammed Nimiri offered his counterpart in a very pleasant manner.

"Allah Akhbar Nimiri." Mohammed replied as he offered him his hand and then asked him with caution in his voice. "What can I do for you sir?" Here was another Arab who he did not care much for, but he was more palatable than Kamal was to him.

"My dear friend Mohammed, I'm here to find out how far along your people are with the mining of the Sinai Desert, sir."

He stared at the Iraqi for a second, displaying his stunned feeling, and he remarked with a trace of anger in his voice. "Mohammed Nimiri Sir, I believe that you have me at a slight disadvantage here, sir. I have no idea what you're talking about, sir."

Ambassador Nimiri grunted as he smiled at the Egyptian and then added. "Oh please Mohammed, don't play me the fool. Did you not think my government would not be included in on an attack against the hated Jews, and the land of the great devil, the United States?"

He merely shrugged as he responded to the Iraqi Ambassador with a snap in his tone. "You seem to know what you're talking about, sir. Perhaps you would be so kind, you can let me know what is supposed to be going on in the desert, sir."

Ambassador Nimiri let a quick flash of anger cross his eyes now as he nearly snarled at the Egyptian. "Mohammed, I know damn well what Egypt is doing in the Sinai Desert, sir. Libya's Delegate, Ambassador Kamal has informed my government before he spoke to yours about the actions in the Sinai Desert. It's the fact that Ethiopia is putting the Dam on the river that any thoughts of allowing Egypt in on our planned attack on Israel, the Sudan and Chad were decided. Now Mohammed, perhaps you'd be so kind as to let me know how your work is progressing in the desert. Or would you like it better if I was to go to President Sadat, and speak to him directly sir? I'm quite certain sure he'd be most pleased to inform me of how it is going."

Mohammed Kheir had to draw in a huge gulp of air angrily, and then he exhaled it slowly before he began to explain to Ambassador Nimiri about how the operation in the desert was proceeding for his country.

After hearing about the operation in detail, Iraqi Ambassador Nimiri smiled broadly as he said to the Egyptian politician. "Good, I knew our brother Arabs the Egyptians, would be a great asset to our holy cause against all evil. You're doing fine work here, Mohammed Kheir."

The Egyptian looked at this arrogant Iraqi politician, and then he grumbled at him in a harsh tone of voice this time. "Ambassador Nimiri, since I have answered your questions to your complete satisfaction, sir. I was wondering if you be so kind as to answer a few of my questions, sir? First, you said your country and Libya has allowed Egypt in on your future plans of attacking Chad and Israel, sir. I was wondering if you care to elaborate a little on that statement, sir. I know most of the plan, so you can fill in any missing pieces for me, sir."

It was Ambassador Nimiri turn to smile as he replied to the staring Egyptian question of him. "Mohammed, I'd be most pleased to fill in any of the missing parts for you, sir. As you know, Libya had a good number of hated Russian defectors finding their way to Libya from the now non existent Soviet Union. Many of the worthless defectors are scientists, and they have brought much of their secret work with them to Libya. The Russian fools have developed a batch of new and extremely dangerous weapons, and some of them are of mass destruction, others, designed to destroy the soldiers and armor machines of their god cursed country.

"Both Libya and Iraq planned to attack Israel and Saudi Arabia, and your country for some time now. The attacks were for revenge on the attack against my country of Iraq. Needless to say sir, we planned to attack these god cursed countries this spring, using these new weapons we have at hand. But when Ethiopia started to cause problems and threatening Egypt's water supply, we decided to see what would develop with this new situation. When Egypt threatened to go to war with Ethiopia, we, myself and Ambassador Kamal that is, decided to allow your country to join forces with our two nations, sir. Mohammed Kheir, I'm most pleased for that decision sir."

He interrupted the Iraqi angrily as he grumbled at him. "Ambassador Nimiri, I know about this part of the operation from Ambassador Kamal. I was wondering if you can you tell me what your country is going to do when Israel is forced to attack Egypt. When we're moving out our tanks and armor into the Sinai Desert, and made a direct threat against Israel? When will we be able, with the help of Allah, to destroy the Israeli tanks and soldiers, sir." He growled with noted sarcasm that meant Ambassador Nimiri better get to the point more quickly for him.

"Yes Ambassador Mohammed Kheir Sir, I'll be most pleased to inform you of what my country will do against Israel, sir. My country is going to join in on the opening attack against Israel when war finally breaks out in this region. We're going to attack her defenses from the rear sir, while she is sending her foul troops and military equipment to support the Jewish state fighting against your country in the Sinai Desert, sir. First we shall destroy that miserable little country of traitors to the Muslim faith, Jordan. My government figures this task should take my soldiers a mere day to accomplish, sir. We'll attack Jordan with tanks and artillery.

"Once Jordan is gone from the face of the earth, we'll then turn our attention and attack Israel at will, and after we start our attack, Israel will be forced to divide what is left of her god cursed Armies. After Israel is destroyed, my soldiers will start their attack against Saudi Arabia, and that miserable little country of Kuwait, as well as send military aid to your country, and Libya, and to any other Arab countries that'll join forces with us in this future war.

"Mohammed, we'll be victorious on all points of this war, and then we'll stop all exports of oil to the United States and Japan, along with the smaller mongrel countries which make up the Baltic Alliance. Then, we'll start numerous terrorist attacks on the hated United States, England, Germany and France, sir. This action will serve to keep these god cursed countries off balance just long enough for both Libya and Egypt to take over the Sudan, Ethiopia, Chad, and any other country we may choose to destroy. In one great sweep of our United Armies, we'll eliminate the black race along with any other Arab country which allowed its blood to be tainted by mixing it with other races of the world, especially the blacks. Soon, the pure Arab race will be allowed to rule all conquered countries. Mohammed, once this is accomplish, we'll at long last be able to turn our full attention towards the once great United States, sir.

"We shall attack that lowly country of filthy jackals with countless waves of terrorist attacks, until her civilians feel there is no place safe for them to hide in the United States. We'll destroy the lowly devils economy, by making the civilians afraid to do anything in their foul country. Then we'll dry up her oil reserves, by attacking the oil wells throughout the country like we did in Kuwait. We'll bring this last great power down to her knees and then we, the Arab countries, will control the greatest power left on the face of the earth, the United States."

Mohammed Kheir was thunderstruck over what he was hearing as he stared dumbly at this madman sitting across from him, as he tried to reason with the man with such wild ideas and dreams of conquest. Shaking his head to clear the cobwebs, he remarked. "What if the United States decides to fight back with her nuclear weapons, sir? I feel the United States will always be a country that could easily defeat any nation she decided to go after, sir."

"Mohammed, you worry yourself over nothing I assure you. Even this nuclear weapons are no longer a threat we fear much from the hated United States. Because we now have the means to attack the very shores of the United States with our own nuclear weapons, delivered no less by Russian missiles smuggled out of the Soviet Union under the very noses of not only Russia, but of the entire world as well. So if the foolish United States threatens us with their worthless nuclear weapons, we'll threaten them right back with our own nuclear weapons. To hit America with a nuclear bomb will be more devastating to them than if they attacked us with five bombs. For one nuclear detonation in the United States, perhaps, say New York City, will kill more people than ten bombs in Iraq or Libya, or even Egypt for that matter. There are more people in concentrated areas in the United States than in the whole of any of our countries."

The Egyptian sat flabbergasted, he could not believe what this Iraqi madman sitting before him was talking about, without displaying the slightest bit of concern for what he and his nation might let loose on the rest of the world. They were thinking about destroying thousands of peoples, even Arabs throughout the world, and just as willing to allow his country be hit with nuclear weapons in return, to strike a minor blow against the United States of America. Once again, he wondered what type of people his country had aligned themselves with.

Ambassador Nimiri continued with his most chilling words of war. "Our intelligence people feel confident the United States will choose not to attack any of our countries with her nuclear weapons. Because if they did, it would surely start the end of the world. I'm quite certain the United States will walk away from this trouble spot, just as they had done in Viet Nam, once it got too hot for the fools to handle. Ambassador Mohammed Kheir, my reason for being at this meeting is to find out how far along your workers were with your operation in the desert, and when Libya is going to start her attack on that nation of mongrels Chad, sir?"

Mohammed sighed deeply and then said with a snap in his tone this time. "We have already made plans to begin our attack against the worthless nation of Chad on October 5th, the start of the Arab fasting days of Ramadhan, sir. This way the Jews will be caught completely off guard because of our fasting period, and they'd never believe we would ever attack on this day. My intelligence people figure it should take the Jews two to three days, before they could be ready to mount any sort of defense against our attack, and by then, we should have our forces in position in the Sinai, and we'll destroy their Armies and armament with the weapons we hid in the desert. This is the best we can possibly hope for, I wish my country would continue to try and find a more peaceful conclusion to their situation then by going to war with the hated Jews."

"A peaceful solution you offer to me? Come Mohammed." Iraqi Ambassador Nimiri shouted angrily as he glared terribly at Kheir. His suddenly loud outburst caused JoAnne to burst into his office from her outer office with her weapon held in hand.

Nimiri found himself looking down the bore of a Glock nine mm pistol, and he was staring into the lovely face of a young female whose eyes were ablaze with anger and hatred against him.

Mohammed jumped to his feet, his right arm extended in front of his chest, as he quickly moved between JoAnne and Nimiri, as he shouted at his female body guard. "No JoAnne don't shoot this foul man. I'm in no danger from him in this room. Ambassador Nimiri has foolishly lost his temper, but didn't lose his good sense. Lower your cursed weapon that is a direct order. Did you not here me woman? I said lower that foul thing now!"

She hesitated for a moment, she took her eyes off Ambassador Nimiri for a brief second, and then looked at Mohammed who was glaring so angrily at her. She took in a quick breath to try and help control her breathing, and then she cautiously lowered her weapon slowly. But all the while, she never once took her eyes off Ambassador Nimiri again. She stood with her arms held down at her sides, but the weapon was still in the open locked in her right hand, and she was ready to spring back into action at a moment's notice. The weapon's hammer was also cocked while she held Ambassador Nimiri in her most threatening stare.

Mohammed Kheir stood between them as he told JoAnne to leave his office immediately.

She did not move right away, she just kept staring threateningly at Ambassador Nimiri.

"Now!" Mohammed yelled, spittle landed on her face because he was so close to her body.

She looked at Mohammed again as she allowed her shoulders to release their tension.

"Now. Please JoAnne." He repeated, this time in a much calmer tone.

JoAnne cautiously backed out of the office, and when the door closed, Ambassador Nimiri found his voice, shaky as it was as he moaned. "How dare you have one of your paid killers aim a god cursed weapon at me, like I was some kind of common criminal Mohammed!"

"She thought you were threatening me, so naturally she felt she was simply doing her job of protecting my life, sir. You're the one who acted uncivilized in my office, sir. Now if you don't mind, I'm a rather busy man, and if you have nothing but complaints to lodge against me. I suggest you take them up with President Sadat, because he is the man who gave me this power, and he's the only person on the face of the earth who can possibly remove this power from me, Ambassador." He stared back at Ambassador Nimiri.

The Iraqi Ambassador bowed politely as he replied. "I guess we're finished speaking at that Mohammed. I'd like to meet with you again, hum, let's say some time in early March. You set the day and notify my office, this meeting will be again to check on the progress of the work being carried out in the desert, and to inform you of our plans and any possible changes in them."

"Very good then Ambassador Nimiri, but you can make the appointment with my private secretary who is in the outer office if you don't mind, sir. Her name is JoAnne, Ambassador. You know, she's the one with the weapon that was just aimed at your person, sir." Ambassador Mohammed Kheir actually laughed and never again looked at Ambassador Nimiri or offered him his hand as he was leaving his office, or the usually friendly Arab greeting as he left his office.

Ambassador Nimiri laughed also as he replied. "It's the first time in my life I was ever threatened by such a good looking assassin, Mohammed. You have a novel idea here, to have such beautiful murderers at your command, sir. It makes dying a pleasure, if you have to die that is sir. Allah Akhbar Mohammed."

"Allah Akhbar Mohammed Nimiri." Mohammed Kheir said without looking up from the paper. He completely ignored most of the words from the Iraqi politician as he left his office.

Ambassador Nimiri bowed again to the non looking Kheir, and then left quietly.

Once the Iraqi politician was out of his office, he placed a call to President Sadat before Ambassador Nimiri could lodged a complaint about how he was treated in his office. After he explained all that had just transpired, Sadat said. "Mohammed, I fear we have aligned ourselves with babies. Because now we have to put up with these inconveniences until we can have a parting of the ways, and stand alone among the great Arab nations, like we once did in the past in the times of the great Pharaohs, when Egypt was all powerful and feared by all."

Before they finished their talk, President Sadat informed Ambassador Kheir to go over to the intelligence command post they had setup. He ordered him to the four separate sites supposed to be nearly completed with the mining operation, and the video hookups needed for the success of the operation. President Sadat wanted him to see for himself what his technicians would see from the fiber optic camera hookups mixed in with the mine fields.

He left his office relieved, and he was followed closely by JoAnne. It took them over an hour and a half to follow President Sadat's instructions, on how to locate the intelligence center.

The Egyptian Ambassador and JoAnne entered the great Mosque housing the intelligence center to their plans, and to also control the Egyptian desert workers. Once inside, their identification papers were checked carefully, and then they were led down a hallway to a room covered from floor to ceiling with computers, video screens and other machinery.

He informed the young technician what he was there to check on, and he was immediately led over to a set of small video screens and computers. He watched as the technician's fingers quickly danced across the keyboard with lightning speed. One screen suddenly came to life. At first, the only thing he saw was a sea of sand on the small screen.

The technician punched a series of more keys and the camera moved slightly, and the road to Katia came clearly in view. On the road, Mohammed noticed two civilian cars speed by the lens, the technician informed him the road was fifty feet away from the camera. Ambassador Kheir made out the year and model of one of the cars and was impressed.

Another camera was cued in operation and it gave a clear view of the same area once the old Israeli Encampment of Gaby. Ambassador Kheir could easily see far off in the vast desert. He was amazed at how clear he could see the entire area he was looking at, and the work going on by the Egyptian workers from the hidden cameras. He watched as this camera quickly scanned the desert until it settled in on a few of the Egyptians working in the sands. He could not tell what they were doing, but he could easily tell the two men both had beards.

The technician pointed to the small screen, instantly drawing Mohammed's attention over to another screen. There he could see a long caravan of camels slowly pass by his view. He watched as a sun burned Nomad, along with his ancient Kashmire rifle looped over his arm, relieved himself in clear view of the lens, and then he went back to his camel. Mohammed saw the camel toss his head back and move its mouth, and he knew it was braying in anger as the Nomad swung the heavy burden on its back. He smiled as the angry camel reached back and tried to nip the Arab on his arm, failing this, the angry beast then sent a long stream of spit right at him, hitting him square in the chest and soaking him with the spittle.

The extremely angry Arab smashed the camel on the side of the neck with a closed fist. A second Nomad came over to the one who just pissed, and more out of habit than respect, the first Arab removed his weapon from his back, and saluted the newcomer by holding his rifle by the barrel to show it was safe to approach him. He laughed aloud this time as he watched this drama unfold, and then he turned to JoAnne who watched the man piss and she laughed. Other Nomads quickly gathered and shared the bitter tea of their great ancestors.

The technician allowed Mohammed to know he could receive pictures from the Khatmia Pass section of the desert as well. This was the most important area to have the cameras observing, because this was where the Jews had setup their major command centers during the Suez

Canal war. The young Egyptian technician made these cameras come to life without being ordered.

Mohammed could plainly see the Khatmia Pass from one angle of the camera, and then as the camera moved again, he immediately recognized Bir Gifgafa. Again, he was amazed at how clear he could see the surrounding areas from over sixty miles away. He through if the Jews were foolish enough to move into their old encampments which they employed during the old Suez Canal conflict. They were in for a great surprise when the enemy soldiers arrived there. Their old encampment and staging areas was going to suddenly become their tombs.

The cautious technician quickly explained to the Ambassador what the Egyptian workers were doing, and how this next trap they were preparing was to be sprung, if the foolish Jew soldiers dared to enter the desert. The Egyptian technician picked up a piece of the detonation strip about a foot long, which he showed to Ambassador Mohammed.

He carefully examined the extremely threatening strip of death. On this small piece, he counted over a hundred of the deadly sharp needles nearly three inches in length, and an eighth of an inch thick. He lightly touched the very tip of one of the super sharp needles.

The technician warned him he better handle the strip with care because the needles were extremely sharp, and coated with a thin layer of porcelain. This enabled them to penetrate steel 3/16th of an inch thick, making many armored vehicles most vulnerable to the pins.

Ambassador Kheir looked at the end of his finger, and noticed a fresh drop of blood on it and he mumbled. "Huh, I see what you mean fool. They are sharp as the devil, are they not?"

The technician saw the slight trace of blood and called out for someone to bring a bandage.

He refused the protective covering, the small prick had already stopped bleeding.

The young technician bragged the Jews would not be able to do anything in the entire desert. Without them knowing what they were up to, and where they were at all times.

"I know more about this god cursed operation than you might believe I do, you desert fool you. So please, answer the god cursed questions I ask of you, and add nothing more to your answer but the absolute truth." He replied as he looked at the bragging man.

The young Egyptian technician put a rather hard expression on his face, and then he replied to the powerful Egyptian politician. "As you wish from me Ambassador Kheir Sir."

"At one of our meetings, there was some talk about some kind of a special hovering weapon, a bomb I believe it was referred to at that time of the conversation, sir. Do you happen to know anything about this new weapon I speak of? How this weapon would be deployed without detection by any enemy planes?" He asked the young technician this time.

The technician instantly puffed up his chest and then he announced proudly to the politician. "Yes Ambassador Kheir Sir, I know of this weapon, and from what I know of it. It's not going to be deployed until the very last days, just before our attack begins, sir. This weapon doesn't need a platform in which to be launch from sir, they're simply fired off from a maneuverable launcher system the size of a jeep, sir. The bombs are launched with the help from a rocket assisted booster mounted on the sides of each weapon. To get the bomb two thousand feet in the air, before the booster is burned out, and then released from the weapon. Then, by using the magnetic and reverse magnetic fields of the earth itself, the bomb can go from two thousand feet, to more than twenty thousand feet, or even higher if necessary. By using the aforesaid methods of propulsion and hovering abilities, Ambassador Kheir Sir.

"Once the weapon reaches the same height as the aircraft are using, it goes into a hover mode for up to an hour before losing some of its altitude. The weapon will hover until the enemy planes enter this area where the hoverers are stationed. We'll wait until the maximum of enemy aircraft are within the range of the weapon. Then we'll electronically explode the bombs with these switches, thus knocking out as many as up to twenty enemy aircraft with one bomb blast. This will enable us to take away the air superiority enjoyed by both the god cursed Jewish state, and also the United States, or any other country which decides to attack us in a retaliation bid, sir. We now fear no nation, sir." The technician smiled at Ambassador Mohammed Kheir.

"Why in the devil would any of the enemy aircraft fly directly towards these hovering bombs and their certain deaths, you fool? I think the pilots would break off the formation and fly in different directions once the flight of bombs showed up on their radar systems, so they can simply avoid the weapons." He asked the concerned looking technician.

"Ambassador Mohammed Kheir Sir, the casing of the bomb doesn't have to penetrate a concrete shelter, or impact on the sand, so it doesn't have to be made out of the usual one inch thick iron casing like all common bombs are constructed of. Much like the two thousand pound bombs the American bombs are made of, sir. Our hovering bombs explode in the air, and this makes it possible for us to use a number of certain types of plastics for the casing of the weapon, Ambassador. The plastic casing takes away some of its power of the blast from the weapon true, but the weapon does fine for our purposes here sir."

"That is fine, but still, if I were a pilot when I saw one of these weapons showing up on my radar, I'd give them a wide berth, and get out of harm's way with my aircraft, you fool you."

"Ambassador Kheir Sir, you didn't give me the time needed for me to finish explaining the operation of this weapon, sir. This plastic shell is mixed with a certain type of rubber, and the curved fiberglass shape that makes the weapon almost impos¬sible to be detected by most modern day radar employed by our enemy warplanes. Combined this with the sharp curved fiberglass shape, and it'll send a distorted image to the enemy's radar systems, sir. Even if our foolish enemy is successful, and they happen to be lucky enough to find a radar that'll clearly detect these weapons. The confused pilot would merely interpret the impulses as false images due to their aircraft flying over the desert, and the rising heat from the sand was creating these illusions they're detecting, or they can also believe sun spots are causing them this problem, sir.

"The aircraft radar will never be able to identify these hovering weapons as a possible threat against them, Ambassador. It does really not matter, either way, the enemy pilot would have no other choice but to completely ignore these believed to be false images until it was too late, and their aircraft will be blown out of the sky, sir. From what I was lead to believe, we could launch a thousand of these floating weapons in less than half an hour. Making it totally impossible for our enemies to get any needed air support, before we can destroy all their Armies in the desert while employing our aircraft and armor to attack their ground forces." The technician stopped speaking, and then looked at Mohammed as if waiting for another question from him.

"How many of these cursed weapons do you have at our disposal in our arsenal as of this time?" JoAnne asked the young man.

Anger instantly crossed the technician's young face. He was a firm believer of customs, and he was stretching it some speaking to this woman with so much of her flesh exposed on her body. But the technician feared the known wrath of Mohammed Kheir more than he feared the ire of the Muslims as he offered. "Enough to do the job for us thank you very much."

The Egyptian politician said nothing over the tone of the man's voice, he merely turned to one of the screens in the room. The others showed some other Egyptian workers from one of the units setting the fuel mines in the soft sand.

A different technician interrupted the first one, and he then whispered something to him which Mohammed did not hear clearly. The technician giving him and JoAnne an explanation went over to a radio, and he contacted a unit working in the desert. The technician pointed to the screen Mohammed watched. After a few words, all work stopped on setting the mines, and the workers made like they were truly searching the area for water. They went so far as to set off a number of small seismic charges on the surface of the sand for show.

He looked at the technician with questioning eyes and a harsh stare.

The technician explained further. "Ambassador Kheir Sir, we were informed the United States has given Israel direct access to one of their spy satellites, so the hated Jews could keep a closer eye on our operation out in the desert from their foul country, sir. The Americans have also sent two other of their spy satellites over us. I guess we're starting to scare the American fools of some concern as well as for the Jews, sir. Well, anytime one of their god cursed satellites makes a pass directly over our workers in the field, we stop them from setting the land mines, and make them look like they're truly looking for water, as you can plainly see them doing now sir.

"The Jew satel¬lite will be overhead this position within ten minutes, and we have to stop the workers for fifty five minutes of work, until the satellite is gone from their position, sir. We have word from Libya about the satellites and their flight path. They received the information from a spy, and the Russians defectors who can detect the satellites while in flight, sir. We don't know how as yet, but when they warn us, we merely put on this show for the worthless fools. We're always well prepared for any emergency, Ambassador Mohammed Kheir Sir."

"I see what you're saying, sir." Ambassador Kheir replied with a slight smile on his lips as he took JoAnne by the shoulder, and picked up a loose pin from the strip and placed it in his pocket. Then he slowly led her towards the door as he offered to the young technician as if it was an afterthought. "I believe we took up enough of your valuable time today. We shall leave you to attend to your work, sir." He turned away, signaling the end to their conversation. His voice taking on the tone that won him enemies whenever he was making a point.

He quickly left the building with JoAnne in tow, and they both got in their car and started off for his private office, so he could make a detailed report of what he had just witnessed to President Sadat. He hated talking to the Egyptian President because he always had that scrambler machine working, and the sound it emitted always made his skin crawl.

CHAPTER 11 – BASE EASY MONEY, ETHIOPIA

Captain Edward Campanelli decided to check on his intelligence people, and see how their instructor from fleet was coming along with their specialized training. Upon his entering the stuffy tent he heard the noise from the computers, the men branded this unit as the Mash Potato Unit. All three officers immediately jumped to their feet and saluted the Captain as he entered the hut. He halfheartedly returned their salute with a frown, he did not mind the salute inside the building, and told the men to carry on with what they were doing before he entered. The officer from fleet informed the Captain his men were doing good, and they were picking up the necessities quickly. He informed the Captain if trouble happen, his men would be ready.

Captain Campanelli stifled the urge to pace around the hut, he really hated having this fleet fag hanging around his base like he was doing. He felt the need to work off some energy building inside him, but there was not any room to pace so he left the tent. He called one of his men outside the structure, his elected spy so to say, and asked him what the young Lieutenant from the Carrier was like, and what he wanted to know about his operation.

The officer quickly assured the concerned looking Captain the Fleet Lieutenant was only interested in teaching them the correct operation of an Intel Command Post, and the Fleet Lieutenant said. "The Captain setup a pretty good network here sir, and it was the lack in his men's training that caused them their short comings. I promise to correct this for you sir."

The Captain allowed the soldier to get back to his work, and then he cursed over what happened to the Marine Corps. Many forced cutbacks were actually forced on the military, and so many great officers were lost due to their forced retirement, or closing of their military bases. Congress was not worried enough about the security of the United States shores, because of the demise of the Communist nations of Russia and Cuba, and the sudden coming around of China to a more peaceful and agreeable nation. There was no powerful threat left intact strong enough to worry the United States any longer at this present time. With all the fighting and small wars still racking the Arab countries of the Middle East. The world did not see much in the way of a real threat to world peace coming from this part of the world as yet.

He was still angry as hell because he felt if enough of the Arab countries ever banded together, they could do quite a bit of damage to the peace of the region, before they were finally brought back under control. Try as he might, he never could understand the Arab world in his mind. Here were for the most part, a beautiful and caring lot of people who believed so strongly in their great religion, and their fellow man's welfare at the same time.

The concerned Captain never saw an Arab walk passed a downed man, be him Arab or not and not offer him some kind of help. He also saw so in the past how Arabs always pitched in and helped other Arabs in need no matter what that need was. How they would do anything for their neighbor's good and welfare. Yet these same caring and loving people, would think nothing about setting off a car bomb, and killing everyone in their path be it man, woman or even child.

Arabs, who always placed their child's welfare before their own life, would kill other Arab children without any thought or consideration. One scene which will forever haunt his mind, was when he saw the Arabs of Lebanon digging through the rubble of a building that was car bombed by other Arabs, and one Arab held the lifeless body of a baby girl by the arm, and he then passed the child down to another Arab man who was crying for the loss of the child's life.

The Captain knew deep in his heart it was only a matter of time before all Arabs finally came around, and they treated life as sacred as the Holy Qu'ran preached them to revere all life. He looked at a young Arab woman as she passed so near him, and found himself thinking how truly beautiful she was, and how smoothly and proudly she walked, even though he could only see her large black eyes through the veil she was wearing, and he mumbled. "Yes, it's only a matter of time before all Arabs live in peace with one another."

Captain Edward Campanelli really hoped Lieutenant Renee Mendoza would be waiting for him when he returned to his tent. He had no worry about the base supplies, because everyday two to three huge transport aircraft landed, and more supplies were stacked up to the rafters in three of the huge metal butler buildings the Seabees had erected for his base stores. He did not like the amount of military hardware, weapons and supplies constantly showing up on his base now though. One of three butler buildings was actually filled to the roof with a horde of military equipment and his building supplies sat left out in the open. He looked to the Dam that was progressing well ahead of schedule, and he breathed a great sigh of relief. He was pleased the civilian workers were doing so well with their construction of the Dam.

The government of Ethiopia wanted the Dam finished in one and a half years from the start of construction, and he felt the Dam should be finished in just over a year's time, if everything continued to go as it was going on at this present time. The portable batching plant the Seabees brought with them was producing concrete at a good rate, as well as the three larger batching plants of Ethiopia. The Captain really liked what he saw so far, here he was in charge of a civilian project, and protecting the civilians with military men and women, and everyone was getting along just fine for the time being. Now, if he could only get rid of this damn fleet fag, he would be set for the entire project. He stopped walking in front of his tent, and took a quick look around and then he disappeared inside.

Mendoza saw him coming and she was ready for him when he reached the tent. She closed the flap of the tent and was laying on his rack naked and oil over her entire body. She looked great in the dull light of the tent. What light there was, reflected off her oiled body, making her skin look like it was covered by a fine layer of small flames. They made love.

Days, then weeks went by. It seemed the peace that Egypt brought about between Libya and Chad was working for now. There had been no trouble for a month, and there was no sign of any trouble in the near future cropping up. Two Aircraft Carrier Strike Forces were pulled off station and they resumed their normal patrols in the oceans. The Carrier Roosevelt was set in place, and would remain there until the Dam was completed and the civilian and military base was close and all personnel were moved from the base. It was Tana Base only air cover. The Marines stationed in the jungle were reinforced twice, bringing their numbers up to just over three thousand highly trained soldiers, with ten added Apache fast attack helicopters and more tanks.

As he peacefully laid on his bunk, he could not help but wonder what the future had in store for this region of the troubled world. Did Washington know something it was not sharing with him? Why were the Marines being reinforced so heavily, and why was his base being subject to numerous flyovers by the heavily armed warplanes coming from the Carrier Roosevelt? He thought how happy he would be when the Dam assignment was over. He knew he was going to have many questions that needed answering. The main one that needed untangling his mind was what he was going to do about his marriage. He lightly stroked her back with his fingertips and understood what his future would hold for him with the beautiful female Lieutenant.

He wondered how his kid would take him leaving his mother and living with another woman. He did not think this was going to be much of a change in his young child's life. In the past three years, he was with his son for a total of just seventy two days. He wondered if his son even remembered what his father looked like any longer, or if he even really cared any longer. The worried Captain laid his head on the pillow and allowed Mendoza give him pleasure. He watched as her head bobbing up and down on him.

The next two days were pretty much uneventful, and he grew extremely bored with his pet project, and he watched the workers toiling on the Dam more and more. It was the only source of any type of action happening on the entire base.

THE PRESIDENTIAL PALACE, CAIRO
MARCH 24th, 1996, 9:35 A.M.

At a special meeting being held between the new Egyptian President Sadat and the Libyan Ambassador Kamal, it was decided they were far enough along with the planting of the land mines and detonation strips in the desert, along with the building of heavy shore defenses were put in place and readied for future action. It would now take Egypt less than a week's time to install the rest of the shore batteries. The time was just right for the first incident to finally take place to set the wheels in motion for the Arab nations.

The Libya government wanted the first incident to start their war, to take place in Chad. Ambassador Kamal wanted to make it look like a patrol from Chad attacked a small village on the Libyan side of the border, and the attackers stole food and assaulted a number of the village women. The Libyan Ambassador promised President Sadat if the attack took place in the borders of Libya, his people would not use the incident to attack Chad right off.

Egyptian President Sadat did not trust Ambassador Kamal, or the Libyan government for that matter. He wanted the incident to take place far away from Chad, Libya and Egypt. He understood it was time for something to take place, if they wanted to convince the world other countries were trying to disrupt the peace of the region.

President Sadat stared coldly at Ambassador Kamal who was showing his obvious displeasure in having to wait for the Egyptian President to give out with his ideas. The Egyptian Leader finally replied in a commanding tone of voice. "I was thinking Ambassador Kamal, if we made the opening incident happen in the nation of Sudan. It'd still be too close to your country, for your nation not to react against it in the same fashion. But don't forget for a moment, your country's first reaction in the past has always been to get even with anyone who threatened your country's sovereignty, sir. If you didn't react in the same manner, the world would think this response quite strange, and they'd come to the most likely conclusion.

"The same one I'd also come up with if I had to think of one. That your country was some how behind this incident, and it'd defeat our purpose. So I think we better come up with a much better incident, yet have it happen far enough away from your country, and mine. So the rest of the world couldn't possibly link us together with the action that happened, sir."

"President Sadat, I think you worry much to much about absolutely nothing, sir. We could make it look like Chad attacked Libya in order to create an incident, and get away with it at the same time." Libyan Ambassador Kamal showed his growing impatience to him.

The Egyptian Leader let this little bit of sarcasm to sail right over his head, for the sake of keeping peace between the two men for the time being as he offered. "Ambassador Kamal, how do you think you can make the world believe the tiny and nation of helpless Chad, who has little resembling any form of an organized Army, would ever attack the much more powerful nation of Libya. Who in her own right is about a super power in military hardware. Think about the arms and soldiers, as well as the airforce that your country has at its command.

"I believe the United States would be forced to think twice before she'd dare attack the military might of your country, sir. So I'd find it awful hard to believe Chad would ever think of attacking your people, Ambassador. Besides, was it not the fact Chad didn't want to fight your country in 1987 that enabled your country to overthrow their government in the first place, and install the government that was ran by President Dedy. Until the overthrown President Habre mustered his forces together to overthrow the government, and get back in power? So you can see why I don't want the incident to happen between your country, and the nation of Chad, sir. I'd be extremely worried about things getting out of hand on us sir."

"In your great wisdom President Sadat, perhaps, you can tell me where it'd be safe for us to create this incident." Ambassador Kamal hissed unenthusiastically and he glared at the Egyptian President. He enunciated his words carefully, respectfully, but not apologetically.

This time President Sadat did not allow the sarcasm to pass without a reply against his stinging tone of voice. "Now you listen here Ambassador Kamal, you're not speaking with Ambassador Muhammad Kheir this time, you're speaking to the President of Egypt, so I suggest you watch your step when speaking to me, or you could find yourself stuck in a compromising situation with your government, sir. Because if you don't treat me with the respect due me, I'll register a complaint with your leader, and he's have your head on a stick without the slightest hesitation, sir. Now, I believe it's self defeating for us to be at odds with each other at this time, sir.

"Both our countries will need each others help in the upcoming future. I think you should keep an open mind in our conversation, and a civil tongue in your foul mouth at the same time, Ambassador. Or I'll have it ripped from your foul body, and then fed to my dogs. You'll keep civil with me until we can agree where this incident will take place, sir. I don't need any further camel shit coming from your evil mouth, or your country for that matter." President Sadat growled as he sat back and glared at Ambassador Kamal as if to emphasize his warning to him.

Ambassador Kamal glared harshly back at the Egyptian Leader and did not break eye contact. Then, a smile slowly spread across his lips as he bowed slightly and then swing his arm down and outward to Sadat as he offered the Egyptian President. "Perhaps you're correct after all, President Sadat. We can ill afford any friction growing between our two countries, sir. Now I see where Mohammed gets his impertinence from. President Sadat, you can trust me sir."

The last remark made him Sadat laugh as he replied with a smirk on his lips. "I'm afraid not Ambassador Kamal. Mohammed is just as impertinence to me as he is with you, sir. As far as my trusting you Ambassador Kamal, that is also another laughing matter. Ambassador Kamal, you're the type of person who'd steal the smell from a goat, if you could get away with it sir."

Both men laughed at the Egyptian President's last remark to Ambassador Kamal as he replied. "I see how well you understand me, President Sadat."

President Sadat suddenly turned serious and then offered with some concern lacing his voice. "I think this opening incident should take place somewhere inside the nation of Ethiopia if I had my way about it, Ambassador Kamal. Maybe even at the Dam being constructed in Ethiopia, say between the Americans and a rebel unit somehow backed by the foolish Chad government."

"Do you not think the finger of blame might be pointed directly at your country, if this attack was to take place where you suggested, sir? Your country has the most to lose if the Dam project gets completed sir." The Libyan Ambassador offered to the Egyptian President.

The Egyptian President replied in a flat tone this time as he was growing rather bored with this never ending conversation. "I know this might be the case Ambassador, but I feel strongly the incident would be far enough away from either of our two countries, to make the world think that we had anything to do with this situation, sir. Besides Ambassador Kamal, as I said before, we'll dress the foul rebels we'll employ in this opening incident in Chad military uniforms, and equip the foul fools only with weapons from Chad. This should keep the cynics off our countries long enough for another incident to take place, which would force the finger of blame to be pointed right at the only country it could possibly be aimed at. Chad."

"Hmmm... I think I can go along with this plan after all President Sadat. When do you think this action should occur?" He replied as he rubbed his chin and broke into his famous sneer.

"I think it should take place say within the next few days or so. Let me see, today is March 24th. It should come to pass a week from today, on March 31st, an early morning attack will do. I think we should also call for more peace talk between Egypt, Libya and Chad after the attack, to show the world we want peace. And only the rebel country of Chad is the true troublemaker in this region. Kamal, do you have the attack force we need to use against the American dogs?"

"I think your call for more foolish peace talks between our countries and Chad is a great idea, especially because I know the cursed President Habre will be in the United States this week, begging for American money. This attack will work out perfectly for our purposes, yes President Sadat, I have a unit of Muslims I can use for this opening attack we speak of. It's a unit of Arabs who were against the Americans and their Allies attacking Iraq. The Brotherhood of Ali. They'd be more than pleased for the chance to attack Americans anywhere in the world. I'll have Chad uniforms made accessible to the foul fools as well as weapons and transportation of the Chad government. I know none of these Arab fighters will allow themselves to be captured alive, and if they are, they'll never talk, even if it meant their worthless lives."

President Sadat rubbed his cheek absentmindedly for a moment as he went into thought and then he replied. "This is very good to hear Ambassador Kamal, since you brought this matter up to my attention, sir. Mohammed informed me he was recently paid an unexpected visit from the Iraqi Ambassador, Nimiri. Where does Iraq fit in this operation sir?"

"Iraq will fit in just fine for our needs during this operation, President Sadat. I shall use Iraq to attack Israel from behind, sir. This action will help destroy the Israeli forces in their own country before they can possibly reinforced the Israeli soldiers we'll be slaughtering in the Sinai Desert. Then I'll sic Iraq on Saudi Arabia once they have destroyed the Jew state, and then Turkey and Iran will also suffer the same foul fate at the same time, sir. This action will split any possible reinforcements sent out to help the Sudan and Chad from any of their worthless Allies."

"Surely, you don't believe for a moment this broken and all but destroyed foul country of Iraq, might be able to beat any of these other foul countries you speak of without our help, do you Ambassador Kamal?" President Sadat asked with much concern lacing in his tone this time as he stared at the Libyan politician for a moment before adding. "Look at what happened to that worthless country when the United States released their military might against the foul fools. Iraq was unable to fight and their worthless soldiers were so scared that the fools surrendered to a helicopter of unarmed news reporters filming them hiding in the sand like flees."

"I don't fool myself for one moment with any such foolish thoughts, President Sadat. I know the Iraqi soldiers will never be able to defeat either of these nations, and I have no intention of helping Iraq when they do attack these nations either, sir. What better way for us to rid ourselves of a most troublemaking country, than by allowing her attack the countries that'll surely band together, and then easily wipe Iraq off the face of the earth for us, sir. Just like the United States should've done during their Desert Storm War with that god cursed nation of Iraq.

"That would have save us the trouble of having to attack Iraq ourselves. President Sadat Sir, you know very well if we help Iraq survive, sooner or later we'd be forced to attack that nation ourselves, and destroy the miserable country once and for all. They're so troublesome a lot of people, President Sadat. So why not allow our lowly enemies to do the job for us, as well as allowing Iraq to keep help from reaching our foes during this upcoming war? This is why I'm more than willing to throw her to the jaws of the hated jackals."

"Once Iraq realizes she's mired in a no win situation, do you not think the Iraqi government and the madman running that foul nation will immediately resort to using their own cursed nuclear or chemical or biological weapons to finish off Israel?" President Sadat questioned him.

"What possible difference would it make to us if Iraq employs nuclear weapons against any of these other nations we want eliminated for our purposes, sir? Once the world sees nuclear weapons being used against these other countries, and they witness the terrible devastation they have unleashed upon certain sections of the world. Do you not think for one moment the great fools will do everything in their foul power in order to try and keep us from using the same devastating weapons against them? I feel if Iraq employs them, the world will do anything, to put a quick end to our conflict with the lesser Arab countries we'll be engaged against, sir." Ambassador Kamal offered to the Egyptian Leader with an ugly sneer on his lips.

"Europe and North America, as well as most if not all the worthless African states will quickly force these miserable mixed blooded Arab countries to settle all their foul differences with us on their own. Thus placing us, our two countries right in the driver's seat, and Egypt will retain the exact amount of Nile River water she always enjoyed and needs to survive, sir." The Libyan Ambassador Kamal stopped speaking and suddenly sneered at Egyptian President Sadat.

"I don't see how you can possibly ignore the fact our two countries are going to be the cause of many of the fellow Arab countries demise after this future war is over with, Ambassador. I wished I was as confident as you obviously are Ambassador Kamal, about the outcome of these most dangerous steps our two countries are undertaking, sir."

"President Sadat, it's something you're going to have to deal with I'm afraid, sir. You have to put all this foolishness out of you mind for the love of Allah. You just worry yourself about being ready to attack on the date we have planned for, sir. Please allow my country to worry about what will happen to certain other Arab countries of the Middle East, sir. We're used to these kind of disturbing thoughts and decisions, and they have little effect on us." Ambassador Kamal glared at President Sadat for his weakness.

"How am I to know if your country doesn't have these same ugly thoughts and plans in store for my country, once we have won our war with these other foul nations we intend to destroy, Ambassador? Is your country going to throw Egypt to the dogs also once we have eliminated the other nations we aim to destroy, Ambassador Kamal?" President Sadat hissed angrily.

"Don't be such a fool, President Sadat. Libya will remember which countries have helped her in her time of need, sir. We'll also protect your country with our lives and military, so please ease your mind President Sadat. Now, I have to get everything ready with the Muslims, if we're going to attack the foolish Americans working inside Ethiopia by next week. You know, I like the idea of attacking them hated fools first. Maybe it'll knock the god cursed Americans off their high horse they're always riding upon in the face of we Arabs. Allah Akhbar President Sadat." Ambassador Kamal said as he stood and extended his hand to President Sadat.

Egyptian President stood and as the two men shook hands he responded. "Allah Akhbar Ambassador Kamal, I wish our countries the best of luck in this up coming war. I feel we might need all the luck. I wonder how many children will end fatherless when this mess is over with."

Ambassador Kamal suddenly laughed as he added. "There you go again President Sadat. Worrying about things that you should not concern yourself about, sir. If you have to beat yourself over the head to feel good then ask how many Egyptian women and children will be fatherless if Egypt is deprived of the water they need to live on. How many of your people will die without water, President Sadat? How many I ask you sir? And what kind of country will you be left with if Egypt doesn't have water? These are the questions you should be worrying about, not what is going to be the fate of a few lowly mongrel Arab states who don't remember they're Arabs, or even care. I'm sorry President Sadat, but I have to go sir. I'll be back with you when our fighters are on their march to Ethiopia, sir. Good-bye President Sadat."

The two Arab men hugged each other, and as Ambassador Kamal left President Sadat's office, he sat down heavily in his chair and put his hands to his forehead and rested his head on them while feeling totally exhausted. For a brief second, President Sadat thought about calling the American Consulate and explaining what was about to take place in this region. He would tell him if they were able to guarantee Egypt water, Egypt would pull out of this alliance Egypt found herself forced to join with Libya. But as he thought about it further, he realized the operation had gone too far to be called off now. He drew in some breath and he silently prayed to the Ancient gods of Egypt's great past for their protection and guidance.

MARCH 30th, 1996 THE TANA BASE,
ETHIOPIA 0650 HOURS

Captain Edward Campanelli cautiously watched as a massive military transport aircraft slowly came in for a landing on his base. Its shape completely blackening the sun from view as the plane flew on its final approach. He played a game of trying to guess what was inside this aircraft as far as military or construction supplies went. He watched as the mammoth plane slowly rolled to a crushing stop, and a portable walkway was instantly wheeled over to the belly door, as the tail ramp of the aircraft dropped, and a mass of Seabees started to unload the plane. The flight crew left the cockpit and were stretching their legs and backs on the tarmac.

He picked up something being held in one of the pilot's hands he had not seen for many weeks. He walked over to the pilot as if in a sort of trance and before he even realized it. He went up to the young flyer and stared at the newspaper tucked under his arm.

The Flight Commander saw the Captain staring at him, and feared he had something crawling on him, or something was wrong with his flight suit until he realized what he was looking at.

"Begging your pardon Captain Sir. But would you like to read this newspaper sir. I'm already finished with it and you can have it if you want, sir? I know you must be cut off out here from the current events happening in the world sir."

Captain Campanelli took the paper greedily, almost pulling it free from the pilot's hand as he grumbled at the fine young officer. "Thanks a helluva lot there Commander. I haven't read an American fucking newspaper for over a month now. It's driving me fucking crazy not knowing what the hell's happening back in the real world, sir. I'll cherish this paper until the ink fades."

The pilot laughed as he asked the Captain how long he was stationed on the base in Ethiopia, and when he was up for some leave time. Then he informed the grinning Captain there was this nice little place in Sicily to go for some R&R (Rest and Relaxation). The Flight Commander offered the Captain a few phone numbers of some clean women as he promised him these women would make his wildest dreams come true. The Commander looked at the Captain obviously not paying attention to what he was saying then he looked at the rest of the flight crew.

A second Lieutenant shrugged his shoulders and then said as he took a quick look at the Army Captain. "Too long in the damn bush, sun stroke I guess if you were to ask me, sir." The four fliers laughed amongst themselves, bringing the Captain back to reality.

"Did I miss something here?" He asked the small group of American flyers.

"No not really Captain, I was just telling you where to go on your next R&R in Italy sir. But I'm afraid you were obviously somewhere else in the conversation, sir."

This made the Captain laugh as he replied. "Right now sir. Believe it or not Lieutenant, this damn newspaper's more important to me than a good piece of ass, son."

This caused the Flight Commander to comment. "Sir, you've been out in the bush too long."

"You're damn right I was Commander." He said absentmindedly as he started off for his tent in a rush. He was already reading the front page of the paper as he walked. The headlines read. "President Cole Is Scheduled To Meet With The New President of Chad." In smaller print it read. "For the third day in a row."

Captain Campanelli quickly turned the next page to read the rest of the story. Chad wanted to borrow one hundred and fifty million dollars from the United States. He shook his head and grumbled at himself. "Yeah, we'll give the lousy suckers all the damn money they fucking need and want. It doesn't make any damn sense to me to give it to them, and yet we'll let good and hard working Americans starves back in the damn States." Another story suddenly caught his attention, it was a story off to the right of the article he was reading. It stated Libya and Egypt wanted to have another sit down meeting with the new government of Chad, in order to keep the lines of communication opened and peace on the table.

He could not believe Egypt was able to talk some sense with the always troublesome Libyan government. The fear of an attack anywhere in northern Africa, was the furthest thing from his mind lately. He went back to the original story he was reading moments before, before getting distracted by the second article in the paper. The one about Chad wanting more money from the United States. It was the same old story told over and over, and he quickly lost interest in the feature all together. As he continued to scan the paper, another article on the third page caught his attention. He cut his teeth in the Vietnam conflict, and he thought as many of the other soldiers did that there were still some American soldiers left alive in the jungles, and this was unthinkable to any serviceman.

CNN was interviewing Hanoi Hanna, and it actually turned his stomach. All he read lately was the poor Vietnam children and people. The papers were flooded with pictures of starving Vietnamese children sleeping on open ground. His blood boiled, because he remembered a few pictures he saw of once proud Vietnam Vets sleeping on the streets of his country, and no one cared a lick about these fine warriors. These poor souls were demoralized from the terrible memories of that miserable war, and the way they were forced to kill so recklessly. Memories that would haunt the troubled Vets for the rest of their lives. Add this to the gutless book written by a once trusted friend, and he was fuming. He cursed as he thought the papers should run the pictures of American Vets sleeping in the streets, alongside the Vietnamese doing the same thing, and see how the people of the United States felt then.

Captain Edward Campanelli felt terrible for his country and the direction she was heading off in. Because he knew he was sent here to stop these people from killing themselves, and yet back in his own country. Americans were still killing each other at an alarming rate now. He was further angered Chad was begging for more money and food from the United States, while good American people were poor, or slowly starving to death in his own country. All of a sudden, he hated these poor people he was sent here to protect from themselves, and to train them to do better for themselves.

Lieutenant Mendoza walked into his tent and offered pleasantly to her Commanding Officer. "How are you doing baby?"

He barely took any noticed of her as he continued to read the newspaper.

She sighed deeply and immediately complained at her Commander. "Oh shit, I see you found yourself another damn newspaper, Edward.

How much did this one cost you, another week's pay, and are you going to get upset by this one like you did with the last newspaper you had, mister? You were a real shit for three days the last time you read the news."

"Yeah." Was the only word she got out of him. She knew him well enough to know any further conversation was going to be a waste of time with the Captain. When he was like this no one could talk to him. She stuck out her tongue at him, and then made an obscene gesture that also went unnoticed by the military officer. Then she left the tent as he continued to read the newspaper. Twice, he tried to put down the paper but he could not. He knew he had other responsibilities he had to take care of, but he was so caught up with the recent happenings back in the States that he could not put it down until he finally got his full of it.

As the Captain read on in the newspaper, he suddenly came across a short blurb about IBM, the Corporation. Stating the Big Blue's stock had finally stabilized at sixty three dollars a share. He shook his head sadly, because he always liked IBM. Living in Putnam County like he did. It seemed to him that no matter where he went in Upstate New York that sooner or later, he passed by a massive IBM complex, from its home headquarters stationed in Somers, New York, to the recently closed down massive location at East Fishkill.

"Yeah, the East Fishkill complex." He growled more than angry about this one memory. He thought back to his past and remembered the angry incident that made him so upset.

In '92, it was the time when the newspapers were full with reports about IBM's trouble, and its future as a world leader in the computer field. IBM's stock was at an all time low of just forty eight dollars a share, and for the first time in the company's long history, it was forced to lay off some of their workers.

It was around this time he was heading for the Poughkeepsie Civic Center so he could watch a wrestling match scheduled to take place between the Undertaker and Stone Cold Steve Austin. He loved the

WWF, it gave him a chance to hide away from reality, and it also made him laugh even though he knew the fights were nothing but an act. He was driving down Route 52, heading for Route 9, when he went shooting passed a police car and he did not think anything of it. Seconds later, he was pulled over and a rather large and sharp looking New York State Trooper who asked him for his license, registration and insurance papers. As he handed the fine looking officer the requested papers, the officer grumbled at him.

"You know why I pulled you over, don't ya buddy?"

He tried his best smile on the trooper as he offered him. "Err... because you wanted someone to talk with, I hope sir." He remembered the officer glaring at him and snapped.

"Where's your registration smart guy?"

"I don't know, it's my wife's car sir. She must have it in her pocketbook I guess, sir."

"Then you're going to have to follow me back to the station sir. I'm going to make damn sure you're legal to drive this car, wiseguy." The officer held onto his license.

Ten minutes later, he found himself standing in front of an even larger Police Sergeant, as the man snapped nastily at him. "You might as well make yourself comfortable, mister. It's going to take a little while to make sure it's your car sir."

He took a quick breath as he looked out the large picture window. Across the road was the main IBM complex of East Fishkill. He could see most of the large buildings were dark. "It's a damn shame they're closing down." He said over his shoulder to the police officer.

"Yeah, the town's gonna really miss the extra tax money they always generated for us, sir. Shit, my taxes already went up this year sir. I hate to think what they'll be next year, when IBM's completely out of here all together, sir." The officer replied as he tapped away on the key board of his computer.

He noticed the police officer was typing away on a Japanese made computer, and he growled at him. "Yeah, and maybe if you guys were typing on a stinking IBM computer, these guys might still be here."

The officer stopped typing and snarled back at him. "Now you look here wiseass. I didn't buy the fucking thing, so back off my ass will ya buddy. What are you trying to be around here, a damn smartass, buster? Tell you what, why don't you just sit there and shut your damn mouth before you find yourself spending the night with us as my guess."

The Army Captain took the angry police officer's advice and sat down and kept his mouth shut for the rest of the time he was at the police station. Ten minutes later he was on his way to the Civic Center, along with two tickets for driving without his registration, and for speeding. He was certain he received the speeder ticket because of his remark about the computer the officer was using at the station. The first police officer was not so interested in the speeder, as he was about the missing registration.

He laughed and went back to reading the newspaper, he glossed over the horoscopes which always made him laugh while reading them. Then he came across the new bathing suits that exposed more flesh than they covered, and he whistled as he looked at nearly bare breasts and barely covered honey spots. He passed over the clothes and shoes section and the likes. He saw the ad for Macy's and was happy the store made it back from the problems they were suffering through. He was heading for the sports pages and did not realize it. Whether he knew it or not, his mind was not going to allow him put down the paper until he read about his one true love. Baseball. The Captain was staunch and passionate follower of the New York Mets baseball team through another very disappointingly past season, and they were out of the playoffs again. But he was already looking forward to another year of following his beloved Mets team.

The Atlanta Braves and the New York Yankees were going to this year's World Series. He felt good at least one of the New York teams made it all the way to the series. This year was the last year Doc Gooden was going to pitch, but he was happy the Yankees acquired Strawberry over the winter. The Mets also added Tom Seaver Jr. to their pitching staff. He could not read and absorb the printed information about the baseball teams fast enough. He knew he was going to read the sports pages of the Daily Times over again until he was finally lucky enough to steal another newspaper from another fly boy or Navy puke sooner or later.

Somehow, Lieutenant John White found out that he had another new newspaper, and he came bursting into the tent on a quest to find out how the Knicks were doing. They were picked to make the playoffs this year, and Lieutenant White could not find out a thing from anyone on how they were doing so far this year.

The Captain looked up at the rather excited man and then asked him. "What the hell are you doing in here buster? What have you been up to, mister?"

"Attending to fucking business man." Lieutenant White offered with a grin.

"Yeah I bet you were mister. Did your business have tits and a box lunch to it, buddy?"

"Ha, don't forget man. You stuck me with those damn Seabee's and civilians fuckers. I never saw so many pains in the ass in one stinking place, sir. How are the Knicks doing man?"

"Oh yeah, I forgot you follow that nigger ball shit. Let me see, yeah, here you go Whitie. The Knicks won their third pre-season game, and they're still picked to go all the way John."

"Awe come on man. Give me that damn thing will ya, you don't know how to read a fucking newspaper right anyhow, Honky. Let me see the damn thing."

"Come on will ya what, when I'm finished with it you can read about your fucking nigger ball."

John White bellowed with a grin. "It's better to follow my nigger ball, than to follow that lily white pansy puff ass baseball you're always following, you stinking Honky you."

The Captain looked at the laughing large black man and laughed himself as he offered. "My God, I believe you're a little prejudice, my old friend."

Again, both men laughed as they bantered back and forth with each other.

"You want a stinking beer John?" The Captain offered as he pointed towards the small refrigerator in his tent, and then he told Lieutenant White. "Help yourself if you want one man, they're cold buddy. I ain't gonna get it for your ass, buster."

"Yeah, I'll get them. You want one I take it?" John asked his Commanding Officer.

Both men could get away with kidding each other in this manner because they loved one another, and knew this was all in fun. But God help anyone else who tried to talked to either of them the way they talked to each other. It was a joke reserved for themselves. If another person tried it, it could cost him his life. Neither man had a real prejudice bone in their body, it was just the way they always bantered back and forth with each other.

Sometimes, Captain Campanelli would slip and call another black man a nigger, causing a complaint to be filed with headquarters. But when the complaint finally reached Captain Campanelli's Commander, he would merely rip it up. Besides, by the time the complaint reached the Commander, the insulted black man knew the Captain did not mean the remark as an ethnic slur, the remark was passed for the soldier's fuck up plain and simple and that was all.

The two men shared a private moment together as they drank their beers.

The Captain broke the entertaining mood by remarking. "John, I was told where to go on R&R by a coupla young flyers today, man. When are you up for leave?"

"Dunno, I think I'm not up for another fourteen weeks or so, man." He replied as he reached for one of the Playboy magazines lying on the floor. He took a second as he thumbed through the pages heading for the color pages pictorials as always. He found the set of pictures he was looking for and then whistled over what he was looking at.

"What's up." The Captain asked over his shoulder as he looked up from the newspaper.

"Man, this bitch Madonna, she's some piece of woman I can tell ya man." He muttered as he slowly rubbed his chin while staring at the almost nude body of the girl sitting on top of a 1948 restored Harley Davidson with nothing on but a leather hat, and knee high black boots with four men surrounding her. "Hey Eddy, I'd walk five miles through a stinking mine field with snow shoes on while under heavy enemy fire, just to hear this bitch fart on the fricking field phone, man." Lieutenant White said as he brought the magazine closer to his face, and then he planted a wet kiss right on her bare backside. Then he laughed one of his whole body wracking laughs as he continued to enjoy the looks of this young woman.

Campanelli looked at this rather large and laughing man and smiled as he grumbled. "C'mon man, you're gonna stick the damn pages together if you keep slobbering all over her ass like that, man. I think you can fuhgedabout any of that kinda shit my friend, you have as much chance of smelling her crotch as I have of winning a date with Miss fucking America. Shit John, what's with you lately buddy, I guess you've been out here too long, man. You really need some R&R, and real soon at that if you're talking like that, fella. I guess I better start protecting my backside some, just in case you decide to attack me man."

He continued to laugh as he remarked to his Commanding Officer. "Nevertheless man, she can still sit on my stinking face anytime, and as far as your stinking ass is concerned. It has nothing to worry about from me man. I don't go that way, it's strictly wine, women and songs for my fricking ass, Eddy. Say Ed, why did you want to know when I was up for leave sir?"

"I need some fucking time off myself, I'm starting to go fucking nuts around here lately man. But I wanted someone to go around with me. Do you mind if my white ass follows you around town for a couple of weeks off, buddy? Are you up for some white ass John? I got some supposed cool numbers from the damn fly boys on me somewhere, man."

"Sure thing my friend, I'll let your Honky ass tag along with me all you want, just so long as you let me pick the girls up this time around, buddy. Shitttt, you remember those last two dogs you called hot that you picked up back in the States. Man, you fucking white guys don't give a shit what you people fucking eat. Hell, the chick you stuck me with stunk bad, man. Yeah, you can come along with me alright, but only if I pick up the women. You know how these European white chicks go for this old Alabama black snake of mine, Eddy. They just can't get enough of this here black snake of mine, buddy." Lieutenant White remarked as he grabbed himself between his legs and shook his member through his pants.

"Yeah, I know how they go for that stinking black snake of yours buster. Maybe one of these day you can tell me how you're able to grow that damn thing so stinking long, good buddy." Captain Campanelli complained at his lifelong friend as he grinned at him.

"Ha, it's easy, you just hafta feed it a constant diet of good looking blondes that did it for me Honky. A steady diet of young blondes will do it all the time fur ya, man." White replied as he rubbed his crotch through his pants as second time.

The laughter caused Mendoza to come in the tent, and she immediately complained. "Oh my God, what the hell happened in here, dammit. Phew, please don't tell me you two shitbirds were having another one of your farting contests, it stinks like hell in here." She waved her hand in front of her face and then she held her nose closed wither fingers.

"John." Campanelli griped with a smile as he pointed to White sitting on the cot with his chin.

"Me, why you little fuck you, what about you, you fucking helped me cut them you know, man." John offered in his own defense.

Lieutenant Renee Mendoza saw John with his hand resting on his cock and smirked at him. "You better be a little more careful with that ugly looking thing of yours, mister. I'd hate like hell to see you getting your fool ass arrested for assault with a dead weapon, John."

All three close friends laughed together.

"Come on over here Maz, and I'll show you how dead this ugly stick of mine is, little sister." John warned her as he wiggled his dick through his pants for a third time.

She slid her tongue out of her mouth which caused John to hoot and holler at her.

"Hey, hey, don't go and try and attack my main squeeze with that damn snake of yours my friend. Or I might be forced to cut the damn thing off on ya, and then I'll put the damn thing in your stinking hand for ya." Campanelli laughed.

"Shitttt man, you and Maz a fucking thing? You gotta be kidding my black ass, Eddy." John looked at his friends and then added while putting on a huge smile. "Well I'll be damn. I don't believe it man. You white people don't care who you slip the stinking meat to, do ya?" He complained as he looked back and forth at his two real good friends.

"Eat your stinking heart out buster. You know damn well you want to get in my pants ever since we first met on our first mission together, mister." She purred sexily, and then she suddenly took off her shirt and threw it at the big black man as she muttered a string of stinging curses at John in Spanish. Then she stuck her breasts in his face, causing more hoots and yells from both men in the tent with her.

"Girl, you do have the nicest set of tits I ever saw in all of my born days. Come back here and let me taste them puppies or yours again." White said as he reached for her again.

She stuck her breasts in his face and shook them, letting each breast get licked.

John's tongue lapped at the hardening nipples as he licked the offered breasts.

"C'mon and knock it off, or you two are going to get me jealous over this crap." The Captain laughed at the two of them playing with each other.

John thought for a second and then he said to the both of them at the same time. "Hey guys, how about we doing a fucking threesome between the three of us. Just think of it Maz. You can have it both ways, and with a black and white dick at the same damn time, honey. Whatdaya say little girl? Do you think you could handle two men at the same time and live through it, little sister? It'll be one helluva blast for all three of us you know sister."

"Hmmm... I think I'd like to try that. I'm up to it if you two are." She purred back at him.

"Whoa, let's not go moving too fast around here you two birds. I like some kink as much as the next person does. But we can't go playing these kinda fun and games like this on base, in the tent. Suppose someone caught the three of us going at it like dogs in fucking heat? No way guys, if we're going to play around like that, I think we better go out to the lake and get far away from the stinking base and the rest of these pain in the asses we have hanging around here. We play somewhere far out of sight if we play at all." The Captain suggested to the two of them.

"Great, I'd really like that man. I haven't been with a woman since we came out to this damn dump." John complained at his two close friends.

Campanelli looked at Mendoza as he shook his head and grumbled at her. "You really think you can take on the both of us at the same time and live through it, baby?"

She laughed as she fired right back at her concerned Commanding Officer. "No problem there mister, I'll put the both of you in the damn hospital if I do."

"Then you got it baby, say tomorrow. We'll pack a good lunch and have a day of some fun and games on the shore of the stinking lake. Heaven knows I could sure do with a day off, and some real fun for a stinking change around here." Captain Campanelli offered.

All three agreed and made it a date for the next day, March 31st. John left happy as hell, while Mendoza remained with Campanelli in the tent. He looked at her again and then smirked at her. "You think you're really up to this kinda shit, baby?"

"Don't go and try and tell me you're getting cold feet on us now, lover? I'm afraid it's a little too late for that kinda shit, my dear. John and I already have our hearts set on some fun and games now, Edward. So don't go and try to back out of our deal on me honey."

"No, no, nothing like that I assure you honey. I just wanted to make sure you knew what the hell you were getting yourself into here with the three of us, baby. You're going to have to satisfy the both of us you know, and I saw John in action more than once in my life, he can really get into it if he wants to honey." Campanelli warned her in no uncertain terms.

"Oh no, you got it all wrong here I'm afraid, honey. It's you two fools who are going to have to satisfy me for a change, mista. And I take a helluva lot of stroking to be happy you know, mista. It's you two guys who'll have to work your asses off tomorrow pleasing me, not me." She offered to her lover with a straight face this time.

"You're starting to scare the shit outta me now baby. Are you really that good you can do the two of us at the same time, and want more than we can offer ya? If you're that good, how the hell am I ever going to satisfy you by myself when I leave my wife for you."

Mendoza looked at him with her mouth hanging open as she cried at her new lover. "You're going to leave your wife?" She said as tears started to run down her cheeks.

"You heard me right young lady. You're going to be mine if you'll have me that is, honey."

She instantly wrapped her arms around him and cried. "I love you, I always loved you since we did that act in Panama. But I never thought I stood a chance with you."

He wiped the tear from her eye, and then he licked it from the end of his finger and said. "Hmmmmm, a little salty, but nevertheless, good. You want to spend the night Maz?"

"You couldn't drive me out of your tent with a stinking mortar attack. Please, can you do me a favor though. Can you for once in your life call me by my first name, that's all it'd take to make me the happiest girl in the world. Try it. It's Renee, remember Edward, Renee?"

"Okay Mendoza, you got it baby." He said with a smirk on his lips.

She looked at him and then bitched at the same time. "You're impossible mista. I guess I can't have everything I want though. But what I have, I'll take with a smile on my lips mista."

"Mendoza, everything's gonna be fine between us just as long as I have you standing by my side, honey." He said to her as he stared her right in the eyes for a long moment.

Lieutenant Renee Mendoza was up well before Captain Edward Campanelli and she quickly got ready for her rendezvous with the two men for later in the day. She had not slept at all the night before. Edward was still sleeping and she silently slipped out of his bunk. She then packed up a knapsack with cold beer, cigarettes, and some pot to help set the mood for the three of them. She was going to head out for the mess and have the cooks make up some extra sandwiches for their trip. She had no way of knowing that John had not sleep either last night. He to was looking forward to this little game of patty cake more than anyone knew. Lieutenant John White loved and missed his wife dearly, but he also liked to have a fling every now and then. It made his love life with his wife reach new heights whenever he was with her again.

She just closed the flap to her knapsack, and then leaned it up against the light wood reinforced side of the tent, and was just about to leave for the mess, when she heard the popping sounds of weapons fire going off in the distance. The distinctive sound of automatic weapon fire could not be mistaken for any other sound on earth.

She immediately dropped to the floor instinctively and in a heartbeat Captain Campanelli was by her side. He automatically reached for his nine mm pistol that always hung over his head while he slept. As he reached he growled at her. "What the fuck's happening out there dammit? I hope those stinking mud Marines aren't fooling around out there, I'll have their fricking asses hanging on a stick for waking me up like this, if that's what they're doing."

As he complained to Lieutenant Mendoza, the warning sirens suddenly blared into life as lights on the base went off, making Mendoza and the concerned Captain duck their heads even closer to the ground out of habit and training.

"What the fuck's going on out there, dammit?" He growled again as he retrieved his pistol and slid the slide back then let it go, putting a shell in the chamber as he picked up the flap of the tent for a look. He turned to Mendoza, she looked scared and he offered. "Hey baby, calm down a little will ya, there's an extra pistol in my footlocker, help yourself."

She crawled over to the locker on her belly while cursing in Spanish as she fished around until she finally found the other pistol and a box of shells for it. She quickly loaded the weapon then she crawled back to Campanelli's side and gave him the rest of the rounds for both weapons.

"You stay here while I find out if those damn mud Marines didn't mistake a stinking Elephant for an enemy Army probe for carp sake." The Captain growled as he slid in his pants and shirt then he crawled out of the tent on his belly, and rolled over to a parked jeep for cover. He leaned against the front wheel and stretched his neck until he was able to see over the hood of the machine, and he looked to where he felt the shooting was coming from. He was unable to see anything that was happening in the jungle where the Marines were known to be stationed.

There were many weapons firing now, and also returning fire was being picked up as well. He could make out the different sounds of weapons being fired. He was certain he heard the Russian made assault rifle AK 78 going off.

Captain Campanelli ducked his head down just as a hand grenade suddenly blew up right near him, and he roared once again at anyone who might be able to hear his words. "What the fuck's happening out there dammit?" The Captain then looked to his left to where most of his soldiers slept, and noticed many of the soldiers pouring out of the wood and canvass covered hut and tripping over themselves as they quickly bunched up near the door of their living quarters. Most soldiers were carrying their M-18s, or the older M-16 rifles.

"Disperse you stinking assholes before one stinking grenade gets the lot of you asses, dammit." He bellowed at them, and then added to his warning to the scared looking young soldiers. "Setup some skirmish lines, and protect those damn civilian workers. Two men together, no more. I want a dozen of you asses to follow me over to the Marine's positions, another dozen of you people will follow behind, and another dozen behind them. I want some of you people to make it out to the jungle and setup a number of M-60 heavy machine guns.

"Set them up to cover all angles of the damn base. And for God's sake, make damn certain of your fucking targets. I'll have men out there, and I don't want you swinging dicks taking us for any fucking enemy and hitting any of us by fucking mistake. I don't know what the hell's happening out there as yet, but evidently we're under attack. Move out, if I see anyone's ass sticking up, I'll shoot the damn thing offa ya myself." The fuming Captain watched as his men rapidly spread out and a number of them made their way to him.

Captain Campanelli's attention turned to where his officers slept, and he bellowed at them this time. "Get the hell out of them damn huts for Christ sake and take command of your troops."

He looked around until he picked up Lieutenant John White and he barked at him angrily. "John, get your ass over to the stinking Intel tent, and see what the fuck's happening around here, dammit. Call the damn Carrier Group and demand some fucking air support over our asses as well, and remind those damn fly jockeys to pick out their stinking targets carefully, man. I don't want any of those fucking birds hitting any of my people out there, mister."

The Captain watched as John sprinted the short distance over to the intelligence tent, and the officers either ran, or crawled to the men and took command of the scared and bunched up kids.

Within seconds he heard his officers yelling orders at the soldiers, and he watched as they headed off in all directions in a rush. He knew enough about the soldiers to get the devils in each of his officers moving, and start the fires of hell burning in their souls, and get his men on the move and take up protective positions until they found out what was happening.

"Get me a fucking helmet and a real god damn weapon for Christ sake." He bellowed as he stuffed the pistol in his belt.

A dozen troopers made their way over to the hunkered down Captain and then they bunched up behind him and the parked jeep. One soldier gave the Captain a loaded M-18, and three extra clips for the weapon. He looked at how the scared soldiers were bunching up again, and hissed at them. "Spread the fuck out I said, god dammit. Didn't any of you assholes hear me, stop holding fucking hands and spread out for Christ sake."

The soldiers followed their orders from their Commanding Officer and they quickly spread out and took cover behind different parked vehicles or stacked up construction materials. Soon, anything that could hide a soldier, was being used for protection by his people. Wood crates, stacks of lumber and steel, all had a number of soldiers hiding behind them and aiming their weapons out towards the dense jungle, and the fighting obviously going on out there.

The Captain sudden darted out from behind the jeep and rushed over to a parked bulldozer off to his left, he was followed closely by seven other soldiers. He plopped down by the heavy blade of the massive machine. An over zealous soldier ran by him while stepping right on his hand as the kid made it safely to a large pile of sand.

"God dammit." He called out after the young trooper who did not know what he had done wrong to get his Commander so angry at him. The Captain then looked to the soldiers who followed him over to the bulldozer. He got their attention and pointed to a small slip trench the Seabees dug for some pipes the day before. He ducked as bullets suddenly buzzed around him like a swarm of angry bees. He immediately realized this was not a joke or exercise from the Marines, and someone was truly trying to kill him.

Captain Campanelli knew he had to move forward, he and his men were sitting duck where they were hiding, and his troops were looking to him to do something. He then glanced over to where he was sure the Marines were dug in. Heavy weapon fire was coming from that area. He jumped to his feet and then offered calmly. "Follow me please gentlemen."

The soldiers moved out and hit the trench together, a few of them fell in the trench and landed on top of one another as they dove into the damp hole, filling the air with a string of curses.

He popped his head up to get his location, and see if he could find out where the heavier fighting was happening around him. He spotted some muzzle flashes going off from the firing weapons, his group was a few feet away from their base perimeter defense now. As the troops hid in the trench, the captain heard claymore going off, and knew the Marines setup their own perimeter defenses. The mines going off meant one thing, the fighting was getting close at hand.

He was really pissed off, because he had not been informed about the defensive lines the Marines had setup. Which meant his men could have stumbled on top of them and been blown to shit. He vowed someone's ass was going to be swinging for this mistake. He heard the whistles from the Marines in the bush as they fought the rebels, or whoever was attacking them.

The Captain ducked just as a mortar round went off directly in front of them, and he turned to the kid hiding by his side and mumbled at the young soldier. "It sounds like a pretty sizable attacking force we have on our hands here mister."

A second mortar round went off ahead of them, and the perimeter line disintegrated, leaving paths for the attackers, or his troops to use. He looked over his shoulder and picked John up adjusting the mortar tube for another shot, and he knew John was trying to blast a way through the wire defense for his bogged down troops to use for a quick breakout and get at the enemy.

He waited for a few seconds to crawl by. His reflexes were aching to do something to burn off some of the adrenaline quickly building up rapidly in his muscles. He finally got his breathing under control as he looked to where his troopers just setup the pair of M-60s, and the deadly kill zone created that the weapons now own. He understood nothing was going to make it through this area and live to tell about it later on.

"Okay, let's help those damn Marines out a little, people." He yelled as he again turned to the soldier to his left, but the kid was no longer squatting at his side, a light red mist stained the air where he once stood. He looked to his rear and saw the young trooper sprawled out in a heap at the bottom of the trench, his right arm sinking slowly to his side. Then his arm came to a rest in the mud as the other soldiers carefully stepped over the body so they could get out of the trench. He cursed as he barked out new orders for his men to follow him as he prepared to move out and let support to the Marines engaging unknown hostiles.

"C'mon! Let's go, we're all going to fucking die if we stay here, dammit." He yelled in a commanding tone as he leaped from the trench. The air was filled with small arms fire and occasional mortar or grenade popping off. Heavy machine gun fire opened up and the Captain knew the Marines were seconds away from hand to hand combat.

As he moved out of the deep trench, he almost immediately came across a downed soldier. This young man, no more than a boy was lying flat on his back, and he looked like he was reaching for the end of an unseen rope dangling just out of his reach. As he struggled with the empty air, the dying soldier called out for his mother to come and help him. As the Captain continued to watch, the boy suddenly began to gargle on his own blood as he continued to cry, "Mother." Soon, the blood caused his words to become distorted to the point where he could no longer understand any of his words.

As the young man's life slowly drained from his body, he flayed his arms at the empty sky while still fighting for the little life left in him. His head suddenly lifted off the ground, and then it banged on the mud created from the blood from his mouth. Finally, he arched his back and then his body relaxed and settled for the last time, as the air rushed from his lungs and causing the death rattle. The fuming Captain looked to where he was sure the enemy was, and he immediately headed in off that direction, angry for the loss of one of his soldiers.

His attention was drawn up towards the sky. A wing of seven F 18 Hornets loaded for bear came in low from the east, and they raked the entire area before him with heavy cannon fire. The jungle came alive as leaves, trees and bushes jumping into the air, along with the occasional body or body parts flung in the sky by the heavy impact of cannon fire on the ground. Colored smoke marked out the area the Marines wanted hit by the attacking American aircraft. The warplanes chopped up the area not marked out by their smoke.

Captain Campanelli's troops took cover near the jungle line, and they watched as the aircraft did their job for them. A pilot flew right over his group of people, and the pilot dipped his wing in response to recognizing them as friendly forces. The planes stopped attacking, and then took up a standoff position just short of the fight zone. One at a time, the aircraft were called in to make a precision attack in a chosen spot, to drive out any enemy forces now dug in, and they were making a fight of it against the Marines. The small arms fire was heavy, and he was certain some of the attackers were too close to the Marines, for the attacking aircraft to fire on them without possibly hitting any Marines on the ground. He noticed the movement to his left, and picked up four soldiers not dressed in American uniforms making their way on his base. Two of the invaders looked like they were carrying some sort of explosives.

The fuming Commander tapped his helmet with one of the extra clips to his weapon to get the attention of his troops, once he got it he pointed at the two attackers cautiously crawling along on the ground. His excited troops starving for a fight immediately went into action by spreading out, and taking aim at the two invaders.

The M-18s spat their little dots of death out, and the two enemy bodies jumped on the ground, pushed along by the rounds ripping into their unprotected bodies. It was the distorted dance of death which occurs when the body's penetrated by bullets.

The Captain's troops moved out without being ordered to, their training taking over as they spread out in the jungle. He was right behind his men, and he laughed as he watched them move. Some of the soldiers were in underwear while others had pants on, and there were a few with just a shirt on. "Sort of gives a new meaning to the phrase 'assholes and elbows.'"

He laughed as he watched his troops move out as a good fighting unit. He was pleased he only had a few women in his command. The last thing he needed, was a complaint to be registered back with command about his soldiers running around with their asses sticking out in the breeze during an attack.

One soldiers opened fire close to the Captain's right side. More troopers quickly fired in the same area, and he cursed as he saw another of his soldiers go flying backwards. Landing hard on his back, and lay still where he landed on the ground, and a red stain quickly spread across his chest. He knew immediately his soldier was dead, because his eyes stared the stare of death. He watched helplessly as a hail of bullets shredded two more of his troops, and then he yelled out. "Medics, get up here on the double quick. I have men down here dammit."

He glared at the jungle. "Sonofabitches!" He roared as he jumped up firing in the direction where the bullets came from that just killed three of his kids. He checked his rifle, he did not notice tracer rounds, but he ejected the half spent clip and slapped a full magazine home. The last time he was forced to use his weapon in anger was in the underbrush of Panama, so he was a little rusty, and he did not realize how many rounds he had already fired off, he chose to play it safe and change the clip in case he was low or out of ammo. He did not want to be caught in the middle of a fire fight with no ammo left in his weapon.

Shooting suddenly broke out to the Captain's left as he was joined by a dozen more excited young soldiers. Some of them cut in front of him in an effort to make him leave the fighting area, but the excited Captain was to in to the fighting to worry about his own welfare at the moment. More troops passed him by heading into the heavy bush firing their weapons.

A radioman with a Prick 25 radio suddenly appeared, and he plopped down by his side and moaned. "Sir, I'm glad I found you. I have the CIC Commander on the line. He wants you sir."

He took the handset and barked into it in an angry tone of voice. "Captain Campanelli here. Go with your fucking traffic, I'm in a hot zone, dammit."

"Commander Owens, Captain. What the fuck's happening over there, god dammit? Who the hell's attacking you, man? Are you sure you have unfriendlies hitting your position, sir? I need some god damn reports so I know how to better respond to this damn situation, dammit." The Commander yelled in the head set as he slammed his fist down on the table in the CIC room.

"I wish I knew what the hell's happening myself sir. All I know is the damn base is under heavy attack from someone, and I'm taking fucking casualties, Commander. It seems a raiding party's attacking us from the south and hitting both the base and construction site. They're well equipped with small arms and some mortars, no armor noted. The Marines are engaging the attackers, and we're lending backup support to the Marines. Commander, where the hell are the god damn helicopters? Dammit, we need some close fire support now, they're all over us sir."

"Probably broke like every fucking thing else we have for Christ sake, sir. Calm down a little Captain Campanelli Sir, I'm dispatching six helos out to you position immediately, sir. It must be the enemy's too close for the Marine choppers to liftoff and support them, or the raiders got the choppers before they could get airborne, sir. Mark your area out well with smoke, and then you're instructed to get in touch with the Marines and have them do the same thing for us, sir. Use green smoke this time to identify your positions. I repeat, green smoke sir. Any area not marked out with green smoke, will be sterilized sir. Stay in the area of smoke.

"Do you understand my orders Captain Campanelli? I have orders from the Chairman of the Joint Chiefs of Staff to protect your civilian population at all cost, and I'll level the entire fucking jungle to do so, sir. An air strike will commence in nine minutes. I repeat to you sir, nine minutes. Keep your head down. Can you see what's happening from your intelligence tent, sir?"

"Intel tent? What the hell are you talking about Commander? I'm right in the middle of the shit along with the rest of my damn troopers, sir. I'm not sitting in any fucking Intel tent, sir. I'm giving orders for a smoke release as we speak, Commander Owens Sir. I have a second radio operator in contact with the damn Marines out in the field, and they have received the same orders to pop off their smoke as well, sir. There, I see the damn Marines marking their positions as we speak with green smoke, sir."

"Captain Campanelli, what the fuck are you doing in the middle of a fucking combat area, sir? You're ordered to get your fucking ass out of there as fast as you can, mister. I can't afford to have you hurt or killed in this mess, sir. I need reliable reports, or I can't help you people, move out of the fucking fighting area now sir, and that's an order. Acknowledge my last order at once as received mister!" The Commander turned red as a beet, as he yelled his order in the receiver, again he smashed his fist down on the table top as he waited for an answer.

"Err... your last transmission came in rather garbled I'm afraid, Commander Owens Sir." Captain Campanelli said as he made some funny noises with his mouth, to try and fake the sounds of his transmission breaking up.

"Don't play that child ass fucking game on my damn ass, mister. I was pulling this same kind of bullshit while you were still just a twinkle in your father's eye, sonny. I'm ordering you out of the fucking fighting area, immediately sir!" Commander Owens flattened his hand on the polished table, overcoming the urge to pound it.

Campanelli continued to make the noises over the radio as he again moved forward with the rest of his troops.

"You have a damn reputation for being a stubborn sonofabitch, Captain. If you don't answer me right now, I'm going upstairs and write your damn name on one of those fucking bombs. And then I'll have one of my flyers drop it right on your fucking ass, mister. Respond before you regret it mister." The Commander snarled into the receiver this time.

Captain Campanelli realized he might have pushed Commander Owens a little to far, so he took the radio and growled into it. "Commander, I have good Intel Officers, and they'll keep the reports coming to both of us, sir. I have no intention of leaving my soldiers while they're under attack, many for the first time in their god damn lives, sir. I can get you much better reports right from here where I'm out in the field, than from my fricking intelligence tent, sir."

The Commander calmed down a little as he replied in a much calmer tone of voice. "I knew you had fucking balls when I first spoke to you sir, but you're not listening to me yet, Captain Campanelli. You're ordered to get your damn ass the hell out of the damn fighting arena immediately, or Ill cut your balls off for you, this isn't a damn request, it's a fucking direct order, mister. Captain, there's no more heroes left in the world. I need you alive sir."

There was a sudden interruption, and the commander spoke to someone else on the ship. He was back to Campanelli and reported. "Captain, I have some new orders for you, sir. You're now ordered to stay where the hell you are and keep your fucking head down. My aircraft should be directly overhead presently, followed by choppers for close in support, and I don't want any unnecessary movement to confuse my pilots, sir. Can you see them yet sir?"

"Yes, yes Commander, I see them coming in now sir. I see at least a dozen or so aircraft, and a number of choppers are coming in right behind them, low to the ground sir."

"Captain Campanelli, tell your damn troops to hunker down right where they are and keep low, it'll be over in a few seconds, sir."

Campanelli bellowed in the second set of headphones for all American soldiers to take cover because a pending air attack was beginning on the enemy positions.

In seconds, twelve F 15E Eagles went into the attack mode, and they made repeated passes over the troubled areas not marked out by green smoke. The jungle again became alive as bombs exploded between the trees and bushes. As he hugged the ground for dear life, he felt like the earth responded, angered by the exploding bombs digging into her soil. The ground the Captain hugged actually lifted up beneath him, and it shuddered as if in an attempt to try and shake the huddled soldiers off her back, and then the ground fell back in place. The Captain found himself being shaken then vibrated along the trembling ground.

Pass after pass from the attacking American warplanes made the earth actually come alive. The Captain heard the shrill whistle of a piece of shrapnel as it flew passed his head around eye level. The jungle was marked by many fires now, as trees were ripped out of the ground, and then hurled in the air from the force of the explosions as if they weighed nothing. Some bombs exploded while still in the air, and the air burst explosions rained down a shower of shards of death on the dug in attackers. The air was now filled with the a new sound, the sounds of the screams coming of the dying and the maimed. Horrible screams filled the smoke clouded air as men, soldiers, were being burned and ripped apart by shrapnel, their screams mixed in with the screams of the living horrified by the brutality war brings.

Many American soldiers joined the screaming of the dying enemy soldiers out of sheer fear of the death exploding with the wild fury of hell all around them. Young men found themselves bleeding from their noses and ears from the concussion, as they went into shock caused by the exploding bombs. Many of the soldiers on both sides were wounded and scraped up by shrapnel and exploding bombs and rounds finding them, and soon the reality of war really set in on the soldiers. Unlike in the movies, here, when a trooper was hit by a bullet or a piece of shrapnel, he did not get up to fight again. Dead was dead in war. Many young soldiers quickly realized Rambo, who was shot many times in his flicks, always managed to get up to fight again, was all bullshit. Here, in a real war, one little piece of lead no bigger than a man's fingernail, killed someone for all eternity. No one who was dead in a real war was ever going to get up again, and share another beer with his friends he left behind.

Reality was a harsh teacher for the young soldiers, and it quickly taught many of the untried soldiers dead here, was dead forever. And the dead would never see their mothers again, or experience the pleasures of lying on the beach with one's lover while sharing sex on the shore.

When the aircraft finished tearing the jungle apart, they backed off to their ordered standoff positions, and allowed the helicopters to move in and finish their job. The Captain watched as the helicopters came in next. They came in in pairs. The war machines looked like huge, angry flying insects, breathing fire and death from their Hughes 30 mm M-230A1 chain guns, and spitting 2.75 mm rockets in a shower of sparks and rapid explosions at the enemy trapped on the ground. It was amazing to watch these weapons in operation.

Captain Campanelli heard what he though at first was rain hitting the leaves, until he realized the sound came from the spent shells from the machine guns of the helicopters, falling through the brush hitting the ground. The choppers never used their hellfire missiles. There was no need to, because the enemy did not have any armor accompanying them on their fool attack. The helicopters ripped apart anything left standing of the jungle with cannon fire, and they also added their rockets to kill any living thing not in the protective ring of the cloud of green smoke.

The bombardment lasted for nearly ten minutes. The strong and burning acid smell of spent cordite was almost choking, as it burned the lungs and eyes of the American troopers on the ground. As the air around them continued to be filled with sporadic small arms fire, and the screams from the wounded and dying. The helicopters quickly took to hovering right over the attack area, and he could see Marines moving around now. One helicopter was overhead and actually following the Marines as they checked on the bodies lying on the ground.

The Captain noticed another helicopter nearly stand on its nose end and shoot straight down to the ground. He looked harder and picked up some enemy bodies being tossed about violently along the ground as the heavy shells pumped into their lifeless bodies, tearing them to pieces. He stared in awe at how the human body was being torn apart by the heavy lead rounds.

Soldiers slowly started to come out of their hiding places to walk through the area of death carved out by the attacking warplanes and helicopters. A wing of six F 15 Eagles, passed just above tree top height. All six aircraft dipped their wings to acknowledge the Marines moving in the open as they flew overhead. Every now and then a shot would ring out, causing the American soldiers to drop down to the ground and aim their weapons in the direction the shot was fire from. Instantly, a chopper was over the area firing at the enemy again.

The grime covered and thoroughly exhausted Captain looked around until he saw who he was looking for. The young Marine Lieutenant was standing by a few tanks parked in the open. There were eleven spent shell casings lying behind the one tank where they fell when fired. The

Captain made his way over to the dirt and sweat covered Lieutenant. He stank of sweat and the stale and filthy water from the slip trench he once hid in.

It was like roaming over the floor of hell itself. Everywhere he looked, there were fires burning or bodies covering the turned up ground that moments before, was lush jungle.

The Marine picked up the Captain making his way towards him and instantly snapped to attention and saluted as the Captain approached him.

"Skip that fucking saluting shit Lieutenant. How many times do I gotta tell ya that shit?" He growled at the young Marine he had a fear of a salute. When he was stationed in the Nam, he was ordered to report to an officer. He walked up to this officer, snapped to attention and saluted the other officer. Instantly, a shot rang out and the officer immediately grabbed for his throat. It was a harsh lesson well learned and remembered by him for the rest of his life. The Viet Cong had setup a number of snipers who observed the going on throughout the United States military bases, or in the field, always looking for officers to kill. They waited until an officer was saluted by one of the lesser troopers in the field. That soldier was then identified as on officer and he was immediately killed. The Viet Cong knew to cut off the head of a snake would make the rest of the snake far less dangerous to deal with, and it would soon die for them.

"What the hell do you think you were doing out there for Christ sake? I told you never to salute me out in the fucking field, dammit." He never told anyone about his fear of a salute, but he always reacted angrily whenever someone showed him this sign of respect out in the field. Once, he even went so far as to slap down a hand heading for a salute to him. He blamed himself for this officer's death, and he never forgave himself for it. He forced his thoughts back to the present time and this new war.

"What the fuck happened out here mister? Who the hell are these scumbags who attacked us, and how come they got so close to the fucking base before we started to fight back, Lieutenant?" He roared as he placed his fear of a salute out of his mind for the time being.

"Captain Campanelli Sir, if you don't mind my saying sir. You smell like you were shot at and missed, and shit at and hit, sir. What's with you sir?"

The Captain laughed as he responded to the Lieutenant's last remark. "I hear you there son."

"Captain Campanelli Sir, I have no idea who these stinking bad guys are, sir. My Intel people are checking for any possible survivors, and the dead for any identification, or for some kind of fucking clue as to who these fucking shitbirds were allied with, sir. It's only a matter of time before we know what the hell's up and who the fuck they are and why they hit us sir."

"How many men do you think were in on the attack against us, Lieutenant Sir?"

"Again sir I have no idea as yet. But I figure there were around a hundred of the P.O.S.'s...."

"P.O.S.?" The Captain asked the young Lieutenant not knowing what he meant by the remark.

"Sorry sir, P.O.S means, Pieces Of Shit sir, battlefield slang sir. I wish I knew what they were up to, sir. I see no reason for this fucking attack, unless Ethiopia's at war with someone, or it could be a tribe trying to take over the country, sir. Right now sir, your guess is as good as mine. I'll know a lot more if we find any prisoners still alive, sir. I know damn well they had no chance in hell of taking over the damn base with such a small group of soldiers, and so ill armed at that, sir. It was more like an exercise or something they played against us, sir."

"Where the hell are your damn helicopters Lieutenant, and how come you didn't employ them during this stinking attack, sir?" The concerned Captain asked the Lieutenant.

"I'm sorry to say this Captain Campanelli, but once again I had to send the helicopters off to the Sudan two days ago for some war exercises with the Sudanese and Iranian troops. So they know how our helicopters act, and react during times of attack, sir. I'll tell you this much though sir, I'm going to make a fucking request to have ten more helicopters assigned to my ass, sir. So I can have a helicopter umbrella over my ass at all times, sir. I promise you this much though Captain, I'll never be caught off guard ever again, not with my ass hanging out in the breeze like this one, sir. Not in this God forsaken fucking country Captain."

"Lieutenant, I'll back you up on your request for those extra helicopters sir, and I..." The Captain started to sound off until he was suddenly interrupted by another young soldier.

A Marine Private came over to the two officers and asked permission to give a report. The Lieutenant gave the soldier permission to speak, salutes were not passed between the two.

"Lieutenant, as far as we can tell, we counted sixty three dead attackers, some were chewed up pretty damn bad, sir. I found many forms of IDs on the dead sir. The damnedest thing though, all the attackers seem to come from or they had some alliances to the nation of Chad, sir. We also found a number of weapons given to Chad from our government, along with a few Russian assault weapons and other crap they armed themselves with. I checked the serial numbers with command, sir. Why the hell would Chad attack Ethiopia, sir? Why the hell would that shit filled little country attack the United States as well, sir?" The soldier asked confused.

"I don't know, but I'm sure as hell am going to find out and if it's fucking true my friend. Then it'll be like Friday night at the fucking fights when I find the scumbag in charge of these lousy bastards, Private.

Captain Campanelli Sir, do you want to come with me while I chew on some asses, sir? I have to call my C.O. and let them know what we found here sir."

"Err... I think I'm your C.O. (Commanding Officer) Lieutenant. But I'll tag along with you just in case I'm not, son. Say Lieutenant, why the hell don't you make your fucking calls from my Intel Post, sir? I think we have a much better setup than you have out in the field at this time, sir. At least we have a fucking Fleet puke that'll get us through all the damn red tape a little faster than you can waddle through it, Lieutenant." The Captain replied to the young Marine.

"Sure thing sir. Do you think they might have any hot fucking coffee at this post, sir? I could sure use a cup of mud, sir. I'm all spent out, sir. Shall we go Captain?"

The two officers headed straight for the intelligence post. An excited soldier ran up to the Captain the moment he spotted his commanding officer coming at him and he saluted him, causing Campanelli to automatically flinch. Then the soldier gave the Captain his report which informed him they had twelve fatalities, and seven wounded in his command.

Captain Campanelli did not reply to this information, he just sighed as he continued walking along while heading for his Intelligence Post. The young Marine Lieutenant noticed the hurt etched in the Captain's eyes as he watched his troopers loading a dead soldier onto one of the trucks, and knew he really cared for his soldiers as much as the Lieutenant cared for his own troopers. The Lieutenant was aware his troops suffered more casualties than the Army forces had. It sucked whenever an officer lost any soldiers, he hated to write the letters to the soldier's family, and he could not help but think it was his orders which might have caused some of the death. He spat on the floor as he followed the Captain.

The two military officers entered the Intel tent together, and they both saw the young new Lieutenant hooked up to the computers by means of several wires, while the other officers jumped up and snapped to attention and saluted the two other officers.

The Fleet Officer spoke while still saluting the grime and sweat covered Captain as he entered the intelligence hut. "Captain Campanelli Sir, the CIC wants you to report to the Flag Ship Roosevelt A-SAP, sir. The Commander's sending out a special aircraft to pick you up and take you out to our ship, Captain Campanelli. He wants a personal report delivered by you sir. I beg your pardon Captain, but I have orders to put you on board the aircraft anyway I have to, sir. I trust that you'll get on board the aircraft and not put me in a position of forcing you on it, sir."

The Captain laughed as he looked at the stress etched in the Lieutenant's face and then he responded. "Calm down a little mister, I intended to go out to the Fleet before. I have a report I have no intention of sending through the normal fucking channels of communications, sir. This will be the best way to relay my information to command, sir. But first I'm going to shower and change into a clean uniform. When is this damn aircraft going to arrive, Lieutenant?"

"Sir, it should be here any second Captain." The Navy Officer reported to the Commander.

"Very good, by the way Lieutenant, how the hell did my two soldiers do in here during the stinking attack, sir? Did they muster up correctly, sir?" The Captain asked as he looked from one to the other of his new sweat stained intelligence officers.

"Captain Campanelli Sir, they both handled themselves well, very well at that sir. They knew where you were at all times, and they also monitored all the incoming reports, and then they transmitted out the right codes and reports back to Command, sir. Then also gave your officers out in the field the correct reports and other controls, sir. I think you have a pretty good unit operating here now sir. I feel my work here is done, Captain. These man here can handle any emergency that comes their way at this point, Captain Campanelli Sir. Sir, I'll be leaving with you sir." The Lieutenant looked to the other officer who he did not recognized.

The Captain saw the look that passed and he offered. "Sorry sir, this is Lieutenant Peter Gates, sir. He's in command of the Marines units stationed in the jungle Lieutenant, sir."

The Lieutenant nodded as he replied. "Pleased to know you sir. Will you be accompanying the Captain out to the Flag Ship, sir?"

Lieutenant Gates looked to the Captain with questioning eyes as he waited for his reply.

"Yeah Pete, I think I want you to come along with me and help me make our report to CIC. Commander Owens' a real bitch when he's pissed off, and he's really pissed off over this attack sir. Do you mind coming along sir? Can your men handle it without you for a little while sir?"

"No sir not at all, I'd like to come along with you, sir. I hear they eat pretty damn good on a Carrier, sir. Heaven knows I can stand a good hot meal with all the fucking trims and fixings, sir. My troops can handle any shit that comes their way for the rest of the day without me, sir."

"I thought you people were stationed on board the Aircraft Carrier, mister?" He asked the young Marine Lieutenant.

The Lieutenant smiled at the Captain as he offered. "I was, I just wanted to go along sir."

The Captain read a number of overlapping reports that were in his in box in the post. He had to do something until the aircraft arrived for them. An out of breath runner was sent out to retrieve a clean uniform, but came back with a uniform which was not much cleaner than the one the Captain had on. He cursed himself for not doing his laundry.

The officers were surprised when the huge CH-53D Sea Stallion hovered for a landing almost right on top of the Intel tent. The Captain wondered how everyone was going to fit in a jet, if that was what the CIC was sending out for him.

The massive Sea Stallion helicopter caused a sea of sand to be kicked up as it came in for a landing to the point where he had to actually turn his face away from the stinging sand pelting his face. A soldier ran the Lieutenant's gear out to the helicopter and threw it in the door, and a sailor quickly stowed it in the chopper. Captain Campanelli and Lieutenant Gates ran over to the helicopter as the Fleet Lieutenant quickly made his way to the chopper right behind them.

He suddenly remembered about Lieutenant Mendoza, and he started to look around what he could see of the base for her. She was nowhere in sight, and he was suddenly worried if she might have been hurt in the attack. The sailor pulled the stalled Captain in the helicopter and asked him with some concern lacing his tone. "Captain, is there anything wrong sir?"

"Yeah, that fucking Lieutenant Mendoza, she's a real pain in my ass lately, sir. Women, they're like fucking frogs, you never know which way they're gonna jump. I didn't see her hanging around anywhere out there since the fucking attack against us started, sir. God dammit, I hope she's all right for the love of God. I wanted to check on her before we left for the damn Carrier, shit. I wonder if we can hang back for a while so I can check on my officers, and see if they're alright." He mumbled at the door guard of the helicopter.

"Sir, we have no time for that kinda shit sir. We have standing orders to pick you up, and then get you out to Fleet immediately sir, if not sooner than that sir." The helicopter door guard said to the Captain as he stared back at the extremely upset looking military officer.

"Who the hell are you buster." The Captain demanded hotly of the much younger man.

Marine Lieutenant Gates told the guard to move off as he pushed the Captain over towards the benches inside the helicopter and mumbled at his commanding officer. "Sir, I think we had better sit this ride out sir, or it could be a pretty rough one for you sir. Strap yourself in sir."

"That fucking Mendoza. She better be all right dammit. Or I'll kick her little ass for her." Captain Campanelli grumbled back at the concerned looking young Marine Lieutenant.

"If you'd like Captain Campanelli Sir, I'll be pleased to place a call out to your base when we land on the Carrier, and you can talk to this Lieutenant Mendoza. I'm sure she's fine sir."

The door guard butted in on the conversation between the two military officers by offering the concerned looking Captain. "Captain, if you want me to, I can place a call back to your base from the helicopter for you sir. That way you won't have to wait until we land on the Carrier, sir. You can talk to this Lieutenant Mendoza fellow right now if you'd like, sir." The door guard had no idea Lieutenant Mendoza was a female officer the Captain was so worried about.

Without waiting for him to answer, the door guard quickly disappeared into the front of the large helicopter. Seconds later, he returned while carrying a headset and he announced proudly. "Captain Campanelli Sir, I have your Intel Post Officer on the line for you, sir." He offered the Captain the headset, and helped him adjust it to fit his head better.

"Yeah, this is Captain Campanelli and I want you to do me a favor and check on Lieutenant Mendoza for me. The last time I saw her was when the attack first started against us, mister. I told her to stay put in my tent and I gave her a pistol, and haven't seen or heard jack shit from her since that time. I want to talk to her. Yeah, I'll hold on son, get it done for me mister."

The Lieutenant placed the headset down and then he called for another soldier and he sent him out to locate Lieutenant Mendoza for the concerned Captain. It took about five minutes for her to be found and then report over to the Intelligence Post, and the Captain was really pissed off over the length of time it took for him to finally be able to speak with her, who was now in charge of his entire base while he was gone.

At last she picked up the headset and snapped in it. "Lieutenant Mendoza. What's your problem, Captain Campanelli Sir? I have a helluva lot of work to do…"

"Where the hell were you hiding at Lieutenant Mendoza? I thought I told you to stay in the damn tent until I returned?" He hissed at her in an extremely upset tone of voice.

"Captain Campanelli Sir, I had my own orders to secure all the pain in the ass civilian workers from the Dam project, sir. Then I took charge of a small patrol and we got ourselves three kills while we were at it, sir. I was loo…"

"I though I told you to stay put in the fucking tent and wait there for my return, Lieutenant Mendoza." He suddenly roared into the radio set at her this time.

She took a deep breath and then she whispered into the headset in an extremely angry tone this time. "Captain Campanelli Sir, you're not my fucking husband, so don't try and start acting like one on me, sir. I can think rather clearly for myself in case you're interested sir, and I can take god damn good care of myself on any battlefield as well, Captain Campanelli Sir." She responded as if insulted and then she said something under her breath in Spanish.

He could tell just from the tone in her voice she was cursing at him in her native tongue and he replied to her over the radio. "Okay, you win this round sister, and I heard that bullshit with cursing me in Spanish again, little Miss Wiseass. Don't start any of that women's lib horseshit on me either again I'm warning you Lieutenant. I'm getting too fucking old for this kinda shit you know. I just wanted to make sure you were all right, that's all. Look err…, I have to make a report to Fleet in person, Lieutenant Mendoza. It might take me the rest of the day to do so at that. So I want you to take command of the base while I'm away. Secure the damn civilians and make certain they're safe, I don't want anyone working on the damn project until after the Marines checked out the area of the Dam. In case the damn bad guys might've planted any booby traps by it. Get the engineers on that. Hey Mendoza, I'm glad you're okay." He said in a soft voice. "Where's Mr. White at, and what's he up too?"

"The last time I saw him, he was running all over the base like a stiff dick with no place to go, sir. No one was spared from his curses, or his wrath at the same time sir. He's really pissed off this time sir." She reported to her Commanding Officer.

This comment caused Campanelli to laugh slightly, as she continued on with her report. "I actually saw Lieutenant White give a kid a hop in the ass, because the soldier was leaning up against a stack of wood smoking a cigarette, and he was not helping out with the other soldiers to secure the damn base, sir. He's in a foul mood I'm afraid, sir."

"Good, I knew I could count on the two of you to pick up my slack for me, Lieutenant. Good work soldier." He replied to his female Lieutenant over the radio.

"Thanks Captain Campanelli Sir, you know you scared the hell out of me by acting like a madman yourself, sir. Running off to war like Gary fucking Cooper, sir. What the hell do you think you are, a damn kid or something sir? I was thinking of popping a cap in your ass myself sir, just to stop you and get you down. Are you okay sir?" She asked him.

"Yeah, I'm fine. I move too slow for any stinking bullet to hit my stinking ass." He laughed, relieved she was okay, and then he added. "I have to go, take care of my stinking base while I'm gone Lieutenant." With this, he broke off the communication.

The guard returned the headset to the front of the helicopter without speaking to the Captain.

The Lieutenant got the Captain's attention. "Your Lieutenant sounds rather excitable, sir."

"You got that right Lieutenant Gates. She's a real pain in the fucking ass lately sir." He replied to the young Marine Lieutenant.

"I'm damn glad they put that call through to the Intel center on the scramble system for you, Captain Campanelli Sir. So Command didn't monitor it on you sir. Or they would've really busted your horns over the personal call over the net sir. A love sick Captain in a stinking war zone sir. I though you were married or something like that, Captain?" Peter laughed slightly as he stared back at the concerned looking Captain.

He rubbed the side of his face as he replied to the young Marine Lieutenant. "Yeah, I'm married alright, but it's not working out the way it's supposed to work though. I'm getting rather tired of making love to her every damn time doggie style."

"Doggie style sir?" The young Lieutenant asked the Captain with some concern in his voice.

"Yeah, doggie style." He laughed over his own remark as he added to the Lieutenant. "Every night I have to sit up and beg, and my wife just rolls over and plays fucking dead on me, mister. I'm going to divorce her when I get back to the States. Then I'm going to marry this hot headed and blooded little Latino Lieutenant Mendoza pain in the ass, sir."

Both men laughed. It took the better part of an hour before the helicopter finally landed on the massive flight deck of the Roosevelt Aircraft Carrier. Both the Captain and Lieutenant were immediately led over to a waiting room while the Fleet Lieutenant made his report to the Commander first. Captain Campanelli tried to keep his arms down at his sides, because he underarms stunk that bad. After another hour passed, the captain was finally sent for and he made his report to Commander Owens.

"Phew." Was the first words spoken by the Commander. Commander Owens was angry as hell and he was also puzzled as the Captain was, as to why Chad would have sanctioned any such an attack aimed against the construction of the Dam, and the United States forces presently stationed there. Commander Owens informed Captain Campanelli he was going to find out the answers to that question even if he had to go to Chad to do so.

The exhausted Captain was led over to the same waiting room he was seated in moments before. Commander Owens quickly made a heated report back to the Chairman of the Joint Chiefs of Staff, and the President of the United States at the same time. The Commander was informed the United States was going to place a stern protest against Chad's government at the next Security Council Meeting at the United Nations.

Commander Owens again sent for Captain Campanelli as he was just ordered. Once he was inside the briefing room again, Commander Owens gave the Captain a little light blue box and said to him in a proud tone of voice. "Err… Captain Campanelli Sir, the President of the United States just ordered me to give you a fucking raise in rank, sir. It seems you have really impressed him by charging into battle like you did, sir. My Lieutenant informed me how you have setup your G 2 unit, and how your men will follow you to hell and back if you asked them to, sir. That's the best any god damn Officers could possibly ask for from their troops, sir.

"Congratulations Lieutenant Colonel Edward Campanelli Sir, allow me be the first one to offer you a drink to help celebrate your rate increase, Colonel. I don't have the right rank, so it looks like you're going to have to use my old birds until you can get hold of the proper rank for yourself, sir. I know it's only a matter of time before you become a full bird Colonel anyway, so you might as well hang onto my Eagles, Captain Campanelli Sir. It'd make me proud if you'd indulge me in wearing my old birds, sir."

The two military officers toasted each other and then Commander Owens offered to the now Colonel Campanelli. "I'm having a number of new uniforms sent out to you at your base, sir. I guess you better get back to you command and see what the devil's going on over there, sir. It was a damn good report and a clean action and AAR (After Action

Report) you delivered as well sir. I wish you would've been a little more careful though with your actions, Colonel. I have a report there were seventeen Marines killed in this attack, sir. Tell your Marine Lieutenant he'll receive the extra ten choppers he has requested also, sir. I'm sorry I didn't have the time to speak with the young man. You better leave so my chopper can get back here before dark, sir."

The new Lieutenant Colonel was led back to the waiting Marine Lieutenant, and then both officers were taken back to the spooling helicopter, which took off the instant they were on board and strapped in their seats. The chopper took over an hour to get out to Campanelli's base. But before it landed, the new Colonel instructed the pilot to make a pass over the war zone. He was amazed at the amount of damage done to the once lush and heavy growth jungle by the wing of attack aircraft in less than an hour of time. Worse yet, the amount of destruction just twelve aircraft could do during a support operation period.

The new Colonel easily picked up a number of Marines picking over a few bodies of the attackers, and they were not being very kind to the bodies either. The Seabee's had one of their massive bulldozers moved in, and it was busy digging a large grave site in the battlefield, and the enemy bodies were unceremonially being thrown into the open pit.

The helicopter landed and Colonel Campanelli was immediately met by Lieutenant Mendoza. He hurried over to his tent, and he took himself a good shot of rye. Then he turned and found himself staring right into the eyes of the very angry looking Mendoza.

"I have a bone to pick over with you, err... Captain Sir." Lieutenant Mendoza hissed in an angry tone of voice as she crossed her arms over her chest, and then she openly glared harshly at her Commanding Officer.

"Hey baby, don't give me any more of that Captain shit if you don't mind. It's Lieutenant Colonel to you from now on baby." He retorted proudly to his female Lieutenant while wearing a huge grin on his lips.

Lieutenant Renee Mendoza forgot about her anger, and she instantly wrapped her arms around his neck, almost pulling the new Lieutenant Colonel down to the ground as she kissed him.

"Calm down some will you please baby. You're killing me here honey. Give me a fucking chance to breathe will ya please." He cried to her.

"Oh, I'm so damn happy Command finally saw you're better than just a mere Captain, Sir." She cried as she continued to kiss the captain all over his face and neck now.

"Never mind that shit for the time being Maz. What the hell's the status of the fricking base? How many troopers did we lose in the damn fighting? And how many stinking attackers were involved on the god damn attack carried out against us, Lieutenant? Did any of the stinking civilians get hurt or killed during the fucking attack, and did the fucking mud jumpers check out the area for any possible booby traps and planted mines left behind the retreating bastards?"

"Colonel Campanelli, we lost fourteen soldiers assigned to the protection of our base sir, and the Marines have lost twenty one other soldiers, sir. All the numbers aren't in as of yet, so it could go a little higher on us once the final tally is completed, sir. We have four soldiers in critical condition, and nine others with wounds ranging from a scratch, to one soldier getting hit twice in the backside, sir. The nine wounded soldiers aren't serious though, sir. The Marines have twelve troopers in critical condition at this present time, and another five not so bad off.

"As of this time, there are no reported civilians hurt or killed during the unprovoked attack, and the Marines have already secured the entire construction area for us, sir. The Marines have placed two of their tanks on ready standby by the working area for protection of the civilian workers at all times, and I have placed a squad of ten extra soldiers there to watch over this construction area, and to help better protect the damn civilian workers on the site, sir. I think we got off rather lucky this time around sir. I don't think we should let our guard down for a stinking second as long as we're stuck out here, sir."

"I hear you loud and clear there young lady, and from here on out for the duration of this god damn construction project these orders will remain in effect, Lieutenant. I want all the fucking guards out around the damn clock during any work on the fucking Dam is going on, Lieutenant Mendoza. We can ill afford to have another such fucking attack aimed against us or the damn civilian workers without being well prepared for it the next time around, dammit. We'll now be on a yellow alert for the entire duration that we're stuck here on this fucking miserable construction project. I happen to agree with you that we got off god damn lucky this time around Mendoza. But I assure you that I'll be much better prepared for the next attack though if and when it comes against us, Lieutenant."

CHAPTER 13

At a special meeting of the Security Council presently being convened in which the nations of the United States, Ethiopia and the Sudan Representatives, filed stern protests against the nation of Chad for its reported attack on Ethiopian territory, and the United States workers stationed on the Dam project in Ethiopia. The meeting was rather uneventful because Chad claimed no knowledge of the attack whatsoever. Nevertheless, it caused rather strained feelings between the United States and Chad. America ordered a stop to all their arms shipments out to the tiny country of Chad as punishment for the attack, and Congress met in an attempt to cut off all monetary aid to that nation at this time, until it was determined if Chad was truly behind the attack on the soldiers and workers in Ethiopia.

At a closed door meeting being held between Libyan Ambassadors Kamal and Egyptian Ambassador Mohammed Kheir. It was decided the attack carried out by the Libyan operatives in Ethiopia caused the desired effect, undermining of Chad's creditability with the rest of the world. The two politicians discussed the feasibility of the next assault. Both men decided the next strike should occur in Sudan, involving the Iranian troops training the Sudanese military. They would stage an attack using the Sacred Brotherhood of Ali a second time. Their loss of men in this attack, made the members of the Muslim radical group more angry and willing to attack again.

Libyan Ambassador Kamal grumbled angrily. "We'll have the attackers on this next mission to also dress in Chad military uniforms again, and set the date for the next attack to take place sometime early in May." He wanted to use May, because of the span of time between the attacks, would give enough time for most militaries to have relaxed their defenses.

Mohammed suggested May 10th should be the date to go on. Ambassador Kamal allowed him to have his way this time around, because on the next scheduled attack and where and when this one was to take place. The third attack would take place and it was going to happen the way he decided it would happen, whether he liked it or not. Ambassador Kamal reached out his hand to Ambassador Mohammed Kheir, who took it and then the both of them shook hands in complete agreement this time around.

"You see Mohammed, we can get along when we keep our country's best interests in mind, as I have always thought we could sir."

"I always have only my country's best interest in mind in any decision I make, or live by Ambassador Kamal Sir." Ambassador Mohammed Kheir hissed angrily at the Libyan Delegate.

"Perhaps you do at that sir." Kamal sneered as he turned and he left Mohammed's office.

The exhausted Egyptian Ambassador sat back in his chair and then he took a quick breath for himself. He hated Ambassador Kamal with a real passion. He reached for the phone to place a call to inform President Sadat of his latest meeting with the always upsetting Libyan politician, and the attack date they have decided on today.

THE EASY MONEY BASE, LAKE TANA, ETHIOPIA

It took the Navy Seabees a week to bulldoze over all the damage that the attacking aircraft had caused to the area. The Seabees also leveled the jungle three hundred yards out in all directions from the Dam project, and also expanded the military base. This action gave the protecting soldiers more reaction time in case of another attack aimed against them, and it would bring the attackers out in the open before they could do any real damage to the Dam, or kill any civilian workers on the site. The Marines were forced further into the jungle to get their cover back.

Lieutenant John White was involved with his troopers, and he did not see his Commanding Officer for at least two days. At his first chance, he when over to Campanelli's tent. The Colonel was sitting on his bunk sharing a beer with a topless and grinning and happy Lieutenant Mendoza. She kept the new Colonel advised of all John's actions all the while he was working with the soldiers.

Lieutenant White gave Lieutenant Mendoza a quick glance as he reported to his Commander. "Captain, I have most of my troops dug in real well, and one out of two will be at the ready for an attack at all times while they man the perimeter wire, sir. I also laid out a number of small arms munitions dumps buried beneath the sand at the best possible locations for their need. Just in case any of my people get cut off during a possible attack, they'll still be able to get at some ammunition and weapons, sir. Also I set up some..."

Lieutenant Renee Mendoza cut in on his report as she struggled into her shirt. "Hold on there for a second will you please, John. I'm afraid from now on, I think you had better address the Lieutenant Colonel by his proper rank around here, sir. Then you better sit down and have yourself a stinking beer or two, to wash away the bitter taste it's going to leave in your mouth, mista. Now that you have to suck up to a half bird crippled Colonel from now on, sir."

John bent his head a little forward out so he could see the Eagles pinned on Campanelli's collar and then he complained. "Sonofabitch, I don't believe this crap for a stinking minute!" He said as he reached out and pulled Campanelli to his feet, and then he placed him in a breath taking bear hug, almost squeezing the air out of his lungs as he went on with his words. "Sonofabitch. Whaddaya mean by that, does this mean I gots tuh salute your lily white ass twice or something, my friend?

Sonofabitch. I'm damn glad someone at Command finally used their stinking head for more than a damn hat rack. Congratulations prick."

John released his grasp of Campanelli's chest, causing him to take a breath to get air back in his lungs as John offered his hand. The Colonel knew better than to put his hand in John's, more than once he was trapped in his bone crushing handshake, suffering the effects for the day. He slapped John's hand away as Mendoza came over with a beer.

As John took the beer he asked. "Why the hell didn't you tell me he got a stinking raise in rank for Pete's sake? Look at you, a fucking chicken ass stinking Colonel. Who woulda ever believed this possible after all these stinking years? Sonofabitch."

Colonel Campanelli roared with laughter as he threw a half empty beer at the back of the huge and retreating man as he ordered him. "Get your black ass the hell outta my fucking tent, and remember this, buster. The next time you have to come in here, you better take off your damn shoes so you don't dirty up my fucking tent any on me, Lieutenant."

John smirked back at his lifelong friend. "Yeah sure, and I'll take a damn shower too and wash behind my ears and brush my damn teeth too." John laughed as he made like he was walking like Igor from Frankenstein as he called out. "Yesum Masur, I gots tuh git backs to my wurk. Rulz iz rulzs yew. Don't gets the whip out, I's do u work without you beat me again Masur." He limped out the tent. Causing all three friends to howl with laughter.

Once John was out of the tent and ear shot, Lieutenant Mendoza remarked to the new Colonel. "You know that man really loves you sir."

"Don't you think I know that, and he knows I love him as well. I feel great my most important Officers love me. But I'm damn glad one of them loves me in a different way." He grumbled as he pulled Mendoza close to him and he kissed her on the forehead.

"No you don't buster! You're not going to get my motor started on me again, and then leave me flat and in heat. Just because you don't have to work any longer for your pay around here, doesn't mean us poor peons don't have to still work for our pay, sir. I have troops I need to check on, as well as a pile of paperwork I have to catch up on over that attack against us, sir. I don't intend to fuck you now, and then have to do my work while dripping and wet all day long, mista. Tonight we'll have time to enjoy our little fun and games, sir." She kissed him as he grabbed for her breasts with both his hands now.

"I said no, and no it is you hot blooded Italian you. Go jump into that cold lake, it should get you out of the mood but fast, sir. Congratulations against honey, you deserve the rate increase, you worked for it sir." She said as she put her over shirt on.

"Thanks a lot Maz, but what the hell good does it do for me to be a god damn Colonel around here. When I can't even order my people to stay here and do my bidding for me. I'm the damn Colonel, and yet you still don't pay any attention to me or my orders, young lady."

"If you're so damn horny then why don't you try and take your pen in hand, and take care of yourself for a change, sir?" She taunted as she left the tent to his calling out. "Fuck you."

"I know that's what you want to do buster, and I said no, didn't I Colonel Sir." She snapped.

The passing days went by without many problems for Colonel Campanelli to handle at the worksite, and no further trouble from the Marines or the local population either. The Colonel left his stuffy tent, and he noticed Lieutenant Mendoza leading her troops through some exercise. He looked in the direction of the Dam, the walls were one hundred feet high, and the generators were already set in place. Within the next week or so, the first phase of the construction would be completed, and they would start diverting some of the water from its original flow. The Dam would then become operational to an extent. They would start producing electricity and use the wedge to divert some water down the man made waterway they had carved deeply into the earth, and head it down into the great Afar Depression, from there the water would follow a natural path to the Desert of Arerge Hererge region of Ethiopia.

The construction of the Dam was at least a full month ahead of schedule already, and Colonel Campanelli looked forward to the day when the water would start flowing down the ravine the Seabees had cut deep in the earth down to the Afar Depression area. The Seabees massive Caterpillar bulldozers worked around the clock, moving millions of square yards of earth in order to make a natural flow for the water to follow.

In his heart, he understood the nation of Ethiopia was going to need the entire flow of the water coming from Lake Tana, to accomplish the feat they were trying to accomplish. He also realized when the water was cut off from the Nile River, the Nile's flow was going to be cut down by over fifty percent of its usual flow. He figured within seven years, the one hundred and twenty seven million acre of water forming the three hundred mile reservoir created with the completion of the Aswan High Dam, would be used up and the Dam would be rendered useless after that time for the sake of Egypt.

Campanelli feared what would happen to the world, if Egypt was forced to fight for her life giving water, he knew Egypt would fight. He was worried about how many other Arab countries Egypt would draw into the conflict on her side if war was released on the earth again. He sent a memo out to the Chairman of the Joint Chiefs of Staff General Weidenbacher, outlining his fears of what he sees coming in the near future, but he never got a response, or follow up from it.

The Colonel watched the civilian workers the day before as his engineers moved the massive wedge shape concrete slab that would force more of the water from Lake Tana into the trench. The concrete groaned in anger at being dragged across the rough concrete surface without any water to use to lubricate the friction for it. He looked at the sun and he figured it must be around noontime, his watched read eleven ten, and the day was April 17th, 1996. He went to his intelligence tent, and told the Lieutenant to get Fleet Command on the horn.

"Colonel Campanelli Sir, I was just about to come out and look for you sir. I have a scrambled message which was to come in from the CIC chamber in ten minutes, sir. You'll need your key to retrieve the secured message so you can read it, sir."

"Shit, I have to go get the damn thing first, mister. I keep forgetting to carry the damn thing with me all the time, dammit." He ran for his tent and opened his safe and removed the key, and then he jogged back to the Intel Post. He showed up carrying the key to show the young and new Lieutenant and immediately pointed towards a decipher machine.

"Colonel Campanelli Sir, you have to insert your key here, near the bottom of the typewriter, and then the report will be automatically typed out by the machine for you, sir."

Campanelli set the key in place and turned it. Immediately, the machine began to type a message, scaring him in the process. The machine was typing faster than he could possible read the report, so he waited until the report was finished by the machine.

The Lieutenant left the tent to giving the new Colonel the privacy he needed to review the report, and he stood outside in case he was needed by the Colonel for any reason.

Another machine started operating, and when he turned and looked at this machine, he noticed pictures being feed out this time. He took at the first one and carefully studied it, it showed many men working in a desert. It looked like the workers were setting some kind of cans in the sand, and then covering them over. The Colonel looked at the rather scratchy shapes on the poorly made pictures with a magnifying glass. The shapes looked like some kind of cans to him and he could not understand the concern over the harmless looking items.

The decipher machine stopped printing and the Colonel quickly read the first of five pages of the report and it started off. 'This is one of the Egyptian units working in the Sinai Desert on their search for a new source of water. Supposedly, they're searching for water in this region. From the looks of picture five, the cans they're placing in the sands could be some form of seismograph charges, sometimes used for locating a liquid hidden under the earth. But on closer examination, our brain thrust think that these items might some sort of a mine, or other type of explosive device being planted for some future use. Most scientists disagree with this summary, they seem to believe the cans are seismograph charges used in the search for water.

'The Israeli government doesn't have any access to this information, because we feel if the Israeli's saw these pictures. They'd probably fear it was a serious threat to their security, and they would bomb the worksite and killing all the Egyptian workers, and start a shooting war between the nations of Israel and Egypt. We're requesting you ask for special permission from the Egyptians to visit one of these so called work units, and remain in the area for a week or more, if you feel the need to gather more information of their supposed project. We'll send you a mine detector system that you can employ without being discovered by the workers.

"We were lead to believe you will receive permission from the Egyptian government to go out with one of these work units by merely requesting to do so, Colonel Campanelli. You're to place a call to Ambassador Mohammed Kheir in Egypt. The phone number is printed below, he'll make it possible for you to go out with the unit. You are to take one fellow Officer along with you to the Egyptian worksite. Ambassador Mohammed Kheir is classified as a friend to the United States, and you'll treat him as such with the greatest of respect at all times.

'Once you have completed your orders, you'll then report your findings directly to Fleet Command immediately, sir. We have to know what the Egyptian workers are up to in the Sinai Desert. Remember, you're a representative of the United States government, so act accordingly Colonel Campanelli. End of communication.'

The Colonel looked at pictures, and all of them showed the Egyptian workers burying a canister of some type. After studying the photos a little closer, he picked up a number of workers burying some kind of strips in the sand also. He looked at this picture under the magnifying glass. It looked like a traction strip of some kind and he mumbled. "Maybe the trucks were having some trouble getting around on the soft sand and they need this crap to help them?" He mumbled to himself after looking at the picture long enough, he felt sure the workers were retrieving the strip, instead of installing them in the sand and leaving them. He reasoned after a truck was probably stuck in the sand, they decided to use this strip as a traction mat to get the truck out, and he merely shrugged off the picture as of little further concern at this point.

Colonel Edward Campanelli called in the young Lieutenant after he placed the report in the flash can and watched it burn to ash. He informed him to setup the phone for a long distance call. The Lieutenant quickly fumbled around with a couple of switches and in seconds he told Colonel Campanelli the line was ready for his use.

The Army Colonel quickly dialed the number he copied down from the report and after three rings, a sweet sounding Egyptian female voice answered the phone. He noticed she had an unusual accent for an Egyptian, and he instantly tried to place it as he asked her to speak with Ambassador Mohammed Kheir. She asked Colonel Campanelli to identify himself for her.

The Colonel quickly introduced himself to her and she replied politely. "Please hold the line while I transfer your call over to Ambassador Mohammed Kheir, sir."

A second later a husky voice said. "Ambassador Kheir, what can I do for you Colonel?"

"Ambassador Mohammed Kheir Sir, how are you today sir? The reason I have placed this call to you today, is because I was just requested by my government to ask your special permission to go along with one of your work units into the Sinai Desert, to observe what they're doing in the desert and see if they have had any success in discovering any water on their toils, Ambassador Mohammed Kheir Sir. My government would like me to observe your operation in person, to see if I could put some of your methods to use in our country, and to also see if some of our methods could be beneficial to your operation at the same time, Ambassador Sir." He offered to the well liked Egyptian politician.

"It does my heart good to see the Americans are open minded enough to say they might learn something from the Egyptian people. I can arrange for you to go with one of my units, Popeye."

Colonel Campanelli was slightly taken back by this Arab politician knowing of his nickname as he replied. "Sir I believe you might have me at a slight disadvantage here I see sir. Do we know each other Ambassador Kheir Sir?"

"I see you have a short memory I fear Captain Campanelli Sir. Yes, we know each other, we had met once a long time ago in a small bar in your Manhattan City, sir. I believe it was around four years ago if I am not mistaken sir. You almost took my head off of my shoulders because I wanted the Dodgers to beat your Mets baseball team in the bar, sir. After you finally calmed down a little, you offered to buy me a drink which you did and we really enjoyed the rest of the ballgame together, Captain Sir. We both got a little more than drunk that night I'm afraid, and I thank you very much for it, sir." He explained happily to the military officer.

Colonel Campanelli quickly searched his memory, but he could not place the man's face, or the incident as he offered to the Egyptian politician. "I'm terribly sorry Ambassador Kheir Sir, but you still have me at a slight disadvantage, sir. I musta gotten really drunk that night, because I don't remember you or the bar or the incident, sir."

The Egyptian politician laughed as he added with a smile. "Don't feel bad about not remembering me, Captain. Because I would not have remember you either, sir. If I wasn't privy to some certain reports I recently read concerning you, Captain. In these reports, you were referred to as Popeye, and that made me remember you and your nickname, sir. It must've been terrible for you to be attacked by a supposed ally to your country without any warning, sir."

"I'm sorry sir, but that's politics, and I stay far away from politics as I can, Ambassador Kheir Sir. I'm a soldier just doing my job sir. I leave the rest of it to people like yourself, sir."

Colonel Campanelli's honesty made Ambassador Mohammed Kheir laugh a little, and he knew exactly why he felt so comfortable with this man and he said. "Captain Campanelli Sir, could you possibly be here by say tomorrow morning at the earliest, sir? I have a work unit scheduled to head out into the Sinai Desert a little after that time, sir. I can hold them back for a little longer until your arrival here in Egypt, Captain Campanelli Sir."

The Colonel allowed the slip of being called a Captain by the Egyptian politician slide as he replied to the Ambassador. "Yes Sir Mr. Ambassador Sir. I certain I can be there by morning's light sir. Can I bring a second Officer along with me as well, sir?"

"Yes, you can bring as many people as you want to take along with you on your visit to my country, sir. We have nothing to hide from our friends, sir."

The two men said their good-byes after Mohammed told the Colonel where to land his plane.

The night went by rather quickly, and Colonel Campanelli and Lieutenant Mendoza did not very sleep much. She was up well before the Colonel and got him something to eat and drink from the mess. She was going to fly the small aircraft because she was a good pilot, and fleet sent a T 2 Buckeye aircraft used more as a training plane than attack aircraft. Unarmed, this plane did not look anything like a military aircraft, the Carrier used this aircraft for a special spotter or recon craft. The small aircraft had plenty of fuel to get from Ethiopia to Egypt. It would have to be refueled in Egypt for her return flight to the base.

Lieutenant Renee Mendoza took a knapsack out to the plane as Colonel Campanelli ate. She, as all pilots usually do, checked out her aircraft carefully as she waited for the colonel to finish his breakfast. Mendoza loved flying, and it was good for her to get back in the chair.

She was starting to get a little impatient, because she longed to be back in the clouds again.

Colonel Campanelli came out of the tent, but instead on coming directly over to the waiting plane. He walked over to a parked blade bulldozer. The female Lieutenant watched as he unzipped his fly and took a leak on the machine's heavy tracks.

She laughed because he was such an uncouth bastard because he did not even turn away from her sight as he pissed on the ground. So she clapped her hands and whistle as he finished.

The new Colonel turned and looked at her and he also laughed as he shook himself vigorously before putting himself back in his pants. But still, no matter how hard he shook himself off, he always seemed to had those last few drops remaining to wet the front of his pants which made him curse and get angry at himself. He then walked over to Mendoza as she kicked the tires of the small plane one last time for good luck. She also checked the front windshield to make certain it wasn't bug splattered.

"Are you ready to get going mister?" Lieutenant Mendoza complained at him angrily.

"Oh, were you waiting for me? You should've told me to shake a leg."

"I thought that was what you were doing when you were shaking your dick like you wanted it to fall off ya." She replied with a smirk.

"Ha ha, very funny little sister." He retorted as he headed up the ladder.

Maz planted a loud slap on his rump, causing him to jump up a step and he looked back at her and complained. "Next time, you get in first so I can return the favor."

"I saw you shaking a leg out there and it wasn't a very pretty sight I don't want to see for a second time. And what are you going to do then if I went first, climb over me in order to get in the rear seat of the damn aircraft, mister? Or do you plan on flying this baby bird all by yourself, Colonel?" She replied back at her lover.

"I probably could fly the damn thing a whole lot better than you can, little Miss Wiseass."

"Hey baby, don't let those little birds you have pinned on your collar go to your head, Colonel Confident. Remember, those birds don't fly with just one wing, mista." She warned, and the both of them laughed as she started the engine of the aircraft.

"I know why you made me get in first, you like to look at my ass climbing up the damn ladder, little sister. I'm just a sex object to you, right Maz?"

"You better stop looking at yourself in the mirror so damn much lately Colonel. I believe you're starting to fall in love with yourself, sir."

The takeoff was smooth and the Colonel sat back in the padded seat and relaxed as best as he could, as he listened as Mendoza humm as she worked the controls of the small aircraft. He really hated flying and he was scared to death as he refused to look out of the cockpit, and he asked his female pilot. "You really like flying, huh baby?"

"I just love it, how about you Edward?" She asked of her Commanding Officer.

"I hate fucking flying with a damn passion but I can take it or leave it. Mostly leave it I guess. I like my fucking feet sitting flat on the damn ground, I feel I'd have a much better chance of living down here. I guess I'll always be a damn foot soldier, honey."

"Edward, I've been going over that attack of last week sir, and the more I think about it sir. The more I can't see any logical reason for the attack to be aimed against our base, sir."

"How's that Mendoza?" The Colonel asked her with some concern lacing his tone.

"What the hell were the damn attackers going after in the first place to cause them to attack us like their did, sir? They had to have known they were in a no win situation by attacking our heavily defended base the way they tried to hit us sir. The asses were out gunned, and we had them out numbered forty to one, not counting the pain in the ass Seabees we have stationed on the base also, Colonel. Edward, say the attackers were able to drive us off the base even for a little while until our support units arrived. What the hell were they going to do then, sir? They didn't have enough explosives with them to cause even some minor damage to the Dam.

"Thinking about it a little further, I just can't make any sense of the damn hit, Edward. Another thing sticking in my craw, Edward. What the hell did Chad think she was going to get out of attacking us? It doesn't make any sense if you were to ask me, sir. The attack seems like it took place just to draw our attention away from another situation which didn't take place for some reason I don't understand, sir. That's the only logical solution I can come up with, Colonel. This attack was some sort of a diversion, and the second attack never took place. All I know is, whoever staged this mess, lost a hundred fighters for nothing, which makes for poor military judgment, and that scares me to death because they were so willing to throw away their soldiers this easy." She held her breath waiting for a reply from her Commanding Officer.

"You know something, I've been giving the attack a lot of thought myself, and I couldn't come up with a very logical reason for the attack to take place either Maz. I must say though, your scenario sounds about right to me, and I never looked at the attack in the same light as you have. I'll tell you what I'm going to do, I'm going to bring your thought up to Fleet Command when we get back to base, honey. Good work there Mendoza, it makes me understand why I keep asking for you whenever I'm sent out on another damn operation, Lieutenant."

She liked to be told she was right by her Commanding Officer, and again she started to humm. Her humming made the colonel relax some, he was having a hard time with flying.

The flight to Egypt took two hours to complete, and when the plane finally touched down, a number of Egyptian soldiers met them and brought them over to a waiting truck. Minutes later, the two American military officers were on their way out in the vast desert, and in an hour and a half of fast and wild driving, they hooked up with the Egyptian work unit. It was extremely hot, over a hundred and ten degrees and the sand actually burned through their shoes. A worker walked up to the Americans and stuck out his hand.

Campanelli shook hands as the Egyptian worker offered in a calm tone of voice. "Sir, my name is Abdul Tamimi, allow me show you our operation please."

Colonel Edward Campanelli followed the young Arab man as Lieutenant Renee Mendoza followed her orders, and she slowly drifted over to where a number of other the Arab men were working. The Colonel followed the Arab over to a rusting old and dilapidated command truck. Inside, the truck was air conditioned and spotlessly clean, and it was loaded down with many computer monitors, scopes and countless gauges. The Arab brought Campanelli's attention to an operating oscilloscope, and then he said to him. "Sir, we're about ready to set off a small charge. Please watch the scope if you will, sir."

The Colonel had no idea what he was looking at, but he did as he was told by the Arab worker.

There was a small explosion just outside the parked truck, and the disruption immediately showed up on the scope as a bunch of dancing lines going crazy. Soon, the lines calmed down until only one of them remained on the scope as a straight line, and the Egyptian worker added. "This is the second time we got a straight line in this area. It looks very good for water to us sir." The Arab laughed as he continued with his words for the American Officer. "Would not it be a kick in the ass if we were to come across oil resting under the ground by mistake, sir."

"Yeah, that's something to laugh about I guess. Finding oil that easily would be a good laugh, buddy" Suddenly, things made more sense as he thought this was a trick to cover up what these sonofabitches were really searching for in the desert, oil. All of a sudden the Egyptians did not look so stupid to him, and he realized it was a good ploy to cover up finding new oil deposits to keep the oil prices high. A big strike would drive oil prices through the roof.

The Colonel looked at the scope as the Egyptian worker called out some orders for the drilling team to setup their rig over the area where they just set off the small explosive on the sand. Then, Campanelli followed the middle aged Egyptian worker outside the truck, and he watched as the portable drilling rig was carefully backed up to the slight depression just made in the soft sand by the small explosion.

"What kind of charges are you using for the sounding test, sir?" Campanelli questioned him.

"Please allow me to show you if you don't mind, follow me sir." The Egyptian worker walked over to a second parked truck at a snail's pace and then he pulled the canvas away to expose a number of the metal canisters as he explained. "Each of these charges are equal to three sticks of TNT, Colonel sir. They're strong enough to reach three miles down into the earth's crust. Deep enough for our purposes and needs, sir."

Colonel Campanelli carefully looked at the small metal canisters, they looked a whole lot different than the ones he saw being buried in the sand on the satellite pictures a few days ago. He reached a little deeper into the truck and actually tried to pick up one of the items up. It was surprisingly light, the ones he saw in the pictures looked more heavy by the way the workers were struggling while carrying them to where they were burying them.

The Egyptian worker pulled the American Colonel's hand out of the truck and nearly growled at him angrily. "Please sir, I prefer that you don't touch any of them items, sir. We had a worker lose his hand when one of these charges went off accidentally."

The American Colonel allowed himself to be lead away from the truck with the charges stacked in the rear of the machine, and he was lead over to an area well away from the other workers, but he was still able to see everything he wanted to see that was going on in the area.

The operation looked legit enough to him by the way the Egyptians were working. It seemed the Egyptian workers were truly looking for water, or at least oil. The rest of the day was long, hot and extremely boring with not much more for him to observe. When the workers stopped for the day, to a man, they all marched over to the water truck and took showers. They gave no consideration to Lieutenant Mendoza's presence, and they showered in the buff while joking and laughing amongst themselves, as they enjoyed their refreshing showers.

Colonel Campanelli busied himself by walking around the worksite moving this can and looking under a canvas, and checking inside some of the other parked vehicles. As he checked a truck containing the charges, he heard a slight commotion over by the showers. "Mendoza." He mumbled and then headed right for the noise.

Some Egyptian workers were angry as hell about something as they waved their prayer books in the air, while others crouched on the sand while watching something and clapping their hands and grinning and enjoying themselves.

The Colonel hurried himself to the shower area and immediately saw Mendoza standing under the showering water, naked as the day she was born. He laughed as he mumbled out loud. "This fucking women's lib shit's going to be the fricking death of me yet, dammit."

Abdul Tamimi rushed over to the Colonel's side and actually began to pull on his arm as he said in a concerned and excited voice. "Sir, you have to stop her at once sir. We have a number of Muslim Fundamentalists who'll kill her for daring to expose herself to the men in this manner, sir. These men stick to the Arab ways, and I have no control over them. Please sir, you have to stop her for her own sake sir. Please hurry, or she could be killed for this terrible insult, sir."

Colonel Campanelli stomped over to the shower and stuck one of his paws in the flow of water and scooped up Mendoza, who kicked and cursed up a storm in Spanish at him.

Tamimi called out for the Colonel to follow him as he headed for a small tent. Campanelli was having a hard time trying to hold onto the wet and squirming and wildly kicking and cursing Mendoza. Many of the Arab workers clapped, while the hard-line Arabs continued to mumbled curses at the insolent young and very daring woman.

Once inside the tent, Tamimi made an excuse and left as fast as he could, because he too did not approve of women using such foul language and displaying her nakedness to the gathered workers outside. And Mendoza was obviously cursing up a storm inside the tent in different languages. Colonel Campanelli put Lieutenant Mendoza down and received a hard slap across the face for his trouble. Her eyes were ablaze as she hissed at her Commanding Officer harshly. "How dare you stop me from doing what I want to do, sir?"

Campanelli slowly rubbed the side of his face and said in an extremely angry tone to his female Lieutenant. "Mendoza, you can't go walking around in front of a bunch of fucking Arab bastards buck ass naked like you are, dammit. It goes against their stinking religious beliefs, you could've gotten your ass killed you know for Christ sake."

She was not to be calmed down that easily as she growled back at her Commander. "If I can't go around naked then neither can they, sir. In case you hadn't heard about it yet, Lincoln freed the fucking slaves, and women are supposed to be equal to you self centered bastard males. I'll be damned to hell if I'll ever allow these damn rag head pricks stop me from doing what I want to do, sir." She glared at the Colonel, and placed her hands on her hips.

"Mendoza, you don't have to go through the damn speech for me again. I know all about your fighting spirit, but you have to remember where you are, dammit. I guess you have to eat some shit like the rest of us bastards, back off some while I calm down the damn Arabs and get you your stinking clothes back for you. Where did you leave the damn things?"

"They're hanging on the side of the water tanker. If the rag heads didn't steal them on me."

Campanelli grunted as he went out to retrieve her clothes, many of the Egyptian workers were still laughing and hanging around as he walked by them, causing him to smile back at them. He found Mendoza's clothes where she said they were, all except for her underpants, he figured they were in some Arab's pocket, who would concocted some wild cock n bullshit story on how he conquered a westerner and took her panties for a trophy.

In minutes he was back in the tent and he threw Mendoza her clothes. She looked for her underpants and when she could not find them, she looked at him who shrugged at her stare.

Neither officer wore a military uniform. Command felt it would be less threatening to the Arabs for the two officers to be dressed in their military uniforms.

She dressed quickly, and then Campanelli said in a commanding voice. "Let's go get ourselves something to eat."

Mendoza followed Colonel Campanelli over to a tent where they sat down, and an Egyptian man brought them some food, everything the Colonel ate or drank had sand mixed in with it. Many of the Egyptian workers leered at Lieutenant Mendoza who glared back at them harshly. Campanelli had to actually grab her arm, or she would have planted one of the bastard right where he stood grinning at her. She looked around and noticed some Arab workers staring at her. She turned to the Colonel who said to her. "Well what the hell did you expect from them after running around in front of them bare ass naked." He smiled at the now blushing Mendoza.

She regrouped quickly and replied angrily. "What the hell gives them the damn right to run around naked, and yet I'm not allowed to sir. It's all bullshit if you ask me, sir."

"Perhaps, but we're in their damn country and these are the fucking laws, Mendoza. When in Rome." Campanelli shrugged and then smirked at her.

Their conversation was cut short by a messenger looking for them, and he came right over to their table. He told Colonel Campanelli that Ambassador Mohammed Kheir requested their presence for dinner, and he was sent to fetch them and bring them back to Cairo.

It took over three hours to reach Cairo in the air conditioned truck from the desert, once there, the two American officers were led to a private office. There, Ambassador Kheir sat behind his massive antique desk. He immediately stood and offered his hand, as they walked into the office. "It seems your presence at the worksite has caused a bit of a stir I was informed, young lady." He said as he held onto Mendoza's hand and looked her deep in the eyes.

She blushed, and Mohammed noticed her embarrassment and offered to her to take the sting out of his last words. "Nothing happens in Egypt without my knowing of it, young woman. Sometimes it's good to stir the blood of my foul and lazy workers up on them once in a while, and from what I was led to believe, you have accomplished this feat for me vastly, young woman." Mohammed then turned to Colonel Campanelli and offered to him.

"So this is the great Popeye I have heard so much about lately, sir. You have quite a following here in Egypt, I don't mind tell you sir. Anytime you get tired of working for your government and want a change in your life sir. I'd deem it a great pleasure to find you a place with mine. You are twice welcome here in the name of Allah, sir."

"Fraid not sir, you know the old saying. 'Once a soldier, always a soldier sir.' But I'm rather impressed with the fine efforts of your people looking for water out in the desert, sir. I was told you have three producing water wells already, Ambassador Kheir Sir." Colonel Campanelli replied to the Egyptian politician politely.

"Captain Campanelli Sir, I fear you might be slightly mistaken here sir. We have nine water producing wells to date, sir. Three of them will produce three thousand gallons of water an hour, sir. If we find more wells with such great yields. Perhaps, and if it's the will of Allah, we'll not miss the water the Ethiopians will take from the Blue Nile River and Egypt. Please enjoy my hospitality while you're visiting my country, sir." He offered proudly.

"Sir, I don't mean to correct you, but I got a raise recently. I'm now a Lieutenant Colonel, sir."

Ambassador Mohammed Kheir smiled as he bowed politely towards the new American Colonel, and then he swung his right hand out and down towards the floor in a sweeping motion. The champagne finally came in and Mohammed took a glass and then offered his congratulations as he toasted the two American Officers. He put his glass down as he said. "I have offered you dinner, shall we go and enjoy a meal together please? I have many delights to shower upon each of you with the great foods I shall offer you."

The trio left the Ambassador's private office together. Campanelli leaned close and whispered to Mohammed Kheir. "Sir, I thought you Egyptians weren't allowed to drink any stinking booze, Ambassador Mohammed Sir?"

Ambassador Kheir smiled proudly as he recited the old American phrase he once heard while visiting a military base back in the United States after he used one of his phases. "There is an old saying here in Egypt, Colonel Campanelli Sir. 'Do not throw stones into a well that you drink from'. But even here in Egypt, rank does have its privileges Colonel Campanelli Sir."

They entered the overcrowded restaurant and the two Americans allowed Mohammed to order the dinners for them, and while waiting he asked the Colonel how they found the work unit in the Sinai Desert, and the work being conducted in the desert.

"As I said before Ambassador Kheir, I was extremely impressed by what I was seeing accomplished by your workers. I don't think there's anything we could improve on I noticed sir. Your workers are doing a great job. They're effective and there is little wasted motion out there. But it was hot, and I give the workers credit for taking the heat as well as they were doing."

"You're most kind Colonel Campanelli Sir. It's good to hear my workers are doing such a good job, sir. Especially coming from an American, makes the compliment all that much more important to me, Colonel Campanelli. May I ask how long you intend to stay in my country for this visit, sir? You're more than welcome to stay and enjoy my hospitality for as long as you wish, sir." He said with graciousness to the Colonel.

"Ambassador Kheir, I planned to stay with your unit for a few days to see if I could offer them any possible improvements to their operation, but I see no need to do this, sir. Since you took me out of the desert, and I see no improvements I can possible offer, there's no reason for me to return. I guess we'll takeoff tomorrow morning sometime for my base if you don't mind, sir."

"Such a short visit from a dear friend. You're more than welcome to stay longer if you so choose, Colonel Campanelli. I shall make arrangements for a private room to be placed at your disposal at the Cairo Hilton, right on the very shore of the sacred Nile River, sir. The room will be yours for as long as you desire to stay in Egypt, Colonel Sir."

Mohammed looked at Mendoza and he offered her in a very polite tone of voice. "I beg your pardon Ma'am. I shall make two rooms available for your stay in my country. It was most inconsiderate for me to just assume you'd be sharing a room together with the Colonel."

Again she blushed, but she wanted to tell this Arab to go and fuck himself. Something about this Egyptian politician bugged the devil out of her, but she could not place her finger on what it was. She suddenly realized she did not trust the man.

They ate and talked sparingly and after they were finished with their meals, the Egyptian told the two American Officers that he had other engagements he must attend to, and offered a taxi to be placed at the Americans disposal, and he left them sitting in the restaurant.

"Let's go for a little walk along the shore of the river, Edward." She suggested with a grin and begging eyes as she looked at her lover and soldier.

They got up and went outside. A cab driver sitting on the sand, immediately jumped to his feet when he saw the two Americans emerge from the restaurant and he cried in broken English. "Sir, this is you cab for night. I shall drive you where you wish to visit, sir."

The two American Officers got in the cab and told the driver to head for the river's edge.

"Sir, I can get you into the Pyramids if you care to visit them tonight that is, sir. I have special permission to allow you to enjoy them all by yourselves." The driver suggested.

"No thanks pal, I just want to take a little walk along the damn Nile River edge." He replied, he had no doubt this driver understood English better than he was letting on. He was positive the man was put at their disposal, so he could keep a close eye on them and also listen to their conversations and then reported to Mohammed over what he hear and observed.

It took fifteen minutes for the cab to reach the river's bank. The ride was constantly disrupted by the driver's consistent beeping of his horn. Gunning the engine and popping the clutch, and forcing the old and beat up BMW to bounce and buck, and the countless angry curses in Egyptian he yelled at the other drivers on the road. Their Egyptian driver completely ignored the traffic lights, or the pedestrians walking alongside the road, or pushing carts across the crowded street at their own risk. Colonel Campanelli could swear his driver even went after a walker, just because he tried to cross the street in front of the cab, making the trip anything but enjoyable for them. Once, his driver even jumped the curb, and actually rode along the sidewalk to get around a slower moving car, a number of shop owners threw debris at their cab, as it quickly sped away at breakneck speed. The drive was sheer mayhem at its best.

The Colonel felt the driver took a long way to get down to the river's edge. He got out of the cab first, followed by Mendoza. Campanelli put his hand out and helped her out of the cab. They walked hand and hand along the sandy bank. He happened to look over his shoulder twice, and noticed the driver slowly following them in his cab on the street, so he led Mendoza closer to the waters and further away from their trailing shadow. When he felt he was out of ear shot of their driver, he asked Mendoza what she felt about the events of the day.

"While you were with that Arab guy who caused all the trouble for us. I afraid I already forget his name, I walked around the work base. A few workers bumped into me I felt on purpose, and at least one of the dirty little bastards actually grabbed a handful of my ass as he passed by me. But I guess that's all part of the job I take it, sir. I checked out a lot of the trucks they had parked at the worksite, and I didn't find anything I thought was suspicious, Edward. I didn't notice any of the workers doing anything wrong or even shady, and no one tried to stop me from looking in or at anything I wanted to see or look at, sir. I noticed a miniature video camera box with a fiber optic coil of wire though. I have no idea what the Egyptian workers would be doing with this type of camera equipment out on a supposed search for water.

"I seriously doubt if they were laying out any sort of intelligence net in the desert for any reason, what the devil would they possibly need it for Colonel? I'm kind of inclined to believe the case was more than likely stolen from someone, and it was being used to carry someone's personal gear around in it while they were working in the desert, sir. This case was the only thing I found a little out of place that made me a little suspicious about the Egyptian workers and what they might be doing out here in the desert, sir."

"Yeah Maz, I didn't find anything out of the ordinary either, but yet they had an awful lot of computer equipment around to be needed for looking for just water. Mendoza, I was thinking about something, let me run this by you and see what you think about my thoughts, honey. If you went into a desert, say looking for oil instead of fucking water, wouldn't you want to keep it under wraps for as long as you possibly could keep it?"

"Why do that Edward? I'd think they'd want to let the world know they were looking for, or finding new oil deposits. Why would they want to hide the fact that they found some oil?"

"C'mon Mendoza and think about it for a few seconds will ya for Pete's sake. If you had any possible inside information on where a new cache of oil was, and you wanted to go out and look for it, yet you didn't want the world to know what you were doing until you were certain the oil was where you thought it was. What better fucking way to do it then by announcing to the world that you were only out looking for some god damn water."

"Why would they want to hide it though? I still don't understand that." She repeated to him.

CHAPTER 14

Jesus Maz, think about it for a second will ya please. If you knew where oil was sitting, you'd want to keep it as quiet as possible for as long as you can. Why you might ask me? Because if you let the world know of your discovery, it'd cause world prices for oil to plummet, and also take away massive amounts of money the Egyptians would get for the new oil find. Remember what happened in Russia when they let out that bogus bullshit story about discovering the largest find of oil ever to be located on the face of the earth. The oil price fell for the next four days straight, causing pure hell for the stock markets at the same time, honey. I think if the stinking Egyptians know where a new oil deposit is, and they're setting up these damn supposed water wells to tap into it as quietly as possible. The next thing you know, those damn water trucks will be heading in the desert empty, and coming back to Cairo full of crude.

"The stinking Egyptians could then allow the new oil to find its way to the world's market in little dribs and drabs, and the world would never know they were paying higher prices for new oil, and there's no shortage in the damn market. Awe, some shit like this anyway I guess. Hell, I don't know how all the stinking economics work around here, dammit. All I know for certain is, if I found a rich new deposit of fucking crude oil in the stinking desert, I'd surely want to keep it quiet for as long as I possibly could. Whatdaya think baby?"

"I think you were out in the desert too long without a hat on, mista. I can't believe you thought up this crazy scenario all by yourself sir. What makes you think it's oil the Egyptians are after in the Sinai? You know once Ethiopia cut off Egypt's water, they're going to need other sources of it if they intend to have enough water for their people. Do you really think they can drink oil? No, I'm going to have to disagree with you on this one, Colonel. I'm not comfortable with this bull story about them looking for water either though. But I have to admit, I have no idea what else they would be up to in the desert." She replied as she looked at the Colonel.

"All I know is, I felt like they were being too damn nice to us, and everything was to fucking clean almost to sterile. Like they're trying to hide something, but then again, I remember they didn't stop me from looking anywhere I wanted to look. Look Edward, I don't know how to explain it. All I know is, I'm not buying this shit they're trying to sell me in the least. I think it was all just a show they gave us to hide their true intentions, and I fear them."

"Do you think we should spend a few more days here then? To see if we could discover anything they might be up to in the damn desert, Maz."

"No Colonel, I think it'd be a waste of our time, because if they're up to something they don't want us to know about, it might take us weeks to find out what it might be, sir. Besides, they wouldn't send us out with a unit working on a secret project. No, I think we went out with one of their units who were seriously looking for water, and that's why we didn't find anything out of place, sir. I wish we could get on a unit we weren't expected to be with."

"Fat chance of that happening. Look Maz, remember when the Israeli's checked out the two Egyptian work units a few weeks ago. They didn't find anything either. The Jews ended up killing a worker and wounding another, and the Egyptians didn't make a real big thing out of it. It seems they're looking for water or oil, not trouble I believe or want to believe that is."

"Colonel, since when wouldn't an Arab, any Arab for that matter not make a big deal out of an Israeli fuck up, sir. The Egyptians should have been crying like children who lost their favorite toy to the Security Council, or requesting help and protection from us, or from the other Arab nations of the Middle East, but they didn't. Like they're trying to hide something from all of us, sir. No, the more I think about it, the more I feel that there's something rotten in Denmark, sir." She warned the Colonel as she stared at him.

"Let me ask you this then Maz? What do you think we should tell Fleet tomorrow? I'm not at all comfortable with all we've seen, or didn't see for that matter, and I'm kinda inclined to agree with you and your thoughts. If they're up to something shitty in the desert, they sure as hell ain't going to let us in on it." He grumbled as they walked the river's edge.

"I have no idea what you're going to tell Command, and I care even less myself if you really want to know, Colonel. In case you don't know it, that's why you have those two little pigeons pinned on your shoulder, and I don't sir."

"Damn, you're a big help around here young lady." He grumbled at his new girlfriend.

They walked a mile from where the cab first let them off. The lights of Cairo brightened the night sky. Campanelli looked around and he spotted the taxi parked about two city blocks before them and he asked his Lieutenant. "Do you want to keep walking or what?"

"Oh please yes, it's such a beautiful night out tonight, Edward. I don't want to be cooped up in some stuffy old hotel room when it's so nice out, honey." She begged her lover.

Soon they were alongside the taxi, and when the Egyptian driver realized the two were going to walk by him, he jumped back in his car and then moved it a little further down the road.

Campanelli noticed the cab was park a quarter of a mile ahead of them again. He pointed it out to Mendoza where their ride was now parked, and it was waiting for them.

"Too bad, I hoped the lousy little bastard would get lost so we could make love on the beach, it's so beautiful out here, Edward."

"You got to be kidding me baby, there's too many fucking people walking around for that kinda shit to go on around here."

"You're not very observant for an Officer you know mister. For your information Colonel, we just passed three different couples making love on the sands tonight sir."

Colonel Campanelli immediately started to look around as he grumbled at his lady. "You're shitting me. Where the hell are they?" He said as he quickly scanned the area.

"Don't do that! Jesus Christ Colonel you're embarrassing the hell out of me sir. Leave them people alone will you please sir. They're only doing what I want to do with you all night now." She yelled at him in a low voice, as she pulled on his arm.

"I wanna see them people doing the dirty on the stinking sand, honey." The Colonel cried as he continued to look around him to see if he could see the people enjoying themselves.

"Take my word for it, they're out there and are having a lot more fun than we are right now."

"Why don't we join them then Mendoza?" He smirked as he smiled back at her.

"With our stinking pain in the ass Arab chaperone sitting right over there watching everything we're doing? I didn't mind taking a shower in front of those Egyptians peckers, but I'll be damned to hell and back again if you think for one second that I'm going to perform in front of the lousy bastards. Besides, I can wait until we get back to the hotel rooms." She laughed.

"Well I can't wait. Since you brought it up to my attention, now I wanna make love to you under the stars." The Colonel snorted as he pulled her close to him and added. "In case I haven't told you today, I love you baby." He kissed her, and then he tried to slid his hand up her blouse.

Lieutenant Mendoza pulled away from his grasp and she warned him hotly. "Oh no you don't mista. You're not going to start my motor running again. I said I was going to wait until we get back to the damn hotel, and that's exactly what I'm going to do, mista. Unless you can find a way to get rid of our little Egyptian watchdog and we can enjoy some privacy." She kept looking at him as she ground her crotch into his groin.

"Is there anything wrong honey? Did I screw up again, baby." He asked with concern because of the way she was staring at him.

"I was just wondering if you could do me a big favor on this night, Edward. Please."

"Sure, just name it and you got it honey." He replied and again he grabbed her breasts.

"Can you say Renee for me Edward?" She looked deeply into his eyes for a moment.

"Yeah, sure, that's easy, Renee. How did I do with it doll?" He grinned at her this time.

"Great. Now that's my first name Edward. Do you think you could call me by my first name for a little while, now that we're getting serious about each other?" She begged of him.

"Sure can Mendoza, err... I mean Renee, if this makes you happy." He said with a grunt.

"It'll thrill me to no end if you call me Renee, Ed." She cried as she smiled at him.

He took her hand in his, and they continued to walk along the water's edge. She kicked up a little sand under her feet as she swung her hand, causing the Colonel's hand to swing along with hers. For the first time in quite a few years, she felt like a school girl once again as the both of them enjoyed the night and stars and the beautiful water of the Nile River.

"Why don't you take off you shoes and enjoy the warm sand baby." The Colonel offered.

"What a wonderful idea honey." Lieutenant Mendoza kicked off her shoes happily, and then she carried them under her arm as she mumbled at her lover. "Hum... the sand feels so soft and warm under my feet, this feels so much better. It's just wonderful Edward."

"Hey, look at that will ya, it's a fucking alligator honey." He cried, as he pointed to what looked like a large log floating in the water some twenty feet away from the bank.

She looked until she picked up the animal floating in the river and then she announced. "That's a crocodile, I don't think Egypt has any alligators in their country."

All of a sudden, their chauffeur slash watchdog stood alongside them out of breath.

The Colonel looked at the young man and said to Mendoza. "So much for the thought of making love in the sand with this prick hanging around. Whatdaya want buddy?"

"May Allah protect you from all harm always, sir. I saw the crocodile in the water and thought you be in danger some. I assigned give ride anywhere you want go, but told make sure nothing happen to you. Egypt very dangerous place to be at night. It would not look good for my government, if American Officer got hurt in my country while visiting here, sir. I suggest leave area right now sir. Insure you safety, I remain you side until decide you leave for hotel where you be safe for night, please." Their excited driver offered to the two Americans.

The Colonel noticed how well the Egyptian's English suddenly improved, the last part of the conversation sounded more like a threat than a warning to him. So he decided he saw enough of Egypt for a lifetime and said. "Okay Sam, drive us back to the damn hotel if you like."

"Sir, my name is no Sam, sir. I Jamal, and I be you driver for all night long if you desire so to it be sir." The driver said angrily back at the much larger American.

The trio climbed into the taxi, and between the gunning of the motor and beeping of the horn and the flood of curses, it took them ten minutes to get back to the Hilton. When they entered, they went over to the main desk. The manager saw them coming and he handed them the keys without waiting for the two Americans to ask for them as he told them the room numbers.

"Sir, your room is One, Nine, Sixty, Eight, it is one of the best suites we have available in the entire hotel, sir. A room for the young lady adjoins yours, the room is One, Nine, Seven, Oh. I hope you'll be very comfortable with your stay here at our hotel, sir."

The Colonel took the keys and then grumbled at the man. "I wish I could get such service at the other hotels we sometimes stay in, dammit."

The manager looked straight ahead as if completely ignoring him and his last words.

Colonel Campanelli shrugged, and then he turned away from the manager.

The two soldiers went over to the elevators and headed for their rooms. When she went into her room, she pulled the blankets from the bed to make it look like she slept in it. Then she went into the Colonel's room and spent the night with him. She told him what she had done and they both laughed over her actions.

At exactly seven o'clock the next morning, there was a light knock on their door.

Campanelli answered the door dressed in the hotel robe, as Mendoza remained in bed.

A young Arab male servant quickly wheeled in a breakfast cart covered with everything possible to eat without speaking to either American Officer.

"Hey, we didn't order any stinking breakfast buddy. You must have the wrong room pal."

"I'm so sorry sir. But this breakfast comes with the compliments of Ambassador Mohammed Kheir, sir." The man servant carefully placed the tray down across Mendoza's lap, and then he gave her a plate covered with eggs, a warm pita bread, and some fresh fruit along with a glass of orange juice and some flowers. He left another tray resting on the small night table on the Colonel's side of the large bed. The servant then handed linen napkins to Lieutenant Mendoza, and then the man servant gave her a leering smile as if to let her know that he was well aware she was not married to the man she was sleeping with.

Her anger instantly rose in her chest as she pulled down the sheets, allowing both her breasts to be exposed. The servant almost choked as she hissed nastily at him as he stared at her breasts. "Eat your stinking heart out you damn pig you." She then stuck her tongue out at the servant, making the man smile as he finished up with what he was doing.

The Colonel saw what she did and when the servant left the room he growled angrily at her. "God damn you Maz! I can hear what the fuck they're saying about us downstairs now dammit."

"I told you before I'm not going to allow these self centered, narrow minded, backassward bastards make me feel like I'm doing something wrong by sharing a bed with the man I love. They can all go to hell in a damn handbag Colonel Campanelli Sir. I'll do what my mind tells me to do, and if they don't like it, they can eat shit and die, better yet, live. I'm..."

"C'mon Maz, change the fucking record will you please. No one is attacking you here, dammit. You have to stop being so damn sensitive all the fricking time whenever someone looks at you the wrong way, baby. Let things pass once in a while will you please, you'll be much happier for it if you do, honey."

"I'll let the nasty looks pass when the lousy little bastards finally give equal rights to their women in this miserable country, Edward."

"Jesus Christ here we go again dammit, why don't you get down off the damn cross will ya please. Someone else needs the fucking wood."

"Yeah, and if you didn't have those damn little birds pinned on your collar, mista. I'd really let you know exactly how I feel about how these damn Arab nations treat their poor women, wiseass." She hissed and cursed the Colonel angrily in Spanish.

"Get off it Mendoza will you please, this is what I mean, dammit. Do you have to be at war with all men all the damn time for Pete's sake? I don't understand how the hell we get along so well, when all you do is attack a man because he might have looked at you the wrong way. Or he didn't ask your permission before he talked to you, or some other bullshit fucking reason for biting a man's fucking head off his damn shoulders. You better back off some, or you're going to end up being a lonely woman in your old age."

"You're not going to leave me are you, Edward?" She suddenly cried as tears started to run down her cheeks.

"No, I'm not going to leave you young lady. I love you too much for that to ever happen, dammit." He grumbled back at her as he pulled her out of bed after removing her food tray from her lap, and then he kissed her as he added to his words. "You have to learn to relax a little and allow things to happen naturally, that's all baby."

"Why can't you ever call me Renee for once in your life, dammit? I don't like baby. I'm not a baby, I'm Renee, Edward."

"Dammit Mendoza, err... Renee. That's exactly what I'm talking about. I'm no threat to you, why the hell are you taking me as one, dammit? Fuck that woman's lib shit will ya please, I want you. Am I going to have to ask permission before I can call you a pet name now for fuck sake now?" He demanded hotly as he pulled away from her.

"How can you ever understand how I truly feel Edward. You were never stopped from joining something just because you were a women, or worse yet, because you were Puerto Rican and a female at that. I was prejudiced against twice as much as most people were in my life, sir."

"Gees Maz, I never thought you'd ever try and use your stinking nationality as a fucking crutch to lean on. Sure you had it rough, but you're strong and you're not alone in that crap. You don't think I was prejudiced against in my life? Let me tell you something sister, you're fucking dead wrong with that thought, girl. With a last name like Campanelli, the first thing that entered a person's mind I was dealing with was, he's fucking Italian, he has to be connected with the stinking mob, or I was some kinda killer. I can't tell you how many jobs I lost, just because my boss thought I was a damn gangster. Hell, it didn't help me a bit because some of my family was connected, but I didn't have anything to do with that part of my family. Dammit girl, I wasn't even allowed to join some of the fricking social clubs, just because I was Italian.

"The fucking military recruiter was an Irish bastard and he told me flat out he wasn't going to process any of my fucking papers, because he felt I had a shady background cause of my stinking Italian heritage. That's why I joined the damn Army, and I know I was passed over a few times for promotion just because I was Italian. Only when I finally took charge of some troopers in Vietnam and saved their lives, and my own as well did I finally get any damn recognition from the higher ups. Now, there's no way in hell anyone could possibly stop me now.

"Why? Because I'm that fucking good, better than most people, and that's the only fucking way to get ahead in this crazy ass damn world of ours, by being that fucking good, sister. Not crying in your damn beer that I was being overlooked because of who or what I was. Mendoza, I never thought I'd ever hear you cry foul because of your Puerto Rican heritage, sister. You're a helluva lot better than that, young lady." The

Colonel growled angrily as he walked over to his side of the bed, and he began to pick at his cooling breakfast.

She looked at his back and snapped at him angrily. "Fuck you Campanelli."

The Colonel spun around and replied hotly at his lady. "No Mendoza, it's fuck you sister."

"I said fuck you because you know you're right, dammit. I know you're right, so fuck you Edward." She offered as she whipped at her eyes with her hand.

"Sure, go ahead, use another of woman's damn crutches now, stinking tears. Why the hell are you crying for, for Pete's sake? Are you giving up on me now sister? Did I hurt your little bitty feelings on you baby. I didn't know you were so damn sensitive little lady. C'mon, you're much better than that, sister. If you're giving up then I don't want to have anything more to do with you, you little pussy you. Where's your damn balls hiding at sister?"

She suddenly flew at him in a rage as she went off in Spanish again. She even tried to strike him with both her hands, but he easily fended off most of her blows, and then he grabbed one of her arms, and he pinned it behind her back when she finally tried to knee him in the balls.

"That's what I like to see from my stinking Officers at all times. Fire, fire in their fucking eyes." Colonel Campanelli laughed and then added to his gripe at his female Lieutenant. "Yes, fire mixed in with a little hatred. A good combination hey Mendoza, true god damn feelings."

"I'm not a damn pussy, you lousy bastard you. I hate you for that last remark mista."

He held her naked body pinned up against his as she tried to kick him in the balls again. But she only managed to knee him on his thigh. But the blow caught his attention though, and he pulled up a little harder on her arm, making her cry out in pain and stop fighting him.

"If you want me to call you fucking Renee then you're going to have to earn the damn right, sister. And the only way you're going to earn it from me baby, is by being a great Officer and a better fucking person to yourself, and to all the others around you, dammit. You treat people like you want to be treated, and you just might get your fucking wish from me, sister. You're way better than anyone else, so stop trying to get recognition for something you're not, lady. Earn it, and you'll fucking get it, dammit. Think it's owed to you, and you're going to end up with the short end of the fricking stick every damn time. You better grow up some baby." Colonel Campanelli hissed in her face as he let her go and he gave a slight shove back.

"You think you're so damn smart mista." She hissed at her Commanding Officer.

"I'm not so damn smart, but what I am, I did all by my fucking self. No one gave me a fucking thing I didn't work my ass for and earn for myself, and I like it that way, sister. You're not the type of person to want something you're not entitled to, baby. So fight for what you want, and don't fucking cry if you don't get it handed to you." He glared at her.

"Do you still love me Edward?" She suddenly asked him with some fear in her voice.

His stance immediately softened as he looked at her and then he whispered. "Come here you little ass you." He said as he put his arms out and she ran into them and he added to his words to her. "You have to learn to relax some honey, not every man's condemning all women you know. Some of us love and respect you ladies you know."

He kissed her on the forehead as he moved some of the strands of hair with his lips. She stayed locked in his arms until she stopped crying, she was trying to get air in her lungs to stop her sobbing. She hated acting like a women, crying when she did not get her way, and that was the way she was feeling at this moment.

"C'mon Maz, let's get the hell out of this damn country and back to where we belong."

She looked deeply into her lover's eyes and then she cried while still naked. "I want to know if you still think of me as a good Officer, sir. Or do you now think of me as just another foolish woman, Edward?"

"No matter how screwy you might act when you're fighting for your damn rights as a woman and a person. I'd never doubt any of your ability at being an outstanding Officer. I'd trust you with my life and wallet, or to think like the professional you are. I'd never doubt you as an Officer for one stinking moment, Maz. We're entitled to take our little day trips every now and then to get our heads back on the swivel. Hell, if we didn't run away from life every once in a while, we'd drive ourselves nuts with all the damn decisions we have to make, knowing one wrong decision could easily cause someone their life, or start a damn war. All you have to remember is when to come back if you take another day trip in the near future. Got that?"

"I see why you're such a good Officer, Edward. You not only brought out all my little devils, but you made me understand what was happening to me. I'm sorry I was so pig headed tonight."

"Already forgotten honey. Let's get dressed and then we can get the hell out of this damn country, Maz. I don't like being away from my workers, or my Command and base for any longer than I really have to, Renee."

The two American Officers quickly packed their stuff and started out the hotel door, only to bump right into their Egyptian taxi driver from yesterday.

"Hey my little Egyptian friend, we're planning to leave your country today, now in fact buddy." The American Colonel offered him with a grin.

Jamal replied just as politely. "I was sent to pick you up, and then bring you over to Ambassador Mohammed Kheir's office. He like to see you before leave our country again sir."

"Fair enough I guess, shall we get going, buddy? We really wanna leave your country my friend." Campanelli replied as he stepped aside and allowed the driver to walk by him.

The two American Military Officers followed the young and concerned Egyptian driver back to his waiting cab. In minutes they were standing in front of the building where they first met with Ambassador Mohammed Kheir. The driver led the way for them, and then he opened the door to Mohammed's private office for the two officers. They were immediately met by JoAnne, his private secretary and bodyguard and also his jailer.

For the first time in his life, General Campanelli actually felt slightly threatened by a female. He did not know why he felt this way, but the hairs on the back of his neck stood up on edge, while he stared at this stunningly beautiful young woman. Maybe it was because of the way she stood, or the way she moved around before him, like a large cat ready to spring on its prey. They followed JoAnne, she looked like she was having a little trouble keeping her breasts in her dress.

Mohammed Kheir came to his feet as the two American Military Officers entered his office.

JoAnne asked if the two Americans wanted any coffee or tea or anything else to drink. When no answer came from either of the officers, she made herself comfortable in a chair so she could oversee the entire office and conversation.

Colonel Campanelli was certain the placing of the chairs in the office was no mistake. He knew this dangerous looking woman was a bodyguard who could easily defend herself very well, and also protect her boss while she was at it.

Lieutenant Mendoza kept looking at the front of JoAnne's dress. She could not believe so much of a woman's breast could be showing, yet still remain inside her dress. She could not help herself as she kept glancing over to see if JoAnne's breasts were going to suddenly pop out of the front of her dress as she breathed or moved in the chair.

Ambassador Mohammed Kheir offered the two American Officers a chair. Once seated, he asked them if they wanted to go out with another work unit into the desert, even though he knew the answer already because the Colonel already said he could not help his workers.

"No thank you Ambassador Kheir, we're planning to leave your beautiful country sometime later on today, Sir. I saw everything I wanted to see on my short visit, sir."

"Oh I was unaware you were planning to leave my country so soon, Colonel Campanelli! That is too bad for me to hear, sir. Surely, you didn't plan to leave my country without letting me know that you were going first, sir. I have many other questions I'd like to ask of you, and I also hoped to entertain you a little longer tonight, sir. I have even rearranged my schedule."

"I'm sorry sir, I didn't know that Ambassador Kheir Sir. It was inconsiderate on my part, but I'm kind of anxious to get back to my workers and Command at the Dam site, sir." Campanelli saw the sour look Ambassador Mohammed just placed on his face at the mere mention of the Dam, and he added quickly to try and ease the sting the Dam project caused the likable Egyptian politician. "I'm sorry sir, I know we're hurting Egypt with this Dam construction, sir."

"Nonsense Captain, err... excuse please me Colonel Campanelli Sir. It's not your fault at all sir. You're merely a soldier doing a soldier's job as he's ordered. That's why we're exploring the desert, so this Dam does not hurt Egypt. I'm quite certain if it hurt us, the government of Ethiopia would understand and do the right thing and release more water to us. I don't think the government of Ethiopia wants to hurt my country in any way shape or form, sir. So don't feel bad for your work. I was going to ask you how it was going on the Dam."

"Ambassador Mohammed Kheir Sir, at this time we're well ahead of schedule by a month at least, and we have diverted some water down the trench to the Afar Depression two days ago, sir. I don't think Egypt will notice the small difference in the flow of water from the Nile to your country, sir." The Colonel knew he lied as he added. "Mohammed Kheir, I was thinking..."

Ambassador Mohammed cut him off by saying. "Colonel Campanelli Sir, Mohammed is quite respectful enough, and I'd much rather be called Mohammed if you don't mind, sir."

"Sure, yes, Mohammed, but please, you can call me Ed, or because you know my nick name already, feel free to use that at any time, sir. If I liked you enough to get drunk with ya then you can use my nick name any time you please, sir."

"I'd like that very much, thank you Popeye." Mohammed smiled slightly back at him.

"As I was saying Mohammed, if you need a hand in your search for water in the desert sir. Or need some of my equipment or engineers for your assistance, all you have to do is get in touch with my government, and I'm quite certain that they'd send us right back to you, sir. I'd be most pleased to help your country in any way possibly, personally sir."

The Egyptian looked at this young American soldier with the strange nick name deep in his eyes for a moment as he replied to the officer. "I knew you were a good man when I first met you in that bar, sir. Any man who can drink as much liquor as you did, and still be able to make friends with a foreigner, and continue walking is an okay man in my book, sir. Do you remember you offered me a place to stay that night, no questions asked. For all you knew, I could've been a mass murderer, or some nut with an ax to grind. But you offered me a safe place to stay that night sir. I think we could have become very good friends once we were sober, sir.

"Popeye, you're more than welcome in my country anytime you want to visit us, sir. I trust you completely sir. Here, take this paper, it contains my phone number, my private number sir. If you ever have to get in contact with me for any reason whatsoever, day or night, call this number and I'll always answer it personally. Either JoAnne, my secretary," He pointed to JoAnne with is chin and then went on with his offer, "or myself will answer the phone. If JoAnne answers, tell her who you are and she'll find me immediately for you, sir."

JoAnne nodded back at him when Colonel Campanelli glanced at her for a quick moment.

Mohammed decided he was going to install his own cut off switch in his scheme, even if his own government was going to install one for themselves. He also understood he had to keep the communication lines open with the Americans, or this war could very easily get out of hand on him, and then destroy the entire world. The concerned Egyptian Ambassador also understood if he could contact Colonel Campanelli, or if the Colonel could contact him at any time if the need arose. They could possibly stop all the craziness which was soon going to grip the Arab nations, and the rest of the world as well in the near future.

Colonel Edward Campanelli took the small slip of paper and folded it in half and then placed it in his wallet. He then reached over and took a paper and pencil and put both of his numbers on it, and he informed Ambassador Mohammed Kheir to use them if he ever needed to get in contact with him for any reason. Both men seemed pleased to know they were giving each other information, information that might save thousands of lives in the near future at that. He handed the paper over to Mohammed who immediately placed it inside his top desk drawer, but not before he looked at the numbers and committed them to his memory.

Ambassador Mohammed Kheir tried to talk the two American Officers into staying in Egypt for a few more days longer, so he could get to know the both of them a little better. But the Colonel would not be swayed by his kind offer. The worried Commander was only interested in getting back to the base and to his people, and nothing short of orders directly from command would change his mind on him at this time.

The Egyptian politician stood when Colonel Campanelli and Lieutenant Mendoza rose to leave his office, and country. Mohammed shook the Colonel's hand and he kissed Mendoza's hand as he politely walked the two American Officers to the door. He led them over to an elevator, and then he waited until they were in the cab, and the doors closed before him.

Ambassador Mohammed Kheir then walked back to his office, entered it and closed the door behind him. He sat down heavily in his chair as he quickly let out his breath in a rush of air. Then he pulled the bottom drawer out and rested his feet in it as he sat back and then placed his hands behind his head, and smiled at his young and beautiful female bodyguard, who remained in his office while he walked the two Americans to the elevators.

JoAnne was waiting for him to return from the elevators.

"Well what did you think of them two JoAnne?" Mohammed Kheir asked of his bodyguard.

"I think the female must be a lesbian or something, because she couldn't take her eyes off my breasts. Every time I looked at the American female, she was staring at my breasts."

"She wasn't the only one staring at them young lady. I couldn't keep my eyes out of your dress. How do you keep them inside it?" Kheir smiled, but she continued with her report.

"I think you can trust this man who is known as Popeye. I know he doesn't think anything wrong is happening in the desert with our foolish workers. I had his room bugged and they made love last night, and then they had an argument about women's rights early this morning. They ate the breakfast you sent them that I thought was a very good move on your part, Mohammed. Then they both came here, sir. They're both very smart, and they made good arguments about equal rights to their women. It was a real pleasure to listen to them arguing like they were doing. I think they'll be most worthy adversaries for us to deal with in the future, sir."

"I think your assumption of the two American soldiers is most accurate about the two of them, young woman. I'll make my report to President Sadat by late afternoon I guess. You're excused please for now." He did nothing until JoAnne finally left the room. Then he sat up and removed his feet from the drawer and opened his top drawer and looked for the paper containing the Colonel's phone numbers. The paper was missing, and he smiled as he quickly wrote the numbers down from memory on another piece of paper, and then he taped it to the bottom of the second drawer of his desk.

He then cursed JoAnne for stealing the paper, but now he knew he could not trust her in the least. He decided he would have to kill her if anything happened, and he had to make decisions on his own. He devised a plan to follow, if war came to his country, and got out of hand, and President Sadat thought about employing nuclear, chemical or biological weapons to help his cause. He would figure out a way to kill Sadat, and pull Egypt out of the war. But for now, he understood he could not possibly enlist JoAnne, or her partner in his plans. He was going to have to figure a way to kill both of the women before they could kill him.

He went over to his chest and removed a pistol, a PPK he was given as a special gift by a British friend he once did a favor for. The weapon had three extra clips with it, plus the one already placed in the weapon. All the clips were loaded, nine bullets in each. He slowly walked back to his desk and buzzed JoAnne who immediately came in.

"JoAnne, I want to start carrying a gun on me. You never know once the fighting starts, if I might have need of one to protect my life with. I don't trust anyone any longer I'm afraid. I have to start worrying about my life for a change I believe. I wish I knew how to use the damn thing though. The Agent who gave me this weapon, never took the time to show me how to use the weapon." He announced to the blonde the moment she walked into his office.

JoAnne walked over to the desk as she offered calmly to the powerful Egyptian politician. "I think you're most correct in your decision to arm yourself, Mohammed. You should be carrying a weapon to better protect yourself from possible attack, sir. It's good to see you're using your head, Mohammed. Here, allow me show you how to break down and clean the weapon for you. Then, I'll happily show you how to aim, fire and reload it at the same time, sir."

He watched carefully as JoAnne broke down the weapon like the expert she was. In seconds she had it torn completely apart. She explained all the pieces to him as she named them as well, and she also showed him how they worked, and where they went as she quickly reassembled the weapon again. She took it apart once more and then she showed him how it went back together. Then she asked him to take it apart and put it back together for himself.

The concerned Egyptian politician had a little bit of trouble at first, and she had to help him reassemble the weapon properly. But on his second attempt, he was able to take the weapon apart and put it back together without further assistance from her. He did it for a third time, and JoAnne assured him he now had it down pat and could take proper care of the weapon.

She then showed him how to insert the clip into the weapon, and then send a shell into the chamber and then how to unloaded the weapon. She also showed him how to aim it properly and had him remove the clip and check the small PPK to make certain it was empty before she helped him aim the weapon a second time. She wrapped her arms around Mohammed's upper body as she helped him steady the weapon in his hands. He could feel her breasts pressed up against his back, and he suddenly reached around himself to cup one of her breasts. She pulled away from his body and gave him a tap on the back of his head as she bitched at him.

"This is serious so please pay close attention to my instructions while I show you something that might save your foolish life in the future, Mohammed." She reached around him a second time and she showed him how to use the sites on the weapon to aim with.

"I think I understand it now. Say how about you and me going somewhere where I can shoot the gun and get the feel of it?" He asked as he turned and looked her in the eyes.

"Sure, come with me please." They both left the office and drove to the desert to a clear place. JoAnne set up a target made from a piece of cardboard she found in the trunk. She again reached around him and helped him aim the gun. "Pow", the shell hit below and to the right of the target.

She quickly explained to him he squeezed the trigger a little too hard, and it forced the barrel of the weapon down a little on him, and she then helped him a second time. This time the bullet nicked the very edge of the small target.

"Now you must try it by yourself Ambassador Kheir Sir." She told him pleasantly.

He emptied the clip of nine bullets rapidly, and only managed to hit the target just once because he allowed the weapon to move his hand all over.

They both laughed at the poor score he accomplished. He then ejected the clip with JoAnne's help, and then he placed another loaded clip in the weapon and cocked the slide and aimed. She helped him a little, she told him to hold his breath before pulling the trigger and squeeze it slow, with even pressure and not pull on the trigger hard with his finger.

The bullet hit close enough to the center of the target to make him cry out. "Yeah."

"Good, good, that was fine Mohammed. Try again please and keep your eyes on the target."

All three bullets hit the target this time as he got comfortable with the weapon. By the time he finished the second clip, he missed the target with just two bullets. He reloaded the weapon by himself this time. When he fired again, every round hit the target. He unloaded the clip, and reloaded the weapon for the fourth time. This time she stood behind him and just off to his left on purpose. She summarized his shooting was weakest to his left side.

He fired off five of the nine rounds, and this time hitting the target every time. He ejected the half empty clip, and the bullet in the chamber, and then he turned with the empty gun in his hand in the direction of JoAnne. Only to see her holding her weapon with both hands and her legs slightly apart and she was aiming her weapon directly at his chest.

The Egyptian politician stopped moving and growled at his female bodyguard. "Is this it? Are you going to kill me now? Is this why you wanted to get me out in the desert alone? Did President Sadat order you to do this to me woman?" Mohammed Kheir asked in a shaky voice.

She slowly lowered her weapon a bit and looked at him over the barrel. Then she lowered the weapon the rest of the way as she replied to the Egyptian politician. "No Mohammed, I wasn't ordered and I'm not going to kill you, sir. It was I was undecided why you suddenly wanted a weapon. I thought you must have something up your sleeve against me, sir. When you wanted to go out someplace private in order to learn how to properly shoot the weapon, I was certain you were going to try and kill me for some reason, sir. I thought you were going to kill me out here in the desert, Mohammed. I guess I don't trust you as yet either, sir.

"When I noticed you didn't use up all the rounds from the last clip, I was certain I was right, and you were going to try and kill me. I'm pleased you didn't try and kill me, because I would've hated to have been forced to kill you, Mohammed. I kind of like you sir. But seeing you with the empty weapon and also the separate clip. I immediately realize I was wrong in my fear, and you just might have wanted to learn how to shoot a weapon for your own protection, which I think is still a very wise idea, Mohammed." She said as she replaced her weapon in the holster on the thigh on her right leg. She exposed as much of herself to him as possible, as a sort of apology for her not trusting and threatening him with her weapon.

He was still shaking as he labored to get his breathing under control some. He did not like looking down the barrel of a loaded gun as he complained at his bodyguard. "I stopped firing because I didn't want to use up all my bullets, I don't know where to get any more. I have no reason to kill you nor do I want to. No reason at all in fact, I'm pleased you're around and protecting me. I never felt so safe as when you're near me, young woman. I decided to learn how to shoot a weapon in case I need to protect myself when you're not near me."

She put her hand to her head and she offered to the Egyptian politician in a calm tone of voice. "I should've realized you might be concerned about extra ammunition for your weapon. You don't have to worry about finding more rounds for your weapon, I'll get you all the ammunition you'll ever need tomorrow morning, Mohammed. This way, we can come back here and I'll get you to the point where you can hit a moving target by the weekend, sir."

As they headed back to their car in silence, he admitted to himself he was thinking about shooting her while they were in the desert, if he was able to get the drop on her. As he thought about the situation, he realized he just worked out an alibi. He was going to tell President Sadat the last time he saw JoAnne, she went off with a stranger, but not before she removed one hundred thousand dollars for his safe. He kept the money there in case he had to bribe someone, or had to pay someone for their services or he any needed information.

Ambassador Mohammed Kheir was certain President Sadat would believe his story when he offered it to him. Besides, what other choice would President Sadat have but to believe him? He would never think he could possibly kill his well trained hired killer, and when he left the body out in the desert, the animals would quickly eat away any evidence overnight for him.

She drove the car, but they both sat in silence for the entire drive back to his office. She did not speak because she knew he was still extremely upset over the fact she aimed her weapon at him a few moments ago. She was wondering what if anything he was going to tell President Sadat, and what was going to be his reaction to her threat against the Ambassador. She suddenly feared she might have overstepped her bounds a little by threatening him like she did. She knew President Sadat gave her the right to use lethal force against him, if she ever felt he was going to betray President Sadat. But how would he react if she killed him while just defending her life from him? She knew his life was more important than hers, and she worked it out until she came up with the only conclusion left open to her. President Sadat would have had her killed if she ever killed Mohammed in self defense.

She decided to make certain there would be some kind of evidence with her at all times, pointing out how he had planned to attack and kill President Sadat. She also put her mind to work on how she was going to get this evidence, even if she had to fabricate it against him herself. In this way, if she ever had to kill the bastard for any reason, she would then be able to save her life with this fake evidence, but just in case she could not find some against the Ambassador. She also decided to buy a universal air ticket, which she could use at any time of the day or night to board a plane out of the country. She had no doubt whatsoever in her mind that Mohammed Kheir would never do anything against President Sadat.

They finally arrived at his office fifteen minutes later and he went directly inside, and she told him she was going to go out to get him plenty of ammunition for his new toy. "Shells for practice, and some of them will be different kinds of shells for yourself protection, Ambassador Kheir Sir." She told him before she left, and Mohammed asked her what the difference was between the two types of different bullets she was picking up for his weapon.

She took a quick breath, happy for the chance to talk with him further. "Some of the shells will be for target practice, and I shall also get you some regular bullets, Mohammed. For your protection, you'll have to keep two clips of brass clad hollow point rounds either by your weapon, or inside it at all times when you're not going to used the weapon for target practice, sir. These shells are much heavier and more powerful than the practice shells, and the hollow points will also flatten out when it hits someone, causing twice the amount of damage and shock as the regular bullets would to the body. I'm also going to pick you up a cleaning kit for the weapon, and I shall teach you how to clean your weapon for yourself, Mohammed. You must keep the weapon perfectly clean if you want it to operate properly for yourself, sir."

He stopped her talking by raising his hand and then he offered after he calmed down a little. "I don't know what you're talking about here with the difference in the ammunition. But I'm certain you do, and I know you'll never do anything that'd ever endanger me. I thank you again for your loyalty and diligence for protecting my life like you are for me young woman."

She looked at him for a long moment while building up the courage to ask him, and then she said in a contrite tone of voice to the still obviously shaken Egyptian Ambassador. "Then do you forgive me for pointing my weapon at you Mohammed? You're not going to tell President Sadat against me? You know the reason why I did it was because I didn't know what you were up to with the weapon you wanted to learn to shoot, Mohammed."

He gave a nervous laugh as he replied to her question. "Yes, I forgive you for your minor mistake, JoAnne. Perhaps, I should've explained myself a little better to you over why I wanted to suddenly start carrying a weapon on my person, before we went out to the desert."

She was still scared and said. "You're not going to tell President Sadat what I did to you?"

"I see no real reason whatsoever to burden President Sadat with any more problems than he already has troubling his mind. It was a misunderstanding plain and simple. I see no sense to make to big a deal out of your mistake. I'm just damn happy you didn't kill me like I though you were going to do. As far as I'm concerned, the incident never happened young woman."

"Thank you so much Mohammed, I'm so pleased that you forgave me for my foolishness, sir. I promise, tonight you'll have a night like no other you have ever experienced. When I get back to your room, I'll call Gail and the two of us will fulfill your wildest dreams, Mohammed."

"The last time you two fulfilled my wildest dreams, it took me two full days to get over it, JoAnne." He laughed as he sat down behind his desk. His laughter quickly disappeared when JoAnne was finally out of his office, and he quickly removed the small slip of paper with the numbers Colonel Campanelli gave him printed on it. He copied them down in his personal phone book, and he used a different name over the numbers so she did not discover his little subterfuge. He was afraid of losing the numbers, or JoAnne coming across the paper taped under the drawer and destroying it on him. Here, left in plain sight, he felt she would never be able to find them. Especially since where he placed the number down in his phone book, was right alongside the Jewish Ambassador's private number and he felt it was a second number for him.

Ambassador Mohammed Kheir then poured himself a stiff drink of scotch and slugged it down in one fast gulp. His nerves were still shattered and on edge from having a loaded weapon pointed directly at him. He thanked his lucky stars that he did not try and kill the bitch as he was thinking of doing earlier in the day. Or he would have been the one who was left behind lying in the sands dying. He did not know what, but something told him not to try to kill her at that time, and to empty the gun before he turned around to face his female bodyguard. The wise Egyptian politician knew how to aim and fire a weapon very well before she showed him. But he had little experience with the use of a pistol like this one. He was slightly familiar with the revolver type weapons though. But this gun was an automatic, and he never used one before in his life.

JoAnne entered the Ambassador's office in about an hour's time. She was carrying a bag with nine boxes of ammunition in it, five boxes were practice bullets, and the other four were the harder hitting rounds going to be use for his self protection.

Ambassador Mohammed Kheir took the four boxes of bullets from her, and placed them in the chest where he kept certain papers and other personnel and important items.

"Here," She said like she was ordering him as she held out four extra clips for his weapon and she informed him. "You'll load these extra clips with the hollow point rounds, and you'll keep one clip in the weapon at all times, and carry two extra clips with you when you carry the weapon on your person for protection, Mohammed. Oh yes, one other thing Mohammed, please make certain that the two extra clips are loaded with the hollow point rounds also."

This last bit of advice made both of them laugh. He looked at her and said to her. "I'm pleased you're on my side. I would sure hate to have you as my enemy, young lady."

She did her best to try and convince herself she might have been overreacting a little when she though she was going to be forced to kill Mohammed, and she decided against trying to produce the evidence to try and frame him for the President of Egypt. She doubted she could ever have killed this man who held his country in such high esteem. She carefully watched him as he struggled and tried to put the bullets into the extra clips. He was so clumsy at it and he was having a hard time, mainly because his fingers were so thick, and he was not used to working with the small bullets either. She laughed, and he yelled back at her. "If you think you can do any better than I'm doing with this cursed damn thing then here, you're more than welcome to try it yourself young woman."

She laughed again as she moved a little closer to him, and then she took the clip from his hand and put the shells in the clip with little problems as she announced to him with a smirk on her lips. "There, you see how simple it really is to do Mohammed."

He was not really watching her loading the extra clips for his weapon, he was having a far better time with looking down the front of her dress.

She glanced back at him, and then complained at the young Egyptian politician with an angry snap in her voice "I hope you're enjoying yourself with acting like a little school child, you great fool you. You know you should really be paying closer attention to what I'm doing here for you, and not dribbling on my tits on me mister. Look at what you're doing, you're staining the front of my dress, you foul pig of a man. Maybe I should take my dress off then maybe you'll stop staining it on me like you're doing, Mohammed."

"I believe I'd really appreciate if you do very much young lady. I can never get enough of looking at your outstanding body you know, JoAnne." He laughed at her this time, the danger of almost being shot to death for some reason made him a little horny.

She hoped he would say that and she straightened up and took off her dress as seductively as she could, to add to his growing desire. She loved having men eat out of the palm of her hand.

He suddenly pulled the naked woman across his desk, knocking the papers and books to the floor with one sweep of his powerful hand as he took her right there on the desk top.

"Oh you wild animal you. I love it when you act like this, taking charge over me really turns me on, Mohammed." She yelled as she suddenly wrapped her strong legs around his rearend, and then she pulled him to her with them, and they laughed as they made love on the desktop.

After they finished making love to each other, JoAnne remained naked for his pleasure as she went back to loading the extra clips with bullets she just bought him. But he was paying little if any attention to what she was doing because he was totally exhausted from their lovemaking experience, and he was just sort of sitting in his chair daydreaming.

When she finished loading the extra clips, she turned and looked at him as he sat in his chair with his eyes half closed. She immediately placed her hands on her hips and glared at him as she hissed at the same time. "Well mister, I see that you were really playing attention to what I was doing for you, fool. I guess you lost all interest in preparing the clips for your new weapon, so I'm going to take a shower, you made me a real mess of me sir.

The Egyptian Ambassador sleepily smiled at her as he remained with his eyes half closed in a dreamy state and a slight smile resting on his lips.

CHAPTER 15 – APRIL 9ᵀᴴ, 1996.

Colonel Edward Campanelli immediately reported to Commander Owens the moment he was back on his base, to quickly inform him of what he observed on his trip to view the Egyptian workers toiling in the Sinai Desert. The report was rather uninteresting and even boring, until the section about the canisters came up for review. Here he tried to assure Commander Owens the canisters were being used in the search for water and that was all.

"Perhaps you can explain why the damn Egyptians are using so many of the damn charges in their supposed search for water in the damn desert Mr. Campanelli?"

The Colonel tried to cut in, but he was stopped by a mere wave of the Commander's hand.

"Hear me out first before you reply, after all I just listened to your summary, mister. My Intel people looked at these damn pictures of the canisters under a microscope if you will, and they feel these items could possibly be some kind of new weapon. Maybe a mine, or something in that family, though we don't recognize the configuration, and it does looks heavy for a land mine. Anyway Colonel, we think we have come up with a pattern to the Egyptian's madness.

"So far as we can tell at this time sir, the Egyptian workers have been looking for water on the exact locations the Israeli Army had setup as their command posts and headquarters during the Suez Canal conflict with Egypt some years back, sir. We find this rather interesting and also quite concerning at the same time, mainly because if there was ever another conflict between Israel and Egypt, and the Israeli soldiers were forced to entered the Sinai Desert. They would automatically head right back for the same exact positions that worked for them in the previous war. Military strategy would demand this of them in any future engagement, sir.

"Therefore Colonel Campanelli, we came to the conclusion Egypt must be preparing for another war with Israel. For now, we have no intention of informing the Israelis of our findings, because, we don't need them to go off halfcocked and start a fucking shooting war with Egypt. We intend to keep a close eye on the Egyptian workers and this situation, and allow them to carry out their little ruse for a while longer, sir. We know of the locations they have worked over, and if necessary we'll stage an attack using aircraft in these areas, and blow them all to hell, and making it safe for the Jew soldiers to operate from these positions for a second time.

"I'll allow the Egyptians to continue their work, at least it'll keep them out of our hair for the time being, Colonel Campanelli. I'll build our strength up in the entire area at the same time. I'm having the Aircraft Carrier Nimitz and her escort ships to deploy at the mouth of the Mediterranean Sea. She's stationed off the coast of Japan at this moment, taking readings from the old Russian radar complex on the Islands Japan's demanding back from the Russians. I feel we're heading full steam for difficulties there as well, Colonel Campanelli Sir. But it looks like the major trouble spot will, as always feared, be the Middle East. Sorry to say Colonel, the nations of Egypt and Israel for some reason this time around will be at war, sir.

"Colonel Campanelli, it'll take the Nimitz four full days to sail to her new standoff position. I'm going to have her entire Strike Force set sail at half steam, so it doesn't look like we're bracing for any trouble in the region. I'll call for exercises between Turkey and ourselves, to give the Nimitz her cover story as to why she's deploying there. What I want from you is, to have your base set on Alert Red. I'll send you a flood of new troops and aircraft over the next few weeks, Colonel. I'm going to have you transferred out to a second military base we're planning for the Sudan, your presence there will cover the buildup we plan for this area as well.

"We asked for added help from the Sudanese government, to fake an attempt at starting up another Dam project on the Nile River to produce electricity. No one gives a damn shit how many little Dams spring up on the river, this one will be just above Kostl, Colonel. This will cover the new troops we'll send to the area. We want to secure a good size military base in this area to operate from. I don't know what's coming at us yet, but I know something's coming, and I intend to be well prepared for it when it does happen, sir. A good example of being prepared was the Desert Storm War Games. We were well prepared there and look what we did.

"We're going to also increase our flyover of the Sinai Desert region, Egypt, and the Sudan by our E 3B Sentry AWACS radar aircraft, to help keep a closer eye on any possible sudden troop movements of the Egyptian and Israeli's and anything else going down in all three of these damn regions, sir. You know Colonel Campanelli, I always thought if trouble was going to start in this fucking region, it'd be coming at us from the damn Libyans. I never figured it'd be the Egyptians who would go nuts on us in this region. Go figure it." The Commander said as he looked at the Colonel while waiting for an answer, or remark about what he just told him.

Colonel Campanelli felt a little uncomfortable under the Commander's harsh stare as he suddenly shifted his weight in his chair, and then he finally replied. "Commander Owens Sir, I don't happen to agree with your assessment, sir. But I understand I'm not as privy to the information you obviously have at your disposal sir. If this is how you're going to call the shots. Then I'll agree with you, and I'll be more than ready for any situation that might crop up, sir. If I'm going to man another military base, will I be able to pick the people I need there, sir?"

"Yes, of course you can have anyone you need or want as extra support, Colonel Campanelli. All you have to do is request them in writing, and you'll have them as fast as I can ship their asses out to your new position, sir. Colonel, I know I'm pushing the panic button here a little, but I intend to be prepared for anything breaking out under my area of responsibility. I think it's far better to be safe than sorry, sir. At your new base you'll be setting up in the Sudan, I'll have you supplied with Abrams M-63 and Abrams 65 Blackfoot tanks with some 152 mm self propelled Howitzer, and M-5 Bradley IFV fighting machines. And as far as any missiles go for your defense or offense, I'll also send you out a number of the MLRS (Multiple Launch Rocket Systems), and the Lance Missile and Patriot systems, in case it goes to hell in your area, sir.

"You'll also have a good number of Apaches fast attack helicopters, more Blackhawk troop helicopters, and CV 22 Osprey aircraft and an E 3A AWACS umbrella, so you'll have advance warning if any attacks are heading your way, Colonel. Your first duty on this new base is to start the construction of an operating airbase in order to accept any fighters and fighter bomber aircraft. Make no mistakes about it for a second Colonel Campanelli, your only duty here is to setup a good working military base, by employing a civilian operation as your cover for this project, sir. Your military people will be ordered to wear civilian clothes as before. Yeah, yeah I know, so don't start with the same shit on me Colonel. I know damn well these men will be treated as spies if arrested by the attackers. But I don't have any intention of allowing your troops get caught. Well, that's all I have for you Colonel, do you have any questions, sir?"

"No sir, I'll carry out your orders the best I can sir. When can I be expecting to ship out, sir?"

"Fine. You'll be notified in due time on any new orders, Colonel Campanelli Sir. That's about all I have for you at this time sir. You may leave if you have no further questions for me, Colonel." The Commander replied as he looked at some charts lying on his desk.

The surprised Colonel stood, and then he saluted the Commander and then left, he was led up to the flight deck and a waiting F 4 Phantom 11, primarily used for reconnaissance, and in seconds he was streaking his way back towards his military base stationed in Ethiopia.

The Commander growled at his Wing Commander to order more flights over Egypt, near the Sinai Desert by the F 117B Stealth Fighters stationed in Saudi Arabia. "I want recon aircraft over Egypt round the damn clock for Christ sake. Order the Navy to put a few of their damn X 117s up also, mister. I don't want to miss anything the damn Egyptians are doing out there, dammit. I can ill afford any surprises coming up and biting me on the fucking ass with this lousy operation for the love of the Christ child. Something's coming our way, because I'm getting a fucking hard on, god dammit. Order the battle cans Missouri and Wisconsin up to join with the Nimitz Battle Group. How long will it take to recommission the Jersey?"

"Commander Owens Sir, the Missouri's a floating museum sitting in a fresh water lake, sir. I know the Jersey went through an overhaul a month ago, sir. I read a report she was guaranteed sea worthy within forty eight hours, but she'll take five days to be refueled, and have her munitions set in place, and loaded with food provisions and crew. The Missouri was fitted with fuel and ammo when she was put to sleep, she'd need provisions and an active crew to be ready for duty, err... say no more than two, three days at the very most, sir."

"Cut the damn orders to the Chairman of the Joint Chiefs of Staff and I'll sign them as soon as they're written up. I want a fucking decision on these requested ships A-SAP, mister. I'll also need those damn weapons if this shit becomes a shooting war where I think it's going to take place, mister." The Commander growled as he stared at the sailor he was speaking with.

"Aye, Aye sir, I'll get on this right away, so consider it done sir." The Flight Commander said as he snapped to attention then he saluted the commander. When no response came, he headed for the radio communications to send his messages out to the Joint Chief of Staff's Chairman.

BASE EASY MONEY, ETHIOPIA

Colonel Edward Campanelli called all his officers into his command post, and then ordered the one Intel Officer out of the tent so he could speak to his officers in private. He quickly informed his people what he was told by Commander Owens, and what was to be expected of them in the near future. He was rather surprised at how many officers agreed with the decisions of the CIC to go on full ready alert on the entire vast military base. Even Lieutenant John White, his usually argumentative black officer readily agreed with the Commander's assumptions and orders, which led Campanelli to believe that trouble was definitely coming his way now. Because John never agreed with command on anything.

APRIL 11th, 1996. 0633 A.M. THE MEDITERRANEAN SEA OFF THE COAST OF LIBYA

A Japanese Cargo ship suddenly placed an emergency SOS call just outside the territorial waters of Libya. The ship let the world know it was floundering, and was in danger of sinking.

Libya immediately responded and dispatched two ocean going tugboats from her shores, to assist with the supposed floundering Japanese ship. The huge tugs hooked up a number of tow lines to the disabled cargo ship, and then they slowly tow the ship towards her port of Bengazi.

CAIRO, EGYPT

On this day, the hawked nosed Libyan Ambassador Kamal leered at Egyptian Ambassador Mohammed Kheir as he entered his office as if he owned the world. He showed up uninvited, begging an immediate audience with the cautious Egyptian Ambassador.

Mohammed Kheir's first thought was to say he was too busy to meet with Ambassador Kamal. But JoAnne pointed out she was told it was important for Ambassador Kamal to meet with him. He glared harshly at her because of her attempted override of his wishes, and then he barked at her angrily. "I guess I have no other choice, send him in then JoAnne."

She quickly followed Libyan Ambassador Kamal into his private office. He looked at her as he growled at the beautiful woman. "I shall speak to Ambassador Kamal in private if you don't mind this time, JoAnne. We have some rather important matters to attend..."

Ambassador Kamal came to her defense by offering to the obviously upset Egyptian politician. "No Mohammed Kheir. Please allow the young female to remain while we speak together, sir. I have nothing to hide from such a lovely young woman as she." The Libyan Ambassador wanted to keep this female killer in his sights, because he did not want her to come bursting in the office if their meeting became a shouting match as the last one had.

She bowed towards Kamal, offering him a good look down the front of her dress and her breasts, which did not seem to want any part of staying within the loosely fitting midnight blue fabric of the dress she wore especially for this meeting between the two Ambassadors.

Kamal took in the lovely sight with a lingering stare, and then he smiled as Mohammed glared harshly at JoAnne, and cursed his luck for being straddled with her as his female bodyguard.

He then turned his attention back to Ambassador Kamal. The formalities were cast aside whenever these two powerful Arab politicians met privately as he nearly barked at the Libyan politician as he stated. "What can I do for you, Ambassador Kamal? I'm extremely busy as you can plainly see for yourself, sir." He grumbled with a deep and disgusted sigh as he pointed to the stack of papers laying on the side of his desk.

Ambassador Kamal glanced in the direction he pointed with his outstretched hands. But he paid no attention to the stack of papers on the desk as he snarled right back at him. "I wanted to warn you of the upcoming events soon to take place concerning our two countries, Mohammed. There's a Japanese cargo ship currently sitting at our capital port of Bengazi."

Mohammed jumped to his feet and threw his pencil at his desk as he suddenly roared at the Libyan politician. "For the love of Allah. Please don't try and inform me that you're now going to start trouble with the yellow devils? Where is this going to end, Ambassador Kamal."

Ambassador Kamal laughed over his childish outburst as he offered him. "Calm down some Mohammed, think of your blood pressure will you please. We're starting no trouble with the Japanese, quite on the contrary Mohammed, the Japanese are working with us. This cargo ship sent out a fake SOS, there's nothing wrong with the ship. But the SOS was sent so we could help her, but in reality the ship was scheduled to port with us. We knew if Japan sent a cargo ship to Libya, other countries such as the United States, England and maybe France would demand to know what was being delivered to us. So my government and Japan came up with this little deception of a SOS, to avoid any investigation or concerns from these other nations, or even a possible attack from these other nations. The cargo ship contains three hundred and fifty cargo containers. Inside each of them is the body of a Mitsubishi T 2R3S Japanese made fighter.

"Each body of these new Japanese made aircraft are armed, and they're equipped with two external fuel tanks. We were furnished with four sidewinder missiles for each plane. We had pilots stationed in Japan for a year now, and they were well trained in how to fly these aircraft. The pilots could out fly most cursed American pilots. The bodies of the planes are to be unloaded from the Japanese ship as a favor to Japan. We're going to let out a story about the ship being damaged by a reef, and was in danger of sinking, and that's why we unloaded the containers. These containers will be stacked on the dock, and using the cover of darkness we're going to transfer the aircraft to box trucks, and move them to hangers at the Bengasi Port by the military airport. There, they'll await the wings and more missiles, sidewinders."

Mohammed was dumbfounded as he stared harshly back at the Libyan politician. He knew Libya planned an all out war involving the entire world as he grumbled. "Ambassador Kamal, how do you plan to get the wings for these aircraft to your country? Fake another Japanese ship in trouble, sir? Come on Ambassador Kamal, if Japan sends more cargo ships to Libya, there will surely be many other countries demanding to know what is truly going on in Bengasi, as you have just stated, sir. Japan is no longer trusted by many other countries of the world, ever since she defaulted on loans, and selling off her real estate in many of these countries."

Again Ambassador Kamal laughed as he offered to Ambassador Kheir in a sharp tone of voice this time. "We have this problem well worked out, Mohammed. Japan is going to be sending a smaller cargo ship, supposedly to retrieve the containers from the ship that had sent out the supposed SOS. This second ship will have the wings for the planes, and even more ammunition and missiles stored inside their cursed hull. We'll empty this foul ship in the middle of the night also. Of course, it's going to be too small a ship to take all the containers back to Japan in one trip from the supposed stricken ship, thus making it possible for Japan to send out a second smaller cargo ship, loaded down with another hundred and fifty more of these warplanes, along with their wings and weapons also. This brings the total of our airforce up to over five hundred of the latest Japanese made fighter planes, but this will just be a start of it all, Mohammed.

"We're also going to have a number of Japanese engineers come over to our country to repair this damage ship, but they'll be employed to put the warplanes together for us, and all the while Japan is sending more workers to my country by ship. They'll be sending even more military equipment and warplanes to us. We'll have a thousand of these aircraft added to our airforce."

"Kamal, why the hell would the Japanese want to help us in this manner for? Libya has never gotten along well with Japan, and they owe us nothing, sir. I'm certain the Japanese knows what could be at stake here. A World War is nothing to be taken lightly by any country."

"That is the beauty of this plan from the start, Mohammed. Japan is more angry at the United States, than she is worried about getting involved in another World War. The Japanese blame the hated United States for her troubles of late, just like the Americans blamed Japan for their ills in late '91. And here we are, sitting right in the middle of the big game, playing both super powers against each other, and having both sides angry with each other, and not angry at us for a change, Mohammed. We'll be able to cash in on their hatred against each other, by getting all the military equipment we need from the foolish Japanese nation. And the West has the balls to call us Arab countries uncivilized, sir. That shows us just how foolish the West truly is with their understanding of us Arab nations, sir." Ambassador Kamal laughed at his own words.

Mohammed looked at the laughing man, he then bitched at him. "Kamal, do you not think there might be some risk you're taking here, with having this Japanese ship sitting at your port?"

"War is war. Any country that contemplates war, and is unwilling to take certain risks is not very serious, and will be destroyed in that war." Ambassador Kamal stopped laughing and then he looked angrily at Ambassador Kheir seated at his desk, and he snapped at him this time. "Mohammed, I told you all I want to tell you about this matter at this time, sir. As you have said a short time before, you're so swamped down with your work you have little time to spend speaking with me, so I shall leave you at this time to your so important paperwork."

Again Ambassador Kamal smiled which was more like a sneer as he added to his words to the Egyptian politician. "I trust you shall inform your President Sadat of what is currently happening inside my country, before he hears it from another source, Ambassador Kheir." Kamal again glared harshly at him as if to warn him he better let President Sadat know.

"I assure you that President Sadat will know everything we have discussed here the minute you leave my office, Ambassador. I keep nothing from my President, sir." Ambassador Mohammed Kheir hissed as he stood and then he offered Ambassador Kamal his hand to shake.

Ambassador Kamal grumbled in an extremely angry tone of voice. "Very well, good bye then Mohammed." As he turned and left, leaving Mohammed with his hand out and he hissed to no one in particular. "Uncouth dung eating jackal bastard you."

JoAnne asked Muhammad from her seat if he wanted her to get President Sadat on the phone.

"No, there are some things I have to do for myself young lady."

She smiled as she got up to leave his office, but not before adding. "Mohammed, I dislike Ambassador Kamal immensely sir. He's an extremely rude and dangerous man with no conscious to deal with. Are we going to party tonight as was promised, Mohammed? Gail is becoming upset lately because we rarely see her anymore. She even threatened to find another couple to party with, Mohammed. I'd surely hate to lose her sir."

He stared at her in silence for a long moment. Then he leaned back in his chair and then he made a steeple out of his fingers, and he positioned it at his lower lip and stared over his locked together fingers and replied. "This offer honors the unworthy. Allah has truly sent you to me on this day. Hmm... Yes, I think it is a good idea, I could certainly stand for some fun and games tonight, young woman. Tell Gail to be at my apartment, hmmm… let's say around eight o'clock this evening. Then we shall start the festivities going young lady." He said with a smile that was half hidden by his fingers as he saw the pleading etched in her beautiful eyes, and he added to his words to her. "Yes, and she can stay the night also if she so chooses."

She almost jumped in the air with delight at the though of sharing Gail's lovemaking abilities again as she said in an excited tone to him. "Thank you so much Mohammed, you have just made my day for me, sir." She just about skipped out of his office.

JoAnne missed Gail, and knew he was not very fond of her. He hated Gail because he had to be watched all the time, even while he slept by either woman, and he kind of took his anger out on her all along. At least he was still making love to her every night, but this was leaving Gail out in the cold, bored with nothing for her to do but be with herself.

He picked up the phone and quickly dialed President Sadat's private office number. Immediately, he heard the sound of the scrambling machine which always drove him absolutely crazy as he said in the phone. "President Sadat, this is Mohammed, I have information."

The world waited for Libya to inform them over what she intended to do with the damaged Japanese ship resting at their port. Many western countries half expected Libya to announce they were going to confiscate the ship for entering her territorial waters. The announcement came that Libya was off loading some of the cargo containers because the ship was in danger of sinking, but Libya was offering Japan the right to come to Libya and pick up the ship containers. She further offered to allow Japan to repair the damaged ship where she was moored in their port, and Libya even offered her assistance to the Japanese government and their workers.

The world powers breathed a little easier over this stunning announcement, and even the United States commended Libya for her decision to allow the Japanese to repair her disabled ship while moored in the Libyan port, and America even went so far as to offer Japan or Libya their assistance to accomplish this feat a little quicker. The United States had no way of knowing this action was a well thought out and planned operation, and Libya and Japan were laughing at the offer of help coming from the West, and the other concerned nations of the world.

THE AIRCRAFT CARRIER USS ROOSEVELT STATIONED IN THE RED SEA

Commander Owens ordered up a number of extra air flights of the Navy X 117B Stealth bombers over the nation of Libya, after the Combat Information Center picked up the SOS call coming from the stricken Japanese cargo ship. The flights were armed in case they were needed to repel any Libyan forces from taking command over the Japanese ship by force.

Commander Owens looked at the first pictures of the Japanese ship being towed towards Libya's second capital city of Benghazi, as they came in from the recon flights he ordered up over Libya. It seemed like the damaged ship was not taken by force, nevertheless he ordered a Strike Force to be ready to fly on the deck of the Roosevelt. The Aircraft Carrier Independence stationed in the Mediterranean Sea, was ordered to deck an Alert Strike Force on her catapults. These alert forces consisted of two attack F 18 Hornets, along with two F 16s to fly cover for the possible attackers. There was a ready air cap of four F 18 Hornets flying cover for all Aircraft Carriers at all times the while the ships were stationed at sea. There were also six Navy divers in the water surrounding the Carriers both day and night.

Three Navy divers were stationed on each side of the Carrier, they were to intercept any enemy divers before they had a chance to place any possible magnetic explosive charges against the ships, whenever the ships were stationary as the Roosevelt currently was. These alert planes from the Carriers, would attack the port at Bengazi, if help was requested from the Japanese sailors. The alert status was lowered when the Japanese ship docked safely at Benghazi, and the Japanese Captain went on Libyan television and announced he and his crew was being well treated, and Libya was a gracious host. Behind the Japanese Captain, stood a number of members of his crew, and all smiled and appeared to be in good health and not threatened.

The ready Strike Force was still sitting on the decks of both American Carriers, but the pilots opened the canopies, showing a sign of a step down in readiness. Commander Owens viewed the latest pictures the stealth fighter aircraft took on their last flyover of Bengazi, and noticed the Japanese cargo ship pushed to the docks by the sea going tugs, and then properly tied off. He saw a number of cranes already busy unload the containers, and placed them on the docks, a move that showed the Libyans were truly worried the ship might be in danger of sinking.

Most of the large cargo containers were placed stacked together, while others were moved over to other locations along the docks for the lack of stacking space. This activity was typical of the workers who had to unload a cargo ship.

Commander Owens shook his head slowly as he mumbled at one of his officers with him. "Who would have ever thunk for one moment that the god damn Libyan's would ever offer help to any country like they just did, dammit." The Commander then ordered a call placed through to CATCC, (Carrier Air Traffic Control Center) and have them order another flyover by the Navy X 117B Bluebirds, so he could have the latest pictures of the situation developing at the Port of Bengasi, and to make absolutely certain that everything was still okay with the Japanese ship and her crew. It was no secret the United States offered Japan military protection.

This pact between the United States and Japan dated back to the end of the Second World War, in which Japan was forbidden to rearm herself militarily, which she never did. Japan produced many other weapons and attack warplanes such as the T 2 Japanese fighter bomber, and a certain number of specialized tanks, but these were to be for her nation's self defense only. The United States signed this pact to better protect the shores of Japan from any possible hostile attack, and to also protect her interests at home and abroad at the same time.

When these pictures came across the Roosevelt's threat board, and the Commander viewed them all, he again shook his head. Because they all showed a lot of activity at the port which was indicative of most dock workers unloading a ship which could possibly be in trouble of sinking.

"Contact the Libyans and offer them our help with the fucking disabled Japanese ship, I want to see if they need anything from us over this damn mess taking place in Libya." Commander Owens ordered the radio operator, as he let out his breath in a disgusted sigh.

In just moments, they received a rather crisp and direct reply which added up to. "Thanks, but no thanks for the offer of help. Libya was more than capable of helping the Japanese with their disabled ship, without the help from the United States."

Commander Owens crumpled the paper up into a tight knob in anger, and then he threw it to the deck and kicked it across the room with his foot as he growled over the nasty reply from Libya. "Sonofabitch, these fucking asses have to keep up a nasty front all the damn time. They never understand when someone's trying to help the lousy sonofabitches. Fuck the damn assholes where they breathe, they can do all the work if they want, but we'll keep an eye on the lousy little bastards, and if they try anything, I'll destroy their country in less than a heartbeat."

BENGAZI, LIBYA

At the Libyan port and secondary capital of Bengazi, the Libyans worked at a fever pitch on rapidly unloading the Japanese ship. The many cargo containers were placed in such a way that the workers would be able to unload the plane's bodies from inside, without having to move the containers around anymore. As the dark of night rapidly set in, a convoy of tractor trailer box trucks moved into position on the docks, without the use of their headlights. Heavy tarps were draped over and between the large cargo containers, and the trailers disappeared under them.

High low lift trucks entered the cargo containers and carefully picked up the bodies of the Japanese aircraft. Then the lift machines moved the aircraft bodies into the box trucks with the help of the workers, pulling and pushing the plane further into the truck. Once a trailer was loaded with the bodies of three planes. It quickly left the sight, and brought the planes over to a number of empty hangers of the military base constructed just outside the city of Bengazi.

USS ROOSEVELT, STATIONED IN THE RED SEA

A quick flyover by a night flight of a X 117 Bluebird aircraft, filmed what it could view of the activity on and around the Japanese cargo ship, and once Commander Owens scanned the pictures. He truly felt it was an emergency unloading operation being carried out by the workers at the Libyan port. There were nine other cargo ships from different nations moored up alongside the docks, and from the actions of the Libyans working on these ships, Commander Owens anticipated no further threat coming from all this night time activity.

A number of tractor trailers made three and even four trips over to the dock, and back to the military base. By dawn, two hundred and ninety aircraft bodies were removed from the supposed Japanese cargo ship, and hidden inside hangers at the base. When light began, all work on the cargo containers stopped until the fall of another night's darkness.

USS ROOSEVELT, STATIONED IN THE RED SEA

During the rest of the day, there were five other flyovers of Bengazi, and their pictorials were sent over to the CIC. Commander Owens sent the batch of photos to his Intel men, there, the photographs were gone over using enhancement machines and magnifying equipment, looking for anything sign of something out of the ordinary. He could not help feeling that the Libyan's were up to something, and he was not seeing what they were doing as yet.

Questions were quickly raised about why the Libyans needed so many canvass tarps to cover over the cargo containers removed from the disabled Japanese cargo ship. Further questions were raised about what the Libyan workers might be doing under those tarps out of the camera's sight. Commander Owens laughed over the last question, he then got angry over all the pictures coming in as he snapped at his intelligence officer.

"What the hell do you think the bastards are doing under those fucking tarps for the love of god? I bet you dollars to doughnuts they're opening up every last fricking container, and stealing anything they get their grubby damn hands on. You can bet your life on that much, mister. I know I would've opened them to see what they had stored inside, and then take what I wanted or needed from them and clear it in my mind as payback for all the help I was giving the Japanese. I want a ship's manifest of what's inside the fucking cargo containers right now."

"Commander Owens Sir, I have a complete manifest from the Japanese ship's cargo. It was sent over to us by the Coast Guard when the SOS was first sent out from the disabled ship, its SOP sir." The young Ensign said as he offered the papers to his Commanding Officer. The papers listed the entire contents of the boxes as tractors and tractor parts. There were also listed some computers, and a ton of video games and other components for the games as well.

Commander Owens laughed as he offered to the young Ensign. "You can kiss all those damn video games good bye." He did not like the fact there were a number of computers listed on the cargo manifest. There was also a second list containing medical supplies. These supplies were scheduled to go to Iraq who was still reeling from the Desert War beating of five years ago.

Again, Commander Owens thought for a moment, and then he mumbled. "No loss if the medical supplies don't reach Iraq I guess." He still felt Iraq should have been bombed right off the face of the earth. He blamed his Commander in Chief for showing them mercy, and stopping the war before the job was completed. He rubbed his stubble covered chin rough as sandpaper, and then laughed as he thought back to that conflict and added. "There's no deal to be made with a damn predator nation. It's either you kill it, or it kills you, it's that simple. Shit, I guess that's why I never entered politics. You're damned if you do, and you're damned if you don't. No matter what your decision was, it'd never please all concerned."

A sailor standing by the Commander whispered to him. "Err... excuse me sir, but what was that you said, I didn't get all of it sir. Were you talking to me Commander Owens Sir?"

He looked at the concerned man for a second, and then he smirked at him. "It was nothing sailor. I laughed at a joke I just remembered from a long time ago, that's all."

The nervous young sailor gave a quick laugh of his own as the Commander looked at one of the many pictures of the Japanese ship lying on his desk.

BASE EASY MONEY, ETHIOPIA

Colonel Edward Campanelli went over to his Intel tent when he was given news of the SOS being transmitted from the supposed disabled Japanese ship. His first thought was Libya attacked the ship for entering her territorial waters. He stepped up his alert on the base, fearing the worse when informed Libya offered help to the floundering ship.

Upon entering the Intel tent he noticed the young Lieutenant, and again he was wired to the computers and he thought of how it would feel to be attached to a machine like this poor soul was. He knew it was necessary because this would stop any possible enemy from compromising his intelligence network if he was able to get into the computers before they were destroyed. Nevertheless, it took a special type of man to be wired up to a machine like this kid was, and he was ready to blow the computers up with the small explosive charge attacked to the computers and if he died in an attack, his last heartbeat would set off the charge.

"How are you doing with the damn computers, soldier?" He asked the young soldier.

"Just fine sir. Colonel Campanelli Sir, I was thinking, every time one of these emergency calls comes up, I have to run to the Intel tent and hook myself up to the damn computers, or they'll self destruct within five minutes from receiving the flash traffic. I'm scared to death one of these times I won't fucking make it in time and come into a Intel tent full of scrap metal, sir."

"I hear that son. What are you suggesting I do about your gripe, soldier?" The concerned Colonel interrupted him and smiled at the young and concerned Lieutenant.

"Colonel Campanelli Sir, what I was thinking was, do you think it's at all possible for me to move into this Intel tent. That way, I'd never be too far away from the damn computers to get to them in time, and they would never destruct unless we're attacked and I set off the charge by either dying, or I set it off manually, sir."

"You sure you only have five minutes to reach the damn computers before they explode, son?"

"I have ten minutes at the most to get myself hooked up to the computers sir, and that's under the lightest of the alerts at that, sir. But if a Red Alert comes in, or a flash message for you sir. I have five minutes to get myself here sir. I have this warning device on me at all times of the day or night, sir." The young Lieutenant pulled up his sleeve and showed the Colonel a small pocket radio device, and then he added. "I really worry what will happen to the machines if I'm out of range, or the battery goes dead on me sir. It's actually cutting into my sleep on me sir."

"I guess I'll give you permission to move your quarters over to the Command Tent if that's really what you wanna do, son. But I'm afraid you won't get very much privacy though by living in the damn tent, son." He offered to the young soldier.

The young man simply shrugged and smiled back at the new and well respected Colonel.

"Okay son, you can move in if that's what you truly want to do. I'll have the Seabees bring over one of their portable heads, and place it to the rear of the damn tent. That way you won't have to go too far to take a stinking dump or leak, Lieutenant. That's the best I can do for you I'm afraid at this point, soldier."

"That'll do just fine for me sir. If it's not too much trouble for you that is sir."

He laughed, here is this guy putting himself out, and he's more worried about it being too much trouble for me as he replied to the young soldier. "It's no trouble at all, you do what you want. Thanks for your concern over this matter, I'll make a note of your request and dedication to duty on your records, soldier. I'm sure it'll lead to a promotion somewhere along the line. The Army likes it when one of its own shows initiative, Lieutenant."

"That's not why I wanted to do this for you, sir. I just want to be in place at the right time if the shit hits the fan, that's all Colonel Campanelli Sir."

"I understand that Lieutenant, nevertheless I'll mark it down on your 201 files, mister. I'm quite certain that it'll help you later on in your career, young man."

The young soldier saluted his Commanding Officer proudly. When the Colonel went over the information he just received pertaining to the disabled Japanese ship stuck in the Libyan port, he realized there was little danger of anything happening to cause an outbreak of hostilities in the region over the situation. He contacted the CIC and was told virtually the same thing.

ON BOARD THE CARRIER USS ROOSEVELT

The Combat Information Center (CIC) on board the Aircraft Carrier Roosevelt was a beehive of activity. It seemed a missile was fired at one of the over flights of Libya by an X-117, and if it was not for some rather quick reactions by the pilot, the Stealth aircraft would have been hit. Commander Owens knew the missile came from Libya and he was steamed about it.

The upset Naval Commander was furious over the attempt to shoot down one of his warplanes as he screamed at anyone near enough to hear him growling. "How the hell did these lousy backasswards sonofabitches even been able to detected our fucking supposed stealth aircraft, and how the hell did they peg a fucking shot at the damn thing at the same time? I'm ordering all the damn flights stopped immediately until I find out how the hell the bastards detected our stealth aircraft. Dammit to hell and back again, I want answers or fucking heads will be rolling."

Flight Commander Richards reported to his Commander. "Commander Owens Sir, evidently the Libyans have one of the old style, low frequency French radar unit left over from World War Two operating in their damn country, and this antique system accidentally stumbled over our flight's signatures. I'm certain it was by just by dumb luck that they found it on us, sir. The Stealth's are equipped to hide and confuse just about all modern day radar units, sir. The only weakness we ever found with the X 117B, was its susceptibility to the old style radar units thought not to be in operation any longer, sir. It had to be by fluke luck the Libyans had this unit in operation, sir. Or maybe they had advance warning or some detection capabilities we don't know about yet sir, and I seriously doubt this second thought for a moment, sir."

"Let me tell you this much mister, until I know for certain if it was just a dumb accident, or if they're able to detect our stealth aircraft, I'm stopping all flights over Libya as of now. I can ill afford to have one of these aircraft falling into Libyan hands. Even the wreckage would give the damn Libyans vitally important information. Maybe even enable the bastards to kill one of the damn things. I want this low level fucking radar unit found, and then rendered useless by our operatives inside Libya. Let them earn their damn money we're paying them for once in their miserable lives, mister." Commander Owens growled at the Flight Commander.

"Damn, I could sure use one of those new SR 91 stealth aircraft, sir. Who ever heard of using a damn Stealth Fighter as a flying camera platform, sir. Captain, what's the status on those new birds and can we get our hands on one of the damn things, sir?"

"Commander Owens Sir, from what I was informed about those aircraft, all the SR-91s are grounded until further notice until they can figure out what's wrong with their guidance systems, sir. At best the brain thrust figures the aircraft flies to damn fast for its computer system to keep up with aircraft when she's in full operation, sir."

"No wonder they call the SR 91 the invisible plane. Any aircraft that doesn't fly, is invisible in the sky and even on the damn ground, Captain. Is there any possibility we might be able to re-commission one of the older SR 71 aircraft? I hate using my Stealth's as a damn recon ship."

"Not a chance in hell of that happening I can assure you, Commander. Even the one NASA has is down for repairs I was informed, sir."

"What about the one that's on display in the Smithsonian, mister?" Owens demanded.

"No good there either sir, the motors have been completely removed from the aircraft, sir. We could never get them replaced in time to do us any good over this present situation, sir."

"Jesus H. Christ, we have nothing but the best equipment in the damn world, and we can't use the damn things when we need them the most. I'd give my left nut to be able to drop a few bombs on Libya, teach those asses they ain't safe in their own beds." The Commander growled, all of a sudden, he felt woozy and checked his implant to see if his time release insulin unit was working. It was working fine, so he sat down and counted to ten before he started again.

"Captain Richards, I want the damn satellite recon platforms to pick up the slack of the X 117s flights I pancake then, sir. I want to deflect some satellite passes to cover the Libyan Port of Bengasi. At least I hope they can't do anything to our damn satellites yet, and I'll again have eyes over Libya in case things get hot there and we have to react against it. I have to know when any threats occur. Get a move on it Captain Richards." Commander Owens commanded as he looked over the reports pilling up on his desk about the missile just fired at his stealth aircraft and he bitched angrily. "God, I can't believe my damn Intel people didn't offer up an opinion about what kind of missile it was the Libyan's fired at our damn aircraft. What's happening to my intelligence operation for crap sake? Get Captain Johnson up here on the double quick. I want to know what kind of missile was fired and now. Stupid assholes."

A SPECIAL MILITARY BUNKER IN LIBYA

Three well aged Russian scientists who defected to Libya last year, linked up to nine Russian satellites in orbit, and now they were able to watch all taking place in, and around the surrounding countries around Libya.

The defectors observed the incoming flights of the F 117 Stealth Fighter/Bombers taking off from Saudi Arabia for most of the day, but when the newer Naval X 117Bs took off from the American Navy Base stationed in Turkey, he made up his mind what he was going to do. These stealth aircraft were much easier for them to track, mainly because of their predictable flight paths, so the old Russian was able to make a pattern to the flights, and then he decided to chance a shot at where he thought the plane should be by a computer worked out time schedule.

The Russian defector lobbed a Snake Missile at the estimated position of the American stealth fighter aircraft. The missile was developed by Libya, long before the Russian defectors came along. The Snake was an anti aircraft missile, which carried thirty smaller heat seeker missiles in her bowels. While in flight, the missile broke up when it acquires her target, and then it sends the smaller and much faster missiles out to destroy the incoming missile or aircraft.

The Russian watched the path of the missile on the scope, from launch to its hunting mode. It easily locked onto the stealth for a second before the pilot took some evasive action, and lost the missiles radar bounce. The Russian decided to blow up the shell of the missile when he lost contact with the plane. He hoped maybe the smaller missiles radar might confuse the pilot, and they could hunt the invisible plane. But the whole exercise went for naught, because by the time the missile exploded, the fighter was out of the area and made an emergency run to Saudi Arabia.

The pilot maintained complete radio silence, until he was well over the Saudi Arabia airspace. Then he announced he was fired on, causing all hell to break out inside of the CIC center.

Even though the Libyan missile fired missed the American stealth aircraft, both the Russians and Libyans took great satisfaction in this action, and they also took it as a major victory over the United States, and their military capabilities. Now, the number of Russian technicians working inside Libya, turned their attention towards the American military bases constructed in Saudi Arabia, to see what the next moves by the American troops were going to be. They were extremely pleased to see the huge steel doors of the special hangers that housed the fleet of twenty five stealth fighters, being closed up and then camouflaged over again. The Russian defector suddenly turned to the Libyan soldier assigned to watch over his charge, and he stared at him in utter disbelief as he announced. "We almost got the damn thing this time sir." The young man cried in an excited tone to the old Russian technician.

The stone face of the Russian traitor showed no spirit in his body whatsoever, because his soul was fighting with his conscience for betraying his motherland, Russia. There was no spirit in his lack luster eyes, they were more like lifeless bits of chipped and discolored glass, reflecting the dead hopes the old man once held dear to himself. His eyes were locked in an old man's face distorted into a mask of pain and fear for his betrayal. The ugly mask was ringed with ruptured veins and small capillaries, and divided by a drunkard's broad nose. He stuttered his words as he though of what to say to the young Libyan guard.

"There will be no more spy flights over Libya by the worthless American aircraft for quite a while to come after this one I believe." The Russian announced with as much enthusiasm as his old body could possibly muster, and then he added to his words. "This action has insured your government the privacy it needs to finish unloading the warplanes from their Japanese cargo containers, without being watched by hated American spy planes." The old man then turned his attention back to the radar scope he was watching moment before.

The young Libyan guard left his ward, and then he headed for a radio to report on the results of the missiles firing at the American stealth aircraft. This was what the Libyan government wanted to have happen, the grounding of the entire wing of the stealth fighters from the United States until they were finished with the unloading of the Japanese cargo containers.

ON BOARD THE AMERICAN CARRIER USS ROOSEVELT

Commander Owens heard the report offered from his Intel Officer Captain Johnson, in which he was informed the Libyans fired a self developed Snake missile at the supposed invisible fighter aircraft. The officer offered his opinion the launch was nothing more than a lucky shot, combined with a luckier guess. He assured the Commander he was confident Libya had no way of detecting the stealth fighters while in flight. He laid out his opinion on how good it was the fighter easily out maneuvered the Snake missile. He confidently reminded Commander Owens the Snake missile was the only real threat we know the Libyans to be in possession of.

"We have pictures of the missile firing, and the launch angle it takes when fired, and action of the smaller missiles when the breakup of the mother missile occurs in flight. The stealth cameras started operating when they detected the plume, and surface heat signature from the launching, sir. This is important for until today, we never witnessed one of these missiles in operation, sir. We can deploy an operational defense against the missiles once we got this film, sir."

"Yeah, I have this file in my hands at this moment, mister. But it almost cost us one of our damn stealth fighters, Captain. If the missile had knocked out the aircraft, I think it would've been a bad trade. What the hell happened to your damn Intel people and network on this one, mister? How the fuck did it happen we weren't informed about this low level radar unit bull until it was almost too late? A unit which costs eleven thousand dollar and made half a century ago almost killed a three quarter of a billion dollar stealth aircraft, dammit. I can't believe this shit for one moment, mister. Is there more than one of these cheap ass radar units out there, and now the Libyans saw they could detect our stealth's with this shit radar system, will they set up more against us, mister? This could render our stealth fighter bombers useless if the shit hits the fan. I know I'd set up more shitty radar units if I knew they could make our spy planes obsolete."

"Commander Owens Sir, we in the intelligence field feel it would be self defeating for the Libyans to setup more of the old radar units, sir. These units are dirty and they also leave a telltale messages as to where the units are located, thus making it easy for our missile's to lock onto their emissions and then destroy the damn things, sir. Commander, although these units are able to detect our stealth aircraft, they react like they can't pick up many other modern aircraft, such as the F 15 and F 16s and 18s, as well as the old Phantom 4s and even the F 111s, because of the use of Ram. (the Radar absorbing materials) throughout the aircraft's structure)

"It'd be suicide on any of our enemy's part to do this, because the old radars need the same conditions as modern units employ, so they'd naturally have to setup both radar unit's together, and the older and easier detectable radar units would put the modern radar units in peril. No sir, I think I'd have to stay with my first assumption which was, this was just a damn fluke, and the missile shot was more luck than anything else, Commander Owens."

"That maybe so Captain, but I don't want to take the damn Libyan military for granted here either, sir. Remember what happened to the Japanese when they took us for granted during the big war, Captain? We ended up kicking their asses all over the damn place, and I have no fucking intention of getting my ass kicked in any future fight, sir. Is there any way for us to block these damn shit filled ancient radar units, from picking up our fricking stealth aircraft, sir? I need these damn air frames to work with sir."

"Yes Sir Commander Owens Sir, there's an effective way of our blocking these old radar units out, sir. We can easily block the old units if we wanted to, the new and old radar unit's alike sir. We can simply airborne an EC 130H Compass Call Jamming aircraft, sir. She's our electronic warfare aircraft platform, and she can jam all known radar units, modern and old alike, sir. Of course, we're going to have to offer these jamming aircraft a fighter aircraft escort because of the low altitudes she has to fly, to accomplish her intended mission sir."

The Commander gave the Captain a harsh glare, and then snapped at him. "This doesn't leave me with much rope to pull with, mister. Err... Captain, I have no fricking intention of starting a stinking shooting war over an old ass radar unit I can tell you that much, sir. If we deploy this platform, it could be construed as an act of war, an invasion if you will of Libya. I just want to jam their low level shit, Captain. I can't jam all their radar units, because we're not at war with Libya. If this aircraft can't jam the low level shit, I can't authorize this mission."

"Commander Owens Sir, I assure you sir this aircraft can concentrate its systems on the low level stuff, sir. It can make it happen so the Libyans will think their equipment's malfunctioning, sir. They'll never know we're jamming the shit outta them sir."

"If you can make this happen without causing a damn war breaking out then I want it done immediately, mister. When I'm certain the old radar units are being successfully jammed, I want the stealth aircraft back in the air." Commander Owens looked at Captain Johnson and then he warned him in no uncertain terms. "I promise you Captain, if I lose one damn stealth ship, you'll rue the day your mother met your father. Get everything in operation, I need those eyes."

Johnson went to the radioman, keyed the mike and ordered the EC 130 in the air and jamming at Megahertz, eleven to eighteen, and no higher than thirty three decibels when they were up.

Commander Owens watched the radar detecting screen that showed the low level transitions being emitted from the old and outdated radar units intensely. In less than an hour, the emissions stared to dance all over the screen and a few seconds later, the screen was nothing more than a mass of crazy acting lines going from left to right with no set pattern to the lines.

Captain Johnson walked up behind the concerned looking Commander staring at the dancing and distorted lines, and he laid his hand lightly on his shoulder as he offered to his Commanding Officer. "Sir, the jamming is in effect as of this moment sir. As you can plainly see for yourself on the screen, sir. This jamming is informing the technicians monitoring the screens there's something wrong with their damn radar sets, sir. The operators will probably blame it on sun spots or something else, and the jamming as I promised you, Commander Sir. Is effecting just the low level stuff, our EC 130's flying low enough so the natural curve of the earth is shielding it from being detected by any of the more modern day radar units in operation, sir. The Libyans have no idea we're causing their current troubles in the least, sir."

"Fine, just what I wanted to hear from you, I want to commit the planes from Saudi Arabia this time. Get those older F 117s ordered up in the damn air, Captain." Owens demanded hotly.

"Commander Owens Sir, I took it upon myself to order the first stealth flights up already, sir. The pilot's instructed to do a high flyover to see if the Libyans can pick him up. Once the pilot's assured of his aircraft's invisibility integrity, the pilot shall then begin making the lower passes, much closer to the targets." Johnson replied confidently to the Commanding Officer.

"Fine, it looks like you have everything under control, so carry on then Captain." Commander Owens offered as he let out his breath in a rush.

Again, the pictures of the men working on the docks in Libya came in from the stealth cameras. The pictures reaching Commander Owens served to confirm the Libyans were doing nothing more than looting the cargo containers, and offering some minor help to the Japanese work on their disabled ship. The United States was not responsible or interested in any looting of Japanese property. America's responsibility was to try and keep Japan free from enemy attack.

Commander Owens smiled pleasantly as he looked at the new pictures coming into the CIC chamber, showing beyond a shadow of a doubt the Libyan workers were obviously stealing everything they could possibly get their hands on out of the many Japanese cargo containers. Commander Owens only worry was about the computers, and if they were going to be able to be used for military applications. He sent an interest memo out to Command and to the Joint Chiefs, to see if they could find out if the Japanese computers could be used for any possible military purposes. If they were, he would have no other choice but to order in an air attack, and destroy the computers before the Libyans were able to put them to use against his forces. The Commander also notified the President, informing him there was no serious threat from Libya over the Japanese ship situation at this time, other than from the computers they were stealing.

President Albert Cole agreed with the Commander's thoughts and concern, he already read a memo from the Japanese government, confirming that there was no problem pertaining to the damaged Japanese ship presently docked at the Libyan port. And Japan was sending special repair workers to get the ship and cargo containers out of Libyan waters as soon as possible. The American President also informed Commander Owens he already informed the Japanese Delegate, he felt the Libyans were looting the cargo containers. The Delegate replied there was nothing he could do to try and stop the looting, and his government had no intention of filing a complaint, as long as they could get the ship, and their seamen out of Libya safely.

After hearing this, Commander Owens ordered yet another step down from a war footing.

THE MILITARY BUNKER IN LIBYA

The Russian defector reading his radar screen suddenly saw it go wild on him. At first, he thought it was some sort of jamming being aimed at his unit by the Americans, but as the screen went crazier on him, he started to believe there was suddenly something wrong with his equipment. He was not too worried though, because the effect was distorting just the low level radar only, his modern radar was operating properly. He was about to shutdown the low level units, when he suddenly received a warning signal from one of the commandeered Russian satellites that a low flying aircraft was paralleling the borders of Libya and Egypt.

Minutes later the well aged Russian defector was warned from the satellite that a number of stealth aircraft was taking off from the coast of Saudi Arabia. He let his Libyan guard know of the launch, and the soldier left the Russian's side and he immediately went over to the radio. Seconds later he returned with orders for the Russian to shoot down the American made fighter plane he was picking up on his still operating radar units.

The Russian scientist pleaded desperately with the Libyan guard controlling him as he cried at the man. "I cannot possibly do as you order sir, because if I were to shoot down this one lone American plane. The Americans would know right off we have other means of detecting their aircraft in flight, and it'd not take them long to figure out we have illegal satellite hookups, and they'll block them against our use, and once that happens we'll be completely blind to any future attacks by the American aircraft. You'll lose the surprise in the upcoming fight your country needs to win this war. So I suggest we allow this American warplane to live. Let them think they have us blind again. It's more important we know what they're up to at all times, than it is for us to kill one of their foul and worthless planes. I implore you to try and convince your government to allow the American stealth aircraft to return safely to his home base in peace, sir." The Russian defector stared back at the Libyan soldier for a second.

"I shall relay your information and request to my government of what you informed me of. For all the good I believe your plea would do for you, old fool. I know once my Commander has made up his mind over what he wants done, he'll never change it under any circumstances." The Libyan security guard replied in an angry tone of voice as he went over to the radio. Seconds later, the Libyan soldier returned and told the Russian his people wanted the American stealth aircraft shot down, period.

The Russian jumped to his feet. This sudden and rapid and rash move making the Libyan soldier jump back a few steps himself, and automatically reach for his sidearm. Then he aim it directly at the Russian's chest as he continued to yell at the Libyan soldier. "I demand to speak with your control immediately, myself young man. It's that important I speak with this Officer at once, soldier!"

The soldier slowly relaxed his grip on his pistol, and then he led the Russian radar operator over to the radio so he could plead his case with his Commander. He handed the shaking old man the microphone when he got through to his Commanding Officer and was informed his Commander would talk to the Russian.

The fuming Russian defector quickly pointed out all the reasons why it was absolutely imperative to allow the American warplane to go safely back to the aircraft's home base in Saudi Arabia. But the Libyan Commander did not want to hear it, because his government wanted the prestige of killing one of America's most prized stealth fighter planes, and he simply would not allow the Russian to possibly talk him out of the order to kill the American aircraft. Just about the time the Russian defector was about to give into the demand of the Libyan Officer to kill the American aircraft, and order a launch of a second Snake intercept missile to destroy it. The Libyan Ambassador Kamal happened to walk into the Command Complex, and he listened in on the end of the conversation the Russian defector was having with the young soldier on the other end of the radio.

The sagging Russian traitor handed the radio mike back to the young Libyan soldier like it weighted a ton, and then he slowly walked back to his radar station like he had the weight of the world resting heavily on his broken shoulders, as he tried to get his breathing under control again.

The Libyan Ambassador Kamal stopped the old man from returning to his post, and suddenly smiled at him as he looked the old man right in his eyes.

The Russian defector instantly recognized Ambassador Kamal, and he smiled at him because he was the man who talked him into coming to Libya in the first place. The Russian defector informed Ambassador Kamal what his government wanted him to do to the American warplane, and he also pointed out the reasons why not to attack the lone American warplane to the concerned looking Libyan Ambassador.

Ambassador Kamal agreed with the Russian defector, mainly because he was still looking after the old man because he regarded him as one of his greatest successes for his country and his position in the Libyan government. Ambassador Kamal suddenly took the radio away from the young soldier's hand, and he spoke in it in a sharp and angry tone of voice. He immediately identified himself to the officer on the other end of the line, and then he told him he ordered a stop to the attack that was ordered against the American stealth fighter plane over Libya at the present moment. Whether or not he liked it.

The Libyan Officer was absolutely livid by the politician's sudden interference into his orders to the Russian fool, but when Ambassador Kamal threatened to have the Commander shot for his insubordination leveled against him. The soldier instantly backed down from his extremely angry stance, and he then agreed with Ambassador Kamal's last order. But not before he cursed the Libyan Ambassador for his intervention of his orders.

Ambassador Kamal made a mental note of this soldier's name, and vowed in his mind he would settle his hash with him later on, after Libya had won the upcoming war against the other nations he wanted destroyed, as he mumbled under his breath at the Libyan Officer. "You foolish asshole with ears." But for now, the angry Ambassador knew he needed all the Libyan Officers he had at his disposal.

CHAPTER 16

The Russian defector watched as the American stealth fighter started its second pass over the Libyan Port of Benghazi. He thought how easy it would be for him to kill this lone American warplane not traveling at its top speed, like it was invisible to his radar system. He was further angered by the arrogance being displayed by this pilot of this aircraft, evident by the way he was flying. The American pilot obviously thought he was undetectable to the Russian or Libyans, because he was flying lower on this second pass.

The well aged Russian defector grumbled he would give up a year's pay from the disliked Libyans, just to see the face of this so arrogant acting American pilot as his aircraft was hit by the missile he would have fired at him, if he was allowed to attack this aircraft. He cursed in Russian for being forced at holding his fire against this American pilot and his warplane, as he mentally warned the American pilot once the shooting started for real, he dared him to try and fly in his airspace a second time.

Sweat dripped down from his forehead and it landed on the small radar screen. He quickly wiped it off with a rag, and then he reached for a cigarette as he watched the stealth aircraft slowly crossing his screen. He looked at the American made Camel cigarette and wished it was a glass of good Russian Vodka. The old defector drew in the smoke deeply in his lungs, actually making his lungs hurt as he thought the United States made the best cigarettes in the world. But he could never afford them when he was living and working for the government in Russia. But here in Libya, he gets them for free for his service to the Libyans.

The American made stealth aircraft was about off his radar screen now, out of the satellite's field of vision as he mumbled angrily at the aircraft. "Go on you way little American warplane. For I shall get you on another day. This much I will promise you, American pig of a pilot." His hatred for the United States was as equal to his hatred of the new leaders of Russia. He blamed them for slowly destroying his country. He wished his country would have attacked the United States with her nuclear weapons, and die a true soldier's death. Rather than dying in the manner Russia was dying, a slow death. Being picked apart by the highest bidder, and the Russian gangsters who controlled most of Russia's vast worth.

It was being taken apart from the United States picking of the best of the Russian scientists who wanted a better way of living. Why the United States never picked him he would never know, but he would never forgive them for what he believed was their error. Now Libya and a number of other Arab nations were bidding for Russian knowhow, and paying top dollar for the scientists and their knowledge, more than the United States ever offered them.

"What has Russia come to, forcing her own once loyal scientists and military officers to defect to these Arab lowly countries." The aged Russian defector was prepared to take Russian top secrets to the United States if the Americans would have offered him a job, as he knew many other scientists had done. He loathed himself for having to work for the dirty Arabs. He vowed to get even with America for not picking him, he blamed Russia for not dying an honorable death, he blamed the Arab for his turning his back on his mother nation. He took another drag from his cigarette. The smoke again hurting his lungs as it filtered deep in his dying chest. "Damn Russia for making me help these dirty animals." He cried as he stared at a blank screen.

BENGAZI, LIBYA

The supposedly disabled Japanese cargo ship spent two full weeks resting at the Port of Benghazi. During this time, two smaller Japanese cargo ships also visited the Libyan port, under the guise of picking up the removed cargo containers from the larger and disabled ship. Both smaller ships carried extra planes, wings, munitions and military capable computers on board their ships. The two smaller Japanese cargo ships were unloaded in the middle of the night under cover of the tarps strung out to cover the unloading. The United States stopped the flyovers by the second week as they lost interest in the situation, and the Libyans were able to work much faster without any American planes watching their operation. The smaller ships were now docked at the Libyan port, supposedly carrying repair workers for the disabled ship, but these workers were the technicians who would put the pieces of the Japanese aircraft together.

By the end of the third week with the supposed disabled Japanese ship still moored at the Libyan port, most of the Japanese warplanes were fully assembled, and also armed and moved to secure cover. Again, using the darkness for cover, the new Japanese fighter planes were then moved out from their hangers covered over by tarps, and then they were moved to other buildings, or hidden under the sand in specially constructed hangers.

Other planes were promised to Libya by the Japanese government. These would find their way to country by way of Yemen and other Arab countries that ship to Libya freely, but were too small for the watch dogs to keep a close eye on most of them. Japan promised Libya it would have another five hundred of their aircraft in their country by the time they finally declared war on the nations threatened by the nation of Libya. And when the war broke out, Japan promised to ship another thousand of their warplanes in the open. Japan further closed a deal to sell a thousand warplanes to Egypt. It was approved by the United Nations.

APRIL 26th, 1996 AT THE PORT OF BENGAZI, LIBYA

On this day, the once supposed disabled Japanese cargo ship was declared sea worthy, many of the Japanese workers boarded the ship as it prepared to leave the Libyan port on April 27th. The Japanese workers needed to finish the final technical hookups on the fighter aircraft and computers and weapon systems, were going to remain in Libya until all the work was finished on the items of war they snuck into Libya.

The American recon satellites instantly picked up the heat signature suddenly being emitted from the massive boilers of the once disabled Japanese cargo ship on their infrared sensor systems. The CIC on board the American Aircraft Carrier Roosevelt was immediately notified the Japanese ship was hot and ready to move out of the Libyan port.

Commander Owens immediately ordered a low flyover of the ship by one of the stealth fighter aircraft, to make certain everything was proper with the Japanese ship. An hour later the pictures came in and the pilot informed the CIC he was certain he was picked up by two different radar systems, but no missiles were fired at his aircraft.

This news bugged the hell out of Commander Owens, because he was concerned his stealth fighter aircraft were no longer undetectable, and he did not like the possibility one bit. He ordered Command to look into blocking the low level radar systems able to detect his planes.

The Japanese cargo ship put up steam, and three tugboats pulled her free of the docks, and by seven a.m., the ship was underway on its own power out to the open waters of the Mediterranean Sea. As the Japanese ship slowly left the Libyan port, it was instantly shadowed closely by the American Destroyer USS Spruce patrolling outside Libya's territorial waters, and when the ship was in international waters, the American ship requested permission to board her and examine the ship's sea worthiness. The Japanese asked the American Navy to inspect their vessel to make certain the Libyans had not planted any bombs aboard her. It took the Americans three hours to sweep the entire ship, and nothing was found and the report was sent to the CIC. The Spruce was ordered to escort the Japanese ship until it was in the Atlantic Ocean, and on her way home.

BASE EASY MONEY LAKE TANA, ETHIOPIA

Colonel Edward Campanelli paid little if any attention to what was going on in Libya at the present time. He was concentrating all his efforts on the construction of the Dam. He knew he was days away from being pulled off his construction project, and then sent to build a second military base in the Sudan. Everything he heard about the Sudan was not good news to hear. He was informed of the terrible heat, the massive swarms of mosquitoes, all sorts of snakes that can kill a person before he was able to get the proper medical care, lions and any other animal that could harm a human being lived there as well. All this, plus the kind of people who trusted or befriended no one, was waiting for him and his troops there.

The Colonel was not looking very forward to going to the Sudan, but if his country needed him there, there was where he would be going without complaints. Every night, he would spend an hour catching up on what was happening in Libya. This was his duty and he gave orders for both Intel Officers to be in the tent during this situation with Libya. The young Lieutenant connected to the computers, was to remain in the tent while the other officer was free to roam and if something came in, he was under orders to find and report to the Colonel. This way, he was free to push the work on the Dam until he was shipped out to the other base construction.

Lieutenant Mendoza was already packed up and living out of her field packs along with Lieutenant John White. John voiced his complaints about having to be moved over to another military base because they just got this base the way they wanted it. But the Colonel knew no matter how much he complained, he would follow him to the ends of the earth if asked too.

Colonel Campanelli put the two Intel Officers on notice they were going to be coming to the new military base with him. By the time he finished this day's work, he was out on his feet, and his clothes were soaked through with sweat and he stank terribly. He strolled into the Intel tent, entered and asked the officer how it was going with Libya.

"Colonel Campanelli Sir, the Japanese cargo ship's under way on her own steam at this time sir. The last report has her in the Atlantic, and the United States escort ship is about to break off her protection of the civilian Japanese ship. Sir, you look a little weathered sir. Why don't you skip the next briefing and hit the sack for some rest, sir. I'll clue you in tomorrow morning and if anything happens before that time, I'll let you know immediately sir."

"I believe I just might take you up on skipping tonight's boring ass stinking briefing, mister. Has Lieutenant Mendoza reported in yet today? I haven't seen her all damn day yet, son." He asked the soldier this time.

"Yes sir, I briefed her about an hour ago on what's going on with the damn A rabs in Libya, sir. No news from the CIC came through though as of yet, Colonel Campanelli Sir. I guess everything's still quiet out there also sir. Why don't you turn in for a while, sir?"

"Yeah, yeah, you're getting worse than Mendoza is lately, Lieutenant. Cut me some damn slack not flack will ya please." He laughed and he was joined by the other officers in the Intel tent as he added to his words. "I'm going to hit it men. Good night."

He left the Intel tent and walked past the showers, and knew he should take one, but he was too exhausted and if he did, he would wake up from the water and never fall asleep for the rest of the night. He dragged his tired and aching body for his tent like a homing pigeon, and just as he reached for the flap, it suddenly flipped open and Mendoza met him in a new nighty she ordered from Victoria's Secret. But as she looked at his half closed eyes and grime covered face, she stepped aside and allowed him to fall into his bunk and she listened to him as he moaned and struggled out of his shirt. He was sound asleep as soon as his head hit the pillow and he got comfortable on the bunk.

She pulled the blanket from under him, not waking the colonel and covered him after she moved his feet on the bunk. She took off his boots and closed the tent. Then she crawled in the extra bunk and fell asleep watching Popeye snooze. She was the first one up and ran to the mess and got his breakfast. He was just waking up as she came in the tent with the food.

"You're an angel baby, I'm fucking starving honey. I didn't eat right all day, dammit." He was barely able to mumble to her as he struggled to get up on one elbow.

"It's no wonder, you were too tired to eat anything last night, sir. I hate it when you work yourself so hard around here, Edward. You better slow down a little bit for your own sake, mista. I don't want you getting sick on me you know my lover and soldier."

"Yeah, yeah Mendoza." Was all he said as he stuffed his mouth full with bacon.

They ate in silence. It was the Colonel who talked first as he moaned. "Gees, I remember you looking awfully good last night Mendoza. Did you have your hair combed differently my lady?"

"Well, I'm glad you were awake enough to notice something was different about me last night, mista. You were so damn tired I don't see how you ever remember anything about yesterday at all, sir." She said as she flashed her soul warming smile at her Commanding Officer.

"If it wasn't your hair then what was it about you last night I remember, yet don't remember."

"I can't explain it, I guess I'll just have to show you what you're trying to remember, my soldier." She got off the extra cot and took off her clothes very slowly and sexily. Once she was naked, she sashayed her way across the small and narrow tent and removed an outfit from a white box with the embossed letters V.S. on the cover.

He stared at her with his mouth hanging opened and his food on the end of his fork when she was dressed in her new negligee. He managed to say despite his mouth hanging open and full of food. "I fell asleep while you were wearing that thing last night? Holy shit, I must have been fucking dead or something to not have jumped your bones in that thing, lady. It's the only excuse I can possibly offer you, honey. What do you call something like that Maz?"

"It's called a lounging suit, Victoria Secrets guaranteed it to raise a hardon on any man who saw me wearing it, sir." She then began to dance like an Egyptian.

"Let me tell you something pretty lady, it works well as advertised honey." The suddenly full of energy Colonel laughed as he stared at her. He had never saw a more beautiful woman in his life, and she was wearing this outfit making her look hot enough to eat where she stood.

She looked at him and then she smirked at her Commander. "Err, I think you can swallow now before you hurt yourself, Ed."

"The hell with this crap. Come here and let me have some sugar baby." He said as he shoved his food tray aside, and then grabbed for her with both paws.

"Hold on there a minute, big boy. I hope you're going to at least take a quick shower, or maybe wash before you get too excited and attack me, mista. You smell like..."

It was too late for a shower or any further talking, he was all over her and she loved it. They rolled from the bunk to the floor, to the other bunk, and then back to the floor and then back to his bunk, while laughing all the time. Their loving making was suddenly interrupted by one of the Intel Officers. The Lieutenant remained standing outside the tent and he called for Campanelli. The Lieutenant knew what was going on inside from the noises he heard.

"Colonel Campanelli Sir. Err... CIC wants to speak with you STAT, sir. I'm terribly sorry for disturbing you at this time sir. But Commander Owens wants to speak with you right now, Colonel Campanelli Sir. He ordered me to find you and report to the Intel tent, sir."

"God dammit, yeah, yeah. Shit, I'll be right with you for Christ sake." He yelled out.

Mendoza was sitting on the floor laughing at the look on the poor Colonel's face, because he was not quite finished with her, and yet he knew he had to go and find out what Commander Owens wanted from him. He looked at her trying to cover herself with her arms.

"Go ahead and laugh. You got what you wanted from me. Look at me, I'm going to have to walk around with this damn pole sticking out." He grumbled and pointed to his stiff member.

This made her laugh all the more as she held him in her wonderful glaze.

"You're really pissing me off lately sister. All I know is you better be here when I'm finished with that pain in the ass Owens. Or I'm going to come out and find you, and then I'll make you take care of this problem here wherever the hell you are on this damn base, sister." He looked even funnier as he tried to stuff his stiff member in his pants.

She started laughing again as she rolled on the floor, and tears came from her eyes. She was enjoying watching the poor man struggle with his stiff member like he was doing.

"Yeah, go ahead and keep laughing at me you little fuck you, but we'll see who is laughing last when I stick this damn thing in your mouth, sister. Then it'll be my turn to laugh at you."

"Oh you think! You're not going to get that thing anywhere near my mouth unless you wash the damn thing off first, mista." She complained as she started to laugh again.

"C'mon Maz, this ain't funny anymore you know. I can't get the damn thing back in my stinking pants, and I have to get going and see what Owens wants from my damn ass, honey."

"Surely you don't think I'm going to take care of that little problem of yours right now, mista. With someone waiting just outside of the tent for you, sir. Here, let me help you get it in your pants, sir." Lieutenant Mendoza offered as she got up and walked towards her lover.

"Yeah, another thing. I'd really appreciate you not using the stinking word 'little', whenever referring to Big Jim and the twin, he's rather sensitive you know, little sister. She didn't mean it Jim." He said as he patted the head of his still rock hard dick.

She grabbed him and tried to forced his member in his pants, causing him to cry out when she tried to fold the slowly softening thing over. She backed off and he moaned. "Shit, I hope the damn thing still works. Crap, you coulda broke the damn thing on me, and then where the hell would I be. You gotta be more careful when handling Big Jim, honey."

The Lieutenant still standing just outside the tent could hear everything going on inside the tent, and he laughed over all the fun the two officers were obviously having with each other. He knew they had to love one another to be laughing like they were, and acting like they were so much in love that anyone seeing the two together, immediately realized they were both in love with each other.

She heard the Lieutenant laughing outside the tent and she yelled at the Colonel in a low voice. "Will you please be a little more quiet for Christ sake, dammit. He's right outside, and he can hear everything that's going on in here you."

"Fuck him, I'm going to get you for rupturing me, dammit. You wait until I get back here. I'll fix you good, you think it's so damn funny now, wait until a little later on, missy."

"Oh shit, look at me shake with fear about what you're going to do to me when you get back here, mista. You're scaring me to death sir." She said as she got up and started to dress.

"I'll fix you real good Maz, I'll fix ya little sister." He laughed and he suddenly kicked the flap of the tent wide open while she tried to get in her pants. She found herself looking in the face of the Lieutenant who instantly turned red with embarrassment.

"You sonofabitch you, will you close that fucking flap please. They're looking at me, damn you Eddy. I'm gonna skin you alive for this shit mista." She yelled at him.

"Are you going to be here when I get back, and are we going to finish what we started here, little sister?" The laughing Colonel asked the blushing Mendoza who let go of her pants and tried to cover herself up a little better with her hands.

"Yes, yes, I'll wait for you here until you get back, you dirty prick you." She bitched at the still laughing Colonel while trying to sound angry at him, but she suddenly started laughing again. She did not mind standing in front of the men on the base naked. In fact, she kind of enjoyed it whenever some men looked at her with nothing but lust locked in their eyes. After all, a woman needed all the advertising she could possibly get for herself. Besides, before the military base was in full operation, everyone took baths in Lake Tana together, and no one wore any clothes as they washed together. So it was not like anyone was seeing anything they had not seen before on her since the base was being constructed. She stuck her tongue out at a young Arab man who moved a little closer to the tent opening, in order to get a better look at her nakedness while she was standing inside the tent.

The Arab man smiled at her gesture. So she put her hands on her hips, allowing her pants fall down to the ground all together as she snapped at the Arab man. "I hope you like what you're seeing, you little fucker you. You better get out of here before I hop you in the ass, buster."

The Arab smiled and bowed his head as he replied with a smirk on his lips. "Oh yes missy, I like very much what I see please. I want to see more please."

Colonel Campanelli walked out of the tent leaving Mendoza with her hands angrily resting on her hips, and the privacy she needed to dress as he closed the tent flap of the tent for her. Then he looked at the Arab man and grumbled at him. "C'mon fella, I'm going to save your stinking life for ya, buddy. You don't want to be standing out here when she comes out of the fricking tent if you know what's good for your ass, the shows over for you pal."

The Arab man shook his head yes and started off for his own work.

The still smiling Colonel slapped the waiting Lieutenant hard on the back, and then offered the officer with a snap in his voice. "C'mon son, we have someone waiting on the damn radio for us. When you get a little older, you better get yourself one of those little babies to help keep you warm at night, mister."

"I'm sure gonna try to get me one of them women, sir. You have a real good lady there Colonel Campanelli Sir." The Lieutenant responded kindly.

"You got that right mister, and I'm gonna keep her all to myself I assure you young man." He retorted with a wide grin plastered on his lips as he started to actually jog over to the Intel tent. When he entered the tent, the second officer called out to him in a rather excited voice as he pointed towards the radio mike so he could speak to the angry sounding Command of the Carrier.

"Hell sir, I thought the Commander was going to have a puppy on us, sir. He's been yelling so loud I thought you were going to be able to hear him all the way back at your tent, sir. He's really amped up and angry as a bee stunk bear, Colonel Campanelli Sir."

"Not to worry bout him, that's the way he is." He smirked as he lifted the microphone and said. "Colonel Campanelli here, what's up Commander Owens Sir?"

"Where the hell were you mister? I didn't know that damn base of yours was so big it'd take you so long as it did for you to get back to me, Colonel Campanelli Sir. I don't like waiting for a fucking minute you well know, sir. You better take a portable radio with you if you're going to be that far away from the damn Command Tent, sir."

"Sorry Commander, but I was attending to duty above and beyond the call of duty at the time you placed this call to me, sir." This response meant only one of two things to a sweat warrior. One, he was either taking a crap, or two, he was making love to someone.

Commander Owens immediately relaxed and then laughed as he fired back at the Colonel. "I read you sir, I hope you were attending to duty under the second code, sir."

This response made Campanelli and the other officers stationed inside the Intel tent with him to laugh as he replied. "Sir, what can I do for you Commander?"

"I want you to be prepared to move out of that mess you created you call a military base tomorrow by Twelve Hundred Hours for the new site of the next base you're ordered to construct, Colonel Campanelli. I'll send a Sea Stallion out to take you over to the place where I want you to setup the new base in the Sudan, sir. I received your so called dream sheet mister, and the extra personnel you requested and they're all approved by Command, sir. You'll have the equipment you also requested and need, and I'll show up at the new fucking base within the next two or three days to check on how things are starting to shape up with the new base, sir. That'll give that lazy ass Seabee Construction Battalion the time to carve out a proper landing site to accept my damn helicopters.

"Colonel Campanelli Sir, I want to show you what I want from your next base, sir. To ensure your security, I'll talk to you one on one at your new encampment. By the way Colonel, when you take Command of this new base, there's a raise in rate that comes along with these orders, sir. You'll be a full bird Colonel as of tomorrow at Twelve Hundred

Hours takeoff time, sir. Colonel, I'd like it if you considered my old Eagles as a personal honor."

"Commander Owens Sir, I'd be proud to accept your old birds, sir. Thank you for the honor, Commander. Sir, I have a small request to ask of you if you wouldn't mind, sir. Since I'm receiving a second bump up in rank, I'd like to have a rate increase for two of my fellow Officers I'm taking out to this new base with me, sir."

"Small request huh mister? Who do you want to increase in rank Colonel Campanelli Sir? I don't know any Officers under your Command who have earned the honor, sir." Commander Owens asked him with a little concern lacing his tone of voice.

"I'd like to have Second Lieutenant Renee Mendoza and Lieutenant John White lifted up to the rank of Captain if it's at all possible, sir." He held his breath while waiting for the Commander's reply, hoping he did not just overstep his bounds with his request.

"I know that old war horse Lieutenant White okay, Colonel. I still get a laugh out of that sonofabitch, a man whose last name's White and he's as black as the ace of spades, damn. But I'm afraid I never met this Lieutenant Mendoza person. Lieutenant White's a good Officer, and if you're putting this Lieutenant Mendoza up for an increase in rank then she must be good as well, Colonel. Yes, I'll trust your opinion and go along with your application for their rate increase of these two Officers, sir. You put in the paperwork, and I'll approve the increases, sir."

"Sir, I was hoping you might be able to pull some strings and push the paperwork through as fast as possible, so they could get their raises along with mine tomorrow morning, Commander." He was certain he was stepping over the line of friendship now, because he was openly pushing Commander Owens with his request for the rate increases for his Lieutenants.

There was a long silence. He could actually hear Commander Owens still breathing on the other end of the phone, and then he finally responded to the Colonel's request. "You know mister, you're really one royal pain in my fucking ass, sir. I heard this about you and you proved it true, buster. Hang on a second while I think about this request of yours, sir." Seconds passed and then Commander Owens was back on the line and he snapped at his officer.

"Okay Colonel Campanelli, you got what you wanted, mister. I'll approve the paperwork from here, and bring the Bars along with me when I show up at your base tomorrow, sir."

"With you sir?" He interrupted the commander, not sure of his last words to him.

"You heard me right Colonel Campanelli, I'll bring the bars with me. I'm going to accompany the Sea Stallion out to your base, so I can give you my birds personally, sir. I'm looking forward to seeing that pain in the can Lieutenant White again. I want to see if that bastard remembers me, Colonel. The last time I saw him, he and another Officer stood before me on a Captain's Mast for disassembling six Japanese Officers when they were on R&R in the mid seventies I think it was in Japan, sir. Hell, he was so drunk, two of my Shore Police had to actually hold him up while I read him the riot act, Colonel. I don't think he remembers the damn Mast, he was so out of it. Don't tell the lousy bastard I'm coming out there, I want to surprise his ass. I can't wait to see his face if he remembers me." Commander Owens laughed.

The day flew by, and he informed the other officers he was taking them with him to the new base, and ordered them to be ready to shove off by tomorrow morning. At Eleven Forty Hours, Campanelli, Mendoza and White stood by the landing strip as the massive Sea Stallion slowly came in view. He never informed either of the other two officers about their rate increases. Seconds later the large helicopter touched down lightly. Commander Owens was the first one off the still spooling machine, and he walked right over to the three saluting officers standing at full attention. He returned their salutes, and then he produced a beaten tab split small blue box that he immediately handed to Colonel Campanelli.

He opened it and saw the highly polished gold Eagles holding arrows with its claws.

Commander Owens saluted the Colonel the moment he took the offered box from his hand and he offered to him at the same time. "I spent half the stinking night polishing those little babies up for you, Colonel. I wanted them to be absolutely perfect for you when I offered them to you, sir. The first time we talked a few short months ago Colonel Campanelli Sir. I considered having you Court Marshaled for not having an intelligence net properly setup on your base, sir. Since that time, I issued you two rate increases and you skipped a rate increase as well, sir. Shows you I can be wrong about a man once in a while I guess, sir." He stuck out his hand and he shook with the much younger new Colonel.

Commander Owens then turned his attention to Lieutenant White and he stared at him for a few moments as he finally groused at him. "I see you don't remember me yet mister. Well Lieutenant, I had the privilege, if you want to call it that of giving you your first Mast many years ago, mister." He said while he chuckled as he presented a box to him and offered his hand to the new Captain as he added. "Congratulations Captain White Sir."

White was dumbfounded as he looked from the box to the Commander then back to the box. He opened it, he then looked to the grinning Colonel.

"What the hell are you looking at me for man? You earned the damn things, mister."

Lieutenant Mendoza got nervous, and when Commander Owens next turned to her, she went weak in the knees. She held her breath when he offered her the same type of small blue box he just gave to the new Captain John White. She took it and looked to Colonel Campanelli who smiled back at her. She carefully opened the small blue box and almost fainted when she realized she was also a Captain now.

Commander Owens turned his attention back at Campanelli and informed him. "A change of plans already, Colonel. Get on board the helicopter and we'll take a quick flyover your new site. I'll drop you off and head back to my ship. A second Sea Stallion will be waiting for you to drop you off at the new base, sir. I'm having half of your damn Seabees picked up, and they'll be shipped out there by the time you return to this base, sir. You can keep them and the helicopter crew as a gift, the helicopter could serve as a mobile Command Center for your ass, sir.

"The Seabee's construction machinery and other equipment will be deployed before they land at the second base. I want and need an operating landing strip, and a secured airfield completed as quickly as humanly possible, Colonel. So I can supply your base properly by air. I want one landing strip in operation within three days at the max, mister. Get on board Colonel."

"In three days you want a landing strip operational sir! I hope you don't think I'm a fucking magician, sir. You want an operational landing strip completed in three days. How about asking me to build you a damn gambling casino while I'm at it for you, sir?" He retorted.

Commander Owens smiled, it was a smile which quickly informed him he would not accept any excuses as an answer from him over what he demanded accomplished on the new base that quickly. He wanted a landing strip in three days out there, period.

The flight took an hour before they were over his site. It was the way Campanelli vision it, hot, sandy and a miserable stretched of land. The helicopter hovered as the door guard dropped a marking beacon, so the second helicopter could find the new site with little trouble. Then the helicopter banked hard to the left and headed back to the old Base Tana.

Commander Owens offered Colonel Edward Campanelli a complete layout of what he wanted the new military base to look like, and then he offered him. "You have six months to make this pile of shit look like a full operational military base sir." Again he smiled.

The day was crazy at best for the Colonel and his crew. They made a second flight to the new encampment. The base was ordered to be named 'Sentry Base' because it was going to stand watch over the Nile River, and the Sudan. For the next three days, Colonel Campanelli was on the go around the clock. The first landing strip was completed on the fourth day of May, and it accepted the first landing of the massive C 5 Galaxy transport aircraft.

Commander Owens stepped off the tail end of the huge aircraft, as the front of the plane slowly raised, and a horde of Seabees rushed up to unload the aircraft from the front end of the massive plane of war. The Commander immediately surveyed the large and new military base and liked what he was looking at. Other Seabee units were already busy constructing the wood barracks for the soldiers and civilian workers, and all living quarters for the officers, wood latrines, and well dug in perimeter defenses for the new base were underway.

Commander Owens was pleased with the progress the Colonel achieved in so short a time. "Colonel Sir." Owens called out to him as he headed down the tail ramp of the aircraft.

The two officers shook hands as the Commander offered to Campanelli. "I have another Unit of Seabees and more construction equipment on board this damn thing. Also, there's a box on board with your name on it, sir. It's for your personal comfort Colonel." Commander Owens suddenly winked at the concerned Colonel as he added. "It's an air conditioning unit mister. Shit, it's hot out here, dammit." He griped as he wiped his forehead with his sleeve and then finished with his orders for the Colonel. "I have three C 140 transport aircraft stacked up with extra supplies for this damn base just minutes behind me, Colonel."

The Commander's aircraft was quickly unloaded and then it was moved away from the only completed operational runway with the use of one of the SeeBees bulldozers, as a second cargo aircraft began to circle the field while waiting for permission to land.

Commander Owens led Colonel Campanelli away from the runway. He placed his hand on Campanelli's back as they walked and he offered calmly. "Colonel, I have a number of Intel reports which lead us to believe there may be some kind of trouble coming our way in the near future, sir. From the reports I read, it looks like Chad's going to start up their crap again on us, sir. I don't understand this course Chad has currently adopted to travel down, but I know if they make any more trouble again, the United States is going to cut off all monetary and military supplies and aid going to the miserable little fucking country. I never thought Chad would ever become the god damn aggressor in this stinking region of the world, Colonel."

"What do you want us to do from here Commander Owens Sir? I trust you have orders for us here, sir." The concerned Colonel asked the powerful Navy Officer.

"I'm glad you asked me sir, I want you to be fucking ready for anything coming down the damn chute at ya if and when it happens, mister. I have three thousand Marines stationed on board the Roosevelt at this present time, as well as twenty Apache fast attack helicopters, and the pilots from the Tripoli, the amphibious assault ship, along with four AV 8B Harriers jump planes all earmarked for this base, sir. Your tanks and artillery pieces and their crews, are in the air as we speak, Colonel Campanelli. I already informed the President that I wanted five thousand extra troops stationed at your base by the end of the week, sir. The President informed me he'd order up the 101 Screamers Airborne here by then, Colonel Campanelli Sir.

"Anyway, your main orders are as follows, Colonel. You have to keep this area of the Sudan operational, or we'll have no active land bases in which to operation from in this entire area if all hell breaks out against us, sir. Colonel, I'm sending you more fucking defensive and offensive equipment, soldiers and personal when I can get my hands on them, sir. These damn military cut backs and base closing have the services cut right down to the damn bone, and closer if possible, sir. I'm sending you a wing of YF 23 fighters, twenty aircraft in all, and the 21st Tactical

Fighter wing will be transferred out to your new base as well, sir. I'm also having some fuel bladders delivered to your base, bury them deep and protected from attack, mister.

"I can't fucking impress upon your ass how damn important this lousy area's going to be to us if war breaks out in this region between Libya, Egypt and Ethiopia because of that Dam construction, Colonel. You'll end up as our first line of defense. If any attackers are successful and drive you out and takeover your damn base, we'll be forced to fight them from Saudi Arabia, and the Aircraft Carriers we currently have stationed around the region at the present time, sir. You know if you have no operational bases on land, you can't possible win a fucking war, sir."

Commander Owens took a quick breath for himself before he added to his orders for the Colonel. "Don't get me wrong mister, we don't have any concrete evidence trouble will happen in the near future as yet sir. But I don't intend to be caught with my damn pants down around my knees for a second either, Colonel. I'd rather be safe than sorry if a situation does arise on us, Colonel Campanelli. Okay sir, I have to get back out to my ship, but I'll send you my Intel Lieutenant again to help assist your people with setting up their new Intel net on this damn base, sir. Colonel Campanelli, I want you to understand this shit right off the fucking bat sir. You're going to be in Command of a Joint Task Force out here sir." Commander Owens smiled as he suddenly extended his hand to the concerned looking Colonel.

Campanelli swallowed as sweat suddenly broke out on his brow as he thought. 'Shit, I'll be in Command of a combined operation consisting of the Airforce, Marines and Army, plus the Sudanese and Iranian military units. It's going to be a global taskforce. His mind raced, thinking about this gift that just fell in his lap, when his thoughts were broken by Commander Owens.

"Colonel Campanelli, you have a reputation for gut instincts and survival, and know how and ability to get the fricking job done you were sent out there to accomplish, sir. You're going to need all your fucking wits and instincts before this operation's completed I assure you sir."

As the two officers shook hands then Commander Owens offered to his military officer as if an afterthought. "Good luck with this mess Colonel Campanelli, it looks like you pulled the duty for this one sir. I know I placed you right in the fucking middle of hell, but I'm certain you can handle it for me, sir. If you need anything, anything at all, place a call out to me and I'll get what you require one way or the other for you, sir." The Commander then turned on his heels and headed back to his waiting aircraft, which was empty and already being pulled back onto the long runway for takeoff as the C 140 was dragged off the runway by a second bulldozer.

"Colonel Campanelli, you'll receive at least three fully loaded down transport aircraft a day for nine days straight. It'll take this many flights to get the equipment you will need to make your new military base fully operational, sir. Good luck again Colonel Campanelli, I'm with you on this one, sir." The Commander started up the gangway, turned and saluted the Colonel. Then he quickly disappeared into the dark bowels of the massive aircraft as the ramp closed behind him.

With a thundering roar and turbulence equal to a small hurricane, the huge transport aircraft started down the long runway while building up full military takeoff speed. He held his breath because he feared the massive aircraft would run out of runway before she finally got off the ground. The aircraft suddenly broke contact with the ground and slowly climbed into the sky as a third military cargo aircraft came in view. The transport aircraft were coming from their massive base stationed in Saudi Arabia.

He mustered his officers together in the field, and warned them in no uncertain terms against allowing any of their troopers to fraternize with the local female population of the area. He also warned the officers the AIDS virus was running rampant in this region of the world, and he did not want any of his troops contacting it because of their own stupidity. He knew his people received the accepted AIDS drugs mixed with their food and drinking water, to better help protect the soldiers against the virus the best it could.

All the soldiers stationed on base were also given boxes of prophylactics, and there were boxes of condoms stationed at every counter and hut you went in on the new military base. Any soldier or civilian construction worker found doing it without protection, would immediately be arrested for destroying government property, meaning their own body, or the civilians were ordered home. Another worry bothering him was all the clouds of flies and mosquitoes constantly flying around his troops both day and night that might infect his people with any number of insect spread disease more than the women. The soldiers were going to have to take quinine to better protect themselves against Malaria, and other diseases.

The concern Colonel warned his officers against many of the other hazards they would be facing in this region of the world, as flies tried to land in his mouth as he spoke. He spat a dead fly out of his mouth and already hating the place with a passion. He turned to the officer in charge of the Seabees and barked at him.

"Lieutenant, I want your fucking men to pay close attention to any stagnant water pools or puddles. Your people are to bulldoze the water over, and if not possible, I want your people to put a skim coat of diesel fuel over the water. That move will help to kill many of these fucking mosquitoes. Your SeeBees are ordered to bury any dead animals or food without having to be ordered, maybe that'll help with some of these damn flies around here. Command's going to send us over a million Dragonfly larvae, once these hatch, they'll help to kill the damn problem bugs off. They're also sending us over electronic bug zappers." He stopped talking as he flailed his hands in the air at the swarm of angry flies buzzing around his head to no avail, and then he growled. "Get your people working on these puddles right now mister. God damn bugs."

He watched as members of the base jumped to work on their assigned tasks. He turned on his heels and headed for his new quarters made of wood this time, and it had the air conditioner running on full blast. He entered the cold hut and went over to his table built by an energetic Seabee, the carpenter even installed a small reading light over the table.

The Colonel mentally laid out his entire base in his mind, and he added some of his own ideas to the layout. He had seven hundred Construction Seabees working around the clock on the airstrips. They had steel mesh lying on the ground just about everywhere he looked, and they were busy packing sand and Portland cement over the mesh to form a hard pack ground, and give a good surface for the sensitive fighter aircraft to land on. He was ahead of his date for completion of the new airbase. He looked to the area of the map which showed his base, he was looking for the area which contained his intel operation. Here, his men were going to be housed in a wood structure, and they had an air conditioner to help keep the computers cool, it did not matter if the two offers were comfortable in the hut. The excuse for the air conditioner was made by the officers, it was needed to protect the computers from heat and moisture.

The Colonel knew he had to protect the intelligence computers from overheating at all cost. The only other place under air conditioning on the entire shaping military base was the mess hut. His two Intel Officers were rather pleased with their living quarter's setup in the hut with the computers. This time though, they were going to have a room for themselves, and the presence of the third Lieutenant from fleet was proving a major plus for their ongoing training. The more experienced Fleet Officer snapped the younger officers into top notch G 2 men.

He looked at the side of a huge mountain in which he was going to carve hard bunkers shelters into, for the protection of their smaller fighter aircraft just in case the airfield came under attack by any unknown enemy attackers. The Sudanese government was cooperating completely with them, and they also signed a pact to allow the Unites States military base to operate for the next ninety nine years in their country.

The Colonel was deep in thought, as he looked over all he had to have completed within the next six months, in order to make his new military base and airfield fully operational. The new Captain Mendoza suddenly strolled in his personal hut and she sat down on his bunk and watched him work for a moment. She quickly grew bored with watching him completely ignore her. he had a TV with a small dish mounted on top of the hut, so she turned it on and quickly started to jump through the few channels they received with the remote, to try and find something she wanted to watch.

The Colonel looked over his shoulder and barked at her in an angry snap because the TV was bothering him. "Do you mind honey. I'm fucking working here, dammit."

"I'm sorry." She shut off the TV and picked up a magazine lying on the floor. It was a six month old Playboy magazine, the only magazine he sort of read. She quickly flipped to the centerfold fold and looked at the rather busty young looking woman smiling at her and she mumbled out loud. "Where the hell do these people ever find these poor women who look like this. I don't think any woman could really look this good without many side trips to the plastic surgeon to make their tits that big, and their face with no wrinkles."

Flash message was transmitted to Colonel Edward Campanelli's Intelligence headquarters. Immediately, the young Lieutenant ran and informed the Colonel he had the Flash call coming in. He ran to the hut to the table and picked up the scrambler phone. A series of loud tones and static greeted his ear, a second later, Commander Owens was heard clear.

"Colonel Campanelli Sir, we received some reliable information there is a pending attack going to occur in your area at or around Oh, Six Hundred Hours today, sir. It's going to take place from the Chad side of the damn Sudan in the lower section, marked CR-3 on your map. Confidence is high, I repeat, confidence is high on this intelligence information we received via special operatives working in the region, sir. Satellite pictures confirm a definite movement of hostiles and military equipment in this area. You're ordered to go to a Red Alert on your base. Repeat Colonel, Alert Red status, sir. I'll send a ready air cap over your entire area, the Commander's call name's Rooster Leader.

"The Flight Commander will have seven Chicks in his protective air wing. The aircraft will remain in your area until I get the 71st Tactical Air Wing shipped out to your position later today for your base protection. Colonel, you'll be ready to refuel and rearm Rooster and his Chicks if needed. I can't send you any flying gas station at this time, so you'll have to refuel them on the ground by hand Colonel. Don't worry, we're behind you if anything goes hot in your area of responsibility, sir. Rooster's Flight will be overhead within the next seven minutes, repeat, seven minutes sir. Good luck Colonel Campanelli." Communications disconnected.

Colonel Edward Campanelli looked at the Intel Lieutenant who turned green as he listened in on the flash message, and then he grumbled at him. "What the fuck are you waiting for mister? Hit the damn panic button, let's wake up some asses around here son."

The Lieutenant jumped at the sound of the Colonel's commanding voice. A heartbeat later the lazy military base was being blasted by the blaring of screaming sirens and soldiers running in different directions throughout the entire massive military base.

Men and women soldiers and equipment were moving around quickly. Gun installations were uncovered, manned and aimed in the air at unseen targets, as tanks were started and helicopters lifted off and hovered in their assigned standoff positions. Captain White ran for the Intel hut and picked up the Colonel standing in front it and asked. "What's up? Whose coming at us sir?"

"Looks like we're in for a probe. I received a Flash from Combat Information Center. They detected movement of enemy troops along the Chad border with the Sudan west of our location." The Colonel and Captain White looked on as seven massive tanks quickly moved out to strategic locations for defense of the base. The artillery nest was a beehive of activity, as soldiers loaded weapons and intelligence computers automatically aimed the cannons for the soldiers. Moments later, the artillery units checked in to inform the Command Post of their ready status.

The tanks were well dug in, and the Rooster Flight Commander was communicating with the base computers. The Seabees were mixed in with the Marines manning the perimeter defenses, and the Airborne moved out to the jungle as the first line of defense. The returning flares to be fired were the color white on this action. Anyone not firing off three white flares was not going to make it on the base alive. They would be classified as the enemy, and blasted by the first perimeter defenders, the Airborne and the artillery units. The first of the outdated but refurbished F 14 Tomcats landed for fuel, it was the flight wing Commander Rooster.

Campanelli ran over to the young pilot and asked him with concern in his voice. "Didja see anything going on out there Commander?"

The Commander instantly snapped to attention and saluted, but Campanelli was not interested in protocol as he growled at the pilot. "Fuck that shit, don't salute me in the fucking field, mister. I asked you if you saw anything moving around out there, mister?"

"No sir, I didn't see very much of anything. At first I thought I might have picked up some movement, but it was inside Chad's borders, and I don't have permission to hit any possible targets located in Chad, sir. We tracked the targets for some time, but they never once came anywhere near the Sudan side of the border. We also noticed a number of muzzle flashes, which indicated to us ground fighting going on, but as I said, all the action happened in Chad, sir.

"We crack the sound barrier over the disturbance to let them know we were around and watching them, sir. They didn't fire at us. Colonel, I'm rather pressed for time, I have to go sir. I have to get back to my Chicks. We were informed the 71st Tactical is just minutes out from base, and should be ready to land as soon as I'm off the ground, that is if you let me get going sir. Otherwise, I might be forced to wait until after their aircraft landed, before I can rejoin my Chicks in the air, sir." The pilot saluted and then he turned and ran to his refueled aircraft. In seconds he was streaking for the sky to rejoin his wing of aircraft.

"I told you not to salute me in the fucking field, you damn asshole you." The fuming Colonel called after the pilot he did not dismiss, but watched him run for his aircraft. He smiled after the young Flight Commander, he liked a man who did what he felt was his duty, and protected his people as this pilot was doing.

He kept a close eye on the sleek Tomcat aircraft as it shot down the makeshift runway with afterburners blasting on full military power. The wings were straight out, but as the aircraft quickly lifted off of the ground and instantly increased its speed, the wings went to the twenty two degree sweep for increased speed capabilities. He watched the aircraft rapidly climb and then immediately go to full power, and the wings went to the full sweep position of sixty eight degrees. The aircraft looked like a large arrowhead shooting through the bright sky. Within seconds, the sleek fighter aircraft was completely out of sight, but the vapor streams continued to mark its heading in the sky. The Colonel went back inside the Intel Center and he listened to the flood of communications carried out between Rooster and his chicks.

"Rooster Flight Leader, this is Chick Three, sir. I just picked up a number of muzzle flashes on the ground off to my right of the aircraft, sir. Over."

"Chick One. I picked up what looked like a small explosion to my left side, sir. Over."

"Chick Five. Rooster Flight Leader. Err.. I'm getting a little low on fuel sir. Over."

"Chick Five, this is Rooster Leader. Hit the deck and get something to drink for yourself sir. Chick Six, go with him for added protection and refuel while you're at it, sir. Over."

"Chick Five. Roger that last, copy as received, heading down for fuel sir. Over."

Chicks Five and Six split off from formation and headed for the hard deck of the new base.

"Chick One. I'm picking up some movement, I believe the movement is a tank. Shit, I got a tank moving through the heavy brush, permission to arm and fire at the mover sir. Over."

"Chick One, this is Rooster Leader. That's a negatory on that request. You don't have permission to arm and fire unless you come under direct threat. Our orders are we can't attack unless hostiles come across the damn border, or we come under attack. Over."

"Chick Three to Rooster Flight Leader. I'm picking up an emergency request for an attack run on what's being called enemy forces, sir. The caller identifies himself as a Captain in the Chad regular Army, and he states he's engaging strong rebel forces heading towards the Sudan border. Should we dip down and see what the hell's happening down there sir? Over."

"Chick Three. Negatory on that request. You're instructed to hold your present position and take a wait and see stance. I'm picking up the same request for assistance sir, which means our Combat Center's picked up the same emergency request call. The ball is in the Commander's corner, we have to wait for further orders. Hit the deck and refuel sir. Over."

"Chick Three. Roger that last as received sir. Going down for some fuel sir. Over."

Colonel Campanelli looked at the Lieutenant who instantly knew what the Colonel wanted and he replied. "Yes Sir Colonel Campanelli Sir, we're picking up the same soldier requesting help from our fighter aircraft, sir. Do you want to help them out sir?"

The second Lieutenant cut in and offered to his Commanding Officer. "Colonel Campanelli, Rooster Flight Leader received Flash traffic from the CIC from on board the Roosevelt, sir. He was instructed not to take any action unless attacked. He was ordered to back off another ten miles from the border. The Rooster Flight Commander's being instructed to use this position as his new standoff point, sir. His orders were now to kill any hostile units who enter this zone of protection from the Chad border region, no questions asked, sir. The Flight Commander's being asked to acknowledge the message which he did. Sir, communication ends at this point."

Just as Campanelli was going to respond to the Second Louie's complaint, the word "Flash," suddenly appeared on the Lieutenant's small computer screen, and he called out quickly to his Commander. "Colonel Campanelli Sir, we have our own Flash traffic coming in sir." The Lieutenant's voice was a little high pitched and rather shaky, betraying the slight fear he was suddenly feeling over all the military action that was taking place now.

"Calm down some son, I need you working with a clear fucking head on your damn shoulders, son. Relax, the action's too far away to get upset over." He said while trying to calm the young man was obviously in his first action, by placing his hand lightly on his shoulder.

The Flash was the same exact communication sent to the Rooster Flight Commander from the CIC stationed on board the Aircraft Carrier Roosevelt. At the end of the Colonel's message he was ordered to stand by for further orders. He looked out the door and saw the a number of aircraft landing from the 71st Tactical Wing. Twenty one planes were rapidly being dispersed by hand along the sides of the runways, as flight crews moved in and checked their aircraft. The 71st was ordered to stand by until needed. The warplanes were refueled, armed and cleaned on the runways, where they were parked.

As the Colonel watched Rooster's Chicks Five and Six aircraft landed. Instantly, the fighters were immediately attacked by a horde hard deck crews who refueled and checked the plane's weapons and engines, while the pilots were given something to eat and drink. Then the aircraft were muscled around by hand and hooked up to the crash carts, and electrical power was sent to the aircraft's engines. Their engines flamed to life, and the jets shot down the runway and ripped into the air on full afterburners. They were out of sight almost as fast as they appeared.

"Colonel Campanelli Sir." The Intel Officer called out to his Commanding Officer.

He turned and headed back inside the intelligence hut, he walked over to the young G 2 Lieutenant and listened to the Commander.

"Rooster Flight Leader to Chicks Five and Six. You two really took your damn time getting back up here to us. I want you two to take up the present positions of Chicks Two and Three while they head off for refueling. Damn we could have sure use a HC 130 Tanker up here that way I'm not caught short handed if hell breaks loose on us, dammit." The leader of the flight complained into his radio.

"Chick Five. I Roger that last, Flight Commander. Chicks Five and Six trading positions with Chicks Two and Three."

Rooster Leader flew closer to the fighting taking place on the ground, while his Chicks held their present standoff positions ten miles back.

Rooster Leader's RIO (Radar Intercept Officer in the rear of the F 14 Tomcat) suddenly reported. "Sir, I see a helluva lot of fucking ground activity going on down there, sir."

"Talk to me Sammy. What are you picking up? I can't see much while flying my aircraft." Rooster Leader called out to his RIO man.

"Commander, I'm picking up a shitload of troop and machine movement down there, sir. Shit sir, I have a radar lock on sir. Something's tracking us at this present time sir. I can't get a good fix on the damn radar signature though as yet sir. So I have no idea what they're aiming at us, sir. Wait, wait, I see something starting to clear up for me sir."

A missile launch warning suddenly screamed to life in the cockpit of the Tomcat.

"God dammit sir, I have a fucking launch detection. I have a missile launch. From its read, it looks like a lousy Russian SA 14 Gremlin missile sir, and its coming right at us at our five o'clock low. Fire ARM missile, she'll lock onto the damn shooter's radar, at least we'll take him out of the equation. Take evasive action or we're going to buy the big dirt farm sir. The SA 14's warhead's seeking, no, no, it's now homing in on us, and it's locking onto us sir. I'm firing off the damn hot bags and flares, sir! I'm firing off the whole deck at the missile, sir."

Captain Meehan pushed the stick down and hard to the right, and his aircraft instantly went into a steep nose dive. His craft went one way, while he turned the other way to see if he could pick up the incoming missile. His attention was torn between the earth his aircraft was heading for at over Mach One, and the yellow dotted flame rapidly closing on his ship at Mach Five. When the missile's warhead locked onto his craft, he pulled the stick to his gut, and the plane pulled out of its deep dive, and then the aircraft shot up in the sky like a dart.

"Fire off the fucking bags right now dammit!" Captain Meehan yelled to his RIO.

Two burning hot bags and six flares ripped off from the wings of the Tomcat, and they headed for the earth. Instantly, the SA 14 heat seeking missile's seeker warhead picked up the much hotter images of the flares, and headed for them at its hellish speed. Sam watched as the missile changed direction, and followed the flares towards the ground, and then explode harmlessly and he informed the pilot. "Missile's done for it sir."

The ARM missile fired from the Tomcat followed the same path the SA 14 missile took, and it exploded on the ground. Killing the shooter and anyone anywhere near the shooter.

"You got his ass but good sir. The shooter's dead. I have a successful impact and kill on the ground, sir." The RIO called out to his Commander.

"Fine, let's get the hell out of here then, we're too damn close to the fucking shooting raging down there, my friend. Hey RIO, next time we come under fire, don't yell so fucking much into the damn radio, man. My ears are still ringing from it buddy."

The pilot put his aircraft in a harsh seven "G" turn to his right, and then headed back to his waiting Chicks stationed at their standoff positions.

A Flash message was sent to Rooster Flight Leader, ordering him to stay back away from the fighting arena, this time he was ordered to shoot any possible hostile movements, even if they occurred inside the Chad border from the CIC Command Center on board the Roosevelt.

Colonel Campanelli said in a low voice which the Intel lieutenant had a little trouble hearing all his words. "Shit, this is fucking bad, it's going to get out of hand on us, and then we're all going to find ourselves involved in another fucking shooting war, dammit."

The awaited attack on the Sudan never did materialize, all the fighting took place within the borders of Chad. The Iranian advisors training the Sudanese soldiers mounted their tanks, and headed for the fighting. But it never came near, or over the border. The fighting lasted most of the day, and it kept the American forces throughout the Sudan on their toes, expecting an attack.

ON BOARD THE AMERICAN CARRIER USS ROOSEVELT

The CIC never ordered a full alert on board the Carrier, but the Commander kept many fighter planes in the air for the entire day as a precaution. The fighter pilots opened up communications with the Iranian and Sudanese soldiers on the ground, and the pilots informed them they were ready to lend any support to them if they came under attack by any enemy troops engaging them on the ground. The defending soldiers were told if any fighting starts, to mark out their locations with red smoke. Any troops outside of the red smoke areas were going to get killed.

The rather upset President of the United States sent a stinging message off to the recently installed Habre government of the nation of Chad, threatening to cut off all military and finical aid sent to the small nation if another military incident took place anywhere in the area along the Sudanese border with that country.

A day later, Libya called for a special meeting of the Security Council, in which she condemned the recent actions of the Chad government, and announced if another incident took place in the region. Libya would have no other alternative but to put her soldiers on full alert. All nations involved with the Security Council, condemned the government of Chad, who protested her innocence over the minor skirmishes that took place.

Japan, who was recently given a vote in the Security Council only as an interested party though, abstained from any voting. Japan was only interested in keeping the tensions high in the area, so she could help Libya and Egypt in their planned upcoming war against the nations of Chad and the Sudan. Japan would back anyone who caused any sort of problems for the United States and her allies. If war broke out in this region, the United States would have no other choice but to get involved as they did in the Desert Storm War, and Japan could then use the Arab countries to do her fighting against the United States for her.

Japan took an even more active role in the upheaval the world soon found itself mired in, mainly because of the heavy pressure being placed on the government of Japan from Libya. The Japanese launched its youth in action, and sent the young out to protest at all United States military bases spread throughout Japan or on Japanese own Islands. No American military bases were spared from the mounting assault from the Japanese youth. Many young threw stones at the American soldiers and sailors, and when three American soldiers were found hacked to death. The United States got up on her heels and complained to the Japanese government. Some heated words were quickly exchanged between both sides, which led to Japan's demanding all American servicemen and warships leave all Japanese land immediately.

The United States jumped all over the chance of finally ending her occupation of Japan, and she quickly closed all her military bases in the region. But secret meetings were held between the United State and Japan, and here it was decided it was in the best interests of both countries for the military of the United States to get out of Japan peacefully.

Japan knew she needed the security that came from keeping good relations with the United States, and she talked America into moving her servicemen no further from Japan than the Islands of Guam, Wake and Midway. As foolish as Japan was acting, she did not get where she stood in world opinion and standing from being stupid. Japan knew if the United States pulled out of their commitment of military protection to Japan all together. The Chinese would attack their country as soon as the last of the United States soldiers was gone from all Japanese lands.

Never once did Japan ever feel threatened by Russia, their main threat was always coming from China, and Japan feared China for what her troops did to that country during the World War, more than they hated the United States. The Japanese government promised to pay the tab for the continued United States protection of her country. Even though the protection was further away from her shores now than ever before.

A further announcement was made in which the Japanese government announced they were sending a second cargo ship containing food and medical supplies to Libya, as a special thanks for allowing Japan to use her port to repair the disabled cargo ship. The other nations had no problem with this offer. But in the hold of the cargo ship there were more Japanese fighter aircraft and missiles, rather than medical supplies and food as offered to the world. The Japanese ship was being shadowed most of the way by an American Frigate. Twice, the Captain of the Barbey requested permission from the Captain to board the Japanese vessel, so the American Navy could check out their cargo, but permission was withheld.

Commander Owens felt all he had to do was forcibly board the Japanese ship in the open seas, with the ill feelings running out of control between the two countries, this action could cause a breakdown of relations all together and my lead to a shooting response.

A EMERGENCY MEETING OF THE SECURITY COUNCIL, NEW YORK CITY, NEW YORK

The government of Chad informed the Security Council President and the other members of the Council there should be no sanctions lodged against Chad, because the fighting took place completely within the borders of Chad. Thus, no threats to another country ever occurred. Then Chad tried to blame Libya for sending the rebels into Chad to cause this trouble.

The Delegate from Libya suddenly stormed out of the meeting, saying this was yet another attempt by the United States to try and blame Libya for something they did not do. The United States paid little if any attention to what Libya had to say, because the Americans were still blaming Chad for the troubles taking place in this region of the world, bringing a promise from Chad's new government to restrain its rebels from attacking any another nation in the region.

CAIRO, EGYPT

In Egypt, the Egyptian Ambassador Mohammed Kheir, sent a message out to Libya, stating he wanted Ambassador Kamal to report to his office as soon as possible. He was informed the Libyan Ambassador Kamal would see him on his return trip from the United Nations meeting within the next two day's time.

A day and a half later, the Libyan Ambassador Kamal walked into Ambassador Mohammed Kheir's office, JoAnne immediately came to her feet at the first sight of him, and she then led him into Mohammed's private office with a smile on her lips. Then she took her place at the far side of the room in her usual chair. Neither man paid any further attention to her.

Ambassador Mohammed Kheir glared harshly at Ambassador Kamal as he snarled at the Libyan. "Ambassador Kamal, your second incident didn't even stir the dust off the floor of the desert, or wake up a sleeping camel, fool. What happened to your great and well feared Muslim fighters? Hell, they couldn't fight off the lowly Chad soldiers by themselves, Ambassador. I don't think the Muslim fighters will be of much help to us when we really have need of the fool, Ambassador." He laughed as to put an emphasis on the insult he aimed at Kamal.

"Mohammed, I bid you not to worry about my Muslim soldiers. They're fighting on the side of right for Allah, and they'll be there and ready to carry out our orders when we have the most need of them, sir. If we were to return to the radical way of the Muslim Fundamentalists, the world would be a far better place in which to live and..."

"Better for who Ambassador Kamal, for who dammit! Women, don't make me laugh, it would set women back to the days of the dark ages in our countries, where their opinions were not considered, or even asked for. Death to anyone who disagrees with their radical religious beliefs. Death to all Arab women who didn't follow all their laws to the..."

"You leave an extremely foul taste in my mouth every time you speak to me, Ambassador Kheir! I curse the foul day my government ever aligned itself to your nation of Egypt. You're a weak man, and in the new world there'll be no room for weak men such as yourself, Ambassador Kheir." The Libyan Ambassador Kamal hissed through clenched teeth as he sprang to his feet as his hand slid under the folds of his robe.

Mohammed also sprang to his feet as his hand shot in the open top drawer of his desk, his hand fumbling for his pistol. "Son of a shit eating dog, I'll rid the earth of you once and for all."

Before either weapon came in the open, JoAnne was already on her feet aiming her pistol directly at the chest of the extremely angry Libyan Ambassador Kamal, as she warned him in no uncertain terms. "It'd displease me greatly if I was forced to kill you Ambassador Kamal, but you're offering me very little choice in the matter, sir. It's my duty to protect Mohammed from all harm, with my life if necessary, sir. Don't remove your knife, or I shall be forced to kill you. Ambassador Kamal, think before you act irrationally sir I warn you." She stood and stared at the hands of Ambassador Kamal, watching for any further movement.

Ambassador Kamal stopped his movement as he looked to this extremely dangerous woman holding her weapon leveled at his chest with both her hands, and her legs slightly spread apart. He looked at the barrel of the weapon, it did not waiver from his chest and he found himself wondering how long she would be able to hold the weapon without moving, or if the weight of the gun would cause her to lower it. For several long seconds his question was answered, until he was certain she could hold the weapon all day if it was necessary.

Ambassador Kamal suddenly relaxed his hand a little, and then he asked her. "May I remove my hand from my robe please, young woman?"

"Make certain it is empty when it comes out of your foul robe, Ambassador Kamal Sir." She warned the Libyan in a combative tone of voice.

Kamal looked to Mohammed who also had his weapon out and aiming at his chest. Ambassador Kamal then bowed slightly as he smiled and then his hand slid out from under the fabric of his robe empty. He held his palm opened to her, so she could see it was empty. She relaxed her shoulders, but nevertheless, she kept her weapon aimed right at his chest.

"JoAnne, that'll do thank you, you can put away your weapon now, please." Ambassador Mohammed Kheir said as he lowered his gun, and threw it back in the top drawer of his desk.

She did not move or lower her weapon as she was just ordered, causing him to yell at her this time. "I just told you to lower your god cursed weapon, and you'll put away your weapon. You'll do it now, or I'll have your bones being bleached in the sun of our desert!"

The female predator allowed her eyes to wander to his face for the briefest second, and she noticed he was unarmed and she offered him calmly. "Ambassador Kheir, I have been ordered to protect your life at all cost by President Sadat, sir."

"I said it's fine, so lower your cursed evil weapon immediately, and get out of my office or I shall have you replaced." The Egyptian politician nearly shouted at his female protector.

Slowly, finally she lowered her weapon, but she never once took her eyes completely off of Kamal's form. She slid in her chair while still holding her weapon and watching Kamal, and for the rest of his meeting she stared intensely at him. Almost daring him to make a wrong move, so she could react against him and end his hatred of her ward.

Ambassador Kamal felt extremely threatened by her harsh and threatening stare and promised he vowed to himself he was going to get a weapon like this female for his own self protection.

"Ambassador Kamal, do you think it might be possible we can be civil to one another, or should I ask President Sadat to intervene and order us what is his desires, fool?"

"That'll not be necessary my friend. I apologize for my poor choice of words, and my poor judgment as well, Mohammed. I guess I'm still rather upset at the terrible failure of the worthless Muslim soldier's more than I thought. Never will I ever allow myself to lose control like this again. I guess it troubles me the cursed Americans have setup a new military base in the middle of the Sudan nation. They're lower than the regurgitated filth of the Vulture."

"What was that you offered, Ambassador Kamal?" He asked as he again stood and stared back at the hated man while he waited for him to reply to his last question.

"You didn't know about this new military base the hated and god cursed Americans constructed in the Sudan, Mohammed? I took it for granted you were aware about this new military base the followers of Satan setup in the loathsome Sudan lands. The great fools stated they were going to locate an area for another Dam constructed along the Nile, and they're using this excuse to setup a new military base there, sir. They think we Arabs are so dumb we don't know their military soldiers are ordered to wear civilian clothes. Or there are many tanks, attack helicopters and fighter aircraft stationed on the worthless new field as we speak, Mohammed." Ambassador Kamal warned the Egyptian Delegate sharply.

He was stunned to his soul as he stopped his pacing and placed his hands on the back of his chair and growled. "This is pure insanity, to dare chance doing battle with the United States over the worthless nation of Chad. Surely, we have to show the fear of Allah to dare challenge such a powerful nation such as the United States, and her military might."

"You're in error with your foul words, this war is not over the worthless Chad, Ambassador Mohammed Kheir. This challenge is over water, water I need not warn you, that you Egyptians need in order to survive in your own country, you great fool." Kamal snarled back at Kheir.

"Does this new American military base in the Sudan change our plans and efforts, Ambassador Kamal? How can we possibly attack the cursed Sudan with these new American troops and military base setup there, sir? I was hoping to have taken all the Sudan and Chad before the United States even had a chance to try and react against our actions in this hatful region. They'll now be involved in the war from the outset I fear, as quickly as we begin our attack against these other worthless nations we have to destroy to keep the status quo in place in the region. I have to inform President Sadat immediately about this new situation you informed me over, Ambassador Kamal." He said as he began to pace his office again.

"No need to panic, this situation with the American troops is just a slight inconvenience that's all. Besides, Sadat has been informed of this and he's not worried about the Americans either."

"I'm not that confident about it, I don't like fighting the Americans. Remember what they did to Iraq. I was hoping to have the major part of the fighting over with before the United States could react. Then we could have allow America come to terms with the other countries involved in this upcoming war. In this way, they would've felt they stopped the fighting and could take their bows, and we'd end up with what we wanted. Your country, with Chad, Niger and Mali as well as most of the Sudan, and we would've ended up with the rest of the

Sudan along with Ethiopia, and both our countries would have been happy with the outcome of this war."

"Mohammed Kheir, you seem to forget one more country that Libya wants, Algeria."

"Algeria!" He cried aloud as he glared back at Ambassador Kamal, and then he went on with is complaint against the Libyan politician. "Algeria is going to help us with this war now. Why on the good earth do you want to attack an ally such as Algeria is, Kamal?"

"Why you may ask of me, Mohammed? Allow me explain this reason to attack them to you then sir. The nation of Algeria is in a real mess, the Muslim Fundamentalists with their fierce adherent to the radical Salafi School of Islam, are completely destroying the foul country slowly, by not wanting to compromise with the present government in power. Yet the useless fools are too weak to take over the foul country for themselves. If we were to take over Algeria, we'll have to put the Fundamentalists in command of that country, Ambassador Kheir.

"This way, the Muslim's will slaughter the remaining Algerians not Fundamentalists, and when this is accomplished, we'll then step in and slaughter if you will, the Muslim and take over a country void of all people. Thus will end another bastard Arab country, Ambassador. There'll only be room for the true, pure blooded Arabs in this new world we're planning to carve out of the dregs of many of these foul Arab countries." Ambassador Kamal said with his eyes ablaze.

Mohammed was shocked as he sat in his chair and then mumbled at the Libyan while trying to control his temper. "Ambassador Kamal, is there no end to your foul deceit, no lows that you'll not stoop to, in order to carry out your evil plans of war in this region? These are Arab people you speak of killing, like you'd kill a sand flea on your foot. I fear what you have in store for Egypt when you have no further use for her in your foul plans of conquest." He said as the anger in him rose anew as he felt the hairs on the back of his neck stand on edge.

Ambassador Kamal laughed his evil laugh again as he offered confidently. "Mohammed Kheir, you're about to witness the birth of the new and pure Islamic power and freedom in the Arab world, sir. Egypt has nothing whatsoever to fear from my great nation of Libya, sir. Your country is of pure Arab blood, and is our long time and proven ally, sir." Ambassador Kamal suddenly glared at him before continuing with his upsetting words. "I have to inform you of the next incident that'll soon take place, that'll place your country with mine on a war alert, sir. I have operatives on call, stationed deep within the loathsome lands of Israel."

"More of your radical Muslim Fundamentalists I guess you mean, Ambassador Kamal?" He hissed in pure disdain for the Libyan politician this time.

Ambassador Kamal completely ignored his nasty remark as he went on with his words of anger. "These Arab Agents of ours operating inside Israel will sabotage one of Libya's ships that'll be scheduled to unload a cargo of silk and tobacco products brought in by special arrangement from the Jew government. The ship will contain certain goods from Egypt as well, and at the same time, more of my special operatives will stir up further trouble in Chad. But close to the border with Libya to force us to react against this military incident. This incident will consist of a number of military probes that'll look like the attackers had come from Chad into Libya, in which a number of Libyan women will be raped, and their men killed.

"This new incident will take place during the early months of August and September in preparation for our opening attack on the two nations of Chad, and the Sudan. In the meantime Ambassador Kheir, your country will move all your military troops away from the Libyan border and move them towards the Sinai Desert. This will cause the hated Jews to rapidly build up their troops stationed on the other side of the Sinai Desert, sir.

"Your Commando Teams already stationed inside Israel being trained by the hated Jews in new military tactics, will immediately request political asylum in Israel. Stating these soldiers don't want to get involved in any further wars being carried out between Israel and Egypt. This way, these specially trained Egyptian troops will be free to roam around behind the Jew's defensive lines and wreaking pure havoc there, by destroying many Jewish fuel dumps and tank refitting and staging areas. If we destroy enough of the tank refitting areas, the foolish Jews will not be able to repair their damaged tanks, and they'll also be unable to rearm them at the same time, sir. The more tanks we can keep out of the fighting, the easier the winning of this foul war will be for us, Mohammed." Ambassador Kamal stopped talking to allow Mohammed to speak.

"Do you really believe the foolish Jews will allow our Egyptian soldiers to remain free to roam around behind their foul defensive lines as you have just suggested when the shooting starts, Ambassador Kamal? Surely the Jews would want to keep a close eye on these soldiers."

"Surely the hated Jews would allow the soldiers to remain behind. They'll think like us. If the Egyptian soldiers didn't want to fight the Jews, they'd surely be allowed to stay behind. So there'll be less Egyptian soldiers for them to fight in the Sinai when the shooting starts."

"I hope you're correct with what I believe is a foolish assumption Ambassador Kamal, for both our country's sakes sir." He replied softly as he slowly lowered his eyes towards the surface of his desk, and then he offered a silent prayer to Allah.

Ambassador Kamal offered his hand to Ambassador Kheir as he said. "I have to leave you at this time sir. I'm due back at a special meeting with President Sadat later on this afternoon. Stay strong and good bye for now. Allah Akbar Mohammed." He left the office.

At the same time Ambassador Kamal stood JoAnne sprang to her feet, and placed her hand on her weapon tucked under her arm, as she stared intensely at Ambassador Kamal, this time she did not take the weapon out. Neither man paid much attention to her to her dangerous actions, but Ambassador Kamal kept a close eye on her out of the corner of his eye.

Once Kamal was out of his office, he could not hide his anger any longer as he swiped the lamp off his desk. He wondered why Ambassador Kamal was having a private meeting with his President, and he was not invited to sit in on the meeting.

JoAnne easily read the anger etched on his distorted face as Ambassador Kamal walked out of his office alone, and she offered him. "Don't allow that lowly dog of a cursed fool get to you Mohammed. He's just a boring ass, and I shall be blessed with great pleasure in taking revenge upon him for the terrible insolence he has displayed towards you today."

He looked at her and then he remarked to her words. "No JoAnne, Kamal is my problem to deal with, not yours. I'll take care of my own problems myself thank you. I hate to have to deal with this dung eating Scarab." He hissed as he started to leave.

She tried to get the Egyptian Ambassador to speak further with her, but she saw it was useless at this point, his mind was else where, and she decided to get out of his way for the time being. She did not want him to try anything foolish now.

PRESIDENTIAL PALACE, EGYPT,
PRESIDENT SADAT'S PRIVATE OFFICE

Ambassador Kamal walked in President Sadat's office fifteen minutes late for their scheduled meeting, and instantly found himself staring at an extremely angry looking Egyptian President, as he snarled at him at the same time he took a seat in his office. "It's about time you decided to arrive for our meeting, sir. I was about to send my guards out to bring you foul head here intact or in pieces I was that angry, Ambassador Kamal. I'm quite certain your President would be most upset with you if he was made aware you kept me waiting, you great fool you."

"Please forgive me, I'm sorry for my delay President Sadat, I was meeting with Mohammed. I still feel we cannot trust the man, I fear he'll betray us when the shooting starts, sir."

President Sadat raised his hand to silence the Libyan Ambassador as he barked at him. "Let us not get in that conversation again. I have Mohammed neutralized, so don't worry about him. I'll know before Mohammed knows if he intends to betray me. My bitch watches his every move. You said over the phone you had information I must be made aware of. What information?"

"President Sadat, my Generals have come up with a scenario. They came to the conclusion that our enemy has forgot what armies are supposed to do. The great fools forgot what they were trained for. The American bastards are doomed, because they fight with political convictions and they fear civilian casualties at the same time. This is the main difference between our two armies and our beliefs. We are true soldiers, because we'll continue to march on, no matter how many worthless civilians we crush under foot. Yet the foolish American soldiers will stop attacking if there's danger of killing too many civilians if they attack further.

"My soldiers have been issued special orders to carry with them, as many civilian prisoners as they can without slowing the speed of their march, as human shields if you will, sir. It has worked for Iraq, and there's no reason to believe it won't work for us, President Sadat. We know the lowly American dogs will not attack our troops if we let it be known we have civilian prisoners in our ranks. This is a Western weakness I plan to take full advantage of, President Sadat. Our foolish enemy will defeat themselves with worry, and fear of killing civilians and becoming embarrassed by their foul news reporters. It'll give us the chance to destroy the great American army, or I'll see the entire population of Chad dead, sir." Kamal smiled at Sadat.

The Egyptian President felt a shiver of pure disgust down his spine as he said with a snap in his voice. "Ambassador Kamal, I cannot believe what I'm hearing coming from your foul lips, sir. These are people you speak about. Arabs. I cannot belie..."

"For the love of Allah. Don't tell me we're going to argue about this decision now. Can't you Egyptians ever go along with the war plans of Libya without crying about them first? This is the break, the edge we needed, to beat the loathsome American soldiers. What are the insignificant lives of the civilians of Chad when it comes to saving Libyan and Egyptian lives? I'll tell you this. They're nothing and that's why we're going to use them for our own best purposes and needs. President Sadat, you must remember it's not I who'll make these decisions, it's the will of the Almighty Allah. I'm merely the instrument to carry out His sacred will, sir." Ambassador Kamal suddenly glared at President Sadat, forcing him to answer.

"I understand this is Allah's will that Egypt does everything in her power to protect the sacred waters of the Nile River Ambassador Kamal, and I find myself being forced to go along with your plane of conquest for the sake of Egypt and her children. But I must also still protest using civilians to protect our fighting soldiers. It should be the other way with our soldiers protecting innocent civilian lives. I believe our soldiers should destroy the enemy on their own merit, and if they can't then we really don't deserve to win this war in the first place, Ambassador Kamal."

"President Sadat Sir, I'm afraid you're a dreamer much like Mohammed Kheir. We'll do whatever it takes to win our battle, and I suggest your people do the same thing if they want to survive in the future times, sir. To kill an infidel is not murder, it's the true path to Paradise." Ambassador Kamal laughed, putting on his ever present sneer, and then he left President Sadat's office without waiting for an answer from him, or being dismissed from President Sadat.

President Sadat glared at the back of Kamal, trying to burn a hole in him with his eyes. He put his head in his hands, and cried to himself. "Phrase Allah, what have I gotten Egypt into."

THE NEW MILITARY BASE SENTRY, THE SUDAN

Colonel Edward Campanelli watched as a massive C 5 Galaxy transport aircraft came in for its landing. He marveled at how these huge planes got off the ground, and flew in the first place. In the past nine days he received four thousand Marines, two thousand Army soldiers and another thousand Seabees. The 71st Tactical Wing with 21 YF 23s were covered with green tarps and sitting, fueled and armed just off the runways. The noses of the sleek fighter aircraft were pointing towards the end of the runway for a fast launch. The crash trucks were hooked up to each of the planes, idling and keeping the fighter aircraft cool and charged and ready to go.

The Colonel found himself in command of a formidable military base. His days were long, and filled with unbearable heat, dust and activity He added to his workload by staying in constant touch with his former base at Lake Tana in Ethiopia. He kept his finger on the Dam project, and did not like having the Ethiopians takeover the security on the base, and construction site.

As far as he knew, the Marines were still stationed in the jungle in Ethiopia, but the main base was being protected by the Ethiopian Army now. Who were busy warring with each other to take any proper security precautions to protect the civilians working on the Dam project.

His thoughts returned to work on his base. The Colonel watched as the transport aircraft was being rapidly unloaded by the air crews, and he marveled at the proficiency of the men he controlled. A mosquito bit him on his neck, and he cursed as he slapped it because he left his battery powered Mosquito Hawk, the tiny sonic repeller machine lying on his desk.

Weeks went by at a snail's pace, and the days never seemed to changed for him. With the oppressive heat, along with the many problem of making certain his people drank enough water to prevent dehydration. The irritation of the incalculable bugs, and the never ending work of unloading the planes continued. The repair of the perimeter defenses, and the blasting into the side of the mountain proceeded at a fever pitch, even though the Colonel could not believe it, the days were getting even hotter. His angry grew with his post until finally, on a hot day in the middle of early June, he declared a complete day of rest for every person on his base.

It was the first day everyone had off on the military base at the same time since their began the construction of the massive base. The Colonel smiled as he watched happy Marines strip down bare, and then jump in the warm waters of the Nile River. A few of the soldiers kept their weapons with them in case a crocodile showed up, or they were hit by any of the many different rebel fractions operating in this region. Further down the river from where the Marines were swimming and having fun, a few of the sweat warriors tried their luck at fishing.

Soon, each soldier caught three of the numerous River Perch, some were of good size. Other soldiers joined the fishermen, and all were pulling in good size fish. Some cooks saw the action, and they quickly setup to clean and cook the freshly caught fish for the soldiers and civilian workers of the base as a special feast. There was laughter and high jinks going on throughout the base. Many soldiers stripped and sunned themselves on the wings of the aircraft parked by the runways, they were soon joined by other soldiers who wanted sun. Colonel Campanelli also had a wing of female flyers stationed on base, who mastered the complicated YF 23 fighter planes.

The female pilots more of less stayed separate from most of the male population and pilots of the base. He heard many of the rumors spreading saying a few of the female pilots were lesbians, and this was why they stayed away from the male soldiers on the base. This did not bother him in the least because he judged the ladies as pilots, and what they did with their aircraft and flying abilities, not by who or how they loved anyone in their lives. Their private life was theirs to struggle with and no concern of his. His love life was far from being great and conventional, and he was not going to throw any stones at anyone else because their lifestyle was a little different than his. But on this day, the women pilots got caught up in all the festivities of the day, and they actually took to sunning themselves naked while laying on the wings of their parked aircraft.

The news that the female pilots were sunning themselves in the nude by their aircraft, rapidly passed through the ranks of the soldiers and civilians on base like a wild fire, and soon every pilot, Marine, Army soldier and male civilian, and even some Arabs working or stationed on the massive military base. Were thinking of any excuse to circulate over towards where the women pilots were stationed along with their aircraft.

Colonel Campanelli was please that the women pilots took all this new attention to them in their stride, ignoring much of the childish antics of the foolish men taking little sneak peeks at them as they sunned themselves. He found himself heading in the same direction to where the female pilots were stationed himself. Once he had an eyeful of the ladies, he went back to see how the fishermen were doing with their chore.

The cooks already carted off many of the large fish the soldiers caught, and they had them cleaned and prepared for cooking, and now the wonderful smell of cooking fish was overtaking the entire base. Many of the locals were hanging around the base for a possible handout of the soon feast. So the cooks setup a number of extra tables on the outside of the first perimeter line, and they gave the natives some of the cooked fish and even soda to drink.

The cooked fish was a meal fit for a king and queen, and it was served on table's setup out in the open on the massive military base. Every man and woman on base had his or her own miniature Mosquito Hawk going off at full blast though. So many flies and mosquitoes did not come anywhere near enough to bother the feasting soldiers and civilians enjoying themselves outside. But the huge swarms of Dragonflies hatched to kill off the heavy swarms of mosquitos were becoming more of a bother, than the insects they were brought over to kill. But at least the dragon flies did not bite the soldiers or spread any possible disease.

Many of the locals were allowed on the new military base to finish off the leftover fish and other items to enjoy, which led to good will growing between them and the American soldiers who invaded their land. Colonel Campanelli was even considering picking out a few of the better fishermen soldiers, and designate them as the base fishermen for the duration of the project to help supplement their meals. They would be ordered fish on every Sunday, so the base could have fresh fish to eat at least once a week for the soldiers and civilians stationed on the base. He figured he could save some food supplies this way, because he realized how rapidly his base was expanding every day, and he was getting more than concerned on how he was going to keep feeding the new soldiers constantly showing up on base everyday.

The day of fishing would also serve another purpose for the troops on the base. It would give them a complete day off from their usual hard work and other duties on base, to enjoy themselves a little for a change by fishing. The day off he called for was good for his troops, and it gave new spirit to many exhausted civilian workers and troops alike.

For three full days, every soldier stationed on the new massive military base was in a good mood and had a new spring in their steps. Even the female pilots were a little more friendlier to their male counterparts lately, and they even began to mingle in with the male pilots for a change. The woman's fighter aircraft wing was given the nickname of, "The Bitches of the Sudan, and the women fighter pilots seemed to enjoy the name the male pilots bestowed upon them."

By the fourth day after the off day, the effects of the relaxing day was lost for the most part to the soldiers, as the future coming days were once again filled with backbreaking work, and suppressing heat and sweat for the soldiers and civilian workers involved with the ongoing construction of the new and massive military base. They also suffered from the never ending attacks on their bodies by swarms of attacking mosquitoes and flies.

CHAPTER 18 – THE ISRAELI COMMAND HEADQUARTERS, TEL AVIV, ISRAEL

One flyover of the nation of Libya carried out by the American Spy Blackbird satellite, picked up a good size movement of troops occurring inside Libya. These discovered soldiers were obviously heading towards the Chad border. Many Libyan soldiers were moved and heavily armed for combat. Before the breakup of the Soviet Union, the Russians sold Libya hundreds of their outdated aircraft and tanks. Seven hundred Mig Floggers, and eight hundred Mig 29-A air to ground support fighter aircraft, along with two hundred Sukhoi SU 24, and one hundred MI 24 Hind heavy assault helicopter gunships add these to the two thousand Mitsubishi T 2 fighter, and Sukhoi SU 25 Frogfoot aircraft Libya secretively got their hands on twenty five of these new planes, and this gave Libya a very sizable and threatening airforce.

Libya also brought over two thousand new T 95 140 mm Russian made tanks equipped with a second turret with a separate 20 mm gatling gun used for helicopter, or most missile interception launched against the tank. Libya also had over one thousand Russian T-85 tanks equipped with a 122 mm cannon, and one hundred Soviet 2S3 152 mm self propelled Howitzers, and the new 2S5, also a 152 mm artillery piece, but with nuclear firing capability also. All this military equipment was brought by Libya through a second nation because Libya was cut off from buying any military equipment until that nation turned away from their terrorist support.

Much of this Russian made military equipment was on the move one way or the other towards the two nations of Chad or Algeria.

Israel paid close attention to Egypt, suddenly moving much of her own war equipment and soldiers around their nation. Hundreds of Russian made T-85, and the American Abrams M-1 and M-1A tanks were making their way towards the Sinai Desert region.

Egyptian flight crews working on their aircraft, armament was also picked up in many photos moved in some of their hard shell hangers, or weapons were being fitted under the wings of the aircraft out in the open. This concerned the Israelis greatly concerned, and the first warning was placed to the Jerusalem Battalions, they were ordered to go on a full war alert.

The latest satellite pictures displayed a number of large box tractor trailer trucks heading to, and parking along the shores of Egypt. Israeli intelligence could give no reason for the sudden truck movements, but whatever the reason was, it was decided it was not good for Israel's interests. The warning from the intelligence units informed the Israeli government.

THE AMERICAN AIRCRAFT CARRIER ROOSEVELT, STATIONED IN THE RED SEA

Commander Owens, stationed in the CIC chamber of the Aircraft Carrier Roosevelt, was examining the same pictures and other information that was being transmitted to his chamber. Command picked up Egyptian soldiers setting up numerous artillery pieces facing towards Israel from Egypt, as well as other troops massing along the nation of Chad from the border of Libya. Libya informed the United Nations they had information of a pending attack from Chad aimed against Libya. The United States took this information on face value, but judging by the past actions committed by Chad, the United States had no choice but to believe Libya, and the United States government did not interfere with the military buildup of troops on Libya's borders.

Egypt also informed the United States they were planning to engage in a number of military maneuvers, starting in late September and lasting into the middle of October. It would be a mock invasion of Israel troops through the Sinai Desert again.

The United States did not like this information because of the mounting tension occurring in the area. But the Americans also knew Egypt was going to hold these military maneuvers in the upcoming months, and were hoping to be invited to join them, but they were not asked this time. The United States sent a memo out to Israel, informing her of Egypt's planned of military maneuvers, hoping this information would explain the sudden buildup of troops from Egypt. Neither the United States nor Israel believed this excuse as the truth though.

Israel asked the United States to join her in her own planned military maneuvers scheduled to start in late October in the region, and the United States readily agreed with the Israeli troop scheduled war games. Militaries from both the United States and Israel started a low level military buildup in the surrounding area of their own. Saudi Arabia was informed of the actions being carried out by Egypt and Libya and became highly concerned, and they requested soldiers and military support from America. All United States troops stationed in Turkey were placed on full alert, and the soldiers were ordered to be ready to be shipped out at a moment's notice.

BASE SENTRY, THE SUDAN

Colonel Edward Campanelli, noticed even more American soldiers showing up on his base lately, and he reminded himself to check on the troops coming on base who were under Captain White's command. The worried Colonel gave the Captain command of these certain troops to get the workload a little lighter for himself, and now he realized the report informing him it was becoming rather hard to feed all the troops was true. Supplies could not possibly keep up with all the troops needs, and what was once a pleasure for the soldiers to fish, and supplement the meals, now become an everyday order, with three hundred soldiers fishing daily.

The Colonel now found himself having to send out hunting parties for Antelope and other different types of deer and wildebeest of the region, to help feed the ever growing number of American soldiers turning up on his new base. Human waste was fast becoming a larger problem than feeding the soldiers for him to contend with. Huge pits were dug by the Seabees, and then planked over, and latrines were quickly erected over the vast pits. Once these pits became full, they were concrete over, and a new pit was dug, and the process was repeated again.

To keep the fly and other biting insect population down, the Colonel received more dragonfly larvae which wreaked havoc on the pests once hatched. The water purifying plant which made the Nile River water fit to drink for the troops, was working at full capacity, twenty four hours a day, and three more of the plants were setup with two other systems placed on order, so he could keep up with the troop's need for clean drinking water.

Over the past few days, the Colonel happened to noticed the amount of fish being caught was way down, and he decided to take a walk over to the fishermen to see what was happening. It was the first time he had gone down to the bank of the Nile River in weeks. He was absolutely stunned when he reached the edge of the water. The spot where he setup his military base along the Nile River was over a mile wide when he first came to the spot, but now the water was half that wide. He walked over to one of the Marines who caught ten fish, and had them lying on the sand after he gutted the fish. He stood by the soldier's side and asked him with concern lacing his tone. "Where the hell's all the damn water going for Pete's sake?"

"Beats the hell outta me sir. But all I know is for the past week or so, the water's been going down real fast, Colonel." The Marine watched as the bobber floated on the smooth surface of the water of the Nile River, as he waited to catch the next fish.

After ten minutes of watching the soldier fishing, he headed for his hut. He was not watching the bobbin, he was watching the flow of water and becoming deeply concerned. It looked like it was flowing twice the speed it had when he first setup his base. He left to make a report to Commander Owens over what he observed of the flow of water.

"Where the hell's the Colonel at dammit?" Captain John White asked a soldier because he was looking for the Commanding Officer.

The soldier replied smartly. "I believe the Commander's down by the River the last I heard, sir. I guess he's trying to walk on water sir."

"Funny wiseass. That was real fucking funny buster, I only wish the Colonel was here to hear that remark buster. If he had, you'd wish you were never born, asshole." Captain White hissed, and then he added. "Aw, the hell with it and you wiseguy." And he went back to his reports after he decided to wait for the Colonel to return to their Command Post.

Colonel Campanelli hurried it up at the last minute, and actually ran into the G 2 Intelligence hut. He knew he had to answer the question of where the water from the Nile River was going. When he entered, only one of the Lieutenants was in the hut. He jumped up and immediately saluted his Commander, but he was instantly waved back to his seat by the Colonel.

"Lieutenant, get me the base Commander at Lake Tana, right now dammit!"

In seconds a voice was on the line waiting to speak with the Colonel. He grabbed the mike and asked who he was speaking to.

"Corporal Evans, sir." The Corporal replied to the Colonel over the radio.

"Corporal Evans, this is Colonel Campanelli. You better listen up to me and listen up real good mister. I'm calling to find out how close you are to putting the Dam on full control?"

"Hell sir, we've been operating on full for the past nine days now Colonel Campanelli Sir."

"Nine damn days! Dammit, why the hell wasn't I fucking informed about this shit before now, buster? The stinking water level up here has to be down by some fifteen feet. Are you letting too much fucking water down into Ethiopia?" He growled angrily.

"Colonel Campanelli Sir, we're only following the orders over here sir. The Ethiopians had us turn the concrete wedge until we were diverting nearly ninety percent of the water from Lake Tana, sir. The water took four days of seeping into the soil before it finally reach the Afar Depression. Sir, the sand absorbed over two days worth of water before it showed any signs of wet, but it looks great now sir. Tons of top soil was also washed down in the Depression as well, Colonel. The engineers are extremely excited with the results of the water, and they figure in the next two years, there should be enough water and top soil in the depression to make this region a productive growing area. Sir, they figure in five years, Ethiopia should have enough food crops growing in the area to feed most of her population. The system's working out real great sir."

"Well soldier, the plan's destroying this entire fucking area up here, mister. I have to make a flyover, I want to see what the hell's going on for myself, buster. I fear we'll have to re divert most of the damn water back to the Nile River, or there'll be one hell of a war within a year's time I can assure you, mister. I'm leaving, so inform the fucking Marines I'll be flying over the damn base, err... say in and hour or so." He released the button flip up and break off his communication. He then ran outside yelling for his female officer. "Captain Mendoza, where the hell are you at, dammit? Mendoza, I need you right fucking now for crap sake."

Heads turned on the base, it was rare for the Colonel to screamed at anyone, he rarely if ever lost his temper, unless someone screwed up bad, and yet he was yelling like he lost the lottery.

Captain Mendoza had her head stuffed under one of the inspection panels of an F 18 Hornet having a bit of engine trouble. She popped her head up and noticed the excited Colonel standing in front of the intelligence hut, and he was yelling for her at the top of his lungs.

She jumped down from the ladder and ran over to him. Renee was scared by the way he was acting, and being in front of the G 2 hut made her more frightened. She feared a war might have broken out by the way he was acting, and she ran up to him out of breath.

"What's wrong Edward? Are we at war sir?" She asked, while coming to a stop while gasping for air and staring at her Commanding Officer.

"Shit, if we ain't we soon will be you can bet the stinking bank on it, baby. Have you seen the stinking level of the fucking Nile River lately, Captain?" He did not wait for her reply as he went on with his excited words. "It's fucking way down, and I'm sure as hell Egypt noticed it by now. They're probably making war talk in their government offices right now, dammit. Shit, I would if my fucking water supply was cut down as much as there's has been by that fucking Dam project I always felt was going to start a damn shooting war once it was finished being constructed, dammit. Maz, do we still have the little fucking Cessna A 37 piece of shit they let us go to Egypt in at our disposal?"

"Yes sir, Command gave the plane to me to use if we had to go some where in a fast hurry, and not use a military threat to get there, sir. It's parked behind the mess hut. Why Eddy?"

"Get it ready for immediate flight, I wanna take a quick flyover the stinking Dam at Lake Tana. How soon can we be ready to leave and get there?"

"She's all fueled up and checked out, and I can be ready to go in less than ten minutes time, Colonel Campanelli Sir." She replied as she smiled at her commanding officer.

"Get it done for me Maz." He ordered his female Captain and now pilot.

She left the Colonel's side and rushed over to the small plane, she did not salute the Colonel who went back to the G 2 hut, and he ordered the Lieutenant to inform Tana Base they were leaving in ten minutes. The Colonel left the hut in a rush and ran over to the small Cessna aircraft where Mendoza had the plane already moving out for the runway. She stopped the aircraft and the Colonel jumped on the wing, and then climbed in the cockpit, half climbing over her in the process. She taxied the plane to the head of the runway.

Colonel Campanelli quickly buckled up as Captain Mendoza slammed the throttles to the stops. The aircraft was soon streaking down the runway while he gripped the handles of his chair until his knuckles turned white. He hated flying with a passion, and lost his stomach as the plane shot in the air. It took minutes before he could look out the window, and then he bitched at his female pilot. "Maz, before you head out, I want you to fly down the Nile River for a mile or so. I wanna see what the hell is really going on further down river if we can."

The two sat in silence as she throttled down to conserve fuel as they flew over the waters of the Nile. The water was so low in some spots wildebeest were walking across the river.

Maz whistled as she moaned to her Commanding Officer. "Shit Edward, would you look at that, I never noticed how low the water was until now, sir."

"You can bet the damn Egyptians did. Let's get to Lake Tana, and see what's going on there."

She banked the plane towards the east and then leveled off at one thousand feet, and headed directly towards Lake Tana. It took an hour with open throttles to reach the lake.

Campanelli drew in his breath in a rush as the enormity of the Dam came in view, it was ninety five percent complete. He watched as the water fell two hundred feet from the gates to the original path of the Nile River. The water was heavy and it looked like it was not cut in its powerful flow in the least. But as the small plane passed to the other side of the dam that fed the waters down the manmade ravine, it was a different story entirely. The heavy torrent of water flowing down this part of the Dam over shadowed the other flow of water to the Nile River by over a hundred times. Here, the vast flow of waters were turned into wild roaring flow and foam, with massive clouds of water flying high in the air around the Dam.

Captain Mendoza put the windshield wipers on the aircraft. The water rolled over and over in a turbulent roar, until it finally transformed into a runaway wall of free flowing liquid mass. Words could not explain the true force of water that sped down the side of the mountain. The roar of the torrent was actually deafening, and the Colonel had to actually open his mouth to neutralize the pressure rapidly building up in his ears.

The small plane was suddenly being wildly harshly bounced up and down and wildly from side to side violently from the roaring force and updrafts created by this heavy flow of rushing water. They drifted down the ravine for a few miles, to where he could easily see many uprooted trees being tumbled around like match sticks in the raging waters, as many animals were also caught up in the powerful flow and drowned and joined the tumbling water.

"Dammit Edward, we're going to have to land pretty soon, sir. I'm getting a little low on fuel, sir." She warned her Commander as she checked her fuel reserves.

"Land then and refuel dammit!" He growled at her, without taking his eyes off the sheer destruction the water was causing to the landscape on its way heading for the massive depression in lower Ethiopia. "Shit, shit, shit, this fucking Dam's going to create all the hell the invention of the damn Atomic bomb caused the world. I hope we can keep Egypt from going to fucking war with this lousy nation once she sees this shit happening. Shit."

BASE EASY MONEY, ETHIOPIA

The turbulence over the Dam was a mess from the air currents produced by the raging water, that caused Mendoza's landing to be rather rough, and making the Colonel turn green and gag, before the plane finally came to a full stop on the old runway. Campanelli was the first one out of the plane, again just about climbing over Mendoza who was still seated in the aircraft doing her last minute landing check off list, this time to get out before he upchucked inside the aircraft. He spat on the ground as she made her way out of the aircraft. She laughed as the stumbling Colonel tried desperately to find his sea legs under him again.

"You almost broke my damn shoulder getting out of the plane you know, mister." She giggled at her Commanding Officer as she watched him trying to calm himself down.

The young and interested Marine Lieutenant Peter Gates, walked up to the still gagging and green Colonel and saluted him as he offered his once Commanding Officer. "Glad to have you back on board the base sir. I heard of your recent promotion, congratulations sir. How do you like how your pet project has turned out, sir? We should have the Dam completed within the next two months or so, with any luck sir. Then I can get the hell out of this God forsaken land and get back to real civilization and begin living again, sir."

"If there's any fucking civilization to go back to mister." He hissed as he spat again.

"Sir?" The Lieutenant asked with questioning eyes of his once Commanding Officer.

"You amaze me mister. Let me inform you of something mister, you can't believe how low the fucking level of the damn Nile River is up by my new military base, sir. Shit, it has to be down fifteen to twenty feet at least, and still dropping rapidly dammit." He stopped talking to allow this latest information to sink in on the Lieutenant for a moment.

"Uh-oh." The Marine Lieutenant mumbled at the still green looking Colonel.

"You're damn right uh-oh mister. You know what the hell this shit means. We have to allow a helluva lot more fucking water down the original path to the Nile River and Egypt. The hell with the damn Ethiopians at this point Lieutenant. We have to divert a damn shooting war instead of fucking water." He snapped back at the Lieutenant.

"I can't do that sir. I don't have the authority to change the flow of water at the Dam, sir. You have to take that up with Command, Colonel. They, and the Ethiopians have the power to do what you ask, sir. And you can bet the bank on it the Ethiopians won't help you in the least sir."

"C'mon with me mister." He said as he walked over to his old Intel tent now a wood hut. The Colonel walked in as if he owned the place, and the soldiers inside immediately snapped to attention. He ignored them and he growled. "Get me Commander Owens STAT!"

The aircraft containing Colonel Campanelli and Captain Mendoza had not gone down far enough to the Afar Depression, so he had no way of knowing what was occurring there. As the runoff of water entered the enormous Afar Depression, most of the water from the first few day's flow instantly evaporated, or it sank into the arid soil and sand of the region. The water that evaporated lifted high in the desert air and forming water laden clouds prowling the vast desert area. The heavy clouds were laden down with vapor and then they would release the water any time when the clouds could no longer contain the vapor. The desert was now being inundated by heavy roaming thunder showers, where an eighth of an inch of rain once fell in a year's time. The showers now flooded the parched sand for as long as the rain lasted in the clouds, and then the water quickly disappeared below the sands, or re evaporated into the air again.

The great Afar Depression was being attacked by these extremely heavy rain showers and storms occurring during the first week as the water flooded down the manmade ravine from Lake Tana. As the water slowly built up in the Depression area, it quickly cooled the hot sand and stones. The steam clouds slowly turned smaller and the showers grew less severe and violent.

The Army Core of Engineers estimated the steam clouds should last for the rest of the year before the danger of a flash flood finally subsided in the area. The clouds would always be in the area because of the high temperatures though. The Engineers figured somewhere in the range of three to five hundred thousand gallons of water a week would evaporated into the air. The Core also hoped the heavy and rain laden clouds would carry some showers away from the Depression into the lower section of desert, helping to fertilize other areas of the region at the same time.

Due to the commotion being caused by Campanelli and Mendoza returning to the Command Post, and meeting with old friends, along with the Marine Lieutenant. The soldier had not place the call to Command stationed on board the Aircraft Carrier Roosevelt as he was ordered to do. He was too busy listening to the many conversations going on between the other officers.

The Colonel suddenly glared angrily as he repeated the request to get Command on the radio. This time, he said it in a much more threatening and commanding voice, which made the young radio operator jump and respond in an excited voice. "Right away sir."

The shocked soldier grabbed the mike and quickly placed a call out to the CIC chamber on board the Roosevelt. In seconds, Commander Owens was on the mike.

"Commander Owens Sir, this is Colonel Campanelli, sir. I have to talk to you right now sir."

ON BOARD THE AMERICAN CARRIER USS ROOSEVELT

"Well how the hell are they hanging Colonel?" The Commander cut in and offered pleasantly.

"Fine sir, but I'm afraid we have a major problem rapidly developing on our hands along the Nile River, sir. With the Dam diverting so much of the fucking water from Lake Tana, the Nile River's water level is going down quicker than was first expected, sir. Commander Owens Sir, if we don't do something and real fast at that sir. I fear Egypt will have no other choice but to declare war on Ethiopia, over the vast loss of water to their lands and people, sir."

"C'mon man, how the hell far can the water level be down Colonel? You sure you're not overreacting a little here, Colonel Campanelli? I'm certain the water's down, but it can't be down as far as you're suggesting, sir. How low is the water?" He asked sarcastically.

"Sir, the water has to be down at least nearly twenty feet back at my base, Commander."

"Whaaat! What the hell are you drunk on me or something, mister? How the hell can this possibly be true sir? The Dam has only been operating for a week now sir. How the heck could the water be down that far already sir?" Commander Owens yelled while catching his breath.

"Commander Owens, it's down at least that much if not more than that sir, and the fucking water's still dropping real fast as we speak, sir." He offered to Commander Owens.

"I'll have my fucking engineers flown out to your damn base by this evening, Colonel Campanelli Sir. I want to know how you got over to Tana and the Dam site, sir?"

"By the Cessna you gave to Captain Mendoza a while back, Commander Owens Sir."

"Great, okay, yeah, err..., Colonel Campanelli, I want you to refuel the damn aircraft and take two belly cans for extra fuel for the damn thing. I'm ordering you to do a quick flyover of the old Atbara River, and tell me what state that damn River's in. Then you'll fly over to the Aswan Dam, I'll clear the flight with the fucking Egyptians from here for you, sir. I want a full report of this region filed by you by no later than tonight mister, on whatever your finding are there, sir. See if you can tell from some of the old water marks on the Dam, and determine just how far down the fucking water down is there. I can assure you Colonel Campanili Sir.

"Heads are going to roll from my engineers for not picking this mess up before you reported it to me, sir. Damn, I surrounded myself with nothing but the best of stinking engineers in the entire fucking world dammit, and one of my Officers has to pick up their damn slack for them. Heads will roll mister, I can promise you that. Get your ass in gear soldier and get me those damn reports. Err... good work Colonel Campanelli, thanks again sir."

The Colonel handed the mike back to the young Lieutenant and then he turned, only to see Lieutenant Gates was gone from the hut. He came out of the hut and Lieutenant Gates instantly ran over to him and reported what he was up to while he spoke to Owens.

"Colonel Campanelli Sir, I saw I wasn't needed inside the communications hut while you were speaking with Commander Owens, sir. So I came out here and made sure your aircraft was refueled and ready for your use, sir. I heard the Commander order you to place two extra fuel tanks on your aircraft, so I oversaw the refit and refueling. Sir, you're ready to take off immediately Colonel. Your pilot's getting something to eat. I suggest you do the same thing sir. I'll have the cooks prepare you provisions, while you're on your way sir. You'll never get back to your base by supper, and you'll be hungry as hell by then, Colonel Campanelli Sir."

He laughed as he offered to the Lieutenant. "I have enough fucking trouble with just flying, let alone trying to eat something while I'm in the damn air, sir. If I did, the crews would have a helluva mess to clean up when we land, mister."

Both men laughed as Gates added. "Sir I'll have the cooks fix you some thing light then, Colonel. Believe me Colonel, when you get hungry, you'll eat even if you were in a boat, sir."

"I've been doing this shit while you were still swimming around in your father's nuts, sonny." He growled at the rather embarrassed young man and fellow officer.

After he ate and had something to drink, he and Captain Mendoza went over to the plane, a care package sat in the cockpit and in seconds, they were airborne again. It took them half an hour to reach Atbara River. Colonel Campanelli stared out of the window in stunned disbelief. The river was bone dry. The bank had already turned to dust in the heat, and the dust clouds whipped down what was once a river, and feeder for the Nile River. Mendoza followed the dry river out to the Nile River. She turned north and followed it towards the Aswan Dam.

All along the river's edge, the signs of a river drying up was prevalent. Dead fish spotted the river's edge, where the fish were caught in tide pools. The water had dried up, leaving dead fish to the birds. Herds of hippopotamuses were forced to crowd together, causing fights between the bulls of the other herds. She pointed to a carcass of a hippo on the shore, likely killed in a fight.

The hippos and villagers were soon locked in war for the remaining water and fish. The hippos were starting to be killed in retaliation for one of the beasts turning over a small fishing canoe and killed the two occupants of the canoe. Many crops of the Sudan were rapidly dying up because the lower water level was no longer able to irrigate the crops.

As the small aircraft approached the Aswan High Dam, there was clear evidence the Dam was opened further to allow even more water down river towards Egypt. The water stained Temples of Philae Island slowly rose out of the waters that usually covered the Temples over completely, except for when Egypt was in times of severe drought.

The small plane headed for the massive Dam. Suddenly, two military aircraft appeared from out of nowhere and took positions on either side of their small Cessna. They were American made F 15 Eagle fighter aircraft from the Egyptian airforce. The two aircraft dipped their wings to inform Captain Mendoza she had permission to freely fly in their airspace.

She immediately opened communications with the Egyptian pilot right off.

The Egyptian with the best command of English, spoke with her over the radio. He ordered her to follow him to the Dam, once there, he pointed out the old watermarks that clearly showed how low the water truly was. By the Dam, she noticed the water that once reached twenty miles out to form the massive Lake Nasser, and reached all the way down to the Sudan, was down to less than half of its usual capacity, and was less than nine miles across at its widest part now. The once great reservoir was drying up rapidly in the heat of the sun, and with it, all hopes the Egyptian people had placed on the massive lake, and the life giving waters of the Nile River. It was their only protection against any times of severe droughts that once plagued Egypt, and almost led to her death a number of time throughout her great past history.

Campanelli looked out the window. Many times since he was sent to this region, he fished this lake and marveled at its vastness. Now he was sure he could see one end from the other. He felt bad for what his creation had done to Egypt as he grumbled more to himself than Mendoza. "Shit, if only we could have left well enough alone dammit, all this shit wouldn't be happening. I bet Egypt's in for another round of earthquakes because of the change in weight."

Captain Renee Mendoza jumped all over him as she heard the words he was saying to her. "Look Edward, we were sent out here to try and save the people of Ethiopia. We didn't foresee the complications we'd be causing to Egypt. But nothing we did is cast in stone yet sir. There are many other options still open to us than there would be if we hadn't built the Dam, sir. All the Ethiopians have to do is move the block wedge, and more water will flow to the Nile River, replacing most of the waters drying up now, sir. I'm quite certain the two countries will be able to work this out together, without having to go to war against each other sir. I don't want you to blame yourself for any of what's happening below us, mista."

The pilot of the Egyptian fighter aircraft, interrupted the conversation by pointing out more of the havoc the lack of water was causing to his nation of Egypt. He showed the second gates of the Dam had to be opened so it could continue to produce electricity, thus lowering the water of Lake Nasser even further. The Egyptian pilot tried to lead the American pilot down river past the great Aswan Dam, so he could point out even more problems created by the lesser water to them.

But she quickly informed the concerned Egyptian pilot she did not have the fuel to fly any further down river. She lied, but she was not going to allow this Egyptian pilot to lead her around by the nose. She told him she was going to have to head back for home for more fuel and some much needed rest. The Egyptian pilot invited her to set down on his base, and he would get her the fuel she needed, so she could fly all the way to Cairo, to see what the Black Arabs of Ethiopia were doing to his country. The Egyptian pilot started to get a little nasty with her, as she had to begged off and head back to her own military base.

At one point, she thought this Egyptian pilot was going to actually try and force her down. During the flight, the Egyptian aircraft took up position directly behind her plane on her so called Six, and she thought she was actually bumped by the Egyptian aircraft.

After a few more rather heated conversations with the Egyptian airman going nowhere fast. A growling threat came from Campanelli, who removed the mike from Mendoza's hand. He warned the Egyptian pilot in no uncertain terms he was going to shove his aircraft up the Egyptian's ass, if they did not back off them immediately.

The Egyptian pilot received a call from his base and retreated, and they allowed the Cessna to turn and head back up the Nile River to

Base Sentry. She found herself having some trouble with controlling her plane properly now, it was constantly trying to drift off to her right side. She was fighting the sluggish controls all the way as she headed for their main base. She followed the Nile River up to Khartoum, the capital of Sudan. She flown over Khartoum a number of time and loved the beautiful sights she observed. She corrected her flight path, and immediately notified the military of Khartoum she was flying in their airspace. Instantly, two Sudanese military planes of Russian construction appeared on either side of her aircraft.

Captain Mendoza asked one of the two Sudanese pilots to check the tail of her aircraft out, to see if they could detect any reason why her plane was flying heavy to her right side. The Sudanese pilot who spoke poor English the best, quickly informed her she sustained some minor damage to her left tail wing. From what the pilot was able to see, she was obviously hit by something in flight, and he offered a possible bird strike might have caused the damage.

She thanked her escort as she continued heading towards Khartoum, but she cursed the Egyptian pilot for tapping her rear section of the aircraft. Campanelli rubbed the side of her cheek with two fingers, as if he knew what she was thinking, and then he offered her. "Maz, I'll send out an official protest to Egypt's government against the Egyptian pilot for bumping our ass like he did. I'm certain Ambassador Mohammed Kheir will be furious at his pilot for taking such a discretion against an American aircraft, honey. Egypt can ill afford any further problems with the United States, especially at this time, honey. You're not going to have trouble landing this damn thing are you baby?" He asked in a troubled voice.

She smiled as she replied to her Commander and lover. "Come on, stop being such a damn crybaby, sir. You're as safe as if you were in the hands of All State, Eddy." She then followed the Sudanese pilots as they led the way for her up the Nile River. She looked out the window and cried over what she saw. "Will you look at that for the love of God, Eddy."

As they continued to fly over the capital city of the Sudan. They picked up a large number of hippopotamuses in the water right in the middle of Khartoum. It was the widest points of the river at the junction where the Blue Nile water from Lake Tana, met with the waters from the White Nile. It seemed like the massive water cows were being forced to gather together to seek the safety of the wider, and much deeper water where boats were trying to corral the massive animals, and then drive them out of the capital area.

The Colonel had no way of knowing three hippos came out of the water, and walked through the very streets of the city. For the most part, the people of Khartoum watched the animals, and they treated them more as a novelty than a possible threat to their lives. Unfortunately, the friendliness ended when a cow suddenly charged a man trying to feed a younger animal, and it killed him. Soldiers killed the hippos and orders were cut to move the rest of the animals out the city limits, even if they had to kill the lot of them to get the job done.

Colonel Campanelli pointed out one of the huge animals attacking a small river boat in the water trailing them, trying to overturn the boat with his enormous head and gapping mouth. A military speed boat turned up from out of nowhere, and the soldiers immediately killed the hippo.

"Rather dumb animals I'm afraid, Eddy." She said as she watched the slaughter of the massive animal take place a thousand feet below her aircraft.

"I guess their first duty is to protect the damn civilians of their capital. I would do the same if I was ever faced with what those soldiers are dealing with." The Colonel told her.

They flew over Khartoum, and then headed back for their base, all the while they made mental notes of the vast amount of damage caused by the rapidly receding waters of the Nile River. Captain Mendoza complained to her Commanding Officer. "Gees Eddy, I see massive swarms of mosquitoes and flies, coming from the drying up waters and dead fish laying all along the River's edge. I don't know how the people are going to put up with the damn pests once they're airborne. I hope the Docs will be able to keep the illness from the pestilence under control."

"Thanks for the stinking warning. When we get back to base, I want fucking booster shots for everyone on the stinking base, from Malaria down to sleeping sickness as well as boosters for the AIDS Virus, and any other crap that can take down any of our soldiers. I don't want any fucking mosquitoes making my people sick while they're on duty in this stinking hellhole. Dammit, if any of my soldiers have to get that stinking disease, I want them to get it by fucking, not from some damn insect flying around them, god dammit." He growled angrily.

"That statement don't make a lot of sense to me, Edward. I think you should be more concerned about the damn shots, more than how your soldiers might get the lousy AIDS virus, sir. Besides Eddy, there's no proof the disease can be spread by mosquitoes, sir."

"I don't give a shit about any of that stinking crap, Mendoza. You believe whatever the hell you wanna believe in, and I'll believe in what I want to believe in, baby. I think it can be spread by the fucking bugs, and that's good enough for me to react against it the way I want to attack it, young lady. I'm telling you everyone gets the damn shots, and that's it, Captain. One of the luxuries of being in Command, everyone has to listen to my ass, even you I'm afraid Maz."

"Calm down a little will you please Edward, I happen to agree with you all the soldiers on base should get the booster shots. It's better to be safe than sorry, just in case the vaccine might protect them against any of these damn bugs. With the water receding like it is, there'll be more mosquitoes we'll have to contend with than ever before, sir. I hope the dragonflies are mature enough to start killing the damn things off for us, sir. We have to remind everyone to take their mosquito hawks with them at all times, sir. I want them protected even inside the buildings of the base. Maybe you better make that an official order when we get back to base, Colonel."

"You're damn right I'll make that order official, and once I get back to the States I'm going to look up the person who invented that damn thing, and buy him a stinking drink. Such a simple item and it works great." He laughed as he shook his head over his last comment.

The Colonel's massive military base came in view. Two YF 23 fighter aircraft came out and took up escort duty from the Sudanese aircraft trailing Mendoza's crippled aircraft. They were from the YF 23 crew, and the women's voices were a welcome sound to Campanelli's ears.

The first female pilot took a quick survey of Mendoza's slightly damaged plane, and then she reported the condition to the female Captain. "This is Red One to Cessna Seven Three. Captain Mendoza, you have slight damage to your tail wing section. It looks like you might have been bumped by another aircraft while in flight, Ma'am. I see different color paint on your rear feathers, honey. What the hell happened to you anyway? How heavy are your controls reacting? Should I call for a crash truck to standby on your landing Cessna Seven Three? Over."

"Cessna Seven Three to Red One. We were bumped into by an Egyptian fighter plane over the Aswan Dam area while in flight. I'm certain the contact was on purpose, they were trying to force us to land with them. I think it might be a good idea to have a crash truck standing by for our landing, in case I have a problem with my landing. My controls are rather heavy, and the plane's not responding to my commands quick enough for my satisfaction, Red One. Over."

"Red One to Cessna Seven Three. Roger that last as received. I'll place the call for you honey. I'll stay to your rear and correct your final approach if needed. Good luck Mendoza. Over."

Captain Mendoza looked to the Colonel who was busy buckling his harness, and then he grabbed the arms of his chair like he was going to rip them off, and held on for dear life. She lightly touched his hand to get his attention, and then she offered the scared acting military officer.

"It's alright Eddy, I won't allow anything to happen to you, I promise sir."

He smiled and replied. "I believe you baby. But you don't mind if I take a few precautions of my own, do ya honey?"

She listened as the pilot of Red One called in for a crash truck to standby for her possible crash landing. Then the air traffic controllers of the base got in contact with the Captain.

"Cessna Seven Three. This is Control, I have you on our screen at this time, Captain. I have been advised of your present situation with your aircraft, Ma'am. You're cleared to land on a direct approach under emergency conditions on Runway Three, Five, Captain. No fly around is required by you at this time, Captain. The winds are at three knots from the south, southeast. No drift or wind sheer noted at this present time along with no gusts of wind noted. Over."

"Traffic Controller, this is Cessna Seven Three. I Roger that last, sir. Coming in on a direct approach for my possible emergency landing. Over."

One minute passed like it was a lifetime for the young female pilot of the Cessna.

"Cessna Seven Three this is Control. I have you on visual as of this time, Captain. Your approach looks good and you're in the proper slot for your landing, Ma'am. You're instructed to increase your speed to one hundred forty five knots, and keep your nose of the aircraft up. Crash trucks are standing by for your possible emergency landing. Runway's foamed down so be careful of possibly sliding off to either end of the hard deck, Captain. Over."

Captain Renee Mendoza looked to the base that suddenly burst into life, a number of fire trucks and other emergency vehicles moved out and quickly lined up along the full length of the runway her aircraft was scheduled to land on. Even the two huge foam pumper vehicles were out and prepared for the emergency landing.

"Roger that last, Tower." She said as her hands glided over the plane's controls like a pianist. She lowered the landing gear and then the flaps as she increased her power to the engines, and then pulled back on the stick slightly at the same time, to keep the nose of her aircraft up. So the plane would not stall out on her as she looked at the runway, and then she held her breath.

"Traffic Controller to Red One. Good work. Cessna Seven Three's fine and is in the pipe for landing at this time. Red One, you and Wild Rider are instructed to veer off and take a standoff position until Disabled is on the ground. Red One, you're to come to a heading of One, Four, Four and use Runway Three for your touchdown as soon as Disabled is on the ground. After landing, you're instruct¬ed to taxi over to Three Niner to Hard Shelter Blackjack four. Over."

"Red One to Controller. Wild Rider and myself will to stay in the air until Cessna Seven Three is on the ground, sir. I want to observe the landing for the pilot anyway sir. Over."

"Controller to Red One. Err... that's a negative on your last request. You're instructed to land immediately, so you're well out of the way for a possible crash landing. Over."

"Red One to Controller. Request permission to follow Cessna's approach to final landing. She's having a bit of trouble flying straight, and I feel I can better correct her flight for landing from my present position, sir. I can correct approach from Cessna's rear. I have a much better field of vision of the present situation from Disabled rear feathers. Over."

"Controller to Red One. Copy that last as received. Permission is granted Red One, I repeat, permission is granted, Red One. You're currently ordered to stay in flight and correct any error in Disabled Cessna's final approach for landing. Over."

"Roger that last as received. Will do as ordered by the Controller. Over sir."

Captain Mendoza heard the conversation going down between Red One and the air traffic controller of the airbase section of the huge military base. She felt better knowing Red One was flying behind her aircraft. She took a deep breath as her wheels were about to touchdown on the tarmac. As she touched down, she immediately noticed a horde of men and women dressed in fire protective gear lining the side of the runway. A thick layer of foam was still being applied to the landing strip, as she came in on the direct approach for the landing.

The concerned sounding air traffic controller came back on the radio again, and he talked to Mendoza as she set down on the runway. When her wheels touched down, she felt the plane slid slightly to her left side, and she immediately corrected the slight slide by hitting her right break lightly. The fire trucks immediately moved out and they followed her aircraft until it came to a stop in the middle of the runway. A man on a loud speaker stared to yell at all the emergency responders. "Crash landing on deck. Okay people, let's get out there and look for fire."

As a mob of firemen climbed all over the small plane, and as the emergency cockpit release was pulled. Red One did a quick flyover, and dipped her wings as a sign of a job well done for the female pilot. She glanced over her shoulder long enough to see the emergency team man handling the pilot and co pilot out of the disabled plane, and she laughed. The female pilot then pulled her stick to the left, and locked on to the heading of One, Four, Four for her own landing. She was getting hot, because she was flying right in the sun's harsh glare, and the rays were heating up her cockpit quickly. She looked out her bug splattered windshield at the rapidly approaching auxiliary runway used primarily for any emergency landing.

At the Cessna landing area, men dressed in silver fire protection suits sprayed CO-2 directly at the engines air intake of the aircraft, as ground crew members also in protective gear ripped open the canopy, and pulled Mendoza and the Colonel from the plane, and dragged the two away from what was being classified as a crash landing. The landing was turned into a training session for the fire control units dying to show off their training skills to their Commanders. It was an overkill operation, a fire did not have a chance of starting with all the foam and CO-2 being sprayed on the small plane, or in the air and on the ground surrounding the Cessna.

Colonel Edward Campanelli tried to break the iron like grip of the fireman dragging him away from the considered plane crash, as it was now being referred to, while Captain Mendoza allowed herself be led away from her plane by a second fire fighter peacefully.

The fireman suddenly and angrily spun the troublesome Colonel around on his heels, and then he growled right in his face. "Look Colonel Campanelli Sir, I understand damn well you're the Commander of the base, sir. But right now your birds don't mean shit to me sir. I out rank you at this time sir, you're on my turf and you will listen to my orders, and go where I lead you, sir. Or I'll plant one on your chops, and then I'll drag your limp ass to safety for your own protection, Colonel. Now sir, allow me do my job and follow me, it's for your own good sir."

The Colonel's first instincts was to glare at the young man, even though he could not see his face clearly through the face shield. He thought about what the young man just snapped at him for a second, and then he smiled and allowed himself be led out of the area.

Once safe and let free from the fire fighter's grasp, Captain Mendoza laughed at the Colonel as she stared at him with a smile.

"What's so fucking funny with you this time, Mendoza?" He hissed at her, knowing he was going to get an ear fill from her, because of his foolish actions with the young fire fighter.

"I guess that poor kid told you off but good and proper, mista. Now maybe you'll start to listen to someone else for a stinking change around here, mista. How does it feel to know you're not the be all that you think you are to everyone around you, mista. But I'll bet dollars to donuts though the poor soldier's going to have to change his pants when he finishes with our aircraft, sir." She continued to laugh as she said something else in Spanish her Commanding Officer did not understand.

"How many times do I hafta tell you to talk fucking English whenever you're speaking to my stinking ass will ya please. I like to know when someone's cursing me out, dammit." He then thought for a second and then added to his words. "Yeah, I guess you're you got a good point there, judging by his reaction when I growled at him. I must have scared the living shit outta the poor fella, but he held up good to my growl." He laughed at Mendoza and mussed. "I have good men under me."

"And women as well you know, mista." Captain Renee Mendoza corrected him and she added at the same time.

"Yeah, and women. Anyway, I'm damn glad that poor kid had the stinking balls to threaten to knock my fucking block offa my damn shoulders for me. Show's me he's more interested in saving my damn life, than the stinking birds pinned on my collar, baby."

She shook her head in complete compliance with the Colonel's last complaint.

After he regrouped some, he rushed for the G 2 hut. He ordered Mendoza to accompany him and listen to his report and make sure he didn't omit anything which might be of importance to Command.

CHAPTER 19 - USS AIRCRAFT CARRIER ROOSEVELT STATIONED IN THE RED SEA

It was Nineteen Thirty Hours, when Colonel Edward Campanelli finally placed his call to Command. Commander Owens jumped on the mike when he was informed it was Colonel Campanelli requesting to speak with him.

"Well Colonel Campanelli Sir, what the hell did you seen on your damn flight out there sir?"

He reported to Commander Owens everything he had witnessed during his flight, and to each revelation, Commander Owens muttered. "Shit, or Dammit." Or he blamed himself for being so sound asleep at the switch over the loss of water to the Nile River water.

When Campanelli informed the Commander about being bumped by an Egyptian fighter plane trying to force them to land in Egypt. The extremely angry Commander finally found a place to vent his pent up anger at. He yelled in the mike, and at his people in the CIC at the same time, screaming that he wanted Egyptian Ambassador Muhammad Kheir on the direct line hookup with him immediately. He was threatening to have the Arab politician strung up by his balls for daring to bump any of his people while in flight, and putting their lives in peril.

The grinning Colonel actually had to take the mike away from his ear, and then allowed the irate Commander to yell it all out of his system.

He knew the reason for the Commander's angry outburst, and it was good for the Commander to get it out of his system.

After a few minutes of yelling on the mike, and at anyone anywhere near him inside the Commander's Command Center. The Colonel finally heard his name being called by the raging Commander. "Colonel Campanelli Sir, sorry for putting you ass in danger with that damn flyover I ordered you to make for my ass, sir. I'll have the damn Arab's head sitting on a platter for this little stunt of his. You gave me a fine report a thorough and complete report which will have the damn bigwigs sweating their asses off tonight, and for many nights to come I assure you sir. Colonel, I'm damn pleased you brought this situation out to the light before the Egyptians did something stupid. Did you meet with the engineers I sent out to your base earlier today, sir?"

"No sir, I just this minute crashed landed, and I came right here to give you my report sir."

"God dammit, you had to crash land your damn aircraft too? Sonofabitch! I'll get even with those damn Egyptian pilots for fuck sake." Commander Owens hissed again.

"Not quite really a crash landing sir. But my people used the landing as a sort of training session, and the damn fools almost drowned Mendoza and myself in fricking foam." He laughed causing the Commander to join him as he calmed down quite a bit now.

"I'm pleased the damn fire eaters took good care of my fucking Officers for me, mister. I shall sent them out a case of steaks for their fine efforts, sir. Give the men a day off too, and a well done for me while you're at it, Colonel. Sounds like you have a good team out there sir."

"I certainly do. Sir, if there's nothing else. I'd really appreciate it if I could get something to eat, I'm starving, Commander." He moaned at Commander Owens.

"I thought the Lake Tana damn base cooks made you up a care package for your flight back to your base, Colonel." Owens fired back at the Colonel.

"Hell sir, I couldn't eat in the damn aircraft if my stinking live depended on it sir. I would've thrown up everything when Maz first banked the damn aircraft to the portside, sir."

"I know exactly what you mean sir, after all these years I still don't like flying myself, Colonel Campanelli. I still get sick when coming in for a landing on the Carrier, or flying through rough air sir. Colonel, go get yourself a meal, sir. If anything comes up, I'll let you know right off, sir. I might pay your base a little visit in the next day or so Colonel, to see what the hell's happening first hand sir. Thank you Colonel for doing such an outstanding job for me sir."

He took it on himself to put the entire base on a stronger alert status. He ordered the military base closed to all non military and civilian personnel, all none essential civilians were not allowed back on base until further notice. He further ordered all perimeter defenses beefed up, even the Seabees were ordered to man the perimeter lines when they had nothing else to do. He also ordered the Marines to stage fake attack scenarios on the defense lines twice a week to discover any possible weaknesses in the systems. Then he turned his attention to the airforce.

Colonel Edward Campanelli ordered a surveillance and ready air cap flown over the base at all times, these flights were to consist of two attack aircraft to do nothing else but look for any possible enemy troop movements in the area surrounding his base. He ordered a first alert crew which forced two F 15 Eagles to be in the air constantly. These planes were to be loaded down for bear, and if called in, they were to attack any targets given to them without question and destroy those targets. The first alert aircraft were to be backed up on the ground by another flight of two ready aircraft ordered to be on a twenty four hour standby for immediate launching stance, and ready to takeoff and engage an enemy at a moment's notice.

He further ordered his two young G 2 officers to monitor all radio and computers communications. He also had a radio installed in his hut from the Intel building, so he could be reached faster, in case a, emergency Flash message came through.

It was no secret he was expecting trouble cropping up from somewhere, and everyone knew if the Colonel was expecting trouble then trouble was coming their way. He was not one prone to hysteria or issuing foolish orders. The guards at the main gate of the base were ordered to shoot to kill anyone who refused to show them their proper papers, or tried to get on the base without permission. The base was closed up tighter than a drum now.

The Army engineers were sent out to plant land and claymore mines in the cleared areas leading to the base, and the Seabee's were put to work by carving out an open trench around the entire base. The weak side of the huge military base was the side facing the Nile River. But the Colonel had no fear of being attacked from this side, because Ethiopia was in that direction. Nevertheless, he doubled the guards stationed along the Nile River side of the base, and he also setup a number of machine gun emplacements along the bank. So the heavy weapons could sweep and overlap their machine gun fire. He also allocated two tanks per every thousand feet of riverbank that ran alongside his entire base. He was taking nothing for granted now.

USS ROOSEVELT STATIONED IN THE RED SEA

Commander Owens was looking over the recent stack of photographs taken by his recon aircraft ordered to fly over the length of the Nile River, starting from the Sudan, and going all the way down to the Delta that reached into the Mediterranean Sea. He was amazed and stunned how far the water had gone down in just ten days of operation at the Dam stationed on Lake Tana. He looked close, he even used a magnifying glass and estimated the water was down some thirty five feet at the face of the massive Aswan Dam. He judged this because he could see the old original watermarks from the past waterline, nearly at the very top of the Dam. Colonel Campanelli's estimation of the reservoir shrinkage was near to being correct as possible. He figured the reservoir to be cut in just about half.

The next three weeks were filled with a lot of added stress for Colonel Campanelli, and the other members stationed on his military base. He felt certain the Egyptians would request an emergency meeting of the Security Council, but it never came through though. Instead, the world watched as the nations of Egypt, Libya and Algeria kept building up their military forces and presence along their borders with the nations of Sudan and Chad. The world felt it was a matter of time before the hell of war was released upon the face of the earth and all her people again.

This heavy military buildup prompted other nation members of the Security Council to request Libya and Egypt come to the Council, and then air their problems presently facing Egypt. And to question their intent for the sudden military buildup inside the two countries borders at the same time. Most other countries thought the Security Council could come to some sort of a solution that could avert a possible shooting war in the region. But Egypt and Libya completely ignored the request and continued moving their military assets around along their borders.

Behind the scenes, a hastily put together private meeting held between the American President, and the Chairman and the rest of the Joint Chiefs of Staff, along with the Central Intelligence Agency Director, the Vice President, Secretaries of Defense, State and Navy, along with the National Security Director, was convened. All members found themselves sitting around a large oak table in the basement of the White House. Three Marine guards were in the meeting room, their duties were to monitor all radio traffic coming in from the Middle East, and immediately inform the President if anything started to go sour in the region on them.

After each of them had taken their seat and had coffee in front of them did the President finally start to speak. "Gentlemen, Ladies, I thank you all for coming to my office on such a short notice. I called you here tonight, because I need your help and advice. I have a fistful of dispatches telling me it's only a matter of time before the shooting starts in the Middle East and Africa region, between the nations involved with this damn mess. I can't believe it has come down to this situation, there has to be some sort of a peaceful solution we can devise, and I'm telling you people here and now, I'm open to any and all suggestions at this time."

"Mr. President Sir," The Secretary of Defense took it upon himself to speak up as he went on with is words without receiving permission to speak. "there's one quick fix solution to this present situation which has been overlooked by all until now I believe." He stopped speaking and then looked to the President for a reaction, and when none came he continued his offering.

"Mr. President, we have three points of concern to discuss, that leads to my solution of this present situation, sir. Point one is as follows Mr. President Sir;" The Defense Secretary paused for effect before going on. "that damn wedge thing installed in the Dam in Ethiopia. It was designed by the Ethiopians, installed by them and never once discussed by any interested nation in that region, especially Egypt. Point two; The Ethiopian government is diverting more water than first agreed to at any meetings held between Egypt, the Sudan, Ethiopia and ourselves, Mr. President. Point three is; Unless we do something and do it real soon, we're going to have one hell of a shooting war on our damn hands. Perhaps one involving every nation in the world, judging by how everyone's taking sides as to who is right and who is wrong in this mess, sir."

"Mr. Secretary Sir, we know the reasons that has led to the present situation we find ourselves mired in, after all that's why we're here tonight. Sir, can you please get to the heart of the matter that you're making here sir? What's your answer to this god damn mess?" The President asked.

"With all due respect Mr. President Sir. There's only one way I know of, to put a quick end to this present situation, sir. We send in a flight of bombers and blow that Dam to dust, sir. Or, we order the Marines still stationed at the Dam site to plant some explosives, and then destroy the entire Dam. Either way Mr. President, that Dam has to go sir." The Secretary sat back and crossed his arms over his chest, while waiting for the screaming to begin.

President Cole stiffened and then groused at the Secretary of Defense. "My God man, that's an act of war we'll be committing against the nation of Ethiopia, one of our few Allies in the entire area. How the hell could we possibly attack an ally as you offered, sir?" The President thought the Secretary was joking with him. That was until he saw many of his Generals nodding in agreement this was a quick answer to the situation. President Cole put his hands to his temples and then applied pressure to them before he spoke again.

"God dammit Mr. Secretary, I believe we're jumping from one fucking crisis to a damn nother, and I'm getting kind of sick and tired of it I warn everyone at this meeting. First with the Japanese cargo ship a few months ago that got dragged to Libya. Then that stupid probe at the Dam site from what we believe were Chad forces, what the fuck's next is going to happen?"

This last remark from the obviously upset President caused the CIA Director to speak up next. "Excuse me Mr. President Sir, but from many of the reports I've been receiving about this situation, we're quite certain Libya had everything to do with that supposed attack on the military base 'Easy Money' and the Dam a few months back, not Chad, sir. We're still gathering the intelligence reports about the attack, but confidence is quite high it was a planned and..."

The President cut off the CIA Director's report by complaining at him in an angry tone of voice. "I don't really care who the hell caused that fucking attack at the Dam at this time sir. All I know is there was an attack at the Dam site, period sir. I can't believe I allowed Ambassador Walters talk me into sending in the Army Core of Engineers to build the damn thing in the first place, sir. I should have had my fucking head examined for myself first, before I ordered this dammit. We should've stayed the fuck out of the damn situation all together."

"Yes sir that's a fact Mr. President, and if we stayed out of this project, the Ethiopians would have built the damn thing anyway, and the way they wanted to build it sir. And we would've ended up in the same predicament, trying to figure out a way to stop another shooting war. But a lot sooner I assure you Mr. President." The Defense Secretary replied as he got angry.

President Cole turned to the Secretary of State and he bitched at him. "Don't just sit there looking at me like someone just took your damn crayons away from you. I need your input sir."

The Secretary was hot and growled angrily as he addressed the American Leader. "This is a bunch of fucking crap if you are to ask me, sir. If we allow the Marines to blow up the Dam. It'll be an act of suicide for them, pure and simple sir. The damn soldiers would find themselves completely cut off, and the Ethiopian military guarding the site would chop them to pieces before we could either get them out of there, or sent in reinforcements to assist them if they came under fire by the Ethiopian troops. I don't think there'll be any fighting in this area. All these shit countries knows the awesome might the United States military has at her disposal. None of these shits are going to dare try and attack one of our Allies, least of all, attack us directly, sir."

The Defense Secretary allowed the Secretary of State finish with his statement, before he started. "We can always support the Marines with the fighter aircraft stationed on board the Carrier Roosevelt, if they come under attack from anyone in the region, Mr. President Sir."

"Jesus Christ, don't be so fucking ridiculous with your thoughts. We'll find ourselves stuck in another ground war, and besides this country's supposed to be our damn Ally, sir. You're being a real ass here at this meeting. We need a much better plan than…"

"Who the hell is being an ass around here Mr. Secretary Sir." The Defense Secretary hissed angrily as he began to stand, causing the Secretary of State to leave his chair as well.

"Enough of this crap, dammit!" The President suddenly hissed at everyone attending the meeting angrily as he continued with his heated words. "Take your damn seats and allow the Secretary of Defense finish his statement. If he has anything else to add to this conversation that is." The President said as he threw a quick glance towards the CIA Director who nodded in agreement with the Secretary's last scenario put forth.

"Mr. President Sir, we know this is the only quick answer to the present situation sir."

The National Security Director spoke up this time, cutting the Defense Secretary's response off in mid sentence as he remarked. "Has the Secretary given any possible consideration to the fact that someone in this damn area might resort to the use of nuclear weapons once the shooting starts? We know a number of Russian missiles with the capability of reaching our shores, has made it to Libya through their black market system, and no one's quite certain what Iraq might still have hidden underground in their damn country for the love of God, sir."

The President turned to his Secretary of Defense and growled one word at him. "Well!"

"Mr. President, make no mistake about it sir, in no way am I advocating war or anything like it in this conversation, sir. As I have stated before, all I know is, if we don't do something and do it quickly, war is what we're going to end up having on our hands in this region of the world, sir."

The President glared angrily at the Secretary as he snapped at him. "You didn't answer my question I put to you, sir. What about the damn nukes becoming a problem for us?"

The Secretary hesitated for a brief moment as he squirmed in his chair, and he tried to gather his thoughts and then he offered. "Mr. President, we have enough of the Star Wars anti missile system set in place to guard the United States against a possible attack from these missiles the Middle East might, or might not have in their possession, sir. I read over the thousands of reports the CIA had accumulated over the years about the missing nuclear warheads and missiles from Russia. Confidence is high there are seventy five Russian long range missiles capable of reaching us from anywhere in the world, unaccounted for in their arsenal. One of these reports, stated most of the missing missiles were destroyed in the fighting that took place throughout Russia back in '93. Am I right sir?" He said as he looked to the CIA Director.

The Director shook his head yes. "That's what we think happened to many of the missiles."

The Secretary then continued with his words in a rush. "Mr. President Sir, we estimated Libya has at least ten of these damn missiles at their disposal at this time, sir. No one knows for certain how many nuclear warheads Libya and Iraq might have in their arsenal between the two nations sir, but these warheads can't reach us no matter how they may try. All we have to worry about are the ten or so long range missiles, and as I already explained this before in this conversation. The amount of the Star Wars System we have circling around the earth, is more than sufficient enough to kill all ten of these damn missiles along with their warheads, before they could possibly hit anywhere in the Continental United States.

"Plus Mr. President, an easy additional fifty more inbound missiles, before we have to start to sweat it out any, sir. I recently read a report on Israel's nuclear arsenal, and confidence is high if either Libya or Iraq decided to try and use their nuclear weapons in the next war. Israel would attack the user with their own weapons, sir. No Mr. President

Sir, I don't really fear the use of nuclear weapons in this region if war does breakout, sir."

"Dammit sir, I wish to hell and back again I was as confident about the use of fucking nuclear weapons as you obviously are sir." The President growled as his mind raced. He was full of anger by the fact that Congress several years back, specifically outlawed the expenditures for additional funds on the space base Star Wars system. The decision was cast because any possible threat of a nuclear attack coming from the old Soviet Union died, along with the country. Simple logic prevailed, no threat from the Russian nation, no Star Wars system needed.

"I want to put this to a vote here. On second thought, I changed my mind. Here's what I want and will have. First, I want the JCS (Joint Chiefs of Staff) to work up an attack plan in case my plan fails. Here it is, I want to get in contact with the Ethiopians, and see if I can talk them into allowing more water to flow back to the Nile River. Yes, I know before any of you point it out to me. If they refuse to allow more water down its original path, we'll all meet here again and come up with another plan of action, short of blowing the damn thing up that's it, people. I don't think Egypt will go to war, sure she might threaten war, but I don't really think she'll attack. At least, I hope to hell that's a fact. To tell you the truth, I'm more worried about Libya starting a war with Chad as she keeps getting her nose involved in this damn thing.

"If Libya happens to attack Chad then all this will all be academic and all bets will be off anyway people. Please gentlemen and ladies bear with me for a few days and let's see what happens. Allow me speak to the Ethiopians first, and see if we can work something out with them peacefully. I'll give the Generals something to sink their teeth in though at this time. Due to the rapid developments occurring throughout the Middle East and Northern Africa, we'll use this present situation as an opportunity to reestablish America's presence in this area.

"Secretary of the Navy, I want you to move some of your warships into this section through the Mediterranean. You pick the ships you want to send in the region sir. General Rossman, you're to pick the

Army and Marine Divisions to be called up to active duty. I'll put all Allied airbases throughout the entire Mediterranean region on full alert, employing the Presidential decree. Okay gentlemen and ladies, let's get the wheels turning, thank you all for your time and patience in this matter today, people." With this, the President of the United States quickly left the room, followed closely by his Vice President and his usual guards and hanger ons.

President Cole spoke to the Ethiopians in a failed attempt to see if they would cut down on the amount of water being diverted to the Afar Depression on their own. But the Ethiopians refused to even consider any reduction in the water flow it was using for their own countries needs. This rejection prompted the American President to offer to build a number of large water purifying plants along the coast of Egypt to help supply the lost water for that nation.

Egypt did not even want to entertain the exhausting idea of using any water purifying plants as a feasible answer to her rapidly growing water problems for her nation. It seemed nothing short of war was going to stop the tensions rapidly building up in this region.

AMBASSADOR MOHAMMED KHEIR'S PRIVATE OFFICE, CAIRO EGYPT

Egyptian Ambassador Mohammed Kheir paced in his office in an extremely agitated mood while waiting for his aide to finally arrive as ordered. He formulated a plan and was ready to act on it. Finally, there was a light knock on his door.

JoAnne allowed the young man in the office, and then she closed the door behind him. She stayed outside the private office this time, because she was aware this aide was used whenever Mohammed wanted to get some X rated tapes from the underground network operating in Egypt, in the dangerous back streets that made up the capital city of

Cairo. She was aware he really enjoyed the filthy things and she gave him this much freedom to enjoy them.

The Egyptian Ambassador Mohammed Kheir directed the young man over towards a chair, and then he walked over to his bookcase and removed a book and leaned it against the wall on top of a small table. He knew he was being spied on by JoAnne from the outer office.

She instantly pulled her head away from the tiny peep hole, the moment she picked up the shadow move before it and she laughed at the thought of being found out by Ambassador Kheir.

He waited until he was seated and then he offered to his aide. "Joseph, I have an important errand for you to run for me. I want you to go to the Army base and see Captain Siyad, don't allow the fool to scare you, he'll bark at you yes, and when he's finished you'll hand him this note and smile at the always angry Captain. You'll then wait till he gives you a small box for me. Place it in the diplomatic pouch and allow no one see what he gave you. You'll then get back here as fast as possible. Do you understand what I'm ordering you to do, young fool?"

The young man replied in a low voice. "I hear and I shall obey my orders faithfully, sir."

"Good, then take these and deliver them to that Captain." He gave the young man the folded leather pouch, along with the hand written note, and then he ordered the young man. "Now be off with you and go with Allah's blessings and protection."

He watched as he left then sat down in his chair. Once he was comfortable he buzzed JoAnne and told her he was not to be disturbed except for the young man's return then he waited.

An hour later the aide returned to Ambassador Mohammed Kheir's office.

JoAnne met the aide in the outer office, and she immediately offered to take the sealed pouch in to Ambassador Mohammed Kheir, but the aide refused to give the pouch up to her. She instantly recognized the leather bag for what it was, and believed she could not possibly interfere with the delivery of the filthy contents. She backed off and allowed the aide to enter Mohammed Kheir's private office alone as she watched him enter the office.

Ambassador Kheir jumped from his chair, and instantly took the small pouch from the scared looking aide as he growled at him angrily. "That'll be all I'll need from you for the rest of the day, get out of my office and inform my girl outside I'm not to be disturbed for any reason whatsoever for the rest of the day." He waited until the aide was out of his office and he locked the door behind him. He knew JoAnne would think it was another one of his nasty sex tapes. So he took out one of his old tapes and put it on the VCR, and put the volume up so she would easily hear the tape running from outside his office.

She did, and then she smiled and allowed her defenses to come down some, now that she knew what the Ambassador was up to in his office.

Ambassador Kheir opened the leather pouch, and removed a new Glock nine mm pistol, and two boxes of ammunition for the weapon. He carefully loaded the clip with the more deadly ammunition JoAnne informed him about when she was trying to teach him how to use the weapon properly. The wise Egyptian Ambassador then set it in the gun and chambered a round into the chamber right off, and then he hid the weapon on top of his desk under some papers. He felt he needed the much heavier weapon for what he had in mind, and he was worried the small PPK weapon might not be heavy enough of a weapon to do the job correctly for him. He sat back and then tried to see if he could see the hidden weapon from the chair.

The weapon was well hidden under the small stack of papers, so no one could possibly see it unless they happened to remove the stack of papers lying directly on top of the new and much heavier weapon, or if they were actually looking for the weapon in the first place. He knew JoAnne would never go rummaging around through his private office unless she had some good reason to do so. He also understood he had not given her any reason whatsoever to miss trust him in the least so far.

The cunning Ambassador allowed the nasty sex tape to continue to play as he went over his future plans, as a cold sweat suddenly broke out on his forehead. He promised himself he would go through with his plan no matter what the outcome was. It was something he understood he had to do for the good of Egypt, and for the future of the world. The tape finished running with a loud snap which brought his mind back to reality.

He actually had to shake his head slightly to force his mind back to the reality he was living through. He understood he had to have all his inner strength set in place if he was going to carry out his troubled plans against the extremely dangerous female constantly guarding and watching everything he did or said, successfully. The deeply concerned Egyptian Ambassador drew in his breath in a huge gulp of air as he got up out of his chair and went over to the VCR and turned it off after removing the tape from the machine. He placed the sex tape with his others and then he returned to his chair and dropped down in it like he had the entire weight of the world resting on his shoulders, and then he tried to get his breathing under control.

The incident that was certain to start the shooting war in the region happened. A Libyan fighter aircraft flying a little too close to the Chad, Libyan border, came under direct fire from anti aircraft systems from Chad border defenders. The Libyan pilot did not return fire as he was ordered, but he did not leave the area either with his damaged aircraft. The pilot flew over the same position of the infraction three more times, until his aircraft was finally mortally wounded by the defenders. The pilot then flew his crippled plane out of Chad's airspace to Libya territory before bailing out, with his unmanned aircraft crashing in the vast desert.

Within an hour's time, Libya had their Delegate to the United Nations demand and received an emergency Security Council meeting, at which time he complained vigorously that Chad ground forces shot down a Libyan civilian aircraft over the desert on a sightseeing flight inside Libya territory. The Libyan Delegate screamed Chad took it on themselves to start a war against Libya. The Delegate further informed the group Libya was not going to wait until Chad military forces invaded Libya, before she took steps to defend herself or reacted against the threat.

"Libya is placing all her military troops on full alert, and the troops are being instructed to attack Chad, if any of Chad's forces fire on any of the Libyan troops sent to guard their border with the always troublesome nation of Chad." The Libyan politician did not inform the other Delegates Libyan planes and ground forces had already invaded the Chad territory.

Certain members of the United Nations begged Libya not to overreact against this supposed unprovoked attack on their civilian plane. The United States immediately offered to institute stinging sanctions against the nation of Chad, with most other nations agreeing to go along with the offer with no further conversation or debate. But the Libyan Ambassador Kamal refused to be soothed by any sanctions threatened against this supposed aggressor nation of Chad.

In the meantime, Libya sent a number of flights of warplanes into Chad air space. The fighter planes attacked any Chad military installations, water facilities, and electric sites situated within the country in easy distance of their border. The capital of Chad, Fort Lamy, received a massive pounding from the attacking Libyan aircraft from military bases Libya setup inside the nation of Nigeria, long before the order to attack Chad was issued by their command.

The Chad government sent protests out to the United Nations, but Libya, Egypt, Algeria, Iraq, Syria, Mali, Yemen, Somalia, Uganda, Kenya, Tanzania and South Africa instantly boycotted the meeting, stating Chad started the aggression in the region, and now Chad was seeking the protection from the Security Council and the other nations of the United Nations for their unprovoked actions leveled against the nation of Libya. These countries let it be known they felt Chad should accept the consequences for the hostile and unprovoked attack on Libya.

The African nations of the Sudan, Ethiopia, the Central African Republic, Niger, Saudi Arabia, Turkey, Spain and even Sicily rallied behind Chad's plight. With Iran voicing sympathy for the Allies, but remaining neutral for the time being. The Congo remained neutral also, but she was leaning more towards Libya's ideals.

The massive attacks were relentless throughout the small nation of Chad. In just three day's time, Chad was reduced to a non existent, and almost completely destroyed nation. The Chad radio was knocked off the air, and hundreds of thousands of Chad civilians were killed in the air attacks aimed at Chad, from both Libya and Nigeria.

In this short a time of combat, Libya was in complete control of the larger towns inside the border of Chad. The Chad cities of Tibesti, Massif, Kebir, and Oum Chalouba, in the first hours of war were completely surrounded by Libyan ground forces, and the cities were being pounded from both the air and ground. The capital of Chad was laid in smoldering ruins, along with the Chad cities of Am Timan and Melfi. After seven days of heavy air and ground attacks against Chad, the only city still offering any further resistance to the Libyan invaders, was Abeche.

Abeche was totally surrounded by a ring of Russian older made tanks and artillery pieces, and shells fell within the city limits like rain, over a hundred rounds an hour were launched against the defenders of Abeche with little regard for the civilian population still trapped within the city limits. The heavy and relentless air and ground bombardment continued both day and night. The Chad city was populated with over a million and a half civilians who flocked there for safety when the other cities and towns of Chad came under the terrible Libyan onslaught.

A mechanized column of mixed Libyan and Nigerian tanks, a thousand strong backed with heavy artillery pieces, form this tightening ring of steel and death surrounding the city of Abeche's border. Libya's warplanes owned the skies over Chad, because Chad's tiny airforce was completely destroyed while still resting on the ground on the opening days of the war. The few outdated and badly neglected planes that got into the air, were unarmed and immediately shot down, or they fled for the safety of the Sudan or any other friendly nations in the region.

Libya's invasion of the tiny nation moved with lightening speed. Chad's tanks were of World War Two surplus from the United States and England, and became mere cannon fodder for the Libyan's more modern tanks and destroyed mostly by the Libyan airforce. Many of Chad's out dated tanks did not even have ammunition for their war machines, and became easy targets of opportunity for the attacking Libyan jets. The Chad tanks were more for show than for fighting.

Libya totally ignored the countless pleas coming from the United Nations to try and stop the terrible slaughter of the civilians of the Chad city of Abeche. When Libyan tanks ringing the city of Abeche began shelling the city proper to a slow death, in much the same way the hated Nazis did to any town they wanted to completely destroy during the old war. The United States saw enough of the terrible slaughter and she began flexing her muscles, threatening to attack the Libyan tanks if the shelling of Abeche did not stop immediately. Many of the civilians from the besieged city were heard begging for help from anyone on a number of citizen band radios.

USS ROOSEVELT STATIONED IN THE RED SEA

Commander Owens sat his coffee mug down on the small metal table in the smoke filled CIC control room of his aircraft carrier. He exhaustedly massaged his forehead, and then he ran his hands slowly through his tight cropped hair as he let out his breath in a disgusted and loud sigh. He then looked over the latest satellite photos taken moments before over the city of Abeche with great interest, as he held them over the light table. After studying the pictures carefully, he growled as his Second in Command. "I want to speak to the Joint Chiefs of Staff Chairman immediately, dammit."

A foolish young seaman lit up a cigarette and absentmindedly flicked the extinguished match to the floor of the CIC, and he also blew smoke into the choking air of the room. Commander Owens glared harshly at the kid, causing him to look down at the match and he retrieved it. He then put it in his pocket, and got out of the commander's sight until he cooled off some. The Commander shook his head as he watch the sailor quickly disappear behind the threat board, and melded in with the other seamen plotting what was taking place inside Chad and Libya.

It took a moment for the seaman to get the ordered hookup patched through to the Chairman. A second General answered the call and informed Commander Owens the new Chairman was busy, but he would be pleased to help if he wanted. The angry Commander cursed under his breath as he told the General about what was taken place on the outskirts of Abeche, and how the Chad civilians were cut off and being slaughtered by the Libyan planes and tanks at will.

Commander Owens outlined his plan on how he wanted to help the besieged Chad civilians. After an hour of conversation, the powerful General had to cut the concerned Commander off by offering him. "Commander Owens Sir, please excuse me sir, but I understand the gist of your plan. I'll present it to the Chairman of the Joint Chiefs of Staff. There's a meeting currently going on as we speak sir. I can cut in and inform the Generals of this present situation, and then go over your plan with them and see want they might come up with to help you out some, sir."

Commander Owens had no choice but to go along with the General on this one. He wished he was sitting in at this meeting though, so he could explain his plan to the General in person.

The two officers hung up, and the General went in the meeting room, and he interrupted the conversations taking place and informed the other Generals of the present situation surrounding the Chad city of Abeche. After an hour of debate in which the Generals agreed something had to be done to try and help the civilians, it was decided General Rossman would give the President a briefing. The Chairman's car was sent for and General Rossman was whisked over to the White House. The meeting lasted an hour, before the General returned to his Pentagon office.

General Rossman informed the Chairman of the President's decision to help, and he informed the General he was to get in contact with the Commander of the Roosevelt, and instruct him his plan's a go for an immediate response.

Commander Owens sat inside the CIC room while drinking from his fourth cup of coffee for the day already, and lighting up another cigar when his phone rang. The Naval Commander instantly jumped for the phone and responded. "I got that, yeah, Commander Owens here sir. Yeah General, good deal sir. Great, I'll get on it right away for you sir, and I thank you for your fast response to this present situation, sir. You did real good for me sir. I'll get the operation in full gear immediately sir. Sure, sure, yeah, I'll keep you well informed of my actions against this damn situation sir. Thanks again sir. This is great General Sir."

When the Commander hung up, he growled at no one in particular working inside the CIC Chamber. "I want a Flash message sent out to Base Sentry STAT."

The Combat Information Center on board the Aircraft Carrier Roosevelt, sent a Flash message to Base Sentry, and Colonel Edward Campanelli was immediately sent for, and he was informed the President made a decision to help the citizens of Abeche get out of the besieged city before it was too late, and they were slaughtered to the last person. Commander Owens informed the Colonel he was ordered to send in a flight of nine YF 23 fighter bombers to attack the eastern end of the city of Abeche. Satellite pictures showed this area to be the lest number of Libyan tanks stationed, so the citizens could escape the slaughter going on therein.

As the Colonel sat in his Intel Post reading the Flash message, small arms fire suddenly broke out on the military base on the Nile River side of the base. The weapons fire was accented by a number of claymore mines instantly popping off. Immediately, the lights went dark as the Lieutenant hooked his arm up to the wire harness coming from his intelligence computer.

Sirens instantly wailed throughout the base as the soldiers made mad dashes for their assigned defensive positions and weapons to defend the base against who was attacking them.

Colonel Campanelli grabbed his M-18 assault rifle and ran from the hut ready to attack anyone assaulting his base, leaving his helmet behind resting on the floor he was that excited. Once outside, he looked around and noticed a number of soldiers running towards the defenses facing the Nile River at the east end of the military base. Most of the weapon's fire had already stopped as he ran in the same direction as the troopers did. By the time he reached the other soldiers, a ring formed in the middle of the ranks. When the group noticed the Colonel running towards them, they immediately opened ranks so he had access to the center of the mumbling group of men and women soldiers. Once in the center, he looked at the three bodies lying on the ground face up. A Marine Sergeant rolled the bodies of the supposed attackers over so they faced up, and he was busy searching the bodies for any identification papers.

"Are they dead, Sergeant? What the fuck happened out here soldier? Who the hell are these lousy bastards." The Colonel demanded hotly of him.

The Sergeant looked up at the Colonel as his hands continued to search one of the bodies and he replied. "If they ain't dead then we'll have to come up with another word for it sir." The Sergeant replied to the Colonel's question if the attackers were dead, before he went on with his finding. "Colonel Campanelli Sir, these three flaming assholes came out of the water carrying fucking satchel charges, sir. We watched them all the way from the moment they were picked up in the damn water, sir. They had no chance in hell of succeeding on their foolish mission that I'm sure was to plant these damn charges." The Sergeant stopped speaking and pointed to the three back packs lying on a mound of sand with a swift movement of his head near the bodies of the three dead attackers, and then he went on with his explanation for his Commanding Officer.

"A good fucking bet these Jerk Bennies were heading for the damn Intelligence Unit, Colonel. Anyway sir, we spotted them swimming from up river sir. We allowed the assholes to come in to see if we could figure out what the hell the dopey dipsticks were up too, sir. Dammit, no fucking ID's on any of the sonofa fucking bitches, sir. Anyway, we allowed them to cut through the defensive wire, and allowed the claymores to stop the dumb fucks which they did, Colonel. We had a few trigger happy asses shoot at them after they were dead, sir. The trigger happy asses killed them a second time sir." The Sergeant growled as he looked at two of his soldiers who immediately put their heads down to get out of the angry Sergeant's harsh glare.

"Their op ended right here where they lay, Colonel Campanelli Sir." The rather large Sergeant hissed as he kicked a body in the face with his boot.

"That's enough of that shit right there, Sergeant. Will someone shut down those damn sirens. Sergeant, bag the bodies and bury them. Take the charges over to the engineers and see if they can determine their origin. Good work trooper, I want security on the damn base stepped up. Put more soldiers on the perimeter lines for defense, Sergeant. Post some extra guards on the damn aircraft and radar units, we go to Red Alert until further notice, mister."

Colonel Campanelli took a last look at the three bodies lying on the sand, and he knew his base was lucky his soldiers were on their toes, and they successfully picked up these attackers before they reached and destroyed their objective on his base. The Sergeant stripped naked the dead men when he searched them which was SOP (Standard Operating Procedure). The Colonel headed back to his Intel Post to check on it. As he walked in, he noticed other Sergeants and junior officers ordering soldiers to their selected guard posts designated under Red Alert status.

He set his rifle up against the wall, and then he plopped down in a chair. He looked at the Lieutenant with the wires coming from his arm to the main computer and offered. "We had a fucking probe, three perps. They didn't make it to their objective which was obvious this Intel hut, I guess you better get the Commander on the squawk box for me, mister."

The Colonel informed the Commander of the recent probe. When he finished with his report, the commander had one comment for him. "This was to be expected Colonel Campanelli Sir."

The fighter bombers were to have an air cover escort flown by ten of the modified F/A 18 A Hornet's from the 71st Tactical Wing. The YF 23 aircraft were ordered to kill as many of the Libyan tanks they discovered hiding in the heavy underbrush surrounding the Chad city of Abeche. Command decided if they were going to attack, they might as well attack everything.

Colonel Edward Campanelli issued the new orders and seconds later, a wing of radar elusive YF 23s Tactical fighter bomber aircraft quickly taxied side by side down the long main runway of his base. A second wing of F/A 18 Hornets fired up their engines with the help of the portable crash trucks, and with plumes of flame shooting from their afterburners, the sleek aircraft shot off the ground seconds later. The YF 23 aircraft circled the field until the Hornets were airborne, so they could coordinate their attack on any enemy tanks and troops discovered in their ordered attack. The YF 23 ATF (Advanced Tactical Fighter) flew at a height of seven thousand feet, while the F 18s flew in at ten thousand feet as their cover and protection. The two wings of American aircraft would not have to be refueled in the air for this entire mission.

The job of the F 18 Hornets was to keep any possible Libyan Migs, and what other fighter planes the Libyans had from attacking the YF 23s fighter planes before they struck at the ring of Libyan tanks and troops, and they dropped their bombs on the enemy emplacements and broke the back of the stalemate, so the besieged civilians of Chad could flee the city.

Campanelli watched the fighter aircraft circle his base, and then fly from view as the second wing caught up to the first wing, he mumbled after them. "I wish I had twenty of those ugly ass fucking A 10A Thunderbolt tank killers stationed on this stinking base for extra support."

His attention was drawn up to the ready air cap aircraft currently taking off. They were the new versions of the F 18 Hornets. The Colonel realized why these planes replaced the old and outdated F 14 Tomcats on many Aircraft Carriers. These newer models were able to make use of the rough airstrips, and short runways for takeoff. Add this to their fast roll and turn rates, and easier maintenance and quick change engines, made the aircraft a natural to replace the aging and extremely maintenance heavy Tomcat aircraft. The plane's engines were the same ones used in the F 16 Falcon planes. The pleased Colonel turned his attention towards a pair of CV 22 Osprey vertical landing and takeoff aircraft sitting just off the airfield, and they were completely covered over by heavy protective tarps to help keep them out of sight for the time being.

The thirty eight foot long rotor blades stuck out of the canvass though. One set of blades were folded over so the planes took up much less room on the base. They were powered by two T406 Allison engines, and having some problems with the blowing sands of the vast desert. This, combined with the up and down air drafts caused by the heat of the desert, resulted in four of the twelve planes crashing, and the grounding of the rest of the aircraft. Colonel Campanelli looked at his feet and shook his head. He was going to miss these planes which could move twenty four tons of military equipment on a vertical take off, and thirty tons from a short runway takeoff.

In addition, it was a useful way to move twenty four fully combat equipped and ready soldiers. The Osprey cruised at a speed of three hundred and forty five miles an hour, faster than his Blackhawk troop carrying helicopters flew at just over one hundred and sixty five miles per hour. "Dammit." Was all he growled as he turned away from the row of parked aircraft.

The Commander of the YF 23 ATF flight was being flown by Lieutenant Commander Joyce Heart. The Colonel heard all the bullshit floating around the base about her, and he knew she might be a lesbian pilot at that, but he did not give a rat's ass about that kind of shit. Heart was the first female fighter pilot from any nation to kill an enemy plane while in a combat situation, and this happened in mid '92 over the skies of Iraq. When the United States, England and France installed the No Fly Zone below the 32nd parallel in the nation of Iraq. To try and help protect the Shiites forced to flee into the swamps of Iraq, to avoid the terrible attacks from the hated Republican Guard of Iraq under President Saddam's control against them. This operation became known as 'Operation Southern Watch'.

The female Commander's call name for this operation was branded as Red One, and her Chicks were called Wild Riders. The F 18 Hornets who flew air cover cap for the YF 23 bomber and attack fighters were known as Foxtrot One through Ten.

"Red Leader One to Wild Rider Two. We're entering the Chad airspace, so let's keep your eyes open lady. We can now be attack by any Libyan forces operating here. Over."

"Rider Two to Red Leader One. That's a Roger as received Ma'am. Over."

"Rider Five. Come up thirty feet please, and close in on my port wing a little Ma'am. Over."

"Red One to Rider Three. Tighten up the formation a little more, you're starting to lag behind a little and I need the full complement of aircraft together. That's better, keep it tight lady."

"All Wild Riders listen up and pay attention. You are now ordered to increase your speed up to Marh One point Four. It's a nice day for a flight, clear and no cross winds to deal with. I feel I can see forever today, ladies."

All the sleek Wild Rider aircraft increased their speed as they were ordered to do. Immediately, the pilots started searching not only the ground for possible targets, but they also searched the sky for any possible enemy attack aircraft trying to hit them from ambush.

Colonel Campanelli remained inside his Intel hut listening to the pilots communicate with each other while in flight. He never missed the thrill of the hunt, and monitoring the pilots made him long to be involved in the action again.

"Foxtrot Leader to all Foxtrots followers. Let the YFs get two miles ahead of our wing. We'll cover their wing from that distance back and we'll climb another thousand feet. Over."

Foxtrot Leader checked his forward looking radar every few seconds, to make certain neither of the flights were heading for a possible ambush.

The much faster YF 23s flew without their radar's systems working, relying on the Hornets to let them know if any threat was in front of them. The YF 23 aircraft were waiting for the last possible moment before finally turning their own radar's on, so the Libya tracking radar units would not have an idea their tanks would soon come under attack. The odd shape of the YF 23 ATF, plus the use of their special RAM acoustics, rendered the plane almost invisible, and extremely hard to locate with most standard radar detection units.

COMMAND BUNKER IN LIBYA

At the main Command Post stationed inside Libya thirty miles away from the border of Libya and Chad, the aged Russian technician suddenly called a warning out to his Libyan guard about the separate wings of American aircraft taking off from the recently constructed American military base in the Sudan. The Libyan soldier actually hated the smell of this old and nasty Russian defector, whose veins stood out on his ancient face much like cracks in old Chinaware, zigzagging up and down his stone cold red face.

The Russian easily picked up the flight of American aircraft as they lifted off Base Sentry with the help of the Russian satellite platform he successfully tapped into, that happened to be in the proper position to catch the planes taking off from the base. He plotted their course and warned his Libyan guard the American aircraft were on their way to attack their tank column operating inside the border of Chad.

Libyan General, Muhammad Sabra was informed of the American aircraft heading to attack his armor, and he quickly ordered the drift bombs to be launched, and had them hover at the height of seven thousand feet. Moments later, the drift bombs were launched from a number of flatbed trailer trucks parked on the sands. It took the bombs eleven minutes to reach the altitude ordered, and then they simply hovered and waited for the fast approaching American planes.

IN THE AIR OVER CHAD

"Foxtrot Leader to Foxtrot One. Come in sir. Over."

"Foxtrot One. Go with your traffic Foxtrot Leader. Over."

"Foxtrot Leader, did you just pick up any blotches on your damn radar in the lower left hand corner of the scope, sir? My radar is acting a little confused and marking these spots. Over."

"Foxtrot One. No, I didn't notice anything moving around in that area, why sir? Over."

"Never mind One. Foxtrot Leader to all Foxtrots followers. Did anyone notice anything showing up on their damn radar units? I make it at least twenty five miles dead ahead of Red One's Flight Wing Aircraft. Over."

"Foxtrot Five. I thought I saw something for a second or two sir. I think it could have been a flock of birds taking off, or something like that I guess, sir. Maybe even some heat transitions coming up from the desert sands, sir. It could be anything at this point sir. Over."

The Foxtrot Leader growled at the other pilot over his radio. "What the hell would any fucking birds be doing up this high, you ass? I'm going to keep my radar on full from this point on, I don't like seeing anything but our aircraft in the air. Foxtrot Three, you're instructed to keep your radar on also and set for full extension, the rest of you people will keep bouncing your radar units on and off as instructed to help confuse the enemy tracking radar's. Birds, shit!"

Foxtrot Leader drew in a deep breath, and then he let it out slowly as he made contact with Red One flight. "Foxtrot Leader to Red Leader One. Come in Red Leader One Ma'am. Over."

"Red One to Foxtrot Leader. Go with your traffic sir. Over."

"Red Leader One this is Foxtrot Leader. Go secure, I repeat. Go secure Ma'am. Over."

"Acknowledged as received, going secure from this point sir." Commander Heart threw a number of switches on her radio receiver scramble system. She listened until the buzzing and clicking tones ceased, and then she spoke to Foxtrot Leader again. "I'm secured at this time, what do you have going for me Foxtrot Leader Sir? Over."

"Red One, I think I just picked up a number of unknown blotches on my radar, they're far out. I never seen anything like them before, and I don't know what to make out of the possible Tangos (Targets). My wing man thinks they could be a flock of birds, I think he was attacked by birds in his damn sleep. I'm going to have him submit himself for a drug test when we land, birds. I don't agree with him. Keep your eyes open. I have a bad gut feeling about this operation all of a sudden." Forgetting who he was speaking to, he remarked. "My nuts are itchy, and that only happens when we're about to get attacked by some fucking enemy. Over."

"That's a Roger on that last report sir. Foxtrot Leader, I sure wish I had such an advance attack warning system like you do, sir. I have to look into getting me a pair of those little things for myself when I return to base, sir. Red One Over." She offered as she laughed over the radio.

Laughter filled the radio as Foxtrot Leader became thoroughly embarrassed at his last remark.

"Can the shit and pay attention to this damn flight." Foxtrot Leader growled in his radio. "I don't want to help the damn enemy locate us before we open up on the bastards, dammit."

Joyce started her long range radar systems up, but she did not read anything on the scope yet.

The YF 23 aircraft were less than six miles from their assigned target area, and closing rapidly in on their targets fast.

"Red Leader One to all following Wild Riders. We're close enough to the target area for the enemy to know we're up here. You're cleared to arm your Maverick Missiles, and light up your long range radar's, switching Master Arm on at this point. All Riders, you're instructed to set missiles on the fire and forget mode for this operation. Our area of responsibility and attack will be a target rich environment, and we're not going to have the luxury of watching our missiles all the way down to target on this one, ladies. We have to rack up the kills real quick if we're going to be of any help to those poor civilians trapped in that besieged city."

Joyce immediately flipped a toggle and she heard the arming whine instantly coming from her missile's seeker warheads as they communicated with her fire control computer on board the aircraft. Strands of shiny sweat soaked red hair slipped out from under her flight helmet that had a red heart painted on top of it. Commander Heart smiled as she stuffed the strands back under the tight fitting flight helmet. She loved her call name of Red One given to her by her female lover who always called her, her Red One. Because of her long, dark red hair whenever they made love together.

She glanced lovingly towards the color snapshot of her girlfriend standing by Red Leader One's aircraft while topless, the picture was wedged on her windshield to keep it in place.

"Red Leader One, Red Leader One! This is Rider Four. I thought I might have just spotted something dead ahead of my aircraft at about the same altitude we're at. One second it was there and clear as a bell, and the next sweep it was gone from my radar scope, Red One Flight Leader. I have no idea if the contacts were real or some form of interference develop by our enemy to employ against us. Confused. Need input and orders immediately, Red One. Over."

"Red Leader One this is Wild Rider Seven. I could swear I just saw something right dead ahead of my aircraft as well, Ma'am. It looked like a sort of garbage can type thing just floating around in the damn sky which is impossible, Red One. Over."

"Red Leader One to all Wild Riders. I see one of the targets to my left side at the same altitude we're currently flying at, ladies. They're definite some form of targets I'd offer. What the hell are the damn things anyway? Anyone able to identify the damn things. Over."

"Red One, Rider Six. I have one of those can shaped objects floating to the right side of my aircraft. I can see at least four more of the damn things in the same area as well. They truly look like cans at that Red One Leader. What the devil do you think they might be, Red One? Over."

"I don't have any idea what they might be, and I don't like the looks of them either. I never saw anything like them before, and I intend to give them a wide birth in case they are some form of weapon aimed at our flight. I'm going to warn Foxtrot Leader in case they're trouble."

"Red One to Foxtrot Leader. We're picking up a large number of garbage type can shape objects floating at the same altitude as we're employing for this flight. I know this might sound a little nuts to you sir, but that's what the damn things look like, sir. Foxtrot Leader, are you picking up anything on your radar?"

"Foxtrot Leader to Red One. That's a negative on that request, Ma'am. I show absolutely nothing showing up on my radar bounces ahead of your flight, Red One. I suggest you switch over to the UHR radar to verify the possible unknown targets at this time Red One. Over."

"Roger that last as received, am switching over to UHR radar now sir. Over." The moment Commander Heart flipped the switch over to the UHR frequency, the sky before her aircraft was instantly littered with countless targets. She counted at least twelve of them in the air, with more targets showing up as she watched, all coming from the ground. She drew in a quick breath as she suddenly yelled out a warning in her radio. "Red One to all Wild Riders. Break off the attack immediately, dump your bomb load and then drop down to five thousand feet and head back to base. I repeat. Break off the attack immediately and drop down to..."

Foxtrot Leader heard the explosions a split second before he noticed them, as the sky a few miles ahead of him suddenly turned into one massive flash of flames in front, and at the same exact height as the wing of YF 23 bomber aircraft were employing. One plane after the other broke up while in flight, and plummeted out of control towards the earth below.

"Foxtrot Leader to all Foxtrots followers. Buster, buster, buster. Your signal is now Buster for this fucking operation. Break left, break left. Go to punch (afterburn) and get your fucking asses up in the damn clouds. Spread out and keep burning fuel. We're under attack. God, did you see what just happened to the Wild Rider Flight? They're all gone sir. What the fuck hit them for crap sake? It looked like the sky just exploded. Foxtrot Leader to Sentry Base. Over."

Colonel Campanelli listened in and immediately keyed the mike and growled. "Sentry Base Command to Foxtrot Leader, come back mister. Over."

"Foxtrot Leader to Sentry Command, sir. Did you see what just happened to the Wild Rider fighters, sir? They were hit by unknown type weapons and the entire flight is down sir. Over."

"That's a Roger Foxtrot Leader. Your signal is now Buster. I say again, your signal is Buster. Break off attack and return to base immediately.

That's a fucking order. Foxtrot Leader, did you see any chutes from our destroyed aircraft before you left the god damn area, sir? Over."

"Negative on that last question Colonel. I see no chutes opening anywhere sir. Over."

"Shit." Colonel Edward Campanelli hissed in the radio as he shook his head slowly.

ON BOARD THE AWACS PLANE JUST INSIDE THE BORDER OF THE SUDAN NEAR THE CHAD BORDER

The E 3A AWACS radar aircraft code named Hawkeye Three ordered up by the CIC for air cover and spotting for this operation, was tracking the American flights heading to Chad. "Sir." A radar operator cried out and then went on with his report to his pilot. "I'm picking up twenty plums on the ground. I can't make out what the hell they represent though sir. I never saw anything like them before sir. They must be artillery shells or something being fired at the city."

"Keep a close eye on that damn area, Airman. We have an attack flight currently in the area and I don't want them to fly into trouble." The Commander ordered back at the operator.

The airman strained his eyes as he stared at the bright orange and yellow scope. Every once in a while he would pick up something that seemed to be floating in the air, just as he was about to call the Lieutenant over to take a look at them, the spots would disappear from his scope.

The Airman watched as the YF 23 flight entered his sphere of his radar control. He easily picked up when the wing of aircraft fired up their radar units, and then he noticed them go to the much sharper UHR radar systems. Once he went over to his own UHR system, his scope was suddenly lit up with many strange looking targets floating at the same altitude as the fighters.

"Lieutenant, hey Lieutenant Sir, can you come over here for a second and take a look at this damn mess I have coming up on the screen, sir. I don't know what the hell to make of them sir."

The concerned Lieutenant looked at the screen and then he asked the rather excited Airman. "God, what the fuck do you think they can be for the love of God, Airman?"

The two operators watched intensely as the flight of warplanes headed directly for the floating blimps, and the blimps even change height as if to better intercept the incoming wing of American fighter planes. The Lieutenant quickly checked the height of the YF 23s on the screen at the bottom left and then he asked the computers to identify the height the blimps were at.

A second passed, and both the aircraft and the blimps were at ten thousand feet even.

"Dammit!" The Lieutenant cried as he reached for the mike and placed a call out.

"Red Leader One, Red Leader One. This is Hawkeye Three. This is an emergency alert status Red Leader One, you're instructed to reply to my call immediately. Over."

"Hawkeye Three, this is Red Leader One. What do you have for me? Come back sir. Over."

"Red One. You're instructed to change altitude. You're under attack by unknown wea..."

"Christ, did you see what I just picked up Lieutenant?" The Airman cried out in alarm to the Lieutenant as he suddenly lost all contact with the entire Red One flight. The radar screen was filled with a bright, blinding yellow blimps of light for a long instant. The radar operator picked up three of the Red Flight fighter aircraft spiraling out of control towards the earth.

"Got one sir, I see a fucking chute plume, sir." The radar operator pointed to a small dot on the radar screen to the Lieutenant standing over his shoulder while bending down so he could see the scope and the small dot a little easier. His hand rested lightly on the Airman's back, and the other hand was sitting on the console for some added support of his body.

The Lieutenant was called over to another computer screen by a second radar operator.

"Lieutenant, the damn Hornet flight veered off to their portside and they're climbing straight up on full afterburners as they complete turns back for their base, sir. They must have seen what happened to the other flight sir." The Airman continued watching the screen, and then he continued with his report to the Flight Controller of the AWACS aircraft.

"Lieutenant, it looks like the Foxtrot aircraft are heading back to base at this time sir, all Foxtrot aircraft seem to be still intact though, sir. Thank God for that much sir. I'm picking up orders for the flight to head back to base as reported, sir." The Airman informed the officer in charge of the operation standing over his shoulder.

"Thank Christ for that much dammit. I was about to order that flight back to base myself, mister." The extremely upset Lieutenant grumbled at the airman.

CIC, ON BOARD THE CARRIER USS ROOSEVELT

Commander Owens placed a Flash message out to Colonel Campanelli stationed at the new military Base Sentry. When he replied to the call, Commander Owens reported. "It looks like we found those missing fucking Russian scientists we were so damn concerned about, sir. I'll bet the damn Libyans hooked up to some of the damn Russian satellites, and that's how they were able to destroy our Red Rider Flight, Colonel Campanelli Sir. I'm certain the damn Russians are responsible for these weapons, and that shot at my stealth recon aircraft a few weeks ago as well. Heads will roll for this one, you can bet your life on that Colonel Campanelli."

Commander Owens ordered Colonel Campanelli not to send any new flights over Chad until he could get a better handle on what these new weapons just employed against his fighter aircraft were, and see how they could possibly defeat them. He let the Colonel go, and then he placed a Flash message over to the Joint Chief of Staff's Chairman, General Rossman. Commander Owens informed the General of the attack on the American warplanes over Chad.

General Rossman sent a message to James Walters, the American Delegate to the United Nations, and informed him he was to demand an immediate halt to the fighting in Chad, or the United States was going to retaliate for the unprovoked attack against her aircraft that were on a recon missions over the war torn Chad city of Abeche. He further stated the flight was on nothing more than a mercy mission to evacuate the civilians from the besieged city of Abeche, before they were slaughtered to the last by the attacking Libyan military forces.

Members of the United Nations immediately condemned Libya for this latest action, and they further demanded her total withdrawal from Chad. The demand fell on deaf ears though.

THE WHITE HOUSE

At a special meeting being carried out between the President and his security staff, the Security Director was reporting. "With all due respect Mr. President, France submitted a plan for the Middle East and its water problem, sir. Looking at the outline, it might work at that sir, if the Egyptians are willing to take a look at it that is, sir."

"What's the new plan you're speaking about, mister?" The President asked with a trace of anger or boredom lacing his voice this time. As he listened to his Security Director explain, his anger peaked and he then snapped another pencil he was playing with in his hands. Instantly, an aide rushed over and picked up the pieces and handed the President another pencil to take his anger out on. Then, the assistant placed the two halves in a box to sell them later on. The aide had quite a little enterprise going for himself. The public was well aware of the President's idiosyncrasy of snapping a pencil when angered, and he collected the halves and sold them to collectors every weekend. His Boss went through at least twenty pencils a week, which brought the assistant a five dollar reward for each prize he sold.

"Sorry Mr. President Sir. France wants to send an Army of their engineers and workers down to the Antarctica, to mine vast amounts of snow and ice from the Ross Ice Shelf, that by the way is named after the discoverer, Jack Clark Ross, sir. This plan utilizes the tapping of the near by underwater volcanoes. The heat from these volcanoes would be used to melt vast amounts of fossil snow and ice into the purest of water, free from many of the modern day pollutants, Mr. President Sir. Once the ice is melted to water, it's to be pumped into converted oil super tankers and transported out to the Middle East to add to their drinking water, sir. The top of the ice shelf is over two hundred feet above the water. It's a sight to see, so I'm told sir."

When no response came from the obviously still extremely upset American President, the Security Director continued. "France wants to construct huge reservoirs in the desert by digging a depression in the sand, and placing thick polyurethane in it. Then pumping the water from the tankers into said reservoirs. The French also want to build over the reservoirs to avoid most evaporation of the water. The plan sounds feasible, but I don't think we can transport enough water quickly enough to avoid war with Egypt." The Security Director announced.

"You seem to be quite certain Egypt's going to join in on this war with Libya, sir."

"I certainly am Mr. President Sir." The Security Director offered the President seriously.

"Dammit to hell and back, that's all I fucking need to finish off my day perfectly for myself, god dammit. I hoped at least Egypt would stay out of this damn mess until we got a better handle on the damn thing. Just how much water's down there on this shelf, sir?" President Cole asked the Security Director.

"We figure there is well over five hundred trillion gallons of usable water trapped in the ice of the Shelf. The Ross Ice Shelf covers a two hundred and eighty thousand square mile expanse, and the ice is a thousand meters thick in most places. But that's not the half of it, Mr. President. Our engineers figure new ice and snow will replace what is being mined almost as fast as we take it sir. The ice replenishes itself at an alarming rate, so there's an endless source of very drinkable water, and with proper controls on the workers, it'll be a never ending source of almost pure water. At least it's a better plan than the one the Saudi's are employing, tapping fossil water and drying up their underground aquifers, producing only forty five years supply of water. Once that's used up, the nations of the Middle East and Northern Africa dies, sir."

"Shit. This operation sounds like it'd be rather expensive to carry off." The President replied.

"Not really, my guys figure it'll cost under ten cents per five hundred and eighty four gallons of water using this method, Mr. President Sir." The Security Director offered with a smile.

"What about the damn desalination plants we keep offering them so they can use the damn water off their coast for drinking, dammit? We could build Egypt a number of these damn desalination plants, and eliminate their water problems once and for all for them, sir."

"Mr. President Sir, we have offered these desalination plants to Egypt, but I'm afraid she didn't hear out of that ear, sir. Besides, the desalination plant operation is quite a complicated and expensive process to carry out. It requires vast amounts of heat and energy to produce a cubic meter of water, at a cost of nearly two dollars and forty five cents per gallon, sir."

"How much is a cubic meter?" The President asked as he let out his breath in a low whistle.

"A cubic meter of water is about two hundred and sixty four gallons, sir. I'm afraid that it's a rather expensive operation for us to produce drinking water this way with the desalination plants, sir." The Director replied.

"I see only one thing to do then I believe, sir. We have to sell the Egyptians on the French plan if at all possible. Send the plan over to Ambassador Walters, and let him get it over to the Egyptian Delegate and see what he thinks of the damn idea, sir."

"Yes sir, I'm on it right away Mr. President Sir." The Security Director said as he immediately left the office, leaving the President looking out the window to his garden below.

CAIRO, EGYPT

The Egyptian government was not the least bit interested in any form of possible settlement at this time, or a plan to ship in fresh drinking water, rather she sent a stinging letter out to the Ethiopian government. Demanding Ethiopia open more of the Dam's flow of water so the natural waters of the Nile would again flow down the same path it has flowed ever since the birth of the earth. Ethiopia completely ignored the abrasive letter from the Egyptian Ambassador.

Egypt immediately retaliated by sending a large column of over three hundred Russian and American built tanks, along with many artillery pieces over to the Sudan, Egyptian border area, and they prepared to invade the country when all their forces were set in place to attack.

Some artillery pieces were starting to show up along the edge of the Sinai Desert as well, which immediately caused the Israeli government to complain vigorously to the Egyptian government. Then to the United

Nations over this latest infraction of the Israeli, Egyptian peace accord. Their complaint did little good as well with either establishment.

Again, the countries that made up the United Nations condemned Egypt, this time for making aggressive actions towards the Sudan and Israel. Egypt's response was to declare war on Ethiopia, prompting Libya and the other Arab nations who already align themselves with Libya in the first place, to declare war on the same countries Egypt had just done.

More words with the United States, caused Libya to withdraw from the United Nations all together, followed closely by Egypt and the other countries that had already backed the two Arab nations. The United States took much stronger steps to this latest response, and they ordered seven of their eleven aircraft carrier strike forces to head directly for the Indian Ocean, and the Mediterranean Sea at flank speed.

England, France, and the United Germany, along with the Baltic Alliance States quickly joined forces with the United States, causing Libya to declare war on any and all other nations who now stood against her in this new war in the region. Many other countries that once offered to back Libya originally, had suddenly refrained from declaring war on the United States and England, but nevertheless they continued with their backing of Libya's actions in her struggle against the other Arab countries she was going to war with.

The United States shared much of its latest intelligence information with Israel, and Israel watched the movements of Egypt's military forces currently operating on the very edge of the Sinai Desert. Finally, when the Egyptian troops and tanks entered the Sinai Desert in force. Israel responded immediately against this action by sending in their own troops and columns of tanks and artillery into the desert from her side of the border.

Israel sent two massive columns of tanks into the Sinai Desert, seven hundred tanks in each column moved out. The Jerusalem Battalion, and the Bren Adan Battalion, entered the Sinai at the same time.

The well feared and respected Jerusalem Unit was backed by the new Merkava MK3 120 mm cannon MBT (Main Battle Tank) built by Israel. While the equally feared Bren Adan Unit was backed by the much older Merkava MK2 105 mm MBT, and the MAGACH 7 MBT, a modified version of the old American M 60 tank, along with the Soltam Slammer, and the Rascal 155 mm self propelled Howitzers, and the older Abrams M-1A tank. A thousand Israeli tanks stood by behind the main line of attack formation, ready to relieve the two battalions if they got in trouble in the desert. Israel was well prepared to engage and destroy all the enemy tanks in the same way they destroyed them in the last war between Egypt and Israel.

When the Egyptian soldiers and military equipment entered the Sinai Desert in force. Israel immediately launched three separate wings of fighter aircraft, containing seventy planes in all, in order start to soften up the Egyptian troops and their present positions. The Israeli fighter aircraft were a good mix of F 18 Hornets, F 15 Eagles, and some of the aircraft were the older but newly refurbish 14 Tomcats, as well as the more obsolete, and retired American F 4 Phantom planes. All the warplanes streaked across the air in a tight formation at just over Mark One, all warplanes were heading directly for the rapidly gathering Egyptian troops and military equipment as they rapidly entered the vast desert.

The Egyptians launched hundreds of their so called drift bombs, given to them by Libya.

Constant AWACS reports went directly to the CIC Chamber stationed on the United States Aircraft Carrier the Roosevelt, who in return would immediately relayed the detected launches of the new weapons to the Israeli forces just entering the Sinai Desert. Israel, being the way she was, did not trust any of this latest information coming from the United States military command, and she basically ignored the United States' warning, thinking it was just another one of the United States' ploys designed to try and delay an attack from Israel against the

Egyptian forces gathering in the Sinai Desert, to try and see if they could stop the war by talking.

Many Israeli tankers stopped their tanks right in the middle of the roads, and they watched as the formations of Israeli fighter planes flew directly overhead their tank columns. An hour into the flight, the first Israeli pilot reported seeing some false images suddenly showing up on his radar scope. Seconds later the horizon was a flash of fire and burning heat, knocking sixty three of the Israeli fighter planes out of the air in an instant. The Egyptian troops did what the Jews thought was their biggest mistake since they chose to fight the Jews back in the '73 war.

The Egyptian forces stopped their advance into the Sinai Desert, and then their military forces were choosing to defend the very banks of the Suez Canal. Israel quickly ordered her leading tanks to head directly for the old Command Posts they once occupied during the old '73 war. Israeli command felt if the Egyptian forces were going to commit the same mistakes twice. Then they will do the same tactics that caused them to win their war with the Egyptian soldiers in the former war in the first place.

CHAPTER 21 - THE COMMAND BUNKER IN LIBYA

Pictures from one of their tapped into satellites reported to the Russian defector, who then reported this new information out to the Egyptian troops operating in the field inside the Sinai Desert. Egypt was pleased with this latest information, because their plan had worked out perfectly so far for them as they hoped it would. The Egyptian forces had strengthened their positions on the banks of the Suez Canal where the troops hunkered down, and then they waited, just as they did during the '73 war with Israel. The Egyptian troops watched the countless reports flooding in of the Israeli tankers and troops retaking the same exact positions they did in the last war they engaged with against Egypt. The box trucks containing the video camera relays, radar and radio controls to set off the fuel mine explosives that the Egyptian work units setup in the sand throughout the desert region before the start of the war against Israel.

The Egyptian trucks moved to position, hooked up the hidden wires to the cameras, and then setup the radio transmitters, which would direct the fuel mines to go off when needed. The Egyptian Command knew full well if their traps in the desert worked as well as the drift bombs, the Jews would be completely helpless to defend themselves against their attacks against them.

Israel was so occupied with the Egyptian military movement she completely failed to take notice of the Iraqi buildup on her border area with that country, until it was too late for her to react against this new threat against them. Iraq had setup scores of Scud missiles, and they aimed them at the Jewish state. For the most part, the warheads were of the high explosive type, but there were twenty specially prepared Scud missiles with nuclear warheads fixed to them, smuggled from Russia. This was to be used as a last resort in the defense for Iraq, and were not to be employed unless Israel broke through the Iraqi main defensive lines against them.

With the devastating loss of so many Jewish aircraft due to the attack of the drift bombs, the Israeli government ordered her tank and artillery to dig in and take up position in previous locations occupied during the war of '73. The tankers were ordered to hunker down and wait further instructions once they were set in position. Egypt had no intention of allowing the Israeli tankers to get too settled in these areas. For the first time in Arab history, an Arabian country had Israel up against the ropes, and Egypt was not going to allow Israel to go that easily.

General Abdul Haidar, Commander of the Egyptian ground forces, watched the video screen from his Command Post, as a hundred Israeli tanks quickly took up defensive positions at the old headquarters at Bir Gifgafa. The Egyptian Commander smiled as he gave the Israeli soldiers time to dismount their tanks, and setup field tents and Command Centers, and feel secure in their old positions. When the first fire was started to heat up field rations for the troops, General Haidar gave the order to fire the fuel mines in a particular firing order of detonation.

The Israeli tanks were not very well dispersed, because they did not fear an attack this far from the Egyptians forces. The tanks were parked within the circle of death the Egyptians had setup with the help of the fuel mines. Forty fuel mines popped off, sending a cloud of liquid fuel in the air, raining upwards twenty feet. The fuel dispersed to a mile in diameter. Raw fuel landed on the parked tanks and troops. Then, secondary explosions went off, detonating the fuel in a white hot blinding flash from the fuel still floating in the air. The temperature inside the circle climbed to three thousand degrees within seconds, killing two thousand Israeli soldiers with the flash fire. Many secondary explosions occurred, as ammunition in the super heated tanks cooked off and detonated. More explosions occurred when ammunition for the artillery started to cook off.

The Egyptian General fired off the detonation strips next against the stunned Israeli soldiers. He could actually hear the soft puffs the exploding strips made, as this weapon finished off any surviving Israeli soldiers who escaped the huge fire balls from the fuel mines. The General heard the Israeli soldiers crying out in such terrible pain. Video cameras showed General Haidar first hand the mines going off, and then a lens clouded over from the fuel landing on it as he stared at the screen with straining eyes. The clouded over camera was still running when the smaller explosions set off the fuel vapor in a massive ball of fire from hell and death.

The camera showed the Israeli soldiers running in all directions while quickly being burned to death, and then the detonation strips going off, and making even more Jewish soldiers fall to the ground, and allowing the spreading flames cover over the down soldiers before the camera finally went dead because of it melting in the flames consuming the Israeli soldiers.

The Egyptian Command Center erupted in wild cheers and this infuriated the Egyptian General as he suddenly roared at his lesser soldiers. "Shut your filthy holes you sons of a lowly jackal, and watch how true soldiers die in war in defense of their own country. These are very brave soldiers dying, dying while carrying out their country's orders and desires. It's a proud way to die, no, for your country and your beliefs. You fools can only hope you're as brave as these proud soldiers dying before your worthless eyes. Respect them and their deaths properly."

A silence swept over the Egyptian Command Post, as the powerful General turned his attention back to the Israeli Post being setup at another of the old Command Post from their past war, this time at Gaby. Here, what looked like two hundred tanks pulled off the paved road, and quickly setting up their Command Post on the hard packed sand flat they once commanded.

Again, the Egyptian General gave the unsuspecting Israeli soldier's time to get comfortable, before he gave the order to set off the fuel mines, but this time he fired the detonation strips at the same exact time the fog mines went off. This action was to try and cut down the Jewish soldier's suffering. The results here were the same as at the other old Israeli post.

This time, the cameras ran long enough for the Egyptian General to witness the first Israeli tanks explode in a shower of sparks and roaring flames, before it clouded over, melted and went black. There was no outburst this time inside the Egyptian command center, as the Egyptian technicians watched in stone silence as the Israeli troop's burn to death and their equipment burn.

Another camera suddenly came on line, showing the Israeli troop's setting up a Command Center at the old post at Tasa. The Egyptian General sat poised as he watched the Israeli tankers dismount their massive machines of war and mill about while lighting cigarettes and talking amongst themselves. He hated killing soldiers in this manner, he felt a soldier should die quickly, by a bullet and not by fire or these painful pins from under the sand.

The Israeli Command Center stationed at El Auja, in the Negev Desert was reeling from the terrible loss of so many of her aircraft as reports filtered in that they were losing contact with tank units stationed in the Sinai Desert one after the other. Israeli General, Amiram Goldblum reached for his radio and requested tank unit Gold setting up at the main Command Headquarters at Bir Gifgafa in the Sinai Desert, but the unit Commander did not respond to the call.

"God dammit Yigal, answer your fucking radio will you please. I need to know what the hell is happening with your troops in the desert, fool." The General commanded him to no avail.

Major Yigal Rosenthal was in command of the Jewish advance tank units in the Sinai Desert.

When the Israeli General realized Yigal was not going to answer, he ordered a flight by a single fighter to do a pass over the position of his tanks, and see what was happening.

The flight was flown by an American made F 15 Eagle aircraft equipped with a video camera mounted in the nose of the plane. As the aircraft flew over the Israeli tank position, the Israeli General and his aides found themselves staring at the video screen in stunned disbelief. Over a hundred Israeli tanks were burning, many exploded from within. Charred bodies of his proud soldiers laid spewed about in the blacken sand, grotesquely forced into the fetal position from the intense heat of the fires and burning ammunition and military equipment. General Goldblum ordered the aircraft to head over the position marked out on his map Gaby, he informed the Israeli pilot that he lost all communication with this tank unit stationed at this site as well.

Twelve minutes later, the video camera reported the same disaster had befallen his tanker column here. Over three hundred Israeli tanks were lost before they even entered the battle.

By this time, the extremely upset and angry Israeli General lost communications with every tank unit he sent out into the Sinai Desert. It was a good decision he held back a thousand tanks at his main headquarters stationed at El Auja. His intelligence had let him down, and he lost nearly two thousand tanks and the supporting ground troops along with those tanks. What he had left in the way of active tanks, was currently gathered behind him. Now he knew what the Egyptian workers were up to in the desert. "Looking for water, shit." He growled to himself.

He felt good knowing his tank refitting and fuel dumps stationed at Beersheba, and at the Oasis Ain Oadeis were still secured, and free from any enemy attack, or so he thought.

The little over two thousand Egyptian Commandos being trained in Israel before the fighting started, immediately requested, and were instantly granted political asylum by the unsuspecting Israeli government, suddenly launched their attack on the Israeli repair centers they were attached to. Three hundred Egyptian Commandos attacked the fuel dumps, refit and ammunition dumps stationed at Beersheba in Israel. They detonated the fuel and ammunition dumps, killed many of the mechanics, and also destroyed much of the military equipment needed to repair the damaged tanks, and refuel and rearm the massive war machines at the same time.

A second Egyptian Commando unit splintered off the first one, and the two thousand Egyptian specially trained troops, attacked and destroyed the fuel and refit areas stationed at the Oasis.

The fuming Israeli General suddenly found himself completely cut off from any and all further supplies and ammunition from his support groups. What ammunition his tanks did have with them, was all they were going to get for quite a while to come. The Israeli General then ordered his tanks to quickly form up a skirmish line along the edge of the Sinai Desert, and they were ordered to dig in and wait for the Egyptian forces to attack their positions.

The rest of the Egyptian Commandos moved further in Israel, and attacked selected airfield at Ashdod, and destroyed military planes, installations and fuel dumps there. The Commandos were moving more up the coast of Israel, attacking any and all military targets and communication centers through¬out the lower section of Israel. They were being dogged by many Israeli units.

The Egyptian plan worked to perfection, and now, Iraq made its move against the Jewish state, feeling the Jewish state was severely weakened by the great Egyptian successes against the Israeli military and airforce. Tel Aviv was the first Jewish city to feel the hatred of Iraq, as three Scud missiles smashed into the ground at Ben Gurion Airport. The destruction of the airfield was complete, as fuel reserves exploded, and many hundreds of civilians were caught in the airport waiting to leave Israel, and they were killed by the surprise and deadly missile attack, and the hellish fire storm which followed the exploding missiles and fuel at the Jewish airport.

The Israeli government turned around what few tanks she had remaining in the middle of the country. To her flank position to try and protect the Israel nation from this massive Iraqi land attack now occurring against them in force. Israel had a thousand tanks form these new lines of defense in their country against the attacking Iraqi troops.

But instead of Iraq attacking Israel, she turned her hatred towards Jordan more. With a force of tanks, fighter planes and troops, Iraq hit many cities in the tiny Arab country. The invasion by Iraqi's elite Republican Guard consisting of three hundred thousand soldiers attacked. The army did not waste their time in the cities. They merely pounded them to dust with heavy artillery bombardments, and air attack, and then the Iraqi soldier's marched through the destroyed city, killing anyone they saw still alive, as they continued their march towards the Israeli border.

It took Iraq two days to destroy the nation of Jordan, and then she massed ground forces, artillery and tanks along the Israeli border. Iraq sent in two waves of aircraft. A wing of Chinese made XAC H7 fighters, which was a mocked up version of the American Phantom F 4, and the Chinese H 5 bombers filled this wing. Thirty five aircraft were in this first wave. The second wave consisted of one hundred Japanese made Mitsubishi T 2 fighter bombers.

Israel was severely damaged, but she was a long way from dead. The Israel military countered these air attacks against her nation by sending up F 18 Hornets which easily intercepted the Iraqi warplanes, killing seventy five percent of the attackers while losing just one third of her aircraft to the conflict. The state of Israel begged the United States, and the Alliance States to send in their aircraft and tanks to help Israel defend her nation from these Arab attacks, but the United States was too busy positioning her aircraft carriers and support ships to defend

Base Sentry from attack. Israel was on her own once again, but just for the time being though.

Once General Goldblum realized the Egyptian soldiers were not going to go any further with her attack against them, but instead the enemy soldiers were going to hunker down and hold their positions in the desert where they had gathered. He sent nearly half his tank reserves to the north to defend Israel against the attack from Iraq. Five hundred Israeli tanks, backed the defenders against the Iraqi's assault. All Egyptian Commando units were caught or killed by this time, but not before they accomplished much of their mission, destroying three fuel and refit depots.

Soon, Israel and Iraqi troops were trading artillery rounds almost nose to nose. Many weapons Israel thought were destroyed in the Desert Storm war with the United States and the coalition forces, turned up again. Scud missiles fell again in Israel with even more damaging warheads than used during the Desert Storm conflict. One modified and heavier missile was capable of destroying five city blocks, most scud missiles were falling in heavily populated civilian areas, flooding roads with fleeing Israeli civilians which stopped many Israeli tanks from getting up to the fighting area. The two countries were fighting to a stand still, with massive loss happening on both sides. Iraq was further plagued by countless attacks by Jordan guerrillas who took to attacking the Iraqi tanks with gas bombs and hand grenades.

Israel traded an aircraft for one of Iraq's planes, and a tank for one of the enemy's tanks, and a soldier for a soldier. The Patriot missile systems were spent out, and Israel was trying to hit the incoming Scud missiles with the hand held Stinger missiles and some remaining F 18 warplanes.

IN THE WAR BETWEEN LIBYA AND CHAD

By the fourth day of the heavy fighting inside the nation of Chad, some form of frontlines between the invaders and the defenders was finally and slowly starting to be established, and Libya appeared to have stopped her swift advance into the tiny country. The Libyan military was still trying to destroy all the defenders stationed inside the besieged city of Abeche. With Chad just about completely destroyed, except for the Chad city of Abeche. Libya soon began to mass hundreds of her tanks and artillery pieces along the border of the Sudan and Chad, and their soldiers were also being strengthened with many soldiers coming from the nation of Nigeria. The Congo now made her military move at this point, and she attacked with lightening speed the African Republic which also bordered the Sudan.

With Libya not advancing her troops any further inside Chad, the low in fighting was welcomed by all countries involved in the fighting. The politicians used this time to bring the fighting to an end by any and all possible diplomatic means.

The massive United States military base stationed in the Sudan, Base Sentry was visited by Lieutenant General Omar Hassan Ahmed el Beshir, the Islamic leader of the Sudan who took over power of that country in an 1989 coup, and he established a strong Islamic law within the country. The persecution of the Christian people in the southern most area of the country had all but stopped in '95, once his control over the country took effect. As the Diplomats did their act with words, the down time was used to flood the vast American military base with more of her tanks and warplanes and defensive weapons. The helicopter wing from the 7th Air Cavalry was sent over along with a hundred Apache fast attack helicopters.

The 127th Airborne Brigade with one hundred AH 1W Marine Super Cobras landed at Base Sentry. Flights of the massive American C 5A Galaxy transport aircraft landed with tanks and artillery pieces, along with plane loads of ammunition for the weapons. It took six months for the combat equipment for Desert Storm to reach Saudi Arabia. But in the Sudan, the massive airlift, accomplished the same feat in just five days of this war. But most of the equipment was already being stored in Arabia since the last war in the Middle East, and it made this task easier.

Some of the massive supplying aircraft were coming under enemy fire from Somalia, as the rebels attacked the Marines sent to Somalia in late '94, after the United Nations troops came under attack in that nation. The American transport planes were coming under fire from Yemen as well as the American aircraft flew over their airspace. No planes were hit so far. However, the Marines stationed in Somalia, there to help protect and feed many of the civilians, were quickly pulled out, and then the United States warships stationed off shore, started to pound the shores of Somalia with their big guns to break the backs of the attackers. Ethiopia then attacked Somalia from the west to support the American actions. The decision to remove the Marines went to the Security Council, who also decided to remove their peace keeping forces stationed inside Somalia. The United States volunteered to evacuate them along with the Marines.

Little known to the United States intelligence, Libya sent in a force of Islamic militants to organize the Somali and Yemen attacks aimed against the slow flying transport planes. Libya supplied the extremists with SAM missile launchers, and computer aimed anti aircraft guns. The American pilots did not take the increased fire seriously, because the gunners had been so far off with their shooting. All this changed when the first SAM missile killed one of the huge transport planes while in flight and heading for Base Sentry.

Commander Owens sent an order out for the recommissioned battleship Missouri to sail to the Gulf of Aden so she could hit Somalia and Yemen with her sixteen inch guns. Accompanying the Missouri was the Buchanan, a missile destroyer and the Destroyers, Hayler, Fletchen and Hancock from the remainder of the support ships of the Missouri battle group. The commander further ordered the Princeton from the Aircraft Carrier Roosevelt support ships to aid in the expanding attack on Somalia. Two Amphibious Assault ships, the Guam and the Inchon were also ordered to aid in the removal of Marines, along with the United Nations Representatives.

The Marine units were ordered to leave behind all tanks and armored vehicles, and they were to render the military equipment useless before they pulled out of the region. The operation was going to be a massive dust off of all United States and United Nations personal, before the guns of the Big Mo opened up on the two small Arab countries. Most medical teams also working in the country, were removed when the fighting started in Chad.

The Marines operating in the capital city of Mogadishu in Somalia came under fire as they waited for their removal from the country. Commander Owens ordered the fighter aircraft from the Aircraft Carrier Washington to fly countless sorties to protect the Marines. The Guam Assault ship was set in position, and the Marines came under the protection of helicopters and AV 8B Harrier jump ships. Two LCAC hover crafts came in and the Marines and United Nations forces piled on board the machines. The eighty eight foot landing craft made eleven trips to remove friendly forces from the area. The massive Missouri took up position and she fired at any enemy position given to her by the Star Light aircraft platform hovering overhead.

The transport planes did not come under any further attack from Somalia and Yemen, and they quickly resumed their original flight path over the two countries. The American warships were ordered to remain in the area until all hostilities came to an end.

Forty two of the total air wing of fifty four F 117 Nighthawk stealth fighter bombers were in place in hard shelters in southern Saudi Arabia. They were equipped with two two thousand pound smart bombs to be used to take out strategic targets and bridges inside both Chad and Libya if ordered to do so. Ten of the super secret F 110 Blue Light stealth fighter bombers which originally gave birth to the F 117s, were also currently being stationed in of Saudi Arabia now. All the specialized aircraft came from the 415th Squadron of the 37th Tactical Fighter Wing.

Libya committed the same mistake that Iraq did back in 1990 against the Coalition Forces. Libya allowed the United States to build up all her troop strength and armament to the point of being unstoppable on the battlefield. Base Sentry was equipped to repel any attacking forces, no matter how large the invading Army might be to attack the base.

Colonel Edward Campanelli watched as the first massive C 5A transport plane almost collided with a second one sitting a little too close to the runway, while waiting to take off. Everywhere he looked he noticed more tanks or helicopters being moved around or armed on his ever expanding military base. The Third Marine and the Fifth battalion as well as the Seventh and Ninth Air Cavalry, along with the First Army were now stationed on his base. His troop strength swelled to well over five hundred thousand troops, and that did not include the pilots, their supporting crews, or any Sudanese and Iranian soldiers going to fight alongside the American troops once the fighting started in their area of responsibility. There were some three hundred thousand Iranian and Sudanese troops stationed along the border of Chad and the Sudan.

Libya was having some serious problems with her allies, Egypt and Algeria. Libya placed even more pressure on Egypt to continue her attack against Israel from the west, but Egypt did not want anything further to do with fighting Israel and her soldiers.

Ambassador Muhammad Kheir felt Egypt had done more than enough damage to the Jewish state, and he did not fear a new attack coming from the Israeli nation for now. When President Sadat was informed the Jews were pulling their tanks and military equipment from the Sinai Desert and send them north, he was positive the Jews did not want any part of the Egyptian troops either. Besides, President Sadat wanted to get at the Ethiopians more than the Jews. It was the Ethiopians damaging Egypt more than the Jews, by taking her water supply.

Libya immediately sent Ambassador Kamal to Egypt, and he argued angrily with Ambassador Mohammed Kheir who stood fast in his refusal to go any further with his nation's attacks against the Jewish nation. Nevertheless Ambassador Kamal continued to pressure Mohammed to attack the Sudan, the two argued until Mohammed finally assured Ambassador Kamal that his country would finally attack the Sudan within the next two days from this day, October 5th.

Libyan Ambassador Kamal listened intensely as Egyptian Ambassador Mohammed Kheir placed a call to the Commander of all Egyptian troops in the field, General Haidar. He ordered the General to pull out most of his tanks, and then aim them in the direction of the Sudan. The upset General resisted this order, saying he had to continue to protect his flank from a possible attack by the Jewish state. But Egyptian Ambassador Mohammed Kheir repeated his orders and used President Sadat as the deciding factor and finally, the Egyptian General relented and he ordered his tanks and soldiers to move out against the Sudanese border as he was ordered.

The United States Intel net immediately picked up the sudden and new troop movement of the Egyptian armor and troops, and they send a message to Ambassador Mohammed, requesting a secret meeting be setup between him and Colonel Campanelli. It was sent through a special messenger whom Mohammed Kheir and Colonel Campanelli knew and trusted, and when Mohammed saw Campanelli's name printed on the memo, he immediately set it up without informing President Sadat or JoAnne. How he was going to pull this off he did not really know, because JoAnne was always around him. He sent his reply message with the runner.

BASE SENTRY, THE SUDAN

Colonel Edward Campanelli received a Flash message from Command, and he read he was ordered to meet with the Egyptian

Ambassador Mohammed Kheir, and he was supposed to inform Mohammed what the United States wanted him to do, to stop some of the fighting taking place in this region. The Colonel was actually looked forward to the meeting.

Libya was having more trouble with Algeria. The Muslim Fundamentalists were giving the government in control of Algeria problems, for their agreeing to support Libya in her unholy war against Chad. The Fundamentalists attacked a number of military bases in Algeria. Military trucks were attacked as they drove through the streets, and planes and tanks were also sabotaged.

Libya did not care what was happening in Algeria, they only demanded Algeria to send her troops to Niger, and to lend their support to the Libyan troops fighting in Chad, as they had promised to do before the war had started. Rhetoric was growing worse between the two Muslim countries, until Libya finally threatened Algeria with an attack, if she did not live up to her side of the bargain, and her troops attacked Chad along with Libya.

Colonel Qaddafi's son was hiding for his life in Algeria for the last year, and now he saw his chance to take control of the present situation. He called for the Libyan people to rise up and overthrow this new government leading the Arab nations down the dangerous path to war and total destruction. The young Qaddafi vowed to reenter Libya and then takeover the government, and then invite his father back to help him run the government of Libya properly again.

This offer instantly stirred up not only the Libyans who did not want to fight, or did not want their country to end up much like Iraq, when they went to war against the powerful United States mighty war machine. But it also served to stir up the Algerian and the Fundamentalists alike. The more moderate Arabs in this nation took up the same call as their fellow brothers, to stop the fighting in all the Arab nations before it was too late to save their country, and the war ended up destroying all the Arab nations of the region.

The fuming Libyan General Sabra informed Ambassador Kamal all this talk against Libya came from Qaddafi's son causing them trouble. He also informed Kamal he was forced to shoot a soldier who refused to follow his direct orders.

Ambassador Kamal ordered the General to hold on and he would settle things with the Qaddafi troublemaker on his own. He called in a spy and ordered the man to kill Qaddafi. The agent looked at Ambassador Kamal with a dumb look on his face that forced the Libyan politician to bark at him. "Do you have a problem with this last order I gave you, you camel eating fool?" he demanded to know from the general as he waved his hand out before him to show the insignificance of Qaddafi's life.

"No sir, but I do fear the repercussions which would surely follow his death though sir."

"You miserable excuse for a dom man. Let me worry about any possible repercussions from the worthless fools of this nation. You make it look like the Muslim fool's killed the young big mouth troublemaker, and I shall do the rest. Get out of my office, you lowly dung eater you." He said as he studied his fingernails in a final dismissal of the agent.

The extremely upset General tried to start his conversation over with the Libyan politician. "Ambassador Kamal, I too fear the death of Colonel Qaddafi's son, and the mayhem that would surely follow his death in many Arab nations which such a dangerous act, sir."

"I don't care one grain of foul and worthless sand about your fears at this time, General Sabra Sir." He hissed angrily while still looking at his fingernails as he continued with his words of disdain. "I want to make plans to attack Algeria drawn up immediately by you, General. Once Egypt finally takes up her part in this god dom war. I want to wipe that miserable country of lowly dogs right off the face of the earth. The hell with the cursed Muslim's, they bore me more than even this Qaddafi pup does." The Libyan Ambassador made a sudden spitting motion, and then he added to his words to his grumbling General.

"Once this war is over, we shall then quickly eliminated all Arab countries who refused to join us in this most holy of wars against the lowly infidels in Africa. Then we'll be left with true blood Arab countries, and the world will have to deal with us as a unified Arab world as it should be, or they'll have to fear our great wrath. I dreamed of a unified Arab nation ever since the hated Jews first entered our beloved holy lands. Draw up the plans for our attack on Algeria right now General, I want them delivered by tomorrow morning to my office. General, are you ready to break out into the Sudan by the two day deadline I gave you sir?" Ambassador Kamal demanded angrily as he stared at the general while waiting for his response.

The General stared at the evil looking Ambassador with a sneer on his face as he replied to the politician. "Yes, I'll be ready to attack within two days, as long as Egypt will attack as she offered. As I told you before Ambassador, Libya and Nigeria will not be strong enough to attack the Sudan and the Americans, but with Egypt's help we will be successful."

Ambassador Kamal's sneer grew into a leer, and then he flicked his hand as if at a unseen fly as again he made the spitting motion and grumbled. "Egypt will be ready to carry out their attack by this time, I assure you General. It's good Egypt will take the heaviest part of the fighting for us, General. It was calculated long ago Egypt will lose two thirds of her soldiers, aircraft and tanks when they finally attack the Sudan, because the American pigs will go after them first. This will give us time we need, and we shall hit the United States forces from the rear, and destroy their supposed super base in the Sudan. Once the Americans are eliminated from the war, we shall then control the entire area, and we'll have a open path to Ethiopia and the Sudan.

"When we have this territory under our complete control, I feel we should then attack Egypt because of her display of weakness in this war. Then Libya alone, will own all the nations of the Sudan, Ethiopia, Egypt, Chad and Algeria. We shall then take their women, and make them produce true blooded Arab children who believe like we do, and repopulate the conquered lands with pure Arabs we shall hand pick, who'll be more than willing to die for Libya and her beliefs. We'll eliminate all subhuman Arabs, and their beliefs in their untrue gods, these filthy and inhuman things they are. The few we shall allow to live will be sterilized, and then we'll use them to do our bidding." The Ambassador suddenly started to laugh over his own words.

The Ambassador's chilling laughing caused the still highly upset General to shudder as he stared at Kamal in stunned disbelief. He remembered the horror stories which his father told him of how Hitler had acted, when he had conquered lands, and he stared at Ambassador Kamal. The General could not help but make the comparison between the two madmen.

The Libyan Ambassador stopped laughing as he suddenly glared harshly at his General and he warned him in no uncertain terms. "What the hell are you staring at now General? You have your god cursed foul orders and you shall follow them out as you have received them. Or I shall have you hanging from the post outside my gate, and your entire family will be branded as traitors to the state. Get out of my office and draw up those plans I want from you General."

ISRAEL

Israel rapidly fortified her lines of defense against the borders along Jordan, and she was prepared for an attack from the Iraqi troops, when Syria suddenly launched her attack against the Jewish state instead from her northern boundary. As fast as Syria attacked, Turkey attacked Syria from Syria's rear. Turkey, aided by warplanes and tanks from the United States bases stationed in their country, hit Syria hard. Syria was getting pounded by the Turkish forces, and they immediately broke off their opening attack against the Jewish nation, she did not have the military forces and equipment she needed to hold off both Israel and Turkey at the same time.

The attack from Turkey was steamrolling over Syria. Waves of American made F 18 Hornets hit military convoys, and a wave of Lance missiles pounded the enemy troop positions. Persian missiles were quickly stripped of their nuclear warheads, and then the missiles were refitted with 10,000 lb. conventional warheads or cluster bombs, and then fired at the Syrian positions.

Within twenty four hours after Syria attacked Israel, their President was forced to bid the war to stop. The Syrian President went to Turkey, and he signed a pact to stop fighting against the Allies, and he was forced to allow Turkish and American forces to cross their land to supply and support Israel. Ammunition poured through Syria, all heading for Israel, in addition to train loads of tanks and warplanes to support Israel and her war with Iraq.

OCTOBER 6th, 1996. ISRAEL

Israel, along with the strong backing from the Turkish and American forces, started a counterattack aimed against the Iraqi troops positioned on Israel's border. The Israeli Command ordered three columns of tanks, along with seven hundred tanks in each, into what was left of Jordan, in an attempt to out flank the Iraqi troops and attack those forced from their rear. All three tank columns were being backed by artillery and aircraft from her Allies.

The Iraqi troops quickly found themselves for the second time in the 1990s, hiding in the ground in their foxholes, as warplanes and artillery shells pounded away at their positions from two separate fronts now. American and Saudi Arabian warplanes launched from the bases stationed inside Saudi Arabia, pounded airfields throughout in Iraq, and aircraft from the Carrier USS America, and helicopters from the assault ship USS Tripoli, flew countless missions over Iraq, pounding her military forces into surrender again on the battlefield.

The two thousand seven hundred pound projectiles which took five one hundred and ten pound bags of gunpowder to fire the massive shells from the sixteen inch guns of the battleships Iowa and Missouri, now began their attack. Each gun hammered away at dug in positions inside Iraq. President Saddam Hussein again, found himself not knowing where to defend his land from first, as his nation was being pounded from all sides this time.

The quick moving Jewish spearheads, easily ripped through Iraq's weakened and depleted defenses, as helicopters landed at cities near Baghdad. Iran was the final straw to break Iraq's back. When Iran declared war on Iraq for destroying Jordan, Saddam Hussein ordered his conventional warheads removed from his Scud missiles, and replaced with the nuclear warheads.

These Scud missiles were the advanced Al Hussein 3s, with a range of eight hundred miles. Mobile launchers were placed on civilian flatbed trucks, and then driven out to pre set launch locations in Iraq's deep deserts. The Iraqis figured it would take twenty missiles to destroy enough of the Jewish state for his liking. The rest of the missiles were ordered to be split up between two different targets, and fired at both nations of Saudi Arabia and Iran. Thirty missiles in all were on their way to launch positions near the Saudi Arabian border, while twenty more missiles headed for the Iran and Iraq border. All the while, Iraqi technicians were working on another thirty warheads, all the warheads Iraq had in their entire arsenal.

An orbiting satellite reconnaissance platform from the United States was first to picked up the sudden movement from the Scud missile transporters in Iraq, and the platform immediately relayed this information to the Combat Information Center stationed on the Roosevelt. The threat of the Scud missiles was not fully realized, because the nuclear warheads were overlooked. Some Patriot missile systems were moved in position to protect the airbases stationed at Riyadh, in Arabia. Israel moved their Patriot systems to protect what was left of Tel Aviv. Commander Owens wished he had a few THAAD (Theater high altitude air defense missile system) scheduled to replace the outdating Patriot missile system available for this part of the war.

Iraq's defenses were rapidly breaking down all around them under the tremendous pressure being placed on the Iraqi military from the Israeli units, and from the attacks to their flanks by the rebel Jordanian fighters. Iraq's government saw the complete collapse of its tanks and artillery units, as thousands of her troops were again forced to surrendered, and the Iraqi Command ordered the firing of the nuclear tipped Scud missiles. The Iraqi Command was not going to lose another war in less than a ten year period. Five missiles were set in place and then fired off.

The Blackbird spy satellite instantly picked up plumes being emitted from the missile engines, and it immediately alerted the Israelis of their firing. As more missiles were setup and fired, different alerts were issued to the Israelis and United States forces in the region.

The first two Scud missiles were easily intercepted, but the third one got through the Israeli defenses. The fifty megaton hydrogen bomb exploded with the force of a star going Nova, and forty square miles of earth once Israel, was reduced to a cinder in less than a heartbeat. A blinding light lit up the horizon and transformed Tel Aviv into a fiery red fury, sounding like rolling thunder, as the massive shockwave rapidly sweep across the desert at subsonic speed. Devastating everything in its path, and leaving smoking rubble, dust and death in its wake. Radiation reached a hundred miles out, offering a slow death for all who lived in the burning death blast. Miles away, camels brayed in anger as they detected the terrible explosion.

The fourth Iraqi Scud missile was also intercepted while in flight, as a fifth missile struck in the Gaza Strip area. Another forty square miles of Israel ceased to exist in this world. There was a sixth missile hit at the third largest Israeli city of Haifa, as the seventh missile struck in the heart of the Pardess Hanna area as the Israeli defenses started to fail the nation.

The Israelis were the first soldiers in the history of the world to feel the devastating effects of a nuclear attack on their military lines of defense. A Scud missile exploded three klicks from the Israeli main guard advance position. Severe heat and radiation emanated outwards from the blast zone at the speed of light. The first humans to die were the Israeli troops caught out in the open. Hundreds, then even thousands of soldiers were forced to dive under parked tanks and armored vehicles for cover from the heat of the blast, adding a few seconds longer to their lives.

Any soldier within five thousand meters of the rolling fireball, was instantly vaporized in less than a heartbeat. Seconds behind the massive heat wave, came the much more destructive shock wave, crushing the chests of the living as well as the dead. Lungs were burned out of their victims, and then ripped from the soldiers bodies by the sheer force of the rumbling shockwave.

The massive shockwave picked up behemoth tanks that were not dug deep in the earth like children's toys, and tossed them through the air as if they weighed nothing. The tankers closed their hatches, leaving thousands of foot soldiers to fend for themselves, while the tanks were transformed into bomb shelters for the tankers inside them. Hundreds of armored vehicles survived the heat wave, followed by the devastating shockwave, especially those dug deep into the sands. But a second heat wave traveling at a slower rate of speed, finished off the remaining tanks and armored vehicles, which survived the first effects of the nuclear blast.

Instantly, the temperature inside the tanks and armored cars, quickly climbed to well over three hundred degrees Fahrenheit, actually boiling the blood in the bodies of the soldiers trapped inside the machines. Ammunition inside the tanks cooked off, as the heat continued to built up inside the steel tombs, exploding the red hot metal death traps, and filling the boiling air with countless white hot chunks of metal from the exploding tanks and armored vehicles.

The shockwave stretched ten miles out from the original blast site, and still strong as it ripped missiles from their launchers, and knocked over lighter weight personnel carriers. The rear defenses of the Israeli army were paying now, as self propelled Howitzer cannons were flipped over on their sides, as rounds went off from the shockwave or fires, adding to the death toll. Many soldiers in the rear area survived the original nuclear blast, with the lessening heat and shockwave, but the survivors were now pelted from the sky by red hot metal bits from the exploding tanks and shells. Some troops were blinded by looking at the deadly flash of the nuclear explosion and the angry, boiling ball of fire and heat, which rose fifteen thousand feet in the sky. Ten thousand Israeli soldiers were dead or dying from this one nuclear incineration.

More of Iraqi's Scud missiles were fired off by the Iraqi troops in the field, and one of them fell on the ancient and Holy City of Jerusalem, and another Scud missile hit in Nazareth. A ninth nuclear tipped missile was intercepted while in flight, but the Israeli defenses were down across the board by this time, because of the nuclear blasts raking the countryside.

Israel launched six of her own nuclear missiles at Iraq before she died completely, and an instant later, Baghdad, Karbala, Rutba, and An Najai disappeared from the face of the earth, locked in their own boiling hot mass of bubbling death. But before the Baghdad government ceased to exist in this world, it ordered the rest of her nuclear tipped Scud missiles to fly at both Saudi Arabia and Iran, but before these missiles even hit the targets. Nuclear tipped missiles suddenly being launched from the United States nuclear submarines Georgia, Alaska, San Diego and Los Angeles stationed in the Mediterranean Sea and Persian Gulf, were fired the short distance towards the very heart of Iraq. All missiles were slaved to strike only the nation of Iraq.

The concerned President of the United States with great despair, gave the final order for the American submarines to use nuclear missiles as a response on any country that used these weapons of mass destruction first. In eleven minutes, forty eight American missiles made their way from the Persian Gulf and Mediterranean towards the heart of Iraq. When the Iraqi government knew the American missiles were launched, orders were issued and the remaining Scud missiles were fired at the lines of fighting soldiers. Jews, Americans, Turkish and Iraqi soldiers, were burned to death in the hellish heat and flames of the exploding nuclear warheads.

Seconds later, the once great land mass which made up Iraq, Israel, Jordan, Syria, and large parts of Iran and Saudi Arabia were laid to waste by nuclear blasts. Once again, the earth was spotted with the nightmarish ash shadows once humans, being vaporized by the nuclear fury.

Sixteen million men, women and children were lost in this devastatingly short period of time of fighting, while six to ten million more people were figured to die within the next two weeks from radiation poisoning, and from exposure to the terrible effects of the many nuclear blasts. Communications were down in the entire region due to the electromagnetic charges, and the heavy disturbances in the air which killed charges in the batteries of the tanks and any other vehicles that were left intact after the nuclear blasts. Communication with most of the American ships and military forces in the Mediterranean area were down across the board.

Communications were expected to be lost for two full days. American warplanes flying less than a hundred feet apart, could not read each other's transmission, because the static filled electronic haze hung heavy over most of the Middle East. Radar and satellite communication screens were a mass of confused lines, and were useless to their operators. Plane radios were filled with ear splitting whines, as if the earth was crying in pain and rage over the deaths of her children, as radio communication centers melted from the heat of the nuclear blasts.

Many other countries of the world were thoroughly outraged by the use of nuclear weapons on the battlefield, and they begged a quick and immediate end to the war in the region. A cease fire was called for with Japan leading the petition, and they were backed by the Alliance States,

China and the United States, England and France. The United Nations offered to send troops in, to try and help guard the present borders of each warring country, until a further compromised settlement could be reached by all nations involved in the fighting in this region of the world.

Both Egypt and Libya condemned Iraq's use of nuclear weapons, and they further announced that Iraq had done so on her own accord, and the rest of the Arab nations were now against Iraq, and what she had done, even though Iraq no longer existed in this world. Libya continued to refuse to end the hostilities, but vowed never to employ nuclear weapons in her conflict with the other nations of the region, but she informed the world she did have such weapons in her arsenal.

Nigeria, as well as the Upper Volta also announced that they were ceasing all hostilities in Africa and the surrounding region. Algeria announced she was going to stop all warfare also.

These announcements infuriated the Libyan command, who was forced to announce she was also going to stop shooting for twenty four hours, to honor the dead and dying of the Arabian countries, and to give the politicians an opportunity to try and settle the fighting with words. Again, Libya blamed the nations of Chad and the Sudan, which allowed a United States military base to be constructed on her soil, this was a serious threat to Libya's sovereignty.

The world did not have the time to morn the massive amounts of death that happened in the Middle East for long, because there was a war still raging on in Northern Africa, which could get out of hand, and more nuclear weapons could be exchanged by either side. England, France and the United States send in a horde of scientists to see if they could help any civilians who might have survived the devastating nuclear blasts. Most of the scientists went to the nations of Israel, Arabia and Iran first. Iraq was put off because she was hit the heaviest and started the exchange.

ABECHE, CHAD. LIBYA'S FORWARD COMMAND HEADQUARTERS

During the short lapse in the heavy fighting taking place inside Chad, Libyan General Abdul el Kadir now found himself staring at a dirt covered captured female American fighter pilot. Lieutenant Joyce Heart stood in front of the Libyan General with her flight suit torn to tatters. His soldiers who found her, raped and tortured her on their own. She was beaten black and blue, with one eye swollen closed, and the only way she was able to stand up, was with the extra support of two Libyan soldiers standing on either side of her, and actually holding her up.

General Abdul el-Kadir stared at the female American pilot in stone cold silence for a long moment, and then he shook his head slowly as he breathed in deeply. The General sat back in his antique chair while resting his elbows on the arms of it, and he made a steeple out of his fingers. Then he rested his chin on them as he looked at this battered American pilot over his hands. He enjoyed a smile as he stared at the obviously terribly beaten American female pilot.

The General suddenly rose, his chair screeched in protest from the change of weight as it was shoved away from him by his legs. He then walked around the desk and sat down on the edge of it and smirked. "Well now what do we have here?" He sneered as his hands separated, and he spread them into a semblance of an uncaring shrug as he smiled openly at the pilot. He took out a dagger and stuck it deep in the antique desktop, actually prying out chunks of wood from the surface as he played with the knife sticking in the wood.

The American pilot suddenly shook free of her captors, and she tried to cover herself with her arms. But the guards grasped her arms again, and they pulled them away from her body.

Commander Heart straighten up the best she could and she hissed at the enemy General right in his face. "I'm a pilot in the United States

Air Force. Your soldiers have committed atrocities upon my person that goes against God, and the Geneva Conventions Codes of Conduct of War. My government will extract a heavy toll on your fucking soldiers for their despicable actions in this war. You'll be hunted down like the miserable dogs you are, and then you'll be..."

The Libyan General jumped to his feet, leaving the knife still stuck in the desk, and he smashed her hard across the face as he roared at her. "Shut your filthy hole, you cursed American shit eating pig you. I care no one grain of worthless sand for the Geneva Codes of War, or for your life, and I care even less for your miserable country, or its empty threats. It's you who have attacked my country, we have never attacker your worthless country." He looked at the terrible condition of the American female pilot. Her uniform was nothing more than mere rags hanging loosely from her sagging shoulders. Her left breast was uncovered, smeared with blood and grime, nothing remained of her uniform pants. He noticed the bruises covering her thighs, and wondered how many of his soldiers raped her and he smiled again at the female pilot.

Libyan General el-Kadir started off talking to the female American pilot with a warning. "You will answer all my questions truthfully, and without hesitation. If you know what's good for you American dog." He hissed through clenched teeth as he picked up the knife, and put it back in its holder, and then he turned his back on the pilot, and returned to his leather chair as the soldiers dragged her closer to his massive desk. He sat and locked his fingers together again. He leaned back in his chair which again cried due to the shifting weight, and he put his legs on top of the desk. His boots marring the highly polish finish of the surface, with one leg draped over the other, he laced his fingers together behind his head as he grinned at the American pilot now. He enjoyed her embarrassment as the two guards kept her from covering up her nakedness.

Heart glared hotly at the General as she tasted her own blood as it trickled down her throat.

After a few seconds, the Libyan General moved. He deliberately dragged his boots off the desk as he leaned forward and came to rest, placing his elbows on the desk and looked her dead in the eyes and hissed again. "Now you cursed daughter of the lowly jackal, you shall tell me how many planes and tanks you have on this base in the Sudan. How many soldiers are stationed on the base?" A ghastly crack of a smile caused the edges of his mouth to turn up.

Commander Heart glared coldly back at the Libyan General as she spat out her words of hatred at him. "I'm Lieutenant Commander Joyce Heart. My serial number is B158 733 345, and I'm in a pilot the United States Air Force." She tried to stand straight while shaking off the grasp of the two guards again, as she stood in front of the grinning enemy General and staring directly in his eyes while showing as much defiance as she could possibly muster in her broken body.

He savagely pounded his fist down on the desk as he glared at her, the sound his hand made, made her flinch slightly. Then he reached out his hand and grabbed her by her hair and pulled her head forward and slammed it down hard on the surface of his desk. The two Libyan soldiers were forced to let her go under the General's pressure. Her nose shattered from the impact with the unyielding oak surface of the desk and she was allowed to sink to the floor.

The two soldiers grabbed her by the arms again and they pulled her back up to her feet. She was coughing and having trouble breathing now, as blood ran down her throat. The General spread out a number of pictures on his desk, ignoring the blood that fell on them from her destroyed nose, as he growled at her this time. "I want you to identify the American Units you see here, and tell me how many soldiers are on this new base of yours, you filth eating pig."

"I repeat I'm Lieutenant Commander Joyce Heart of th..." The American pilot began again, but she was instantly cut off in mid sentence as the General roared at her.

"God damn American bitch pilot." The Libyan General screamed in her face, it was only with the greatest restraint the irate General prevented himself from pounding the desk a second time in rage. He felt any sign of rage on his part was a sign of weakness before this hated female American pilot. He reached for her hair again, and this time he ground her face in the pictures still lying on the desk. Then he lifted her head by the hair so her eyes could focus on his face, and he shook it violently. With unbelievable force he dragged her body across the desk with one hand, and he ordered one of the his soldiers to hold her arms on this side of the old desk. Two other soldiers grabbed her legs and they pulled them apart on her.

"American Dog, you shall come to regret your cursed folly for not answering my questions when I ask them of you. Allow me introduce you to my soldier Camel. You're in for some rather interesting times I assure you, if you continue to defy me and refused to answer my questions, pig." He laughed while holding her head up, and shaking it by her red matted hair.

A Libya soldier slowly walked to the front of the desk, and then he rested his hand lightly on her back as he began to laugh at the terribly battered American female pilot.

"American pig, allow me show you why we call this man Camel." The General hissed at her, and then he laughed aloud. "Camel, will you show this pig why you are called the Camel."

The man slowly and confidently moved directly in front of her face as the General held her by her hair and he actually forced her to look at what this man was doing right in front of her face. Camel then pulled open his robe, and exposed himself to her which caused her to gasp in fear.

His penis was huge, long and thick, and he was hard as a rock as his member hovered right before her face.

"American shit eater, please allow me to explain the peril that you are trapped within to you. Camel here, has received his name because when he makes love to his camels, they cried out in both pain and delight. As you can plainly see for yourself why the poor camels cried out in such pain and delight. Allow me to warn you pig, unless you answer all my questions truthfully, Camel is going to stuff his manhood up your ass, and he will tear you in half with his proud member. Then you'll find yourself crying out in pain much like his camels always do. Alas, two short hours with this Camel here, and piss will run from your foul and painted eyes. So for your own sake American Commander, I think and I also suggest you better think, and then you better cooperate with me completely, or else. Now speak you American dog you."

Camel walked to the other side of the desk and he stood behind the spread apart female pilot.

In a trembling voice the female American flyer cried out defiantly. "My name is Commander Joyce Heart, and I'm a Lieutenant Commander in the service of the United States and..."

Again, the General slammed her face hard into the surface of the desk, and then he grumbled at her. "Suit yourself pig of an American flyer. I shall show you the weakness in your cursed country for allowing a mere women to enter into a man's world. War is no place for a female pig, especially one who is going to be interrogated in ways no man could be interrogated. Camel, will you do the honors to this pig for me." He ordered as he held her head over the desk.

Camel pulled up the pilot's rearend, and then he slapped her hard on the rump with his hand.

"I don't want to do this to you because you're a soldier in your government's employ and as such, you should be respected as the soldier you are. But respect has nothing to do with it, I need the information you have locked within your foul head of an infidel. And I assure you, female pilot, I shall get this information from you one way or the other, fool. So I ask once again Commander, you'll not like Camel's play thing, so answer my questions, woman!"

"This is against the Geneva conve..." Her warning was turned into an ear piercing scream as Camel did as he was instructed when the General nodded to him. She passed out from the pain.

Cold water was thrown on her body lying across the desk, and as she regained consciousness, the General pulled her up by the hair, closer to his face until she was just inches from his, and she could smell his vial smelling breath, and spittle landed on her face as a further insult. "Are you now willing to tell me what I want to know, or should I have Camel enjoy your pleasures for a second time? He's ready to go again as you can plainly see for yourself, American infidel."

In a surprisingly strong voice, Commander Heart hissed through clenched teeth at the Arab General. "I'll see you rotting in fucking hell before I tell you anything, you piece of shit you."

The General screamed out in a wild rage as he slammed the female pilot's face into the oak desk twice this time, knocking her unconscious again. General el Kadir grew bored with the female pilot as she slumped down to the floor a second time, when the two other Libyan soldiers released their hold on her battered body. He walked over and looked out of one of the windows to the streets of Abeche below, and watched as his soldiers put countless Chad civilians against the wall, and shot them dead. He smiled, because he knew in his mind he would soon break this American female pilot's spirit, and prove to the world that war was no place for women, because they were so easy to get military information from.

CHAPTER 22 – AMBASSADOR MUHAMMAD KHEIR'S PRIVATE OFFICE IN CAIRO

The scared Egyptian Ambassador Mohammed Kheir was sweating as he watched the clock slowly passing the time away. He was a few hours away from his scheduled meeting with Colonel Edward Campanelli, and he did not know how he was going to get away from JoAnne, unless he used his plan. Finally, he called her into his private office, she found him sitting behind his desk as he announced the moment he saw her face. "JoAnne, I'm rather nervous on this foul day, and I need something to take my mind off all this killing and pressure."

She smiled proudly, because this was the first time in quite a while the Egyptian politician actually asked her for sex. Gail left them, and moved to Ambassador Kamal's employ as she replied. "Let me see what I can do for you Mohammed. Would you like a little head, it might help you relax some I believe." She used the Americanism 'Head', for the offer of oral sex.

"I think that might just do the trick for me young woman." He replied with a smile as he moved slightly away from his desk and then waited for her to do what he requested from her.

She walked over to him while opening her blouse as she walked, and then she knelt down before him and slowly undid his pants and pulled them off his legs, and then she placed them at the side of his desk as she took him in her mouth. Ambassador Mohammed Kheir had all he could do to keep his hands from shaking so. He let her get into her act for a little while before he finally reached out with his left hand, and carefully pulled her head up and down on himself, helping her which made her moan with delight and she increase her speed on his manhood.

With his right hand, he cautiously searched for the weapon and found it, and then he carefully pulled it out from under the pile of papers which hid the weapon from her sight. When the gun was firmly in his hand, he suddenly grabbed her and pulled her up by the hair, pulling her head off his shaft, and he smashed the barrel of the weapon against her forehead. Sweat poured down his face, and his hands shook as she smiled at him with her eyes closed.

He pulled the trigger before she could reacted to what was happening to her. Mohammed was deathly afraid of this young blonde woman. His chest shook violently with the effort to breathe.

The sound of the gun going off was deafening, and the force of the bullet hitting her forehead, ripped her head out of his grasp, and he was left with holding a hand full of blonde hair entwined between his fingers. The top of her head was splattered on the wall feet from him, as her body came to rest crumbled at his feet. Kheir's body trembled from relief of killing this extremely dangerous woman. He looked at the bloody blonde mess and took a huge gulp of air. He noticed his shaking hands, and then he looked at his blood covered legs and instantly grew weak in the knees, almost collapsing down to the floor. He breathed in deeply in an effort to try and gain some control over his body again. Finally, his body responded to his orders.

It was a good thing she had removed his pants, or they would have been covered by her blood. He got up and wiped the blood from his legs as if it was burning him with a damp towel, and then he pulled on his pants and dragged her limp body over to the small closet in his office, and he quickly stuffed her inside it. Then he cleaned the blood from the wall and carpet as best he could, using more paper towels and coffee, and then he wrote himself a letter in which he said she was going to be gone for a few days to visit her sick mother. He signed the memo with her name, and okayed the fake request with his own signature. Then he calmly left his office for his scheduled meeting with the American Military Officer.

The Egyptian and American were supposed to meet in Nasta. He had no way of knowing Colonel Campanelli had been in the town for over six hours already, and he was being protected by the Egyptian Fundamentalists, who wanted the fighting between the Arab states to stop. Captain Mendoza and Captain John White were with him as support.

NASTA, EGYPT

The small Egyptian village was sheer mayhem at best, the oppressive closeness of the heavily overcrowded streets was unbearable with confusing noise coming from the horde of passerby's, and their feeble attempts at overriding the constant chatter and yelling of the merchants hawking their wares, and screaming at the walkers. The noises coming from car horns and revved engines was making it nearly impossible to even think clearly in the village. The mass of beggars, old and young alike, countless barking dogs, and screaming chickens added to all the havoc, and made the hair on the back of Campanelli's neck stand on edge. His head pounded as the street vendors and shop owners, bellowed louder than the next, while trying to be heard over all the noise while contending for the attention of any of the streams of buyers who walked by the stalls, that lined both sides of the narrow main street of the small Egyptian village.

Colonel Edward Campanelli breathed a deep sigh as he was lead to a safe house to wait the arrival of the Egyptian Ambassador Mohammed Kheir. The Colonel felt extremely nervous, because he swore he felt he was being watched, ever since first arriving in the tiny Egyptian city. He got the word, Mohammed Kheir had arrived in Nasta for their private meeting.

THE CITY OF ABECHE, CHAD

When the extremely upset Libyan General could not get any useful information from the female American pilot by using Camel's persuasive means, he also resorted to the use of an electric cattle prod, electrical wires hooked to her nipples and sex organ, which proved useless in getting the pilot to talk. General el-Kadir smiled as he thought about the female flyer and all her screams. He knew he was going to start the process over again, first with Camel and then the cattle prod, and if these methods did not work, he had made up his mind to use fire.

Maybe burn the bottoms of her feet, this method always seemed to have the desired effect in the past for him. The General used the cattle prod as a cane as he slowly walked around his office and admitted he was enjoying hurting this young and pretty American female pilot. He smashed the cattle prod down across the desk, he was dying to get back to his interrogation to try and break this strong female American pig. He rubbed his chin and decided he was going to give her some time to be alone with her pain. An hour later, he had her brought back up to his office. After another session with Camel, she passed out again. As she was revived and stretched over his desk again, the Libyan General received a message from his Commander in the field.

Libyan General el Kadir's interrogation of the female American pilot was interrupted by a communication coming from General Sabra, the Commander of the attacking Libyan forces. The Commanding General informed his officer that he wanted the General to break out and attack the Sudan in two hours time. He also informed General el-Kadir that Egypt was going to attack Sudan in that time or maybe even sooner and he had to be ready to move out as well.

General el-Kadir had no idea of the meeting being held between Ambassador Mohammed Kheir and Colonel Edward Campanelli, and now Mohammed was on his way to meet with President Sadat. In addition, orders were given to Libyan General el Kadir for a second Libyan army to head for Algeria. This attack was going to take place at the same time.

PRESIDENTIAL PALACE, CAIRO

After the meeting with Colonel Campanelli was completed, Mohammed returned to Cairo, and he walked into President Sadat's office unannounced. President Sadat stood with his eyes ablaze and he barked at his arrival. "Where is your cursed female bitch bodyguard, Mohammed? I don't want you to move a muscle without her being by your side, fool!"

"JoAnne had to go visit her mother, she's extremely ill and is dying I am afraid sir."

"The filthy infidel pig, she picked the worst possible time to go away from your cursed side Mohammed, your life is in extreme danger every second this cursed war goes on. You couldn't talk the worthless female out of going to visit her mother till this war has come to a conclusion, fool?" President Sadat said with suspicious eyes cast on Ambassador Kheir.

"I'm truly sorry, but you know how women are when it comes to their mothers, my President." He replied as he shrugged his shoulders and spread his hands apart at the same time.

"Yes, and I'll see to it that you're assign another god cursed worthless bodyguard until your bitch returns to your side, Mohammed. To what do I owe this sudden visit to my office, sir? Would you care for a cup of tea, or a glass of bottled water to enjoy, Ambassador Kheir?"

Ambassador Mohammed Kheir looked around the office, there was only one bodyguard still standing inside the room, two others were stationed just outside the door of the President's office. He looked at the guard who stood over the shoulder of President Sadat, and the guard instantly nodded slightly at him. He turned his attention back to President Sadat who was staring directly at him, while waiting for the reply to his question. "Did you happen to fall asleep Mohammed?" he growled in anger at his Ambassador.

"I beg your pardon sir. I was trying to find a polite way to phrase this, but there is none. We better pull our support of Libya before it's too late, and Egypt gets destroyed as Iraq and Israel."

President Sadat instantly jumped to his feet and bellowed at Ambassador Kheir. "You should choose your words with greater care, when addressing them against me Mohammed."

When he did not back down from what he thought as a threatening stance, President Sadat savagely screamed at him. "There'll be no Egypt if the black Arab countries continue to cut off our vital water supply against us, you cursed fool. You know this true Mohammed. I'll not pull any support from Libya, I was about to issue orders for our troops stationed on the border of the Sudan to attack that worthless country of lowly animals. And attack is exactly what they are going to do. Now, if there is nothing more you have to talk about, you better leave before I have you shot as a traitor. Get out of my office, fool!" President Sadat demanded hotly.

When he refused to move, President Sadat instantly turned to his guard and warned him in no uncertain terms. "Fool of a jackal, you'll throw this son of a goat out of my office now, and then you'll order the guards outside to arrest him, is that clear, fool?"

The Presidential security guard did not move a muscle, he just stared straight ahead of himself.

President Sadat bulked up his shoulders and then he stomped over to the guard and slapped him hard across the face and yelled at the same time. "I have just issued you an order for you to throw this filthy shit eating pig out of my god dom office. And you will do as I have just ordered you, or I will have you shot for disobeying my direct orders, fool. What the devil is wrong with your mind? Are your ears full with camel dung that you do not hear my orders, god dommit!"

The Egyptian security guard ignored the slap, and smiled back at President Sadat, and then actually turned his back on the man as he continued his ranting at him.

President Sadat turned red as he roared. "What treachery is this being displayed against me, the leader of Egypt?" He growled as he turned to Mohammed. His mouth hung open when he looked down the barrel of his Ambassador's pistol being aimed at him.

"I believe you lost all control of yourself, and of our country, President Sadat. I shall take over Command of the Egyptian Presidency, and I shall stop this war myself. Please, make this easier on yourself to contend with by doing what I tell you, or I shall kill you where you stand, sir. Make no mistake about it President Sadat, I will kill you if forced to."

Sadat's eyes were wild as he roared again at Mohammed. "How dare you aim a gun at me, you son of a lowly jackal? I'll have your head freed from your foul body, and then fed to my dogs after I have used it for a piss pot. It's a true friend who will stab you in the front. It is written, follow the cursed Vulture and he will surely lead you to death, Mohammed."

"What do you expect from the people who prey upon each other like snapping dogs as they attack an antelope? I bid you to stop moving towards me if you know what's good for you, President Sadat Sir." He warned, but Sadat did not stop. When Sadat was just a few feet away from him, he pulled the trigger. The bullet hit Sadat in the upper arm.

"How dare you shoot your President, you cursed infidel!" He bellowed as first he was pushed backwards a few steps from the force of the bullet striking his body, but once he got control of himself, he lunged at Mohammed while growling at him in anger.

Mohammed Kheir fired two more times in quick succession, striking President Sadat in the chest with both rounds. Sadat's body stopped as if he was just smashed in the chest with a hammer and he slowly sagged to the floor, he then fell dead at his feet.

The security guard crossed the office and pulled on Mohammed Kheir's arm, and quickly ushered him towards the radio, he keyed it in and informed the Ambassador it was President Sadat's private hookup to all his troops prepared to enter the war against the Sudan. Any word coming from this radio was considered law by all Egyptian troops in the field.

He took the mike and issued an order for all Egyptian troops to stand down and stay where they were currently positioned. He ordered an immediate end to all hostilities in Egypt, and gave further orders for no soldier to leave Egyptian soil under any circumstances. The troops were ordered to protect the lands of Egypt from attack by any country, these orders included attacks from Libya. He sent a message which had no meaning to his troops in the field, but it meant everything to the Americans. It simply read. "Wet Work Completed."

The Egyptian troops did not have to be told twice to stop fighting, because they already lost their will to war further. General Haidar was greatly relieved when he ordered his tanks to turn away from the Sudan and Sinai Desert, and aim their cannons towards the country of Libya.

ON BOARD THE AMERICAN CARRIER USS ROOSEVELT IN THE RED SEA

The Combat Information Center on board the Roosevelt picked up the message sent to the Egyptian soldiers. Commander Owens understood immediately what the code words, "Wet Work Completed," meant to him. It was a term usually employed by CIA agents for a successful assassination and he mumbled to his second in command officer. "Mohammed must have killed Sadat. Get a Flash message out to Colonel Campanelli, and inform him our offer was accepted. Mohammed's now in Command of Egypt, and he's stopping all further hostilities. Sonofabitch, the fucking Colonel pulled it off for us, dammit. Send the message and include orders to attack the enemy forces from Libya still attacking Chad. Let's knock Libya out of the batters box. Inform him he has orders to go all the way. I have no intention of making the same mistake with Libya they made with Iraq. Let's do it soldier. Order a attack with all Allied forces."

"Commander Owens Sir, we just received a report stating Libya just attacked the nation of Algeria moments ago, sir." A soldier suddenly cried out to him.

"Good. Get a message out to the government of Algeria, and inform them we're willing to help their country battle against the Libyan attackers. Tell them all they have to do is request our help, and they'll get it plain and simple, dammit." The Commander replied.

The sailor sent the message out and seconds later, a request was sent for help from Algeria.

Commanders Owens looked at the threat board then barked. "Where's the Nimitz stationed?"

A sailor pointed out the Nuclear Power Aircraft Carrier Nimitz was sitting off the coast of Morocco at the present time while waiting to deploy her aircraft into the theater of war.

"Outstanding, I want you to issue orders for the Nimitz to go to an Alpha Strike immediately. Tell her Captain to launch all attack aircraft. Inform her Captain he can use Algeria's airspace now. Ah, here's the Carrier Independence, tell her to go to Alpha launch as well. The Iwo Jima's to send her helicopter force out against Libya. I want to hit Libya from all sides this time. I'm committing six AC 130 H Spectra gunships to this mess. Three will protect the strike force from the Independence, and the others will protect the strike force launched from the Nimitz.

These damn gunships will kill those drift bombs shits they used against the pilots of the YF 23 flight. Any word on the missing downed pilot yet, dammit?"

When no one answered, Commander Owens continued with his orders to his people. "I want four EC Compass Calls up. Every bit of their damn communications are to be scrambled and knocked right out of the fucking air on the damn Libyans. I don't want Libya to have FM, AM or even Microwave communication capabilities any longer, mister. I even want the damn TV and telephone communications knocked out also. Order the Nighthawks up. Their targets are to be all bridges, roads and communication centers, as well as all military bases inside Libya. The first hours of this damn operation should be a target rich environment, so let's make bombs count for the most damage as possible against our damn enemy. The F 117s did it for us in Iraq, so now they can do it in Libya and Chad. Is Colonel Campanelli back with his Command yet?"

"Yes sir, the Colonel reported he was back at the base at this time, Commander Owens Sir." Was the call from another seaman stationed inside the CIC Chamber.

"Good, get him on the squawk box. I wanna pitch a bitch at him." Commander Owens yelled.

Seconds later, the Colonel was on the radio speaking with his Commanding Officer.

"Good to hear your voice again Colonel Campanelli Sir. It looks like you done it for us with the damn Egyptians, sir. Egypt's out of the war as of this time sir, and I want you to attack the Libyan troops operating in Chad. Libya's currently hitting Algeria, it's a two front war for them fools now, the damn asses will never learn. Break out and push the fucking Libyans back to Libya. I have the Carriers going in an all out launch, Colonel. I'm giving you the call, use your troops well, sir. It's your game to win sir. Go and get the bastards, Colonel Campanelli."

"Will do as ordered Commander Owens Sir." The excited Colonel replied as the radio went dead from the other end. He called his officers to his command hut and held his briefing. "Gentlemen, you know me, but in case there happens to be someone who don't, I'm Colonel Edward Campanelli, and I'm the man here." His introduction was more than enough to silence the last conversations still filling the briefing room when he first entered the room.

"A warning to all of you gathered inside the Command Hut. I'm the one you have to fucking worry about here, not those sorry ass sonsofbitches wearing them damn bathrobes, and aiming their fucking weapons at you people, dammit."

Laughter instantly swept through the meeting room.

The Colonel grinned confidently, even though his thoughts were with the pending invasion. He held up his hand and the laughter quickly subsided. "Enough." He growled and silence was instantly restored as he began issuing his orders. "Listen up people, this is important so let's get things under way. First off, the Marine's objective here is speed. Speed and shock. The Marines will be our forward or raiding parties for this operation. They're too quickly close in on any enemy lines, and force a breakthrough at a number of different points of positions. Here, here, here, here and here marked on your funny papers (maps), people."

Campanelli pointed to the six locations printed on his map as he added to his words. "These breakthroughs will prevent the enemy from reinforcing their lines and closing the gaps on us. You men are going to maintain a single focus until you reach the rear defenses in the Chad city of Abeche, and cut off as many Libyan seasoned troops between the Marine and Army forces. Remember, a soldier's duty is to wage war. Total, all out, devastating, savage war. If we forget this for a second, hesitate, or show the enemy forces mercy, it could stop our momentum and cost us the damn war. You're cleared to shoot anyone who even looks at you the wrong way.

"This is no Viet Nam here by any meaning of the words gentlemen. There is one helluva an enemy Army out there who is hell bent on doing everything in their power to try and stop your forward progress in this mess. Any tanks or troops you come across will be hostile in nature unless identified otherwise. Chad's air, armor and ground forces are completely destroyed, so take it for granted any troops you happen across in that nation will be enemy, and you'll act accordingly against them. A word to the wise gentlemen and ladies, every bad thing God has placed on the face of this earth, is gathered in these damn jungles we'll soon be invading.

"Snakes, lions, dogs, the list goes on, so be extremely careful out there. Getting back to the attack, yeah, I know before any of you birds bring it up to my fucking attention. Civilians. Yes civilians, none combatants, shit happens targets will be involved in most of the engagements we'll soon be involved with, they always are. Keep reminding yourselves of your duty and orders and continue your advance. You have to try avoiding killing the none combatants as best you can but you cannot allow them to stop your actions that might endanger you or fellow troops.

"If you need an artillery response in a certain sector of your area of responsibility, and civilians are thought to be present, you're going to have to bite the bullet and call it in no matter the results. Your first responsibilities is to your troops and this operation. You need troops to fight and stop these nuts, and you can't do it with civilians. If it makes it any easier for you people to carry out your orders. Remember this, the enemy's slaughtering the civilian population of Chad by the hundreds, maybe even thousands as we speak. As ironic as this might sound to you, the faster we keep moving, the more civilian lives we'll save.

"Now that's been discussed, I'll not speak of it again, you people will have to handle this situation the best way you can as it crops up in your area of responsibility plain and simple. Your Gods see what is happening, and they'll forgive you for any actions you will have to result to stop the damn slaughter of the civilians of this poor nation. We're fighting a just war here. Anyone who thinks this might get to him or her and you people might not be able to issue orders that might cost civilian lives, speak up now and I'll have you replaced immediately."

No hands went up, and no one spoke out from the gathered soldiers.

"Good, that's it for this subject then. Now people, the first wave of Marines are to keep moving as fast as they possibly can, heading directly for the enemies rear defenses and supply depots and supply lines, stopping long enough to destroy anything they can't be easily out maneuver or overrun by them. Once the Marines are in the enemy rear flanks, their orders are to destroy all enemy artillery units, food, water and military and fuel supplies, and any other enemy support troops they happen across which should be made up of their lesser fighting troops and support units than are manning the front lines at this time.

"It's the Army's orders to stand and fight the bulk of the enemy troops on the Libyan lines until the Marines actions in the rear takes effect on the front line enemy troops and their will to continue fighting. Remember gentlemen, speed. Another reason speed is so important to this damn operation is, I want as many of our troops invading behind the enemy's lines to keep the nuclear question from becoming an attractive option for the lousy Libyan Command to consider as an option. We don't want to have happen here, what happened to Israel and Iraq. We're not positive the Libyan's have the damn bomb, but it's a good bet they do, dammit.

"So I feel if we have enough of our troops behind their fucking lines, the damn fools would be less apt to resorting to the use of these weapons of mass destruction, if it means destroying their own stinking armies to get at ours. The Army will dig out those enemy forces the Marines left behind, so don't stop unless you get bogged down, and if you do get bogged down any, call in. and I'll immediately sent air out to annihilate any of your fucking obstacles blocking your forward progress on the battlefield, dammit. Base Sentry's our assembly area for all American, British, French and Russian forces involved in this damn war.

"Major Hawkins, here is where your fly jockeys come in to play in this mess. The area of Chad and Libya's land surface has been sliced up into thousands of neat, little Kill Boxes. You have a copy of the block identification numbers, so your pilots won't have any trouble identifying the fucking attack coordinates once issued to the pilots. This tactic was developed during the damn Desert Storm action, and it worked rather well there. That's why we're going to rely on the same system here, but with one change mind you. The kill box grid will be a fifteen square mile block, but here we'll assign two fighter aircraft to each box instead of one as before.

"Major Hawkins, your aircraft are going to be called into a certain section. Will you men pay close attention here dammit, this is important and if you're fucking around back there, then you're not paying attention to my orders! Major as I was saying before I was interrupted by those assholes, your aircraft will be called into these boxes of death as needed. Their job is to destroy any and all enemy targets they come across. Ground forces will have communications with your aircraft at all times, and the ground forces will direct the aircraft to the targets that need sterilization. After the aircraft have destroyed the targets, the pilots be free to roam their block and hunt at will. Make fucking certain your fly boys don't hit any of my troops. Major, when it comes to your bombers, they'll work the same grid pattern with one difference.

"Each bombing block will be cut into fifteen neat little one mile square blocks, and there'll be four bombers assigned to each one section of that block. Your bombers will do a checker board pattern of bombing if called upon to assist any of our troops on the ground, sir. One will do blocks one, three, five and seven, while the second aircraft patrols two, four, six and eight and so on. This way, if the enemy tries to jump in a grid the first bomber missed, the second bomber will pick up the lousy bastards and do them in. Remember people, any ground unit can draw from air cover any time needed, and your fly jocks better be there and respond when needed, Major. You got it sir?" He warned and added at the same time. "I don't want any swinging dicks or bouncing tits cut off from air support because he or she's from a different service."

"Aye, aye sir." Was the response from all the soldiers gathered at the meeting.

"You bet you fucking ass it's, aye, aye, people." He hissed back at the soldiers

Some nervous laughter broke out over his last remark.

The Colonel allowed the laughter for a moment, and then cut it off by going on with his orders to his troops. "We have to attack any and all enemy intelligence systems unilaterally. Without eyes on the battlefield, the fucking enemy are blind and shit. Captain Williams Sir, you're to employ the Fifth Air Cavalry, sir. This is your job mister, get the Apaches up and attack enemy communication, or spotters' positions. Use everything at your Command to accomplish this order, I'll give you the 74th "C" squadron if needed, sir. You can store the extra aircraft in your arsenal, they're being held in reserve so use them wisely, sir.

"Captain White's Command is going to consist of the 3rd, 5th, 9th and 12th Marine Divisions, sir. You'll Command this entire operation from my fucking helicopter command center which will be hovering over the battlefield at all times, Captain. The Marines are going to spearhead the opening attack against the Libyan forces, backed by columns of tanks, squads of helicopters, artillery units and any fighter aircraft they need employed. The 10th, 16th, 19th, and the 22nd Marine battalions will head up the second wave of attack, led by Captain Joseph Salsiccia hiding in the corner over there. I see your fucking ass hiding over there mister."

Everyone attending the military briefing room looked to the Captain and then laughed at him as most of them nodded towards the grinning Captain.

"Army units from Red One's First Army with a joint effort from the 1st, 5th 7th Air Cavalry units will coincide the attacks with the Marines as back and mop up operation forces. Their helicopters will lend support to the Marines. If a call comes in from any unit, Marine or Army, I want to hear two fucking air units requesting permission to lend a hand, is that clear? I don't want anyone's ass caught hanging out in the open unprotected for any length of time, dammit. We're all American troops whether they be Marines or Army, and will be supported by either Marine or Army helicopter cover, period. The Apache and Super Cobra or Snake helicopters are going to coordinate their support operations with the Bell OH-58 Kiowa helicopter, nick named 'The Black Eye' for those who aren't very familiar with this system, I'll explain some. The Kiowa has a massive sight mounted above the main rotor hub and the blades to the Jesus bolt.

"This sight finds and points any enemy targets to our helicopters or artillery units. The Bell helicopter system employs infrared, laser and real time television optics to aim their weapons at the stinking bad guys. The eye can find any fucking enemy targets, and yet remain safe from attack by hiding the body of the helicopter below a mountain ridge, in a tree line, or behind a stinking building, whatever cover the pilot can find to protect his airframe. Then she allows the sight optics to stick above her hiding place, and light up the enemy targets for our attack.

"I don't want any fucking crying about support like in the damn Desert Storm War witnessed. Captains Mendoza, White, any Officer who can't get the job done when we need it done, is to be immediately replaced. Even if you have to use a noncom to replace the damn Officer, if he or she's willing to carry out whatever is asked of him or her. Here is the attack plan people." Colonel Edward Campanelli said as he quickly spread out a map of the area to be attacked.

"One more thing John. Your advance units can draw any extra units they might need at any given time, from the second or back up attack units being held in reserve for this operation. Especially to move the wounded back to the rear area for medical care. I don't want your men stopping their advance for any fucking reason, sir. You got that Mr. White?"

"Yes sir loud and clear sir." The Captain replied to his Commanding Officer confidently.

"Good, see to it then, Captain. Well that's about all I have for you people, any questions, ask them now." He looked around the gathering and then announced. "Yeah, the Captain with his hand up. I don't recognize you, but what's your question quickly, sir?"

"Yes sir, my name's Captain Billy Houston Sir, I'm with the 7th sir."

The Colonel cut him off and asked the man. "Is there any relation to Sam Houston, mister?"

This remark caused everyone in the meeting to laugh as they stared at the soldier.

"Sorry sir, no such luck Colonel. Sir, my question is as follows sir. Does Command have any idea what we're coming up against in terms of enemy troop strengths and equipment, sir?"

"Yes, John's gonna fill you people in on those statistical numbers, but since you asked, sir. We figure the enemy has somewhere in the vicinity of five to seven hundred and fifty thousand troops in the field. We estimate the enemy have up to three thousand seven hundred tanks, with two thousand artillery pieces. The aircraft is put at over a thousand fighters, and two hundred Mi 24 Hind attack helicopters, but our fighters will cut those figures down quite a bit before we go in action against the enemy forces. Well, that's about it for me for the time being. Captain White, I'll leave you to answer any further questions the troops have and finish up for me, sir. Thank you gentlemen and ladies, that's all I have for now. Good luck people." He said as he saluted the gathering of officers and then left the meeting.

The meeting broke up quickly, as the officers and junior officers hurriedly folded up their maps, and placed their notes in their leather carrying pouches and secured the information they were informed about over the meeting. Many conversations started as the Colonel left the smoke filled briefing room after turning the control of the officers over to Captain White. He laughed as he heard John already screaming at his captive audience.

Campanelli did not get far before he glanced over his shoulder and noticed a number of helicopters lifting off, and staff cars leaving at speed, carrying the officers to their troops to prepare for tomorrow's opening attack. He thought John finished up sooner than expected, and he dismissed the other officers. He entered his quarters only to find a technician working on his computer. The man started talking when he saw the Colonel enter his quarters.

"Okay sir, I really need to know what you did to it in order to start my damn repairs on the damn thing, sir." The technician asked as he stared at the Colonel's damaged computer.

Colonel Campanelli looked at the engineer and sort of smiled as he offered in a sheepish tone of voice. "Emergency repair order number one."

"Oh gees sir, you didn't go and kick the damn thing on me again, didja sir? Sir, you can't go kicking the damn thing around all the time and then expect it to keep working for ya, sir. You gotta treat her with a little love sir." The technician wailed at his Commanding Officer.

He smiled again as he smirked at the upset technician. "I don't expect the damn thing to keep working for me, mister. That's why I have you on board my fucking base, mister. How soon before you get the damn thing back on line for me son?"

"Ten minutes at the most I believe sir. Colonel Campanelli Sir, I'm going to get you a kick board so you lay off of my damn computer some, sir."

"I'd lay off of the damn thing if it was a little easier to operate son." The Colonel retorted.

LIBYA

The Libyan Ambassador Kamal placed a quick call to his operatives working in the nation of Somalia, he informed them the American planes attacked his forces destroying the Chad city of Abeche. Ambassador Kamal told his operative to launch the attack against the American warships stationed off the coast of Somalia in the Red Sea.

Alarms instantly went off all over the Aircraft Carrier Roosevelt, as excited sailors ran for their battle stations. Over the loud speaker a voice screamed at the sailors. "General Quarters, General Quarters. All hands man battle stations. We are under attack by four fast moving surface craft heading for the Strike Force. General Quarters. This is not a drill, all hands man your battle stations. All fire control personnel, man your posts on E, K and R decks."

Commander Owens looked to the officer in charge of the threat board and asked him in a concerned tone of voice. "Whatdaya have for me son?"

"Commander Owens Sir, radar reported picking up four fast moving small speed boats heading in our direction, sir. They're presently fourteen miles out and heading directly at us at thirty five knots, sir." The officer's voice was high from fear and concern.

"Alert Cardinal Flight Leader to intercept said targets for us. Launch Ready Flight. Instruct them to join with Cardinal Flight in case they have to attack any enemy surface vessels coming at us. Move two of the damn big boy destroyers between us and the damn speed boats, mister."

The alarms continued to wail its mind disturbing screech inside the CIC chamber, as the smoke filled room was instantly bathed in the dull red lights, which warned everyone on board the massive ship that they were under attack by enemy forces.

"Jesus H. Christ, will someone shut down those fucking alarms for Pete's sake. How the hell does anyone expect me to think, or issue fucking orders if no one can hear me over that damn racket, and get me some real lights on in here dammit, so I can see what the hell I'm doing in here for Christ sake and miracles." The Commander growled at anyone who could hear him complain inside the CIC Command Center.

The alarms went off as the regular lighting was placed back on line in the CIC Chamber.

"Cardinal Leader, you're instructed to head for coordinates, Zero, One, Three, Three. We have four inbound surface ships, intent, unknown at this time, but believed to be aggressive in nature. You're instructed to buzz said ships, in an effort to turn them away from the Fleet. They're thirteen miles out and heading for the command ship, if they break the Eight Mile Red Zone, you're instructed to attack and destroy said surface craft on your own call, Cardinal Leader."

"Cardinal Leader. Acknowledged, leaving Air Cap area to intercept the surface ships. Over."

"Roger that. Conn, launch Ready Able Flight and inform the Flight Commander they're to link up with Cardinal Flight and intercept said surface craft. Over."

A second later, two usually land based F-15 Eagles shot off from the bow of the massive flight deck of the Roosevelt and streaked towards the clouds.

Commander Owens listened to the communications between all four of the early alert pilots.

"Ready Able Leader to Cardinal Flight Leader. We're on your six for backup sir. Over."

"Ready Able Leader, glad to have you on board and protecting my stinking tail feathers, sir. I have four small inbound surface targets locked on, on my forward radar sweep sir. Over."

Ninety five seconds later, Cardinal Flight Leader and Sparrow were circling over the four incoming surface craft.

"Cardinal Leader to Safe House. I see four, twenty foot speed boats, I repeat, four speed boats. Two have tripod mounted 60 mike mike machine guns mounted on board the bow of the small craft, sir. The other two surface boats have large boxes stacked on their deck. When the boats saw us approaching them they immediately scrambled and headed off in different directions, but they have since corrected and straightened out their course, and are once again heading directly for the Task Force. Over."

"Safe House to Cardinal Flight Leader." Commander Owens growled in the radio as he nearly roared into the mike. "Buzz the lousy sonofbitches once. Shake them up some Cardinal Flight Leader. Don't fire on them lousy bastards unless they fire on your aircraft first, or they break through the Red Zone of the Carrier security defenses, sir. Over."

"Roger that last as received Safe House. Am going to let them know I'm pissed off at them sir and see how they react to my being pissed off at them, sir. Over."

Cardinal Flight Leader and Sparrow Flight trailer did a low flyover, breaking the sound barrier directly right over the four small speeding water craft. The boats reacted quickly to this new threat from the American warplanes flying over them. Two of the smaller boats opened fire with their 60 mm machine guns on the passing American warplanes.

"Holy shit. The stupid bastards opened fire on us, dammit. Sparrow, get up in the fucking clouds for cover. We'll regroup at three thousand feet." The two aircraft shot into the clouds.

Commander Owens heard his aircraft came under attack, and he immediately gave the order for the aircraft to arm their weapons. But he told the radio operator to inform the pilots to hold their fire on the surface contacts, until they knew for certain what the inbound boats was up to.

"Safe House to Cardinal Flight Leader. You're cleared to arm and lock on, but hold your fire until further ordered. Let's see if they got the message and they have turn around sir. Over."

Commander Owens called over his shoulder to another sailor working inside the CIC of the Roosevelt. "Threat, how far out are the damn surface boats, and what is their direction sir?"

"Nine miles out and still coming directly at us at this time, sir. The destroyers are taking up position between us and them as a defensive protection for the Carrier, sir."

"Shit, I wish we had a lot more water out here dammit, I don't like being so close to fucking land with my ship. Dammit, we're out of fucking time and patience, tell Cardinal Flight Leader to splash the damn targets. I say again. Splash the targets."

Cardinal Flight Leader heard the order from the Commander and grumbled. "It's about fucking time. Sparrow, pick out a target for yourself sir. We're going after the two with machine guns mounted on them. Able Leader. You got the ones with the boxes. Good hunting sir. Over."

"Roger that last as received. Am starting bombing runs over the targets as of now sir. Over."

Cardinal Leader watched the two Eagle aircraft arch down, and then head right for the boats then he and Sparrow did their own dive on their ordered targets. Immediately, the small speed boats Cardinal Leader and Sparrow were diving on, opened fire on the attacking aircraft as they suddenly veered off in different directions on the surface of the water.

Cardinal Flight Leader lit up the small water craft with his radar, and then he fired a Harpoon missile at his leading target. And within heartbeat later, the fast surface craft exploded. Sparrow hit his target. Then, the two aircraft did a victory roll over their two kills.

Ready Able Flight Leader along with the second aircraft Able Two opened fire on the unarmed boats with their cannons. Instantly, one of the small water crafts exploded with the thunder equal to the forces of an overdue thunder storm and disintegrated in a cloud of debris.

Able Flight Leader suddenly veered up and off to his right side in order to avoid the powerful force of the blast, and then he bitched in his radio at the same time. "Dammit, what the fuck did them sonofabitches have on board that damn thing man?" He said as secondary, thunderous explosions followed the first one.

Able Two opened fire on the last surface craft still heading directly for the command ship of the fleet. It too erupted into a massive explosion and clouds of flames and smoke.

The three pilots informed Cardinal Leader of their kills and he immediately reported to his command. "Cardinal Flight Leader to Safe House. Splash four sir. I repeat. Splash four. Secondary explosions detected. Looks like the nasties were up to no good here sir. Over."

"Roger that. You did good, real good sir. Cardinal Flight Leader, you and Sparrow Flight are ordered to deck down on the Carrier. Able Flight Leader and Two are instructed to replace you as air cover over the task force. I'm dispatching an A 7 refueler to top off your fuel tanks, sir. I want to see you two pilots as soon as you are deck down. Well done sir."

"Acknowledged my last orders as received and will comply Safe House. Over."

Commander Owens listened as Cardinal Flight Leader quickly informed Ready Able, he was to replace him as the ready air cap stationed over the carrier. Then he looked to the threat board officer and he reported. "Sir, the board is clear, nothing out there at this time sir."

He leaned back in his chair and reached in his pocket and pulled out his last, bent and sweat soaked cigar as he moaned. "I had all I'm gonna fucking take from these lousy asses. Back her off another twenty four miles from shore. Put her rear in the shipping lane, and warn off any other civilian shipping until further notice, the Gulf of Aden and the Red Sea's closed to all commercial shipping. Any ship entering the fifty mile defensive zone no matter what her origin, will be fired on first, and then questioned. I'll not lose a ship because we were waiting for a ship to ID herself to us. Put it on the radio, and I don't give a shit whose nose gets bent outta fucking shape by the last order." The Commander left the CIC for his stateroom.

When Cardinal Leader landed, the pilot headed for the stateroom. He banged on the door.

"Yeah, come on in Commander. Ah Chet, come in and sit, smoke if you like. Coffee if you need a cup, sir?" Owens offered and then asked as he nodded towards the coffee pot. "So, how was it up there mister? I'm please you got all four of the nasties."

"Commander Owens Sir, the nasties were packing one helluva shitload of explosives on those four damn boats, sir. Plastic explosive I bet ya sir, it was some kind of explosion, followed by a few extra pops, sir. Cannon fire from our aircraft set the mess off, or they might have set it off themselves once they saw us closing in on them, sir. Who knows, who the hell really cares how it popped off, as long as it popped off and killed them before they could hurt the Task Force, sir. The damn bastards would've done a helluva lot of damage to our shipping if they popped them damn things off alongside one of our ships, sir. A good thing they decided to fire at us first, Commander. Sir, what would you have ordered if they didn't fire on us first, sir?"

"I would've had you buzz them until they did act against us first, young man. The question is academic now, because they would've entered the Red Zone by the time you were set to buzz them for a second time, Chet. Whatdaya think I sent you two pilots out there for. Hell, I knew if anyone could provoke a fucking attack, you surely could mister."

"Commander Owens Sir, I don't know how to take that last remark from you sir." He said as he joined the Commander in quick laugh over the Commander's comment.

"Chet, you think this was a damn suicide mission these four assholes were out on, or was it just a fucking probe of our defenses and intentions, sir?"

"It was a suicide mission without a doubt sir. They were heading right for the ship. They knew what they were doing sir. These A rabs are nuts, suicide opens the gates of Paradise for them."

Owens smiled at his pilot as he said. "Err... It's good for us they couldn't control themselves when you buzzed the lousy bastards. I'm damn glad they made the first move against us my friend. You saved me a hell of a lot of paperwork on this one sir. There was no way they were going to get passed the damn destroyer defenses though. Chet, I want to increase the ready air cap over the entire Task Force. Put another two aircraft up at all times, with two more resting on the catapults ready for immediate launch. I ordered the Task Force to back off another twenty five miles from shore, to give us more time to react in case these assholes try another attack on us again. These damn A rabs are going to learn they should've stayed perched on their damn camels and never should've challenged the might of the United States."

"Sir, my pilots are really strung out. Can I pull a few extra pilots from the Strike Force, sir?"

"You gotta be shitting me mister. I need every pilot I have. You have to get by with what you have. I'll see if I can draft a couple of pilots from the Constellation. She's in the least dangerous area that's the best I can do for you. Do me a favor and get another set of aircraft up, okay sir?"

"Yes Sir Commander Owens Sir." He said without much enthusiasm in his tone.

"You're dismissed sir and thanks again Chet. You did real well up there for me son."

THE CHAD, SUDAN BORDER

At exactly Zero Six Hundred Hours on October 8th, 1996, artillery from the 7th battalion, 13th artillery opened fire on the well dug in enemy Libyan lines. The sun was not quite up, and the darkness seemed to add to the destructive power of the powerful shells hitting the ground. Three hundred pieces of artillery opened fire, as cannons from the 3rd Marine Division joined in. Off in the far distance, the ground actually turned into a mass of flying earth, flames and crumbling trees, as body parts and shell pieces rained down on the heads of the entrenched Libyan soldiers. Over one hundred helicopters joined this massive attack, as Apache fast attack helicopter Hellfire missiles found the dug in enemy tanks and artillery pieces, and destroyed them where they lay.

Combined American, English, French and Russian aircraft streaked through the brightening sky, delivering their own harbingers of death to the enemy below, as the bombs fell from planes to high to even be seen clearly by the naked eye. B 52s moved in next, dropping tons of dumb bombs on the Libyan fortifications and troops. Smart bombs were dropped from the nearly invisible F and X 117s, as the B 52 dumb bombs were dropped to kill just soldiers and military equipment, and cause mass confusion in the enemy lines. Two bombers were hit by lucky shots from Russian made SAM missiles launched by the Libyan defenders at the attackers.

THE COMMAND BUNKER IN LIBYA

The well aged Russian technicians were tracking a wing of American and French attacking aircraft, just as they entered the air space of Algeria, and they sent up two hundred of the drift bombs to intercept the incoming planes. This time, the American orbiting reconnaissance platforms knew what to watch for, and they immediately informed CIC they detected the small tell tale puffs of smoke the drift bombs emitted when they were fired off from the ground.

The launch was detected by the satellites, and CIC ordered a pair of AC 130 H gunships from the First Special Operations Air Wing to intercept the new weapons. Well before the fighter aircraft and bombers reached the area containing the drift bombs. The two gunships easily picked up and then opened fire on the multiple targets. The horrendous fire power from the two on board 20 mm Vulcan Rotary Cannons, destroyed all the drift bombs in one attack.

One of the Bluebird satellites monitoring the area of the conflict, sent a Flash message to CIC informing Command it detected three plumes from missiles fired towards the ships stationed in the Mediterranean. The threat computers inside the CIC picked up the missile plumes when attention was called to them. It was determined to be three supersonic missiles fired at the American warships stationed in the Mediterranean.

In seconds, all communications with the Aircraft Carrier Independence were lost as the three missiles ripped into her metal frame. Calls flooded in from the support ships reporting the Independence exploded, and no radar picked up the inbound sea skimming missiles. The missiles traveled a few feet above wave height to hit the ship without radar detection.

One of the pilots successfully got his plane off the flight deck of the crippled Independence just moments before she was hit. Horrified, the pilot watched as bellowing smoke and roaring flames came from his stricken ship, as he circled the Independence, carrying out his last orders to marshal off of the ship's fantail. The pilot stared in stunned disbelief as the super structure of his mighty ship suddenly exploded from below, causing the Independence to list heavily to her starboard side. Flames leaping up from the remains of the super structure spread out quickly across the entire ship as she burned unchecked.

The warplanes still sitting on the massive flight deck loaded with missiles and shells, caused secondary explosions on flight deck of the

Carrier, as the lapping flames touched them, racking the full length of the Independence. Flames, smoke, pieces of planes, the ship and body parts went flying into the air. The Independence was ripping herself apart from mid ship outwards.

The pilot was joined by the few other planes that successfully got off the Independence before she was hit by the enemy missile. His radio came to life and he was instructed to carry out orders to head for Base Sentry, and then take orders from command there. "Good luck," were the last words he heard as he headed out with one last glance towards the Independence. He watched as the great ship shook and shuddered from more of the follow on explosions on and below deck. He cursed as he aimed his aircraft towards Libya and his revenge.

The Commander turned his wrath loose on a Seaman who had the misfortune to be standing at attention in his field of vision. "What's this fucking shit out there mister? Are you telling me that both our damn anti missile defense systems were shut fucking down on the Independence at the same damn time, buster? I find this rather hard to fucking believe mister. Heads are going to roll for this one, that I can promise you buster. Why the fuck did we spend so much money developing these damn defensive systems, the Hard Rock and Starlight systems, if these damn assholes with ears leave the god damn things shut down during hostilities, dammit? Don't those asses know we're at fucking war, man? God damn this shit any how."

Owens turned red as he stopped yelling long enough for him to catch his breath.

"Commander Owens Sir," An officer suddenly interrupted his raging Commanding Officer as he reported to him. "The Independence was scheduled for a refit next month at the end of her tour in the Mediterranean, sir. But when this war broke out, her orders were changed due to demand for her aircraft in the field of battle, and her best defense against a possible missile attack against the ship were her two Phalanx systems, as you well know sir. The two CIWS (close in weapons systems) operate at a maximum range of just two Kilometers to zero feet, sir. The stations were situated one each on her bow and her stern of the ship, sir."

"Shit, shit, shit." Owens growled angrily as he demanded to know what kind of missile was fired at, and had hit the Independence. He checked his pocket for another cigar.

After intensely analyzing the latest photos coming in from the satellites, it was determined it was a French made ANS missiles that struck the Independence about mid-ship, and its supersonic speed instantly rendered the missiles all but invisible to the ship's usual detection systems. The Commander cursed the French for selling the damn missiles to the Libyans.

There was a deafening hush clouding over the entire CIC Chamber as the horror of the loss of the Aircraft Carrier Independence was realized. A second officer, this time from the Carrier Roosevelt, contacted the few aircraft that successfully got off the deck of the dead ship and the ready air crap aircraft, and informed them their IFF (Identify Friend or Foe) units were to be switched over to the shade blue, for this attack on Libyan military targets.

THE SUDAN, CHAD BORDER

An eerie silence was almost thick enough to be touched by the hands of the American soldiers hiding in the heavy bush on the very edge of the jungle, bordering Chad from the Sudan side of the border. Moments before the invasion of the nation of Chad from the Sudan was to take place. This sudden silence was more disturbing than sound to the charged up and excited troops. Missing was all the shrillness from the wild animal's cries, or the high pitch, lyrical songs of the bird population, cutting through this odd, thick, stillness which always seemed to fall over the battlefield just before an attack was to take place between the two warring sides.

Radio chatter started as the Captain listened in on the many conversations taking place now, as the troops prepared for the opening attack on the dug in enemy forces.

"Move Iron Hat Two Seven over some seventy five yards to help out with the FnG's (fucking new guys) of Lion Company at A-Four, Four, Three, near the frontline immediately. They're going to need all the extra help they can possible get when the shooting starts, sir."

"Iron Hat Two, Seven. Move to reference A-Four, Four, Three over seventy five yards to lend extra support to Marine Company Lion Three. Over."

"Iron Hat Two, Seven to Command. That's a Roger, hauling ass now sir. Iron Hat out."

"Iron Hat this is Lion Company. Bill this is Carl, glad to have you on board. I feel we're going to need the extra help. How's your wife old buddy?" The young and green Marine Lieutenant asked as he tried to use the conversation to help calm down his nerves a little.

"Hey stupid, that's a fucking real world question you asked, buster. I won't answer personal questions over the fucking open net asshole. Stick to orders and shut up, asshole."

Most disturbing to the Allied soldiers prepared for attack were the insects. Almost as if they knew of the up coming events, their constant buzzing, whirring, clicking, chirpings and biting was muffled and far off in the distance now, well out of harm's way. The Captain ducked his head down, actually forcing his face into the soft sand as the huge 155 Howitzer cannons suddenly opened fire as one on the entrenched Libyan soldier's lines five hundred yards before them. The bone jarring recoil from the massive cannons shook the ground on which the Captain was hugging the earth for dear life. He actually had to force himself to look up as three formations of American fighter aircraft streaked by through the morning sky overhead, all heading for the enemy troops stationed inside the nation of Chad.

"Iron Hat to Hot Shot. I need an immediate fire mission of HE (High Explosive) and Wily Pete (White Phosphorus)to dig out the enemy forces blocking my fucking advance, Hot Shot. My funny book lists map reference as Delta, Foxtrot, Ready, Ready Foxtrot, Tango. Say back."

"Iron Hat, this is Hot Shot. Am aiming High Explosive and White Phosphorus rounds at said coordinates of Delta, Foxtrot, Ready, Ready Foxtrot, Tango, correct as repeated? Over."

"Roger that. Correct as repeated. Iron Hat out." The soldier replied in the radio.

"On the way Iron Hat. Out of the tube." The artillery rounds landed in the area requested.

"Hot Shot this is Iron Hat again. Listen up. Correction, up fifty, left twenty. Fire for effect."

"Roger that. That's up fifty, left twenty, correct? Am firing for effect this time out. Out."

"Roger that, correct as stated. Fire for effect. Keep it coming until I call you off target. Over."

The artillery rounds were corrected, and they were now coming in hot and heavy on target.

A voice came over the radio. "Man, art's (artillery) really putting the bang on the bastards."

The dark horizon flashed an angry bright yellow from countless artillery rounds exploding. Soon, fires lit up the tree line in a dreadful light, adding to the fears of the American soldiers about to go into combat against a yet unseen enemy force.

"Hot Shot this is Dragon. We have a number of enemy troops inside our fucking perimeter lines. Request illumination rounds fired off at Delta, Delta, Ex-ray, Three, One, Three. Over."

"Roger that, Delta, Delta, Ex-ray, Three, One, Three is target area. Bright Light's on the way, Dragon. Stay low, hell's on the way to visit your area, Dragon."

Captain Salsiccia saw the Star Burst rounds exploding two hundred feet in the air, lighting up the sky and ground below, not to far to his left. More artillery rounds landed nearby the troops.

Again, Captain Salsiccia was forced to hunker down as he said a silent pray as he muttered more to himself than anyone within ear shot of him. "If only we damn humans were as smart as these dumb animals are, and we knew enough to leave the damn area before the fighting started. Then no one would have to die on this hot, stinking fucking morning in hell."

The noise of war was deafening, as it rattled the very fillings in his teeth. The Captain looked around him in the hastily dug, shallow foxholes, at the many scared faces of the young soldiers he could see in the brightening morning, and shook his head sadly as he mumbled. "I have to apologize to your mothers, because so many of you are going to die in this fucking jungle today. So damn far away from home." For some reason, Captain Salsiccia was feeling a little sorry for himself, his thoughts were suddenly interrupted by more artillery firing off.

A soldier suddenly yelled out at the top of his lungs. "Incoming! I got incoming coming in."

This remark caused an instant argument between the soldier, and his foxhole buddy.

"What the hell do you mean incoming, you asshole you. That was outgoing if I ever heard outgoing, stupid. Didn't you pay any fricking attention in class you stupid dip stick you?"

"Bullshit man. That was incoming if I have ever heard incoming man."

A second later while the kids continued to argue with each other, there was an explosion forty feet behind them. Both men stopped fighting and looked at one another, and then they both yelled in unison. "Incoming." And the two soldiers ducked down in their shallow pit. There, they began arguing with each other again.

"Who is the asshole now, asshole? I told you they were incoming rounds didn't I man?"

"Shut up stupid! It was a lucky guess on your fucking part man, that's all it was man."

"Lucky guess my stinking ass buddy. I told you it was incoming rounds coming in on..."

Captain Salsiccia had enough and put a quick end to the bickering. "You two shitbirds, put a fucking lid on it before I kick ya in the ass to hell and back." The angry Captain knew many of his people were going to die, but he learned a long time ago not to allow the deaths to effect him. He spent half his life trying to make himself believe his troops were assets to be cherished when possible, but sent to their slaughter when necessary.

All the Marines hunkered down and they went back to listening to the cruel sounds of war.

The Captain ran over his orders in his mind as the ground shook under him again. He drew in a breath, put his whistle in his mouth and then he gave three loud, ear splitting blasts on it, and then he yelled out to his troops. "Okay people, that's our cue to go to work, good luck. Watch out for any man traps setup against us out there." As he moved out, he saw three Altair RPVs propeller driven flying wing type, pilotless drones sent out over the battlefield. It contained real time television and data fed back and down link systems on board it.

ABECHE, CHAD

The original Libyan plan of attack scheduled against the Chad city of Abeche as their assembly and jump off point in their plans to attack against the Sudan and American military base. Hundreds of Libyan, Algerian and Nigerian tanks, artillery and armor, along with thousands of reserve troops, gathered in the rubble of Abeche, waiting for orders to advance against their enemy. The Libyan troops were told that the American forces would never risk their lives and equipment for the Sudanese or Chad people. The American presence in this region was being classified as defense purposes only, and a possible deterrent to Libyan's attack against the Sudan. The Libyan command preached this belief to their foolish soldiers. But now the American Marines were attacking and on the offensive against their troops, the morale of the Libyan soldiers was down, and this put their defense lines in disarray and unorganized.

AMERICAN FORCES ATTACKING FROM THE SUDAN

American men and women now soldiers soon to be baptized by the blood of war, quickly moved out as one. Their war paint set in place, screaming as they jumped to their feet and then they charged wildly at the Libyan lines as a fighting, well trained unit of soldiers.

The excited Captain Salsiccia yelled out in a commanding voice. "Okay people let's saddle up, let's haul fucking ass, move out. Move, move, move it. It's time to get bloody on this one. Get your asses up and in fricking gear and get at the fucking enemy, dammit!"

As Captain Salsiccia and his troops moved out, his mind wandered to his men, the Ranger's Delta unit of thirty seven highly trained men and women he sent to Chad three weeks earlier for covert actions to sabotage the major bridges, communications and supply lines of the enemy troops. His Rangers checked in every night via special satellite hookup at Twenty Four Hundred Hours to receive further orders, and inform command of any possible enemy troop movements and strength they discovered during their covert actions. On the information the

Rangers had gathered, three wings of American warplanes started their attack this morning.

Throughout the three weeks the Rangers operated in Chad, the Captain was sure he heard explosions which credited them to the Rangers actions. He remembered the final orders he issued to the Rangers unit as they started on their mission towards Chad. The Captain ordered the Marines they had to keep their eyes open for any downed American pilots. They were to pick up and protect any flyers they came across. He shook his head as he mumbled. "War sure is hell."

Three separate Marine Units headed for the Libyan lines packed inside M113 Armored Carriers, M2 Bradley Fighting Machines, Lav 25 Canadian 25 mm cannon, and hundreds of HUMMVIE troop movers, and also moving out on foot for the enemy lines.

After a long run Salsiccia pulled up, out of breath and cursed himself for going it on foot, rather than riding inside one of the armored command tracks. He could tell his artillery was dominating the exchanges just by the sounds of his big guns. The still out of breath Captain had his radio operator running close by him. As he took his little breather, he listened in on more of the chatter going on over the field radio again between his troops.

American spotters were directing some tank movements and positioning artillery fire.

"Sergeant Mason, move the 5th mechanized unit over to that small tree line to your left. You're instructed to stop on this side of that small crest. I saw some enemy troop movements taking place near that dirt road, so keep your eyes open for any trouble, guys."

"Second Platoon, listen up. You're instructed to move your entire Unit just south of the dirt road ahead of you and take cover there and wait for further orders."

"Seventh Platoon, you're to cover the north end of the dirt road for Second Platoon."

A frantic voice cut in. "Fifth Mechanized, enemy tanks, I have enemy fricking tanks heading for the damn dirt road by your position. Three of them. Do you have them in sight yet?"

Cannon fire was the soldier's answer as Captain Salsiccia heard it coming over the open radio key and he tried to locate where this action was going down near him.

"For Christ sake, get the stinking mover before he gets away on us, dammit! Get the fucking mover, he getting away from your ass dammit! Waste his ass will ya man!"

"Calm down some soldier." Came over the radio, followed by even more cannon fire.

"You got'em. Seventh Platoon your unit is cleared to move out. Second Platoon, cover the Seventh's advance, and then follow and prepared to engage the enemy forces."

Another call came in from a second excited soldier. "We need many fucking anti tank weapons, or air support and we need it right now, dammit, now!"

A different voice cut in and bellowed at the talker over the radio hookup. "Okay soldier, this is control, calm down some, we got ya ass covered, buddy. Give me the exact coordinates you need hit son. Air's on the way your location but I need those coordinates first soldier. Over."

The Captain handed the radio operator the phone and ordered. "Let's go."

The soldier moved out to catch up with his company. Just as he started out, a command setup infantry fighting vehicle came up to him. The Captain and radioman jumped on board the track machine. Captain Joseph Salsiccia was glad for the lift, realizing how out of shape he was in. After a short ride, Salsiccia's track came up to where a firefight had taken place. The Captain ordered the driver to stop and he climbed out of the track. Now he knew why he chose to go on foot. He was in a Bradley, the M-3B1 altered to be a Command vehicle, equipped with computers and communications. The turret was moved to the front of the machine, and it had four hatches on top for the commander to stand and see what was happening outside it.

Just before he climbed out of the M-3B1, the gun erupted as the gunner fired at some enemy soldiers running towards the tree line. The acrid waste of cordite from the spent shells, added to the poisonous mixture of exhaust, and the sweat trapped inside the tightly closed track machine.

After the heavy firing had ended, he opened the hatch and jumped out of the track. The Captain was pleased to be out of the track, and able to stretch his legs for the moment. He took in huge mouthfuls of fresh air. The smell from the spent shells and carbon from the machine's diesel exhaust stuck to his face and sweat soaked uniform, making his stomach actually turn on him. Suddenly, the Captain yearned for a steaming hot bath, to wash away the terrible smell of battle and death coating his body. The landscape turned into something that was found only on the moon. The land was dotted with hundreds of craters from artillery rounds and exploding bombs from the aircraft, and everywhere he looked, small fires were burning out of control.

The Captain cautiously walked forward towards the continuing sound of fighting. He passed by a decapitated, burned out hulk of an American Blackfoot main battle tank, its automatic feeding chain hanging over the side of the blacken tank, and there were a number of unexploded rounds still caught up in the chain track. The turret rested some ten feet away from the twisted main body of the massive war machine, like a distorted modern art sculpture done by a drunken artist. A silent testimony to the ferocity of war. He touched the fender as he peered inside the burned out machine, the bodies of the tankers were removed. He understood no one could have possibly survived the terrible blast by an obvious anti tank missile. There were dead lying on the ground by the tank, but they were covered by bloody Army green tarps.

The Captain thought. 'Shit, all this stinking destruction, and still no sign of any enemy troops yet'. He stood in total awe of the terribly devastating effects of war, but he was immediately brought back to reality, when someone nearby him suddenly yelled out.

"There, over there stupid. Shoot over there will ya for the love of God. There's some stinking enemy soldiers moving over there and they're trying to get position on us, soldier."

Salsiccia fired in the direction the yelling soldier pointed to. As fast as he fired, he saw a soldier instantly go down. His first sight of the enemy. His track pulled up alongside the winded military officer, and the driver growled at the exhausted officer huffing and puffing. "Captain Salsiccia Sir, you have to get back inside the damn machine sir. We have to go right now sir. They just broke through to the city of Abeche, Captain Salsiccia Sir."

As the second wave of Marines, along with some Army Units caught up with the advance units bogged down on the outskirts of Abeche, the fighting became intense. The backup troops set up artillery, and added their fire power to that of the Marines, as planes dropped its ordnance on the entrenched Libyan soldiers, left behind to cover the retreating troops heading back to Libya.

Soldiers from both sides got lost in the manmade fog created from thousands of weapons, tanks, artillery and bombs exploding and firing at the same time. The air was fast becoming unfit to breath, from the gases of explosions, burning wire, plastics and bodies. The smoke was getting so thick at one point around Abeche, both sides had to stop firing at each other to allow the battlefield to clear some so the warriors could see each other. The fear of being killed by friendly fire was on every trooper's mind as they fought on, and every soldier from both sides understood how easily this type of accident could happen to them.

By the time the second wave of Marine troops finally reached the crumbling frontlines of the Libyan defenders taking severe punishment from the attacking American forces, they were appalled at what they discovered waiting for them.

546

CHAPTER 23 – CAPTAIN SALSICCIA'S COMMAND VEHICLE

Captain Joseph Salsiccia was back in his track and on the move again. As his track passed by another burned out hulk of a massive M-65 Blackfoot tank, he looked at the destroyed metal monster. The side of the machine was completely missing. Suddenly, the concerned Captain had an overpowering feeling to duck back inside the safety of his track, and close the hatch as if this action would protect him from a possible missile strike on his vehicle. He fought the feeling of hiding, knowing he needed his full range of vision to better spot any possible trouble before it hit him, or any possible ambush the enemy might have set up against him and his troops.

The radio was getting overrun by countless soldier's gripes and requests for added support. The soldier's main gripe was they were cursing the fine sand being kicked up by the tanks and armored vehicles. The sand got into everything, eyes, clothing, boots and machinery, clogging the air filters on the heavy machines of war. There was a dispatch stating two helicopters crashed due to sand getting into the intake ports of the engines, but the worse complaining was over the food. Everything the soldiers ate or drank, was mixed in with the fine sand, causing their gums to bleed. Many troops' asses were sore because every time they took a dump, it was like shitting out sandpaper. Add this to the ever present mosquitoes and biting flies as large as bees, and there was not a soldier around who was not ready to kill someone or thing.

As Captain Salsiccia's track machine passed by the destroyed tank, his attention was drawn to what he mistakenly took to be a burned chunk of tree stump lying on the ground near the tank. He stared at it until he realized it was a charred body of a tanker. He grew sick to his stomach as he forced his attention to the center of the road again, vowing not to look off the left side of the road at any more of the wrecks for fear of what horror he might see next.

"Driver, let's get the fuck out of here but quick, mister." Salsiccia called out from the rear of the track. He was getting sore from the constant jostling and banging around his body was absorbing inside the metal monster. His body was becoming black and blue from head to toe. He ears rang from the almost unmuffled whine from the track's powerful engine.

He was a tanker like his father before him was, and he was always pushing his troops, sometimes, beyond all exhaustion, in an effort to make his battalion the best. His soldiers were well known for their hard work, training, maintenance and standards of perfection and tactics. His battalion was outstanding when it came to hitting, or outmaneuvering the enemy troops. The Captain relied very heavily on his Sergeants, which made his battalion sought after by many NCOs and recruits. He was a private man who cared dearly for his troops.

The Captain was married and he had two children, a devoted Catholic who attended Mass every Sunday when he could, and he made certain his children went to church. He never cheated on his wife, the thought never entered his mind, he was happily married and he played life by the book. If he decided to do something, he saw it through to the end no matter what it was or involved. His one great memory, besides the birth of his children, came when he was on R&R in Rome. He bumped into the Pope. The Pope was pleased to meet him, and he shook his hand and talked to him both in English and Italian for nearly an hour, before leaving the Captain's side.

His armored personnel carrying track machine slowly pulled in a hastily put together refueling, repair and rearmament depot. As his track came to a bouncing stop, he noticed repair personnel working on seven tanks in various degrees of damage. The workers were stealing parts from one damaged tank, to repair the other six not so bad off, in hopes of getting them back in the war. The tankers from these tanks being repaired, sat under trees far away from the workers. They were either eating or sleeping, and a few of them were busy writing letters. The area stank of fuel, exhaust and body sweat. Salsiccia came out of his track machine and laid down across the hot fender. It felt good to lay down, even if it was on a hard metal surface covered over with bolts and rivets which dug into his back and shoulders.

The radio operator let the rear ramp of his machine down to air out the inside of the track. The Captain was suffering from a splitting headache from all the exhaust he ingested. The exhausted military officer sat on the steel hatch and checked his radio, and cleaned the dust from the surface of it. No sooner did he closed his eyes, enjoying the heat from the sun's rays and fresh air, than did a jeep type humvee pull up alongside his track.

"Excuse me sir, are you Captain Salsiccia, Sir?" The soldier called out while still sitting inside his vehicle.

The still thoroughly exhausted Captain did not bother to look at the soldier speaking to him as he replied in a grumpy tone of voice. "Yeah, why?" He barked back at him.

"Captain Salsiccia Sir, you're instructed to report to the Command C.P. (Command Port) immediately sir. The Regimental Commander was killed in a sudden air attack a few minutes ago, Captain. You're instructed to take Command of all Allied ground forces operating in the field at this time, sir. The brass hats are meeting over there sir." The Sergeant quickly pointed towards three armored vehicles parked in a sort of a circle.

"You mean the damn Battalion Commanders, right mister?" He snapped angrily at the soldier as he openly glared at him for bothering him.

"Err... yes Sir Captain Salsiccia Sir. Excuse me sir, all the Battalion Commanders are meeting over there and your presence is commanded, sir."

The Captain sat up with a groan and then swung his legs off the side of the track, and then jumped down from the fender. When his feet hit the ground, he stopped. He looked at his track, on the reactive armor, there was a deep blackened scar that bent two of the protective plates, and about cut through a third one. The nasty scar stared back at him in mute testimony at how close his track had come to being destroyed. The stunned Captain now knew his track was singled out by an enemy shell, and he thanked God for allowing the reactive armor do its protective job, or he might not be here thanking his God for his life.

He lightly touched the jagged rip in the armor plating out of morbid fear of how close he came to death, while cutting his finger and covering two fingers with black ash and he mumbled. "Lord Jesus Christ's love." He moaned as he pulled his hand away at the feeling of pain from the slight wound. He looked at the small trace of blood on his finger, and immediately wiped it on his pant leg, as if his finger had just burned him.

"Shit." He growled angrily as he walked over to the gathering of military officers at the makeshift hastily created Command Post by the parked vehicles.

The radioman stayed behind with the track, in case he was needed by crew for something.

When Salsiccia reached the other officers, one of them looked up from the map draped over the front of a track and offered as soon as he saw the Commander. "Colonel Campanelli was informed of the death of the Regimental Commander, and he picked you as the new Regimental Commander to replace him, sir. Congratulations sir, you're the main man now sir. Word has it, you're going to be promoted to Major Sir, as soon as the orders are cut by Command. Anyway, here's what we got going so far sir. We forced a good size breakthrough here and here, in the enemy's lines and the Third Marines are pushing like hell right to the center of the town, sir.

"Incoming reports have it the enemy's pulling back under our heavy assault, sir. Other reports state the enemy's leaving soldiers behind to act as a sort of rear guard to slow us down, long enough to enforce their with¬drawal, sir. We're massing troops and armor here, to make a major push here and here in pursuit of the retreating enemy troops, sir. This action should break the back of the enemy. All Battalions are rested, fed, armed, and good to go on your Command, sir. The airforce knows their routine as well sir. Orders have been passed by the Commander before he was killed, so we're well prepared to engage. All we need is your word and we're off, sir."

The reporting officer stopped speaking just long enough to catch his breath, and to give the Captain a chance to respond to the information he just offered to the man.

He turned his arm. It was hurt from the banging around he received in his track.

"Are you hurt there sir?" The officer doing all the talking, asked him.

The Captain rubbed his arm and bitched back at the other officer. "Yeah, I was wondering, do you think it might be possible for me to get my hands on one of those new rubber tire command vehicles for a change, sir? I'm a little sick and tired of being bounced around like a rag doll inside the damn track machine I was issued, sir."

"Not a chance in hell of that happening sir. The only one on the entire continent is the Colonel's personnel Command Vehicle, sir. He'll never get you one of the damn thing Captain."

"What about his partner in crime, Captain White. I think is his name mister?"

"Nah, you'll be wasting your time there as well sir. He'll never help you out without the Colonel's okay. Hell, he so far up the Colonel's ass, he could tell what he had for breakfast, sir."

This remark made the gathering of officer's laugh. The three other officers allowed this officer do the talking for them.

The Captain glanced at the large sand table map equipped with plastic tanks and soldiers to help mark out the different Allied troops and armor operating in the field. It was carved in the ground in front of one of the parked track machines. He took out his map, he quickly unfolded it and then laid it out over the other map in order to mark down all the new the information, and new troop locations he was lacking. After studying the map for a few moments longer, he pointed at the site of the old building. "Here's the key gentlemen, once we get our main forces to this location. We'll be in complete control of the whole stinking city. Where the hell's the leading elements of Marines stationed at this time sir?"

"The Marines are positioned here sir." The officer pointed on his map lying on the table.

"I got it sir. If this doesn't work, in my next life I'm coming back as a squirrel, and I'll climb up your pant leg, pal. How long do you think it'll take me to get from here to there?"

"About seven minutes at the most I'd say sir." The same officer replied confidently, and then continued to offer to the new Commander. "Recon's up and taping away sir, so by the time you get out to the leading elements of this operation. You should have all the latest updates, pictures and data about the enemy troop's strength, and where they're presently positioned and where they might be pulling back sir."

"Good, send the word out to all Unit Commanders. We attack in full force in fifteen minutes. We have to help support those damn Marines who broke through already. I don't want them getting cut off to where we might lose them in this mess, dammit. So let's move out gentlemen." The new Commander of all ground forces offered as he quickly refolded his map, and then he replaced it in his leather holder and ran back to his waiting track.

The driver saw Salsiccia coming at him and he called out to the Commander. "All fueled up and good to go sir."

"Good, then let's get a move on it mister. Head for coordinates C-Three-R by One, One, Three on your map, mister. We have soldiers out there who need help so move it." He growled at his drive as he climbed on board the vehicle.

"Will do sir as soon as you're on board the track, Captain." The track operator pushed the button, and the rear hatch quickly closed up. The dust covered track's motor roared to life as the excited Captain was slammed up against the side of the steel machine when it suddenly lunged forward, and the interior of the track instantly filled with the smell of exhaust once again.

"Take it easy will ya for the love of God, dammit. I want to get there in one stinking piece man." The Captain grumbled as he righted himself inside the rapidly moving vehicle.

The driver laughed as he called back to the Captain. "So you wanted to be in the armor sir."

THE MARINE ADVANCE UNITS

The breakout went forward as was decided by Command, destroying any and all Libyan lines of defense, as the heavily supported Allied forces rapidly pushed forward with lightening speed, and massive troop strength and movements. Many of the Libyan defenders had already pulled out of their defensive positions before the major push by the American forces started against them. But before the enemy forces left the all but destroyed Chad city of Abeche, the Libyan soldiers killed all the remaining civilians from the area they were holding as prisoners.

A Marine Lieutenant thought he witnessed everything there was to see when it came to war, and its ugly effects. He believed he saw the worse of the worse, until he crossed over the crumbling Libyan lines and entered the Chad city of Abeche. He was shocked to his soul to see the cold, calculated butchery of the civilians left lying in the streets, and along many roads leading out of the city. He remembered the impersonal attacks on the civilian population from the artillery, aircraft and missile attacks which did not actually see their targeted civilian death.

But here, along the narrow roads of Abeche lay the butchered bodies of thousands of civilians, men, women and children, killed in a most cold blooded manner. Many of the civilians were killed by soldiers who stood right before the civilians as they were murdered, close enough to actually feel and hear the fear in their voices, and to make direct eye contact as the soldiers killed the helpless civilians. They were butchered standing side by side and left where they dropped. The scene made even this battle hardened officer shed a tear over the mass murder, as he spat on the ground in an attempt to try and get the horrible taste of the bile out of his mouth. The American Officer immediately ordered pictures of the murders to be taken, and then sent out to command to inform them of what they were finding out in the field in the Chad city of Abeche.

Soldier after soldier looked at the butchered bodies, shaking their heads in stunned disbelief. Some of the harden soldiers cried as they vowed to take their revenge for the slaughter of these helpless civilians. One thing any opposing Army did not want to have happen, was for the fighting to get personal. A soldier with a purpose during battle was a man on a mission, and a soldier on a mission would never stop until he did what he had set in his mind to do.

A new anger arose within the ranks of the rapidly advancing Marine and Army Units, as the soldiers dogged the heels of the retreating Libyan soldiers. A few Libyan troop stragglers were captured, and by the time the American soldiers got the captured Libyan fighters over to their commanders for interrogation, the prisoners did not look too healthy.

The Marine Advance Command had to issue orders on the conduct of all American soldiers who came across and took in any enemy Libyan prisoners. In the first three hours of the hard hitting operation, the Marines and Army backup units fought their way to the outskirts of Abeche which was a hundred miles into Chad. Here, the Libyan armies decided to dig in and make a good fight of it against the American soldiers. The fighting was extremely intense, as both armies traded artillery and weapon fire with each other. The next hour of fighting was bloody.

Well over a hundred Libyan tanks were blown apart from the aircraft and helicopter attacks launched against them, as well as from the quickly advancing American and allied tank and artillery fire coming from the Marines, and their backup Army and allied units.

ON BASE SENTRY

Captain John White quickly leafed through the countless dispatches flooding into the CIC Center of the base, and then he reported to Colonel Campanelli. "Say Colonel, I have the first initial casualty reports coming in sir. The 3rd and 5th Marine Units are reporting casualties are heavy, that's all. Err... the 7th Air Cavalry puts their casualties at around twelve percent, no word from any other units in the field as of yet, sir. Sonofabitch, will you look at this stinking shit sir? One of my troopers just got mauled by a stinking lion, can you believe that shit Colonel? A fucking lion chewed up one of my troopers, like we don't have enough to worry about."

The Colonel looked up and snapped at his Second in Command. "Put the stinking injured soldier in for a Purple Heart. He was mauled in the line of duty, Whitie."

"Thank you sir, will do sir. Other soldiers killed the damn thing before it got away. I have more reports coming in right now sir. Damn, I have six troopers bitten by poisonous snakes. Like my men didn't have enough shit to worry about out in the damn field of battle, now they have to fucking worry about damn snakes and lions and other crap like that man."

"War sucks the big one Johnny. The same thing holds true for these soldiers also, Purple Hearts for the lot of them, mister. Put the paper work through and I'll sign off on it, John. Is that all you got for me John?" The Colonel asked his lifelong friend as he smirked at him.

"No sir, I have a shit lot of other crap to go over with you at this time, Colonel Campanelli. The 4th, and the 21st Mechanized Army units are screaming for replenishing main mount tank and artillery ammunition, sir. The speed at which they're consuming this shit up is horrendous and staggering sir. I'm having one hell of a hard time with trying to keep up with the damn shit as fast as they use it up on us, sir. I'm having small arms ammo being sent to the front line."

"I hear that, but we have to resuppy our stinking equipment on the frontlines if we want to drive the fucking enemy forces the fuck out of Chad, John." The Colonel grumbled as he sort of laughed and grunted at the same time as he went back to reading is own report.

"Here's another dispatch that just came in, Eddy." The Captain mumbled as he shuffled through the stack of papers and then reported. "Hot damn! The Rangers successfully destroyed most of the enemies' lines of communication and rail, and they're further reporting they picked up nine of our pilots shot down behind enemy lines, sir. I also have a number of complaints about traffic control problems. It reads, I have two columns of tanks currently being bogged down off the damn main road, and they're allowing the civilian traffic out, in our safe areas sir."

"Jesus H. Christ John, if you can't move the stinking civilian traffic off the damn road by normal means, steal a fucking blade track from the damn Seabee pain in the asses and push the damn civilian traffic the fuck off the road. I need those fucking tanks moving now, dammit!"

He looked at the Colonel with concern clouding over his eyes for a moment.

"Yeah, I know they're stinking civilians, but I have a damn war on my hands I have to try and control, John. I don't care how the fuck you have to move the damn civilians the hell outta the damn way of these troops and armor. Just get my tanks moving again, dammit! Any more shit I gotta look afta sir?" The Colonel asked his Second in Command with concern.

"A few more to go yet Colonel. The Marines are wreaking pure havoc on the enemy support infrastructure. The enemy can't get their fuel or ammo out to their stinking defenders sir, or even communicate with them either. They're about cut off cold sir."

"How is our own support infrastructure holding up on us sir?" The Colonel inquired.

"Err... we're having some minor problems here ourselves with hooking up our supply trucks with the advance tank columns in most need of refurbishment, and the spearhead of ground forces, sir. What the hell's happening is many times one of our supply trucks pass by a column of tanks, they're stopped, and these tankers commandeer the requested supplies from the front line forces. Leaving the other column who is in most need of supplies without them sir."

"What the hell are we running here for the love of God? A first come, first fucking serve operation or something? John! You have to get the damn supplies out to those stinking tankers who need it the most as fast as you can, man. I don't care how you do it, even if you have to put armed guards on the fucking supply columns, mister. In fact, the tankers on the frontline have top priority over any lagging tank units moving for the damn frontlines. Is that all you have for me now, John?" He mumbled as he went back to his maps.

"Yeah, that's about it for now, Colonel." The Captain replied with a snap in his tone of voice, but his words fell on deaf ears as the Colonel pored over his maps again.

The Allied casualties mounted up quickly in the field. The Marines lost twenty tanks, nine Apache helicopters and three Cobra fast attack helicopters, sir. Twelve aircraft were also downed due to the heavy fighting occurring near the still besieged city of Abeche, Colonel. The Marines were bogged down and forced to actually go from house to house, in an effort to drive out any hidden Libyan snipers or lagging behind soldiers from the shattered buildings or piles of rubble. In many instances, the fighting became hand to hand combat, a soldier's worse fear.

The Libyan troops dug deep foxholes in the soft sand from which they fought bitterly from. The American Marines had to fight for every square inch of Chad they wanted to take over. Artillery and aircraft were forced to destroy what was left of the civilian buildings in the all but destroyed Abeche to dig out the enemy still hiding in the city. The Libyan soldiers setup local defenses, trying to keep control over the two main roads along with the small air field at Abeche. The Libyan defenders were trying desperately to break, or even slow down the rapid Allied momentum. But the American forces passed through these enemy defenses like they did not even exist. The enemy forces were beginning to become overwhelmed on all points now.

The Marines watched as columns of thick, black smoke arose from the city, when the aircraft attacked and dropped bombs on the Libyan forces. Helicopters moved in and made the Libyan tanks pay with their lives, as well as attacking any Libyan soldiers they happened across. These attacks and softening up of the Libyan units, helped to keep some Marine casualties down.

Abeche was under constant massive air and ground bombardment, for over three hours before the Marines finally entered the city proper. The civilian death was appalling, as the Marine units were forced to fight from corner to street corner. By the fourth hour of heavy street fighting and sniper hits, the Marines sat in the middle of the Chad city, and the operation has taking on the shape of a cleanup and help the injured and dying civilian's action now.

Most of the fighting was coming to an end with small pockets of resistance still holding out against the American onslaught. Thousands of Libyans, Nigerians, Congolese and Upper Volta soldiers were giving up and being taken as prisoners by the rapidly advancing allied forces.

The Marines finally broke in and took over the complex General Abdul el Kadir had occupied as his headquarters, and turned the building into a prison. In the makeshift cells in the basement of the building, the Marine soldiers found evidence of terrible torture of the civilian population, taking place in the building by Libyan soldiers who interrogated the civilian prisoners. Captain Joseph C. Salsiccia ordered the entire complex to be cleaned up and checked out for any possible surviving American prisoners who might have been taken captive by the enemy troops.

The rubble covered streets of Abeche were layered with bodies of the dead and slowly dying civilians. Thousands of civilians were killed or left wounded by the retreating Libyan soldiers, as many more thousands of civilians were killed, or wounded by the American heavy artillery and aircraft bombardment, or from the heavy strafing by the American aircraft of the Chad city.

From what the Marines were able to piece together, it was quite evident the Libyan soldiers had hordes of civilians with them as they pull back, and they were using them as human shields to hide behind them. When the civilian shields reached the point of uselessness to the retreating Libyan soldiers, they were merely slaughtered and left lying where they had fallen to the ground.

As the Marines quickly setup their own Command Center inside the old governor's palace, and the once headquarters of the Libyan General. They searched throughout the ground floor and basement area of the structure. Every nook and cranny inside of the structure was checked out for the most likely place for any hidden explosives, traps, or any Libyan soldiers who might have been left behind to cause the advancing American soldiers more problems than they were already suffering though. It was in the damp, dingy cellar two Marines found what was left of Lieutenant Commander Joyce Heart, she was chained to a wall in a stone cell with no windows or good air. One Marine worked on the rusted chains that held her body to the stone wall with his K bar knife, as the other soldier quickly ran off to find his Commanding Officer, and report to him what they found down in the basement of the building.

Seconds later, Captain Salsiccia stood in the doorway of the tiny cell stunned at what he saw. He stared at a fellow soldier who was barely recognizable as a human being. She was chained naked to the wall. The Captain turned green at the sight of her, and he almost upchucked and then bellowed out in a roar. "Get her down from that wall dammit! Get her off that wall, she's a soldier. Get her down now dammit!" He yelled as he pushed the soldiers gathered behind him out of the cell, and barked orders to the men pushed in the hall.

"You two, get the hell out of here and get me some medics, and a female soldier down here to help her, A-SAP. I want a heater brought in here as well as some food and water. Dammit, get me some doctors down here on the double quick." The Captain glared at the soldier who jumped in action, and ran down the narrow hallway to carry out his orders.

The Captain turned his attention back to the cell as some of his soldiers pried and pulled at the rusting chains, until they were finally free of the stone wall. A cot, along with some blankets was brought down, and they were left sitting in the middle of the tight hallway, as the fuming Captain ordered the shocked soldiers to carry the female commander's broken body to the cot. A female Corporal came up to the Captain's side, and the angry officer glared harshly at her for a moment, as the soldiers carefully laid the Commander's bloody body down on the small bed. The Captain was trying to make certain the soldiers were treating the injured soldier properly.

"What the hell are you waiting for Christ sake Almighty. Cover her up, you ass. What do you think you were down here for dammit." He hissed in her face as the female Corporal jumped at the force the Captain used in his voice on her.

The Corporal covered the bloody body of the flyer with a blanket brought down by the soldiers along with the bed. The Captain turned to the soldiers who helped get her body from the wall.

"You two soldiers get the devil out of here on the double. You two guys are ordered to stand at the foot of this damn hallway, and not allow anyone down here unless he or she's a damn doctor, or female soldier trying to help with this wounded soldier. You got that order?"

The two soldiers shook their heads in the affirmative as they ran down to the end of the hallway, and then they took up their positions as ordered by the Captain and waited there.

"One more thing for you people before you get the hell out of here, dammit. I want you two men to find a way to get these damn chains from this injured soldiers wrists." He called out after the running and still fuming soldiers.

The angry Captain turned to his terribly injured female flyer, he stared in stunned disbelief at the broken form of the soldier lying in so much pain on the cot. He carefully moved some strands of red matted and filthy hair from her grime covered and swollen face and mumbled to her in a soft tone. "What the hell kind of animals would do what they have done to this soldier, and still call themselves soldiers." He looked at Commander Heart, and he promised her he would get even with the bastards for what they had done to her, as he recalled a rule of soldiering his father once told him.

'Son, a soldier never breaks the rules of engagement, until the rules no longer work for them.' He looked into the lifeless staring eyes of this female pilot and he said to himself, but loud enough to be heard by anyone standing near him. "The rules no longer work here, dammit."

As other American soldiers continued to search the basement complex of the governor's mansion, they came across even more evidence of the calculated butchery the Libyan soldiers visited upon the civilian population of Abeche. They found the remains of flayed bodies, bodies hacked to pieces, one piece at a time while still alive. Other bodies were found burned beyond recognition. The female population of Abeche were not spared this terrible degradation either. Many female bodies were found burned, cut up, or tied in such a position that it made it impossible to breath properly, thus causing a terribly slow and very agonizing death.

A few female survivors were found. One sat in her cell and continued to scream at nothing. Another was barely able to speak, but she told stories that made the combat hardened soldier's skin crawl. She told a Chaplain her tormentors tortured many women to death, like children torture animals with sticks, fire and electric, just to hear the women scream until their lungs gave out on them. Many women were raped by the Libyan soldiers.

Two Army medics ran down the hallway to the pilot lying on the bed. One absentmindedly pulled the covers away from her body, with little thought he was exposing the Commander. The Captain grabbed him by the throat as he yanked him to his feet and yelled in the medic's face.

"This is an American soldier who suffered enough indignities at the hands of these stinking lousy criminal soldiers! You'll keep her body covered as best you can all the while you work on her, or I'll skin your stinking ass alive, mister. You'll treat her with the greatest of respect at all times, or I'll have your balls for breakfast, mister." He growled angrily as he gave the medic a hard shove back, and then he carefully covered his female pilot with the blanket again. The Captain then looked to another female soldier who walked down the hall towards him. "You, I want you to get this soldier some clothing, so if these medics have to uncover her again, she'll have some dignity left to her, dammit."

"Where am I to find these items you're requesting sir?" The scared female soldier asked and made a gesture with her shoulders as she spread out her hands.

"I don't care if you have to rip them off the back of a civilian, you get them. I want her covered now." He stared at the female as she undid her blouse and slid it on the pilot.

The Captain looked at her standing before him in her brand offered her. "Very good Corporal, you're an outstanding soldier and a true friend. What's your name?"

"Corporal Pat Kelly, sir." She replied to the angry looking Captain in a calm tone.

"It's now Sergeant Kelly. You stay with the Commander to insure her dignity is protected at all times, Sergeant." With this said, Captain Joseph Salsiccia started down the long hallway in silence and anger. When his back was turned to his men, a tear suddenly escaped his eyes, and it ran down the side of his cheek. He wiped at it as if his body had just betrayed him. He returned to his new office, and there he found two Intel soldiers going over the thousands of files the Libyan soldiers left behind on their flight from the besieged and destroyed city.

"What the hell's going on in here dammit? Who the hell authorized this bullshit? Who in the Sam hill are you two birds?" he bellowed, glad to have someone to finally yell at.

The Intel Officers, startled at the Captain's sudden appearance and anger, jumped to their feet at attention and saluted him as one of the soldier's responded to his question. "Captain Sir, we found a wealth of important information in here sir." The taller of the two soldiers replied with a half smile on his lips as he turned his back on the Captain, and then he pulled open a file drawer filled to overflowing with reports, lists of supplies each Libyan division had. Along with many troop strengths and tanks and artillery pieces each enemy division had in their command.

"A wealth of important information Captain Salsiccia Sir. The flaming assholes didn't even have the smarts to burn their own damn files before taking off, sir. A simple flare thrown into each of the drawers would have done the job for them, sir. We caught them with their damn pants down sir. Look at all this stuff we found in here sir." The officer said as he pulled three file folders packed with papers out of the drawer, and then held them out to the Captain and added. "Sir, we have found the complete operational plans of the Libyan Army, and how they were planning to use them against us, sir. It's one hell of a find in here Captain."

"I can't read that shit, that's why I have you birds." The Captain looked at the soldiers standing at attention saluting him. He wiped at his chin with a hand covered with blood from his pilot.

"Sir, you're hurt Captain. Do you want me to get someone to look after your wound for you, sir?" One of the Intelligence Officers warned as he pointed at the Captain's bloody hand.

He looked at his blood covered hand and shuddered, he picked up a sweat covered shirt from a Libyan soldier who left it behind when he ran from the advancing American soldiers. He wiped at the blood as if it was burning his hand, rage instantly took over his facial expression as he barked savagely at the two Intel soldiers.

"I want you two guys to do me a favor, I want you to tear this place apart until you find some papers on the rotten sonofabitch who was in Command of these bastards who hurt the civilians downstairs." What he wanted was the name of the Libyan Commanding Officer, so he could take out his own revenge on the bastard for his injured flyer down stairs in the basement of the building, Lieutenant Commander Joyce Heart.

"No problem with that request Captain Salsiccia, we already have the name of the Libyan Commander for the enemy soldiers stationed here sir."

The Captain glared at the them. "Who was the rotten bastard who did this crap to my pilot?"

"Captain Salsiccia Sir, the Libyan Commander's name was General Abdul el Kadir, sir." The obviously lead Intel Officer reported proudly to the angry looking Captain.

"Good, that's great, you just earned your pay for the month, mister. I want a memo sent out to all Company Commanders on the ground. I want it to read as follows, exactly the way I'm saying it to you, mister. I just placed a bounty on this sonofabitches ass, and I'll add my full months pay to the pot myself. Any sweat warrior who brings me this bastard's ass in alive or dead, will get an instant rate increase and a month off in Morocco for his or her trouble, soldier. I can't tell you how much I want this lousy bastard's head locked in my damn hands for just five moments, people.

"Cut those orders out this moment, and I'll sign them immediately. I want this scumbag before he gets back to the safety of his own country, and I'll never get my damn hands on the sonofabitch again. And I warn you mister, if I do get my hands on this bastard then it looks like I'll have to take my anger out on his troops, do you get my drift?" he rarely if ever cursed, but he was so upset about his female flyer that he forgot about his usually polite and Christian mood, and he was cursing with the best of them now.

The newly the appointed Sergeant Kelly, cautiously walked into his office as the Captain was still screaming at his two intelligence people. Captain Salsiccia immediately picked up her come in, and he stopped yelling at the two as he glared and barked at the new female Sergeant. "What the hell are you doing in here young lady? I just gave you an order for you to remain with my injured pilot downstairs, soldier!"

"Sir, Commander Joyce Heart has expired to the terrible wounds done to her body, sir. She was hurt too badly to recover sir." Sergeant Kelly suddenly broke down as she continued on with her report. "Sir, you should have seen what these lousy animals done to her body sir."

"That's enough of that bullshit, get hold of yourself soldier, that's an order. You're a fucking soldier, so start acting like one dammit. I don't want to hear any more of that kind of shit around here ever again. Leave my office at once, get the hell out of here, dammit! Before you go, see to getting her body shipped out to the Roosevelt. Find a uniform for her, even if you have to have one air dropped specially from the damn

Carrier. Top honors and all the stuff that goes along with any fallen soldier. She's to have it all before she's shipped out of here."

One of the confused Intel Officers suddenly interrupted the Captain's conversation with the Sergeant and offered him calmly. "Captain Salsiccia Sir, is this the female American pilot the Libyans had locked up downstairs, sir?"

"Yeah, Lieutenant Commander Joyce Heart, why do you ask me that question, mister? She was one of my people, dammit. Do you have something on her you found in this office? Did you find something on her in any of those damn papers you have there, mister." He demanded more than he asked his young Intel soldier.

"Captain Salsiccia Sir, I was going over some of the reports pertaining to her interrogation at the hands of the Libyan soldiers, sir. According to the ones we came across, she didn't break during any examinations carried out against her, sir. We came across a total of twelve separate dispatches covering the interrogations carried out against her person by the Libyan interrogators, sir. The dirty bastards did just about everything one soldier could possibly do to another human being, to try and get vital information from that poor soul, sir. Electric, fire, physical, sexual and mental assault, you name it sir and it was used against her, sir. Sometimes, these interrogations lasted for hours, sir. You name it sir, and the scumbags did it to her in their effort to break her down sir. She must have been a real strong one sir."

"You know she was strong, too strong if you were to asked me, sir. I can't tell you how many arguments this pain in the ass trooper caused me with Command, when she first filed for active duty with my unit, sir. A female pilot, a bitch lover, shit. I hate to have a women in a damn combat situation for this very reason. You can tell the bastards raped her, this is what I was trying to warn her and Command about. I liked this bitch. Shit, she had brass ovaries the size of my hand, dammit." He suddenly turned away from the other two officers and looked out at what was left of a stain glass window, in an attempt to try hide a tear in his eye. Instantly, he noticed all the bodies of the slaughtered civilians still lying in the street below him, and he asked the officer he was speaking with. "Do we have anyone working on getting rid of all those civilian bodies all over the place out there, dammit."

"Yes sir." Was the call from one of the soldiers who was in his office along with him.

The Captain had some technicians setting up computer terminals and communications as they turned the destroyed room into a first rate communication network. His staff officers setup map tables as orderlies quickly cleaned up all the debris from the space. In a matter of a few short hours, Captain Joseph Salsiccia was able to speak to any battalion or Command Officer out in the field. His Command Center had taken great shape and was ready to work for him.

A runner out of breath came in the Captain's office. He was ordered to report a situation to the Captain in person. The soldier snapped to attention and saluted as he began his report. "Begging your pardon Captain Salsiccia Sir. Sergeant Wyndham sent me here to report to you personally, Captain. All our divisions are on the march again, sir. We got bogged down for a short time on the outskirts of Abeche, sir. The retreating Libyan forces destroyed two main bridges spanning the River Nice, sir. We had some minor trouble here sir, because we had no bridge laying equipment with our division, Captain Salsiccia Sir. The Combat Engineers are with the advance Marine units, sir. The Sergeant put in a request for a Unit of Engineers and a bridge layer, because the field maps showed two more small rivers we're going to have to cross, and he wanted the equipment with him as his troops advanced and he can keep moving at..."

"Will you get through with this endless report of yours before I die of old age for Pete's sake, mister. I have other work to do, and your dragging this damn report out is stopping me from completing my other duties of command." The Captain interrupted the soldier's report as he bitched at him, and then he added with a snap in his voice. "You can tell your worried Sergeant he'll have his damn Engineers out to him by no later than this afternoon. They might be there by the time you get back to him, mister."

The soldier started speaking much faster this time as he went on with his report for the angry acting Army Captain. "A number of tanks swam this river easy enough sir, but they were having trouble transversing the other side of the steep river bank though, sir. The bank was muddy and soft, and the tanks were sinking in the earth and then dragging their bottoms on the bank, which stopped the machines from moving forward, sir. Seeing this, the soldiers were stopped from swimming any further tanks across the narrow and shallow river. Then a Seabee with the unit came up with an idea in the field.

"The Seabees dumped three eight foot wide, by twenty four foot long ribbed heavy metal covert pipes in the river. They then filled over the pipes with earth and stone, and forced a usable road over the water, sir. The pipes allowed the water to flow underneath the road, and left the makeshift road intact. Sergeant Wyndham's branded the Seabee unit traveling with his troops as the 'Smart Bastards Squad' sir." The soldier tried to laugh, but it did not impress the angry looking Captain very much though.

"They better be stinking smart bastards if they're tagging along with any of my people out in the field, mister. I want you to tell this Sergeant Wyndham of yours he did good with forging that river like he did, and keeping the tanks moving at the same time, soldier. But first, I'm ordering you to go over to the Officer's Mess and grab yourself something hot to eat, mister. You eat your fill before leaving to get back to your troops out in the field. You'll tell anyone who challenges you in the Officer's Mess that I gave you special permission to eat there, and then get back to your troops. How is the fighting doing up there mister? I'm not receiving very many reports on how it's going up there, soldier." He asked the soldier this time.

"Captain Salsiccia Sir, there is a helluva lot of crazy ass A rabs that were sent on their way to that big tent in the sky, Sir. They're still trying to fight us with little success, sir. Any time the enemy try and make a stand against our troops, they get the shit kicked outta them, sir."

The fuming Captain absentmindedly drummed his fingertips on the map, and then he turned to a report coming in over his computer terminal. He did not notice the soldier salute him and then quickly leave his office.

The Captain did not like staying locked up in the governor's palace in the Chad city of Abeche while coordinating his troop's actions out in the field, and their supplies and aircraft attacks on the Libyan units. His heart was with his troops on the battlefield, and that's where he wanted to be, right in the thick of the fighting with his troops. He completely blotted out the chatter from his staff in the office with his mind, as they ordered up troop movements onto the field of battle, as he concentrated his attention on the teletype report coming into his field office.

CHAPTER 24

Rapidly converging on the nation of Libya were all the fighter and bomber aircraft being launched from the Alfa launch from the Aircraft Carrier Nimitz. These aircraft quickly linked up with twelve planes that was able to launch off the Independence before she was sunk by a Libyan missile attack. All the pilots from the stricken ship had no idea the carrier started her slow slide under the sea. The eighty six aircraft launching from the Nimitz were over Algeria when Sleepy Eye, an AWACS E 3A radar aircraft, picked up a number of enemy fighters taking off from Libya with the intent on intercepting the aircraft launched from the Roosevelt.

"This is Sleepy Eye to War Child Leader. You're instructed to come in sir. Over."

"War Child Leader to Sleepy Eye. What do you have for me sir. Over."

"War Child. We have at least thirty Gomers taking off from the hard deck of Libya at this time, believed to intercept your flight, sir. We see more Gomers moving around on the hard deck, taxiing for immediate takeoff, sir. Keep your eyes open for any incoming hostiles, sir. Over."

"Roger that as received, will do as instructed. Thanks for the information Sleepy Eye. Over."

"War Child Leader to Bunker One. Did you copy that last transmission from Sleepy Eye, sir? We have a mess of Gomers coming up to play around with us a little, sir. Bunker One, you're picked to take the lead with your wing of Hornets, and work over all incoming unfriendlies, sir. Break them up good and proper for us while we continue on with our mission, sir. Over."

"That's a Roger on last order as received sir. Bunker One's moving up to the lead to intercept the bad guys before they attack the wing of aircraft from the Roosevelt, sir. Over."

Bunker One was the Air Wing Commander, or AWC. Bunker One did not like the AWC. Tag. So he made sure most of the men under his Command referred to him as just Bunker One.

"Sleepy Eye to Bunker One. I have a positive read on many enemy radar tracking our flight, sir. They have you locked on their attack radar as of this moment, sir. Suggest you light up your own radar and let the Gomers know you're aware of their flight and are ready to fight them, sir."

"Roger that last as received. Bunker One to all bird followers, we might as well turn on our long range radar time. They know we're up here and are prepared to engage us people. Over."

"Bunker One to Snowbird and Richmond. You two are to move up with me as my Wingmen. Looks like we're going to have to earn some of the money that the Navy has been paying us all these years. We have some Zappers coming to play with us, pilots. Over."

"Snowbird to Bunker One. Have you looked off to your damn left side yet sir? You see that fucking smoke out there in the sea, sir? It has to be coming from the Independence sir. Over."

"I copy that last as received Snowbird. Just think about it, we have the lousy scumbags who did this crap coming up to pay us a little visit, sir. Let's go and pay the damn cocksuckers back for what they have done to the Independence, people. Over."

"Snowbird to Bunker One. You got that right sir. Let's go get the lousy bastards. Over."

"War Child to Starman. Drop back five thousand feet, and allow the forward fighters take care of these Gomers rapidly moving in on us, sir. Keep an eye out for Tree Clipper and his wing of Intruders, they should be well below us about now, sir. Over."

"Starman to War Child. I already picked up Tree Clipper and the rest of his wing of Intruder followers on my IFF (Identify Friend or Foe) sir. I know exactly where they are sir. I'm also picking up twelve orphans from the Independence on the IFF as well sir. They're coming in from the north, and they're all fighter bombers and have reported they're armed with bombs and missiles, sir. I think they should linkup with your flight wing for this opening attack, sir."

"I hear ya there sir. That's a good idea you come up with sir. Do it sir. Over."

"War Child Leader to incoming flight of F 15 E Eagles from the Independence. Over."

"Nugget to War Child. Yeah, I read you five by five sir. I have no home nest to return to once this mission is completed sir. I have been instructed by CIC Command to drop my eggs on the already pre-assigned targets, and then my flight has been ordered to report back to Base Sentry for further orders and support them if necessary, sir. Over."

"War Child to Nugget. You're instructed to linkup my Wing for support of this operation, sir. You'll drop your eggs on your pre assigned targets as suggested, and then continue on with previous orders sir. Good to have you with us, sir. Sorry about the Independence man. You have two options, you can deck down on the Roosevelt, or head for Base Sentry, sir. Over."

"Yeah. But the rotten bastards who did it ain't gonna be pleased to have us visiting with them, sir. We want payback for the Independence, sir. Over."

"This is Sleepy Eye to Bunker One. Listen up people this is important sir. Your Gomers are coming at you from below and off to your left side at eight o'clock low. Are you picking up the enemy Wing of Gomers on your radar units yet, sir? Over."

"Bunker One to Sleepy Eye. Roger that last. I have fifteen positive Gomers on my read as of this time. Moving out to intercept the bastards, sir. Over."

"Sleepy Eye to Bunker One. Good hunting then sir. Give them hell for us please sir. Over."

"Bunker One to Snowbird. Nine aircraft in, and nine aircraft under. Attack the bastards from the sun, light up your attack radar now on the bastards to help confuse the Gomers. Do you have a positive identification on our incoming unfriendlies, sir? Over."

"Damn bugs." One pilot suddenly growled in the radio, complaining about splattered bugs covering his windshield. It was one of the A 6 Intruder aircraft flying at just four hundred feet above the hard deck, so they could intercept the enemy targets from below.

"Yeah, flight crews are going to have a hell of a time with trying to clean these damn planes up for us after this mess for our next mission I tell you, sir." Another Intruder pilot responded as the other fighter pilots listened in on their conversation.

"Tree Cutter to all Intruder followers. Cut out the bullshit on the damn radio for fuck sake, we don't want to help the fucking enemy locate us by means of bullshit radio chatter, people. Keep radio silence, zip lip this mission dammit, people. Over." The lead pilot of the attack ordered the rest of the pilots in his flight wing.

Instantly, the Intruders radios went dead silent.

"War Child Leader to Bunker One. I thought we had it tough on this fucking mission sir, at least we can see where the hell we're going for Pete's sake sir. Over."

"Bunker One to War Child. Don't worry about that crap sir. We're all going to have it pretty bad ourselves soon enough dealing with these damn Gomers coming up to play around with us, sir. Any one get a positive I.D. on those bad guys coming at us yet, sir? I'd sure as hell like to know what kinda enemy aircraft we're going to be dealing with on this one, sir. Over."

"Snowbird to Bunker One. I can't make out what type of fucking aircraft they are yet, sir. Their configurations are all wrong sir. From the looks of the bastards, they look like some kinda Japanese shits, but that's impossible sir. How could they get Japanese aircraft, sir?"

"Shit, dammit, this is Richmond. They are those new Jap aircraft I've been hearing so much about lately, sir. They're those fucking Mitsubishi T 2R3s fighter shits we were informed the Japanese were developing. Jesus Christ, another fucking war and here we go again, fighting Mitsubishi Zero shits. Just think about those poor Americans motherfuckers driving them fucking Mitsubishi cars back in the States once this shit gets out, man. I'd sure hate like hell to be one of them when the American people find out we're fighting the Jap Zeros again, sir."

"I hear you loud and clear on that one Richmond. Over." Bunker replied with a quick laugh.

Another pilot who did not identify himself growled in his radio. "This is one major league fucking bullshit and bad manners gig, man. Someone is going to pay hell for this shit. Over."

Their conversation was cut short as one of the pilots of the Wing announced in an excited voice. "Tally, tally, tally. Many Tangos (Targets) in sight. Engage the Gomers."

Bunker's aircraft looked like a flock of migrating birds that just spotted food, and charged at it.

"Bunker One to all aircraft followers listen up. Tally ho. Fire Phoenix missiles. Fox Three, Fox Three away. Remember everyone, don't yell over the damn radio people. Over."

"Fox Three call." Came screaming over the radio as eighteen F 18 A/F Hornets fired their long range Phoenix missiles off at the rapidly closing in enemy fighter planes. Thirty six missiles charged after forty Japanese Libyan planes. Twenty of the American long range missiles easily found their intended targets, but the incoming Libyan planes were being reinforced by another Wing of thirty aircraft as a follow on force. They replaced the downed Libyan aircraft and continued heading right at the fast approaching wing of American fighter aircraft.

"Starman, this is Bear. I have three stinking bogeys off to my port side, sir. Fox One, fire. Bingo, scratch one bad guy sir. Over." A radar guided missile instantly found its target fired at.

"Furball!" Was the next call to come in over the radio suddenly being jammed by excited pilot chatter, meaning a multi aircraft major engagement was taking place in the air over Libya.

"Bunker One to Bunker Three. You have a fricking Zapper on your tail feathers, sir. Pull up Bunker Three, and I'll take care of him for you sir. Pull up, pull up, damn you, pull..."

The silence meant only one thing to the American flyers. Bunker Three was downed.

Bunker One's HUD (Heads up display) system was set on air to air combat mode, as his aircraft rapidly closed in on the enemy aircraft. The clear plastic display lit up like a Christmas tree, and a white circle came in view in the middle of the screen, identifying the spot of kill for his missile firing. The thin shape of the Japanese made F 2 fighter aircraft entered his HUD display screen from the lower right hand corner as a red triangle. He adjusted his plane's flight until the Zapper's aircraft was caught up right in the very center of his target circle.

A second circle suddenly appeared, a red one came in view on his screen as a low buzzing started in his cockpit, indicating his target was zeroed in for the kill. A loud electronic whine from his missile's warhead started next, informing him his warhead was locked onto the enemy target and ready to fire, as he watched the enemy pilot put his aircraft in some emergency radical evasive maneuvers now. A loud warning alarm sounded in the enemy plane's cockpit, informing the pilot he was currently under attack and about to be killed in flight.

The Zapper started a series of hard jinking to his left, and then pulled his aircraft up, and then off to his right side and down, the enemy pilot added a series of radical, and well calculated turns in a useless effort to try and shake off Bunker's attack against his aircraft. The Bunker pilot matched the enemy pilot's every maneuver for maneuver with the running enemy plane before he locked on his missile for the kill shot. All of this was for naught, because the enemy pilot knew he was as good as dead as the alarm in his plane continued to shriek in his ears.

Bunker One did a sudden hard corkscrew dive at the Zapper, as he pressed the button on his flight stick, and a Sparrow missile instantly dropped off his wing from the right rack, making his plane jump a bit from the sudden change of weight. Bunker continued to watch the missile as the weapon rapidly closed the gap and hitting the Zapper in the right wing area, and the enemy's aircraft explode in flight. Bunker One actually felt the slight shockwave from the explosion, wash over his wings as he struggled to stabilize his own plane now. Then he growled in his mike. "Splash one bastard. Over." As Bunker One then leveled off his aircraft while adding more power to his engines, as he picked up the nose of his plane for more speed.

"Splash another one."

Bunker One instantly searched the sky around him until he picked up another dark smudge presently staining the crystal clear bright blue sky. Indicating to him one more kill for his side. A frantic voice suddenly called in on the radio to all pilots as an override report.

"Check six, check your six." (The American aircraft had to check their rear for any possible Bandits trying to get position on them).

"Check Six, Check Six! Check your fricking Six man!"

Bunker keyed his mike. "Bunker One to all birds. Don't yell over the stinking radio. I can't make out what the hell you're saying, and if I can't understand you, I can't help you. Over."

A pilot replied in a nasty tone of voice at him over the radio. "Fuck you asshole."

Bunker One shook his head as he laughed over the other pilot's rather colorful response.

"Bandit to your left Bunker Two. Head's up man. He's trying to fucking lock you up for a kill man. You better do something and do it fast or he's gonna have you for fucking supper, man."

"Dan, below you buddy, a Zapper coming at ya man. On your four o'clock low, four o'clock low, he's coming in on you from your port side, man. Get the hell out of there before he does ya ass in, Dan. Do some of that flying shit you were taught man. Shit."

An explosion was heard over the radio in most of the American planes engaging the enemy.

"Two more Zappers at your twelve o'clock high. Over." Another pilot offered on the radio.

"Two o'clock, two o'clock. Get the dirty bastard man." Still another pilot said in his radio.

"Hot shit. Snowbird just got one Bandit for himself people. Over." Another pilot reported.

"Bingo. Good shooting Bunker Seven Sir. Over." A pilot said to another one while in flight.

"Fox Two, Fox Two fired away. Fox Two on the way man. Scratch that fucking Zapper from the score card, people." Another pilot said over his radio this time.

"Bunker Nine, Bunker Nine you got a fucking Bandit heading for your tail feathers, sir. Check your six, check your six, he's closing in on you real fast sir. Over."

"I'll take care of the lousy bastard for you sir. Fox One fire away. Fox One hunting sir."

"Bunker Four. You have a shit on your tail end, get up in the damn clouds man. Over."

"Coming in at your three o'clock low to break off the Bandit from your six, Bunker Four."

"Fucking Japanese shits anyhow dammit." A pilot grumbled angrily over his radio.

"Good shooting, you got the bastard Richmond, keep it up sir. Over."

When the Japanese warplanes were positively identified, and as the pilots notified Commander Owens of the new Japanese aircraft presence in the air war, he became hot. He stormed around the CIC room cursing anyone or thing that got in his way. After a few minutes of his blowing off some steam, he sat down and ordered his radio operator to get the Chairman of the Joint Chiefs of Staff on the phone, because he wanted to see what they were going to do about the Japanese fighter aircraft in operation by the Libyans over their country.

AN EMERGENCY MEETING BEING HELD AT THE WHITE HOUSE

Minutes after explaining about the sudden appearance of the Japanese made Mitsubishi fighter aircraft being employed by the Libyan pilots, General William Weidenbacher informed the Commander he would handle this present situation from the Pentagon. The General hung up and instantly sent for his car. In minutes, he was sitting in the Oval Office in front of the extremely upset President dressed in his bathrobe, and he was rubbing his eyes with both of his hands. The President's hair was a mess, obviously, he had not taken the time to comb it before the unscheduled meeting. The General understood his condition, because it was not every day the Chairman requested an immediate audience with the President, especially this late at night. General Weidenbacher could not remember if he used the word emergency in his request.

Even before the General started with his report, the concerned Security Director came in the Oval Office unannounced, and quickly took a seat to the left of the ancient desk without uttering a word. Then he placed his attaché' case down between his legs and smiled at the President.

The President nodded to him and then spoke. "This better be damn important General Weidenbacher Sir. I have had one hell of a long day today as it is, and I'm dead tired, mister."

"I wouldn't have bothered you sir, if I didn't feel this was extremely important situation for you to be made aware of, sir. Mr. President Sir, as we speak, the first wave of our fighter aircraft are engaging the Libyan planes over their own air space, sir."

The President cut the powerful General off in mid sentence as he suddenly looked down at his watch and then announced. "Yes, and they're right on schedule at that General Weidenbacher Sir. Surely, you didn't wake me up to tell me this shit, sir? Am I detecting a sort of a tap dancing going on around here General Weidenbacher Sir? What the hell are you trying to say, come on and spit it out man, and dump all the garnishing too while you're at it as well, General Weidenbacher. I'm old enough to take some bad news sir." President Albert Cole remarked with obvious anger creeping into his voice as he openly glared at this military officer this time.

"No sir, give me a second please Mr. President Sir. The first wave of our attacking aircraft were intercepted by over forty of the new Japanese made Mitsubishi fighter aircraft sir, and our radar aircraft detected and reported quite a number of these same type Japanese aircraft were spotted resting on the hard deck, waiting for immediate takeoff against our aircraft, sir." The General stopped speaking to allow this new information set in for the American Leader.

The General decided and then he turned to the Security Director to see if he wanted to add anything in on this conversation, he was just smiling back at him.

President Cole was extremely upset over this stunning new information about the Japanese aircraft supporting the Libyan airforce. He suddenly pushed his chair away from his desk, and stood and began to pace in front of it while popping his knuckles. He stopped pacing, pulled his chair back to the desk and sat heavily in it and picked up a pencil and began playing with it.

"Are you absolutely certain about this report, General Weidenbacher? What the hell am I asking you, of course you're sure of it, or you wouldn't be here, General." President Cole stared at the General as the pencil in his hands suddenly snapped, and the President asked. "What do you think General? Are we going to be able to beat these new planes in this war, sir?"

"Without a doubt about it sir. Before I came here to give you this latest report, I was informed that our aircraft had successfully killed twenty of the damn things with only three losses to our own aircraft, Mr. President Sir." He reported to his Commander in Chief.

"General, I don't care what it takes to overpower these damn planes. You have the power to use all fourteen Carrier Groups if you feel you may need their aircraft. Just get the job done sir."

President Cole turned to the CIA Director who entered the Oval Office along with General Weidenbacher, and with a grunt he growled at him. "You have been awfully quiet about this shit mister. What the hell do you have to say about this present situation, Director?"

"Mr. President Sir, I think you should speak privately to Prime Minister Ito from Japan, and see what the hell he has to say about this shit. If he refuses to react properly to this information then I think we should consider declaring war on the Japanese nation, sir." CIA Director John Raincloud offered to the President of the United States.

The President was stunned by his Director's last remark, and how simply it was spoken by him as he leaned back in his chair over the force of the statement. Then the President announced for all to hear at the meeting. "Declare war on the nation of Japan? No way in hell will that ever happen mister. I don't want to react too hasty here, not yet at least, Director Raincloud Sir." President Cole turned to his right and he spoke to an aide. "Get me that bastard Gershiro Nangaku on the damn line, I'll straighten his ass out right now for him, mister."

"Mr. President Sir, you have to be extremely careful how you speak to him, sir. He's not a pleasant fellow to deal with when he's in a good mood sir, and this will bunch his undies sir."

"Gees, there goes another Christmas card I won't be getting this year I guess. If you think he's hard to get along with now, just wait until you see me in action against the prick, mister. Let's make this a conference call. Wake Ambassador Walters, apologize to him over the ungodly hour we're calling him. Tell him it's a matter of extreme important. Get going young man."

The President looked back to the General and stated to him for a moment before announcing. "General Weidenbacher Sir, I believe you better get back to your office, in case you're needed there by any of your people, sir. Thank you for staying on top of this current mess for me General Weidenbacher Sir. I'll let you know how I make out with the Japanese Ambassador, sir"

Weidenbacher stood, he shook the President and Director's hands, and then left the office.

The CIA Director sat in total silence along with the President and the rest of the members of the meeting. The stillness was suddenly upset by a loud crack, as another pencil the President was twirling in his fingers, paying the price of his anger instantly snapped, while he was waiting for Ambassador Walters to call him back as he was ordered to do.

President Cole turned to the Director and remarked to him. "Hell Director Raincloud, this is a new turn of events I never expected to happen sir. Do you think I might get a..." The President's conversation was suddenly cut off by the shrill ringing of his private phone.

"Yes, hello Ambassador Walters Sir, I'm terribly sorry for waking you so early this morning sir. I have an emergency on my hands, sir." After he explained the situation, Walters responded.

"Mr. President Sir, I'm glad I was home to take your call, sir. I'm available to you twenty four hours a day, every day sir." It was all he could think of to say at the moment.

Just then, his other phone rang. "That has got to be the Japanese Delegate, I'm going to place this call on the three way conference line, so you can hear all his words, Ambassador Walters. Hang on for a moment Ambassador Walters." The President picked up the receiver and set it in a cradle and then began speaking. "Ambassador Nangaku Sir, I'm sorry for the early hour, but it has come to my attention my aircraft in Libya are coming under attack by Japanese made fighter planes, sir. What do you have to say about this stunning situation, mister?"

"Mr. President Sir, I'm afraid I don't think I care very much for your tone sir."

"I don't give a rat's ass what you think about my tone, Ambassador. I have American boys dying because of your damn warplanes that somehow got in the hands of the Libyan airforce, sir. How the hell did the damn Libyans get a hold of these new fighter planes from your country, mister? Your country signed the pact not to sell military equipment to any Arab nations, sir. Am I to take it Japan broke this pact your country agreed to, sir? Before you answer my last question sir. I have to inform you I've been advised to declare war against your country by my military advisors over this new situation, sir."

There was a moment of dead silence on the other end of the phone, and then the Japanese Ambassador replied to the American President extremely angry tone of voice. "Mr. President Sir, you'd consider declaring war on my country, sir? Japan, one of your long time trusted Allies for all these years, sir. Please Mr. President, I beg of you, don't act in haste against my nation, sir. I can assure you Japan has not sold any advance fighter aircraft to the nation of Libya, sir. Maybe they received them through China, or by some other means, Mr. President Sir. I promise you sir, I shall find out and report back to you sir."

"Please Ambassador Nanaku, let's not bring China into this situation now, she has enough of her own problems to contend with, sir." The concerned and upset American President replied angrily at the obvious attempt to shift the blame from Japan by the Ambassador.

Ambassador Walters read trouble coming and he cut into the conversation and offered. "Mr. President Sir, I'll send a message to the Prime Minister of Japan, and ask him to attend a special emergency meeting of the Security Council, I'll request to assemble tomorrow afternoon."

"Tomorrow afternoon you say Ambassador Walters. My Prime Minister could not possibly be here in the United States to attend this emergency meeting in such a short period of time, sir." Ambassador Nangaku cried as he turned his attention back to the American politician now.

"I'll have him picked up by the SSR 74 supersonic aircraft sir." Ambassador Walters offered.

"Mr. President Sir, may I speak with you privately? Off the record sir." Nangaku asked.

"It's a little too late for any privacy meeting around here sir. What's on your mind Mr. Ambassador Sir?" The American President snapped nastily in the phone this time.

After a long moment of strained silence, the Japanese Delegate spoke calmly. "Mr. President Sir, I know how the Libyans got their hands on our fighter aircraft, and I can assure you we have been doing everything in our power to have them returned to my nation, sir. Mr. President Sir, do you remember when our cargo ship had that problem off the coast of Libya a number of months ago, sir? The ship was loaded with these aircraft. They were to be offered to the Israeli government in hopes of a quick sale. You understand what state our economy is in sir."

"Come on, get on with your damn words man. My time and patience is rapidly leaving my control, sir" The President demanded of the Japanese Ambassador.

"Very well Mr. President, the Libyans stole the aircraft from the ship's cargo containers, sir. My government has issued a strong complaint and demand for the aircraft to be returned to my country, and Libya has promised to give the aircraft back to us, sir. That was the reason we didn't inform the world of the thief. But as you can plainly see, the Libyan government have not done as promised Mr. President Sir. Japan is not to be blamed in this matter Mr. President Sir." The Japanese Ambassador to the United Nations offered in his own defense, yet the sound of his own words proved he did not truly believe what he was trying to say as well.

The CIA Director was shaking his head no, as the President spoke again to the Japanese politician. "Just say I happen to believe this yarn you're spinning here, Ambassador Nangaku. How come Japan decided to lie to us about the damn cargo this ship was carrying?"

"Because Mr. President Sir, we felt you wouldn't believe our story as to how the Libyan government stole the advance aircraft from my nation, sir. I assure you Mr. President, my nation has exhausted all avenues to try and have these aircraft returned to my country, sir"

"How many of these damn fighter aircraft are we talking about here sir? How many of your aircraft do these sonofabitches have in their possession, Ambassador Nangaku?"

"I believe it was eight hundred planes in all they stolen from us, Mr. President Sir."

"Jesus Christ Almighty sir. I think you're a damn liar, Ambassador Nangaku Sir."

Ambassador Walters cut in again to try and stop a confrontation from happening between the two powerful politicians as he offered. "Mr. President Sir please, we're talking here, sir. Let's try and keep it that way. Ambassador Nangaku, I'm sorry, but the President is only reacting to the heavy loss of our fighting men and women to these stolen aircraft of yours, sir. Mr. President Sir, please allow Ambassador Nangaku and myself to settle this situation our way, sir."

"Don't you dare apologize for anything I said Ambassador Walters Sir!" The President growled and then thought for a moment and added in a little calmer tone of voice this time. "Very well, you two settle it your way. But I want Japan to demand her planes back or they better be prepared to declare war on Libya themselves, if they know what's good for them, sir."

"Mr. President Sir please. Allow me handle this one sir." Ambassador Walters cried again.

"Ambassador Walters Sir, I'll leave this mess in your more than capable hands, sir. I have to apologize to you sir. I'm sorry I had to wake you at this ungodly hour. Good night Ambassador. You'll keep me advised on the outcome of this situation with Japan, sir. I want those damn aircraft out of the hands of the Libyans, or destroyed to the last, dammit."

"Yes Sir Mr. President Sir, by all means I shall sir. Good night sir."

The President hung up without further words for the Japanese Delegate, leaving him steaming but fearful on the other end of the line.

The American President turned to the CIA Director John Raincloud and barked at him in an extremely angry tone of voice. "Well what the hell's wrong with you all of a sudden, the damn cat got your tongue or something around here, Director Raincloud Sir? I thought you would've had an awful lot to say about this latest situation and you kept your mouth shut, sir."

"They're lying through their fucking eye teeth at us sir." The Security Director replied angrily.

"I needed you to tell me this shit, Director. I think we better get this information to General Weidenbacher so he can react accordingly against it. Eight hundred planes, those lousy bastards. After this mess is over with, I'm going to settle my hash with Japan."

"Sanctions?" The Director asked quietly as he stared back at the President for a moment.

"Never mind sanctions mister. I'm going to destroy them and their country."

"Sir, if we come down too hard on Japan, they could always retaliate against us Mr. President Sir. Right now we have them trapped between a rock and a hard place…"

"Retaliate?" The President growled back at him this time, and then he went on with his angry words to the powerful Director. "I'll give them fucking retaliation against us mister."

"Yes sir, they could dump dollars, securities and liquidate stock holding they have in our stock market, and harm many of our businesses that way, sir. Which could cause the rest of the nations to dump American properties as well, and put us in one hell of a depression state, sir."

"Yes, they could do this and more I guess sir." The CIA Director offered and then he continued with is offering. "But they'd finish off their own country in the process if they go this route against us, sir. We have studied this case scenario, and we feel strongly the Japanese government would submit to certain sanctions, especially after what I just heard said, sir. I feel we could come to an understanding with Japan, behind closed doors given half a chance sir."

"Behind closed doors is bullshit mister, if we have their asses dead to right as you just offered for God sake. Then we should drag their ass's right through the fucking mud in the open for every one to see and hear what they have committed here, sir." The fuming President hissed at the Director, and then he complained bitterly. "Gentlemen, I'm afraid we're getting a little off track around here for the moment." The President snapped angrily this time at everyone attending the meeting.

"Mr. President Sir, Japan does have its place in the pulse of world affairs, sir. This shit can all be worked out peacefully a little later on, and restitution paid and sanctions leveled at the nation of Japan. Mr. President Sir, the Japanese government is going to..."

"Don't you think you should get this latest information out to General Weidenbacher as quickly as possible, sir? So he can send it out to General Campanelli so he can direct his forces properly to deal with this latest situation. I want to be left alone for now please. But I want to be kept well informed about this mess at all times."

"Yes, of course Mr. President, once I speak with General Weidenbacher and find out what he intends to do about these damn Japanese aircraft we're engaging in the skies over Libya, I'll be back to you immediately afterwards and report on what he's ordering his troops out in the field to do to combat this situation, Mr. President Sir." The Security Director stood like he had the weight of the world resting on his shoulders, and he put out his hand to shake hands with the American Leader, but the President's eyes were closed, and he was rubbing his temples with both hands. He actually looked like he was praying. The Director decided and left the office as quietly as possible, followed by the second aide.

Even CIA Director Raincloud kind of left the office as quietly as possible as not to disturb the seemly upset American Leader.

CHAPTER 25 – IN THE AIR WAR OVER LIBYA AND ALGERIA

Bunker Two's hit, his fricking aircraft going out of control, and he's going down in a flat spin, dammit. He popped his glass, he's out of the disabled aircraft, I see a chute from him, sir. He's out okay and drifting down fine and slow and he's giving us the thumbs up signal, sir."

"Bunker One to all birds. Stop the damn yelling into the radio all the time dammit. How many times do I have to warn you people about that shit. When you yell in the damn radio, it makes other communications go right down the damn shitter on us. Over."

Bunker One suddenly picked up an enemy Zapper trying to get position on Bunker Four's aircraft, and he immediately made his move to assist Bunker Four, and get the Zapper at the same time, before he got a kill on one of his planes. Bunker One hit his afterburners and his aircraft shot forward at breath robbing speed, and he came up below, and quickly got position on the enemy plane on his six. When he heard the tone being emitted from the missile's seeker warhead, he knew he had the bad guy in his sites. Bunker One fired his Sparrow missile off and in less than a heartbeat later, the T 2R3 Japanese made Zero instantly exploded while in flight.

"Splash another Japanese bastard." Bunker One announced in the radio as he watched the enemy plane break up in the sky. A contrail streak from an enemy Sidewinder missile suddenly flashed by his cockpit a few feet before his aircraft and instantly vanished in the distance.

Bunker One was furious as hell at himself, because he never picked up the missile coming in on him at eye level. Bile built up in his mouth and he swallowed it and it made his stomach burn and grow upset at him, because he knew if it was not for dumb luck, he would be dead about now. He was covered by sweat as he breathed heavy in his oxygen mask. His hands shook from the near miss from the deadly missile. He frantically searched the sky for the shooter, but before he even located the enemy plane his radio came to life.

"Bunker Four to Bunker One. I got the lousy bastard who just fired on ya dead in my sights, sir. Firing now sir. Over." The other pilot offered to his Wing Commander in an excited voice.

Bunker One looked to his portside just in time to see Bunker Four fire a missile, and a running T 2 almost instantly exploded in a cloud of smoke and flame, as it quickly disintegrated while in flight, and the pilot announced in his radio. "Bingo, splash another fricking Zapper."

"Bunker One to Bunker Four. Thanks for your help on this one sir. If he was a good pilot, I'd be on my way to hell by now. I owe you a beer when we get back to the real world. Over."

"Bunker Four to Bunker One. No problem sir, I'm only here to serve sir. Over."

Their conversation was cut short by three attacking enemy Zappers. Bunker One was forced to bank hard to his starboard side, and then put the nose of his aircraft down, and increase his speed at the same time as he went into a heavy "G" turn. His ears pounded, and he had to yawn to relieve the built up pressure and pain in his ears, but this did nothing to relieve the pain the hard turn caused in his chest. After he completed the hard turn and increase speed again, he pulled the nose of his aircraft up, allowing the climb to bleed off some of his air speed. Bunker One continued to climb to get a position on an enemy plane, and he immediately fired his 20 mm cannon as he dove into the fighting. He got some help from Foxtrot One.

"Foxtrot One Leader. Attacking from your nine o'clock level flight sir. Over."

Radio protocol was all but forgotten because of the fever pitch of the wild dog fight taking place in the air. Another eighteen American aircraft now joined the fighting. They were YF 23s fighter bombers returning from a bombing run, and they were making fast work of the slower Japanese warplanes. Their call names were Foxtrot One through Eighteen.

"Foxtrot Three. Fox One fired off. Fox One away and seeking a target, sir. Over."

A Sparrow missile crashed into a fleeing T 2, and the plane instantly exploded in flight.

"Switching to cannon fire now because there are too many friendlies to employ my missiles further, sir." A Foxtrot pilot who did not identify himself, called in on his radio.

Another bandit exploded while in flight, and the severely damaged aircraft quickly went down.

It took some time, but General Weidenbacher informed the Commander about the number of Japanese made fighter aircraft they would be facing in this action, and in return he had to inform Bunker One of the situation.

"Commander Owens to Bunker One. Listen up son this is important to this present situation, you have a total of eight hundred T 2s to contend with. Over."

"Eight hundred fricking Jap planes, sir. You got to be fucking around with me sir."

The radio was full of other gripes from many of the angry young American flyers now.

"Man, you got to be shitting me here sir." One pilot bitched into his radio.

"This is bullshit, I can't wait till I get back to the real world and tell the public about this shit."

"God damn this shit man. I want some stinking blood from these damn suckers, people!"

Bunker One put a quick end to the complaining by growling in his radio at the other pilots. "Knock the shit off for Christ sake, we have a fucking job to do, and this makes it just a little bit harder for us to accomplish our mission, that's all. Tighten up formations. Commander Owens Sir, can you get me any information on these damn planes that might help us defeat them, sir?"

"Will do as requested sir." Was repeated back to him over his radio this time.

"Bunker Seven. Get your ass out of there man, you have three Zappers closing in on your seven o'clock low. Get up in the damn clouds, and hide there until help arrives, will ya?"

"Bunker One, Bunker One, this is Sleepy Eye, sir. You have another large flight of Gomers taking off from the hard deck below you, sir. Do you copy traffic Bunker One? Over sir."

"Not now Sleepy Eye. I have my stinking hands full here with the damn shits in the air already, sir. Stay off the damn air for now so I can communicate with the rest of my pilots, sir. Over." Bunker One bitched at his security blanket flying in the air out of the firing.

"Foxtrot Five get your ass in there and help Bunker Seven out right now man."

"Foxtrot Two to anyone. I'm hit, I'm hit, no power, engine's are dead, I'm going down."

"Foxtrot Two. Punch out, punch out, eject, eject, eject! God dammit!"

An explosion dotted the heavily vapor streaked sky just as Foxtrot Two exploded in flight, before the pilot's cockpit canopy popped open and he escaped his dead aircraft. The pilot was unable to get out of his plane in time and he went down with his bird.

A voice suddenly growled angrily in the radio to the other American pilots engaging the enemy aircraft. "Foxtrot Two didn't make it out of his fricking plane in time, dammit. These bastards are gonna pay big time for that one I assure you people."

More T 2s took off from the deck armed with orders, they were to go after the fighter bombers before they could drop their bombs on Libyan ground targets. Thirty planes took to the sky.

"Bunker One, Sleepy Eye. Flash, Flash, Flash. Enemy takeoffs have been detected, I repeat sir enemy takeoffs have been detected. From the angle of their approach, it looks like the new batch of Gomers are going to ignore our fighter planes, and go after the bombers against us this time sir. The Roosevelt's going into an Alpha Launch at this present time. Her Alpha Strike force is ordered to help you, and hit Libya from her rear. ETA's two hours, I say again, ETA's two hours away. No help to you, your fight will be over by then sir. I suggest you drop down to Angel's Five Thousand Feet, and regroup your fighter wing to try and help defend the bomber aircraft, sir. I'm calling for a emergency buster signal for your attack at this time sir. Over."

Bunker One interrupted Sleepy Eye's communication with him as he barked at him over the radio. "Fuck your damn buster signal mister. I have no fricking intention of turning my stinking tail feathers to these damn Jap Zero shits and bug the hell outta here, sir. Over."

"Take it easy with your communications with me, sir. Remember I'm on your side Bunker One, sir. I'm only trying to help you guys out, that's all sir. Over."

Bunker One overrode the orders for the buster signal being transmitted from the AWACS aircraft Sleepy Eye, as he ordered the rest of his pilots to continue engaging the enemy aircraft, and then he concentrated all his efforts on the air war still raging all about him.

"Richmond to Bunker One. I count six, no, correct last, seven Zappers ganging up on the F 111 flights, sir. They cut one free from the rest of the pack already sir. Shit, they got that one dead sir. Some Foxtrot aircraft are coming in to try and the aid some of the bomber planes, sir. The damaged EF 111s tail section's disintegrating while in flight. She's heavily smoking, there she goes, she's out of control now sir. She's had it sir. I'm going to follow the EF 111 until separation time. There it goes sir, the separation has been completed sir. Look at that shit man." Richmond said as he watched the entire cockpit of the disabled plane with both pilot and co pilot inside it, free falling through the sky as the body of the aircraft suddenly exploded in flight. The cockpit had a good lateral drift, controlled by two fins on the back of the assembly. The pilot stared at it until the chutes finally opened and controlled the free fall of the cockpit.

"Bunker One. Have radio contact with the pilot inside the separated EF cockpit, sir. They're reporting the both of them are alright and in fine shape sir, and the transponder's beeping away for them already, sir. The pilot informed me he was going to drift out to the sea for easier pickup by Angel rescue. He's kind of worried about being taken a prisoner if they land on land, sir." This remark did not surprise any of the fighter pilots, because they all knew the cockpit assembly of the EF 111 would float, and act as a life raft until pick up was accomplished.

"Angel One Helicopter rescue's in radio contact with the downed pilot already sir. I'm breaking off my contact with the pilot's sir, and I'm coming back up to get back in the fighting, sir. Over." The pilot of the Foxtrot aircraft reported to the commander of the flight.

"Bunker One to Richmond. Roger that last. Do you think they'll make the sea okay? Over."

"Easy sir. He's drifting lateral a quarter of a mile towards the sea for every half mile she drops down sir. At this rate Bunker One, she should come down at least seven miles out to sea, sir."

"Good, get back up here then. We need your aircraft sir. Over." Bunker One ordered as he ended communication with the Richmond pilot. Bunker One knew he was going to need the electronic jamming the EF 111 afforded him. He shrugged as he thought, what else can you do.

The Flight Wing of EF and F 111s came from the 474th fighter wing stationed in Texas, and they were sent out to the Carriers for their electronic protection, and their attack potential of enemy targets. Once they finished their flight, they were ordered to land in Saudi Arabia.

"Foxtrot One Leader, Bunker One Commander. Call all of your Foxtrot fighter aircraft together sir, and have them regroup at five thousand yards behind my group, sir. Over."

"Bunker One to Starman and War Child Leader. Pickle off your eggs, (bombs) and then get up here and help us fight these lousy bastards off. That's a direct order people. Over."

"War Child to Bunker One. I already issued the order to jettison our bomb load, sir, and then we're coming up to help you out with this new batch of attacking Gomers, sir." The War Child pilot immediately reported to Bunker One.

"Bunker One to War Child Leader. Stay low and start your attack on this new wing of Zappers from underneath the Damn bandits, sir. I have all Foxtrot aircraft dropping behind us to help confuse the enemy radar, sir. Then all Bunker followers will pull a four "G" to our right and up, leaving all Foxtrots aircraft to a attack the Gomers head on, while we loop over and then attack them from above while your aircraft attack the enemy formation from underneath the damn Gomers, sir. I hope to catch them in a damn vice this way sir. Good hunting people. Over."

Bunker One lost four of his wing of attacking aircraft, which left his wing with fourteen still active aircraft. Foxtrot One lost three planes which left him fifteen remaining, taking up position to the rear of Bunker's remaining F 18 Hornets. Bunker One read his radar and counted fifteen bandits in the air while he read another possible thirty enemy aircraft still coming up from the deck. This gave the bad guys over forty five attacking aircraft again. Bunker knew he had thirty fighter bombers coming up to attack the underbelly of the unaware Zappers. If the enemy did not reinforce again, he would still have them outnumbered, and this gave him the upper hand.

Bunker One checked out his missile rack, and noticed he had two Sidewinder heat seekers, and one Sparrow radar control missile left on his aircraft. He had a full cannon magazine left though. He watched his screen cloud over with a mess of incoming bandit hits. The T 2s fighters were equipped with four Sidewinder heat seeker missiles each. Bunker One called out to his pilots to follow his call, as the two formations hurled at each other at near Mach Two speed.

"Steady up people. We have to keep an eye out for any possible leakers, too many enemy fighters coming at us to get them all at one time on this charge. Over."

The two formation of American planes were less than five miles apart now, and he still waited.

"Three miles out now, steady up people. Keep it steady people. Over."

Bunker One picked up a number of plumes on his scope from launch of the enemy Sidewinder missiles and he immediately barked in his radio. "Release all countermeasures, break right and get up in the damn clouds for cover, dammit." Were the orders from Bunker One.

The countermeasures consisted of a number of flares to be fired off by the fighters as they turned tail from the wing of attacking bandits. The unbelievable heat generated from a hundred burning flares and hot bags attracted the heat seeking Sidewinders, which chased many of the countermeasures to the ground. Ten Sidewinders picked up the turning Bunker aircraft and gave chase. But the retreating aircraft had such a jump on the missiles they burn out before they could catch up to the fleeing planes. One by one, the missiles lost control and fell to earth.

Bunker took the aircraft under his command through the four "G" turn, and then they leveled off after the planes climbed three thousand feet as ordered. Bunker One was well above the large wing of Libyan attacking aircraft now. In his scope he located the fighter bombers gathering up in position below the attacking bandits, and the flight of YF 23 tactical fighter bombers were heading right at the unsuspecting Libyan attackers. Bunker One looked in his radar and picked up another wing of American aircraft linking up with War Child's group. Another ten planes in all rapidly closed ranks with the other aircraft. Then he remembered about the aircraft flying with them were from the Aircraft Carrier Independence.

The attacking enemy Libyan aircraft did not know which wing of planes to attack first, but the American planes that were head on with them got their pick. It was a fatal mistake committed by the attacking enemy pilots, because while their attention was glued on the oncoming YF 23s, the fighter bombers and F 18 Hornets attacked their incoming wing of enemy planes from their twelve o'clock high and six o'clock low. The Hornets swiftly ripped through the T 2 formation from the top, killing five of the enemy planes with one pass, while the attacking F 15 Eagles completed their attack from beneath the Libyan formation. Killing nine of the remaining enemy planes, and trading places with Bunker's aircraft once on top of the Libyan aircraft, before the remaining few Libyan warplanes had a chance to disperse and protect themselves.

"Tally, tally, tally." Was the call coming in over the American pilot's radios, as the wing of F 18 Hornet fighter aircraft began the first of many attacks on the surviving enemy planes.

"Bunker Four. Bingo, I got one people. He's going down for the count man."

"Bunker One to Bunker Four. You have a bandit on your tail feathers, get out of there fast."

"I have the bastard dead in my sights sir. He's history sir." Was the call from Starman.

Shot Gun, who received his tag name by shot gunning beers at the officer's club, put his F/A 18 Hornet into a sharp dive and then he quickly lined up on the rear of the once attacking Zapper. As he killed the enemy aircraft, two other Zappers jumped his tail.

Starman was Shot Gun's nearest help. "Hey Shot Gun, get the hell out of there for Christ sake man. You have two Zappers closing in on your damn tail end from your nine o'clock low, man. You better get the hell out of there before you're history in this mess, buddy."

Shot Gun did not have a chance to start his jinking maneuvers in an attempt to avoid the attacking enemy planes before they finally opened fire on his aircraft. They both hit Shot Gun at the same time, raking his cockpit with bullets and causing his right engine to smoke up and instantly flame out on his aircraft. He jumped as the shells and canopy plastic sprayed all around him inside the cockpit. He was slightly disoriented when the smoke quickly filled his cockpit, but he could successfully escaped through the many holes shot in his canopy which blew most of it away and he finished breaking the rest of the canopy away with his hands.

Shot Gun felt something warn running down between his legs. He looked down and he saw a mass of dark liquid quickly pooling at his middle section and lap. He felt his chest and found a hole ripped in his flight suit. Blood was pouring out of the ripped opening. There was little pain from the wound though to him. His mouth suddenly went dry and he coughed, everything around him abruptly seemed to take on a slow motion dimension. His senses grew numb on him, first his sense of touch escaped his control. Then the color in his eyes faded from his vision as everything slowly turned to a black and white hue in his mind.

He suddenly felt like he was falling, and he looked down at his hands and tried to focus on them at the same time. His hands were still locked on the stick of his plane's controls, but he could no longer feel it, or his hands. His mind angrily ordered his hands to pull back on the stick of his aircraft, but his arms would not respond to his commands. The injured pilot coughed again, this time sending a fine mist of blood all over his cockpit and instrument gauges through the torn oxygen mask. Operating out of pure instincts and his training, he next reached for the ejection handle stationed under his seat, but his hand would still not obey his command to grab hold of the handle and pull back up on it and send him out of his aircraft.

A scream was still ringing in his ear phones, but his mind could not decipher what the screaming was about. He suddenly had an over wheeling desire to relax and let go of his stick as everything grew dim, and then black as his head suddenly slumped forward, and it came to rest on his chest. The Hornet headed point first right at the ground like a flaming dart.

The screaming in his deaf ears continued in an excited yelling.

"Shot Gun! Pull up, pull the fuck up man! Eject, eject, eject. Get the fuck out of there you sonofabitch you. Do something man. Shit, shit, damn. Good bye my old friend." The pilot of the trailing aircraft mumbled as he watched the disabled F 18 Hornet aircraft until his attention was forced back to the fight arena, as Bunker One ordered over the radio.

Bunker One looked over his shoulder in time to see the Zapper threatening Bunker Four, disintegrate in a cloud of smoke and flames. No chute appeared in the sky, informing Bunker the enemy pilot did not make it out of his aircraft alive. He then watched as Starman's sleek F 111 plane pull up, and a T 2 enemy fighter immediately take up position on his six.

"Starman, you have a Bandit coming in on you on your five o'clock low from your tail end sir, get up and out of there dammit! Turning to get position on the bastard on you sir."

"No need to worry Bunker One, the Preacher has this viper dead in his sights already, sir. He's mine to take out of the picture, sir." Another America pilot informed his Air Commander

He kept a close eye on the action as the Preacher's F 111 chased after the running T 2. He fired his 20 mm cannon and the T 2 aircraft instantly broke up as the shells ripped through its body, and the plane instantly plummeted out of control towards the earth. He picked up the white plume of a chute as the enemy pilot got out and drifted slowly towards the ground.

Bunker One picked up another enemy aircraft go after one of his Eagle bomber planes, the enemy plane quickly got position on him and easily kill the American warplane. He pulled his stick back and gave chase, but he noticed Richmond's plane come out of the sun and instantly get position and fire a Sparrow missile at the enemy plane, and then heard the call on the radio. "Fox One away!" And saw the Japanese made aircraft explode. This time there was no chute in the sky, and he knew this pilot did not made it out of the aircraft alive. The rest of the enemy bandits pulled back, and tried to regroup as they turned back towards their country of Libya and headed down for the hard deck, admitting to the American pilots they won this round.

Bunker One called for all American aircraft involved on the attack against the Libyan aircraft to immediately regroup behind his lead aircraft, and they follow him up to the waiting HC 130 fuel tanker aircraft presently circling over the nation of Algeria. The warplanes which sustained the most damage in the battle, or were the lowest on fuel were given top priority to refuel first. The modified gas tankers could fuel up to five aircraft at once. He watched as two planes were forced out of his formation, and they both plummeted towards the earth out of control. He watched until he picked up three chutes open, and then he breathed out when he knew the pilots got out of the disabled aircraft before they crashed into the ground.

He found himself wondered how many of his planes would make it back to the Carrier Nimitz safely. His ragtag formation flew at three quarters speed back for the Nimitz when they were fueled up. Out of the eighty six planes launched by the Nimitz, sixty one circled the ship. One Hornet, and one of the F 15 Eagles were damaged and smoking, they were given first landing.

A damaged Hornet was the first aircraft to land on the waiting carrier. As the aircraft lined up with the flight deck of the Carrier, the pilot got a sudden red warning light, meaning his tail hook was not locking down and setting in place. A Bolter was called for the damaged plane, and the aircraft was instantly waved off of his landing as the trap was quickly set up for an emergency crash landing into the nylon and wire barrier of the Aircraft Carrier.

All planes resting on the flight deck of the Carrier ready for launch were brought below deck on the main elevator, as the damaged warplane started to come in again. Two helicopters were launched, and they hovered off to the side of the Carrier at the ready to pick up any pilot who had to do a blue water divert, by ditching in the water. The Landing Officer or LSO talked to the pilot of the damaged Hornet as he came in, he showed the pilot the location of his wings with a pair of red paddles and he barked in his radio at the same time at the pilot. "Up, come on and get that nose up or you'll stall the damn thing out, that's it, a little up, a little more sir. Your landing gear looks good. Okay sir, you got the ball. Land, cut your engine. Sir, pick up the nose and cut your engine now sir. Down, that's it. You're down and home free sir, good job sir."

The damaged Hornet hit the flight deck hard and it instantly crashed into the trap wire barrier. Immediately, alarms wailed on the Carrier as the Deck Officer yelled over the speaker. "Crash on deck, all hands emergency, crash on deck. Let's get out there and look for any hidden fires people." Two small fire trucks and a horde of deck firemen dressed in their protective fireproof silver outfits, instantly climbed all over the damaged plane, and they immediately pulled the semi unconscious pilot out of his aircraft, as other firemen shot CO 2 into the crashed plane's intakes. A flight deck fire truck pulled up and it quickly pushed the crippled plane off the side of the deck and into the water, as the deck crews quickly removed any possible debris from the flight deck, and the cables were lifted to receive the next waiting aircraft for landing.

Smoke poured out of the heavily damaged Eagle, and orders were issued for the pilot to do a blue water divert and ditch in the water. Deck hands watched as the disabled F 15 Eagle glided down to the surface of the water. Instantly, the Angel helicopter was hovering over it and a diver jumped from the chopper twenty feet to the water to assist the pilot out of the rapidly sinking fighter plane. When the pilot was hooked to the chopper by the retrieval wire the deck hands on the carrier cheered. It took an hour to get all the planes to deck down on the Carrier.

Captain Ray Taylor of the Nimitz Aircraft Carrier called for an immediate debriefing, and when the pilots gathered in the flight room, the concerned Captain wanted to know what each of the pilots had observed about the Japanese aircraft. The first and most important question asked by the commander, was if any of the T 2 Japanese made Zero's might have been flown by possible Japanese pilots during this last engagement of the enemy aircraft.

Most of the American pilots thought the enemy planes were all being flown by the Libyan pilots because of their radio jabber picked up, and the extremely sloppy way the enemy aircraft attacked their formations. Bunker remembered two planes he felt maneuvered too good to be flown by any poorly trained Libyan pilots. The more he thought about it, the more he was convinced that these few aircraft had to have been flown by Japanese pilots.

Many American pilots were angry as hell that they had to go up against the Japanese made planes. Prompting the Captain of the Nimitz to offer he remembered the many talks he had with his father, and when he told him how he fought against the Japanese Zeros during World

War Two. He cursed as he said he hoped he never came across another Zero as long as he lived. He promised the pilots he would get answers on how the planes suddenly turned up inside Libya.

The debriefing lasted a little over an hour until the Captain was certain all his pilots were accounted for one way or the other, and he had successfully gathered all the information he needed on how the T 2 planes handled, and their weaponry performed during the attack. The pilots were fed then ordered to sleep. The Nimitz was being refitted with planes she lost from the USS Andrew J Higgins, in preparation for another all out alpha attack against Libya.

The nuclear Aircraft Carriers the George Washington and John F. Kennedy were ordered out of the Indian Ocean, and they took up their new position stationed in the Red Sea. They now had orders to lend support and fighter aircraft to the Roosevelt's attack group, and her support ships with their next attack scheduled on the nation of Libya. The planes launching from the Roosevelt had attacked Libyan airbases, while the Libyans were paying attention to the air war raging over Algeria. Massive damage was done to the city of Hass Messaoud, from the bombs jettisoned from the American bomber planes, so they could better defend themselves against the attacking enemy T 2 Japanese made Libyan fighter planes.

Thousands of tons of bombs landed on and all around the small town, killing well over a thousand men, women and children. The government of Algeria understood why and how this accident occurred. The Muslim's did not condemn the death of their civilians, as long as the United States made Libya pay for her crimes against the rest of the Arab world. By the morning of October 9th, 1996, and with the help of the other Aircraft Carriers, the Nimitz air power was increased to two hundred and forty planes for the upcoming attack on the Libyan forces.

The hell Libya started when she first attacked the small nation of Chad, was not going to stop because of the darkness of night. Two flights of the stealth F-117 Nighthawk aircraft, and one wing of the stealth F 110 Bluelight planes, which gave birth to the F 117, took off for the coast of Libya from their hard shelters stationed well inside Saudi Arabia. Each wing of attacking American aircraft consisted of twenty one planes equipped with two powerful GBU 10E/B two thousand pound laser guided smart bombs apiece. Three MC 130 Combat Talon aircraft dropped the so called Daisy Cutter, the fifteen thousand pound bombs on selected Libyan hard shelters thought to be hiding more small Japanese fighter planes in many areas of the nation of Libya.

The almost completely invisible F 117 Nighthawks and F 110 Bluelight stealth fighter planes to any radar detection, would be forced to refueled over the nation of Egypt, and a second time while going over what was left of the nation of Israel, on their way back to their base stationed in Saudi Arabia. But the attack from the F 117 and F-110s were well worth the effort and the in flight refueling need twice for the aircraft. The main Libyan Command headquarters, in addition to many of her fuel depots and armor bunkers, were scheduled to be hit during this latest flight of the stealth fighter planes over Libya.

Many Libyan fuel depots were not going to make it through the night. The stealth fighter bombers would be over Libya at exactly twelve o'clock midnight. This timing was absolutely essential to the American Command, because it would stop any Libyan military personnel from sleeping the whole night long, and a tired soldier is an already defeated soldier. There was no radio communications from any of the pilots. Each pilot knew his target, and they knew the exact route to and from their targets. That was all the pilots needed and wanted to know.

The Nighthawk aircraft split up while in flight, and each of the stealth aircraft then began their own attack on the secondary capital city of Libya, Bengasi. Four of the Nighthawk planes dropped their bombs dead on the military base stationed in this city, and the communication Command Post, and the power of the explosions was felt miles away from the impact area. The F 110's targets were all the bridges in the same region of Libya. The Libyan cities of Al Marj, Zawiyat al Bayda and Suluq felt the massive power of the Nighthawk heavy bombs. The second flight of the Nighthawks hit the border towns of Pico Bette in Libya, as well as the military installations stationed all along Sarir Tibasti, and the two cities inside the nation of Chad that had been taken over by the invading Libyan troops, and then occupied by them.

The Libyan cities of Aozou and Bardai felt the full wrath of the American stealth warplanes. What was so devastating about these night attacks was, no one could tell where and when they were going to come under attack, until it was too late for them to react to the attack, and they were hit by the invisible American aircraft. A number of bombs being dropped on this night, successfully caught many of the small T 2 Japanese made fighter aircraft on the ground, or trapped inside their hangers, or even sitting in the open on the runways of the airports under attack. Two hundred enemy planes were destroyed by the night attacks, with two airports along with a number of military communication centers inside Libya.

The two thousand pound bombs dropped by the Nighthawk and Bluelight aircraft, were all of the smart bomb variety directed towards their targets by special TV guidance systems during the day, and by an infrared aiming and guiding system during the night raids. As the massive and devastating bomb hit the ground, it left a crater eleven feet deep, and nearly sixty feet wide, and the heavy percussion from the GBU 10 E/B laser guided bomb could damage tanks and military vehicles as far away from the blast as a hundred feet. The heavy use of the smart bombs was employed by the United States command to try and help minimize the death and destruction that would soon be suffered by the civilian population of Libya. The collateral damage was always reported to the world, but always during wartime, many civilians died in the middle of the night by these such attacks, nearly a thousand Libyan civilians died on this night.

The Libyan defenders did not lay down and die under the heavy pounding and devastating bombing attacks they were receiving coming from the overwhelming American forces attacking their country. After the first bomb fell on Libyan soil, the sky over the twin Libyan capitals of Bengazi and Tripoli, was quickly filled with heavy anti aircraft fire, or Triple A fire. Effectively lighting up the entire sky more than it did during the American attack on the capital of Iraq during the Desert Storm war. Libyan civilians and military soldiers alike, were killed on the ground by the super heated shrapnel returning to the ground from thousands of feet up from the anti-aircraft shells and missiles exploding in the night sky over their country.

Libya's command also ordered up a number of their new Japanese fighter aircraft to try and intercept the Nighthawk and Bluelight aircraft, they successfully located one of the stealth planes, and though they did happen to shoot it down, the pilot stayed with the aircraft all the way until he was over the Mediterranean Sea. Before he finally ditched the super secret aircraft into the water, thus securing the secrecy of the F 117 stealth fighter bomber for the time being.

This attack was the first successful action taken directly on Libyan soil to date since the war first started in the region, and it did not sit very well with the Libyan government, or their civilians. But this attack was far from the last one which was going to be visited upon the people and military units of Libya. The massive B 52H Stratofortress bombers were just taking off from their land base stationed inside England, and they were heading directly for Libya, just as the first of the F 117 stealth fighter planes finished up with their attack against the Libyan military forces, and they headed back for their bases inside Saudi Arabia to refuel and rearm, and then prepare for their next attack against Libya. To this point, the B 52 Stratofortress bombers were used solely to attack the Libyan army presently laying siege at the Chad city of Abeche, but these orders had just changed for the pilots of the massive warplanes.

Twenty of the massive B 52 bombers took off loaded down with over sixty thousand pounds of conventional bombs stored inside the belly of each of the enormous planes. The bombing of Libya had just started in earnest, and it was not going to stop until the end of the war was finally realized by all parties concerned in the war. Both day and night Libya was scheduled to be heavily pounded into total submission, much like Iraq was in her war with the United States and her Coalition forces.

The mighty Stratofortress plane's targets were many strategic bridges and roads running throughout Libya and upper Chad. These were targeted in an attempt to try and slow down the heavy flow of military supplies and equipment needed by the Libyan army to maintain their strangle hold on the occupied areas of the nation of Chad.

The stealth fighter aircraft would again be back over the skies of Libya by dawn of October 10th, just as the B 52 bombers finished up with their attack against Libya. The massive bomber flights were constantly being monitored by the American satellite platforms, and all Libyan troop movements were also being monitored in much the same way, so the American warplanes would know exactly where, and when to attack the military convoys, or the troop positions for the best possible results of their bombing runs against the enemy forces inside Libya.

Matters grew much worse for the Libyan government and their military personnel and civilians, and also for their Russian defectors and helpers.

RUSSIAN SATELLITE TRACKING STATION A3R

Inside the Alliance State of the Ukraine, one of the loyal Russian soldiers whose assignment was to monitor the six screens of the bank of forty Russian spy satellites presently operating in space. He noticed a sudden drain off of information being siphoned off from the satellite UV 41. He immediately called his supervisor over to his side, who leaned over the concerned soldier's back, and he watched the screen intensely for a few long seconds. It took a few more moments for the lead supervisor to read off the numbers being spun at a fantastic rate of speed on the bottom of the tiny computer screen, to realize that someone was actually tapping the information coming from the Russian spy satellite. The thieves were being given the same exact information that the Russian soldiers were receiving. The stunned supervisor quickly place a call to his next in command, who in turn contacted his

Commander, until the phone was finally picked up in the UKGBA. The Ukrainian equivalent of the KGB.

The angry sounding UKGBA Officer ordered the channel to remain open until one of the other technicians was able to pinpoint exactly where this information was being sent to by their compromised satellite. In less than an hour's time, the officer had the exact location of the stolen transmission. It was in the small town of Dahra inside the nation of Libya. The UKGBA Officer immediately ordered this satellite to be put to sleep for the duration of the Libyan war, until the fighting was completely over in both Libya and Chad. One of the Russian technicians asked his supervisor if the Libyans were able to gain access to this one satellite on them then could they possibly tapped into the other five satellites observing this certain area of the world.

The special officer snapped his fingers as he stared at the concerned looking technician. He then ordered all six specialized spy satellites to be put to sleep until further notice. The wise supervisor then reached for a phone, and he informed his supervisors of what they had just discovered happening to one of their spy satellites.

This new information prompted an immediate call from the President of the Ukraine to Washington. As the President of the Ukraine informed the President of the United States what they discovered happening to one of their special satellites, and the emergency steps they adopted to prevent any further stealing of this vital military information from them that was going over to the Libyan command structure stationed inside Libya. The American President placed an immediate Flash call to the CIC Center on board the Aircraft Carrier Roosevelt, and he then informed Commander Owens the Libyans were now totally blind of any such further attacks by his warplanes against them on their soil. The President complimented Commander Owens on his being able to deduce the Libyan command must have had some sort of access to a Russian spy satellite flying over the region, to be able to react against his attack so swiftly and successfully.

Commander Owens could not keep the smile from crossing his lips at the knowledge he was absolutely correct all along. He could not wait to disconnect from the President so he could get on with his moving his attacking forces around to better positions of attacking the Libyan forces. He was pleased, because he felt he was able to attack Libya without having to worry about them having access to valuable satellite information on his troops and military equipment.

CHAPTER 26

The well aged Russian defector monitoring the Russian spy satellite screen inside the Libyan command station, almost jumped from his chair as his screen suddenly went dead right before his eyes. The Libyan soldier assigned to watch this Russian technician, instantly ran over to his side as he cried out. Both of them stared at this blank computer screen. The Russian cursed as he tried everything in his power to try and re establish the linkup with the dead satellite. Nothing he did worked, and he soon realized they must have been discovered by the Russian technician controlling the spy satellite in Russia, and now they were cut off from the satellite's help.

The upset Russian tried to hookup to one of the other five Russian satellites he was aware to be in this area of the world. Every channel or hookup he tried, remained blank as he pushed keys on the key pad from his memory to give him access to an orbiting Russian reconnaissance platform. After more than an hour of trying, the angry Russian finally turned to the Libyan guard and said to him. "My friend, we have been detected and cut off from all satellite feeds."

The young Libyan soldier glared at the old Russian as he asked him with concern straining his voice. "Old Russian fool, you can no longer talk to your dom spy satellites?"

The Russian shook his head no slowly as he let out his breath in a sigh of disgust.

"Son of a lowly desert dog you! I'm not your friend in the least, and my government has no further need of you and your cursed services, or your foul presence within my faithful country, you evil jackal." With this said, the Libyan guard suddenly pulled out his pistol, and then he shot the Russian defector in the head as he growled at the old man as he fell to the floor.

"This is the fate of anyone who doesn't help my government in her time of great need. We should've never offered our hand to you Russian jackals " The Libyan left the communications shelter in a huff to report to his Commander of the loss of their satellite communications.

Libyan Ambassador Kamal, still hold up in Benghazi was asleep at the Hilton Sands hotel when the first two thousand pound bomb suddenly hit the airbase just outside town. He was knocked completely from his bed, and landed hard on the floor from the powerful concussion. His female bodyguard Gail, ran into his room and saw him lying on the floor and she announced in an excited voice. "Sir, we're under attack from American bomber planes. I believe you better go down to the basement area for your own safety, Ambassador Kamal Sir."

"Under attack you offer to me, desert witch? It has to be the cursed Americans and their cursed warplanes which hide from our worthless radar and anti-aircraft weapons."

Gail cut him off by adding to her warning to the Libyan politician. "Ambassador Kamal Sir, we have to go at once to the basement of this building if you wish to remain alive, sir." She cried just as a thunderous explosion occurred in the direction of the Bengasi airfield.

The fuming Libyan Ambassador Kamal allowed himself to be pulled up and out of the room by the scared female bodyguard. He stopped to dress, and then he headed to the basement, but he stopped and instead, he left the building and stood out in the middle of the street as the sky overhead lit up from the flash of flack shells exploding in the heavens.

Gail tried to get Ambassador Kamal to come to the basement with her, but he was completely mesmerized by the flash of fireworks exploding overhead in the night time sky. She was the first one to hear the bits of white hot metal from the flack shells falling back to the streets and she actually forced him by bending his arm behind his back, to go to the basement to wait the end of this latest air raid against Libya. But the air raid never ended, for no sooner did the F 117s, and 110 stealth fighters and Navy's X 117s leave the skies over Libya, than they were immediately replaced by a wing of heavy B 52 bombers, who started their attack on the Libyan city. He found himself having to stay in the hot, dusty basement filled with screaming women and their children for the rest of the night until the air raid finally ended.

The next morning, Ambassador Kamal woke dirty, hot, sweaty, sore and still worn out because of the heavy bombing of his city kept him up most of the night, and he was in a most foul of moods. He smelled, and he was exhausted from the lack of sleep, he was angry as hell as he ran up the debris covered stairs to his state room in the hotel, in order to view the damage done to the bombed out city by American air raids last night from the seventh floor. The capital of Bengasi looked undamaged. Most of the damage was done primarily to the two airports, both the civilian and military airports was laid to ruins by the attacking American warplanes.

Vast columns of thick black smoke and flames bellowed high into the air from the Japanese made fighter planes destroyed and scattered about along the runways. Many military installations were likewise destroyed or burning also. Ambassador Kamal looked out to the sea, he picked up a column of smoke from the debris of the American Aircraft Carrier Independence still burning, and knew where he was going to aim his anger for these latest air raids against his country, as he continued to watch the bellowing smoke. He picked up the dust covered phone and to his surprise, it still worked and he placed a call out to his Command Post, which was somehow left intact. He was able to tell the soldier who answered was standing outside the structure.

He quickly explained that he wanted more missiles fired at the god cursed American ships helping the disabled warship they hit yesterday with missiles. In fifteen minutes, three missiles were launched at the American targets. All three missiles went undetected until they found their assigned targets. The USS Taylor, a Missile Frigate, and the USS Spruance, a Destroyer, and USS Barbey were left smoking and sinking in the sea.

Other American warships immediately raced in to help any of the survivors of the stricken ships. Out of over seven hundred personnel on board the three American warships, one hundred and two survivors were recovered. Reports of the attack on the United States ships flooded into the Combat Center of the Roosevelt. Commander Owens ordered all American warships within range of the Libyan missiles to pull back, until they were well out of range. The pilots on deck of the Aircraft Carrier Nimitz waiting for their takeoff orders, were quickly informed of the disasters, and the news filled the pilots with a new resolve. The flyers from all the Carriers stationed in the Red Sea were advised of the attacks against the American warships. All were preparing to takeoff on their missions over Libya, and they were really pissed off now.

BASE SENTRY IN THE SUDAN

Colonel Edward Campanelli was informed of the latest attacks on the American ships stationed in the Mediterranean as he prepared to launch his aircraft on their attack of the Libyan soldiers, and Libya. Libya was to be hit by aircraft from the Nimitz to Libya's west, and also by the carrier planes to the east stationed in the Red Sea, and from Libya's south by planes coming from Base Sentry. Libya was set to be ripped apart from three different directions at the same time. All this, coupled with the ongoing attacks by B 52 Stratofortress, F 117s and the F 110 bombers, would prove to be a long day for Libya, and her defenders and civilians.

BENGASI, LIBYA

As Libyan Ambassador Kamal watched, he picked up three heavy columns of thick smoke rising slowly over the Mediterranean Sea. He smiled to himself, feeling he revenged himself for the attacks by the American warplanes against Libya last night. But his smile quickly faded as his attention was suddenly drawn behind him to the military section of the docks stationed at Bengasi's seaport. What looked like hundreds of bombs were exploding along the docks, detonating ships tied to the docks, and wiping out the entire dock installations and storage facilities. Seconds later, the dock ceased to exist in this world. He could actually hear more bombs whistling through the air as they fell in the distance by the docks.

The bombs were falling for the first time on the main capital of Libya, Tripoli. Ambassador Kamal witnessed with anger the smoke raising miles into the sky over the capital. He observed his attacks on the warships, caused the Americans to retaliate by hitting the main capital this time. The first time since he started his war, he thought of calling an end to the fighting. His thoughts were to save as much of his country as he possibly could, before it looked like Iraq at the end of her war with the American soldiers and their country. He picked up the phone and placed a call to his President, but the capital was still under heavy attack, and he did not answer his call. He replaced the receiver angrily and then stared out the shattered window in stunned disbelief as even more bombs fell on his country. He was able to detect at least three more wings of American warplanes coming in from the sea to attack his country.

UKRAINE, NEW RUSSIA

The new but rather weak government of Russia sent out information they had on the strains of chemical and biological weapons once under development in the old Russian regime. These new strains were developed by the State Union Scientific Research Institute for Organic Chemistry and Technology at Number 23, Highway of the Enthusiasts in Moscow, and they were believed smuggled out of Russia by a number of missing Russian scientists evidently working for the Libyan government now. The break¬through in this extremely deadly class of Toxins came under the Floriant Day Light Time program that had began in early 1993 inside Russia.

The Enzymes DH50 was designed to be launched at night, because it was very sun sensitive. If inhaled by any person, that person would dehydrate, and it forced the host to drink water, but the host will never get enough to satisfy his thirst. Death occurs by the host actually drinking themselves to death. This weapon has a very short life span because of the sun light, ultra violet light kills the Enzyme immediately upon contact. The second weapon was far more dangerous, and the Russians feared it so much that they stopped any further development of the new weapon, when the Russians realized just how unstable and uncontrollable the weapon truly was.

This Biological weapon was code named Crimson Code One. It was a strong Millie toxin, which caused the hosts blood vessels in the brain to rupture, causing an agonizingly slow and extremely painful death. This toxin lived on itself for five full days before it finally slowly died off. The life expectancy of the infected host was just ten hours after infection. The deadly Toxin could be inhaled, or absorbed through any exposed skin to the Toxin. A plastic skin of just 3/32 of an inch thick would protect the skin of a person in any effected area. It was an airborne contaminant, which could be picked up from contaminated surfaces through the skin.

The fear the Russians had of this new strain was that the Millie Toxin was highly susceptible to extremely dangerous mutations, which caused any further work on the Toxin to be stopped instantly. It was well noted in one laboratory experiment that the Millie Toxin changed into a dangerously stronger Toxin base which would not die off, and became a stronger Toxin with a shell casing called a glass shine, which also attacked the nervous system of the body.

The President of the United States sent this new information on along to his military command structure stationed at the Combat Information Center on board the Aircraft Carrier Roosevelt. At once, Commander Owens immediately issued orders for all chemical and biological weapons protective gear to be issued to all ground forces currently engaging in the fighting area. No one was certain if Libya had these extremely deadly weapons of mass destruction in her arsenal or not, but Commander Owens did not want to take any chance of getting any of his people hit by these chemicals. While not being well prepared to defend themselves against the possible attacks by these horrible weapons of mass destruction.

The massive C 5 Galaxy transport aircraft landed one after the other at Base Sentry safely, and many pallets of radiation and germ protective gear were quickly unloaded from the huge planes, and the officers in turn, immediately issued them to all their foot soldiers stationed on the military base and the soldiers out in the field of battle.

An article that was printed in the Asali Shimbum, a Japanese state own newspaper stated.

DATE/TIME 10 09 96, 2:35 P.M. EST JAPAN:
AFTER CLOSED DOOR MEETINGS HELD BETWEEN
JAPAN AND THE UNITED STATES AND MEMBERS OF THE
SECURITY COUNCIL AND UNITED NATIONS MEMBERS,
JAPAN DECIDED UPON HERSELF TO DECLARE WAR ON
LIBYA OVER THE THEFT OF JAPANESE PROPERTY STOLEN
FROM HER DISABLED SHIP.
JAPAN WILL BE SENDING BOTH HER NAVAL
DESTROYERS TO FIGHT ALONGSIDE THE ALLIED
FORCES CURRENTLY ENGAGING THE AGGRESSIVE
ACTIONS TAKEN BY THE LIBYAN MILITARY. AS ALWAYS,
JAPAN PRAYS FOR AN IMMEDIATE CESSATION OF ALL

HOSTILITIES, AND A RETURN TO A PEACEFUL STATE IN THIS REGION OF THE WORLD.

The memo failed to add Japan was giving the United States all the information she had on the T 2R3 fighter planes. This knowledge would enable the American pilot's job of killing these Japanese developed planes a whole lot easier to accomplish. Japan also agreed to pay for half the entire cost of the war in Libya.

BASE SENTRY IN THE SUDAN

Colonel Edward 'Popeye' Campanelli's ground forces were ordered to go into action before the American planes started their next attack on the nation of Libya. The Colonel was airborne in his huge Sea Stallion command helicopter, with radio communications linked to all troops operating over the field of battle. He watched angrily as a number of his ground units moved out from the besieged capital of Chad, Abeche. The fighting was extremely heavy, and the American soldiers were finding themselves bogged down once again. This time near the small Chad city of Bilyine, where the troops encountered fierce resistance coming from Libyan defenders. The advance American units of the Third Marine Division were hard hit. He listened to the sounds of war over his radio as he ordered up even more reinforcements in action.

"Call OPS for some extra air support." A Marine yelled in his radio.

The Colonel listened to the Marine's requests for help and moaned. "Richie, what the hell's the closest air of ground support units we can get over to those trapped Marines, dammit?"

"The 27th Mechanized Infantry Division's the closest unit we have to them, sir."

"Then get them over there on the double quick mister. I'm committing my backup reserve troops as of this time. How long for the reserves to get up there and assist these Marines out?"

Captain Richie took a few seconds as he quickly looked over the map on the makeshift table in the helicopter, and then responded to his Commanding Officer. "An hour at the most for those troops to support the other units, Colonel Campanelli Sir." The Captain cringed as he announced the time to the Colonel, knowing full well it was going to set him off again.

"A fucking hour! Aw C'mon for Christ sake man. You gotta be shitting me for fuck sake, Captain. No way in hell will that do in this instant, Captain! The fighting will be over with by that time mister." Colonel Campanelli yelled back at the Captain.

Captain White offered up to try and get some of the heat off of the other officer. "Colonel Campanelli Sir, air support's on the way."

Another call came in over the radio from the Marines trapped below the Colonel.

"Bravo One. Bravo One. Take the First Squad on point duty, Second Squad take up all fucking flanking positions. Bravo, Bravo, come in Bravo One. First Squad, what the fuck's your present status people? Shit, claymore's popping off. First Squad, where the hell are your people at, dammit? Report in immediately, god dammit. Over!"

"Bravo One, First Squad reporting in, we're getting our fucking asses kicked out here sir."

Colonel Campanelli could actually hear the small arms fire going off in the background over the radio report. He was pleased someone had the smarts and left the radio open. More small arms fire went off. Suddenly, someone cried out in terrible pain over the radio linkup.

"I'm hit. Oh God, I'm hit. Sweet Jesus, God it hurts. Help. I'm hit. Oh God, oh God."

The scared soldier who spoke on the radio moments before, spoke to the fallen Marine this time, as he ripped open a field compression dressing, and used it to hold pressure on the man's chest, to try and stop some of the heavy bleeding as he bitched at the wounded soldier. "Come on man and take it. You can take it buddy. You got to take the fucking pain man."

"God, oh Christ Almighty I'm bleeding. Oh God it hurts so much. Please help me man. It hurts, oh God, oh God I'm gonna die, Oh God Jesus it hurts! I don't want to fucking die, don't let me die man." The wounded soldier was begging another soldier to help him.

"Knock the shit off will ya for fuck sake, you fucking crybaby you. You sound like a damn honky, man. Medic, someone get me a damn medic up here on the fricking double quick man. I got a downed soldier and he needs aid immediately, dammit."

"Oh God it hurts." The wounded soldier continued to cry out in both pain and fear.

"Don't you fucking ice out on me nigger. Come on man, don't you fricking die on me mother fucker, or I'll kill ya my damn self man. Come on sucker, come on, shit, shit. Come on man you gotta fucking stay with me here man, dammit. Medic, where the hell are you at, you stinking bastard you." The other black soldier cried out towards the Heavens above him as he held the wounded soldier in his arms as he slowly died on him.

Another voice over the radio came in as he ordered the soldier helping the downed soldier. "Get out of my way soldier and let me get at him man. Come on man, you have to let him go Marine. You have to get the fuck out of my way so I can see his situation man."

"It's too fucking late sucka. You! You lousy bastard you! You sure took your ever loving sweet ass fucking time with getting here, motherfucker. You let the nigger die on me Homes."

"Hey man that's not fair Marine. I have other wounded to care for ya know. He's not the only wounded soldier we have in this war I hafta look after my friend." The medic complained in his own defense as he tried his best to bring back the dead Marine.

"Fuck you sucker, you took your time with getting here because he's a fucking brother, and you're a stinking snowball, man! You coulda saved his fricking ass if you got here a lot sooner man, and you really wanted to help save a brother!"

Colonel Campanelli could hear a slight scuffle going on between the two soldiers, and another soldier must have stepped between the fighting men and growled at the both of them.

"Knock it off. Joe, the medic's not the enemy here man. He's doing his damn best with the wounded he hasta look afta, man. The enemy's out there Bro. We can't fight ourselves. Remember sucker, Marines don't fight Marines, Homes."

"Yeah, yeah, you're right man I guess. Sorry brother." The angry Marine offered the medic.

The two men hit closed fists twice. Then the white medic wiped at a trace of blood from the corner of his mouth. It came from a rap in the face from the other soldier who lost his buddy.

More automatic weapons fire broke out and cut off the Marines speaking to each other.

A Lieutenant whose name the Colonel did not catch came over the radio. Colonel Campanelli looked to Captain John White who merely shrugged back at him, because he did not get the officer's name either. He listened as the Lieutenant spoke to his men.

"Bravo One, Bravo One. First Squad, First Squad listen up this is important, people. You're instructed to fall back, haul ass back to defensive position five clicks to your rear, and then hold there until further ordered. We need this position held at all cost. Read me First Squad?"

"Loud and clear. It's about time we're ordering these soldiers to fall back and regroup. Over. Saddle up people, we're moving the fuck outta here double quick. Take him with us, Marines don't leave their dead behind. Watch your fucking spacing whole we move. Let's go."

Small arms fire could still be heard being fired off over the open radio hot and heavy, as the Marine Units gathered up and quickly moved off to their new positions.

A shout suddenly bellowed out over the radio. "Watch your fucking fire people. Pick out your damn targets better. We got friendlies out there so be careful, dammit."

Another shout came in over the radio. "Take up the slack people! Dammit, where the hell are you shitbirds hiding at for Christ sake? I need some fricking help out here man. Dammit Lieutenant, I have many Zappers off to my left side, and they're trying to cut my units off, what the fuck should I do about them sir? I need some stinking orders man."

The excited Lieutenant's voice came back over the radio and he ordered the upset soldier. "Straighten up soldier, you pulled the fucking duty, buddy. Look sharp man, you're to lay down a suppressing fire while you pull back to a safe zone, man."

A frantic voice cut in over the Lieutenant's voice as he yelled over the radio. "Copy, copy. Bravo One, Bravo One, we're cut the fuck off sir. No time to bug out now dammit, we're trapped man. Lock and load, let's fucking rock with these scumbags, shitbirds."

Heavy small arms weapons fire was heard over the open radio as Colonel Campanelli listened in on what was happening on the battlefield below his hovering helicopter.

Another call came in over the open mike by an excited sounding soldier. "Requesting E-vac, emergency pickup immediately. Dust off is needed, I repeat, emergency dust off is needed right now man. I have lots of critically wounded down here, and we have to get the wounded soldiers the hell out of here before they buy the big dirt nap, dammit."

Another voice barked over the open radio this time. "Negatory on that emergency pickup man. Your position is still compromised by the enemy, I repeat, your area is compromised. Soldier, buck it up some and try to fight your way out of this mess, if you want to live mister. Air support is on the way to you as we speak, you're instructed to hold your present position son. Hang in there for a few moment longer before the fly guys get here. Over."

The hysterical voice came back again, actually screaming in the radio now. "Fuck you, we're getting slaughtered over here. We're moving out so I can save some of my damn troops now. Everyone, move it move it, get it going, drag the wounded with us."

Campanelli heard enough and he cut into the conversation himself. "Bravo One, Bravo One. Marine, this is Command Ops, listen up fellow. Where is your Commanding Officer at soldier?"

"The Second Louie's pushing up god damn daisies in the fucking mud, and I don't intend to join him, sir. We're pulling outta this area toot sweet Commander."

The Colonel cut off the scared soldier as he barked at him over the radio this time. "Listen up soldier, you're Commanding NCO, buster. You and your swinging dicks are instructed to hold your present position, your position is vital to this operation. Trust me son, help is on the way to you and your fellow troops as we speak. You're ordered to fire off flares and yellow smoke to mark enemy position for attacking aircraft. You're too..."

He was cut off by the excited Marine. "Tanks, tanks on our flanks, where's the Dragons? We got fucking tanks engaging our asses, get the Dragon shoulder launch missile."

There was five loud whooshes easily heard over the open radio which came from the firing of the anti tank weapons. Seconds later the excited voice was back on the radio reporting to his Commanding Officer again. "We nailed all three of them suckas, their fricking history Colonel. I think we can now hold our present position until air arrives on sight and save our asses, sir."

He looked to Captain White and then he asked him with some concern in his tone. "Where the hell's A.A.A.D?" (Airborne Anti Armor Defense).

Captain John White flushed at his sudden anger aimed directly at him. He quickly scanned the map, and then he reported back to his Commander. "Sir, the 82nd Airborne is already committed on map sector Thirty Three-R Colonel Campanelli Sir. They are engaging enemy forces trying to hold a bridge against them, sir." Captain White pointed to the map.

The Colonel got angry all over again as he snapped at his lifelong friend and second in command with him this time. "Where the hell is the damn ready air cap then for Christ sake? These damn soldiers need some help down there right now dammit."

Captain White quickly opened the radio and snapped in it. "OPS to Over Shield. Your target is Green Goose. I repeat, your target is Green Goose, sir. The target area is marked out by flares and yellow smoke. Coordinates are as follows, M One, Four, Three at Seven, Seven, One, section Three. Marine Units are bogged down at this time, and they're taking rather heavy hostile fire, sir. I repeat Over Shield, heavy weapons fire by enemy ground and armor is ripping up my god damn units on the ground, sir. Where the hell are you birds at for the love of God?"

"Over Shield to OPS. We're ten minutes away from your called in target sir. Over."

"You better get a damn move on it mister. You people are moving like old folks fuck. I have soldiers cut off down there who need your fricking help right now buddy. Over."

"Roger that last as received OPS, we're going to full push now sir. (afterburners) Over."

In a southern drawl the young American pilot cried out in the radio. "This is Major Robert E. Lee to all Over Shield pilots. You're cleared to go to full pop at this time. We're ordered to get a move on it gentlemen. On my mark go to afterburners. Mark, mark, mark, hit ignite." Robert E. Lee let out with a Rebel yell over his mike which was in tune with the blaring song he was playing on his portable radio inside the cockpit of his aircraft. Billy Idol's "Rebel Yell," which Major Lee always had playing whenever he was flying on a combat mission.

One Over Shield pilot complained about the bugs getting smashed on his windshield.

Lee cut off the pilot's bitch as he replied. "Keep your mouth shut or you're going to eat some of the damn things. We have a mission to run and until it's done, enjoy the fucking bugs, man."

All the pilots part of the Over Shield flight laughed except for the pilot who was doing all the complaining. "The bugs are so heavy they're getting in my engine ports and cutting down power and speed. Can we go above the damn things for a while before they stall out my engines?"

"Nagitory on that last request. What the hell did you expect, you're flying over a damn jungle, mister. We have no time for any of that kind of shit. We have to help those fighting soldiers on the deck out double quick. Think about those poor helicopter jockeys flying right on the stinking ground, and what they must be going through with the damn bugs, man."

When Captain John White finally finished up with his message to the young pilot leader of Over Shield Flight, Colonel Campanelli looked at the tall black man as he laugh at him and then he added. "Like old folks fuck, huh John? Where the hell did that come from, mister?"

He shrugged as he smiled back at his Commanding Officer.

Captain Richie cut in to the conversation between the two officers and offered. "John, I'm moving in two reserve divisions to help out with support for those trapped ground forces, sir. The 7th Light, and the 17th Air Assault backed by choppers to help out the damn Marines, sir."

The Colonel looked at the map as the Captain spoke and he noticed these divisions were the closest ground forces to get any ground support to the trapped Marines. "Good call Richie."

John was pissed, the Army was under his command. But once he thought about it, he calmed down. They were Americans and soldiers were in trouble and needed help, no matter who sent it.

The fighting was getting worse as Colonel Campanelli listened to the soldiers on the radios.

"You want some, come get some, get some, come get it sucka. I'm waiting for your ass."

Heavy machine gun fire was heard as the soldier fired and yelled at the same time on the radio.

Another voice yelled out at the top of his lungs. "Trigger time, fire, fire. Come get some."

"Get your ass in the fricking grass man." A third soldier called out as he fired at the enemy.

More yelling over the radio was easily heard by the officers in the helicopter. "Your in the shit now sucka. We got us some real damn combat going off over here people."

"Get down get down, oh shit." A startled voice suddenly called out to the other soldiers.

"Over Shield, this is Bravo One. Over Shield listen up this is important sir. Have direct eye ball contact with you at this present moment sir. We're spotting a number of enemy tanks stationed over at sector Seven, One Three A in your funny book, sir. I repeat Over Shield Commander, Sector Seven, One Three A on your maps, sir. We have five, no, correct that last, six targets out there at the time sir. The tanks are being backed up by an estimated company strength of enemy foot floppers. Get the lousy bastards off our ass's man. Our troop location's marked out well by green flares sir. Your targets are the god damn tanks, work over the god damn tree line, and the fucking right side of that dry gully for us, sir. Over."

"Over Shield Commander to Bravo One. I see you all, I have a good visual on the flares." Lee did a quick correction, and his aircraft instantly lined up on the manmade smoke cloud, and the first enemy targets he picked up. Currently trying to make it to the safety of the trees once his wing of aircraft were detected by the enemy troops. Lee had some problems spotting the targets because of his speed, but he refused to slow and become an easy target for the enemy weapons. Over Shield's Hornet was equipped with Maverick missiles for close in ground support. Some of his planes carried the CBU 55b cluster bombs for anti troop combat on the field.

Major Robert E. Lee checked his Heads Down Display, (HDD). All six enemy tanks lit up on the clear plastic display unit as six small red dots. Lee targeted the two tanks in the lead for his first bombing runs on the Libyan war machines. He hit the master arming switch for his Maverick missiles. The missiles warhead cried its low arming whine, as his targeted tanks made a beeline straight for the protection of the trees. He lowered his portable radio so he could be heard, and then yelled over his mike. "Fire one, fire two."

In seconds, the first enemy tank erupted into a ball of roaring flames and sparks and bellowing smoke on the ground, killing the tank along with its five man crew. The second tank was also hit, but the missile only knocked off the right track, and Lee was forced to fire another missile at the disabled tank. It too exploded as two of the tankers got out of the disabled machine alive, and made it safely to the trees before the tank died in a shower of sparks and flaming death.

As Major Lee's aircraft pulled out of his attack angle, he looked over his shoulder as the second Over Shield aircraft fired and killed two more of the enemy tanks trying to get out of the attack area alive. He leveled his plane off as the third aircraft dropped two cluster bomb units on the hostile foot soldier supporting the tanks. The ground between the enemy troops flashed into a sea of bouncing sparks, as razor sharp shrapnel ripped into the trapped enemy soldier's bodies. The forth plane started his bombing run on the enemy forces, and killed the last remaining enemy tanks on the ground, as he regrouped with his flight wing, and they ripped the tree area apart with heavy cannon fire and their remaining air to ground missiles.

In ten minute's time the entire support operation was completed for the trapped Marines. The American aircraft attacking the enemy troops and armor could be heard over Command's radio as massive explosions were occurring, when the pilots were requesting more flares to be fired off, to correct the enemy positions for the pilots and attacking aircraft.

Major Robert E. Lee did a low flyover the Marines with his weapons quiet. He noticed a few American soldiers moving around as they cautiously came out of their hiding places. He dipped his plane's wing at the troops while doing a victory role over the battlefield.

The Marines in return waved back at the planes as they headed off in the sky above them.

"Over Shield Leader to Bravo One. Come in sir. Over." The lead pilot radioed in.

"Yeah, this is Bravo One man. Go Over Shield Leader. You did real good for us down here sir. I own you a beer when we get back to the real world, sir. Over."

Major Lee ignored Bravo One's offer of a beer as he replied. "Bravo One listen up sir, this is my plan. I'll cut free two of my fighters so they can get back upstairs and refuel. My wing man and myself will stay overhead until they return, this is so we can keep an active ready air cap over your troops and position at all times, until our backup aircraft come and relieve us of this duty. So we can rearm our aircraft and return your position, sir. When they get back, my planes will protect you all until the helicopters arrive on position and relieve us from our support of your ground forces. If trouble comes your way, you all are to mark out the area with red smoke this time around, and then get the hell out of the way, and we'll do the rest for you my friend."

"Yeah, that's great man. I got you loud and clear man, red smoke and fricking flares for marking smoke. You got it man. Thanks for all your help man."

"You got it Bravo One, and I think I'll take you up on that offer of a beer, friend. Look, one of my aircraft will be in constant contact with you and your people all at all times, until the Rotary airframes come in, man. All you have to do is leave your key open, sir. Over."

"You got it man. Thanks again for your help Over Shield. We owe you big time sir. Over."

Colonel Campanelli cut in this time and he offered to the pilot of Over Shield. "Command OPS to Over Shield Leader. Well done here mister, well done sir."

Major Robert E. Lee smiled proudly over the message coming at him from OPS Command, as his two aircraft circled the once trapped Marines at just five hundred feet up. Six Marine super Cobra attack helicopters instantly headed in to take over the ready air cap protection over the exhausted Marines operating on the ground. The six helicopters were scheduled to reach the Marine's present position within twenty minutes or so.

Major Lee monitored the evac helicopter communications. They were hovering just outside the attack area until Over Shield secured the entire area for them. Then they would quickly move in and then pick up the wounded soldiers and get them to help. The Med-evac helicopters were communicating with the Marines on the ground already. Lee looked to his left and picked up the choppers quickly move in. When it was evident the attacking aircraft beat back the attacking enemy Libyan forces, the Marine got on the radio and they sounded a lot more professional.

"Get those damn flares fired off, mark out the trouble spots for the damn fly boys up there people. Get some squads out there, sweep and clean the area. I want the kill teams sent out as well. Tell easy targets to look for any blood trails and drag marks on the ground. I want a good body count on the damn enemy this time around, people. Any prisoners found out there are to be cared for and questioned. Set fire teams up. You people betta get your damn act together, or I'm going to giant shit on your fucking face, soldiers. You! Call for some stinking evac helicopters to come in. I want all our wounded the hell out of here before we get hit again by the lousy bastards. I think our stinking friends will be back as soon as they can regroup and get some reinforcements aimed against us, if they can man."

A radio call suddenly cut off the Marine issuing the orders to the other soldiers for a moment. Then he was back on the radio. "Fire green flares off to mark out an LZ Landing Zone for us. The stinking Dust Off birds are on the way in to collect our wounded, people."

The Colonel looked at Captain White and remarked. "Colorful little bastard isn't he, Johnny? A couple of questions for you though John. What the hell did the damn soldier mean by a kill team sent out and easy targets, sir? I never heard that remark before, sir."

Captain John White looked a little embarrassed as he quickly explained the soldier's remarks. He tried to show little emotion in his words as he offered his commanding officer. "Sir, 'Easy Targets,' means the point squads usually hit first by any enemy attack. The other remark's a battlefield slang, sir. It means a team of soldiers, sometimes consisting of up to five troops depending on the size of the attacking forces, are sent over the battlefield to kill any wounded enemy to badly chopped up or damaged to help and save, sir. Or the wounded soldiers were armed and still trying to make a fight of it against our people, sir. It's a humane way to deal with the seriously wounded enemy, sir. And of course, Dust Off helicopters are the medi-evac teams."

The Colonel could not help the nasty look he gave Captain White, as he stated in a rather heated tone of voice at him. "I knew that shit, I'd kinda like to try and save all the wounded soldiers if we can, no matter whose side they're on, Captain White Sir."

"So would I sir. But sometimes it just ain't possible on such a fast moving battlefield as this one is shaping up to be, sir. As the old saying goes for all soldiers engaged in war, Colonel. War is hell sir. Say Colonel, you have to raise that Captain you appointed Regimental Commander to Major. You sure you didn't pick this guy out because he's Italian, sir?" Captain John White asked in a joking manner of his Commanding Officer.

"C'mon John, you know me much better than that mister. I don't raise anyone unless he earned a rate increase, mister." He replied seriously to his Captain, and then he continued with his words to the officer. "I'll tell you why I picked this prick out for a rate increase sir. The first time I ran into him, he was still a wet behind the ears First Lieutenant. He was a young pup, dumb and full of cum and just starting out in the service. He had everything to prove and he wouldn't listen to anyone's advice. He always took wild ass chances, sometimes really dumb ones, sometimes they worked out well for his ass. Nevertheless, he made a name for himself with these deeds both good and bad. The brass liked the kid because he showed balls.

"Shit, I'm getting a little off the track here John. Anyway, the first run in I had with him was on a battlefield during a War Game operation. I think it was in '85, he was ordered to get through my lines and secure a vital, simulated bridge and road leading to the bridge. Our War Games were taking place in Kentucky in the dead of summer. The plains were dry earth that kicked up a massive fricking dust storm whenever a tank passed over it. But the mountains were covered with heavy brush and trees, which kept the ground damp and dust free.

"The Captain had a hundred tanks, and forty support vehicles, humvee's and other shit in his fucking Command. I had twenty pieces of artillery, backed by thirty five tanks, and I don't remember how many other fucking support vehicles. There was no way this little punk kid was going to get through my damn lines of defense, and I was dying for him to just try it against me. If anything, just to prove to this young puke that he wasn't as good as he thought he was.

"But the little bastard proved me wrong, here is what the sonofabitch did to me and my forces. He split up his forces into two different attacking groups. He committed thirty of his tanks for a frontal assault on my defensive lines, and he put most of his support vehicles in on this attack as well. He had his men cut down a number of stinking trees and tied the damn things to the back of his tanks, and they went back and forth along the damn plain. The dust kicked up by this stunt made me think he committed his entire fucking force on this dumb frontal attack against my troops. My men laughed at this asinine move as they prepared to rip his attack force to pieces. A typical mistake that's usually made by an over aggressive kid so I thought. Anyway, my artillery opened fire a few times and we picked off a few of his tanks, and we laughed again. The damn kid was keeping his tanks far enough out of our range to make the total kill. All his ink rounds were falling well short of my position, and we laughed more at him and his troops.

"I checked out the terrain in the mountains and my engineers assured me the damn area could never possibly be used by any sane man as an attack angle against my forces. Evidently this kid wasn't sane. He sent the rest of his tanks along with two blade, armored engineer vehicles up the side of an impossible mountain slope. The blades cut a rough road which the tanks used to get to the peak of the mountain. Once there, his forces came across an old, over grown fire road not used in many years. Hell, it didn't even show up on any of my stinking maps. He used this old fire road, and was able to make good time on the damn thing against my troops. He crashed five of his tanks on the rugged road, and caught some hell for that shit. Well anyway, it took his tanks three hours to get behind my lines. None of my spotters picked up this movement either. We were all too busy laughing at his tanks going around in circles out on the plain. We laughed, knowing their troops were being choked to death by the thick dust cloud they raised.

"This damn kid brought this tanks right down the mountain hidden from our view by trees and folds in the mountain side. You know, there was a ravine up there, and his men dragged a Biber bridge layer along with them. Don't ask me how the fuck they ever got the damn thing through the trees, but they did. Once the kid got his forces on the plain he split them in half. He sent forty tanks in an attack, hitting my flanks. They lobbed so many damn ink rounds at us, the air was nothing more than a red and yellow mist. They caught us flatfooted John. We were finally able to fight them to a stand still though. That was until they attacked us with the tanks from the frontal position. We were forced to split our fire power in half in order to try and fend off both of his attacking units, it was too little and too late and they easily over powered us.

"I was completely helpless to stop him with the force I still had operational behind to protect the damn bridge. We were fighting for little over an hour before I saw the green flare fired off, and then I knew he had taken the fucking bridge out from under my ass.

"General Weidenbacher was acting as an observer over the War Games, sent a jeep to take me out to the compromised bridge. The full Command Structure were laughing at me now. This young punk ass Lieutenant sat on his ass on a damn tank drinking water from a canteen, and daring to snicker at my lousy ass. Oh sure, I was mad as hell at this lousy little bastard who bested me in the damn war games. But I was also happy this kid beat me as well which is no small feat mind you, sir. It showed me this new generation of young soldiers understood the idealism of tactics on the battlefield. It made me feel real good because I was teaching tactics, both in the classroom and out on the field. I was convinced they were paying attention.

"I didn't like having to wear the back end half of a damn jackass medal for the week, showing everyone someone made a horse's ass out of the teacher, but what the hell he made me look like an ass in the games. Needless to say, we became close friends, he was always coming to me with new attack scenarios, and we worked them out together. In fact, I'm using some of his stinking tactics in my operation right now. That's why I picked him for Regimental Commander, John."

John smiled at the Colonel as he remarked at his old friend. "Sounds like he's qualified to me sir, especially if he beat you in the war games, Ed."

"You're damn right he's more than qualified for the position of Commander, John. I'm damn glad you reminded me about his raise, sir. I'll get to the paperwork when we get back to base."

It was extremely hot inside the helicopter which prompted John to offer as he wiped the sweat from his brow. "Damn, this is the type of stinking day that makes me want to spend it with a good book and a hot young blonde while soaking in the pool, sir."

Colonel Campanelli looked at the smiling black man and remarked with a queer look on his face. "Since when can you read anything without it having a shit load of pictures of naked women in the damn magazine, mister?"

John laughed again as he added in a smirk. "Who the hell said I can read, Colonel?"

He went back to looking out of one of the windows of his command helicopter. He shook his head as he thought of the foot soldiers dying in the mud below him, and he grumbled at the Captain. "You're right John, war certainly is fucking hell, sir."

The Colonel wondered how any mother would ever put up with war. How she could possibly allow her children to get slaughtered this way in the mud. The concerned Colonel really thought it was about time to get a woman in the Presidency. He knew if any mother saw what these poor kids were going through as they battled the Libyan soldiers, they would surely place a quick stop to it one way or the other. His thoughts came back to the present and he said.

"John, I don't really think I like how long it took the fucking air support to catch up with my advanced front line ground forces, dammit. The soldiers were out there way too long with their asses hanging out in the open. From now on, I want air to fly a ready cap over all assaulting ground units, tank them up in the air if you have to, sir. I don't want the damn fly boys to wait until they're called in for any god damn ground support. By that time it could be too late, and I could lose too many of my soldiers needlessly." He looked over a land nature had obviously turned her back on, and man was ripping apart in the heat of battle.

The battlefield was heavily dotted with countless burning Libyan tanks and armor which sent thick, black columns of smoke over their destroyed remains. Some destroyed tanks burned alone, while others burned in small clusters of destroyed war machines, a grotesque testimonial to being caught out in the open by artillery, Apache helicopters, or air attacks. Bodies could be seen lying nearby many burning tanks, burned beyond recognition. Every where he looked, the colonel saw bodies as fires cooked off the ammunition inside the tank's shattered steel shells.

The Colonel stared at the awesome movement of some American troops and track vehicles moving across the war scared surface of the ground below him at his command. It was an unbelievable sight to behold, as vast columns of death crawled slowly along the ground now devoid of most trees, brushes or life other than that of the allied soldiers under his command. The terribly pot marked surface of the ground was dotted with many small fires. These long columns of allied soldiers and military equipment were grinding anything they came across to dust under horrendous fire power and the tracks of their machines. Colonel Campanelli suddenly noticed a number of massive tanks and armored vehicles had their hatches latched open.

This was a sure sign that the soldiers were in full control of the battlefield now. He looked over much of the theater of war covered by deformed shapes of once enemy fighting machines. This sight filled him with sheer fear. A new fear he never felt before in his life, as he thought about what man's great technological feats could do to man itself. He wondered how long man had left to live on this earth. Something was seriously bothering him about what he was seeing, and then he finally realized exactly what it was.

The confused Army Colonel did not like the way the tanks and support vehicles were starting to bunch up on him in the field of war. He watched a flight of Palvo 111 armored plated helicopters move in, and they started strafing the battlefield with three rotary machine guns. He took a quick breath in, and then he reached for the mike and barked into it. "Command OPS to lead tank column, coordinates as follows, Five, Seven Two area C-One-R."

"Yes Sir Command Ops, this is Second Lieutenant Ralph Backman, sir. What are your new orders, Commander Sir?" A command soldier asked his Commanding Officer.

"Your tanks are starting to bunching up too close together Lieutenant. Aren't you keeping a damn eye on what the fuck's happening behind your ass, mister? Spread those damn things out better or I'll have you hanging by your toes." The Colonel growled in the mike.

"Aye, sir. Err... yes sir, I'm giving the orders out immediately sir. Sorry for the mess up on my part sir, it'll not happen again I assure you, Colonel Sir. Scrap Iron Leader to all track trailers. Your orders are to spread out. You people are moving in too close to each other. You're bunching up on me, dammit. Repeat order and execute same immediately."

Colonel Campanelli monitored the tank commanders repeating their order to spread out their machines more, and then he watched as the tanks did as they were just ordered, and they quickly began to spread out to the proper distance between the fighting machines, and their follow on support vehicles, and the foot soldiers also moving behind the armor.

"That's much better there asshole." The Colonel said to Captain John White who did not respond because the remark was not directed right at him. The Captain was too busy with monitoring the radio and moving the plastic models of tanks and soldiers along on the battle map mounted inside the large helicopter Command Center and bitched. "This shit sucks the big one."

"Excuse me sir?" John looked up from the map and replied in a confused tone.

"Nothing John, I was just kind a thinking out loud, that's all my friend." Colonel Campanelli said as he again looked out the chopper window to the battlefield below him.

John joined him by the window, he then tapped the concerned Colonel on the shoulder and pointed to five soldiers moving slowly between, and checking out the dead Libyan soldiers laying on the ground where they fell, and he announced in a flat voice. "Kill teams sir. Those soldiers pulled the shit end of the stick of any engagement, sir. They have to decide who is worth trying to help and who is so badly wounded they have to place an end to their suffering, sir."

"Shit. Let's get back to our base, I want to pick up Maz for the next part of this damn operation. I want her with me the next time we head out sir." The Colonel growled, but before leaving he wanted to speak to the soldier he listened to during the attack against his position.

John snapped back at the Colonel. "Those fucking guys were scared shitless there man."

Campanelli looked at John with anger blazing in his eyes as he growled at his next in command in an angry tone of voice. "Where you ever combat fucking scared John?"

"Yeah, I'm fraid so? More times than I care to admit to Colonel." John replied to his friend.

"I was to my friend. I was so fucking scared I couldn't even control my water and I pissed myself. I don't blame them poor kids in the least for being scared, sir."

The Colonel stopped talking to John and he then picked up the radio mike, and talked to the young Marine soldiers who was with the radio throughout the entire attack against the dug in enemy soldiers on the battlefield. "Marine, this is OPS Command, what's your rank son?"

"I'm a Corporal sir." The soldier replied to his Commanding Officer over the radio.

"It's Sergeant now buster. Listen up soldier, you and your pack of swinging dicks and bouncing tits down there done real well for yourselves, mister. You can give your troops a well done from Command Ops and from myself as well, mister. Over."

The massive Sea Stallion suddenly banked hard to its left as the helicopter headed back to Base Sentry, to refuel the machine and also pick up Captain Renee Mendoza, along with any needed supplies for themselves, before the next attack occurred on the field. Colonel Campanelli squirmed, his shoulders ached from the tight seat buckle straps that dug into them.

USS NIMITZ HEADING FOR THE MEDITERRANEAN SEA

On board the massive Aircraft Carrier the Nimitz, the fighter planes were launching in the wind for the next attack on the nation of Libya two at a time. The pilot named Bunker One stood by as the Flight Chief readied his aircraft for him. The Chief sent a stream of spit towards the deck, colored red from the large chaw of tobacco he chewed on as he screamed new orders at his overworked crew workers. "If I told you people once, I told you damn shitbirds a hundred fucking times now to keep the damn shrouds on the fricking missile points until the damn aircraft was ready for immediate launch from the flight deck, dammit." The Chief's bark instantly upset the moment of stillness on board the massive Carrier.

The flight crew immediately busied themselves as they raced around the parked aircraft. Checking out anything of the planes they could, to avoid the Chief's harsh and angry glare. Because now that he spat, no one was sure which path his anger might take next against them.

When the F-18 Hornet was prepared for launch, Bunker One quickly did his last walk around his aircraft, checking out the missile mounts, tires and anything else he checked on his plane, before he lifted off the Carrier. When he was satisfied the aircraft was ready for flight, he climbed up the ladder into the cockpit while it was sitting resting behind the foul line of the flight deck, and maneuvered himself into the hard padded, specially contoured seat. He removed the four safety pins from his ejection seat, counted them to make certain he had all four pins out correctly. Then he stored them in the special container pocket designated for them.

His Flight Crew Chief followed him up the ladder, and helped the pilot quickly strap himself into the seat. The Chief helped Bunker plug in all his wires and hoses, which were the umbilical cords that hooked him up to the brain center of his aircraft. Bunker One checked his two engines, and when they reported they were idling after being powered up from the crash jumper machine. He signaled and his deck crew quickly disconnected the electric cable and air hose, supplying high pressure air to turn over his powerful engines. Seconds later, he had the engines idling at over seventy percent full power.

Before the elderly Chief climbed down the boarding ladder, he yelled to Bunker One over the deafening roar coming from the powerful jet engines. "If you mess up my fucking bird mister, I'm going to mess you up so damn bad you're going to look like a fucking Flamingo sucked threw a damn engine port, mister. Remember sir, you only have to fly the damn things, I have to repair the fricking things when you and the rest of your damn fly boys mess them up on me, sir. Good hunting today sir. Give them hell for my ass, sir!"

"I'll take good care of you little baby for you Chief." Both men laughed this time.

When the old Chief was clear of his plane, Bunker One slowly eased the throttles of his aircraft forward, and the plane slowly moved out from the so called foul line parking place on the fight deck of the carrier forward in response to the lighted wand movements of the yellow shirt taxi director. The Bunker One pilot cautiously moved his aircraft's nose wheel carefully over to the correct alignment with the waiting catapult hookup set in the massive flight deck of the carrier. He immediately stopped his forward movement of the aircraft, and then he watched the Flight Deck Sergeant as he called the plane forward very slowly now.

The crew sarge called him up with two fingers swilling in the air, he then put his hand up in order to stop Bunker One's plane forward movement again. A green shirt deck crewman doing a duck walk, and sometimes actually crawling under the still slightly moving aircraft until it finally stopped, and then he quickly hooked up the metal toe bar harness coming from the front wheel of the aircraft, over the catapult head in the flight deck. A second green shirt held up a small chalk board denoting the Hornet's thirty six thousand, four hundred and forty nine pound military takeoff weight. He checked the numbers with his log, and then he gave the thumb's up signal to the concerned green shirt. The catapult was set to the proper weight and his plane was ready for immediate launch from the flight deck of the Carrier Roosevelt.

The Crew Chief looked at his young pilot from the deck of the carrier. The eerie glow coming from the many dials and cockpit lights, made the pilot look almost luminescent, ghostly.

"Hornet Flight, Delta, Victor, Lima, One, One, Seven, you're cleared for immediate launch at this time sir. The wind's coming out from the south at three, four, seven, at speed seventeen knots, repeat seventeen knots. Give'em hell for us back here on the flight deck Bunker One. We're all with you inside that cockpit sir."

"Delta, Victor, Lima, One, One, Seven. Roger last sir, and I'll make you damn proud of me on this operation sir." Bunker One offered confidently, and then saluted the Captain, and then the colors displayed proudly on the ship, and then he saluted the Deck Crew Chief and his Sergeant immediately snapped to attention, and then he returned Bunker One's salute just as proudly.

The Deck Sergeant suddenly twirled his fingers swiftly in a circular motion in the air, and then Bunker One knew he was finally ready for his launch from the carrier flight deck. He gave him the thumbs up signal in reply to the Deck Sergeant.

The pilot then closed his canopy and quickly advanced his throttle controls to the stops, and instantly hit the afterburner switch, bringing both the engines of his plane roaring to full military take off power and life. He kept his eyes glued to the series of red lights from the launching officer's control bubble stationed built right in the center of the flight deck set between the two catapults. Suddenly the lights went from blinding red to a soft green glow, indicating a clear launch signal for the pilot and his aircraft.

Bunker One instantly felt the awesome power being emitted from the aircraft's rapid power buildup, until he finally let go of the brakes, and then the steam catapult head immediately shot him and his aircraft forward in the air. His F-18 Hornet went from zero to just over one hundred and fifty knots within four seconds, and the sheer force of the launch actually pinned him against his seat. A heartbeat before he launched, the pilot checked the thirty cockpit gauges and dials of his aircraft. He raised his landing gear when his plane clear of the massive flight deck of the carrier and shot in the air.

Then he allowed the nose of the aircraft to rise up to a good ten degree angle, and he held it as he trimmed off his plane, and the fighter aircraft continued to accelerate and climb at the same time. When his air speed reached three hundred knots plus, he raised his flaps of his aircraft, and then dropping the nose of his aircraft down to level flight and he headed off for the fan tail of the massive carrier. In order to wait for the rest of his flight wing of aircraft to link up with him, and then they can head off for the battlefield.

The few aircraft still waiting for the rest of the wing to get airborne, had already linked up with Bunker One and the aircraft marshaled off the fantail of the Carrier while waiting for the rest of the flight wing to be launched from the flight deck of the Carrier. It was a sight to see as all the aircraft took off side by side from the Carrier two at a time, and a third plane shot off from the angle deck catapult system at the same time. Soon, the first Wing of F 18 Hornet fighter planes were heading towards off to strike at the nation of Libya again.

For the second time since his Wing of aircraft were ordered to engaged the enemy forces in the nation of Libya, Major George Bunker was placed in command of the fighter planes consisting of eighteen F 18 Hornets, and another eighteen YF 23 Tactical stealth fighter aircraft in this attack flight. The twelve well aged A 6 Intruders were already launched from the carrier twenty minutes before Bunker One's flight was airborne, and the attacking Intruders were better organized in groups of four, and they were already flying over the target area, busy attacking any radar of the enemy communication centers controlling the dangerous enemy SAM missile systems. The moment the enemy forces lit up their missile tracking radars to intercept the American aircraft while in flight.

The Wing of Intruder aircraft orders were to knock out as many enemy attacking SAM missile systems they possibly could uncover, in order to help minimize the hits by the missiles against the incoming American fighters and bomber planes.

The Intruders did this by putting their own aircraft up as targets for the enemy missile systems, and when any enemy SAM tracking radar systems locked onto their planes. The Intruders would instantly fire off an AGM 65F Maverick missiles, which would immediately zero in on the enemies tracking radar system signal, and then the missile would follow the signal right down and kill the system where it sat on the ground.

USS ROOSEVELT STATIONED IN THE RED SEA

On board the American Aircraft Carrier Roosevelt, Commander Owens stood on the freezing cold, wind sweep Vulture's Row section of his mighty warship. The observation deck on the super structure of the center island. He was wrapped up in his heavy Navy blue watch coat, and he was watching proudly as his aircraft were taking off from his flight deck two at a time from the twin main steam powered catapults. The planes launching from the Nimitz and also the Roosevelt at the same time were receiving their commands from the AWACS control plane, Overseer. Which circled well over the target area at fifty thousand feet.

Bunker One was informed just before his takeoff from the Carrier by Command that this operation was going to be a 'Zip Lip', or a radio silence operation to all aircraft involved in the current attack aimed against the enemy forces operating inside Libya. Except for his lead aircraft, and the large Overseer AWACS control aircraft, until contact with the enemy planes had been established. Then the American attacking aircraft will be on their own to engage the enemy aircraft as they deemed fit and fight it out with them.

Bunker One started his communications off by bitching in his radio to the controlling AWACS plane communication officer. "Bunker One to Overseer. What the fuck's happening with those damn Intruder aircraft, sir? Where the hell are they hiding at for Christ sake sir? I'm already picking up a number of enemy radar hits aimed at my Wing of aircraft, sir. Are they doing their fucking job yet as ordered, sir? I'm can't fucking believe how many stinking radar bounces I'm picking up hitting my aircraft at this present time sir. Over."

"Overseer to Bunker One. The Intruder aircraft have already done their assigned job for their first flight attack against the enemy units operating in Libya, sir. They're now heading back to the nest for refueling and rearming as of this time, sir. They'll be back in the air doing their act as soon as they're properly topped off with fuel and rearmed, sir. Sorry sir for not informing you of this fact earlier in your flight than this time, sir. But I'm afraid we're the ones hitting you with the radar bounces sir, in an attempt to try and get a good fix on all your aircraft in formation, sir. But make no mistake about it though for a moment Bunker One.

"There are still plenty of enemy missiles and flack units still active and very much alive ahead of you and the rest of your attacking flight, sir. Bunker One, be advised that your group of aircraft is forming up very well behind your six at this present time, sir. I see no stragglers detected behind your lead aircraft from my present position sir. You have a rather Loose Deuce formation setting up well behind you sir. Your flight's shaping up very well for contact with any Gomers at this time, Bunker One sir. Over."

Bunker One looked over his right shoulder and quickly picked up the aircraft from his flight wing and noticed how well they were forming up behind his six, as just suggested by the Overseer Commander. His Wingman was already set in position off to the starboard side of his aircraft, some ten feet below his plane's present position, and he was also giving him a number of rapid visual hand signals of his intent while in flight. The second pilot wanted to make certain that his Flight Leader knew exactly what he was going to do, once they finally make contact with any enemy planes waiting for them to attack the nation of Libya, and any enemy troops spotted operating on the ground.

Bunker One's flight wing was going to be a little more than fifteen minutes ahead of the much heavier and slower traveling bomber aircraft still being launched from the two carriers involved in this present air raid over Libya. The reason for this was, if all his fighter aircraft got in any trouble over the target area. The bomber planes could very easily dump their bomb payloads, and then they could turn their bombers into fighter aircraft, and also help fend off any possible attacking Libyan fighter planes which the American pilots had now branded as Zappers during this new war, and for this current operation.

CHAPTER 27

As Colonel Edward "Popeye" Campanelli's command helicopter safely landed on his massive military base branded Base Sentry, he immediately picked up Captain Renee Mendoza. He also listened in on a new report just coming in over the radio of the spooling helicopter.

"Area secured." In a soft and thoroughly exhausted voice, he also heard the Marine add to his report. "We need some damn body bags, let's get them tagged and bagged people."

ON BOARD AWACS PLANE, OVERSEER FLYING
OVER THE MEDITERRANEAN SEA OFF THE COAST OF
LIBYA

"Overseer to Bunker One Sir. You're currently less than twenty minutes from your intended target area at this time sir. Over." Overseer, the AWACS Aircraft Commander replied to the leader of the attacking American fighter group.

"Roger that last Overseer sir. Starting my final, turning to course Zero, Two, Two. On my mark! Mark, mark, mark, commence turn. He we go Chicks, good luck. Over."

The entire wing of attacking American aircraft turned as one, as Bunker One lead the way for the rest of the aircraft.

"Overseer to Bunker One. We're picking up some rough air ahead of your flight, sir. I'm afraid you're in for some serious bounce in a few minutes, sir. Over."

"Roger that last as received sir. Thanks for the warning about the bad air ahead of my flight, Overseer. I need all the help I can get from you people on this damn operation, sir. Over." Bunker replied to the Commander of the Overseer AWACS aircraft.

Bunker One to Bunker's Two through Eighteen. We're in for some chop ahead of us so be prepared for it. We're less than twenty minutes out from our intended target area. Over."

"Overseer to Bunker One. Fifteen minutes seven seconds out from your intended target area at this time, sir. Be advised, your flight is now showing up on the enemy radar systems at this point forward, sir. I suggest you turn on your long range intercept and attacking radar at this time sir. There's no sense in trying to hide from the enemy any longer at this point, sir. Over."

Numerous puffs of white smoke from the drift bomb launches was instantly detected from the hard deck. Four AC 130 Gunships immediately closed in on the cloud of slowly drifting hover bombs coming up to intercept the American fighter aircraft.

Overseer remarked to inform the Commander of the Fighter Wing. "Bunker One Leader, the Gunships are moving in and they're engaging multiple drift targets coming up from the ground, sir. Damn, the Gunships are really working now on the damn things sir. Over"

"Bunker One to Overseer. I hope they can clear the entire fricking area for us before we're forced to engage any enemy aircraft coming up from the hard deck, sir. Over."

Moments later a report came in from the Flight Commander of the gunships. "Leadhead to Overseer, target area is cleared of any drift weapons. We and Ghost Rider's staying in area just in case the Zappers make another launch of the damn weapons. Tell your fly jockeys to keep an eye open for us. I don't want to be one of those friendly kills if you know what I mean. Over."

"Overseer to Leadhead. That's a Roger on your last report Leadhead. I'll surely inform the other attackers of your presence still in the strike zone sir. Good job sir. Over." Overseer replied to the lead pilot of the three gunships hovering over the target area at this time.

The Commander of the AWACS aircraft immediately reported to the Commander of the attacking Fighter Wing. "Overseer to Bunker One. Nine minutes to target area, sir. Air is clear of any possible drifters. Be advised Leadhead and Ghost Rider aircraft are intending to remain in area in case another launch of the damn things are committed, sir. That's two Gunships hovering in your intended attack area, sir. Keep eyes open for them, Bunker One. We're picking up many Zappers taking off from the hard deck, and more enemy aircraft taxiing to takeoff positions on deck sir. You're going to be rather busy in a few minutes, sir. Good hunting sir. Over."

"Roger that last information sir, Bunker One to Foxtrot One. Payback, many Zappers are on their way up to play around with us a little sir. Pair off and get up high. I want your wing of aircraft to come down at the damn Zappers from the sun. Over."

"Foxtrot Leader to Bunker One. Taking my Foxtrot aircraft up to the sun now sir. We have your high top covered for this attack against the Zappers, sir. Over."

"Payback to Crow. Let's get up in the sun and wait for any possible hostiles to enter our zone of responsibility, sir. We have top cover for this mission sir. Over."

"Roger that last as received, taking my Foxtrot followers up along with me for extra top coverage sir. I'm not picking up any enemy targets as yet on my attack radar sir. Over."

"Overseer to Bunker One. Be advised I'm currently picking up multiple enemy targets to my left a thousand feet below your fight wing. I count forty enemy targets launching from the hard deck. Be advised, a second wing of Zappers are currently forming up a mile behind the first wing of enemy aircraft coming at ya, sir. Looks like they're taking a fucking lesson from us."

"Roger that last Overseer, Bunker One to Starman. Fire Phoenix missiles sir. Let's thin the rotten bastards out some for us before we engage the bulk of enemy aircraft. Over."

"Roger that as received, fire Fox Three. Repeat, am firing Fox Three missiles now, sir." The Starman lead pilot replied in his radio in an excited tone of voice to Bunker One.

Thirty six missiles instantly fired off from the American inbound fighter planes, twenty eight of the missiles found their intended targets, leaving just fourteen enemy Tangos (Targets) left to continue their attack from this first wave of Zappers. Fourteen Zappers never stood a chance to attack Bunker's more powerful Wing of fighters. Payback's eighteen YF 23s came at them from the sun, and they killed them off before they counter attacked Bunker's wing of aircraft.

Bunker One watched attentively from his present standoff position as the last of the enemy aircraft were killed off in the quick and hard hitting air war, as it slowly plummeted towards the earth as the destroyed enemy aircraft began to break up while still in the air, as the destroyed plane began to tumble through it helplessly. The Bunker One pilot noticed the enemy pilot never got out of the destroyed plane in time to save his own life.

"Bunker One to Payback. Get back up in the fucking sun and wait in case we're jumped by a second wing of Zappers, sir. Overseer's tracking another enemy wing of maybe up to forty Zappers presently coming at us. I think this time they'll be ready and waiting for us, sir. Over."

"Read you loud and clear on your last Bunker One. Taking all my birds back upstairs to take high top coverage of this operation for a second time, sir. Over."

"Overseer to Bunker One. Be advised sir, I have a Flash message coming in for you sir. We're presently picking up a wing of enemy aircraft that evidently went out to sea, and they're now trying to sneak back in, and seem like they want to attack you from the north side of your formation, sir. Sneaky little bastards they are sir. I take it as possibly fifty hostile inbounds are flying at Angel's Thirty Five Thousand Feet, be prepared to engage them at this time sir. Over."

"Bunker One to Overseer. What's the fucking ETA from the supporting aircraft from the Carriers Roosevelt and Washington, sir? Over." Bunker one wanted to know.

"ETA of support aircraft are seventeen minutes out to your intended target area at this time from the two Carriers, sir. Closest Flight Wing to you for any added support are the YF 23 group with fifty four aircraft in their formation, sir. The Commander's of the Flight Wing are Watchdog with thirty one pups, and Silk with eleven Angels in her Flight Wing, sir. Over."

"Commander Silk? What the hell is a Commander Silk god dammit, Overseer? Over."

"That's a Roger on that one Bunker One. Commander Silk, sir. She's a damn good fighter pilot sir, and she has an all female Wing of eleven birds equally as good as she is, sir. I wouldn't mind having her group protecting my ass in a stinking dogfight, Bunker One Sir."

"Bunker One to Overseer. How soon can I make fucking radio contact with the other fighter aircraft, sir? Over." The flight leader of the Hornets asked the Overseer Commander.

"Two minutes plus zero, you're three minutes away from the target area at this present time sir, and one minute out from engagement of the second Wing of inbound Zappers, sir. Over."

ON BOARD THE CARRIER ROOSEVELT

Commander Owens anxiously sat inside of a smoke filled CIC room, sweating heavily as he took a slug of cold coffee from a cup a seaman found for him. The air filtration system had been unable to keep up with the heavy cigarette smoke trapped inside the overcrowded Command Chamber. The concerned Commander listened in to his pilots as they engaged the enemy planes for the second time since the beginning of this latest attack mission launched against Libya. Subconsciously, Commander Owens cursed the Japanese made aircraft locked in deadly fights with his warplanes and pilots. There were so many of his pilots speaking at the same time, he was having a hard time following what was truly going on in the air over Libya.

Commander Owens turned and faced a Yeoman First Class standing to his right side, and said to him in a sharp tone of voice. "Pipe me through to Overseer immediately mister."

The Yeoman keyed the mike and hooked up to Overseer then handed Owens the receiver.

"Overseer Commander, Commander Owens! What the hell's going on up there for the love of the Christ child? How does it look, sir? Are we going to get driven off?" His voice was almost drowned out by the Seamen manning the threat board as they called to each other, marking current positions of detected enemy planes in correlation to the attacking American aircraft.

"Overseer to Command. It's one hell of a mess up here sir. Gees, there goes ahead on mid air collision between two aircraft, an enemy and one of ours I'm afraid, sir. Yes Commander Owens, we're slowly beginning to take control of the situation sir, but there's still a hulluva lot of enemy aircraft left to deal with, sir. We're having some serious trouble with directing the attack, too many aircraft in this circus at the same time, sir. The enemy planes are turning into courtesy targets for our pilots, sir. Their pilots suck at what they're trying to accomplish here. We're forced to take a back seat and allow our pilots react to eyeball contact and attack against the enemy aircraft. We're gonna win this one sure as hell Commander."

Commander Owens grunted as he replied to Overseer's report. "Good, that's great to hear sir. Well I guess that's it for now, sir. Keep me informed Overseer Flight Commander. Over."

"Will do as ordered sir. Overseer Out sir." The command pilot of the AWACS aircraft replied to the Commander running the entire operation in the air over Libya.

Commander Owens gave the phone back to the Yeoman and turned his attention back to the radio chatter of his pilots still engaging the enemy aircraft over the sky of Libya.

No sooner did Overseer issue the warning than the American pilot Sandman called out in an excited tone. "Tally, tally, tally. I have many Zappers below my aircraft. Multiple contacts sir, we have a environment rich target sightings, people. Let's run up the fucking score against the lousy bastards. Tally Ho Bunker Birds, let's go get the bastards. Yeehaw."

"Don't yell over the damn radio I told you people before, dammit." Bunker One bitched at his pilots again as they mustered to engage the new wing of enemy targets.

"Eat me man." One of the other pilots replied over the radio back at his Flight Commander.

The eighteen Hornets attacked the second wave of enemy Zapper aircraft, as the YF 23 aircraft hovered outside the attack area, and the F 18 Hornets broke up the enemy formation. While the Zappers were trying to get top positions over the faster moving F 18 Hornet aircraft, the YF 23s attacked them from out of the sun's harsh cover. All eighteen of the YF 23s attacked as one.

The Bunker One Commander easily picked up the YF aircraft coming in, because he was aware of their intended attack, and the three Zapper aircraft explode while in flight. The Libyan pilots had no idea who just attacked them or from what direction the attack came at them. Some of the Zapper aircraft chose to turned and run in an attempt to try and save their aircraft and their lives, their inexperience as pilots showing under the terrible combat conditions. Bunker One and the rest of his wing of aircraft went on the attack against the fleeing enemy aircraft.

"Snowman. Heads up sir. You have a stinking Zapper coming in on you at your nine o'clock high. Watch it, watch it sir, he's getting fricking position on your fucking ass sir. He's getting fricking position on you dammit, do something sir. Get the hell outta there before he tags you Snowman. That's an order sir. Move off to your port side and I'll try and get him for ya."

"Bunker One. He's ghosting my ass on me man. You have to get this motherfucker the hell off of my Six for me sir, or I'm a fucking goner for sure sir. I can't shake the lousy sonofabitch off my ass sir. Get him the hell off of me for Christ sake, sir!"

"I've got you, the Zapper's mine." The pilot Richmond announced as he immediately fired a heat seeker missile at the enemy aircraft trying to ghost Snowman. "Fox Two, fire."

"Watch out, a fucking SAM missile coming in at five o'clock low man. Now they're trying to get us with SAM missiles, dammit." An excited pilot suddenly roared over the radio.

Bunker One pulled up five hundred feet and looked down at the nearly one hundred and twenty aircraft currently buzzing each other at near supersonic speeds, while firing death at each other in an all out effort to try and kill one another. For the briefest of seconds, there was a sort of low in the fighting. Bunker One pilot thought it must have been because there were so many aircraft crisscrossing the area, neither side wanted to fire for fear of hitting one of their own planes. This low lasted a few seconds before the heavy firing started all over again.

Bunker One started his attack at a sharp forty three degree angle, and he easily hit a Zapper coming in from his top rear side. Bunker One's 20 mm cannons rounds easily ripped through the canopy of the enemy plane and the soft shell of the aircraft, as the enemy aircraft instantly went into a half roll, and then it headed out of control towards the earth below. Another Zapper plane started to get in position on

Bunker One's aircraft, but even before he could call out for help, he heard the most sexiest voice come in over the radio, low and sweet and yet commanding.

"Don't trouble yourself a bit about this little nasty, sir. Silk's on the job and this Zapper's going to meet his maker, sir." Commander Silk offered over her radio to Bunker One.

Thunder roared from her 20 mm cannon as the shells instantly ripped into the side of the T 2 Japanese made enemy plane. It suddenly burst into flames as it quickly disintegrated while still in flight. Bunker One felt a heavy thump to the tail section of his aircraft, and he immediately checked his gauges, everything still showed normal enough at this point. But his control stick was suddenly getting a little heavy in his hand, and he had lost some of his air speed, and in a dog fight, speed loss could very well spell his death. He immediately took himself out of the fighting arena, as he headed for the cover of the clouds above him to get a better fell of his plane.

"Silk, are you still there?" Bunker One complained in his radio as he looked for her in the air.

"Silk's still here honey. Who are you sir? Identify yourself at once please, sir."

"Bunker One to Silk. Commander, can you check my tail feathers and see if they're still there. Suddenly, I have a rather heavy stick on my hands, and I'm having some trouble controlling my level flight at the same time." He grumbled as he searched the sky for Silk's plane.

Silk did not reply as she quickly closed in behind the possibly damaged Hornet, and then she checked out his aircraft and reported to the concerned pilot. "Bunker One, you have a hole in your left section of your aircraft about the size of a baseball, and it looks like there may be some damage to your body near the middle center low of the aircraft, sir. The exhaust is still clear though sir. Are you going to bug out and head back to the barn for a repair deck down sir?"

"Hell no, I'm not leaving while my guys are still locked in the fight of their lives, Commander. I'll stay high until I get used to the way the controls are handling for my aircraft, and then, if I can I'll get back in the fight myself. Silk, you better get back to your Angels. They need you more than I do now. Good luck to you, and thanks for your help, Commander."

The American pilots forced the fighting closer to the ground, this was so the bomber aircraft could fly over this engagement, and then attack their assigned targets without the enemy fighters harassing their attack flight. Bunker One's pilots kept the horde of enemy Zappers too busy for them to notice any of the bombers moving overhead them.

Bunker One was in a good position to see the bomber aircraft flying overhead, and he gave a thumb's up sign to them as they passed by him. Then, he looked to the east and easily picked up the other wing of bomber planes presently closing in on their targets also. The F 117 stealth fighter/bombers were doing a great job, as they dropped their two thousand pounders on any enemy shore batteries still in operation in and around the capital of Tripoli. To try and put a quick end to the threat to the American ships being targeted by the French made missiles.

A BUNKER INSIDE LIBYA

A fuming Libyan General was losing his voice as he tried to shout over the thunder of the exploding missiles and bombs invading the capital of Libya. The command bunker was sheer mayhem as phones rang incessantly, radar operators and military aides called out the constantly moving positions of the attacking American warplanes, and then directing the aiming of intercept missiles at the attackers to their country. But just as quickly they countermanded the orders because of the fast shifting American planes. The Libyan command did not have the technology or the training to keep up with so many attacking enemy aircraft at the same time.

The extremely angry Libyan General was being overwhelmed as his bunker was suddenly hit by a sea launched American Harpoon missile, destroying half of the Command Complex. The submarine launched Harpoon and Tomahawk missile barrage was joined by a massive Naval bombardment, as the American warships moved even closer to the coast of Libya now, and the naval guns and missiles opened fire to take some heat off their attacking aircraft.

THE AIR WAR RAGING OVER LIBYA

Bunker One's attention was drawn to the seven F 15 Eagles as they started their own bombing run on Libya, and they dropped down towards earth. He was sorry the government discontinued making the older Tomcat aircraft. He thought this a poor decision on their part, but nevertheless he was happy they stationed some of the Eagle aircraft on the Carriers, to replace some of the decommissioned Tomcats. When the Eagles started their bombing run, the sky was instantly streaked by contrails coming from the Russian made SA 11 Gadfly SAM (Surface to Air Missile) missile systems. Hundreds of missiles were fired off at the wing of attacking Eagle aircraft.

Bunker One noticed one missile hit an Eagle in flight as he just released his bomb load, and cursed at the loss of the plane and its pilot. Many missiles went wild and missed the attacking American planes, because there were so many aircraft crisscrossing the sky, the missiles did not know which aircraft to lock onto first. A second Wing of Eagles went into their bombing run, as a third and fourth Wing sighted up their own bombing runs and then waited to attack.

Colonel Campanelli listened in on the attack going on over the air of Libya.

The American Eagle pilot known as Rum Runner suddenly cried out in his radio. "Pickling, bombs away sir." He let go of his ordnance, and twelve laser guided five hundred pound bombs being controlled by a hovering F 111 plane pulsating the target area by illuminating it with infrared signals, headed for their targets. The bombs started for their targets from a release point of seven thousand feet. Rum Runner again yelled in his radio. "Bomb zeroing in on target one, a direct hit. Enemy target's gone sir. Second target is illuminated, pulsating recorded. Hit, positive kill on this target. Next up." After he was certain his bombs hit their targets correctly, he pulled back on his stick and placed his aircraft into a hard five "G" turn to his right side.

Everything went incredibly fast as it was ordered. Below Rum Runner's retreating aircraft, a thick column of smoke marked the remains of a shot down Eagle on the hard deck. Behind the twin tail section of his Eagle, the world seemed to have exploded as Rum Runner shot up in the sky at breakneck speed. His plane shook and shuddered from the air displacement caused by his exploding bombs, and the number of secondary explosions happening below his plane. In an instant, Rum Runner found himself holding on to the stick with both hands to continue to control of his aircraft, as he worried if his Eagle was going to be shaken apart in flight from the violent rocking it was receiving. When he finished his turn, he looked back and forth over his shoulders for any possible attacking enemy Zappers who might be in his area hunting him.

One of Rum Runners bombs was ear marked for an aircraft hanger constructed on the outskirts of the huge military base stationed at Bengasi. This bomb landed right in the center of the huge hanger, it exploded and sent a fireball some four hundred feet in the air. The Rum Runner pilot had no way of knowing it, but he just killed forty three of the T 2 Japanese made fighter planes packed tightly inside the large hanger, in an effort to try and save the planes from the American air attack. Bombs also landed in the civilian sector near the military base as well. American intelligence warned the CIC the civilians were moved out, and the Libyan military was taking to hiding the T 2 fighter planes inside the garages of the civilian homes.

Eagle bombers took to dropping low and strafed the civilian garages once they dropped their bomb loads, sending plumes of smoke and flames bubbling hundreds of feet in the air, as the hidden enemy fighter planes exploded in the confines of the garages. This attack killed one hundred Japanese fighter planes while still sitting on the ground. The American pilots had no way of knowing how successful their air attack was. But soon, the pilots notice the older Russian Mig 29's coming up, and they quickly realized their success with the latest attacks against Libya. The enemy was quickly running out of the far better built and much newer Japanese T 2 fighters.

The American EF 111 planes started their jamming efforts, which pounded out high energy impulses to help confuse any incoming enemy missile radar tracking systems, causing the SAM missiles to go off their intended targets. Missiles flew wild until they finally ran out of fuel, and then fell back to the earth, landing on the city and surrounding area, adding their explosions to the force of the air raid currently taking place above the city. The Eagle bombs were dropped then many of the planes joined the dog fights, and they attacked the thinning enemy aircraft. Bombs were aimed and hit most of the active SAM missile sites, refit camps and the Libyan troop locations. The EF 111 plane's jamming worked out to perfection, as just five of the Libyan SAM missiles were able to locate their targets, and killed three American planes.

Now, some of the enemy Zappers pulled off the dog fights to aim their efforts after the more important American bomber planes, who did not drop their bombs as of yet. The American fighter aircraft quickly gave chase after the enemy fighter planes going after the bombers.

Bunker One looked for the flight of YF 23s which were his fastest aircraft still engaging the enemy aircraft, he picked up Commander Silk's plane going after a Zapper, low and off to his portside and grumbled in his radio. "Bunker One to Silk. New orders for you, Ma'am. Take your Angels and go after the damn flight of enemy fighters who pulled off, and are now heading after our damn bombers. Protect those damn bombers at all cost, Commander."

"Got ya and I'm on it Bunker One. Angels up let's go. Follow me and pick out your easy targets ladies. We have to protect those bombers."

Bunker One's damaged aircraft was still hovering over the air war and he watched as Commander Silk and her Angels peel off the fight, and they head right for the Zappers. His attention was suddenly drawn back to the fighting raging just below his wounded aircraft.

"Dutchman, Rebel here sir. You have a stinking Zapper on your five o'clock low. Get the hell out of there and get up in the clouds for some cover, sir. Over."

"Sandbagger to Dutchman. I got the bastard for you sir. No need for you to worry about him. He's about to make it to Paradise to be served by his 76 virgins, man."

"Rebel to Sandbagger. Check your six, check your fucking six. You have your own Zapper to worry about. He's coming in on you at your seven o'clock low and has a good track on you sir."

Another pilot that did not identify himself cut in. "I'll cover the Dutchman's backside sir."

"Bunker Three will cover Sandbagger sir." The new pilot and plane went after the Zapper.

"Roger that last as received Bunker Three." Bunker One offered back in his radio.

"Snowbird to Bunker One. I have three fucking Zappers closing in on me from my tail end sir. Shit, I need some stinking help here real fast, or I'm going to be history, dammit sir."

"I got that one Bunker One. Snowbird, this is Watchdog along with three Pups, sir. Coming in from your three o'clock level flight, sir. Keep your eyes open and call your shots for us sir. We'll take care of them attacking Zappers for ya good and proper, sir."

"Watchdog, you better get your ass in gear, or I'm done for it fella." The scared pilot known as Snowbird excitedly announced in his radio to the Watchdog pilot.

Bunker One cut in and ordered the other pilots angrily. "Stop yelling into the damn radio For Christ sake. I can't understand a word you're saying when you yell like this. Snowbird, calm down a little sir. I see Watchdog's in position. There, he's got two of the Zappers already sir."

"Roger that last as received sir." Snowbird replied to the pilot helping him out.

The radio was jammed with attack orders and firing commands and counter orders and the likes. One second a pilot yelled out. "Fox One!" And a Sidewinder missile instantly streaked through the air after its enemy target. Then, another pilot would call out in an excited voice. "Fox Two!" A Sparrow missile pierce the air on its way to its target at just over Mark Five.

Everywhere the American pilot Bunker One looked, he picked up another of his aircraft engaging an enemy in a wild dog fight. He cursed as he noticed a YF aircraft explode while in flight, and saw the Zapper pull off the exploding plane and do a roll over, indicating a victory.

"Sonofabitch." Bunker One yelled at the victorious Zapper, helpless to do anything about his kill because of the damage to his plane. But just as fast, another YF aircraft closed in and gave chase to the rolling Zapper and easily killed the plane while he tried to evade the American craft.

Bunker One suddenly cursed his luck at how slow and heavy his Hornet was handling and flying. He looked to his portside and noticed Commander Silk and her Wing of aircraft finally caught up with the moving enemy Zappers going after the bomber planes. He kept watching as Silk's YF aircraft skillfully went into a sharp arch, as she aimed her plane directly at one of the running Zappers, a thousand feet below her and off to her starboard side a little.

Commander Silk yelled in the radio. "Fox Two, fire!" And a Sparrow missile blasted in the air, and it instantly locked onto the fleeing T 2 enemy fighter aircraft, and in less than a heartbeat the enemy plane exploded while in flight.

Bunker One smiled as he watched proudly Commander Silk's sleek plane pull off the destroyed enemy aircraft, and then instantly go into a tight victory roll of her own, as she moved away from the debris flying in the air from the destroyed enemy plane.

"Angel Three to any friendly out there. I have two Zappers locked on my tail, people. I need some damn help over here real fast people." Another pilot cried in his radio now.

"I got you baby, he's all mine honey." Was the call and Bunker One watched as a YF went into attack arch, and the plane fired off a missile at one of the Zappers on Angel Three's tail.

Silk went in a three "G" turn to her portside to get in a better position on the second fleeing Zapper. Bunker One watched as Commander Silk use her 20 mm cannon on the enemy plane. One quick burst of twenty shells started his engine on the port side to smoke and flame out as the enemy plane instantly lost altitude, but the pilot still controlled the damaged plane while in flight.

As he watched the female fighters do their act, a call suddenly came in over the radio. "Seven Bears, this is Black Cloud. I'm getting a little low on petrol, people. I'm being forced to break off my attack and then head for a flying gas station, or I'm going in for a little swim, and the water's too damn cold to enjoy a quick dip, sirs."

"Tenspot to Seven Bears. I need fuel as well sir. Over." A second pilot reported.

The radio was suddenly flooded with the same call in by a number of pilots. Many of the attacking American warplanes were getting low on fuel and even weapons.

Bunker One looked at his own fuel gauge and then he smiled because he still had plenty of fuel remaining, but he remembered he was no longer in the battle, so he was conserving his fuel. He reached for his radio just as the Overseer radio operator cut in and remarked.

"Overseer to Bunker One. I estimated your plane's fuel consumption at the present rate of engagement sir, and after computing it I took it upon myself to call the Gas Stations in a little closer to the fight arena, to better service your aircraft, sir." The Commander of the Overseer AWACS plane reported to the flight leader.

Bunker One responded to the report coming in from Overseer as he announced. "Bunker One to Overseer. I didn't plan to stay over the damn target area this long, sir. What the hell's the coordinates of those flying Gas Stations, sir? Over."

"Overseer to Bunker One. The refuel tankers coordinates are stationed at Zero, Three, Three B by Five, Four, Five L sir, at about a mile and a half off to your starboard side, hovering at a height of Angel's Forty Three Thousand Feet, sir. I have them dropping down to Forty Thousand Feet for an easier fuel transfer for your starved fighter aircrafts, Bunker One. Over sir."

"Got it Overseer. Bunker One to all follow on fighter aircraft. If you need fuel, it's waiting for you at coordinates Zero, Three, Three B by Five, Four, Five L at your Forty. (Forty thousand feet) Six Gas Stations, so there's no waiting. They take credit cards and or cash, so have them at the ready in you need fuel, people."

The Commander of the AWACS aircraft cut in again and reported to the Commander of the attacking American aircraft. "Overseer to Bunker One. Be advised sir, I have twenty Nighthawk aircraft coming in your present position at Angel's Fifty Five Thousand Feet, sir. So don't confuse them for any Gomers coming in to attack your starved aircraft, sir. Over."

"Roger that last Commander. Thanks for the information Overseer. Will keep my eyes opened for the incoming Nighthawk Wing. Over."

The Eagle bomber planes that successfully dropped their eggs on their assigned targets, were coming up and forming up with the fighter aircraft from Bunker One's Wing, to add their strength to theirs, and to get some kills of their own for a change.

A number of Zappers had to break off their own attacks because they were also running low on fuel, and the enemy planes did not have flying gas cans to refuel them while in flight. The fighting was coming to a quick end as many American planes went into a tight formation, and started for the waiting fuel tankers, and then back to their Carrier bases to rearm their planes.

Bunker One decided to top off his fuel tanks as well. As he began to ease his damaged fighter plane up and under the portside wing of the massive tanker aircraft, his plane fought him all the way. The boom operator on the tanker called out to the Bunker One pilot over his radio in a concerned tone of voice. "Thirty feet from the hookup sir. Twenty feet now sir, up a little to your portside. Ten feet, ten feet, you look good sir, looks good keep coming straight in now sir. Hold it there sir, there it is sir, hookup's completed and successful sir. Good job sir."

Like a hungry bass coming to nibble on a baited hook, Bunker One's aircraft hooked up to the fuel feeder pod floating in the air before his aircraft from the transport plane. Seven hundred pounds of fuel was instantly transferred into the small fighter wing's fuel tanks from the nose refueling receptacle pod in a matter of minutes.

The boom operator came back on the radio and he reported to the pilot of the Bunker One aircraft. "Fuel transfer is completed sir. Disconnect complete. I'll send my Wingman out to clean your windshield, sir. Don't forget to tip him, he's a good worker sir."

This remark brought some laughter from the air crew aboard the refueling tanker, as well as from some of the fighter pilots waiting their turn for refueling. The huge refueling tanker was nicknamed Tiger in the Sky, and their motto was, 'The hell with a Tiger in your tank, try a little Tail in the air'.

Bunker One understood all the aircraft would have to refuel in the air once more before they finally reached the safety of their Carrier bases. Many attacking American planes were out of missiles and ammunition, which caused a stop to most of the fighting. The air refueling went off without a hitch, and on the trip back to the Carrier, Bunker One lost five more of his aircraft in his formation from damage received in their air engagement with the enemy aircraft.

Four of his planes were forced down from the damage to their aircrafts sustained in the fighting over Libya, and one plane went down when his aircraft just plain quit on its own on him due to the hard flying the pilot put his aircraft through during his engagement. The five planes went down over Algeria, and there was a good chance the Algerians would find the pilots, and take good care of the down flyers who escaped from their failed planes by bailing out.

Bunker One was trained to handle any such emergencies with a plane in trouble. He had graduated from the Navy Strike Training Center at Fallon Springs Naval Air Station in the Nevada desert, many years ago. He was drawing on all his training to get his crippled fighter back to the carrier while still in one piece. The though of not getting his plane back to the carrier had never once entered his mind. His training would not allow that though to enter his mind.

Out of sixty six American aircraft that took part in the attack on Libya from the Carrier Nimitz, forty seven of the planes returned safely, with seven aircraft receiving enough damage that the planes were pulled out of any further action until the aircraft could be repaired. Bunker One lost count of the enemy kills, because everything was happening too fast to keep decent count on the downed enemy planes. The Americans piled up over two hundred and twenty five enemy planes downed. This number was a total number killed by all the American aircraft in the attack, including the planes from the other two Aircraft Carriers stationed in the Red Sea.

The forty five remaining American fighter planes marshaled in a holding pattern behind the Aircraft Carrier Nimitz, and the damaged planes were given top priority to land first on her deck. Bunker One immediately notified Pri fly control tower that he was having some trouble with his control stick, and he was also requesting landing priority. It was immediately granted to him and he was the fifth plane given permission to deck down on the waiting Carrier.

Bunker One fought the stick of his aircraft more and more as he tried to hold his position in the formation as he slowed down his speed a little. His arms ached him from the heavy pressure he had to keep on the stick control, because the plane wanted to drift off to her right constantly on him. Bunker One's stick was no longer self centering itself, and he was forced to hold the stick in the flight position with both hands. A task which proved to be rather difficult due to the plane's constant wanting to drift off to the damaged side of the aircraft.

The Payback pilot was keeping a close eye on his Commander and his plane, and he easily noticed the amount of trouble he was having with keeping the plane's nose up, and holding the plane in level flight. Payback flew right up behind Bunker One's aircraft and looked to see if he could see any further damage done to his injured plane. There was no other damage noticeable, and he concluded the damage to the plane was mostly internal and he reported to Bunker.

"Bunker One, Payback, sir. I just checked your six and noticed no other damage visible to your airframe, sir. Your exhaust is still good and clear sir. Do you want me to follow you in just in case something let's go on you while you're trying your landing attempt on the Carrier, sir?"

"Negatory on that offer Payback. I don't want you or anyone else anywhere near me or my aircraft, just in case something goes wrong with my aircraft on my landing attempt, sir. If I go down, I don't want to take anyone else with me, dammit. Over."

"That's a read Bunker One. Be prepared to punch out and do a BWD (Blue Water Divert) if your aircraft let's you down sir. Backing off your six, you're up next sir. Good luck sir. Over."

The Air Commander gave him emergency status, and he asked Bunker if he wanted the barrier.

Bunker One refused the offer of the barrier wall, he was staying in constant contact with Carrier Air Commander stationed in the Pry fly. It had a forest of radar dishes and antennae growing from the top of the super structure. It was where the Air Commander controlled the launching and recovery of the carrier's aircraft. The Air Commander turned Bunker One's landing attempt over to the LSO (Landing Signal Officer of the deck) now.

The voice of the LSO came over Bunker One's radio in a commanding tone. "Happy Hour to Bunker One. State problem sir. I need to have the latest update on the condition of your aircraft. Be advised sir, if I don't like what I'm hearing sir, I'm going to order you to punch out and ditch in the sea, sir. I can't allow your damaged aircraft to threaten my Carrier, sir. Over."

Bunker One had to go through the list of damage to his plane to the LSO all over again.

"Happy Hour to Bunker One. Your main mount, (Landing Gear) is down and seems to be properly locked in position at the present time sir. Do you have a green light for your tail hook lock down warning sir? You're looking real good for the landing at this time sir. Over."

"Roger that last, I have a strong green light for the tail hook lockdown, sir. The tail hook's down and set locked in position sir. Over."

"Good, let me see sir. You're coming in rather sloppy and low, sir. Suggest you pick up your nose a little, or you're going to stall out and make a helluva mess on my flight deck, sir. Cut down on your drifting too while you're at it for me, sir. You're sloppy, very sloppy sir."

"I'm trying my best with this damn thing sir. She's handling heavy on me sir. My plane's constantly pulling off to my starboard side, and she's wanting to dip low on sir. She's killing the shit out of my stinking arms, sir. I never knew how heavy this plane was on the arms until this time, sir. It's like driving a car with the power steering out, sir. Over." He reported back to the concerned LSO Officer.

"Bunker One, do you wish to declare an emergency at this time sir. Do you want the crash barrier set up for your landing sir? Or do you wish to abort your landing and ditch in the sea, and I'll send the helicopter Angel One out to pluck you out of the water nice and neat as slick as snot, sir." The LSO Officer replied to the pilot who was having trouble with his plane.

"Negative on that shit, I can land her sir." Bunker had no intention of crashing into the barrier like some damn rookie, or punching out and ending up in the water by the side of the Carrier. He would ditch in the water before he went for the crash barrier on the Carrier.

"Very well then Commander. I need no further radio communication from you at this present time, sir. You're to listen to me and do whatever I tell you, and not what you want to do with your aircraft, sir. Get that nose up and go to full power for two seconds, sir. This action will force the nose of your aircraft up sir. Good, that's it, now sir, move the stick to your left for good line up with the flight deck, a little more, more. That's it, hold it there sir. Okay Commander, you're there, you're in the grove sir. Three quarters of a mile out, call the ball. That's it, that's it. Number Three arresting wire's your target for landing sir. Come in on full power sir, paddle contact now, dump your fuel, come on sir. Touch down! You're home, very good, you get thirty five points for your landing, you hooked number three arresting wire, Commander. Welcome home sir." The LSO Officer cried out, pleased with the commander's landing.

His damaged fighter slammed hard on the angled flight deck, his tail hook kicking up a small shower of sparks as it snagged the number three arresting wire pulled tight across the metal surface of the flight deck. The sudden harsh stopping of his plane almost threw his head threw the windshield of the fighter plane. The Flight Chief was the first one up the ladder, after he pulled the emergency release handle which opened the canopy from outside the plane. He pulled the quick release buckle for the harness straps locking Bunker to his seat inside the fighter.

"Sloppy, very sloppy there Major Bunker Sir." The Flight Chief grumbled at his pilot as he immediately set the four locking pins in the ejection set to disarm it, and then he added to his bitch against the exhausted looking young pilot. "Jesus H. Christ sir, you looked like a fucking cherry trying to land his plane for the first time on a Carrier, Commander. Look what you did to my damn bird sir, and you told me you were going to take good care of her for me this time sir."

The Flight Chief growled as he spat another red stream of red tobacco juice down the side of the ladder, and then continued dumping on his young pilot. "You're lucky you didn't crash my bird on that sloppy ass landing of yours, sir. Or you woulda had to get out of the wreck all by yourself, sir. I wouldn't have helped you out any sir. Come on, get your fat ass up will ya please. This damn thing can still go pop on us you know sir." The concerned Chief snarled, as he almost pulled the pilot free of the stalled plane, seat and all with the power in his arms.

A firefighter tried to spray his CO-2 extinguisher in the air intakes of the damaged plane, hitting the older chief and Bunker with some of the spray as he fought the heavy bottle of CO-2.

"Watch it will ya, you fucking asshole you!" The older Chief snarled as he and the pilot almost stumbled down the narrow ladder. Once on the deck, Major George Bunker stepped back and looked at the damage to the main frame of the aircraft. A hole the size of his fist was ripped in the engine section of his plane and there were seven bullet holes in the fuselage.

"You're a damn lucky little bastard that's all the damage you did to my fricking bird on me sir, you damn amateur you." The Chief then laughed as he placed his hand heavily on Bunker's sweat soaked back, and then he smiled at the stunned looking flyer, as he skillfully and quickly lead him away from the damaged plane.

"Hell Chief. You had me more scared of what you were going to do to me if I damaged your damn aircraft, than what any damn enemy pilot could do to me out there sir." Bunker laughed also as he followed the elderly Chief away from his aircraft.

"You're damn right there Major Bunker Sir. I gotta go along with my hurt bird sir. You did real fine with getting her back to me in one stinking piece, sir." The elderly Flight Chief said as he tapped the side of the damaged plane lightly with his hand, and then he followed it as the fighter plane was being manhandled by some of the deck crew workers to the main flight deck elevator stationed right in the middle of the Carrier flight deck. All the while he was walking with the plane, the Chief constantly screamed out a string of orders and spat red spit out at the same time at his flight crew workers, who instantly started going over every inch of the damaged fighter plane. Both inside and outside as it slowly disappeared below the flight deck as another aircraft started its landing run on the Carrier flight deck now.

Bunker One was quickly ushered right over to the so called Vulture's Row of the Carrier to where Captain Taylor watched the landing of his planes on the flight deck of his Carrier.

"Coffee." Was the only word Taylor said to the sweat soaked pilot dressed in an overcoat.

George Bunker took the steaming cup of coffee in both hands, savoring the heat from the cup as he gulped down a mouthful of the hot liquid, and then finally relaxed a little for himself.

"How bad was it George? It looked pretty bad from what I was able to tell about the engagement." The Captain asked the flyer with some concern as he finally turned to look at him.

"Tough Captain, it was pretty bad up there sir. We lost a lot of good flyers today sir. I never saw so many damn aircraft in one spot in my entire life, all shooting at each other and wanting to kill each other, sir. It was so thick up there that I shot a missile at a Zapper, and it ended up zeroed in on a different T 2, killing that plane instead, Captain Taylor

Sir. I saw three mid air collisions, and you can bet the bank on it there were more that I didn't notice sir."

The Captain cut off the Major's report as he asked the exhausted looking fighter pilot. "How soon do you think you can be ready to attack Libya again, sir?"

"Today sir?" He asked the Captain with a surprised tone in his voice as he stared at him.

"Yes today. Look mister, I have the damn enemy on the run at this time, sir. They couldn't get all their damn fighters and interceptor aircraft off the ground because of the bombers we had attacking them, and I'm a firm believer in showing no mercy to your enemy once they're down and out for the count, sir. I don't intend to allow any of my enemy to live, because enemies left alive today, will only come back to fight us on another day, sir. What the hell good did mercy do for us in Iraq for Pete's sake? Not a bit of good Commander. No, the safest option here is the complete annihilation of the enemy, sir. Never allow your enemy to return as an enemy. Remember that sir. Now, when will you be ready today, sir?"

"I guess it'll take at least two hours in order to refuel and rearm my the fighter planes before we can possible be ready to reengage the enemy planes over Libya Captain Taylor Sir, and then I'll need another aircraft for myself, and a number of my other pilots will need new air platfo..."

"I'll have your aircraft replace for you myself sir, and I have nineteen new ones stowed below deck already refitted and refueled, and ready for immediate flight, sir. I just need a few extra pilots to fly the damn things for me sir." The Captain remarked as he eyed his young pilot.

"That's an understatement if I ever heard one there, Captain Taylor Sir. I need a few new pilots to replace the ones I have all fatigued out, sir. I don't want some of the pilots back..."

"That's bullshit and bad manners, you're over stepping your bounds with me here, as well as our friendship, mister. If I tell you to get your ass back in the shit then that's exactly what you're going to do mister, and you'll take all the damn pilots who returned, along with you sir. This is war, and I need your planes pounding the living shit out of Libya and her damn ground forces and aircraft. Now, see to your men, Major. Make damn certain that they have something to eat and catch some rest while they can sir. I want all the pilots to meet me in the wardroom in one hour, one hour for a briefing Major. You got it sir?" The Captain hissed at the pilot.

Bunker placed the cup down on the stand, snapped to attention and saluted his Commanding Officer. Then he turned on his heels and went below to check on his pilots, and to get himself something to eat, and maybe rest as best he could before he had to see the Commander again.

THE SEA STALLION HELICOPTER HOVERING OVER THE BATTLE FIELD IN CHAD

Colonel Edward Campanelli was riding inside his command chopper as soon as the helicopter was refueled, and he had himself something to eat. This time Captain Mendoza accompanied the Colonel and Captain John White to the battlefield. For the moment, Colonel Campanelli's forces were consolidating their actions, and the troops were also preparing for their next breakout in the field of battle. The Colonel was going to commit all his troops, aircraft, helicopters and military equipment this time, in an all out attack and effort against the Libyan defensive forces. His supplies had finally caught up to his advance troops, and they were refitted, fed and had plenty of fresh water to drink and bathe in. The soldiers were also pretty well rested up, and they were ready to fight again. His helicopters spooled on the deck, armed, and ready to go off to battle.

Colonel Campanelli looked to Captain Mendoza, he then smiled at her as he announced in a calm tone of voice. "I want you to control the damn pain in the ass Marines on the ground for me this time, Mendoza. John, I want you to control the backup Army follow on support units and equipment this time around, while I'll Command the damn choppers and aircraft needed for this breakout attack, sir. I'm not going to allow any of our damn troops to get caught with their stinking asses hanging out in the damn wind like the last time around, sir. Captain Richie's staying behind this time to take care of the base for my ass."

Captains White and Mendoza were smiling back at their Commanding Officer while staring at him for a moment like they both knew something he did not know.

"What the fuck are you two jaybirds laughing about around here, dammit? You two are acting like I'm some kind of a damn adulterer or something. What the hell is with you two birds anyhow, dammit?" He growled at the two of them while he waited for either of the two to reply to his last question aimed at them.

Captain White laughed as he said to his lifelong friend. "Colonel Campanelli Sir! Adultery is what happens when a sneaky ass Irish bartender puts fucking water in the damn whiskey on you, sir. I was smiling because I'm damn happy we're all together again, and I like it that way, sir. You two are the only friends I have in the real world. I guess what I'm trying to say to you two guys is, I love the both of you sir. Heaven knows why though sir."

The Colonel did not know where this comment came from, and he looked to Captain Mendoza for an quick answer, but she was smiling from ear to ear while looking back at John. She suddenly reached over and wrapped her arms around his neck, and pulled him to her and she hugged, and then kissed the smiling big black man as she said to him while smiling at him. "I love you too Johnny." She kissed him again as she added to her words. "I knew I could count on you. I'd like to know if you would like to be our best man at our wedding, John."

Captain Mendoza turned to Edward who shook his head in approval of her choice, and then he glanced at Captain White who was smiling back at him.

He laughed a good hearty, soulful laugh as only he could laugh, and then he grumbled at his two dear friends as he slowly shook his head no. "Sonofabitch, you two jaybirds are really going to do it huh? You two are really going to tie the damn knot, huh? God dammit, I don't think the stinking world's ready for the two of you getting together and popping out some kids, but what the hell. I'd be god damn pleased to be the best man at your wedding, friends. Man, I wouldn't miss this for all the stinking tea in China, my friends. Sonofabitch. Who the hell would have ever thunk it possible, dammit?" He repeated as he stared at both of his friends this time, while wearing the biggest grin Colonel Campanelli had ever seen in his lifetime.

CHAPTER 28

Colonel Edward 'Popeye' Campanelli told the two other officers now trapped in his Command helicopter that his attack was going to be coordinated with the air attack presently going on over the nation of Libya. He called this attack, 'The final blow to the enemy'. He explained he had some inside information that Libya was planning to attack Egypt next. This would put Libya right smack dab in the middle of a three front war, as well as sustaining continuing attacks from the sea, now that the stealth aircraft were able to knock out most, if not all the shore missile systems on the Libyan defenders. He was quite certain this attack would finally break the back of the Libyan soldiers, and they would surrender and put a quick end to the war.

The massive Sea Stallion Command helicopter was flying at three thousand feet now, it was early afternoon as the Colonel watched as a large number of his fighter aircraft streak across the air as they started what was believe to be the final assault on the dug in Libyan troops still operating in the nation of Chad. Forty five American attack aircraft in all, stormed in on the Libyan defensive lines. Twenty Apache fast attack helicopters also moved in for the kill and they concentrated their opening attack on finding any hidden tanks and artillery pieces, and the helicopters quickly and easily took them out with their Hellfire missiles and heavy cannon fire.

The Colonel's helicopter hovered over the units of Marines as Captain Renee Mendoza issued orders to the ground soldiers, and support orders to the soldiers stationed below. With such an onslaught by over five hundred tanks and artillery pieces, and two hundred thousand troops from the Marines and Army Units. The hard pressed Libyan defensive lines flounder, and then they crumble all together under the heavy pressure mounted against them from the American forces.

Captain John White moved in his Army Units, and with the seventy five thousand troops joining the fight. The Libyan defenders were quickly overwhelmed on all fronts, and they started to withdraw in mass confusion. There was little surrendering from the Libyan soldiers though, because there was still a lot of fight left in these well trained and tried soldiers of the battlefield.

As the Marines continued their opening attack, the Libyan defenders staged a desperate counterattack aimed at the middle of the attacking Marine Units. But this counter action was short lived, and was quickly crushed by a joint attack by supporting aircraft and helicopters.

The American warplanes owned the air behind the enemy lines, and they were wreaking pure havoc on the Libyan supply lines and reinforcing soldiers, and the Libyan soldiers quickly found themselves completely cut off from any further military supplies or reinforcements.

The Libyan airforce who supported their troops on the ground during their takeover of the nation of Chad, tried to attacked the American warplanes. These attacks consisted of the old and outdated Russian made Floggers and Foxhound aircraft, but the Libyan pilots and not the planes, were no real match for the American pilots and their aircraft. This led to a complete failure of the Libyan air support, and the American aircraft easily started to pick and chose their enemy targets on the ground at random.

A new line of defense was quickly being established by the retreating Libyan soldiers at, and around the Chad city of Ennedi. Here the retreating Libyan troops dug in and they fought back, they were being supported by what was left of the enemy planes, armor, artillery and helicopters. It was Libya's last stand before being completely pushed out of Chad and back into Libya.

The Libyan soldiers were using everything they had at their disposal in order to try and stop the wildly charging American forces. One hundred and fifty MI-24 Russian made Hind anti tank helicopter gunships were hard pressed into action now.

The first wave of enemy attack helicopters caught some Marine forces a little flatfooted, and the helicopters chewed up thirty American and allied tanks, before the Libyan helicopters were finally driven off by the backup YF-23 aircraft from Base Sentry, and a regrouped wing of Apache helicopters attacked the enemy helicopters and easily killed forty five airframes.

The Marines stopped their forward advance and then they dug in to ward off the heavy attacks from the Libyan choppers and ground forces. The fighting was particularly bloody with both sides trading artillery rounds as close as one hundred yards apart. Ammunition expenditures were greater than ever expected and getting more ammunitions to the front lines was a problem.

Colonel Campanelli listened in on the flood of incoming reports as requests for artillery shells and other forms of ammunition came in from the many of the American units stationed on the frontlines of the fighting. He suddenly looked at Captain White, but even before he could growled at his second in command, John replied to his unasked order of his Commanding Officer. "I'm working on it as best I can for crap sake, all I can tell ya is it's on the way sir."

As the American Command helicopter hovered over the massive field of battle, John tapped the Colonel on the shoulder as he pointed out of the port window of the helicopter at some new troop movement taking place below them. This time his attention was drawn over to the six large C 17 transport planes nicknamed 'Flying Trucks', as they slowly circled over a certain section of land being held by the Marines inside the nation of Chad.

"Supplies and ammo coming in by the stinking pound at this time, sir. I told you I was on it sir." John said while smiling proudly and informed his Commander.

One of the massive aircraft suddenly left the formation that was being escorted by a Wing of fifteen F 18 Hornets and the much larger aircraft came down for a rough landing in the field.

The Colonel looked to the ground and realized the plane was going to try and land on a messed up narrow dirt road. He was having some trouble seeing all of the dangerous looking makeshift landing strip, and then he complained at his second in command. "That fucking nut's not gonna try and land his damn aircraft there, is he John for crap sake?"

The Colonel grumbled at his second in command, but he did not wait for the answer as he ordered the pilot of his airframe. "Pilot, get us up, I wanna see this fucking act. Take the helicopter up another five hundred feet so I can see everything happening below us, dammit."

The Sea Stallion lifted so smoothly it was hard to tell the craft had changed its altitude. The Colonel and John watched as the incoming plane performed. It took two minutes for the Flying Truck to align itself properly with the narrow strip. Campanelli drew in his breath and warned John in a huff. "The damn road's not wide enough for the aircraft. Its wings are going to hit the trees and be ripped apart before the damn thing lands. He's going to crash, the damn fool!"

"Have a little faith in the pilot sir, he seems to know what he's doing with the landing Colonel. He'll get down okay sir. But even if he doesn't, as long as the damn supplies gets to the troops, the plane and its crew are expendable for this damn mission, sir." John replied smartly.

Without knowing it, both the Colonel and Captain held their breath as the plane came in. He leaned in a subconscious move to help the pilot maneuver his massive plane for this dangerous landing he was attempting. They both watched in complete silence as it slowly touched down. As the aircraft carefully touched down, it was instantly lost in a bellowing cloud of dust until it could no longer be seen by either of the officers stationed in the helicopter. All that was visible of the landing was this moving cloud below them. By the time the cloud of dust finally settled down, the Colonel noticed the plane already being unloaded by the troops.

"Damn." Was the only word muttered by the concerned Commanding Officer.

The Marines quickly finished unloading the aircraft, and then they pushed the empty plane by hand so it was aligned properly with the widest part of the road, and then the pilot revved the engines. In a minute, the plane was off the ground and heading for the sun. It stayed low and banked hard to the left to keep out of the way of a second C 17 preparing for its landing.

Colonel Campanelli watched with concern as the second incoming aircraft quickly lined up with the narrow road, and then set down as the plane before it had done.

"God damn John, those damn pilots are good, real good sir. I'd never have tried to land a fucking plane that big in so tight an area if it was up to my ass, sir. Shit, I'd never have believed the damn things would ever be able to set down on that road safely, sir. I thank my lucky stars Congress didn't cut back on the whole order of the damn C 17s. Do you have any idea how the hell many of the damn aircraft were made anyhow? Twenty I believe was it?"

es sir, twenty planes, and we have them all of them under our command, Colonel. I'd like to see a C 5 Galaxy try and land in such a tight spot, Eddy." John offered with a smirk.

C'mon John. You know damn well the damn C 5s are almost twice the size of the C 17. That was what all the hubbub was about back in '94. Why do we need the C 17, when we have so many C 5s and other shit available. The C 5s would have had to air drop their damn cargo, but the troops would've received their supplies, sir. Well John, that's why we need the damn C 17 to fit in these tight ass places, and get the stinking supplies to our troops safely. I wish some of those crybabies could see these babies in fucking action, sir. Maybe then they wouldn't be so quick with their grips of trying to stop us from updating our services for Pete's sake."

"Sir, it's also the pilots skill too you know Eddy." John offered as he tried to protect his pilots.

"I know that for cripe sake, mister. Jesus John, I know the pilot makes the damn airframe, sir. But on the other hand, there's an argument the plane makes the pilot also, mister." The Colonel smiled at John and then he went back to his maps and charts.

ON THE BATTLEFIELD IN CHAD

On the battlefield, first, the Marines would probe the Libyan defensive lines, but they were quickly driven back by sheer force of the enemy troops and weapon fire. Then the Libyan soldiers would try and probe the Marines lines only to be driven back themselves as savagely.

A stalemate on the field of battle was evident between both warring sides, with neither side able to take the advantage of this situation, and neither side was willing to commit the necessary troops to the slaughter to cause the breakthrough that was needed by both armies.

The Colonel saw what was happening on the field of battle, and he called for another air attack on the entrenched Libyan defenders, in order to try and produce the needed breakthrough for his troops. Because he knew his soldiers were dying defending their lines, and he would much rather his troops die on the offense, than on the defense. He ordered twenty B 52 bombers up to attack the Libyan lines. Colonel Campanelli was immediately informed the requested attack would occur in twenty minutes. He ordered the Marines to stand down and wait for the air raid to start, the fighting calmed down as the Marines received the orders, and they held off some.

The Colonel stared at the radar screen, looking for the first sign of the incoming massive B 52 bomber aircraft. An airman whose job it was to read the scope, picked up the planes first, and he quickly pointed them out to the Commanding Officer. The large blimps on the screen left no doubt that these blimps were the enormous bombers coming in. he watched as the incoming aircraft flew towards their assigned targets. Finally, the bombers circled the area, and then they lined up into their bomb run on the enemy positions below. He saw on the screen the planes leap up almost five hundred feet, and knew immediately that the bombs were released by the planes, and they were just reacting to the sudden weight change in the aircrafts.

The bombers immediately headed back to their base in England, without waiting around to see all the destruction their bombs had just wrought on the enemy lines of defense. The Colonel ordered his helicopter to move in closer to the ground, so he could see the bombs hit their targets. Campanelli was not prepared for the terrible destruction which occurred. Each bomber dropped sixty thousand pounds of dumb bombs right on the Libyan troops and their lines. One million, two hundred thousand pounds of high explosives landed directly on the Libyan defenders.

Colonel Campanelli stared in stunned disbelief as he watched buildings instantly disappear in the thick clouds of heavy smoke, flames and explosions. Proximity slow fused rounds from the artillery added to the overwhelming destructive power to the bombing, as the shells detonated twenty feet off the ground, showering the surviving enemy troops with white hot shards of steel traveling at super sonic speed. Ripping the enemy soldiers apart as they hid in their foxholes. As the Colonel watched bombs smash the earth, another radio communication came in on him.

"Blue Eight Two Leader to all Trailers. Split up and head for pre arranged targets. Over."

The Colonel pushed the keys on his computer keyboard, and the description of Blue Eight Two flashed across his screen. Blue Eight Two was a code name for the massive bomb the six MC 130 Combat Talon transport planes carried. It was the fifteen thousand pound ordnance nicknamed the 'Daisy Cutter', in the Viet Nam war. Back then, the bomb was used for clearing large areas of jungle for an instant landing zone for helicopters, and the slick troop transport choppers. The bomb was going to be used differently here, the massive bombs were going to be dropped on the Libyan troops for their shock value against the enemy troops.

The concerned Colonel listened to all the communications coming from Blue Eight Two flight commander. "Two minutes plus two seconds from targets."

"Roger your last as received sir. Maintain your present heading and altitude sir. Over."

Seconds later. "Over the target area. Tail door open and ready for release of the weapon. Bomb's away, the weapon is launched. Turning to get out of the target area. I'd give a weeks pay to see the faces on those lousy bastards when these babies go pop on their asses, sir. Over."

"Roger that last as received sir. Cut out the crap, and turn to your new heading of Three, Three Four, and reform up there with the other five MC 130 transport planes, and then you're flight is instructed to return to your assigned base to rearm if necessary, sir. Over."

"Roger that last as ordered sir. Am turning to heading of Three, Three, Four as ordered and then am returning to my assigned base for possible rearmament, sir. Over."

Again, the Colonel turned to his computer to see where Blue Eight Two's target was. Once he got the proper coordinates, he ordered the pilot to head closer to the target area for a second time. He wanted to see the effects of the massive bombs falling from 35,000 ft on the enemy positions. Triple A fire filled the air as the Libyan gunners tried their best to hit the large lumbering aircraft as they showed up on their radar scopes. His Command helicopter did not come under any enemy triple A fire, because he was flying low, and the gunners concentrated all their efforts on the threat coming from the huge bomber aircraft. Small arms fire bounced off the side of the helicopter's armor plating every once in a while though, but it cause little concern to the pilot of the command staff traveling inside the massive airframe.

Eight seconds later, Colonel Campanelli helicopter was hovering where he wanted to be, as he put his binoculars to his eyes and focused them in on the target area. Instantly, there was a massive and blinding explosion resembling a small nuclear blast. The shock wave crashed in the side of the helicopter, and it shoved it forty feet off course. The pilot did not wait for orders as he instantly changed course, and headed away from the area before the other bombs hit.

"God damn!" The Colonel groaned as they headed to their original position over his troops.

"Did you see what you wanted to see so far Eddy?" John asked his Commander with concern.

He glared harshly at him as he snarled at his close friend. "Too much dammit, John."

The rest of the flight was done in stunned silence. They got back to their original position as the bombing of the enemy troops continued. In seconds, all he could see was a huge dust cloud as bombs from a second wave of B-52 bombers continually struck the ground. His helicopter again felt the effects from the bombing, as his pilot was forced to bank left, and then to the right to stay in the air, as the helicopter bucked and bounced from the terrible shock waves.

He hit his forehead on a metal brace attached to the side of the helicopter more than once, as he tried to see exactly what was happening in the heavily raising cloud of dust below him. By now, all bombs hit the ground, but the earth was still being assaulted by hundreds of secondary explosions, as enemy tanks, planes, fuel dumps and ammunition exploded. Colonel Campanelli could not believe any soldiers could possibly survived this heavy pounding as he watched even more shells and bombs still assaulting the surface of the earth in this massive bombardment. But he also knew there would always be many soldiers who would be left alive to continue to fight on, somehow there always was soldiers left to fight on in this madness of war.

After the bombing and much of the heavier fighting came to an end, it would be estimated that over nine hundred Libyan soldiers lost their lives in this latest attack, add this to the one hundred thousand civilians who also perished, and you could realize the sheer size and scope of the battle that just took place on the battlefield below the command helicopter.

As the massive dust cloud started to settle down a little, Colonel Campanelli noticed the carnage created by the heavy bombers. The face of the earth was covered with debris and pieces of human beings. Hundreds of stunned, staggering and exhausted Libyan troops roamed the battlefield aimlessly, surrendering to Marines who moved in to what was left of the once Chad city all but completely destroyed. As the Marines interviewed some prisoners, they accused the American forces of using tactical nuclear weapons against them on the battlefield. The bewildered enemy soldiers confused the massive Blue Eighty Two bombs as nuclear weapons, and this confusion caused them to give up rapidly to the advancing American troops.

Bulldozers and bladed engineer tanks from the 72nd Combat Engineers were put into action, cutting roads through all the debris. So American tanks and troops could get to the center of the city. The Marines came under intermittent small arms fire from snipers whose job it was, was to delay the American troops forward advance on Libya, until the retreating Libyan soldiers could muster a defensive line much closer to their own border and better military supplies.

The Libyan soldiers knew full well that the American troops would continue their forwards advance and invade their country of Libya, and this gave the enemy soldiers the resolve to fight to the death with a new heart and inner strength. The terribly staggered Libyan soldiers would do whatever was necessary to try and stop the American troops where they were, because they did not want the infidels to enter their homeland. The Libyan snipers were doing well, and the Marines were getting bogged down a few times, and they were forced to wait for tanks to come up to root out the hidden snipers. This slowed the Marines advance down to a snail's pace, and it gave the Libyan troops time to setup a better defensive line at the town of Tekra.

The path the Libyan troops took to get to Tekra, was laid heavy with mines and countless mantraps, and it kept the American engineers rather busy disarming the traps. Hundreds of enemy snipers dug in along the route to hamper the Marine's forward progress down. The Marines now found themselves fighting for every step they took towards the Libyan border.

The American soldiers would come under fire from a stray Libyan Mig fighter, or a Hind helicopter which managed to evade the American aircraft protecting the United States soldiers on the ground, radar or missile defenses by flying in low and hitting the Marines and then trying to make a fast getaway. But these enemy aircraft rarely did much damage, because they were instantly pounced on, and killed as fast as they showed up by the ready air cap flown over the American troops, by the YF 23s or the F 18 Hornet fighter planes who owned the sky.

John's receiver came to life as a dispatch rapidly typed out on his terminal. He tore the paper free of the machine and then announced to his Commanding Officer. "Uh-oh." He then handed the page over to the Colonel and offered. "Eddy, you're not going to like this report any, sir."

Colonel Campanelli quickly read the report and cursed angrily. "Dammit, I can't believe this shit for a moment, John." The suddenly angry Colonel instantly typed a message to be sent out to all ground troop Commanders. It was a strong¬ly worded memo. 'To all battalion and Divisional Commanders, you will be held strictly responsible, as will any other American soldiers guilty of instances of undisciplined actions or infractions of military laws, committed against the civilian population or against any surrendering enemy soldiers'.

All Field Commanders who received this last report, knew this warning was aimed at the rape of any female citizens by allied soldiers under their command or torture of any enemy prisoners.

THE CARRIERS USS NIMITZ AND THE USS CONSTELLATION

The massive Aircraft Carrier Nimitz finally entered the Mediterranean Sea, and once she was certain all the enemy missile batteries once defending Libya were destroyed. The Aircraft Carrier Constellation, at full steam since the day before, caught up with the Nimitz and her support ships. Both Aircraft Carriers entered the Mediterranean Sea almost side by side. The Nimitz and Constellation were going to combine their awesome air power in another Alpha attack aimed against Libya. Their attack would be joined by the aircraft due to be launched by the Carriers Roosevelt, Washington and the John F. Kennedy, along with the aircraft from the 82nd Airborne, who had replaced the 27th Tactical Wing stationed on Sicily just days before.

IN THE SKY OVER LIBYA

Two wings of F 117 Nighthawk and F 110 Bluelight aircraft attacked Libya as the carriers prepared to launch their opening attack, as a third wing of Navy X 117 aircraft strained to catch up with the other stealth fighters groups. A wing of twenty seven massive B 52 bombers was going to overlap the Nighthawk aircrafts attack. Commander Owens decided he did not want any time to elapse between the continuing air attacks being carried out against Libya.

Bunker One, Major George Bunker was sore as hell as he painfully climbed back into his waiting Hornet aircraft, and then he waited to be the first aircraft launched from the Carrier deck. It was near one o'clock in the afternoon when they finally started this latest air attack against the nation of Libya. The American aircraft would have to refuel over Algeria again, but much closer to the Libyan border this time around. This was because the Nimitz was stationed in the mouth of the Mediterranean Sea, and she was much closer to the Libya coastline now.

As his aircraft was being hooked onto the catapult cart, a jet blast deflector instantly raised out of the flight deck directly behind his aircraft. Bunker One was again plastered in his seat as the catapult built up launch speed power, and then fired his plane in the air. Side by side, one after the other, his Flight Wing shot off the flight deck of the Roosevelt. The planes instantly marshaled off the fantail of the Carrier, and then they waited until his entire Wing of twenty F 18 Hornets formed up and again headed directly towards Libya. This attack was scheduled to be carried out by five hundred and seventeen planes, and they were going in for the kill this time. The Compass Calls were up and jamming away at all Libyan communications for fifteen minutes, and ten of the dreaded AC 130 H Spectra Gunships were on the prowl, looking for any possible drift bombs being launched to destroy the attack American aircraft.

As Bunker One and the rest of his Flight Wing climbed up to 35,000 feet, he noticed a number of thick columns of smoke raising over what he took to be the main capital city of Libya, Tripoli. Which indicated to him the Nighthawk aircraft and B 52 bombers were hard at work attacking the Libyan city. He could easily pick up flack bursts still going off in the sky. But this time, the flack was no where near as heavy as it had been earlier in the day. This was another indication the bombing was having its desired effects on the Libyan military defenses.

Bunker One looked to his rear and he noticed some of his planes were forming up behind the Nimitz, and mumbled to himself from sheer exhaustion. "C'mon you fricking assholes, you know god damn well that you have no chance of continuing this stinking war. Do the smart thing and put it to an end will ya, and start saving your soldier's damn lives. You guys can't possibly win this damn thing so put a stop to it and save your country from further destruction."

Flight Commander Major George Bunker looked at his instrument panel of the plane. His course was set at Zero Three Niner. He really loved the Hornet, and the freedom of the air it afforded him as he presently flew his aircraft towards his assigned target. His IFF (Identify Friend or Foe) system was already marking out all the American warplanes in the air this time in white. His headset was alive with technical rhetoric, and the fears of many of the young pilots. Their talkativeness was as irritating to him as was the voice of an auctioneer's babble.

Bunker One looked out of his canopy as he started to fly over the land mass of the nation of Algeria. It was a beautiful, bright cloudless afternoon that was soon to be marred by the death he supported under the wings of his plane as he quickly closed in on his assigned target again.

The AWACS Aircraft Overseer was set in place as three of the radar jamming Compass Call aircraft, and the Spectra Gunships were already plastering away at hundreds of the drift bombs launched as soon as Bunker One's wing entered the Algerian airspace, and they came up as contacts on the Libyan radar systems.

The trailing EF 111's started their jamming as other F 111s formed up on the bombing runs.

The Commander of the Overseer aircraft opened his communications with Bunker. "Overseer to Bunker One. Your gas cans are presently stationed at Angels Thirty Six Thousand Feet, and they're waiting to refuel your aircraft as needed sir. You're fifteen minutes away from your intended target area as of this time, sir. You have two Flight Wings of Nighthawks operating at Angels Forty Five Thousand Feet, so pick out your targets carefully, sir. You also have twenty A 6R Intruders in groups of four, working at Angels One Thousand Feet, killing all active enemy radar units, so keep your eyes open those aircraft, sir.

The Carriers Roosevelt, Kennedy and the Washington are launching an Alpha Strike Force, and their aircraft should be over the target area in an hour after your attack begins, sir. A one two punch if you will. Luck Bunker One."

"Bunker One to Overseer. Read you loud and clear on your last report sir. I'll keep my eyes open for the Nighthawks and Intruder aircraft, sir. Starting my refueling run now sir. Over."

"Bunker One to Snowbird and Richmond. End all radio silence now, take your birds up and start your refueling as instructed. When your aircraft have completed their refueling operation. Sandman and myself will lead our birds up to refuel. Over."

"Bunker One to Foxtrot Flight Leader. You're ordered to refuel up next after we have finished our refueling operation, sir. Over."

"Roger that last communication sir. Understood all as received and will comply sir. Over."

"Bunker One to War Child. You're up next to top off your fuel tanks after the Foxtrot aircraft are finished their refueling operation, sir. After you're fueled up, then Starman and the rest of his birds will begin their refueling operation next, sir. All birds are to regroup to form formations, and commence our opening attack on our assigned targets in this order, sir. Over." As he broke off his umbilical fuel feeder from the refueling aircraft, his radio came to life.

"Bunker One, Overseer Commander here sir. I have many Zappers coming up from the hard deck preparing to play with you a little, sir. I'm picking up at least forty enemy aircraft in all, I say again, forty enemy planes in the air as of now, sir. I'm further picking up to another possible forty enemy aircraft still on the deck taxiing to lift off positions at this time, sir. Good hunting sir. Will advise if detect any other hostiles taking off from the hard deck sir. Over."

"Roger that, Overseer. Snowman and Richmond. You're up first. Soften them bastard up and Sandman and myself will attack with our birds from the sun at your two o'clock high, sir. Over."

"Bunker One to Bunkers Two through Five. Let's get up in the damn sun and prepare to engage the enemy aircraft from their twelve o'clock high. Sandman, follow my air wing when you're done with your refueling sir. Let's get them this time around gentlemen. Over."

THE LIBYAN DEFENDERS

Libya sent up her second and third string pilots against this latest attack from the American aircraft, because most of her better trained pilots were already killed or missing in action. These lesser trained pilots coming up, were less of a threat against the American pilots, and they amounted to be no more than mere targets of convenience for the much better trained American pilots. The kills for the American pilots mounted up quickly. Their radios were alive with calls.

"Fox One, fire. Fox One away." One of the pilots announced in an excited tone.

"Target acquisition. Vector at One, Three, Zero. Over." A second pilot said in his radio.

These reports meant that the enemy planes were falling victim to the American aircraft. Now, the only protection Libya had left to her defense were the anti aircraft guns, and some active SAM systems still working. When a SAM radar was lit up, or a missile launch was detected, the missile site was instantly killed just as quickly by the low flying wing of Intruder aircrafts. The SAM missiles were becoming less of a threat against the American pilots and aircraft.

FIGHTING IN THE NATION OF CHAD

The ground war inside Chad was going exceptionally well for the American and Allied troops involved in the ground fighting. Colonel Campanelli's ground forces were rapidly driving forward, pushing the

Libyan ground forces back into Libya for the first time since the war started. The only problem that the concerned Colonel still milled over in his mind was, he really did not realize how many times he wished he had some of the old A 10A Thunderbolts Warthog aircraft. The old Warthog airframe was the real workhorse of the Desert Storm war, and it compiled such an outstanding kill rate of tanks and armor vehicles in the Iraq war. Even though the Apache and Sea Cobra helicopters were doing a great job for his ground troops. The Warthogs were much faster, and they could support the ground troops much quicker and with heavier weapon systems.

The Colonel thought, 'Shit, if this is the only problem I can come up with, I can live with it easy enough god dammit'. As he smiled when he heard Mendoza call in the radio for a squad of Marines to move up, and support another squad of grunts engaging some enemy troops.

FRANCE'S HELP.

A number of French scientists were working carefully with the samples of the Crimson Code Millie toxin given to them by the Russian government. The scientists conducted a number of rather detailed experiments, exposing various animal populations of Arab countries involved in the fighting, the toxins to learn the effects on them.

Well into one experiment, a sudden and startling discovery was made. When the deadly toxin was exposed to the ruminant Antelope family included the small Spring buck, Eland, Kudu, Giraffe, Gerenuk, Steenbok and Kirks dik dik, who recycled their food by chewing the cud to extract more of the protein and minerals from their food. The toxin effects on the Herbivore stomach in the omasum where a chemical reaction would take place in which the toxin mixes, and then changes the digestive fluids, causing the animals an extremely slow death.

Once the animal was dead, the chemical makeup of the toxin continued to change until mutating, and then go from a short life expectancy of five days, to an unlimited life expectancy. Surviving scavengers who would rip open the stomach of the carcass, would cause the mutating toxins to become airborne again, and this time much lighter than the first strain of the toxin released, thus extending the contamination and wave of death.

The French scientists came to the conclusion that if Libya ever employed the terrible toxins on the battlefield, they would contaminate the entire world in less than a year's time. The fearful scientists immediately informed the United States about their stunning findings, and the United States started their own experiments on the toxin, only to come up with the same conclusions.

The President of the United States was informed of the findings, and he called for a emergency meeting of his entire security cabinet, along with all Joint Chiefs of Staff. The meeting was long, and sometimes extremely heated, and almost came to blows a few times between two angry Generals so intent with protecting their troops on the ground in the fighting arena. When the Chairman of the Joint Chiefs of Staff announced the United States would have no other choice but to resort to the use nuclear weapons to instantly sterilize any possible affected areas, if Libya resorted to the use of any of these chemical and biological weapons on the battlefield.

A memo was sent out to the Libyan Delegate to the United Nations, in which he was ordered in no uncertain terms to attend a specially called for meeting of the Security Council being held at this moment. He was informed no excuse would be accepted for missing the important meeting. A second memo was included, informing the Libyan Delegate that the police would be dispatched to bodily bring him to the meeting if needed.

Here, the concerned and upset Libyan Delegate was informed of the findings of the French and American scientists. The Libyan politician did not believe the information he was being offered at the meeting, but he did say he would inform his government of their sudden fears. The new Libyan Delegate assured the Security Council that Libya did not have any such weapons of mass destruction in her arsenal and if she did, she would never resort to using them on the battlefield.

After the security meeting was over, the Delegates from the United States, France and the Alliance States of Russia met in a secret meeting. All three nations agreed if Libya dared to employ the toxin weapon during this war, each nation would fire nuclear missiles at the affected area, even if it caused the entire loss of the continent of Africa.

The President reissued orders for all American troops to be issued the chemical protective clothing and independent breathing apparatus. American tanks were self contained, and once they were closed up tight, no chemical or biological weapons could possible get at the soldiers hunkered down inside the tanks and armored vehicles.

THE COMMAND HELICOPTER

Colonel Edward Campanelli had just received more orders for the NBC (Nuclear, Biological and Chemical) protective gear to be issued to all ground troops under his command for a second time, but his most pressing necessity was clean drinking water for his troops. His foot soldiers were making great strides in the fighting on the battlefield against the Libyan soldiers, and taking huge chunks of land as they rapidly chased after the retreating Libyan troops right back into their own country. His supply lines were stretched to the absolute limit, and they was having an extremely hard time with keeping up with the rapidly advancing American and Allied soldiers on the ground. To make matters even worse for his attacking soldiers, the Libyan troops were destroying all water wells and reservoirs by blasting and poisons the water.

Elements of the 3rd and 5th Marine Divisions being backed by over seven hundred tanks, and M 992 Field Artillery Support vehicles carrying ninety extra rounds each of ammunition for the tanks, instead of ammunition for the 155 cannons. The advance units of the attacking

Marines had a Libyan Army of some fifteen thousand enemy soldiers completely cut off from withdrawing and trapped, or getting to any of their much needed military supplies so they could keep fighting the American troops. The Libyan troops were being pounded from all sides by heavy artillery, and constant aircraft and helicopter attacks. The Libyan troops who were caught in this trap for nearly an hour of bombardment, were getting slaughtered and their forces finally relented and raised the white flag, and instantly the Marine troops quickly moved in, taking prisoners and disarming the bewildered and battered and confused Libyan troops.

News got back to Captain Salsiccia that the Libyan General, Abdul el Kadis, who had tortured his female pilot, was captured alive in the ring his troops enforced around the trapped Libyan army. He immediately issued orders for the Marines to have the wanted Libyan General brought back to his command post, alive so he could have the pleasure to interrogate him personally .

CHAPTER 29 - LIBYAN COMMAND, TRIPOLI LIBYA

The President of Libya read the copy of the latest Japanese report which Japan stated it had just declared war on Libya herself. The Libyan leader angrily threw the paper down to the floor as he screamed at one of his aides. "Add another enemy to the ever god cursed growing list of Libya now. I should have known better than to ever trust the lowly yellow infidel devils from the East. I shall enjoy my revenge upon all their lowly cursed heads, and visit pure hell on their foul and worthless country as well for this betrayal against my country and her civilians."

Libya was completely cut off from all military reports over the fighting in Chad, because the American Compass Calls and EF-111 aircraft were jamming everything across the board on the Libyan troops. The twin Libyan capitals of Tripoli and Bengasi were under constant heavy air attacks from the carrier aircraft as well. The Libyan President looked out from his bunker thirty five feet underground through a specially designed telescope, and he noticed all the heavy and almost countless columns of smoke rising over Tripoli. He cursed angrily as he turned to a General and growled at him and demanded. "Where the devil is that lowly dog eater Kamal at?"

"Sir," The General began to offer as he instantly snapped to attention, and then added to his reply. "he's supposed to be at a special meeting currently being conducted at the United Nations, but he has sent his Second in Command to the meeting. He is at..."

The Libyan President hissed as he cut off his officer's reply. "Get a message out to that great dung eater of a fool. I want him to be standing here before me in the hour's time, or it'll be your head that'll pay the price for your failure to carry out my order properly, General."

"Sir, it'll take over two hours for him to possibly arrive here sir."

"I told you I wanted him in one hour's time, General. You dare to offer me he cannot be here as I have just demanded? You will send my private jet to get him. I want him here, General."

"As you have demanded it shall be my President. I shall dispatch your private jet to pick up the Ambassador, and then bring him here as you have just demanded by you, sir."

This small jet landed right in the midst of a heavy American air raid raging on at the civilian airport stationed in Bengasi. Ambassador Kamal was waiting at the airport for the plane arrive to pick him up after he received the order for him to report to his President. The small private aircraft was an unarmed civilian plane, and it had large red crosses painted on each wing, plus one on each side of its tail, and at one point, an American F-18 Hornet spotted the lone plane, and it immediately started an attack approach against it. But when the pilot recognized the red crosses, he immediately pull off and allowed the plane to live. The pilot was not certain this Libyan plane had anything to do with the Red Cross services or not, but he was not going to take any chances on knocking down a possible Red Cross aircraft no matter who was inside it.

The aircraft picked up Ambassador Kamal and on its way back to the capital of Tripoli, it was once again picked up by another American fighter plane. But the Libyan aircraft was allowed to live again when the American pilot picked up the large red crosses painted on both sides of the plane in question. The small aircraft landed on a leveled plain near the President's bunker. Ambassador Kamal was led over to the bunker, and to the angry waiting President.

Immediately, the two politicians locked into a rather heated argument. The Libyan President was blaming Ambassador Kamal for giving him the wrong information about the American resolve in the fighting for Chad, and this new threat presently coming from Japan.

Ambassador Kamal tried to blame the two nations of Algeria and Egypt for their overwhelming situation, because the two rebel nations had pulled out of the fighting on them. As they argued, a report got through the American jamming.

Many of the Libyan owned by Japanese built T 2 fighter planes were now trying to land in Egypt, in order to try and escape the terrible onslaught of Libya. But the Egyptians had taken to shooting any of the Libyan aircraft down as they entered the Egyptian airspace, rather than to allow the fleeing Libyan pilots and planes asylum and safety in their country. Egypt was so upset that Libya had talked them into this war, it hated Libya more than they hated the Jews now.

The Libyan President went absolutely wild as he suddenly announced he was declaring war on both Egypt and Algeria. The Libyan Leader ordered the declaration to be sent out immediately. Ambassador Kamal did his best to try and talk the fuming Libyan President out of attacking Egypt, but the extremely upset President would not back down from his latest order.

As the air raid over Tripoli slowed down, and with the decrease in American attacks against Libya, more war reports finally started to filter through the lessening jamming. The EF 111s stopped jamming, and more reports from Chad got through to the Libyan Command Structure.

The Libyan President was shocked at the terrible reports that he was reading about his soldiers surrendering by the thousands to the rapidly advancing American and allied troops. Chad was all but lost to him now, and the Libyan units were taking up defensive positions all along the Libyan border, in a feeble attempt to try and keep the American troops from invading their country. Bombs fell at random throughout all of Libya as a harassing action was being carried out, in order to stop many civilians and soldiers from getting any rest, or possible regrouping to offer the American troops any possible military resistance.

Egypt received the declaration of war from Libya, and Egypt immediately responded to this threat by declaring war against Libya.

This latest report made Libyan Ambassador Kamal cringe with both fear and anger. He understood full well with losing Egypt as an ally in this war, and having that nation declare war against Libya. All was lost and it was only a matter of time before Libya fell to the terrible onslaught of the American and ally forces attacking his country from every point of the compass.

The bombing over Libya slowly came to an end, as Bunker One and his wing of fighter aircraft headed back for the carriers for armament, fuel, food and some rest. The planes from the carriers stationed in the Red Sea were late getting to the target area, due to a problem with the weather. The HC 130 tankers moved, and Overseer was not notify of the change in position of the refueling tankers, and did not inform the attacking Wing of aircraft from the two Carriers. So this added to the loss in time and these planes were over an hour late getting to the target area.

The Libyan President slowly calmed down and he listened to Ambassador Kamal's words. He tried his best to find a way out of this present situation. He asked the Libyan President to put a cease fighting order out, but the irate President immediately refused this idea. Ambassador Kamal kept at it though, because he understood any further fighting by them was just a waste of time and human life. The Libyan President seemed to be wavering slightly, and just as Ambassador Kamal thought he had the President convinced to stop the fighting, the second phase of the attack from the later American warplanes started, and two hundred bombers hit the capital city. The Libyan President's bunker shook by powerful bombs landing nearby it.

Tripoli was picked to sustain the brunt of this latest air attack against Libya. The heavy pounding made the Libyan President angry as hell as he tried to look out the telescope, but it was destroyed in this bombing. This made him even more angry as he turned to Ambassador Kamal and snarled at him savagely. "I have been thinking, obviously the cursed war is lost to us, but I'm not through fighting yet. Order the firing of the chemical weapons. We have to do something to try and stop these cursed foul American dogs from attack my country."

Ambassador Kamal started to sweat as he stared, measuring this man who was going to destroy so much of the earth if his last order was obeyed by him, and he offered to his President with deep concern lacing his voice. "Sir, I've been reading all the latest reports about the weapons the hated Russian fools have been working on in our country, sir. These evil weapons are highly unstable, and they could cause far more destruction to the world, than any nuclear weapons possibly could. I had hoped you would not employ them in this war sir."

"I'm not interested in your worthless opinion or what you might have read over this weapon of mass destruction, you lowly son born from camel dung. I have followed you valueless advice before, and I now find myself on the verge of losing this war, and my country, because of your foul and misleading words and encouragement, fool. Launch the cursed missiles at Chad, Algeria and Egypt as I ordered you to do. If Libya has to be destroyed in this loathsome war, then so be it, it's Allah's will. But the rest of these lowly mongrel Arab countries will also die along with my nation, you jackal. I want the missiles launched no..."

"Mr. President, could we just employ the DH30 weapon instead? Think of the affects this weapon would have on the battlefield, sir. It would kill many of the loathsome enemy soldiers, but also, it would wound many thousands more, and this is more important to us. Because a dead soldier is dead, but a wounded soldier puts much more pressure on the American infrastructure of war capability, sir. This wounded soldier becomes a burden to the attacking soldiers, the wounded fool has to receive immediate medical care, and then evacuated to a nearby hospital. There he'll require even more medical care, where as a dead soldier puts no additional burden on the war makers and their ability of continuing their attacks on our soldiers and nation, sir.

"Mr. President Sir, a wounded soldier can make all the forward movement of the enemy troops stop completely, as they have to make many preparations just to get the wounded soldiers back to the rear for medical care. Enough wounded soldiers could entirely cripple an army's forward progress all together on the battlefield. Then, we could possibly overtake what is left of the enemy soldiers still standing on the front lines, and possibly still win this war my President."

"No! That's no good for my wants you lowly jackal of a fool. What possible good is our future as a nation, when you show me roads I can no longer tread upon, jackal. You are a traitor to your own intelligence, Ambassador Kamal. I shall hear no more of this from your foul and dung filled mouth, Kamal! I want to use the Crimson Code weapon, and I demand it deployed immediately by your own god cursed worthless lips, Ambassador. I've been told this one weapon is the worst of the lot of loathsome weapons the Russian dogs have brought to us, and I want to do the most possible damage done as fast as possible to our enemy, and these foul nations who have turned their back on us at our time of great need. This way, the world would want to stop all the foul fighting, and we'll be able to stop the war on terms that are much more favorable to us. Now, order the launch as you were ordered you great fool you."

Ambassador Kamal glared at the President, and for an instant he briefly considered killing him. With him dead, the soldiers would want to stop the fighting immediately. The President glared as hard at Kamal as a soldier stepped up and aimed his rifle at him.

"That'll be all I wish to speak with you Ambassador Kamal. Get those missiles going."

The Ambassador left the angry Libyan President's office in a huff, he was sorry he had to leave his bodyguard, Gail back in Bengazi. Sudden, he felt extremely threaten as the two soldier followed him closely. The Libyan Ambassador went over to the radio operator and ordered him to open up direct communications to the Russian launch command center operating in Libya. He then ordered the Russian who responded to his call to launch of the Crimson Code missiles. He gave the blank eyed Russian the list of enemy targets he wanted destroyed by these missiles, and then he dropped the mike to the floor and mumbled to himself. "May Allah have mercy on my foul soul, and for the souls of all Libya."

The guard laughed as he aimed his rifle at Ambassador Kamal's head, and then he pulled the trigger. His head splattered on the seated radio operator. The guard then went back into the President's room and informed the President that Ambassador Kamal was dead. When he was certain the Ambassador was dead, a second soldier immediately killed Gail in Bengazi.

The old Russian defector did not blink an eye as he ordered the SS 21 Spider mobile missile launchers up on full alert as if he was ordering some food to eat. Before the war started, the Libyan troops moved twenty of the Russian made mobile missile launchers down nearer the Chad border, and another twenty near the Egyptian, Sudan and Libyan borders. These launchers were hidden away for possible future needs if the war started to get out of hand for the Libyan President and his troops. The missiles had nuclear warheads installed on them, and two chemical warheads were also stored with each of the hidden missile launchers.

The nuclear warheads were quickly removed from the point of the missiles, and they were immediately replaced with the new chemical warheads containing the Crimson Code on the long range missiles. The target area was quickly set in the guidance computers of the missiles, and the camouflage netting was then removed from the missile launchers to allow a clean launch of the weapons. The cities of Ennedi, Biltine and Abeche were targeted inside Chad, as were the cities of Khartoum, Atbara, Malha and Sufyan inside the Sudanese nation. The Egyptian cities of Cairo, Qina, Aswan and Ash Shabb Oasis were also targeted inside Egypt by the Russian missiles. Libya was unable to aim any missiles at the nation of Algeria, because it was too far away from where the hidden missiles were stationed at at the present time.

A report was sent back to the Libyan president that the missiles were ready for immediate firing, and they were waiting for his final order to launch them at their assigned targets.

THE SEA STALLION HEADING BACK TO BASE SENTRY

Colonel Edward 'Popeye' Campanelli's Command helicopter headed back to his military base stationed in the Sudan, because most of the ground fighting was about over inside the small nation Chad. The command helicopter was flying at just five thousand feet, and the Colonel, and Captains Mendoza and Captain White were celebrating the apparent end of the fighting with a drink. As they were heading back to the base, the Colonel suddenly heard the pilot curse, and he got up and went over to him to see what was wrong with him all of a sudden.

The pilot looked over his shoulder at the concerned Colonel standing right behind him with his hand actually resting lightly on his shoulder, and he complained to him. "Sir, we have a leaker, and we were picked up by the trailing enemy Zapper's radar, sir. I have no chance in hell of out running the bastard sir. I'm calling for some help sir. You better take your seat and buckle up, and prepare yourselves for a possible crash landing, if this lousy sonofa fucking bitch fires a missile at us, Colonel. You better inform the other two officers back there also sir. It's going to get pretty hairy up here if this bastard attacks us, sir."

The Colonel went back to his seat and sat down heavily, and then he buckled himself in the chair and looked at Captain Mendoza and Captain White, and then said to the both of them. "We have some trouble. It seems a stinking Zapper's coming after the damn chopper."

Captain Renee Mendoza stared at her Commanding Officer and lover with disbelieving eyes, as she quickly buckled herself tight in her chair.

"Baby, it looks like we're going to get our ugly asses a little bloody on this one. The pilot's trying to raise some help for us, but I don't think any will get here before it's too late."

Captain Mendoza stared at the Colonel for a long moment, and then she snapped back at him. "What's so ugly about my ass mister? You didn't seem to have much of a problem with my ugly ass this morning as I remember right, sir. Now, you want to curse my ass, sir."

Colonel Edward Campanelli and Captain John White laughed as the Colonel took Captain Renee Mendoza's hand in his, and then he tried to comfort her by offering in a calming tone of voice. "Don't worry about it baby, everything's going to be fine honey. We didn't go through all this hell only to get beat up after this mess is just about over with, dammit."

The huge helicopter suddenly veered off harshly to its starboard side as Colonel Campanelli heard the rounds from the attacking enemy T 2 ripping into the side of the wide chopper as the inside of the helicopter instantly went dark, and then the flames, sparks and smoke replaced the light. The pilot was doing his best to try and avoid many the bullets, as the co pilot could be heard yelling into the radio for help from any American fighter aircraft still operating in the area. The co pilot finally reached a pilot named Duster, who quickly informed the co-pilot he was on his way to help them, but it was going to be too late to help them out.

On the second pass, the enemy plane had the chopper dead in his sights and as he fired, the rounds actually ripped the chopper apart. The pilot looked at the bank of switches and gauges flashing red, and he knew immediately they were going down, and going down hard at that. There was a small explosion in the rear of the chopper, knocking out the tail rotor, and the pilot instantly lost all control of the helicopter as she went into a spin on the pilot.

The Colonel heard at least three of the warning alarms still screaming inside the confines of the burning helicopter, and he immediately realized they were going down. He tightened his hold on Captain Mendoza's hand as he tried to see her through the heavy smoke rapidly filling the troop area, as the helicopter rolled hard to its starboard side, and then headed at the ground a hundred feet below them. The pilot controlled the chopper as best he could, but it still crashed hard into the ground on its port side with a heavy thud.

The stunned Colonel watched the helicopter come apart as if it was happening in slow motion before his eyes. The heavy wood map table crushed in on itself, as the papers and charts went flying through the interior of the crippled helicopter. Heavier smoke quickly filled the now tight compartment as the Colonel desperately looked for Mendoza through his tearing and burning eyes, as the heavy smoke burned them, and he gagged on the thick smoke.

By the time the massive helicopter settled on the ground, it was lying on its right side, with roaring flames pouring out from the engine compartment area of the downed helicopter. The confused Colonel ended up actually suspended in the air while he was still buckled tight in his seat, some twelve feet off the ground. He struggled desperately with the thick safety harness still trapping him in his chair. He looked off to his left, the seat once containing Captain Renee Mendoza was gone, completely ripped right out of the floor boards of the destroyed and burning helicopter.

He looked through the wreckage in fear, he was terrified he was going to see Captain Renee Mendoza being burned alive in the wreckage. But all he could see through the heavy smoke and flame was the wooden map table crumbled up and crushed on the far side of the helicopter, and it was starting to burn in the fire now.

"Mendoza!" He roared as he struggled desperately to free himself of the confining harness. "Mendoza!" He called out a second time as he reached for the edge of the open door, and then he pulled himself over to it. He stood on the handles of his chair, his upper body already stuck outside the burning helicopter. The Colonel frantically looked all around until he located his closest friend John, he was out of his chair and his eyes were wide and wild, and they showed he was petrified, and his face was covered with grim and sweat.

John was sitting directly across from the Colonel before the crash, now his chair was almost turned completely around in the other direction. The Captain was able to free himself from the chair and in a flash, he too was standing in the opening of the helicopter doorway, gasping for fresh air as he gasped and tried to speak to his Commanding Officer at the same time.

"Mendoza, where the hell are you at god dammit!" Colonel Campanelli yelled back into the bowels of the burning helicopter, and then he added to his angry words. "You got to get the hell outta there before the damn thing blows up on us, damn you anyway girl. Where the hell are you for the love of God? C'mon Mendoza, we gotta get the hell outta this fucking thing!"

"Eddy, you hafta get the hell out of the damn thing yourself man. She's gonna blow on us sir!" John yelled in the concerned and extremely upset Colonel's face over the roar coming from the flames rapidly eating its way through the interior of the all but destroyed helicopter.

Colonel Campanelli ignored the concerned and excited Captain, and he started to climb back into the burning death trap to try and find Captain Renee Mendoza.

"Oh no you don't buster. You're not going back in there as long as I'm at your side, mister. We're getting the hell outta this damn death trap right now buddy." John said as he forcefully grabbed Edward's arm and then he tried to pull him out and away from the flaming wreckage.

The upset Colonel would not leave the burning wreck, and he actually tried to savagely yank his arm free of John's tight grip, and then look for Mendoza in the wreckage.

Captain White was slightly hurt from the crash, but he continued pulling on the arm of his Commanding Officer as he screamed at him again. "C'mon Eddy will ya please! You have to get the fuck outta here before she blows up on us man. C'mon, dammit Eddy, C'mon sir."

The Colonel still refused to leave the burning helicopter, as he yelled out once more into the flaming helicopter. "Mendoza, where the fuck are you, you pain in the ass you. Mendoza!"

Captain White again pulled on Edward's arm as he bitched at him. "Colonel, you hafta get the hell out of this damn thing right now. It's no fucking good man. Mendoza's gone on us sir. C'mon will ya man and get the hell outta here before she explodes on us will ya."

Colonel Edward Campanelli turned and glared savagely at Captain John White as he roared right in his face. "What the fuck do you mean by that load of shit buster? What the hell are you trying to say man? Whatdaya fucking mean Maz is gone? Fuck you, she ain't gone nowhere you!" He hissed harshly at John as he actually shoved his friend back, and then he broke free from his grasp and struck the big man in the face with his fist.

John easily shook off the force of the punch, and then he snarled angrily at his confused friend, trying to get him to leave the burning hulk. "Sir, Ed, when the plane hit us, his shells hit the left side of the chopper. I'm sorry, but she was on the left side, sir. I saw her take hits in the chest sir. She's gone sir, you hafta get the hell outta here, now."

Captain White was joined by the pilot, and together they both pulled the stunned Colonel up and they nearly threw him out of the burning wreckage. John more or less picked his friend up with one arm. He was built like a defensive tackle, and he could have had his pick of any pro football team if he decided to play pro ball.

The stunned and confused Colonel was on his feet in a flash, as John and the pilot jumped down from the side of the crashed helicopter next. They immediately grabbed the Colonel as he made another move to go back into the burning aircraft, to look for the missing female Captain. He fought both men off as he called back at the flaming wreckage. "Mendoza, goddamn you, you bitch you. Mendoza get the fuck outta the damn thing will you! Renee! Renee!"

The three exhausted and battered soldiers stood for a second, and they stared at the wreck as the fire rapidly ate through the underneath of the crashed chopper like a cancer. Parts of the once great war machine caved in on itself, as it continued to burn unchecked.

"She's gonna explode dammit." The pilot screamed as he rushed for cover from it.

The two officers dragged and more of less carry the Colonel away from the burning chopper as it suddenly exploded in a flash of flames and bellowing smoke. The three soldiers landed hard on their asses from the force of the explosion so near them. Captain White placed his arm on his friend's shoulder, as the Colonel continued to stare at the wall of flames with unblinking eyes, as if he was trying to will Mendoza to walk out of the flaming wreck as he whispered. "Renee."

He was filled with a terrible grief as he turned to John and then cried at him, his tears cleaning paths through his soot covered face. "You know I loved that girl, John. Renee was going to be my wife as soon as I was able to get a divorce from my wife, my friend."

"I know that Eddy. You two were made for each other, man. But you gotta get a hold of yourself now sir. She's gone sir. You gotta let it go sir. You have to let her go man." John said as he put his hand on the Colonel's shoulder and then he pulled him to him in a gentle hug.

The pilot of the helicopter cut in as he talked over the survival radio. He made contact with home base, and requested an immediate dust off pickup, he gave their coordinates, and was instantly informed that an air rescue helo would be dispatched immediately, and arrive on site in less than twenty minutes. The pilot was as upset because he lost his co-pilot and navigator in the attack as he informed the two officers what had just transpired.

Campanelli did not hear a word the pilot said to him, he was still staring at the flames as if he expected Mendoza to come walking out of the wrecked chopper with her ever present smile.

COMMAND HEADQUARTERS. LIBYA

The Libyan President was still fuming as he gave orders to the Russians to fire the missiles.

Nightbird One was the first observation satellite platform to pick up the sudden plumes being emitted from the missile's launch. And it immediate Flash an emergency warning across the CIC threat board on board the Aircraft Carrier Roosevelt.

The excited Commander Owens immediately informed the American President of the detection of a number of missile launches. The concerned President asked the commander if he was certain the missiles contained possible Biological weapons. Commander Owens confirmed his own thoughts about that possibility, and the President gave out with a deep sigh, and then he thought for a few moments as he remained silent on the other end of the communication. Then he gave the orders to launch the nuclear weapons to sterilize the soon to be biological contaminated areas on impact. The shaking American President ordered Commander Owens to broadcast the NBC (Nuclear, Biological and Chemical), warning to his military forces in the field, warning all Allied soldiers to take cover and get in their protective gear.

The Commander ordered all his fighter and bomber aircraft to break off their present attack orders, and then they were ordered to head for the barn immediately. He then ordered all in flight fuel tankers further out to the Mediterranean, and had the attacking fighter aircraft to go out to meet them, in order to get the smaller attack aircraft out of the soon to be blast areas, and save as many of his pilots and aircraft as he possibly could.

Moments before the Libyan missiles hit their assigned targets on the ground, Flash warnings were transmitted out to all military combat operations and command centers, warning them of the pending possible biological attacks aimed against them, followed by the nuclear sterilization hits ordered up by the American President. Hundreds of thousands of military personnel immediately went underground, as tanks closed their hatches, and the hard shelled aircraft hangers were closed up, to better protect as many of the soldiers on the ground as humanly possible. Hundreds of thousands of other soldiers were going to be caught out in the open, and they would soon die most horrible deaths. These soldier were classified as acceptable losses to the present situation. The few to protect the many. This was the only way to try and stop the spread of the toxin from getting into the Middle East, Europe, and then the rest of the world.

The President was deeply distressed by his latest order to launch the nuclear tipped missiles, but he also knew it was the only hope the world had to survive this terrible weapon of mass destruction. Other missiles from the three nations in agreement to launch missiles to end the threat were also aimed at Libya, in an attempt to try and eliminate the threat of any future trouble from this country. President Albert Cole also ordered his American submarines to their launch depths. He transmitted the list of targets to be hit by their nuclear tipped missile warheads, and he picked the two submarines to launch the initial opening attack against the few nations involved in the fighting. The Bridgeport, a submarine support ship assigned to the Roosevelt Task Force, was stationed a thousand yards off the stern of the massive Aircraft Carrier, and the New Orleans, also in the support group protecting the Missouri on station in the Red Sea.

The American President got in contact with the Captain of the Bridgeport himself, and he gave him command over the missile launches. The Commander of the submarine was informed if his two submarines missiles could not hit all the intended targets, he was in power to employ any other submarine missiles to get the job done for them. In this case, the missiles from the two submarines the Tennessee and Idaho, stationed seven miles off the coast of Libya, were ordered on a standby to launch alert. The American Leader informed the skipper of the Bridgeport, that Commander Owens will inform him of the targets going to be hit by the Libyan missiles, and he wanted these targets hit by nuclear warheads immediately afterwards, to burn off the possibly deadly biological weapon before it spread from the impact areas.

ON BOARD THE AMERICAN SUBMARINE BRIDGEPORT

The Captain of the submarine received a deep water warning, he immediately ordered the submarine up to antenna depth. Hull popping noises flooded the interior of the Bridgeport, as pressure on the hull decreased rapidly when the submarine came up to its proper antenna depth to receive further orders from Command. Once at station, the Captain received the Flash traffic from the President of the United States through the COMSUB communication secured system. The message came through as a garbled mass of numbers, jumbled letters and crazy symbols. The Captain stood over the shoulder of his Boatswain's mate, with his hand actually resting on his shoulder, as he quickly converted the mess into a readable message for the worried Captain of the submarine.

When the Boatswain's mate finished deciphering the message, he handed the unscrambled memo to the waiting Captain. He turned his back on the mate and read the report in silence. After he finished, he turned to the mate looking up from the paper ashen, and stared at the young sailor whose face was a mask of fear.

"Shit, I never dreamed it would've ever come down to this kind of shit, Boatswain. Sound General Quarters mister."

Instantly, the submarine's intercom screamed to life as the orders were bellowed out over it for the crew. "General Quarters, General Quarters. All hands man your battle stations. General Quarters. General Quarters, this is not a drill, I repeat, General Quarters this is not a drill. All fire watch personnel man your stations. General Quarters, General Quarters."

Whistles, sirens and a number of loud alarms resounded throughout the entire length of the submarine, as scared Seamen and officers alike ran in all directions, dressed in life preservers and helmets as they scrambled to their battle stations, and then the crew prepared to launch their missiles at their ordered targets.

The Captain took over the Conn. His XO (Executive Officer) stood by his right side as the very confident acting Captain checked over his charts, and the XO confirmed the launch orders for him. "Helmsman, rudders amid ship." The Captain yelled over his shoulder, and then he added to his orders to the Helmsman. "Take her up to launch depth immediately mister."

Dead silence quickly spread throughout the entire ship as each man and woman on board analyzed the meaning of the last order. Each crew member remained silent as they waited to hear the next orders as the Captain prepared to launch his missile compliment.

There was a slight hesitation from the sailor to the last orders, which caused the Captain to turn and look at the scared Helmsman, and then he growl harshly at him this time. "Helmsman, I ordered rudders amid-ship dammit!"

The Helmsman actually jumped at the forces in the Captain's voice in his chair, as he cried out. "Rudders amid-ship. Launch depth Aye Captain."

The Captain moved over to the launch control center, and then he carefully inserted his gold plated brass key into the panel. The XO moved over by the Captain's side, and then he inserted his key and looked at his skipper and waited his next order.

"On three, you'll turn your key sir." The Captain warned him. "One, two, three. Turn."

They turned their keys together. Instantly, a panel slid open, exposing a computer keyboard.

"Launch Control Officer, take up your position immediately please." The Captain ordered.

Once the officer was seated in front of the small keyboard, the Captain continued with his next orders. "Here's a list of our assigned targets for our full complement of missiles, put them in the damn computer, and then leave the key open. CIC from the Roosevelt will transmit the code word to launch. 'Sterilize'. Once this word is passed, launch. Is that clear mister?"

"Yes Sir Captain, once Sterilize is transmitted, I launch the birds, sir. Understood Captain." The officer snapped back, trying to sound confident of his orders and his reply as well.

"Are you certain of your present orders mister?" The Captain demanded to know from the concerned looking officer.

"Positive of my orders as stated Captain." He replied to his Commanding Officer.

"Then get it done man. I want you as cool as a cucumber during this launch, mister." The Captain added as he let out his breath in a rush.

The launch control officer pounded the keyboard, as the skipper turned to the radio operator and ordered him. "Open up a channel to the Orleans. I want the Captain on the horn."

A few seconds later the Captain of the New Orleans was on the horn and the Captain of the Bridgeport asked him in a controlled tone of voice. "Ray, how the hell are you doing sir?

"Fine Captain. What's up sir? I've been monitoring all communications, Captain."

"It looks like we pulled the shit duty for the day, Ray! You up for the mission sir?"

"Understood. I was afraid of that crap coming down the chute when this damn thing first stared, sir. I'm ready to launch on a moment's notice on Command, sir."

"Ray, here's a list of the selected targets my missiles are zeroed in on sir, with more to come as needed, sir. Copy these down, and here's your list of assigned targets, Captain. Code word to launch is, 'Sterilize'. I repeat Ray, 'Sterilize'. I control the game. If we can't get all the fucking targets with our full compliments of missiles and warheads, I have the power from the President of the United States to order in additional submarines closest to the targets to launch their missiles. All Allied submarines involved in this operation are ordered up to launch depths, sir. I have the Tennessee and Idaho waiting on standby in the Mediterranean, in case we need their Units to finish off any possible targets we can't get at with our missile systems, sir.

"Ray, once you launched your compliment of missiles, you're cleared to get the hell out of the area before it gets hot on us, sir. I'm to stand by, and order in any additional launches if needed to complete my orders as issued, after the initial missile launches have been calculated. Skipper, once you fire off, go deep and bug the hell out of the area, sir. Good luck on this one, Ray. The order to launch is on my shoulders alone, sir. I'll do all the answering to God. Spin them up at this point sir." Captain Pat Hamilton ended his communication and then he turned, only to see the many scared faces of his crew staring back at him.

The skipper took a breath then offered to his crew members. "Any personnel who feels he or she can't do this job asked of them speak up now, not when the missiles are flying. I'll have any man or woman who so desires, relieved of duty immediately." He stood for a second.

Two men stepped forward with their heads hanging down and they waited.

Captain Hamilton stared at the two men as he rubbed his head and then he offered. "Okay, I guess you two are relieved of duty. You're confined to your bunks until this mess is over with. Thank you for your honesty. Master at Arms, will you escort these two gentlemen to their bunks, and assign a guard to watch over them until this current emergency has been completed, sir."

"Conn to Captain, reporting we reached launch depth, all missiles are spinning up as of this time sir." The Navigator cried out the warning to his Commanding Officer.

"Launch Control, target positions are set in the computer, and the birds are locked on, sir."

"Very good, stand by for further orders then, people. We have to wait for the orders to launch from Command." The Captain answered.

"How long before we start shooting sir?" The XO asked his skipper in a concerned tone.

"They'll let us know in due time I guess sir. I'm still hoping they don't order us to launch."

ABOARD THE COMMAND AIRCRAFT CARRIER ROOSEVELT

The concerned Commander of the Aircraft Carrier sat inside the CIC center while drumming his fingers nervously on the surface of the metal table, while feverously moving the cigar around in his mouth with his teeth. Suddenly his threat board tripped on him. The upset Commander looked to his satellite uplink computer. Instantly, the machine came to life as a number of sheets of paper were spat out of the machine at lightning speed.

A Yeoman ripped the paper free of the machine, and handed it over to the Commander. Even before he looked at the paper, he knew what it read. Because the threat board was already tracking twelve missile trajectories from Libya, heading towards the Sudan, Egypt and the small nation of Chad.

As the Commander read the latest satellite report, a second satellite uplink computer screamed its metallic talk. He knew this one was backing up the information from the first satellite, and the Commander barked at his crew member. "Okay Yeoman, let's do this mess by the fucking numbers. Do you have all target locations for missile impacts, mister?"

"Yes Sir Captain, they're already plotted in the launch computer sir. We know exactly where they are coming down Skipper."

"Good. Transmit the target areas out to the Bridgeport so she can target her missiles accordingly. End the transmission with the Code Word 'Sterilize'. Repeat the Code Word so I know you understand it."

"Sir, the Code Word is Sterilize as was ordered sir." The Yeoman replied to the Captain.

"Good, transmit the order to the Bridgeport immediately son." The Captain ordered.

"Aye, aye sir. It's on the way out as we speak sir." The Yeoman remarked as he sent out his traffic as he was just ordered to do.

ON BOARD THE SUBMARINE BRIDGEPORT

Less than a second later. The threat computer on board the nuclear powered submarine the Bridgeport, screamed to life as it rapidly printed out the impact locations of the intended missile strikes. The last word the computer printed out was 'STERILIZE', in capital letters. The launch control officer immediately entered the locations to be targeted by their missiles.

The Captain stood against the periscope tube sweating, with the XO standing at his side. The skipper was pleased the tube was cold to the touch. He waited for what seemed like an eternity, when the radio speaker almost scared him to death. He jumped when the speaker overhead screamed out the orders.

"Sterilize. Repeat, the Code Word for this operation is Sterilize." The message echoed throughout the entire submarine.

The Captain shoved his weight off the tube with his shoulders and stood erect, and then he barked out the order in a booming tone to his crew. "Launch all missiles! Let them fly."

Every seven seconds, the submarine shuddered from within, as another missile was fired at a target stationed inside Libya, Egypt or the Sudan. In under three minutes, twenty four nuclear tipped missiles were flying at their ordered targets. The American missiles would hit the same targets the Libyan missiles were slaved to, at about the same instant the Libyan missiles hit.

The crew of the Aircraft Carrier Roosevelt stared at the calm sea's surface in awe, as missile after missile broke the surface of the water and then ignited their engines in a tail of flames, and then the missiles shot off in the sky after their targets.

"Conn to sonar. Where the hell's the damn Roosevelt stationed at dammit? I need her exact position on the surface of the water, mister" The deeply worried Captain asked the sonar operator with concern.

"Sonar to Conn. The Roosevelt's positioned Twenty Five Hundred Yards off our port bow, sir. She's upping power as we speak, she doing turns to six knots, Captain. I guess we must have scared her a bit when we fired off our birds, sir. Support ships are clear also sir."

"Navigator. What's our present position of the damn Task Force, mister? I want to know where all the damn support ships are positioned." The Captain requested, the last thing he wanted to have happen was one of his birds making contact with one of the surface ships.

"Skipper, we're on bearing, One, One, Four sir. We're doing turns to twelve knots, needed for the launch control of the missiles, sir. Course is, Two, Six, Six, and clear of the task force sir."

His XO stared at the skipper while waiting for any further orders. Usually, after a launch was completed, the submarine was supposed to head deep and hide until the damage was calculated. So far, the Captain did not issue the order to dive the submarine yet.

The skipper looked at his XO and smiled at him as he asked. "You scared any sir?"

"Yep. Scared as hell I'm afraid sir. But it won't stop me from doing my duty though sir."

"Good, me too. We're ordered to stand by our present station, and control any further launches if needed. Rig for silent running, order SQ. We can do that much at least until we run from the fucking area, dammit."

"Silent running, aye Skipper. SQ, Quick Quite is the current orders for the boat, sir." The XO ordered the crew.

"Sonar, keep your ears open mister. I don't want to get hit unprepared dammit."

"Torpedo room. Load all tubes with Mark Forty Eight, and Ark Fifty torpedoes, and stand by to fire the damn things off if we come under attack from any possible enemy shipping or warships in the area, mister." The Captain ordered in a commanding tone of voice.

The Captain then turned to his crew and offered. "I suggest we all better make ourselves comfortable, we're going to be here for a while. Radar. What's the status on those birds?"

"All birds are away perfectly, running true to target as ordered. No drop offs detected as of yet sir. The first bird is set to hit in one minute, plus seventeen seconds from now, sir."

"Good, keep me informed of their flight paths to target at all times, mister."

"Aye, aye Skipper. Will do as ordered sir." The radar operator replied to the Captain.

"Sonar. You should be able to pick up the impacts. Let me know when you hear anything."

"Sonar to Conn. We're still maintaining contact with all surface ships. They're holding their positions, sir. No sign of any action going on upstairs as of this time. Sir, I'm picking up another launch going off. It has to be the Orleans launching her birds at her targets, sir."

"It's about time they launched their missiles dammit." The skipper growled.

"Counting. Twenty four. All twenty four missiles are away and flying true at this time sir."

"What the hell's she doing now? Is she preparing to get the hell out of the area, mister?"

"The Orleans' flooding ballast as we speak, Skipper. There she goes, she's heading deep at full power at this time sir. Luck Orleans."

"Okay, right full rudder. All ahead two thirds, come over to course, Zero, One, Three. Get up to periscope depth, I want to see what the fuck's going on up there for the love of God. It has to be one helluva mess by now, mister."

"Right full rudder, ahead two thirds. Coming to new course of, Zero, One, Three. Periscope depth, Aye sir." The Navigator responded to his latest orders from his Commander.

The skipper looked at his XO a second time, and then he said. "Now, we stand pat and wait further orders from Command. Okay people, quiet down. You all did well on this mission so far. The smoking lamp is lit, smoke if you got them, people."

The submarine was filled with many concerned and excited conversations, as the crew whispered to relieve their tensions.

As the fleet of missiles hit their assigned targets, large sections of Chad, the Sudan and most of Egypt, and all of Libya were instantly erased from the face of the earth forever. What was left, was rake by a searing, wind whipped overwhelming shockwave, and the intense heat of the nuclear storm raging on the surface of the earth.

PRESIDENTIAL PALACE, CAIRO, EGYPT

Egyptian Ambassador Mohammed Kheir, was sitting in his new office in the heart of Cairo, heard the soft thud as a biological tipped missile landed in a yard a few buildings away from the Palace grounds. The Ambassador looked out of the window as the missile suddenly exploded while laying on the ground. It was not a powerful blast, more like a pop than an actual explosion. He immediately noticed a heavy green mist raise from the debris of the missile. The stunned Ambassador stared, and the cloud quickly spread out. A number of the civilians who ran over to see what landed in their backyard, immediately fell to the ground while rolling on the floor in terrible pain, twitching and convulsing. Blood poured from their gaping mouths, noses, ears and eyes as they stopped moving.

Mohammed ran away from the window as he screamed out. "Chemicals." And he ran to the front door, and out to the street and away from the missile strike. He looked in the sky and easily picked up a vapor stream coming from another incoming missile and he cried. "Shit!" Was all he was able to cry out before the American missile exploded three thousand feet above ground. Moments later, Cairo, and the surrounding area lay in ruins from the air burst nuclear blast, and the incineration that quickly followed, but the toxin was also killed off by the intense nuclear heat from the explosion.

When the missiles stopped flying, and the terrible effects of the nuclear blasts subsided, a hoard of scientists quickly descended on what was left of most of these destroyed countries. The scientists were dressed in their extremely heavy protective nuclear and chemical and biological protective clothing and separate breathing apparatus while looking for evidence of any of the toxin still living. In one section of the Sudan, two missiles were called in when some of the toxin was found still alive and active in the area the scientists were working in.

Rescue workers were sent to Egypt, the Sudan, Chad, as well as Iraq, Israel and Jordan, to look for any possible survivors, and to start to bury or burn the massive amount of dead. This section of the world would take seventy five years to get back to a near civilized state.

THE CRASH SITE OF THE COMMAND HELICOPTER

Colonel Edward Campanelli did not feel the pain from his burned hand and fingers, nor did he feel any pain from the many minor scrapes and cuts he received in the helicopter crash. All he could think about was Captain Renee Mendoza, as he stood silently by and watched as the rescue workers carefully removed what was left of her body from the smoldering wreckage of the torn and twisted command helicopter.

Her body was carefully placed in the long black body bag, and it saved him the pain of seeing what the bullets and fire had done to her once exquisite body and face. Captain John White, with his arm wrapped up in a sling, and bandages on his face and other arm, stood alongside his Commanding Officer and dear friend.

The Colonel angrily kicked at a small pile of sandy soil as the rescue workers took the body of a female officer from the wreckage of the helicopter, and they carried it over and placed it on a waiting helicopter.

"Take it easy with her body or I'll kill you two fucking assholes, god dammit! She died in the service of her country." The Colonel growled at the stunned rescue workers.

"C'mon Eddy, we have to get the hell out of here and back to safety ourselves, sir." John said as he pushed up against the Colonel's side with his body in an effort to move him along some.

"Yeah, I guess you're right John. There's nothing else we can do here any longer buddy."

The two exhausted and battered soldiers slowly dragged their feet to the spooling helicopters in total silence, they both leaned on each other for warmth and comfort. John tried to lead Edward to the spooling rescue helicopter without the bodies resting inside it, but he ignored the lead and climbed in and then sat down alongside of Captain Renee Mendoza's body.

John followed him in it. The helicopter lifted off in a cloud of blowing sand.

"God dammit John, I can't believe she's gone on me man. I thought I was finally going to get my damn life straightened out for myself, and now this shit had to happen to us. I had it with this crap John, I really had it this time I tell you man. I'm getting the fuck out of the damn service, I can't take this shit any longer, man. This stinking lifestyle sucks the big one man." Colonel Campanelli growled as he leaned his head back until it rested on the cool metal side of the helicopter. As he put his head back he closed his eyes, but no matter how tight he kept his eyes shut, a tear escaped and it slid down the side of his grime covered face. All the while, the Colonel kept his one good hand resting softly on the black plastic bag where Captain Renee Mendoza's head was. Keeping her company.

John looked at his friend not knowing what more to do or say to him. He lowered his eyes and stared at his feet, giving Edward as much privacy with Mendoza as he could offer him, he shook his head sadly over the loss of the female Captain and dear friend.

The grieving Colonel, along with the charred bodies of Captain Renee Mendoza, the pilot of the command helicopter and the cabin airman, and what was left of his command was quickly evacuated back to his military base, that had sustained little effects from the nuclear and biological blasts that decimated the area near the massive military base.

As many of his military units checked in, Colonel Edward Campanelli was able to determine how many casualties his Command suffered on the theater of war. His private grief had to be placed on the back burner for the time being, as he looked after his surviving troops, and their military equipment.

It was estimated well over seventy thousand American soldiers were killed from the biological, or the nuclear attacks on the battlefield, with another ten thousand soldiers expected to die within the next few weeks from exposure and radiation poisoning. So many civilian deaths were estimated, but no one really wanted to fix an exact number on the actual deaths of the civilians, in the affected nations of the Middle East and North Africa. But in just twenty days of fighting, there were more death in this single war, than all previous wars combined, including the Civil War, and a fifth of the world's surface was now devoid of all human and animal life for a hundred years to come.

CHAPTER 30 – COLONEL EDWARD CAMPANELLI'S HOME, CARMEL, PUTNAM COUNTY NEW YORK STATE

Colonel Edward 'Popeye' Campanelli was left so devastated by the terrible death of Captain Renee Mendoza, that the Joint Chiefs of Staff were actually forced to relieve him of his present Command, and of his active duty. The stunned Colonel went home to his wife who had never knew he was gone in the first place, as a One Star General this time. But General Campanelli also knew he was only marking time with his wife, because Captain Renee Mendoza was too big a part of his past, and her memory was going to be to big a part of his future. The new General knew he would jump at the next assignment his government offered him, and he would use this in his search for another Captain Renee Mendoza, and a new life for himself.